A brutal slaying in New City, New York,
along the banks of the

DEMAREST KILL

*A home-town tale of reminiscence, friendship,
obsessive love, betrayal and murder.*

a novel by
FRANK EBERLING

DEMAREST KILL
a novel by Frank Eberling
©1999, 2000, 2006, 2014, 2015 by Frank Eberling

Third Edition, June, 2017-Many thanks to cousin Bruce Rogers for revisions.
Printed in the United States of America
ISBN-10: 1535127732
ISBN-13: 978-1535127738

Learn more information at: www.frankeberling.com

WHAT ADVANCE READERS ARE SAYING:

"A combination of a highly detailed, yet fictitious memoir, with a murder story set in a small town with small town secrets."

"Even if you didn't grow up in this area, you are still likely to connect to the feeling of the times."

"For those of a certain age, this is our story."

"A murder mystery wrapped inside a would-be memoir takes the reader back and forth in time."

"A time-capsule of an era, sharing both the euphoria and the heartbreak provided by the times."

"If you grew up in New City during the 1950s and 1960s, you won't want to miss this. I can't even begin to count the memories it triggered."

"The most heart-wrenching coming-of-age novel I have ever read. The surprise ending caught me completely off-guard and serves as a vivid reminder of what a great loss-of-innocence some of us went through."

"I was totally unprepared for the ending. I cannot stop thinking about it."

"Having walked these same woods as a child I was taken back to a special time. How lucky we all were."

"Filled with period details and period sentiment."

"What happened to the generation after 'the greatest generation'?"

"The lives of a child piano prodigy, an artist, and a fifth generation New City boy are intertwined in this marvelous murder mystery novel that is both pastoral and horrific."

DEMAREST KILL

a novel by
FRANK EBERLING

The genesis of all art is the pursuit of the irrecoverable.
— John Fowles

Some spend their lives building for the future.
Others live it trying to reconcile the past.
— Unknown

Just because it happened to you, doesn't make it interesting.
— Dennis Hopper

Frank Eberling

CHAPTER ONE

THE DUTCH GARDEN
NEW CITY, NEW YORK

Monday, 8 a.m.
October 16, 2000
Age 54

It started with a dead body.

It almost always starts with a dead body. At least for me. Or, for that matter, anyone else who works homicide cases. With all the players who work this detail, whether it's the Town of Clarkstown beat cops who arrive first, or the Rockland County Sheriff's detectives who may be next to arrive, the County Medical Examiner who usually gets there before I do, and finally me, from the investigators' office of the District Attorney, it almost always starts with a dead body. It makes sense. No dead body, and our little meetings would have no reason to convene.

I've seen more dead bodies than I want to think about. How many? Not as many as someone in my same position twenty five miles down the Palisades Parkway in Manhattan, but plenty for a small-time guy like me in a small town like New City. After a while, they all seem to look the same. Twisted in their final struggle on earth, faces in a grotesque pleading, reaching out for who knows what, some reprieve or moment of mercy that is never going to come. Some are bloody and battered, their faces smashed in from having the life beaten out of them by a loved one. Others bear gaping black/red ugly gunshot holes. I've seen them all, some dressed in homeless clothing, others in formal attire, nurse's uniforms, chenille bathrobes, even cops' uniforms. The common denominator is the look of finality they all bear. It is the end of something, some dark, sinister secret that has finally caught up with them. Now, no matter how much you want to, no matter how much you try, you're not going to wake them up. Some person, usually someone they've known, can't take it anymore, and in a moment of anger or passion or lack of caring, they let it happen.

Some of the time it surprises even the murderer, and they want to take back their evil act. They cannot believe that they can't rewind the clock even five seconds. The most frightening aspect of it all is how very commonplace it all seems to look. It's almost with a shrug of your shoulders that you arrive on the scene, knowing before you get there how ugly it's going to be, yet somehow so ordinary, so tedious. You grow immune to the horror.

But this one was going to be different. Some sick feeling deep down inside me just told me that the moment the call came during my walk into work that morning. It was all too close to home. All too familiar.

For starters, the body was found just south of the Rockland County Courthouses, a mere few hundred feet from where the judges' chambers are, where the probation offices and District Attorney's offices are, and within a hundred feet or so from where county prisoners were held in tiny jail cells until the recent past. It was just a brisk detour from my office early that crisp, clear autumn morning. As I walked into the empty courthouse parking lot off Main Street and walked to the south corner, I marveled at how blue the autumn sky was.

Behind the Courthouse is a small county park known as the

Dutch Garden. It was funded by Roosevelt's Works Progress Administration, designed by Mary Mowbray-Clarke in 1934, and built by Italian bricklayers from Haverstraw and local volunteers. It's a narrow, flat piece of grass just two acres in size, extending south from the Courthouse parking lot and bordered by an elaborate brickwork wall, now covered in ivy and weeds. On the north end, closest to the Courthouse, is a brick building, a tea house, with ornate frescoes, showing wear from the almost seventy years of weathering since it was built. The open-air, slate-tiled building has a hearth and fireplace inside, and was once the site of afternoon teas for the ladies of the garden club. It was turned into a County Park in 1968.

Inside the ornate perimeter brick wall are small garden plots once filled with daffodils and forsythia and peonies and lilac and miniature pansies of dark purple and gold in the early springtime, and marigolds and geraniums in the summer. Yew and arborvitae, shaped and pruned over the decades into topiary animals, separate the beds from the brick latticework. Now, in mid-October, of all the flowers, just the hydrangea survive. White all summer, their pink tinge was always a signal that it was time to go back to school.

On the southwest end of the grounds is a slate-roofed brick gazebo. In all, it's rather an odd sight to see, this small, perfect garden, adjacent to the county jail. Over the years it has had its ups and downs of care and maintenance, of use and neglect and abuse.

During the early 1950s, my mother held her Girl Scout meetings there on spring afternoons, while I, about five years old at the time, looked on in amazement at her commitment to "her girls." I can still hear the echoes of my mother's footsteps as she led her troop over the gravel walkways, bordered by hens-and-chicks, on a tour of the begonias and peonies that were so plentiful at the time. She was teaching them the meaning and import of being a good Girl Scout, as she stood before them, tall and true, trying to maintain her dignity in her one tweed jacket.

Each week when my mother met with her troop they stood at staunch attention at ceremonies where Brownies evolved into Girl Scouts, where Girl Scouts were told the criteria for merit badges and dreamed of becoming homemakers. The girls had walked beside her, hanging on her every word, eager for her smile and look of approval.

In kindergarten and first grade our teachers took us on field trips to wander among the flowers and butterflies and snakes. Later, in the early 1960s, when I was in high school, vandals knocked over the brick walls and the grounds were left to grow wild in milkweed and sumac and Queen Anne's lace. Over the next few decades, it was adopted by one, and then another well-meaning group, trying to maintain its composure and sense of history, while my little town swelled and forgot its past.

Now, at the turn of the 21st Century, The Dutch Garden is maintained just enough to keep it at its minimum beauty. Court-house workers use it to eat their bag lunches and catch a few rays during the first few weeks of Spring Fever. I had only been in The Dutch Garden a few times over the last years, usually on specific dates of the year.

If you stand in the gazebo on the southwest corner, the one known by the old-timers as "The Summer House," and look out to the west, the plateau drops off sharply into a dark, deeply wooded glen that engulfs a slow running brook that flows northward among the rocks, winding its way past the Dutch Garden above it, then under the wooden pedestrian bridge that joins the old Court-house and County Jail and the newer Annex.

From there, the brook flows under New Hempstead Road, into a culvert that runs underneath North Main Street, or old Rte. 304, and underneath the parking lots for the first bowling alley and supermarket in town that were built during the late '50s, before it exits the culvert and heads its way north through the old "Squadron A" Farm property. Running parallel to North Main Street, it winds its way through what was once horse pastures and old Senator Buckley's weekend retreat. The Senator's place provided a fishing hole for the boys "on the list." The stream then flows toward Christie's Airport, a grass strip, two-hangar airport that provided local aviators a place to hang out, and for the swells from the Dellwood Country Club to fly in on weekends.

Most of these landmarks are gone now, surviving only in the memory of those who grew up here, wandering the fields, exploring the woods, fishing the ox-bows in the shallow creek. Before the Palisades Parkway came through in the early 1950's and turned this sleepy little farm hamlet into a bustling, high-priced bedroom community, it was a little piece of paradise. When the New York Thruway and the Parkway ripped their way into the gentle rolling hills of Rockland County in those sleepy, post-war days, it took just a matter of a few years to change New City from an off-the-beaten-path, 19th Century farm town into a Post-World War II enclave to raise baby-boomers.

The brook, known as "The Demarest Kill," ambles along slowly, unrushed in its northbound flow, before it joins in with the Hackensack River and dumps into Lake DeForest over near Haverstraw, just this side of High Tor. For many years, the Demarest Kill was mine. I owned it as only a young boy can own a beloved piece of land.

One of the tiny tributaries that eventually feeds into the larger stream, bordered the field behind my family's homestead on South Main Street. I could follow the tiny creek from my back yard and wade downstream through the old Florion Estate, and the newer Damiani compound. There it was dammed up for a swimming and ice skating pond for the kids, and then, north of that pond it formed yet another millpond, the ruined dam of which still remains near the south end of the Dutch Garden. It eventually flows into the main fork of what is called The Demarest Kill.

The Demarest part of the name comes from a pioneer family who settled this area before the Revolutionary War. The second

part of the name comes from the language of the early Dutch settlers. "Kill" is a Dutch word for "small river," or "brook."

Yes, Demarest Kill was my domain growing up in New City
in the late 1940's, the 1950's and the early 1960's. I was lord of
the river, emperor of all that I beheld in its path. We built huts
and forts along its stream banks, floated rafts made of old doors
lashed to inner tubes and played Huck Finn, searched for fresh
water springs and the crawdads that inhabited them, and swung
from bank to bank from the sinewy vines that criss-crossed the
water hanging from the majestic elms and oak and maples that
towered over the banks and provided a deep, dank canopy. A
stand of birches graced the western bank and we climbed to the
tops, threw our legs out, and let them swing us down safely to
the ground, just like Robert Frost's farm boy had done with New
Hampshire birches.

My hours of play on the Demarest Kill and the surrounding
hills and vales were endless, and as I explored its banks, I was
subconsciously discovering what it was like to be a young boy
alive in a perfect world, in a perfect time, in a perfect town. I
experienced the joy unencumbered by introspection. It would be
years before I came to that profound revelation, after many years
of reflection, on the importance in my life of that relatively small
plot of ground that stretches behind downtown New City.

My father had grown up and lived here and my grandfather
and great-grandfather and great-great-grandfather, five generations in all. They had all waded barefoot in The Demarest Kill on
a summer day in our perfect Elysian Fields, beginning almost a
century before I was born.

The family homestead still stands on the top of the New Hempstead Hill, overlooking the new Court House and the Highway
Department. At one time the land was all owned by my ancestors;
including the portion of the Demarest Kill that runs behind the
Courthouse. When it was my turn to roam and stake claim to the

territory, on property no longer in the family, our stream-wading adventures always ended in the Dutch Garden.

It's hard to see that little town I grew up in anymore. It's dissolving like a long-ago memory that you try to reach out and grasp as it slips away into the mists of fading memory. The crowd rushes past you in the opposite direction, jostling you, as you stand on tiptoes looking backwards, trying to keep the memories in sight. But before long, they have pushed you downstream and around the bend and you can no longer see where you came from, no matter how you struggle. Eventually, you give up trying and let yourself go with the momentum of the water. It's easier that way, and a lot less exhausting than wading against the current; walking your way back upstream toward a place that no longer exists.

It's especially hard to see that little bygone town when you see what I see on a regular basis. Even harder still when you make a life-long, conscious effort to forget that happy childhood. Happy memories only make you soft and vulnerable. I will testify to that, Your Honor.

So it was with great interest that I heard that a body had been found face down in the Demarest Kill right behind my office building that first morning.

Someone had desecrated my childhood playground with some evil, vile act, and I was taking it very personally. I had been called on my cell phone while walking to work that morning at 7:30. It was now just a few minutes before eight o'clock.

As I walked from the tea house toward the pergola that led to the gazebo, I ducked under the crime scene tape, and skirted the brick wall, stooping to pick up a remembrance from the past. Where the walls had crumbled, a piece of brick, the size of a child's building block was covered with mortar, from where an artisan disguised as a mason had stacked it against an adjoining brick sixty-five years earlier. Absentmindedly, I put the fragmented relic, a souvenir of my past, in my jacket pocket, and walked south to the gazebo.

The dead body first appeared to be that of a young woman, a teenager, perhaps. It first seemed she had been killed in the gazebo, forty feet up above in the Dutch Garden, and then rolled down the embankment, where the body had come to rest at the water's edge, half in, half out of the Demarest Kill. A depression in the newly fallen red and gold leaves could be seen where the lifeless form had tumbled down the hillside, kicking up twigs and mud, picking up sheer, dead-weight momentum, as it skidded and somersaulted down into the stream bed.

When I arrived, several minutes later than the others on the crime scene task force, they were still taking pictures of the body as it had been found, forty feet below me down the embankment. The usual team was there. Ron Faber, from Clarkstown Police Department's road patrol had been just about to end his graveyard shift. Ron was the first on the scene after the call came in from a jogger. Two homicide guys I had known for years were diligently taking notes and walking the nearby ground, inspecting it for any minutiae of evidence. David Sherman and Ray Cicci were originally from NYPD homicide who had taken an early retirement, left the City for good, and moved upstate to work with the local department. Another ten years and they would be double-dipping in the State's retirement fund.

Dr. James Capobianco represented the Medical Examiner's office. Jimmy and I had gone all through school together ever since his family had moved here in the first wave of "City people." We were "Townies." Like many of those kids who shared my childhood, we were almost like brothers. We both may have had closer friends growing up, but we were among those who had never permanently moved out of town, and now we were all like many an extended family. Maybe we didn't see each other on a regular basis, but when we did we could pick up a two year-old conversation as if it had been a moment ago. Even those who remained behind but didn't want to be a part of that family could hardly escape that reality.

Every once in a while I would bump into a classmate from high school that I hadn't seen in years. Unlike those who had moved away "temporarily" to go to college and then had never come back home, we were all just kind of "around" all the time. I had moved away for over four years to attend college in Florida, and to do a hitch in the Army and some traveling, but I had eventually moved back and never left home again.

With the new guys, we had built new friendships. Ray, David, Jimmy; we all knew one another from years in the law enforcement trenches together. We trusted and respected one another's judgment. Most of the time it was the endless drone of petty crimes. Once in a great while, a homicide. Not that New City, or Clarkstown, or even Rockland County had that many homicides over the years, but the ones we did have, we had worked on together; a bank robbery, suspicious suicides, the Brink's robbery in 1981. Mostly domestic violence stuff, and the last few years, crack-related murders, and what we called "stupid murders."

Now, I stood in the hexagonal gazebo staring down at the crime scene forty feet below, unlike any other murder scene I had ever been on before, unprepared for what we were about to discover.

Part of the brick latticework from above had tumbled down into the stream where it now lay, untouched. I followed the footpath north as it sloped gently away from the victim's fall, zigzagging my way down the hillside switchbacks. It had rained for two days before. Then, this morning the skies had cleared but the enormous tree trunks were slick black from the rain and I could almost feel their coolness on my cheeks as I passed each one. These trees, too, were old friends.

As I approached the small group on the investigative team that surrounded the body and obscured it from my view, they barely lifted their heads to nod and acknowledge my arrival. I was usually there just for back-up, or follow-through for the District Attorney's Office. Making sure that all the "i's" were dotted and the "t's" were crossed so we could build a strong case without any loopholes some smart-ass defense attorney could walk through later on.

We all stood there, our badges hanging on leather wallets draped from the kerchief pockets of our suit jackets.

"What have we got, guys?"

David was the first to answer. He stood, then looked down at what had once obviously been the statuesque shape of a vibrant young woman but was now contorted and twisted from the roll down the hillside through the leaves and mud. While Ray snapped the crime scene photos David circled the body as he spoke.

"Not to belabor the obvious, but nude white female, age undetermined, although from this viewpoint, I'd say late twenties, early thirties." He was looking at the shapeliness of the body, now devoid of any sexuality in its current state. With these guys there was none of the crude jokes or gallows humor that you often hear about and that I have seen for myself when in Manhattan while shadowing homicide detectives there. The television shows love that kind of snappy repartee. My guys were professional.

Jimmy picked it up. "Cause of death: Too soon to tell. I can't see any gunshot wounds. We'll take a closer look at her skull when we get her on the table, get her hair out of the way. From the looks of things, I'd say she was tossed or shoved off the gazebo up there," gesturing to the brick structure up and over his shoulder without turning around. Here, he paused to look at his watch. "Probably sometime after dark last night. Her neck looks snapped. Probably from the fall, I'd guess at this time, but it's conceivable that it could have been broken somewhere else by whomever."

I had to ask the stupid question. It was all part of the job to play devil's advocate. "No chance of an accidental fall…." I looked up to the gazebo, never really looking closely at the mud and leaf-covered body.

"Think about it. Naked in the Dutch Garden after dark, this time of year? Prancing around in the gazebo? Lost her balance and rolled down the embankment snapping her neck? A remote possibility, I suppose, you know, lovers' quarrel after a quickie? More likely, she was pushed. My initial hypothesis? Killed somewhere else and just dumped over the edge here. We still have to go over the gazebo a lot more closely."

Ray looked around. "If she was killed here, whoever did it took her clothes from the body at some point before she rolled down the hill. See all those mud smears on her shoulders and buttocks that would have been otherwise covered? And then they took those clothes when they left. There's nothing up there."

I looked up again to the hexagonal brick building. I had spent hours playing in that shelter, the Summer House, smoked my first cigarette there at the age of ten with a bunch of the other neighborhood boys. These bricks were a part of my history.

Jimmy seemed to be reading my mind. "Less than two hundred feet from the Courthouse parking lot. Was she led here? Cajoled? Seduced? Forced to her death scene above? Or was she already a dead body carried from the parking lot? We won't be able to tell until we get her back to the morgue and do some work and take a closer look around up above."

He stopped, as if trying to prolong the next inevitable step. "Well, let's look at her face. You wanna help turn her over?"

We all glanced around instinctively. We were alone, no members of the press had shown up yet. The only sound was the slight breeze moving through the leaves and the familiar gurgling pitch of The Demarest Kill. The small group circled around the body where it lay twisted, wedged among the rocks in the stream bed. I put on rubber gloves like the others had already done. My ears were filled with the sound of the water rushing over the rocks, as it had done for thousands of years since the glaciers retreated. The bubbling effervescence, affected only temporarily by summer rainstorms and springtime snow-melt, had not really changed since my childhood. It was like listening to an old familiar song. The notes remained the same. The tempo changed with the seasons.

The victim's dark hair on the back of her head was muddy and matted from the stream bank. Her pale skin was smeared with grime and debris from her roll down the hill. What had once obviously been an attractive woman had now been reduced to just a slab of muck-covered meat. Like other such crime scenes, my partners and I went about our duties objectively, trying to overlook the dull routine of it all, despite the fact that we knew just hours ago, this had been a live human being, living who-knew-what kind of lifestyle? Seeing so much of this, you become hardened, immune to the indignity of it all. After a while you learn to cut off your emotions. You have to for your own self-defense. You feel sorry for the victim to a point. Glad that it's not you, or anyone you know for that matter. You put away the subjectivity and try to remain focused on who did this, and why, and try to forget the sickening ache beginning to build up in your stomach.

A slight breeze blew overhead, and I could really smell autumn for the first time that year. It's a fresh smell, filled with wet earth and crisp leaves and moss and wood smoke and cooled just to the right temperature by arctic currents coming in from Canada. Like a shot of smelling salts, the fall is a slap in the face to the memory sector of your brain and its pungency pulls out all the files of wading through leaves along Maple Avenue to get to New City Grammar School, or raking backyard leaves into a pile and kneeling to light a smoldering fire, or listening to Doc Carney's post-touchdown trumpet solos during the home football games of the Clarkstown Rams, or parking on "The Hill" on Low Tor with a girlfriend and watching the sun disappear over the Ramapo foothills.

Fall in New City has a visceral quality about it that cannot be explained. It's part of what eventually drew me back home just a few years after my college career ended abruptly down south.

There were, through the years, other, better career opportunities for me elsewhere, but none offered an autumn in New City, to be able to walk my woodsy domain, drive the serpentine South Mountain Road, or climb High Tor on a perfect fall day to look down on my town to behold all before me. If it weren't for the dead body at my feet, that very day I might have even played hooky from work to make the climb up High Tor that had become an autumn pilgrimage for me.

Above us, the squirrels, fattening up for the winter ahead, seemed to gather in the amphitheater of tree branches above to watch. I half-knelt and touched the woman's near elbow. Rigor mortis prevented us from easily turning over the body, and when we did, it was in some grim imitation of a stiff play-doll, a mannequin. Her elbows and knees and shoulders were locked in right angles. We flipped her over and Jimmy reached down and brushed the mud-caked hair that had covered the woman's face.

He made the sign of the cross. "Jesus Christ… Jesus Christ… Jesus Christ." Later, when thinking back on that moment I realized what Jimmy had expressed was not an expletive. It was a prayer, an anguished plea for mercy uttered in complete desperation. With an ashen, sickened look on his face, Jimmy turned and stared at me.

I looked at the woman's face and muttered. "Fifty-four." It was the only thing I could manage to say. The air had been sucked out of my lungs.

David turned to me, confused. "What?"

Jimmy and I exchanged looks once again.

"She's not in her 'late twenties, early thirties'. She's fifty-four." The words seemed to get caught in my throat.

"How in the hell can you tell that by just looking at her?" But I think he realized what my answer would be even before he finished his question.

By that time, I had stood and was walking away from them, taking a few paces upstream, staring off into the brilliant reds and yellows that were being blindingly lit by the morning sun. I was trying to catch my breath, retain my composure. I was losing the battle very quickly.

Jimmy answered for me, looking at my back for a reaction to what we had just discovered. He knew our history. He turned to David and Ray. "We all came up through school together. Her name is Beth VonBronk. She's married to Rainer Klein."

It was a name they all recognized as the locally-based developer of internationally-known shopping malls.

In my almost twenty-five year career with this office, I prided myself on never once having done anything in public even close to what could ever be construed by a peer as "unprofessional." But now, at that moment, that record seemed unimportant. I had segued from a part of the law enforcement team to a bereaved onlooker. I turned back to her body and collapsed to my knees in the stream bed. I lifted her head in my hands as I had done so many times before and in some futile attempt to restore some dignity to her face, swept the wisps of hair from where the mud had pasted them to her forehead. But suddenly seized with grief, my shoulders shook with uncontrollable sobs. Over forty years' worth of memories scrambled to take first place.

Jimmy slipped on the rocks, almost tumbled in his already soggy Florsheims, then regained his balance as he stepped to put his arms on my shoulder. "Ah, Jesus Christ. Will....Will? I'm sorry Will." David and Ray stood before me, confused by the scene, wondering what to do. I knew what they had immediately surmised. It was a cop's worst nightmare: coming upon a murder scene or an accident scene only to discover the victim is a member of your family, one of your own, perhaps from a circle of friends.

But then, before anyone could answer, Ray turned toward the parking lot behind the Courthouse Annex. "Ah shit. Here comes the vultures. Ron, finish up that crime-scene tape around the perimeter. A wide perimeter, wider than usual. Include the bridge and the tea house. When they find out who this is, all hell's going to break loose and we don't want any stampeding herds. Close off the entrance to the Garden as well. Get on the radio and get some help over here, right now."

A television reporter and a videographer were making their way slowly upstream from the Courthouse bridge, trying not to get their feet muddy. The woman was in high heels, dressed to cover an inaugural ball not a murder in a stream bed. She and her camera guy carefully made their way through the poison ivy and over the slippery rocks on the stream's edge. Ray yelled downstream and blocked their view with his outstretched arms. "Hey, this is a crime scene. You wanna keep your distance here. We'll come to you. Just hold it right there. Get back behind the bridge."

"Come on, Will, let's take a walk." Jimmy lifted me from my elbow, but not before my fingertips lingered on the dead woman's cheek and mouth as I touched her lips one final time. As I tried to regain my balance, I fell forward in the water, bracing my fall, wet to the elbows. I clutched the stream bed, grasping for balance, my hand clasped around a flat rock the size of a matchbox. Without thinking, or perhaps because of my emotional state, I picked up the flat stone and squeezed it in my palm as I stood to walk with Jimmy.

"Come on, Will. They'll be here in a second. We gotta get you out of here. They can't see you like this."

With our backs to the reporters, Jimmy led me upstream to begin the charade of looking for evidence, while David and Ray kept the press at bay. Within twenty feet we had passed from view behind a stand of yellow leaves from a low maple branch.

Another few feet and we were almost out of earshot. "Jesus, Will. Who would've believed it?"

I was fighting to pull myself together, to get a public face on, in the eventuality that the others would follow us down the path. A hundred feet away we could still hear David and Ray being cops, raising their voices, warning the interlopers not to enter the crime scene area, waving them back to where Ron was draping a plastic yellow tape to block their path.

"Back up! Back up! You're in a crime scene," I could hear him insisting, all politeness now out of his voice. "I'm not gonna say it again."

Leaning on the tree for support, the flat rock from the stream bed creasing my clenched palm, I looked up at the brilliant blue sky beyond the red and yellow autumn canopy and tried to get Beth's face out of my mind. A face once filled with such youthful exuberance and happiness and hope. Now, a face covered with muck and dead leaves and the detritus of a recent storm. I snorted in a few breaths of air in an attempt to catch my breath.

"Will, I'm so…..sorry. I don't know what to say." Jimmy searched for his words. "Are you gonna be okay?"

"I don't think so."

"When…..when was the last time you saw her?"

His abrupt shifting of gears from condolence to investigation stunned me, and he saw it on my face and he regretted his question immediately. I thought back over the years; the days of daily life with Beth; later, the emptiness when she married and moved away. In the ensuing years, my life had been miserable without her. I strained to answer his question.

"It's been awhile. Bumped into her in town. Almost a year ago. Right around Christmas time. I was having lunch at Tor's." I mentioned an old luncheonette across the broad front lawn of the courthouse. The lunch counter had been there for decades but it hadn't been called "Tor's" for years. Only an old timer would know what I was talking about.

Jimmy's eyes explored my tear-stained face.

In fact, I had seen her a year ago this up-coming Christmas at the lunch counter in the Fagen Building, just across the street from the Courthouse. As I stepped up to the cashier to pay my bill for lunch, she was there beside me, paying for a greeting card. In recent years, when we had coincidentally bumped into one another in public, her attitude had always been the same: fake-friendly, as if greeting an acquaintance instead of someone she had known since fifth grade, a man she had once loved and lived with, shared intimacies with. Let's not get into any meaningful conversation, her attitude had always implied. Keep it light, a slight air of annoyance in her voice, mixed with condescension and dismissal. That, and a sense of superiority, pity, maybe even contempt, (or was it fear?), knowing that she was speaking to someone who had loved her far more than she had ever loved him, and who couldn't seem to let it go and move on with his life. She had smiled and suddenly remembered a pressing engagement as she received her change from the cashier.

"Love to stop and talk, but you know, the holidays."

Then she was gone. I was still shaking by the time I had walked back to my office that day. The encounter had made me feel like a stalker.

"Jesus Christ, Will. I'm so sorry." Jimmy was one of the few people in town who still would have even known that her death would make such a difference to me. Family ties do that.

We stood in silence for a moment while I regained my composure, Jimmy standing guard at the bend in the path. I took a few steps and gazed above to where the trail disappeared behind a slight grade and into the autumn cover. He finally stepped alongside me and we both looked southwest toward the rise in the distance. We were far enough away from the crime scene now, so that the only sounds we heard were the scraping of the crisp leaves above in a gentle wind and the rushing of water over rocks in the stream bed. Like a brother who is too close, he seemed to read my mind as I stood staring ahead upstream. The path disappeared up a slope and curved off to the left. We both held our gaze in that direction, trying to piece it all together individually. We stood that way in silence for a full two minutes before he spoke. His glance up the path, and his conclusions, had apparently matched mine; two men facing southwest.

"You can't go up there, you know."

His statement didn't surprise me, really. It was so obvious we were both thinking the same thing. What else would I be thinking about, standing there, staring off up that specific path along that particular stream bed? Still, it took me a moment to answer.

"I'm going."

"Will, wait until Ray and Dave can go with you. If Tom's got anything to do with this, you could blow this case."

"I want to talk to him."

"Will, it could cost you your job. He's eventually going to have to talk to all of us, so why don't you just wait?"

"I know it could. I just want to talk to him."

"I guess David will have to track down her husband and tell him, too. That is if he doesn't already know." Jim's statement was loaded. "Did her husband know that you and Beth had been.... friends...over the years?" He was trying to be delicate.

"Sure. No secret. No problem. We were just kids then. It was a long time ago."

"Over thirty years now?"

"Thirty-two years. It was a long time ago," I repeated.

"It was only yesterday, Will."

"Yeah, Jimmy. I know. *Only yesterday.*"

"Right." He nodded, put a comforting hand on my shoulder, then turned to leave. He had only taken a few steps before he turned back to me. "You don't want to lose your job over this. You go up there and that's what will happen. I'll try to buy you some time. I'm really sorry, Will. Beth was such a beautiful soul, so, I don't know, *spiritual.* I know how you felt about her."

"Thanks, Jimmy."

He reached out to give the perfunctory hug, then turned and walked back toward the crime scene, to Beth's dead body.

It was a simple, two hundred yard walk up that grade and around the bend, following closely along the stream bed. A simple walk. Yet I couldn't seem to take the first step. I was frozen in that spot, unable, or unwilling to head away from where Beth's body lay. To walk upstream on the Demarest Kill that morning, I knew I would be forced, against my will, to take a journey into my past and face things that should have been long-forgotten. It was a journey I had resisted taking, struggled so hard for a long time not to have to take, and now I was presented with a very harsh reality. I knew I was risking serious reprimand, if not dismissal, for what I was about to do, but I had no choice. I had to talk to Tom. It was either that or stay behind as Beth's body was lifted from the water and taken to the morgue. I couldn't bear to watch that.

Sometimes facing the past is the hardest thing you ever have to do. It forces you to confront mistakes; forces you to re-examine and second-guess missed opportunities; admit your priorities may have been wrong, and accept that maybe you could have not wasted your life as you have. Worst of all, the best, happiest memories of the past only underscore what a failure you have become, of all the unfulfilled, unkept promises you made to yourself.

With the small, flat stone in my hand that I had pulled from the stream bed underneath where Beth last lay, I walked away from the Dutch Garden, away from the lifeless form of Beth Von-Bronk, following the Demarest Kill upstream toward the bend in the path that disappeared into the trees, back to the boathouse and back in time thirty-two years to find Tom Hogenkamp.

I looked behind me. The stream rushed away from me as if toward the future, while I hiked back into the past.

AUTHOR'S NOTE: While reading CHAPTER TWO, I would recommend going to GOOGLE MAPS and inputting "New City, New York." Zoom into the map until Lake DeForest Reservoir fills up the right side of the screen. Click the plus sign(+) twice more, and you will see Demarest Kill County Park, the Demarest Kill flowing northward.**

CHAPTER TWO

THE DEMAREST KILL

The Demarest Kill begins in a trickle of springs bubbling up from the earth over near New Valley Road, half way to Nanuet, and winds its way northward through what was for many years, the rolling pastures and fields of Native American, then Dutch, then German, and then Norwegian farmland. As it passes along, it is remarkable for going unnoticed for so long. It's not until it approaches the outskirts of New City that it begins to take on historical significance. At least for me. Maybe farther upstream, another little boy had once played on its banks and dreamed of floating downstream to an unknown future. The narrow brook flows unhurriedly, pausing from time to time in its journey, to spread out and rest in a wide pond formation, as if to provide some boy a new, hidden place among the willows to swim or ice skate or fish or skip stones on a late, May day.

Near Middletown Road the Demarest Kill passes through a wide marshy area. Back in the 1930s Dr. Davies dammed it up, brought in a few truckloads of sand and a diving board and called it Davies' Lake. It was a favorite teen-age hangout all during the War and into the early 1960s. Open from Memorial Day until Labor Day Weekend, hundreds of kids would go there to swim and lie on the narrow sandy beach. Occasionally, a few of the boys would nonchalantly wander off toward the bath house and peer through one of several strategically placed holes drilled through the thin plywood wall that separated the men's and women's dressing rooms.

Several phenomena brought about the eventual demise of Davies' Lake. The polio scare during the 1950s and the arrival every summer day of busloads of "City people." Local people stopped going, convinced that the polio virus was being transported into our town from New York City on a Red and Tan bus. Davie's Lake disappeared in the early 1960's, was filled in, and lay dormant, awaiting sale for residential property. Now, kids ride their bikes on a street located where I learned how to swim; where I learned the secrets and mysteries of a woman's body while sharing a peephole with a line of other eleven year-old boys.

But the stream still meanders its way northward behind Cropsey's Farm, under Middletown Road and into New City Park. There, a colony of Norwegians founded the New City Park Lake Association in the 1920s at the site where farmers had dammed up a low-lying marsh earlier with a sluice-way for a mill wheel. The mill house and narrow channel are still there for those who know what to look for. What catches the eye now is the waterfall next to where the diving board used to be. Those same Norwegian families dominated ownership and control of the lake through the early 1960s when I was a lifeguard there for a few summers. With lake access restricted to homeowners in New City Park, the membership kept strict control over who and who could not swim in the lake or even ice skate in the winter when it froze over.

For years before I became a lifeguard, I was always there as a guest of one of the members and my summer days were filled with the sounds of rock and roll music from a half-dozen AM transistor radios tuned to Big Dan Ingram on WABC giving the weather report as "Peter the Meter Reader and his wife, Fat Pontoon, and her weather balloon"; the *thwuppp*-bounce of a child on the diving board, and the roar of the water passing over the dam. Nighttimes, before we were all old enough to drive, New City Park Lake was the scene of many a make-out session on the picnic tables under the pines and in the shadows of the clubhouse.

After it spills over the dam, the stream cuts through the rocky hillsides and glens on its way northward to downtown New City. Running parallel to what is now known as Little Tor Road, it flows through the backyards of a dozen or so homes before it enters the old, original Florion Estate.

The Florion Estate, as I remembered it growing up, was ten acres of rolling farmland. The majestic white house had been given the name "Dove Cottage," after Wordsworth's hideaway in England's Lake Country; a place of solace. The house itself stood on a bluff overlooking pastures, as my own ancestral homestead did farther to the north. The top soil here, although rich and deep, is littered with almost solid rock, providing an endless supply of building material that became available, as the early settlers cleared the land and planted their crops.

The open fields are bordered by stone walls assembled by farmers in the years leading up to the Revolutionary War, and later repaired by Civil War soldiers returning home to New England after that war, soldiers desperately looking for work as they passed through the area. Some of the early homes and out-buildings are also built from the readily available stones.

Dove Cottage, as the Florion Estate house was known, is of faux English Country Manor Design. Florion was an impresario and orchestra conductor who married his lead singer and later started a popular radio show. Florion had built it in the early 20th century with old family money and radio money. At the bottom of the hillside on which it stood, before the open pasture takes over, three acres were filled with rows of Concord grapes, and MacIntosh, crab apple, and pear trees.

On the southwest corner of the estate, as The Demarest Kill flows north toward Dove Cottage, it arcs northeast at the base of the hill. It then circles behind the hill through a canyon wall on the west side that rises up to the back yards of the homes built across the top of the ridge line when Florion sold off part of the estate in the late 1950s. A fifty-foot sheer drop awaited those who strayed too far beyond those back yards. Now, it acts as a wall, blocking the sun as it makes its daily trip westward. The stream rolls on behind the mansion through deep woods, feeding its way through the footprints of several now-empty millponds, before it snakes its way due north again.

Bordering the Florion property on the southeast was one of many smaller tributaries that would eventually join together with the Kill and flow through the Dutch Gardens. On the east bank of that small tributary, my grandfather had built a small farm for himself, where he labored when he wasn't working as a mailman or handyman at Dove Cottage. It was on his small farm, which straddled the narrow tributary and ran east to South Main Street, where he and my grandmother had built a home. Later, when my parents were married, they lived in the house with my grandparents and it is where my brother, Francis, and I were raised.

On the back of the hill behind Dove Cottage, in a small valley, the Kill converges with a series of other, smaller, streams to form one larger stream. At that junction, farmers in the late 1700s had dammed up those streams and formed tiers of cascading millponds, designed to power stone-mills created to grind their grain and corn. Very little of their workmanship remains behind, save a few crumbling dam walls covered in vines.

The most widely known millpond is the only present day survivor. It is situated behind the County Sheriff's Office off

New Hempstead Road. When I was growing up it was known as Greenberg's Pond for the man who owned the estate house on the property. The pond was filled with pickerel, perch, trout, and bass, and was patrolled by a guard named Jim, armed with a shotgun and accompanied by a great German Shepherd. The Greenberg's Pond mill dam still remains, with the spillway emptying to the south and then circling to the east to join the northbound Demarest Kill.

Near where that stream convergence occurs is the site of the original, second mill pond, Simmonds' Pond, now long gone and grown up with thick sugar maples and oak trees.

If you were to look carefully, you can still see the remains of the dam of that second pond. Now it's just a stack of tumbled boulders, similar in appearance to a stone wall, but larger in scale.

On the south hillside, once the shoreline of Simmonds' Pond directly behind the rear of Dove Cottage, and separated by one hundred yards of deep woods, there is a two-story boathouse, another vestige that remains to offer evidence of a larger body of water that is no longer there. Made of indigenous stone and with a slate tile roof, the boathouse juts out from the hillside facing the Demarest Kill stream bed and what was once the large pond formed when the dam was created. The boathouse architecture is what I call Bear Mountain CCC, because it reminds me of the stone buildings constructed along Seven Lakes Drive in Harriman State Park by the Civilian Conservation Corps in the closing days of the Depression, on the eve of World War II.

With a sloping roof and a deck on all sides, a boathouse is an unusual sight to come upon in the middle of a woods where there is no longer a pond. It's the opposite effect of swimming to the bottom of the man-made reservoir up in Doodletown to find the remains of an abandoned town submerged, when the Lake Welch reservoir was dammed up.

Here, on the Demarest Kill, the pond is gone, the water has dried up to a stream bed. A boathouse now hangs over a hillside, literally left high-and-dry, where the millpond shore once was.

Farther north along the stream bed, the newly revived Kill converges with yet another tributary. The stream that flowed past my family's back yard, expands into Damiani's Pond, and flows over yet another area spillway until it meets up with the Kill, just a few yards south of where it passes beneath the brick walls of the Dutch Garden and the gazebo.

It was there, in that verdant triangle of woods bordered by ponds and brooks and streams and tributaries, that I spent almost every daylight hour, summer or winter, of my young boyhood. Between Kindergarten release at midday and dusk, I would wander. All through my New City Grammar School years until the start of high school, I was lord of my domain. It was then that I came to love those rocky hillsides and stately trees and rolling pastures.

It was there, in those impressionable years that mold a young man into the person he will become, that I formed the childhood bonds with my fellow explorers, sneaking onto Greenberg's Pond for swimming or fishing or ice-skating in winter, wading through the streams and springs in search of crawdads, exploring the woods and generally living the life of an adventurer. Here in this dark canopy where no parents trod, we were true woodsmen: Davy Crockett, Daniel Boone, Natty Bumppo, Lewis and Clark. I cannot count the life lessons I learned there.

We were exceptionally lucky in that the owner of the Florion Estate had a grandson who was our age. His name was Tom Hogenkamp, and he was my first and last best friend. We were inseparable from the age of ten until the end of our college years when our paths inevitably diverged, a demise in a friendship that was caused, at least partially, by the same war that pulled our very country irreparably asunder.

But until then, his friendship provided us free access to the pastures and vineyard and orchards that belonged to his grandfather. There, we climbed the apple trees and stuffed our shirts, pants, and stomachs with Concord Grapes and pears and MacIntosh apples. We yanked up the raw rhubarb from the garden, rubbed the dirt off on our shirts, chomped down on the celery-like stalks, our faces screwing up from the sour taste. We flew our kites, and later our remote controlled model airplanes in the open pastures of Dove Cottage belonging to Tom's grandfather.

Playing behind Dove Cottage, we skirted the small, one-headstone cemetery that holds the remains of a prisoner from the New City jail, a victim of the influenza epidemic of 1918. And beyond that, approaching The Demarest Kill near the bottom of the hill, was the stone boathouse we used as a playhouse, left abandoned, standing on a dried-up shore of a phantom millpond.

When the pond forever emptied with the collapse of the dam after a week of torrential rains in the 1920s, Tom's grandfather had enclosed the bottom entryway and boat slip and made it into a downstairs area. The large upstairs area, with its wooden floors, stone walls and exposed beam ceiling, was a gigantic playhouse for us all.

During hot summer nights, the kids in our group would sleep within the screen window enclosure, tell ghost stories and listen to the night sounds around us; listen to the peepers and the locust; listen to the rush of the Demarest Kill.

I have since traveled all over the world, but the sound of the peepers and the exact pitch of the rippling of the Demarest Kill, are sounds I can summon from memory at any time.

CHAPTER THREE

THE BOATHOUSE

Monday, 9 a.m.
October 16, 2000
Age 54

I hadn't been to that boathouse in over thirty years. But like it or not, my forced journey back in time was beckoning me to its threshold.

The boathouse could, of course, be reached by parking along Little Tor Road and walking in through the woods from the west. Or for that matter, driving right up to Dove Cottage near Muller Court and parking in the driveway at the crest of the hill next to the mansion, and walking down the path on the far, rear slope. But since I was already along the Kill path, I decided to take the most scenic route.

Looking down, the path was now partially obscured as if no other town boy had bothered to follow in my footsteps in the ensuing years. My feet followed a memory of their own, retracing old steps they hadn't trod in so many years. It was all familiar to me still. Although my town had changed so drastically in the past forty years, my Demarest Kill, it seemed, had not changed at all. Overgrown perhaps, with tree branches stinging at my eyes, but it was still the same in most respects. A chipmunk, cheeks stuffed with winter forage, watched me pass. Had I seen his ancestors in my childhood? My feet seemed familiar with the terrain, memorized from thousands of treks in my boyhood. I could have closed my eyes and made it to the boathouse, my feet never once stumbling over an exposed rock or root in the pathway.

I glanced up to see the remains of an abandoned tree platform. A deer blind, perhaps? One day up there, while in the second grade, my brother and I watched silently as a fawn walked slowly beneath us, unaware of our presence. We always referred to it as, "The Last Deer in Downtown New City," although the deer population would continue to flourish all over Rockland for many years. The skeletal remains of the platform hung from the tree like an icon of my childhood. What boy had put it up there? Was it from the 1920s? 1930s? 1940s? Perhaps even my own father had built it during his childhood in these woods.

Looking down as the muddy path veered to the southwest, I saw the first of the footprints. I knelt to examine them more closely, being careful not to have mine conjoin, and glanced back over my shoulder to estimate the distance to the crime scene. Two hundred yards?

No Indian scout here, but they looked fresh, like the impressions of jogging shoes heading *toward* the crime scene at a brisk clip. Then, a little farther west, closer to the boathouse, similar imprints heading *away* from the scene, but this time walking at a normal pace. It had rained the night before, bringing the cooler air. These footprints had been made since midnight. I would have to send a crime scene crew to take impressions before it rained again, although that was not in the forecast any time soon, from the look of the deep blue sky above.

Keeping my head down toward the imprints I walked onward reluctantly, toward my destination, and back into my past. Snatches of earlier days kept floating through my memory. It's like catching the distant sound of music playing, tilting your head to try to recognize the melody, attuning your ears, until finally, a familiar phrase reaches you, and your hearing seems to become more acute. The farther upstream I went, the closer to the source of my memories I came. It was an unfamiliar, unwanted feeling, and I fought to shake it off. I didn't want to relive the memories. The deeper into the woods I hiked, the deeper into my past I descended, until, without realizing it at first, I really was hearing music. Like trying to recognize the tune, I stopped, tilted my head and listened closer. It was the sound of piano music, faintly at first, then the closer I got to the boathouse, the louder it became. I recognized it instantly, to my own disbelief. A surprise, but really no surprise at all. A Chopin Nocturne: *Opus32, #2 in A-Flat Major.* How would I recognize that so easily, you might wonder?

I stayed there, listening, overwhelmed by the events of the last hour. The last twenty-four hours. The last thirty-two years.

How could I have done what I did to Beth? Suddenly, it was more than I could bear and I sank to my knees again, sobbing, reaching out to the familiar roots that crossed my pathway; grasping onto the trunk of a tree in an embrace to catch my fall.

"My God, my God. What have I done? What have I done?"

Standing, I staggered. Was I staggering backward or forward?

I was thrust into a movie about my own life and I was hearing the soundtrack refrain, signaling a scene change to a flashback. Such an odd sensation, almost surreal, yet there it was. But then, when I was fewer than two hundred feet from the boathouse deck, the music stopped abruptly in mid-phrase. Had Tom heard me coming? Sensed it somehow?

Overhead was the caw-caw of crows, and a jetstream line across the blue sky. No traffic could be heard as my town came awake behind me.

When I turned the final bend, it was as if I had taken a step back in time. The boathouse looked exactly the same as it had that last eventful, fateful day I had seen it during the autumn of 1968. Not one stone, not one splinter of wood appeared to have changed. The only thing I did not recognize at first was the man sitting on the bottom step of the deck that surrounded the second story. His eyes were fixed on me as I approached and it was his eyes that gave him away. It was Tom. Be a best friend with someone for twelve years, then not see him for thirty-two years creates a certain dichotomy. Like me, he was fifty-four. Had I aged so dramatically? The hair was thinner and beginning to gray, his face had aged, there were lines, wrinkles, like mine, I'm sure, but his eyes were the same. But they were also red, like he had been crying. Like I had been crying, but for a different reason.

At the bottom hem of his jogging shorts, extending down to just above his left knee, was deep scarring.

"They sent you? Irony isn't dead, after all."

"What do you mean?"

"You're here to ask questions about Beth. I didn't expect a social call after thirty-two years."

"How do you know about Beth?"

"Who do you think called it in? I found her this morning on my run."

That explained the jogging shoes' footprints.

"I'm not allowed to talk to you about that."

"What do you mean?"

"Someone from homicide will be here to question you. I won't be able to work this case. Conflict of interest."

"So what are you doing here?"

"I wanted to see how you were doing."

"We live in the same town, and after thirty-two years you decide to drop in and pay a social call. Am I correct so far?"

"I've wanted to before. It's just that it always seemed so... awkward."

I stepped forward to shake his hand. "How are you?" He ignored my gesture.

"If this is not official business, I would like you to leave my property."

"Tom, I...."

"Aren't you going to read me my rights first?"

"Tom....."

"I am a suspect, right?"

"It's way too early for anything like that.....Tom..."

"So now that Beth is dead you decided to come see your old pal, Tom, to see what he knows about what happened."

"Tom, that's not it at all..."

"I don't know anything about it. I didn't kill her, if that's what you want to know. I had nothing to do with it. I was jogging and I found her body and I called the police with my cell phone to tell them there was a dead body in the Demarest Kill. I talked to them briefly at the scene and then walked back here to wait for them to come and question me some more. But I'm telling you again, I didn't kill her."

"When was the last time you saw her?"

"Are you asking for personal reasons or as part of the investigation?"

"I'm not going to be allowed to ask you any questions regarding the investigation."

"So does that mean you're not going to read me my rights? I didn't kill her. I want you to leave this property right now or I'm going to call the police." He pulled a cell phone from the hip pocket of his jogging shorts and held it aloft.

As if by telepathy my own cell phone rang. It was Ray. He was furious.

"What are you doing?"

"I just came to see him. He's an old friend. I didn't know he was the one who found her."

Ray's anger grew. "Do you realize your presence there with him could jeopardize this entire investigation? You have to leave there immediately. You haven't said anything to him have you?"

"No. I just wanted to talk to him."

"Hang up and leave there now. Don't screw this up on us, Will. You know the drill."

"I'm leaving now."

"Do you know what kind of car Beth drove?"

"I have no idea, why?"

"Hang up and leave. Now, Will."

I hung up and looked to Tom.

"You lied to him," was all Tom said.

"What do you mean?"

"You said we were old friends."

I left him sitting there.

CHAPTER FOUR

COMING HOME

Monday, 10 a.m.
October 16, 2000
Age 54

Autumn is my favorite time of year. It always has been. The air is so clean, the skies so glorious. The brilliant colors, the smell of the wet ground and the burning leaves. A crispness in the air that chills your skin and tingles your nose. It has always been a time of exhilaration. But it has also always been a time of such great sorrow for me. It's something I cannot explain. It seems as if the earth is trying to tell us something, that it is tired out, worn down, and wants to rest, like a frail old woman after a lifetime of toil.

If anything, for me, June, not November, should be a time of sorrow. Not like other boys, who await the warm spring days of June with anticipation of the summer days to follow. Yes, it is the arrival of June that brings a deeper sadness for me because of what happened to my brother Francis one beautiful June afternoon. That one June day, just a few days after school let out for the summer after the fourth grade, will always be "Francis' Day" for me.

My brother Francis and I were born two years apart; Francis in the closing days of WWII in 1944, and I in 1946, the first of the baby-boomers.

As we grew up, Rockland County and New City were just coming alive in the post-War growth that was taking place in the country. Our parents, children of the Depression, had fought the good fight and won WW II. By 1945-1946, they were home and wanted to start families and enjoy the good times. Life was indeed good, even living on the modest salary of a mail carrier. Within just a few years The New York State Thruway and the Palisades Interstate Parkway bisected Rockland County, and provided Manhattan-ites with an escape route. New City, once a mostly agricultural community and haven for artists, seemed to explode with new people; "City People."

The New City Grammar School, sufficient to hold the children of three generations of my family, became overcrowded. Our kindergarten was held in the Methodist Church basement on Maple Avenue. Once designed to be the County Seat's main thoroughfare, Maple Avenue was thick with the giant sugar maples, and my brother and I walked the four blocks through heavily shaded canopy to classes every morning. In the fall, it could get waist deep in fallen leaves. He would leave me at the church steps, tussle my hair, before continuing down to Demarest Avenue east, past Vanderbilt's Pond and Vanderbilt's lumberyard in the old railroad station. Then the final leg up the dirt road hilltop to the rear of the old schoolhouse.

And as our town grew up, my family's history, dating back over 100 years, seemed to diminish in significance. The name meant something to the old-timers. For the newcomers, it held little import.

Now, leaving the Florion Estate, heading toward the home of my childhood on Main Street, I decided to go "the front way." It had been years since I had driven or walked this route, even though I had lived near here most of my life. It was the shortest route to my mother's house, but I never approached it from this direction since I had to walk past the forty homes that had been built here in the late 1950s. I made it a point to always circumvent the houses built there to somehow preserve my image of what it looked like before.

From the boathouse I crossed over the Dove Cottage hill and down toward the "new houses" to Muller Court. Coming down Twin Elms Lane, I crossed the Demarest Kill tributary that ran behind our house and turned south on Capral Lane instead of heading east toward Main Street. It was an easy decision, based on a thousand boyhood trips. I could have closed my eyes (I seriously thought about it), and made the trip from sense-memory, knowing how many steps to take, knowing when to turn, knowing when to lift my knee higher to avoid tripping on a curb. Yes, I could have closed my eyes, but then if I did, I would have had to deal with the disappointment of what I saw when I opened them. I would have wanted it to be like back when I was ten years old again, not in the present. I would have had to deal with that disappointment on top of what I was already dealing with on this day. And so I didn't close my eyes as I walked, and my hips and knees and feet recognized the repetitive motion of having walked this trip so many times in my childhood.

At the rear of our property there was a gate between two lilac trees that served as an arbor. On either side, stretching north and south, was a massive forsythia hedge. The bent, sinewy branches, loaded with delicate, pale yellow flowers, formed tunnel-like crawl-spaces in which a boy could hide. I swung the old gate slats open and walked past the apple tree and through the field toward the house.

Now overgrown with saplings, once the small field had served as a baseball diamond for the neighborhood boys. My father had carved it out of what remained of his own father's vegetable garden plots after his old man's death when I was seven. A little work had turned it into a playable ball field. Nothing fancy, just functional, yet precise in its accomplishment. My brother and I spent half our early grades there with my father and the neighborhood boys.

At the crest of the hill, behind home plate, I passed alongside two long-abandoned chicken coops and a still-functioning outhouse. My grandfather had used it while working his garden plots, and later the kids used it during our baseball games.

A meticulous gardener, one of my earliest recollections was watching my grandfather stand, swinging a hoe, as he surgically removed the weeds from between his vegetables. The rhythmical music of the "chop-chop-chop," as the broad blade struck against the rocky topsoil are among my earliest auditory memories. "Let the blade do the work. Let the blade do the work," he said in syncopation with the hoeing, lifting the hoe and then surrendering to the weight of it as it fell into place.

As I approached the house, the maple tree my brother Francis and I had claimed as our own was now a brilliant yellow and red smear, and to my left stood my grandfather's barn. Once used to stable the horses that pulled him and his small carriage on his mail route, the barn had fallen into disrepair. I walked past, brushing my fingertips along the pitted paint.

As if having been given a warning of my arrival, my mother met me at the back door as I walked up the sidewalk to the steps of the back porch. I fell into her arms and found myself sobbing for the third time that morning.

Marion Summers, my mother, was just sixteen years old and a new graduate of Spring Valley High School in the fall of 1936. The Depression was in full swing, and her father, who worked as a bank courier in Manhattan, found her a job in the accounting department at Lord & Taylor's Department Store near his bank. Every morning, brown lunch bags in hand, my mother and her father would walk from Hillcrest into downtown Spring Valley. There, they would catch the 7:00am Erie Suburban Line passenger train that linked Suffern to Manhattan. They would return home on the evening 7:10 train.

My father would rise early and walk to the New City Depot, where Vanderbilt's Lumberyard now sits. The train, nicknamed "The Dinkie," was part of the New Jersey and New York Railroad Line, and it jogged southbound from the New City spur through Durant and Bardonia, parallel to Rte. 304. The train would stop long enough at the junction in Nanuet for the riders to disembark and join the commuters on the Erie-Spring Valley main line.

On one of those trips, my father, among many enroute to New York University to study, caught my mother's eye as he got on the train in Nanuet. She was captivated by his shyness. One day he sat in front of her and picked up a Yiddish-language newspaper left behind by another passenger. He held it upside-down and pretended to read it in front of her. She lost her composure, laughed, and they fell in love on the train during that first fall semester after her high school graduation. When he graduated from NYU two years later, they got married and settled into two rooms in my grandparents' home on Main Street. He got a job as an accountant at Lederle's pharmaceutical plant in Pearl River. They planned to build a house on the vacant lot next door to my grandparents' house. But after saving every penny for three years, Pearl Harbor was attacked and my father joined the Navy.

My mother told me she didn't see my father for the last two years during the War. Just before he left for that last time, my brother was conceived on the last day of the last furlough. When my father returned in 1945, it was as if his body had been taken over by another person. He was so different she barely recognized the boy she had fallen in love with on the train. The young scholar had found out what the world was really like during a two-year hitch on a destroyer in the Pacific. I was conceived in the comfort she tried to give him in those post-war days, while she tried to breathe life back into the young man she had once known.

Upon his return, my father settled into his new job at the Post

Office. He had given up accounting for good, and taken a job similar to his own father's. He couldn't concentrate on accounting after the War, he told my mother. I was born a year after VJ Day, on August 15, 1946.

Growing up, I remember an emotionally detached mail carrier, devoted to his namesake son, my brother, while paying scant attention to me. An accurate impression? From talking to others who knew him during this period of time, my observations as a five year-old boy were accurate.

My mother was devoted to her husband and two sons. She lived a selfless life, without a moment's thought for herself or her own emotional needs.

And so it was now as she tried to comfort me in what she understood, as only a mother can, my deep sense of loss over Beth.

"My poor boy. How you have hurt for her for so long. Maybe now that she is at rest you can find some peace for yourself."

Her words, meant only to comfort, had me on my knees again, and I felt like a schoolboy. After a few moments, I was able to regain my composure.

"Why don't you go see Father Carrick? Maybe he can help you get past these feelings. He has been very kind to me in my time of need."

She was forever the optimist. I hadn't been to church in thirty years except for the occasional baptism, wedding, or funeral in town. But I would be the dutiful son and go see the family priest to make her happy.

"Okay, I'll stop by."

"But take a moment to see your brother before you see Father Carrick. You didn't stop this morning on your way in to work. You know he loves to see you."

The mention of my brother, as always, brought a rush of mixed feelings. Next to Beth, there had been no other person in my entire life that I had loved more completely. And as now with Beth, this love of mine had been suffocated in tragedy. As I stood before my mother, for yet another time that day I wanted to cry out in anguish for a love that knew no bounds, but a love that could never be returned.

"Sure, Mom."

The dining room off the living room was separated by ornate sliding pocket-doors of oak-and-leaded glass. I walked to them and slid them open. What had once been our family's dining room had been converted into a convalescent room. A hospital bed was in the upright position, supporting my older brother Francis. His pale, frail body was slumped to one side and he was aimlessly watching a silent game show on the small television at the foot of the bed. Drool rolled from the corner of his mouth and onto the pillow. When I walked into the room his entire demeanor changed and he seemed to come alive from his almost semi-comatose state.

As I stepped to the bed, Francis broke out into excited, ani-malistic, grunting laughter, accompanied by a mild thrashing of his torso. He broke into a wild smile that tore my heart apart. I reached down to hug him and hold him and comfort him and stayed that way for several minutes until he calmed down and drifted off into a deep, peaceful sleep. I held his hand, kneaded it with mine, as I had seen my father do on that day so long ago, knowing there was no hope, but powerless to do anything about it.

I released him gently, once again losing control of my emo-tions as I had that morning on the Demarest Kill about Beth, and moments ago with my mother. What kind of life is this he is lead-ing? I pondered this for the millionth time, slipping into despair at the feel of my brother's hand. This is not even a human life.

My mother stepped up behind me and whispered. "Go see Father Carrick. Please. Talk to him."

I never bothered to ask her how she knew Beth was dead. What would she have said? Who had called her early that morn-ing? Was it on the radio news? Television? It couldn't have been. Too soon, and they would not have identified the name of the victim that soon to the press.

CHAPTER FIVE

THE HISTORY OF MUSIC
IN NEW CITY, NEW YORK:
PART I

1956
Age 9

Back before it was called "Rock & Roll;" back when it was still called "Louis Jordan" and "Wynonie Harris" and "Big Joe Turner" and "Amos Milburn" and "Charles Brown," my brother and I were indoctrinated into the music that would become Rock & Roll by my father via his small radio that sat on the shelf of his electronics workshop in the basement of our home on Main Street in New City, New York. The bench was where my grandparents had stored their apples and pears in the winter and sharpened their ax to chop firewood on a pedal-driven grinding wheel for fifty years. My father had set up a workbench upon his return from the war, pieced together ham-radio sets and AM tuners for friends in town so they could listen to their music. To my brother and me, it was just music that we listened to, fading in and out from WOV-AM way over on the right side of the dial.

But then, after the music had been absorbed and cleansed

of all veiled references to carnal acts and filtered through white sensibilities by early February of 1956, and it was ready for the consumption by the general population, it was loosed on the American public.

Oh, sure, those pioneer musicians had spent years in the trenches playing a new form of music that no one had really given a name to. And sure, maybe Jerry Wexler had labeled it R&B and Alan Freed was supposedly the first to call the music "Rock & Roll," but he really wasn't. But those are stories for another time. For me, Rock & Roll was born on the night Elvis Presley first appeared on our television set during The Dorsey Brothers' Television show. My mother, my father, Francis and I sat at the Philco, spellbound in the dark room. My mother didn't know quite what to make of it. My father recognized it as a re-creation of the music he had been listening to for years in the basement on his hand-made radio.

After that night, the lives of my family and friends would never be the same. How could we have not recognized the power of the radio and television in those early days?

We had heard rumblings for at least a year or two. All over the country, something was happening, a giant was awakening, and the impact would put a questioning look on the faces of our parents and a new sense of exhilaration and camaraderie between friends.

One day we were listening to Patti Page singing "tweedle-dee-dee-dee, it gives me a thrill," on *Mockingbird Hill*, and the next we were walking around school with our hair slicked back, checking for sideburns potential, wiggling our hips while strumming a string-less, tennis racket guitar.

Francis was enthralled by what he saw on television. He spent hours at the mirror, twisting his bangs into a Bill Haley spit-curl. The morning after the Dorsey show, our father drove us to Barker's corner in Bardonia. It was the closest place to New City where you could buy a record. We bought our first 45 r.p.m. *Heartbreak Hotel*. We spent a lot of time down at the end of Lonely Street that spring.

We were rarely out of earshot of a radio. From 6am to 10am we listened to the antics of Ted Browne and the Redhead on WMGM-1050. She was the 50s version of an earlier, Gracie Allen scatterbrain.

Later in the morning we listened to Zeke Manners on 1010-WINS.

At night it was spin the dial back to 1050 to catch Peter Tripp's YOUR HITS OF THE WEEK on WMGM.

Along with the other rites of passage of our youth, the music became our anthems.

During that music-filled springtime, as Little Richard, Fats Domino, and Chuck Berry embraced our lives, it was just weeks away from "Francis' Day."

CHAPTER SIX

"FRANCIS' DAY"

June, 1956
Age 9

Up until the time I was ten years old, my brother Francis was my boyhood hero. He was the neighborhood *wunderkind.* As much as a young man of twelve can be, Francis was the perfect All-American Boy. An athlete, a gentleman, a scholar. A Boy Scout without the uniform. He took pride in being good. His sense of honor was developed early, and in some ways it made him seem so much older than he really was. He protected me and gently guided me through the typical traumas of kindergarten, first- through-fourth grades. I loved him and idol-worshipped him as only young boys can do with the person they want to grow up to be like. At that age, loving my older brother Francis was my entire life.

When my father was not walking his mail route, the two of them were inseparable. I was always the tag-along. In my father's eyes, the love, the pride for my brother was so apparent, that any other younger son might have been jealous. Not me. I saw my father as just another worshipper at the same altar. I watched from afar as he taught Francis how to hook a worm, holding the wriggler gingerly in his left fingertips while impaling it precisely with the hook pinched tightly between his right thumb and forefinger. It was a skill Francis later showed me. During our soap box derby days, they built a crude racer out of baby carriage wheels, some scrap lumber and a nail keg we found in our barn. I stood and watched as my father pulled the contraption up to the top of Third Street hill and pushed Francis toward infamy. He coasted down toward Gerken's Apple Orchard, the wind blowing his hair like a WWI aviator. My father watched, smiling quietly, while my brother laughed with fear and exhilaration.

The same with stilts. My father built a pair of stilts from more scrap lumber, and without hesitation, stepped up on the blocks and twisted and wobbled his way down the sidewalk between the catalpa trees as if he had been in the circus for years. My brother and I, having never seen my father with his guard down, laughed on the lawn until our bellies ached at the sight of his stiff-legged steps. Francis tried it, starting from the rear stoop, he climbed on board and following my father's coaching, tap-danced his way into the hedge the first time, collapsing into a pile of giggles. The next try he got farther; the next, farther still. And so it was later, when he taught me stilt-walking. We called them "The Seven League Stilts," after a boys' mystery novel our father had read to us.

The Daily Adventures of Francis and His Younger Brother, Will, took us across our brook to the Florion estate. As boys, we knew that the Florions were an old couple that had been a famous radio duo during the 1930s. They entertained the masses, he conducted an orchestra and she sang and played the piano. During the War they had been USO regulars along with Bob Hope. Now they were old, retired, wealthy beyond the imagination of anyone who lived in New City. With few exceptions, they lived in solitude in Dove Cottage; the old mansion on the hill.

During the first thirty years of the 20th Century, my grandfather had worked as a mailman, and when he retired from the Post Office, he did odd jobs around the Florion estate. Yard work, truing cabinets and door frames, raking leaves. Before he passed away, I remember watching him through the heat waves created by a burning pile of leaves on the front lawn of the estate. He wore wide-wale brown corduroys and a plaid flannel shirt with wool vest. He patiently worked his pipe with a knife and then swept a small pile of leaves into the controlled burn. He was silent that day, as in all my memories of him, rarely speaking to his son or grandsons who watched him work. My father seemed awkward raking leaves in the presence of his own father, waiting perhaps for a conversation that was to never be, never to commence.

What was my grandfather thinking during those times of silence, that *made* the silence that prevented that conversation that was never to come? Was he thinking of other days, walking through the woods in the 1890s when he himself had been a boy, wading the shallows of the Demarest Kill, while throwing out a hook and worm? Trapping otter and beaver for their pelts to make a little pin-money? Losing a precious silver dollar at the New City racetrack at the annual New City Fair?

After a while, Old Man Florion came out and slipped an envelope into the watch pocket on my grandfather's vest. "Got the brood with you, I see, Francis."

My grandfather nodded as he raked, ignoring his son and two young grandsons.

Mr. Florion continued, "You know, when we had our radio show…." his words blended together, and I inhaled the smoke of the cooking elm leaves as they smoldered at my feet.

When I was seven, my grandfather would die on the Florion property, falling from a ladder while grafting a new branch on a crab-apple tree in the sweep of the Florion's front lawn. Like my grandmother, who had died ten years before I was born, he was working at a job that he loved. My grandmother had died in those late days of the Depression while volunteering as a gardener at the Dutch Garden. My grandfather had found her near the sundial, face down in the flowers she had just planted.

We did not find out until another few years went by that the Florions had a secret we had not known about. A grown daughter with a son of her own, my age. A boy named Tom Hogenkamp. But that story is for later, for now I must recount, as I have every day for myself for the past forty-four years, the events that transpired to result in "Francis' Day"; events that replay in my mind like the lyrics to a song that won't stop playing, until it drives you to distraction, madness even.

"Francis' Day" started like any other. Spring stayed late that June. I had just finished fourth grade and Francis had completed sixth. It was our first day of summer vacation after the weekend. We spent the morning lying on our backs, staring up at another brilliant blue sky mottled by the leaves of the sugar maple above us that served as our fort, our pirate brigantine, our playhouse. That maple by the barn was our hangout, with cool, shaded grass on a path with a gentle slope. From the maple's treetop branches we had spied the onslaught of the Iroquois and Ramapaugh, or the buccaneers who threatened our very existence. We hid in the leaves, climbing up the mast ropes disguised as sinewy branches, bouncing upward with each step.

Now, the grass was chilled at our backs and the air was mild and fragrant with peonies. The damp smell from the sod beneath confirmed for us the earth was truly being reborn, just as it had promised weeks earlier with the arrival of the daffodils that lined the driveway fence in a blaze of rich yellows.

Later that day we aimlessly wandered the brook behind the house, looking for water spiders and crayfish. At such times we would stroll down the path past the baseball field our father had cleared out of the weeds that were allowed to grow when his own father's garden had become overgrown. Had he done it as a diversion from his grief or as a way of moving on for his sons?

My father was not much on gardening. The garden tools he used were originally used by his own father and grandfather, that had been brought earlier from the family farm at the top of New Hempstead Hill.

Francis and I walked past the sumac patch and the apple tree and forsythia hedge and the arbor of white and lavender lilac, the still fragrant grape-like clusters of the Whitman tree, now brown in late spring.

We passed through the narrow opening in the trellis that served the outermost perimeter of our ballpark. From there it was just a few steps through overgrown weeds before we came to our brook at the far extremity of our property. On the other side of the brook, the Florion estate began.

In those days, the brook's water was clear from the springs that fed it just a few hundred yards to the south. Like the Demarest Kill it would eventually join, our brook also flowed north. We sat on the embankment and stepped in wearing our old sneakers, the ones with the holes in the canvas and the ankle patches ripped off; too worn to wear for anything except gaining a foothold in our stream-bed meanderings.

If we had been a few weeks earlier, we would have seen frog eggs, their gelatinous mass filled with caviar-like B.B.'s, or later, hundreds of tadpoles. Now the frogs that would eventually grow into a lovely green iridescence were at an in-between stage. Still pollywogs, but with black legs lengthening and tails shortening as they metamorphosed into frogs. *Ontogeny recapitulating Phylogeny*, as it had for millions of spring days before, right in front of our astonished young boy eyes. It all had become part of the breathtaking wonderment of being a boy in that particular place, alongside a tributary of the Demarest Kill, in that particular time in history.

Occasionally we would see a crayfish. They were more for

novelty value than for anything else. We caught them as a prize, then released them unharmed. In just moments, Francis had caught two. Water spiders by the hundreds, Daddy-Long-Leg-like in appearance, skated across the surface tension of the water.

We walked up and down the brook a dozen times that day, Francis telling me about his own experiences in the fifth grade, the grade I was about to enter. Every season had a boyhood ritual attached to it. March was marble month. Intricate games were played in the gravel playground of New City Grammar School on Old Congers Road, beginning on March 1st, when the month roared in like a cold, wet lion. Thirty-one days later, tournaments completed or not, the marble playing would end abruptly, as March ended like a lamb. There was no explanation for these rituals starting and stopping, just traditions passed down year after year. Had they been in effect during the War? Had my father played marbles in March in that same gravel playground when he went to school in the same building, thirty years earlier? My grandfather, who also attended the same school almost sixty years earlier?

On this summer day, it was now getting close to four o'clock and we both silently anticipated the arrival of our father, home from his mail route. Every day at four o'clock he would leave the Post Office next to Kienke's grocery store across the street from the Court House and walk home. Every day at ten minutes after four, he would turn the corner in the drive and greet us both with a hug and animated stories of his life on the "Chisholm Trail." That's what he called his mail route after watching an old Hopalong Cassidy movie with us on the new Philco television set in the living room.

Thinking about Francis absentmindedly as the afternoon wore on, I lost my concentration reaching for a crayfish. I slipped and fell, and attempting to prevent splashing headlong into the water, I sat down hard in twelve inches of water, twisting my ankle badly.

I screamed with the sharp pain and Francis rushed to my side to comfort me. In a swoop, he picked me up in his arms out of the stream and carried me past the lilac arbor and forsythia hedge. His walk was determined, but without panic. He was caring for me. Still in pain, I began to relax. My older brother, Francis, would make it right, I knew.

As we reached the top edge of the field, in a place where the first baseline dugout would be if we had built such a dugout, he did something I couldn't explain then. Can't explain now. Was it to catch his breath from carrying me? Our forward motion stopped and he hesitated, almost as if someone had called his name and he suddenly turned around and faced the brook. Held in his arms, I looked in vain for what he was looking for, but his eyes just followed the white baseline of lime dust my father had pinched out between his fingertips from an old coffee can kept full of it in the nearby outhouse. The lines went all the way from home plate to first base; from first to second; from second to third; and back to home plate. Why had Francis looked back at the brook at just that moment, like a child leaving his home for the very last time, taking inventory of the small details so he could remember them later? Had he heard something? Was he trying to remember something? Had he had some sort of premonition? Francis stood there another second, staring toward the brook, as if posing for a portrait of himself holding me aloft, a Bill Haley spit-curl falling down on his forehead, before I became impatient with my pain and jostled him from his reverie, and then reluctantly, he turned and continued carrying me up the slight grade past the chicken coops and the blue spruce alleyway and the barn, up to the grassy slope past our maple tree and to the back porch stoop of our house.

There, he lowered me to the top step and rolled up the cuffs of my wet dungarees, offering words of comfort as he worked. I was his younger brother. He was my protector. Gently, he pulled off my high-top sneaker, then rolled down my soaked white sock to examine the swelling.

Within minutes he had distracted me from the incident with his joking manner, and the pain seemed to disappear beneath his probing fingertips. I remember the concern on his face. I don't remember the pain of my ankle. He had learned his compassion from my mother, I suspect.

He rubbed my hair and told me to go down into the basement and get out of my wet clothes.

"Don't make a mess for Mom," were the last real words he ever spoke to me. Later, I would reflect on the irony of his statement.

I didn't find out the exact details of what happened while I was changing my clothes next to the old hand-wringer washing machine in the basement until the police arrived later that night to talk to my parents.

Next to our house lived the Hessian family. Their Victorian-style house and adjoining barn were mirror images of our house and barn. The four buildings had actually been built by my grandfather in 1906, within two years after my grandparents, as newlyweds, had bought the vacant property from the Florion land holdings. The two lots had remained in my grandparents' name for thirty years. Then, during the Depression, after my grandmother died, my grandfather had sold the adjacent lot as income property. The duplicate house and barn had changed hands several times since. Despite the financial gain, it was the worst mistake my grandfather ever made. Our barn had served as a horse stable for my grandfather's mail route until almost 1920. Then, the downstairs served as a garage and workshop, and the upstairs was filled with family furniture and storage boxes from the previous fifty years. His old mail carriage had been hoisted up to the second floor to the hayloft on a block and tackle that still hung from an iron spike in the top floor doorway. Most of our yard and house and barn were kept as impeccably neat as when my grandfather was alive. At least as well as could be expected under the circumstances.

The twin house next to ours had fallen into disrepair. The identical barn in the lot adjacent to ours was filled with the leftover trash of twenty years of landlords and tenants, who left behind the items they either no longer wanted or couldn't afford to take with them, or had simply abandoned and were later moved out to the barn by the new tenants.

The current residents of the house were the Hessian family, who had recently purchased it when they moved to New City from Sloatsburg. They were a tightly knit family, their ancestry dating back to the Revolutionary War.

Both the Hessian parents in the house next door were alcoholics. Mrs. Hessian was a slatternly housewife who drank beer all day long. Mr. Hessian was a carpenter by day and a terrorist to his two young sons by night. The boys matched the ages of Francis and me. Marvin was a husky twelve, a bully in training, constantly punching people, as if out of control. Calvin was in my class. Slight in size, quiet and withdrawn, he was the perfect target for his brother's uncontrollable punching and verbal abuse. Calvin's nickname was "Sparrow." He had adopted the name of a bird for reasons I would not find out about until we were older.

On "Francis' Day", while I was still in the basement in search of dry clothes, Marvin had walked over to see if Francis wanted to play. Tailing behind him in a fearful wake, Calvin stood off to the side. Hide-and-go-seek, the current rage, was a game we played for hours on end, capitalizing on the lush shrubbery in the yard that my grandfather had planted for my grandmother during the first twenty years they had lived there. The rules were simple. The well-house in our front side yard was home base. Any place on the two properties was in-bounds and fair game. The barns, but not the houses, were also fair game.

What happened next varies, depending on the telling and the teller. When Francis agreed to play, Marvin shoved Calvin to the ground and yelled, "You're it, dip-shit! Start counting to….300. And make it slow!"

"No swearing," Francis quickly retorted.

Calvin hid his eyes on the well-house door, rubbed his sore shoulder, and started counting to 300 out loud. Marvin whispered to Francis, "Follow me, I've got a great place you can hide."

If only I had fallen in the stream a few minutes later, if only I hadn't shaken Francis from his reverie on the edge of the ball field, if only I had asked him to carry me down the cellar steps and help me take off my wet clothes, if only Calvin had only counted to just 100. *If only.* Just another few minutes and both our fathers would be home from their respective jobs as carpenter and mail carrier. That's all it would have taken to prevent what happened next.

Marvin led Francis to their barn. Inside it was dark, with sunshine cutting swaths through the dust motes sharply angled by the golden, four o'clock-hour sun. The barn was filled with the skeleton of a 1948 Plymouth convertible, stacks of old magazines covered with the distinctive smell of dried rat droppings, tables cluttered with rusty tin cans filled with nails, and greasy nuts and bolts. And a 1930s Kelvinator ice box.

"Get in here. He'll never think of looking for you in here."

Inside the Kelvinator, the racks had been removed in preparation for Mr. Hessian converting it to a smoker for the venison he anticipated shooting that next autumn up in the Catskills along the Neversink River. He had made the old ice box air-tight with putty to keep the smoke in. The door opening and the compartment were just the right size for a boy of twelve like Francis. The door stood open as if in a welcoming embrace.

Marvin slammed the door closed on Francis, turned the latch and spun around to find his own hiding place outside. As he stepped into the bright sunlight, he ran smack into his father's chest. The carpenter stood swilling an almost empty quart bottle of Rheingold. The impact knocked the bottle to the ground and it smashed on the round flat stone that acted as a threshold and door-stoop to the barn.

"Goddammit! Look what you done. What are you doing in there?"

"I ain't doin' nothin."

"I told you to stay away from that smoker."

"I didn't touch it."

"Goddammit. I'm gonna teach you a lesson."

I heard the shouting as I hobbled up the basement steps to rejoin Francis, my dry clothes quickly pulled from the basement clothes-line.

Instead, I saw Mr. Hessian's huge hand encircling Marvin's shoulder as he forced him toward the house, repeatedly shoving him to the ground then yanking him up.

As they neared the back porch, my father rounded the corner from the front sidewalk and stood silently watching the spectacle before him. He put his lunch box on the ground.

Marvin was protesting. "I didn't do nothin! I didn't do nothin!"

"Shut up!" was followed by a slap to the back of the head from Mr. Hessian that knocked Marvin to the ground.

He shoved Marvin up the three stairs of the back porch and into the house. The sound of Marvin's bare knees sliding across the porch deck made a fierce squeak, burning off the skin from the momentum as he slid.

My father stepped forward. "Mr. Hessian. I don't think…."

"Mind your own goddam business." He raised a finger in my father's face. "I ain't gonna have trouble from you, now, am I?"

My father took a step backward. A look of calculation crossed his face, as if he were trying to decipher a complicated algorithm against the clock.

Mr. Hessian jerked Marvin through the back porch door and it slammed behind him. A split second later, the screen door slapped shut, bouncing twice before coming to rest in a final punctuation.

Just as I turned to look at my father, we heard Sparrow at the well-house for what seemed like the first time. He spoke the words slowly, searching, oblivious to what was transpiring right next to him.

"298, 299, 300! Here I come, ready or not. Anyone around my base is *it* !"

From inside the Hessian's house we heard a belt slapping a bare behind and Marvin's screams.

Sparrow looked sheepishly to my father and me, suddenly aware of the disturbance. "What happened?"

My father finally finished the calculation and realized there was information missing from the equation he struggled to solve. He snapped his head to my direction, a sudden look of panic on his face that he was trying, unsuccessfully, to contain. "Where's Francis?" As if he were prescient.

"I don't know. I was in the basement."

He tripped over his black lunchbox on the ground and ran to Sparrow and knelt down in front of him, gently putting his hands on the boy's frail shoulders, showing him he meant him no harm. "Where's Francis, Calvin?"

Sparrow started trembling at my father's touch. "I don't know. We were playing hide-and-go-seek. I was 'it.' He's hiding somewhere."

My father stood quickly and scanned the tree-filled yard: an infinite wealth of possibilities where a young boy could hide. Underneath the giant blue spruce branches where the bows swept the lawn? Buried in the tall columns of the clipped arborvitae, standing as still as statues?

"Francis!" he yelled, calmly at first.

He hesitated a second and all we could hear was the slapping of Mr. Hessian's belt and Marvin's sobs.

"Francis! Come on out. Game's over."

Silence filled the afternoon. Or maybe I had just tuned everything out.

"Answer me, son. I need to talk to you."

When there was no answer, my father stepped to me and spoke very distinctly. "Go get your mother."

Before I could turn and run inside, my father was heading for our tiny baseball diamond. Just past the barn on the north side of the path were the outhouse and two chicken coops, long-abandoned. At the outhouse he looked down into the cesspit. In the chicken coops he paused to look in each one, afternoon light spilling in the windows, lighting up the columns of dust motes of dried out chicken manure.

At the forsythia hedge he knelt and peered into the long yellow tunnel we always crawled through. Back on the path, he shielded his brow with his hand and scanned the north sumac patch and then to the south by a grape arbor, heavy laden with late-spring fruit.

"Francis? Francis? Francis!" Each successive call more plaintive.

I ran inside and found my mother seated at her old Singer, sewing a dress for one of Mrs. Florion's society events. The white satin squeaked in her fingertips, as she pushed it through the chrome presser foot that held the needle and drove the bobbin for each cross-stitch.

"Mom! Come outside. Dad wants you."

The look on my face, the sound of my voice, must have told her something was wrong. She brushed past me and bolted for the back door.

Down in the field my father raced from shrub to shrub, looking behind each one. His eyes swept the line of tree branches above, looking for Francis' dangling sneakers. How much time passed as he seemed to run in desperate circles? I don't know. All I know was that it was *enough time* to do the damage.

My mother ran to meet him at the entrance to our barn.

"What's wrong?"

"I need to find Francis."

"What's wrong?"

"I need to find Francis. I need to find Francis. I need to find Francis." He could no longer hide the panic in his voice as he paced in circles.

He brushed past her and into our barn. From outside, I could hear his footsteps, first on the cinder floor, then bounding up the stairs to what had once been the hayloft. Each step he took, he called my brother's name. He must have glanced at his father's mail wagon, sitting dormant in the corner; must have peeked inside for the crouching son he sought, into the blackness of the tiny cab his father had spent the first half of his entire thirty-year career sitting in, delivering the mail.

I followed my mother into the darkness of the barn in time to watch him stumble down the stairs three at a time. "Look for him. Look for him."

My mother and I spread out to the corners of the bottom floor. As I looked out the cobwebbed window, my father was heading toward the Hessian's back porch on the bound.

I limped outside to join him, sensing I needed to be there to somehow, I didn't know how, protect him from Marvin's father. I would do it, sprained ankle or not.

"Where is he?" he called as he tore open the door.

"I ain't gonna have any trouble from you." It wasn't a question. A statement of fact from Mr. Hessian.

"Where is he, Marvin? Where is Francis hiding?"

Marvin's nose was bleeding, his right eye blackened and swollen shut from where his father had apparently back-handed him, but he managed to blubber out, "He's in the barn."

"I was just in the barn. He's not there. Where is he, Marvin?"

"I said I ain't gonna have any trouble from you. You're gonna get out of my house now. Your kid is your problem."

My father ignored Hessian. "Tell me where Francis is, Marvin."

There was a hesitation, then, "He's in our barn. *Our* barn."

"Why you little….I told you to stay outta there."

"Don't hit me. Please don't hit me anymore. I didn't do anything. Please don't hit me anymore. No more hitting." Marvin's words trailed off in a hopeless blubber of sobs.

My father ran through the screen door and out of their house and past me. "Francis!" The screen door, once again, added the punctuation with two slaps against the lintel.

I followed my father on the run, my ankle screaming in pain. Two more slaps of the screen door.

On the driveway, the gravel beneath his feet gave way and he slipped, fell flat on his face. When he stood up, gravel stuck to his chin and cheeks and he brushed them off. He regained his balance and continued to run. I would later recall, "Francis' Day" was only the second time I ever remember seeing my father run.

He ran into the Hessian's barn and peered into the darkness. I joined him at his side and then my mother followed. It took a moment for our eyes to adjust to the light. By the time they did, my mother had joined us. My father raced from one dark corner to the other. "Francis, Francis. The game is over. Francis, where are you?"

He bounded up the staircase and was back down again before my mother and I could really even see.

At the bottom of the staircase he looked around hopelessly for a split second before the instant horror of the Kelvinator caught his eye. "Francis!"

When the ice box door opened my brother sprawled forward and was caught in my father's embrace. His arms were limp spaghetti and his face was wet and as gray as the coal cinders beneath our feet.

My father stood cradling Francis and bolted for the door. "Call Dr. Cohen," he called over his shoulder to my mother. Then, to me, "How long was he hiding?"

I couldn't answer him. Five minutes? Ten minutes? I had no sense of time. I had been in the cellar changing into dry clothes. *Enough time. Sufficient time.*

As my mother raced for the house, I followed my father as he first stopped to breathe oxygen into my brother's depleted lungs. Then he disappeared at the end of the driveway at a full sprint, my brother's arms flailing loosely at his sides, as if the wings of a young bird trying to ascend, then collapsing.

The tears started to form in my eyes as the realization of what had happened and the resulting unknown began to sink in. As fast as I was as a runner, with my sore ankle, by the time I reached the end of the tall hedge that lined our driveway, my father was already running north down the white line in the middle of Main Street. Two cars had pulled to the curb to let him pass.

Somehow thinking my brother could hear me, I screamed out, "Francis! Francis! Wait for me!"

At the crest of the hill by the Esso Station, my father again stopped to force air into Francis' lungs. Then he disappeared as he began his descent down the gentle slope into downtown New City.

I didn't realize it at the time, but when he disappeared over the crest of that hill, my father would never really return home. Oh, he would come home every night for another eleven years and sit down at the dinner table with us, but that afternoon was really the moment when he left my mother and me for good.

By the time I reached the crest my father was running past The Rexall Drug Store and Fred Steinman's General Store. My lungs were burning and my side was stitched as I watched him run up the sidewalk under the horse chestnut trees to Dr. Cohen's office. My ankle was getting numb.

The front door was still open on the once residential Crafts-man-style house that had been converted into a Dr.'s office. At the entrance I hesitated, then walked slowly down the polished oak floor hallway and peeked into the examination room. My brother lay on the cream-colored, enameled steel table, an oxygen mask over his face. The only sound in the room was the hiss of the oxygen tank. My father was on his knees, massaging my brother's hands and kissing them, touching them to his own cheeks as if, somehow, to pass life back into the little boy he loved so much. Something eclipsed his face and I wouldn't realize until later what it was.

Seconds later, I heard the police siren wailing as it pulled to a stop and Billy Zeliech stepped out of the car and raced toward the open door. I backpedaled out of his way as he made his way into the room.

"Ready?" was all he said.

Dr. Cohen picked up the portable oxygen bottle connected by tubes to my brother and my father picked up Francis in his arms as he had done before. They ignored me. With Zeliech leading the way they raced to the police car. Dr. Cohen got in the back seat holding the oxygen tank, followed by my father carrying his son. The siren became louder as the police car pulled from the curb, and the last I saw of it as it disappeared down South Main Street enroute to Suffern Hospital was my father kissing my brother's face and talking softly to the lifeless form he held in his arms.

My brother survived that day, if you can consider that his life for the next forty-four years was any life at all. There is a name for the damage the lack of oxygen did to his brain, to his central nervous system, but I can never remember what the name is, or perhaps I've blocked it in an attempt to deny and ultimately reverse what happened. After being in a coma for two weeks, he lived the last forty-odd years in limbo, a semi-vegetative state, responding to external stimuli, able to recognize voices and faces, but unable to communicate in any meaningful way. At the age of twelve he went back into diapers and into the constant care of my mother for the remainder of his life.

My father didn't survive. It was all downhill from there. Perhaps if he hadn't experienced two years of combat in the War he would have made it. Since he never spoke about what he witnessed in the North Pacific we'll never know. For some it makes them stronger. For others it depletes any defensive emotional resources they might have once had.

Every afternoon after "Francis' Day," he would return home from his long walks for the Post Office and join Francis at his bedside in the dining room that we had converted into his bedroom on the ground floor. It was easier that way. No stairs for anyone to maneuver. There he would patiently provide two hours of physical therapy.

Following a light dinner, my father would go into Francis' room again and close the heavy wooden pocket doors with their leaded glass windows, and sit on Francis' bedside reading aloud to him. My father worked his way through the green leatherette-bound Mark Twain series, then the complete Charles Dickens. Then the Booth Tarkington novels, starting with the Penrod series with Herman, Verman, and Sherman, and reading his way through Alice Adams and The Magnificent Ambersons. Then he started on The Hardy Boys. He saved the best for last when he read his favorites and what would become my favorites, when he read the Jerry Todd and Poppy Ott boys' adventure series by Leo Edwards. Those stories about a group of good-natured Midwestern boys from the imaginary town of Tutter, Illinois in the 1920s had kept us spellbound while growing up. The town of Tutter reminded us of New City, as I'm sure it reminded my father. A safe place where kids could grow up without fear and where neighbors knew and spoke to one another, when life was simpler and without care. A world slowed down.

When he finished the Jerry Todds and Poppy Otts, he started all over again. All the while, Francis lay propped up on his pillow, a slack-jawed blank stare of hopelessness on his face. And all the while I sat curled up on the carpet outside the dining room, listening to my father's voice vibrate and rebound through the flowered living room wallpaper. I can still hear his voice reading those stories to Francis; and, I always liked to make-believe, reading them to me. I can still hear his voice reading as Pudd'nhead Wilson, or as Jerry Todd in *The Rose-Colored Cat,* or as Poppy Ott in *The Seven League Stilts.*

After, when Francis drifted off into sleep, my father would put the book back on the shelf, tuck in his older son, and silently leave the room. He would walk out onto the porch fronting Main

Street and St. Augustine's Church, standing with his hands in his pockets. Then he would walk off into the darkness beginning the second long walk of the day that marked his routine for the rest of his life. He would walk the night away; walk the streets of his own boyhood hometown; up North Main to Zukor Road, over South Mountain Road west to Rte. 45, and down 45 to New Hempstead Road. I would only figure out later why he walked this particular, very specific route; walk until three or four or five in the morning most nights. Then he would return home, sleep until six and rise to be at work for the long walk of his Post Office delivery route by seven.

The nightly routine continued, unchanged in hours but rotating in sequence and direction, all through my school years, and even after I went away to University of Florida. Two long walks a day. Why did he do it? I asked myself that every day for years. One walk to earn his living, the other walk to somehow earn his right to remain on this earth while his mind slipped away in grief.

Then, eleven years later, while I was a junior at The University of Florida, my mother frantically tracked me down one night to tell me that my father had died. He was struck by a car while crossing the street at three in the morning on his return home from his nightly-walking-pilgrimage-toward-oblivion. The driver of the car was drunk and fled the scene on Main Street outside the New City Pub, across from Steinman's General Store and Dr. Cohen's office.

CHAPTER SEVEN

ST. AUGUSTINE'S CHURCH
NEW CITY

Monday, 11 a.m.
October 16, 2000
Age 54

Now, forty-four years after "Francis' Day," and thirty-three years after my father's funeral, I left my brother sleeping and turned off his television with the remote control.

"Why don't you go see Father Carrick?" my mother asked, as I left my brother's room.

Father Carrick had been a priest across the street at St. Augustine's since the mid-1950's. He had taught me to be an altar boy, had coached my C.Y.O. basketball team, spoke at my father's funeral, and had been a symbol of stability in a community in flux for all of those years. Now, he must be in his mid-to-late seventies, I guessed.

"Maybe he can help you get past these feelings. He has been very kind to Francis and me in our time of need."

It had been thirty-three years since I had last stepped up the stone steps into the sanctuary at St. Augustine's for any meaningful visit. I have tried to forget about the most significant day. It was the day of my father's funeral. But as I would discover some-time during my growing up years, I have a difficult time forget-ting. When people ask me how I remember some detail from my past, I try to explain to them, it's not that I remembered it, it's that I've never forgotten.

The first time I saw Father Carrick is a story I remember well. A cool spring morning with the flower beds around the sidewalk yellow with daffodils and the smell of freshly mown grass in the air. The front of the vine-covered building was alive with new-born wren-chicks being fed early-bird worms by their early-bird moms. Or perhaps that first memory was really the amalgamation of a hundred Sundays, growing up and attending early Sunday morning Mass with my mother and Francis.

My mother is a devout woman, and I would watch her closely as she would change when she walked through the church door. It breathed life into her, or perhaps it was just hope that filled her chest. Francis and I would rise early, at the sound of the three big bells pealing from the bell tower made of Rockland County stone for the seven a.m. Mass, and get ready for the eight a.m.

We never missed a Sunday with my mother. Across the street, on the wide front porch of our house, my father would wait for us, while doing the Sunday Times crossword puzzle.

St. Augustine's Parish has an interesting history.

The original New City Grammar School was in an old build-ing on Congers Road that would later become the original For-ester's Hall, then St. Augustine's Church, and by the 1950s, Doc Goebel's Veterinary Clinic.

In the 1890s the huge new, two-story school was built on the hill on Old Congers Road, just to the east. At first The Forest-ers moved into the abandoned school house. When The Foresters moved out of that Congers Road building, St. Augustine's moved into it.

The new Foresters' Hall, by then located at Third and Main,

was a social hall. As a boy, my father had watched movies at the new Foresters' Hall, directly across the street from our house on Main Street. The movies were provided by an itinerant projectionist who made the rounds from town to town, hauling heavy film cans, putting up the projector on a card table in the rear of the room, and bringing Hollywood to New City via a bed sheet hung on the far wall.

Later, The Foresters' Hall on Main Street became St. Augustine's Roman Catholic Church, dressed up in stained-glass windows and a steeple and bell tower made of stones culled when clearing the adjacent field. For a second time, the Catholics had followed the Foresters in New City; followed the Foresters twice and tried to carry on the reputation of that location being a social gathering spot for the community.

Now, walking through the sanctuary doors of St. Augustine's brought back a rush of memories of days of being an altar boy with Francis and then later, with Tom.

The first fraction of a second I ever saw Father Carrick sums up his entire career. It was his first day at the church, in 1952, a young, vibrant priest, still in his mid-twenties, having been reassigned from The Bronx. It was almost exactly four years to the day before "Francis' Day."

Have you ever seen a priest running down a basketball court full speed in a black cassock with thirty-three buttons that reached down to his ankles? Father Carrick. He drove in for a lay-up during a practice match, incongruously, his black P.F. Flyers squeaking loudly on the church basement floor, rosary swinging from his neck in wide circles, as if to give anyone trying to block him second thoughts about getting too close. After the lay-up, he blew the whistle signaling the end of practice, but no one wanted to leave. We wanted to stay with vibrant newcomer, Father Carrick.

"Boys," he said, "take a knee." We did what we were told and huddled around him silently, expectantly. To this day, I've never seen anything like it. We were transfixed by his presence, trusted his authority, hung on his words that were tinged with just a trace of the map of Ireland and tempered with a Bronx accent.

"The Lord is in every one of ya's. Remember that when you are on the basketball court. Remember it when you step out into the street or into the classroom, or when you're flirtin' with the ladies. Especially when you're with the ladies. Always treat 'em with the respect they deserve." That drew a few stifled giggles from the pre-teens in the group before him.

"He lives in ya, you're His representative out there, so don't let Him down. We all owe Him that much. Always remember that boys, till yer dyin' day when you'll get to meet Him in person and touch the hem of His garment."

He stood and made the sign of the cross to bless us. "So, enough of my preachin' this first day of mine. Go and do good deeds." His black Irish eyes had sparkled that day, as he smiled down at me and Francis. He was a take-no-shit guy from that very first encounter, but his heart was filled with love for us all. Being in his presence made us all feel safer, somehow. We never wanted to leave his side.

Now, when I entered the sanctuary, seated in the front row, as if waiting for me, was Father Carrick, idly fiddling his rosary. As I walked down the aisle toward him he rose from the pew. I hadn't seen him in probably two years, except in casual passing during his Christmas visits to Francis and my mother. For the first time that I can remember, he was beginning to show his age. With his commanding presence and his white hair combed straight back, he could have been a movie star, had his life taken another direction.

"Will."

"Father Carrick."

He made the sign of the cross. "May the Lord bless you in your time of sorrow, my boy."

"Thank you."

"Would you like to pray with me?"

The idea seemed preposterous, but I knew he was trying to help.

"Sure."

He sensed my discomfort. "Okay, Will, maybe just a talk first, then."

"Sure."

He led me across the sanctuary to a small hallway and to his office. It was sparsely furnished, but the desk was a foot deep in files and papers and future program proofs; strategies to save souls.

"I'll be honest with you Will. This might be my greatest weakness as a priest. Trying to help people who have lost a loved one. I'm not very good at it, so please be a little tolerant if what I say doesn't work right away."

"No, you're doing fine."

"Lyin's not gonna help you now, Will. There's nothin' gonna make you feel any better any time soon. Not a thing I can say or do. And yourself not bein' a believin' man anymore, any talk about the Lord from me would probably just make you feel worse."

"You're probably right about that."

He shrugged his shoulders and rubbed his eyes hard with his fingertips. "You loved that poor girl for such a long time. I know it's gotta hurt real bad."

I thought back to the first time I met Beth. "Is over forty-four years a long time?"

"You know, Will, your Mom has been worried about this situation with you and Beth for some time. She knows how you feel, how you spent practically your whole life loving someone you were never gonna get back. A woman married to another man."

"Was it that obvious?"

"Only to all of us who know you like we do."

"No fool like an old fool."

"No, no, Will. You can't do that. Don't ever give yourself

short-shrift for your feelings. You can't punish yourself that way. You fell in love as a young man with a beautiful young woman in the bloom of both your lives. It's all part of God's plan for us. There wouldn't be any human race if God didn't give you that feeling in your heart, and well, down below, too. It's nothin' to be ashamed of. What you felt in your heart, there's not a person alive who would fault you for that. It just didn't turn out like you wanted it to and you got hurt real bad for a very long time. A lot of people got hurt by it.

"But, there comes a time when, and maybe now's that time, when you gotta finish your grieving for her and try to find a new life for yourself. A man grieving for a lost love as long as you have, it's just not healthy. I've known you a long time, son, and I know God wouldn't want you to suffer any longer than you already have. You've got to promise me that when you're through with your grieving in a few days that you'll try to see to it that you let the past slip away to a place where it rightfully belongs.

"Now, I'm not saying you have to forget Beth, or stop loving her. I want you to go home and cry until you can't cry any more. And then you just might want to think about kind of sealing those feelings up tight in a little box and tucking that box away in a corner of your heart somewhere. Somewhere, where you know where it is, and how to get to it, so once in awhile you can open it up and think about her. But on a day-to-day basis, it will be tucked away in that secret spot, hidden away so you can get on with your life. Does any of that make sense?"

"What did you mean that 'a lot of people got hurt by it'?"

He stood and walked to the stained glass window that looked out onto the rear parking lot behind the school. It had been the Little League Field for a few years in the early and mid-1950s, and later it became the site of St. Augustine's parochial elementary school.

"You know, Will, God has given me the privilege to work with his children for many years. Over those years I have tried my best to earn that honor every day. It's such a blessing to watch all of the young people I have worked with grow up into fulfilled adults, with children of their own. I now work with the grandchildren of some of the kids I first worked with, you know, your crowd.

"But I must be honest with you, Will. Of the thousands I have worked with, of the millions of good memories, none of those kids have meant more to me than you, your brother Francis, Tom, and Beth. The four of you meant more to me than any others. Those are the days that God blessed me the most. As I grow older, the days I look back on with the fondest feelings are those few short years."

He looked out the window for a brief moment and I felt like he was in a confessional confessing something to me.

"When y'er brother Francis was hurt, I thought I would die inside. I saw what it did to your mother and father. Where was God that day? I asked Him that. I asked God that point-blank. In my anguish, I demanded of Him to *tell me where He was* at that moment, leavin' your brother unprotected like that. The only thing that kept me together was knowing that I had to be strong for you and your family. Your mother. Then, later, when you and Beth and Tom grew older and went away to school, my heart was broken again. I prayed for the day when you would all come back to New City and grow into adults within my purview. So I could watch you all become…happy. Happy in your own way. I know I'm not supposed to feel that way about my children. I'm supposed to be impartial and treat everyone equally. But I was guilty of being selfish.

"And when you came back for those summers, I thought I would see my dreams come true. But then Tom went off to fight in that despicable war and came back broken, and you went back to Florida for those years. I didn't ever think I would see my 'kids' together again.

"And then that day, that day that…" He hesitated, searching carefully for his words as if they were hiding somewhere out on that Little League Field that wasn't there anymore; that hadn't been there in years.

"That dreadful day that three young friends, who had loved one another so much, all decided not to see one another again…."

Here, he stopped, his back still to me, his head hung down, he whispered. "You were all my children, and I failed you all. I failed you."

I stood and walked to his side. "Father Carrick. No."

"Yes, Will, I failed you all. I was charged by the Lord to protect his little ones and I let you all down. I wanted to do so much to help, but you went off to Vietnam and later ran off back down to Florida. Beth ran off to the City and began her own world travels. I should have done something, to bring you all back together; you belonged together, but I didn't. It was so cowardly of me."

"You couldn't. You couldn't leave here."

"I tried to do the best I could, I could see how you were all hurting. And Tom…."

Now his anger prevented him from crying.

"What they did to that young man over there in that place, to all you young men. It was a betrayal on an unimaginable scale."

"I saw Tom this morning. After….when I left Beth…."

"I know."

"How do you know?"

"He called me. He said you came to see him this morning for the first time since the autumn of 1968. Said you were his best friend and you live in the same town and you didn't go see him even once in thirty-two years."

"I know. I know. I guess I was embarrassed. I didn't think he wanted…"

"Tom and I have become close over the years. There was no one around when he came home broken in mind and body and spirit like a pile of discarded twigs. He came to Mass every day. Every day, confession. Every day."

"Wow. That's a lot of confessing."

"Oh, my, yes, Will. A lot of confessing. A lot of confessing for someone you probably only remember as some straight-arrow, white bread, goody-two-shoes, who wouldn't hurt a fly. A lot of confessing."

"What do you mean?"

He turned from the window and sat down on the thick leather chair behind his desk. "I think I've said enough for today. Why don't you come see me again in a few days. We'll talk some more. Maybe you'll think about prayin' with me then."

"Sure."

"Until then, go home and have a good cry for the only woman you may ever love in this life. Be thankful for the only woman who ever gave you comfort and joy and solace and hope. Cry for her. Cry for yourself and your loss. You deserve it. Get it all out. Get it all out good and once and for all. Don't let anyone deprive you of it or take it from you. But promise me that when you're finished, you'll put it away in that little box and hide it in some hard-to-get-at part of your heart, and try to get on with your life. Your mom, she's worried about ya'. And the Lord, He doesn't want you to spend the rest of your life mournin' over Beth. We've seen enough cryin' around here to last a lifetime."

He stopped, and hesitated before he continued, as if to catch himself from revealing something too personal. "I want the cryin' to be over once and for all."

"Okay."

"I'll be prayin' for you Will."

"Thank you, Father Carrick."

"Prayin' for us all."

CHAPTER EIGHT

ROCKLAND COUNTY COURTHOUSE

Monday, 1 p.m.
October 16, 2000
Age 54

It was now time to face the music at the office. I knew they would all be there so it was time to get it over with. I walked down to the Courthouse and turned up the three steps to cross the broad lawn.

The Rockland County Courthouse is the third County Seat building to be on the Main Street site. The second one held Saturday night dances in the basement where my grandfather, a local farm boy, met a girl from Manhattan visiting her relatives in New City. They were married in 1904. That second County Courthouse burned down in the early 1920s.

When the Courthouse was rebuilt in 1928, they chose a transitional Beaux Arts/Art Deco architecture. On the broad, front walk is a classic statue and on the north and south lawns are WWI and WWII monuments, respectively. Along the building's façade are tower lights each supported by four bronze tortoises.

Inside, the cigar smoke from over seventy years has accumulated and adhered to the marble and dark wood walls and mixes with the smells of furniture oil and floor cleaner, and sometimes, the smell of justice.

As you open the heavy brass doors, you face an oil painting on the far wall depicting Rockland County as it was 150 years ago: farmlands and woods and streams and dirt roads.

I walked up the marble staircase on the left and down the south corridor to the District Attorney's Office.

At the front desk Jeanette nodded a hello and then another nod to where I knew they would all be waiting.

Inside the interior hallway, District Attorney Barry Henion stood, the most impressive thing about him, the width of the suspenders not-at-all necessary to keep his pants from falling. His predecessor, now retired, had been the one to hire me, twenty-four years earlier. Henion was talking to Jimmy when I entered and they both looked up.

Barry walked forward, his hand extended. "I'm sorry to hear about Beth. Why don't we all go inside?

By inside he meant the board room with the long oak table where his team planned their prosecution strategies.

"Your timing is perfect. We're about to get started."

In the board room were all the players that would be needed to prosecute this case, in the eventuality that Beth's murderer was found. Carl Betts, an investigator with the D.A.'s office and my immediate supervisor, David Sherman and Ray Cicci, the homicide investigators from Clarkstown's Police Department who had been at the murder scene when I arrived earlier that morning, and Jimmy, representing the Coroner's Office.

Barry was running the show. "Jeanette, you can start recording. Before we get started, I want everyone to understand, and I mean everyone to understand, that although Will can listen in on the meetings, he can in no way take part in the investigation because of the possibility of conflict of interest. As you all know, Will knew the victim for over forty years, as well as the primary witness Tom Hogenkamp, who found the body on his morning jog, and called it in.

"So Will, whereas I understand that you have a personal interest in this case and I can appreciate that, under no circumstances are you to implicate yourself into this investigation in any way, shape or form. Is that understood? I don't want you talking to potential witnesses, I don't want you going around asking questions, I don't want you doing anything to jeopardize this case in any way. Are you reading me here?"

"Loud and clear. You wanna give me a list of who you don't want me to talk to?"

"This is no time to be a smart-ass Will. I think you know who I'm talking about here. I'm willing to write off your little *tete-a-tete* with Hogenkamp at the boathouse this morning as a chance encounter in the woods. Any more of that and it's you and me going to the mat."

"Is he considered a suspect?"

"I didn't say that, but he is a witness. He found the body."

"Isn't that a coincidence?"

"Could very well be, but that's up to us to find out and not you. Standard process of elimination will no doubt clear him. Let me be quite clear about this. You may observe this investigation, but in no way are you to get involved in it. No freelancing. Got it?"

"I got it."

He turned to the others at the table. "Do I make myself clear to all of you about Will's involvement in all of this?"

There were silent nods. I got the feeling this had all been discussed at great length before I had arrived, and what I was seeing now was a repeat performance for my edification.

"So, Will. Jim tells me you've known Beth since the fifth grade.

"1956."

"And you were once in a romantic relationship with her?"

"Last three years of high school, all through college, until late 1968."

"And she was married to her current husband when?"

"Spring of 1971."

"And then they moved out of New City?"

"In and out. Europe for a few years. Hong Kong for about ten years."

"Did you see her during those years?"

"Since she was married? Just by chance encounter. Driving down the street, whatever. Small town, bump-into stuff."

"You saw Beth almost a year ago at Tor's Luncheonette across the street?"

I looked at Jimmy and he nodded.

"Yes, that's correct. And as far as Tom goes, I know it was a mistake on my part talking to him this morning, but he was an old friend of mine and I hadn't seen him in years and I…"

"No matter. Just as long as you understand you are to have no further contact with him until he is cleared as a suspect."

"I understand."

"I know you 'understand' it. That's not what I'm saying. I'm *telling* you that you are to have no further contact with Tom Hogenkamp. I need your word on this."

"You have my word."

"You understand that your contact with him this morning has the potential to seriously compromise this case, depending where it winds up?"

"Yes, I understand."

"Okay. Then let's proceed. What do we know? Carl?"

Carl Betts was a beefy investigator working for the D.A.'s office. He was smart, thorough and efficient, despite the first impression many people had of him. He shifted uneasily in his chair and in his suit. He had recently lost forty-five pounds, but was still wearing a tubby-suit from his former life.

"Ray, Dave, and I contacted her father at his studio on South

Mountain Road this morning as soon as Will and Jimmy identified her."

Barry was looking over the shoulder of his secretary as she took notes on a steno keyboard and monitored the back-up recorder. "How did he react?"

"He collapsed on the floor. I got the idea that it was real. "

I thought back to the first time I had ever met Beth's father, a famous sculptor who lived on South Mountain Road.

Barry interrupted my thoughts with another question for the investigative team.

"What about the husband?"

"Rainer Klein," Ray answered.

"The developer, right?"

"Yeah. Dave and I tracked him down through his Manhattan office. He has an airtight alibi in Hong Kong for the past seventy-two hours. There are witnesses, even security videotapes from the casinos and offices he visited to confirm it. No way it could have been him, unless you have his private jet involved, shuttling him back and forth. We're checking flight plans now. We have the local police verifying everything. He's enroute back here, as we speak, on his private jet. He's air-tight."

Most people considered Rainer a slime ball. He was a greedy pig of a land and shopping mall developer from Holland, with development interests all over the world.

"So, married almost thirty years?" Barry looked at me.

I tried to keep it impersonal. "Yeah. Beth met him at the gallery where she worked in downtown Manhattan when he stopped in to look at some art work. He was well known in New City, by reputation at least, for years before that. He's the guy who bought up the out-parcels of the Florion Estate from Tom's Grandfather in the late 1950s and built those houses on Twin Elms Lane and Capral Lane. Klein courted her with his riches and she succumbed to his charms and they were married about a year later."

"He's what, twenty years older than her?"

"Twenty four."

"Okay. Anything from autopsy yet, Jimmy?"

"No, give us a few more hours. We're working...."

"Wait a minute Jimmy." Barry interrupted Jimmy to dismiss me. "Will, nothing personal about this. We've worked too many of these together. I know you're probably feeling crazy right now about all of this, but you've got to step back. You're a friend and probably the best guy we got here, but I'm not going to allow you to hurt us or this investigation. I can't let you do that. So get out of here and take the rest of the day off. Tomorrow. Take tomorrow off, too. Come back Wednesday."

I got up to leave.

"And Will. Don't come sniffing around here looking for information or go rogue on us. This isn't some TV cop show. We'll call you when we need you."

"I got it. I got it."

As I left I couldn't help but feel like a suspect along with Rainer and Tom. Who else was out there? Someone who knew her? Some random chance encounter? Someone recently released from jail, where they might have seen her take that path from their jail cell window in the old courthouse jail? Who else even knew she frequented that path?

I followed Father Carrick's advice after I left the office. I headed home to take a nap. I walked slowly south on Main Street, waving to my mother as she sat on the rocker on the big front porch facing the street.

"I'm going home to rest."

"You and Delores come for dinner tonight if you want."

I nodded to my mother and continued north to Collyer Avenue then west to New City Park. As I walked I thought of my beloved Beth and how we had all met in the fifth grade.

CHAPTER NINE

THE HISTORY OF MUSIC
IN NEW CITY, NEW YORK:
PART II

Summer-Fall, 1956
Age 10

The rest of the days in the summer of 1956 between my fourth and fifth grade years, after "Francis' Day," seem to have transpired in a silent blur. Marvin and Sparrow disappeared for the rest of the summer, hiding out in the Ramapos with other family members, I would find out later, taking daily beatings from their father.

At my house I was alone that summer, truly alone for the first time I could remember. I tried playing in the baseball field and in the streams and woods behind the house, but without Francis leading, the adventures were empty. Anyone seeing me during the long days of that summer would have seen me walking along the paths adjacent to the streams, twirling a switch, singing to myself and recreating or inventing conversations with Francis; conversations from the past about life, conversations which never took place about the ensuing battle or conflict we were about to encounter as we continued our march of conquest over our domain; conversations with Francis I knew I would never have again.

One day in late August, during such a conversation I was having out loud with myself, I looked up to see a young man watching me from behind a tree on the opposite bank. I was startled by his presence. How long had he been watching me? I knew immediately it must be the grandson of the Florions we had heard stories about.

"Hi. I'm Tom, the new kid. I live up in that big house on the hill. You wanna play, or hang out or something?"

We stood looking at one another across the narrow tributary of the Demarest Kill, and more than any other time since "Francis' Day," I felt terribly afraid and lonely. So instead of answering him, I turned and raced back to the safe haven of one of my grandfather's abandoned chicken coops. Although they had been swept out, the smell and dust of chicken manure from years before still hung in the air. I wasn't ready yet to play with anyone else and I curled into a corner and cried for my brother and the life he was living. But most of all, I cried for myself and the loss of a brother who had been stolen from me through carelessness and fear and the unpredictable randomness of chance.

All that summer I tried to stay out of the house as much as I could. The sights I saw and the sounds I heard were unspeakably oppressive. Emily Dickinson once wrote a poem that describes *"the silence in the house, the morning after death."* It's the only way to describe what was going on in my house. There was no conversation between my father and me. He was almost as comatose as Francis, as if he had taken on his beloved son's muteness. About two weeks after the incident they had brought Francis home from Suffern Hospital, where we had both been born. But he was never really my brother again. He was just some organism we had once all loved who would never be the same. Between my father and my mother, the conversations were few, the words hushed, as if anything they said might be overheard by Francis, or a neighbor, or me.

It wasn't as if I didn't want to be around Francis or had stopped loving him. I loved him even more. It just hurt too much to be with him, to see him the way he was. As much as I felt bad for him and the life he would never have, I mourned for myself and the fact that I would never again have an older brother to play with. I had been cheated by life. He had been stolen from me and I couldn't face the pain.

My mother's words to me were few, except to say that things had forever changed in our lives and we were all going to work together to make the best of it.

Father Carrick came by to see my father, engage him in prayer, but my father was beyond that. During the daytime, every daytime, Father Carrick would come again and say mass for Francis, the little altar boy whom he had taken under his wing and was grooming for possible priesthood before that tragic day that took him from us.

And meanwhile, my little hometown of New City was beginning to grow up around us.

Just two years before, the ability to travel from the metropolitan area of New York City to upstate had changed dramatically. Under President Eisenhower's leadership, The New York State Thruway bull-dozed and dynamited its way north through Rockland County toward Albany, and then west to Buffalo. Not long after, the Palisades Interstate Parkway that would make commuting possible between the George Washington Bridge and Bear Mountain was completed. It made it easier for the thousands of drivers who'd previously taken the train or the Red and Tan Bus Lines, or Route 9-W to the city. With commuting made that much more convenient, thousands of City families began to explore the suburban countryside. And when they discovered the beauty of Rockland County and New City, and realized the ease of the commute, New City went from a suburban outpost to a bedroom community in a matter of just a few years.

In just one year, 1955-1956, class sizes had doubled and the school on the hill on Old Congers Road that had been built before the turn of the Century that my father and grandfather had both attended was now too small to handle the hordes of newcomers. Neighborhoods and boundaries were gerrymandered in ways never thought possible before because they hadn't been necessary before.

From first through fourth grade, I had attended classes at New City Grammar School on old Congers Road. It was the same school my father had attended thirty years earlier and my grandfather, sixty years earlier. My fourth grade class had thirty-four students. But by the end of my fourth grade year, attendance had risen dramatically with the influx of "City Kids," and fifth grade would be split into two sections. Kids on the east side of town would attend the old school.

Fourth and fifth graders who lived on the west side of town and from Street School up on Zukor Road would attend classes in makeshift classrooms fashioned out of two large basement playrooms in the Damiani house on Twin Elms Lane. It was a large, modern, brick residence built several years before on the bottom of the bluff beneath where the Florion mansion stood. Built into the side of the hill as it was, the main living quarters were on the first floor, if approached from the front. If approached from the rear, the cavernous, empty basement opened onto a parking lot. The Clarkstown School Board rented the entire basement for the fourth and fifth grades. They were perfect accommodations. Spacious, well-lighted rooms paneled in knotty pine, with adequate restroom facilities. Isolation from the rest of the growing New City Grammar School student body gave us a feeling of being special, as if we were an advance team sent out to explore the unknown.

But best yet, a large rolling field for playing our recess games adjoined the classrooms. It was a perfect environment for a fifth grade boy, since it was so close to my beloved Demarest Kill.

Several important things happened in those first days of fifth grade. Tom, the boy along the brook who had extended an invitation to play earlier that summer was seated next to me when class began. There was an awkward silence between us during the first class day, but as school ended, he stood and lingered after the others left and shyly offered his hand for me to shake. He was tall and thin and had long curly blonde hair. Even then he was muscular with an athlete's physique.

"I'm Tom Hogenkamp. You're the guy I saw down by the brook that day."

"Yeah."

"You live over by that tiny little ball field. My grandfather told me your grandfather worked for him. He said your dad made the ball field after your granddad died. You wanna hang out or something? I can go home and get my mitt."

"Yeah, sure."

That afternoon I followed him across the field and up the hill to Dove Cottage. We walked around the back to the pantry door and walked in through the narrow hallway to the kitchen. A woman that I first thought was a nurse because of her starched white uniform smiled at Tom and offered me a hello. In a thick, German accent, she said, "And who might your friend be?"

"I'm Will."

"Of course, you are Francis' grandson. I used to see you in our yard when you were just a little one. I knew your grandfather for many years."

I merely nodded and hung my head.

"So, there will be milk and cookies for two this afternoon, then?"

"Yes, Frau K. Thank you." Then, turning to me, Tom said, I'll go upstairs and get my glove. You can keep Frau K. company."

There was silence in the kitchen as she prepared the snack.

Then, softly, she spoke. "Your grandfather was such a good man. I'm sorry you didn't get to know him better. I don't know how we could have kept things going around here if it wasn't for him, he's been such a help to the Florions. He planted every tree, even the vineyard in this yard, shaped every bush like a Michelangelo. And inside here? He kept us ship-shape."

I thought of the boxwood outside on the expansive lawn, each shrub crisply trimmed; the fruit trees heavy with apples and pears. I looked around the kitchen. I knew my grandfather had done woodworking and fix-up stuff on the side, but what I saw hadn't prepared me for the extent of his craft.

Frau K. caught me examining the cabinetry.

"You remind me of your grandfather. He re-built those cabinets a hundred times after he first built them. He couldn't keep his eyes off his work when he came in here. He was a perfectionist."

"Did he do all of this?"

"Oh, yes. All by hand, like in the old country."

I stood to inspect the mitered joints. Every one was tightly sealed against the next.

"It's a shame your father didn't follow in his footsteps."

I remember thinking of what my father was going through at that point in our lives.

"And your brother. How is he now?"

I was surprised by her question. How did she know? I had no idea adults routinely talked to one another about things like this.

"He was in a coma for two weeks. In Suffern Hospital. He's home now. Getting better," I lied.

"I'm so sorry. He was such a nice boy."

"Yes, ma'am."

Tom came bounding down a circular staircase on the other side of the kitchen with his baseball mitt. The first glimpse of the mitt didn't prepare me for the fact that I would think of it often in the coming years, for the rest of my life. There seemed to be handwriting on it in ball point pen.

"I'm ready."

After the milk and cookies, we were off, walking the fields and woods between the mansion on the hill and my back yard. We crossed the Demarest Kill tributary together for the first time that day. It was to be the first of countless crossings over a lifetime. Although, of course, I didn't realize it at the time, it was a rite of passage.

After school that first day of the fifth grade was the beginning of a close friendship that would last for twelve years.

To a certain degree, all great athletes share many traits. The shape of their torsos, the proportion of their shoulders and waist, the ratio of muscle to body fat. Every move effortless, natural, without strain or anxiety. My brother Francis had moved in this way, and so now did Tom. That afternoon, as we tossed the ball between us on a ball field that was already showing signs of neglect in the two months since "Francis' Day," I saw it all in him. In so many ways did he remind me of Francis, that it was almost painful to hang around with him. Although Tom and I were just weeks apart in birth dates, he was far more mature for his age, deceptively so, from the way he carried himself and with the demeanor he spoke to everyone, even the adults in our lives. It wouldn't be very long before Tom began to replace Francis as my role model in sports, in school, in life.

At first I resisted the feelings because they made me fearful, and later angry over my loss and angry over the fact that I was allowing a new friend into my life. It was a reluctant transfer of influences, one I both rejected and embraced. I wanted things to be the same with Francis, but knew they could never be. Tom stepped in to assuage the pain at the critical moment when he was needed.

As the sun was going down on that first day of our new friendship, we sat resting our backs on the poplar trunks behind home plate. He stared into the setting sun.

"My parents are in Europe."

"That's cool. Are they on vacation?"

"Not exactly."

"What do you mean?"

"They're living over there."

"How come you're not living there with them?"

"I don't think they want me there."

I didn't know what to say, so I said nothing.

"They don't know that I know that. I heard my grandfather on the phone talking to my father. My grandfather told my father that he and my grandmother would take care of me and not to bother coming back if that's the way he and my mother felt about it."

"I'm sorry."

"You don't have to be. My grandparents are really nice people. They treat me like I'm their own child."

"Still…."

"I guess they have important stuff to do over there."

"Don't you miss them?"

"Not too much anymore. I really haven't seen them much since I was five. That's five years ago."

"Where have you been?"

"Boarding school in New Hampshire, mostly, Phillips Exeter Academy."

"What's boarding school?"

"It's a school where your parents send you when they don't want you around."

"Huh. Why don't they want you around?"

"I don't know. I haven't been able to figure it out. I guess I made them mad or something."

"I'm sorry."

"You don't have to be. I love my grandparents very much and they love me. That's why I'm living here permanently now. They want me with them. And with fifth grade within spitting distance right next door, what could be more convenient?" He laughed lightly.

"I guess you're right."

It was the last time I ever heard Tom mention his parents. I would find out only years later he would never see them again in his lifetime.

"Anyway, I gotta go home. They're expecting me home soon. I gotta go help Frau K. get dinner ready. Practice my piano."

"Piano?"

"Yeah, I take lessons from Yolanda Mero."

"Who's that?"

"You'll meet her someday. She's friends of my grandparents. She's a concert pianist. One of the best in the world. But she makes me practice three hours a day."

"That must be a pain."

"Not really. I like it. So, you wanna be friends?"

I shrugged at the directness of his question. "Sure. I guess."

"Okay, then."

We stood and he slapped the side of his thigh with his baseball glove. There was writing on it I noticed again, but I couldn't make it out.

There was an awkward silence between us for a moment before he spoke again. He was looking toward the stream and the setting sun. His face and hair were painted golden.

"I'm sorry about your brother."

"That's okay. He's gonna get better soon."

I truly believed that with all my heart and soul. I would believe it until months later, when late one night I couldn't sleep and snuck downstairs to lie beside my brother's still form in the hospital bed in the dining room. It wouldn't be until then that I would accept what I should have known that very first moment when I saw my father lift my brother from the Kelvinator. The boy with the ashen face and the arms as frail as a bird's wings that he carried off down the street was never coming back to us in any way.

It was only when I accepted that, cuddled beside him on the bed in the dining room, that I could finally let go and say goodbye to him. Say goodbye to all the fun that we had had together, to all that he had taught me, to all the adoration I had given him. Say goodbye to the endless days running the bases, chasing the pop flies, hooking worms, going on expeditions through the woods, the Dutch Garden, and wading the Demarest Kill. It was only then that I could say goodbye to my childhood forever and begin to move beyond the pain a ten year-old boy hides in his heart; begin to grow up and forge a new friendship with Tom Hogenkamp.

CHAPTER TEN

NEW CITY PARK

Monday, 3 p.m.
October 16, 2000
Age 54

I had turned off my cell phone as I walked home along Main Street from the District Attorney's Office toward New City Park. I didn't want to talk to anyone anytime soon. I could have gone south on Little Tor Road, but I wanted to vary the trek as I did every morning.

On Collyer Avenue, past the funeral home, I turned toward the west and walked up the hill to New City Park. On Lake Drive I stopped to look at New City Park Lake, its surface dappled in early midday light, dotted with yellow oak and maple leaves drifting lazily toward the spillway. We had all spent so many hours there as kids.

No matter where I walked that day I would have seen a place full of ghosts, so I just turned into the parking lot and walked down the lakeside path that skirted the eastern perimeter to the south end of the lake. My little cottage sat nestled in a blaze of fall colors, fronting the water near the small lighthouse on the south shore.

So many days spent at this lake. So many stories. So much history.

Every kid has to have a swimming hole. Ours used to be Sweet Clover over on Long Clove Road. Just the name alone, Sweet Clover, evokes a simpler time; a place to lie down and nap on a warm summer day and dream of wild horses galloping in slow motion alongside the stream at sunset. But in the mid-1950s Sweet Clover had been consumed by the flooding of the Lake DeForest Reservoir. The kids had to find a replacement, and New City Park Lake was one of the lakes of choice, out of the perhaps dozens of choices we could have made.

No, it didn't have a swift running brook feeding it and it wasn't covered completely by a canopy of trees and no it wasn't hidden from view like Sweet Clover had been, but we needed a place to swim and we found it.

At the north end of New City Park Lake was the dam that kept the water back from the north-flowing stream and served as a deck for the two-story clubhouse. It had been built as a grinding mill and an ice house to store the ice, prior to being sold for ice-boxes in town, before electric refrigeration became widespread. The clubhouse was where parties were held in the summertime and deck chairs and picnic tables were stored in the wintertime.

All the lakeside cottages had been built in the 1920s by the Norwegian immigrants as summer weekend places. Later, they had been winterized and the permanent Norwegian colony was established.

By the 70s most of the pioneers were all gone and their children had moved off to other places and the cottages were sold to both outsiders and to people like me who had fond childhood memories of the place and wanted to recapture it all by living there themselves. That's what I had done in 1978. Two years after I started work at the District Attorney's office I had saved enough money by living at home with my mother and brother that I put down a fifty percent deposit. Within a few years I had paid it off, living frugally. Before then I had met Delores, an English teacher at Clarkstown High where I had attended and later taught. She had her own place with her mother, but moved in with me. So now we shared its cozy quarters that had a big kitchen window that looked across a small back lawn to the lakefront.

As I turned off the lake path to cross the back lawn, I stopped to take a look at a small patch of the grass, hallowed ground, now growing dormant with the season, and stared down at it. Just a tiny piece of earth, that held so much meaning for me. I squatted down and touched the earth at my feet, spreading my hand on the cool, dry grass trying to soak up the memories; touching it in either hope or fear that it would suck me back in time to a night so long ago.

I stood and walked in the house before I lost control again. Inside, the house was silent as I climbed up the narrow staircase and fell into the bed that I shared with Delores for the last twenty-odd years. I landed face down in the pillows, and as the smell of autumn drifted in through the open screen windows, I began to follow Father Carrick's orders and I drifted off to sleep and dreamed of my Beth.

I awoke with a hand on my arm. It was Delores. She was in her teacher's school clothes and sat on the bed next to me, stroking my face. Her long dark hair fell toward me, and for a moment I thought I was still dreaming. Delores was an Honors English teacher at Clarkstown High School, where I had graduated in 1964, and had later taught there for a few years in the mid-1970s. She had grown up in Haverstraw and graduated from Haverstraw High before going off to SUNY Potsdam on a scholarship. We met in the teachers' lounge and started hanging around together, but it was a year before we eventually started dating after partying with the same crowd. We just drifted together; left behind by our-selves in the lonely hearts' club otherwise known as the teachers' lounge, through attrition more than anything else. Since then, we had spent the better part of twenty years living together.

I looked at the clock. It was almost four and the shadows were lengthening along the lake and into the bedroom.

"I heard at work. About Beth. I called your office. I've been trying your cell all day."

"I turned it off when they told me to go home.

"Why didn't you call?"

"I was going to. I didn't want to disturb you in class. I fell asleep."

"I'm sorry Will. I know how you felt about her."

"What do you mean?"

"Look, Will. This is really no time to argue. I don't want to argue anymore. I know because ever since I've known you, you've been wearing your heart on your sleeve for her."

I was still groggy. "Really?" Even to myself I sounded on the defensive.

"I know this is rough for you Will, and I don't want to give you a hard time. I just want you to know I feel bad for you and I'm here for you if you need me."

I looked in the eyes of the woman I had been living with for years and felt nothing. I was thankful for her patience and kindness and understanding, but all I could think of was Beth.

Delores stood, and smoothed her dress against her legs and narrow frame. "Why don't you go back to sleep? I'll make some dinner and wake you up later."

"Okay. Yes. I want to go back to sleep."

CHAPTER ELEVEN

THE HISTORY OF MUSIC
IN NEW CITY, NEW YORK:
PART III

August - September, 1956
Age 10

> *They say for every boy and girl*
> *There's just one love in this whole world,*
> *And I know I've found mine.*
> *Young Love*

Written by Ric Cartey
and Carole Joyner
Performed by Sonny James

Starting immediately that summer after "Francis' Day," and before fifth grade, I inherited Francis' paper route. I would get up before dawn and walk to the sidewalk where a tied-up bundle of the *Rockland Journal News* would be on the curb, having just been thrown from a passing truck that looked like it could have been used by a milkman. For the next twenty minutes I would wrap them in rubber bands, the snap beating rhythm to my hands' work as they folded each newspaper. I tossed each one into a giant muslin bag my mother had sewn for Francis two summers before. I would sling the bag across my shoulder while riding my bike.

Then, as the dawn broke over Third Street, I would be off, perfecting my toss's accuracy with each passing home. Down Main Street to Collyer Avenue and west to New City Park. All up and down the side streets and hills of New City Park, then north on Little Tor Road to Phillips' Hill Road. It didn't take me long to realize that some of my route duplicated my own father's mail route and his father's before that. On Saturday mornings I would collect my bills and by the end of the day, my mother would have an additional six dollars in her household account, most often in nickels and dimes. She would give me back a dollar for my allowance. It was all worth it for the seclusion my bike rides offered me. It was meditative.

I would reflect on that same route many times as I traveled over the familiar roads with two classmates who would become new friends. For a dozen years they would be my best friends and soul-mates. We would bike this same route as a trio countless times.

Fifth grade was all new to us. One shock was that we had our first male teacher; Cornelius, "Pete" Dennehy, a war veteran, Ivy-Leaguer, educated on the G.I. Bill, and settling into a new home with his young wife. With him came his Brooks Brothers suits, his pipe, and his Socratic teaching methods. We started every day by reading aloud the front section of the New York Times that was delivered to the basement with copies shared by all the kids. Our world was expanding exponentially in more ways than we could imagine.

In addition to befriending Tom, something else happened that first week of fifth grade in that knotty pine basement. I first saw a young girl who would steal my heart away from me that very first week and would possess my mind and my soul until the morning I saw her face down in the Demarest Kill forty-four years later.

Even in fifth grade Beth VonBronk was tall for a girl our age, almost as tall as Tom and me. She was thin, with long shiny dark hair brushed back and kept in place with blue barrettes. Her olive skin was flawless. She was the most beautiful girl I had ever seen in my life, and even though at the age of ten I didn't fully understand the long-term implications of all of that, I sensed that there was some abstract, life-affirming meaning to it all. Her mere presence had some physical impact on my entire being. I started to perspire, and I swear I could taste metal in my mouth as my heart and chest filled with warmth I had never felt before. The biological urges responsible for human procreation throughout hundreds of thousands of years went into full swing before I could even realize their ramifications. It literally made me light-headed, all in the fifth grade.

She was escorted into the room by the school's elementary guidance counselor and introduced to Mr. Dennehy. After a brief, hushed conference, he put his arm on her shoulder and spoke to the class.

"I would like everyone to say hello to Beth VonBronk. She lives on South Mountain Road. For the past few years she's attended Street School. But as you all know, with New City growing so quickly, Street School has become grades one through four, exclusively. All of her other former classmates from up toward Zukor Road and the Dellwood Country Club are going to the other fifth grade in the regular New City Grammar School building.

"Please make her feel welcome. Beth, why don't you have a seat next to, let's see. . . Will, and we'll continue our discussion on the Mid-Atlantic States?"

She walked down the aisle toward me, her blue-grey, cloth-bound loose-leaf binder clasped to her flat chest and just before she sat down in the vacant chair she did something that lasted but an instant, but would forever change my life. She looked at me and smiled, shyly. *Just one smile.* Her eyes were brown, almost black, darker than any I had ever seen before. And that smile. It lasted but a second, perhaps longer, since I couldn't look her in the eye for more than a split second. But it was a smile and a glance that changed my entire life. I looked up again nervously and she had not broken eye-contact with me. She was waiting for me, daring me to make eye contact with her.

"Hi." She *kept smiling.*

I nodded, quickly turned away.

So there it is. A two second event in the eternal, infinite, time-space continuum that would direct the rest of my life's path. It would affect every decision I would make forever after.

Her voice shocked me and all I could do was grunt in response and look at my open textbook map of "The Mid-Atlantic States: New York, New Jersey, Pennsylvania, Maryland, and Delaware."

During recess she boldly walked right up to me.

"So, you're Will."

"Yeah."

"I'm Beth. Thanks for sharing your book."

"Yeah."

"Have you always gone to school in New City, or are you a new kid?

"No. I'm a regular. A native, I guess. My father went to school in New City and so did my grandfather and great-grandfather."

"Wow. My father and I live on South Mountain Road."

"Nice place."

"How about you?"

"Main Street."

"North Main?"

"South Main." There was a difference. An understatement on my part.

South Mountain Road and the area around Lake Lucille was an artists' colony, starting back in the 1920s. I would soon find out Beth's father was a famous sculptor who in the post-war years of the Jackson Pollock era had taken Manhattan by storm and who was now hob-knobbing with other South Mountain Road habitués like Maxwell Anderson, Burgess Meredith, Lotte Lenya, and soon, Ernie Kovacs. Beth's mother had died years earlier, but it would be a while before we found out the details.

Just that one smile and my life would forever after be changed. And yes, there were the black, patent-leather shoes with the white ankle sox. When she was seated next to me, my face was on fire, my throat tightened, and I didn't know what was happening to me. That was the start of the next forty-four years.

She was a beauty. Loving, passionate, but, I would find out far too late, unforgiving. Not that I could ever blame her for that. Perhaps pragmatic or self-protective would be better word choices.

CHAPTER TWELVE

NEW CITY

September-October, 1956
Fifth Grade, Age 10

I like to think of fifth grade as a year when I really started to grow up and see the world. There was the loss of my brother's companionship, and the slow awareness and acceptance that I now had to face the world alone. But this fear of loneliness was quickly being overcome by the events that began to reshape my world.

It was during Mr. Dennehy's readings of the New York Times every morning, that began to make me aware of the center of the universe that existed less than thirty miles from where I was sitting. It was exciting to know that there was a place so nearby that literally invented so many aspects of our culture. Just a few miles south was the world's largest financial district, big thinkers who made decisions that changed how people lived and what they bought; the heart of the music industry that was producing the music that we loved, Broadway, filmmaking, and the pioneers who were spreading their wings after the birth of television and were experimenting with the relatively new medium in ways never thought possible before.

It was all right there just a few miles away and many of those people now commuted home every night to our little hamlet that was now becoming a bedroom community. Prior to this year, as far as I was concerned, New City was just a pleasant little village, having descended from a farming community. Now, we were on the outskirts of Metropolis.

And what were the events that shaped my new thinking as my beloved brother lay flat on his back, a few hundred yards away, discovering his own new little world that only existed between his ears and nowhere else?

Sometime in the beginning weeks of fifth grade, in keeping with the end of Major League Baseball season, our teachers held a cross-town rivalry baseball game played at the neutral field behind the Dutch Garden, where the parking lot for the Highway Department and the new County Courthouse sits. There, in the back yard of the Eberling Shoe Factories of the late 1800s, a mountain of gravel overlooked the baseball diamond, home to generations of softball games and holiday picnics with sack-races and pie-eating contests. As the years wore on, more and more of it would become parking for the new Courthouse additions. Where the feet of young girls and boys trod on their way to baseball and three-legged-races' glory, there now sits just a parking space for the County Clerk's sedentary paperwork shufflers.

The fifth graders from both school fifth grades, now rivals, marched down Main St. in our high-top sneakers with the rubber patches ripped off, gloves dangling from the bats we shouldered, and turned into the Courthouse parking lot and down the hill across the wooden bridge toward the field. We stopped at the springhead to get a drink of cold spring water from an iron pipe that came out of a cave-like opening made of fieldstone by some early farmer who had discovered the spring. The pipe emptied into a small pool at our feet and then flowed lazily east toward the

Dutch Garden in a stone sluice-way filled with fresh watercress. Could it have been an early mill run providing power for the farmers' grinding stones? Probably.

At one time I could have led you to a dozen fresh springs in New City, where as younger boys we had stopped to sip the ice cold, clean water. Now, many of them were covered or diverted or polluted with fertilizer or septic tank run-off. A young boy today, assuming they still explore these woods and fields in New City, wouldn't even find a trace of my watercress filled spring sluice-way.

That game on that day had pitted kids who had played together since kindergarten and were now on opposing teams. Was there more to the distinction than just geographical boundaries, or were there some other factors at play here? In some subtle way, the division of the class was a portent of the future, a shifting of gears we never even noticed until much later.

I don't remember the final score, or even who won. I was too distracted by the new faces in the other class, and how much many of my former classmates had matured in the few short months since I had seen them at the end of the fourth grade.

Toward the end of the game, some parents began to show up, and after, sandwiches were served by some of the moms and our girl classmates. Beth had packed a picnic lunch for Tom and me, and as I sat and watched the two classes mingle, I felt lifted away, watching it all from an observer's post on the thirty foot-high pile of gravel.

The next big event in our lives almost defied description by a fifth grader. Tom's grandfather called my mother to invite me to accompany them to Ebbets Field in Brooklyn to watch the Dodgers play the Phillies on Sunday, September 30, 1956. Of course Beth was invited, too. Tom's grandfather even offered to bring Francis in his wheelchair, but my mother said no.

With Max as chauffeur, Mr. Florion sat in the front passenger seat. The three of us rode in the back like royalty. Beth wore jeans and a Dodger's cap she got from her father, her shiny black hair pulled into a pony tail hanging from behind, trendy years ahead of her time. Tom and I had our gloves with us, ready to catch a foul ball. I stole a glance to try to read what he had written on his glove. We drove down the Palisades Parkway through the gorgeous seasonal colors just beginning to change, across the George Washington Bridge. It was the first time I ever crossed the Hudson or even seen Manhattan, as we drove over to Brooklyn.

At Ebbets Field, Tom's grandfather was greeted like a celebrity that he had recently been, and our reception was like nothing I had ever experienced. As we stepped out of the limo and Mr. Florion escorted us through the gates, a press photographer stepped forward and called out. "Mr. Florion, a picture please!" Mr. Florion stood behind us, arms outstretched over the three young kids in his charge and said "Cheese," then "Thanks, Eddie. You know where to send it." I never gave that photo much thought until years later.

In the stadium, every usher, every vendor seemed to know him as we were led to the head of the queue. The crowd parted as we walked to the front of the line and were escorted to box seats along the third base line behind the dugout. It was one of the last games before the closing of the 1956 season. And who were those Dodgers who played on that particular Sunday? Only one of the best teams ever fielded. PeeWee Reese, Duke Snider, Jim Gilliam, Jackie Robinson, Gil Hodges, Carl Furillo, Roy Campenella, Don Newcomb, among others. Legendary names that defined the sport during this golden era. Thanks to Tom and his grandfather, we were able to witness them play; we were able to witness history. The Dodgers beat the Phillies, 8-6. In a few weeks, the Dodgers would face the New York Yankees for the World Series.

Later that fall, Mr. Dennehy allowed us to listen to the World Series on the radio during class hours, something unheard of before in our school experience. When I came home and told my mother, she asked me to relate the news to Francis. I sat on the edge of his bed, and in an as animated way as possible, did a play-by-play of each game's highlights. Did he understand what I was saying? He never took his eyes off of my face.

What we didn't know was that the Brooklyn Dodgers would abandon Ebbets Field a year later and move to Los Angeles after the 1957 Season; after they played in the World Series in 1956 and lost to the New York Yankees. It was demolished in February of 1960.

It was also during this year that Beth and I learned more about who Tom really was and his hidden secrets, his piano playing, the history of his grandparents. But nothing of his missing parents.

It was during a long, dazzlingly beautiful fall Saturday afternoon in fifth grade, not unlike the day when we would find Beth's body so many years later, that Beth and I would discover how truly talented our friend, Tom, was.

As was our routine then, we had met in the Dutch Garden, and walked through the woods to the back of the Florion estate. Just as had happened to me earlier that day on my way to Tom's, we could hear the piano music playing through the woods. We thought it was a record player. We were wrong.

Frau K. met us at the back door and ushered us in as she had other times in the brief duration of our friendship up to that point. We were a half-hour early, and she met us with a "Shhhh! You mustn't interrupt his practices. His grandfather insists."

She led us through the kitchen and up a rear circular stair-case into a drawing room, where Tom sat seated at a Steinway, alongside his grandmother and Yolanda Mero. It was Tom who had been playing the beautiful music, led by the index finger on his right hand, that we had heard earlier in the woods and would later be able to recognize as Rachmaninoff's *Piano Concerto in D Minor.*

Beth's eyes lit up in wonderment and she turned so quickly to me we almost both started laughing. But then she caught herself and we looked on in quiet amazement as Tom continued to the closing crescendo. It was like the index finger on his right hand had commanded, "Follow me," and the rest did as ordered. The sounds of the piano strings lingered as he held his foot on the sustain pedal and the legato echoed off the walls, enroute to our woods behind his house. The intensity on his face, the sight of his fingers racing across the keyboards like the wings of a hummingbird in flight. How did they know where to land?

On other days, when the weather was crisp Beth and I would sit behind the mansion in the small cemetery under the blaze of autumn, and listen to Tom practice for hours. The small, solitary headstone in the tiny plot, with O.B.W. engraved into the granite was our waiting room. Beth's nickname for the deceased, "Old Bird Watcher" stuck for many years afterward, and would serve as a reminder to Tom's constant practice.

It also served as a reminder to Beth, something she had never shared before.

"My mother's buried in a place much bigger than this. A mausoleum in Brooklyn. Greenwood Cemetery."

"I didn't know. I'm sorry."

"I hardly even remember her. She died when I was three. She was hit by a bus crossing the street in Manhattan. People said she was in a hurry and wasn't paying attention. Anyway, that's why my father moved out here to the country. He didn't want me to have to worry about traffic. He wanted the solitude."

"I'm sorry."

"It's okay. We go see her grave every Easter weekend. That's when it happened."

"I'm sorry."

"You don't have to say that anymore. My father is a good dad. He takes care of everything. Him and the hired help. We have a woman like Frau K. who helps out."

It would be one of the only times Beth ever mentioned her

mother. But every time we came to the O.B.W. spot, I knew she was thinking about her, thinking about what it might be like to have a mother in her life.

CHAPTER THIRTEEN

THE HISTORY OF FIRE
IN NEW CITY, NEW YORK:
PART I

Age 10

Memorial Day, 1957, was on a Thursday. They had not yet designated that all Memorial Days would be celebrated on the last Monday in May. That year, the Memorial Day Parade was on Saturday Morning.

Beth and Tom and I sat on the front porch roof of my house on Main Street, having climbed out the front bedroom window. It was a grandstand seat, as the parade made its way from the American Legion Hall near Demarest Avenue down Maple Avenue past the nunnery and the rectory to Third Street where they turned west, then north on Main past my house to the Courthouse steps. As the parade passed by before us, the old fire truck from the 1920s led the way, with a driver and the Grand Marshall seated above him on the hoses. "Link" Blauvelt was seated at attention, facing forward, trying to cover his true emotions with stiff pride and a smile. He was blind.

There is a long proud history of the New City Fire Department. It started in a building on Maple Avenue across from where the magnificent new building stands today.

Old photos show the determination and commitment on the firefighters' faces as the volunteers pose in navy blue wool uniforms, caps pulled down, silver buckles and buttons shining. Just out of frame was a brass band getting ready to strike up some Sousa to celebrate the taking of the formal photograph, my grandfather had once told me. In some of the pictures, the band can be seen wandering in the background of the shots, indicating it might have been taken during some sort of celebration; the brass instruments gleamed in the spring sunlight.

If you look on the plaque in front of the fire house today, it's like taking a roll call of my ancestors. They helped found the New City Fire Department, they were there, volunteering their times and their lives to serve their friends in the small community.

The call would come into Eberling's Market next to the courthouse and Kit would run across the street to the station. He'd crank up the fire siren and the volunteers would drop the reins of their plows or throw down their hammers and saws or stop the needle on their sewing machines in the shoe factory, and race to the firehouse and hop on the engines as they pulled out of the firehouse.

On July 4th weekends in the 1950s, full of WWII spirit, they would hold the Firemen's Carnival in the firehouse parking lot and the night would light up with the lights from the hoop-toss booths, games of chance, and the sounds of a calliope. I would throw ping-pong balls toward the necks of tiny fish bowls holding drowsy goldfish, that would survive the trip home in a plastic bag, only to be dead the next morning.

I would place my dime on the oil cloth mat filled with numbers one through thirty, and listen to the clicking of the wheel-of-fortune as the leather strap ran over the finishing nails that marked its circumference. We'd eat hot dogs until we got sick and we rode the Ferris wheel high above New City rooftops on our way to a faraway star-field. We'd hope the giant wheel would slow to a stop while my brother, and later Beth and Tom, sat swaying with me in the very top bucket, looking down at the crowd below, a hundred different scenarios being played out in every corner of the lot, all lit by the stringer lights that formed the perimeter of the parking lot, and from our viewpoint on high, resembling a scene out of Pieter Bruegel's *Children's Games.*

Then we would cut through the alley next to the Fagen Building and dash across an abandoned Main Street and run over the Court House lawn. The Dutch Garden would be quiet then, the only sound the far off calliope from the carnival complementing the glow of arcade lights on the eastern sky of Maple Avenue behind the bakery. We'd sit on the steps of the tea house and eat fried elephant ears and moan from our full stomachs.

Later, we'd all walk up North Main past Squadron A and stand in an empty field to watch the fireworks display.

But at the end of that fifth grade year, the Memorial Day Parade was led by a blind volunteer fireman from The New City Fire Department. He lost his eyes fighting a fire two years earlier that resulted in the death of one of my third grade classmates.

In 1954, during that Christmas break of third grade, we went through an exceptional cold wave. In the middle of the night, Francis and I had heard the phone ring, heard the sirens, saw my father grab his overcoat and race out of the house, yelling "Schriever Lane." It was the first time I had ever seen him run. "Francis' Day" would be the second and last time I ever saw him run.

He turned south and ran down Main Street to rendezvous with the trucks. Francis and I ran down to the baseball field where we could see the flames above the treetops to the south and then ran through the swamp along the brook behind our house to the back yards of the houses on Schriever Lane.

We stood there half at the edge of the woods, while flames filled the frigid night sky, watching from a safe distance, as my father helped unspool the heavy hoses from the back of the truck.

We had never seen him engage in such heavy, frantic labor. In the air was the blanket of black smoke, the smell of burning wood, and we could see flames billowing through the windows. Someone, the landlord perhaps, had replaced a burned out fuse with a copper penny and the overheated wires against the dry wood near the fuse box started smoldering and then the house acted like a tinderbox fueled by the screams of frightened children. As we watched the house become consumed, Link Blauvelt came half-crawling, half-scrambling out the front door, a child in his arms, his eyes squinted shut tightly. Three other firemen, including my father, raced to his side to pull him and the little girl to safety. That fireman was later to be grand marshal of the parade. He had pulled the body of the little classmate of mine from underneath her bed where she had been hiding from the flames while her house was burning down. She was already dead when he rushed her down the smoke-filled staircase, but he couldn't have known that. On the way down, his heart racing with hope, he was hit across the face with a burning banister dowel and blinded before he reached the bottom of the staircase.

He had crawled the rest of the way on his hands and knees, cradling poor Michelle to his chest.

Francis and I stood at the edge of the woods, my classmate stretched out on the ground, dead. My father, in his fireman's boots and fire coat and helmet, saw us and turned us away. There was no more he or any of the others could do for little Michelle.

A crowd had gathered within minutes and in the crowd I saw Calvin and Marvin and their father watching, the orange glow of the flames lighting their faces. Marvin was smirking.

Later, when the fire was out, our father, wet and shivering in the bitter cold, walked us home in silence. I kept staring straight ahead and it wasn't until we turned up our sidewalk that I looked over at him and saw that he had tears running down his cheeks. Were the tears for little Michelle, or for the realization that it could easily have been one of us? Maybe it was because he had seen enough death in his lifetime, far more than his share, I would find out in the years to come. When daylight broke, they would find the scorched remains of Michelle's brother, where he had hidden under his bed in fear, as if the mattresses and bedding could protect him from the searing heat as they had done from the bitter cold only moments before. Where had the parents been on this angry, freezing night?

There were to be many fires in New City, both before and after the one on Schriever Lane. A statistical anomaly? More than our share?

In the early part of the 20th Century, the barns of my great-great uncle were torched, along with his smoke houses, and even his brother's shoe factory. Later, in my lifetime there would be the Elms Hotel; New City Grammar School where my grandfather, father, and I had all gone to school; the New City Park Lake Clubhouse; the Squadron-A Barn near downtown; the Verdin Mansion on North Main; later, a horse stable. And there was to be one final arson in this New City story, one that both destroyed and exposed long-lost secrets.

CHAPTER FOURTEEN

NEW CITY

Spring, 1957
Age 10

As we grew older, our guardians seemed to understand we needed to explore our world, and the best way to do that was on our bicycles. I knew a little of the local geography, Tom not as much, but he was learning. Beth knew her neighborhood up around South Mountain.

It was during these late spring days in the fifth grade that we learned more of the geography of our beloved New City.

On our bicycles, packed with fishing poles, our woven creels were filled with night-crawlers we'd picked from the rich soil of my front lawn by flashlight and kept moist in used coffee grounds. With our lunch bags on board, our journeys would begin. We would head north on Main to Congers Road, and ride east past the grammar school on Old Congers Road, then past Clarkstown High School and down the hill and toward Lake DeForest, where only years before Francis had taken me swimming at the creek on Sweet Clover Farms.

From Sweet Clover we would head north on Ridge Road to

South Mountain Road and head west to Lake Lucille for another quick swim before moving on. We'd take a quick detour through Dellwood Country Club on Zukor Road for a third quick swim in the pool, compliments of Mr. Florion, then circle back to South Mountain and west to North Little Tor Road.

We would turn south on Little Tor and pedal past Collyer Avenue and turn into New City Park Lake. There, we would talk to the lifeguard we knew, take a swim, eat a sandwich and move on to Davies' Lake and Chestnut Grove School where we rested on the stone steps and snacked. Then just before the Palisades Parkway, we would head east on Germonds Road, go past the cemetery, across Main Street to Parrot Road.

We'd follow Parrot Road to Strawtown Road, head north on Strawtown past French Farms until we hit Congers Road, westbound again for the home stretch. At Brewery Road we headed south to Gerkin's Apple Orchard for a cold drink of apple cider and then west on Third Street, walking our bikes up the steep hill to the top and then coasting all the way down to Main Street and right into my driveway.

I don't know how many times we made that bike trip. I do know that I have taken it a thousand times in my memory, and quite a few times for real since then. When I think about what it was like then, compared to what it is today, my heart sinks.

Every child in New City should be allowed, maybe *required* to make that bike ride. It is the genesis of understanding New City and its history.

One day during that spring of our fifth grade, Beth and Tom and I were walking through the Dutch Garden, aimlessly wandering down the path that criss-crossed the embankment south of the wooden bridge.

At the gazebo we bumped into Marvin and Calvin. They were hanging out with some other guys, and when we came upon them they looked guilty as if they were going to do something and we had caught them.

Marvin reached brazenly up into the rafters of the gazebo and pulled a pack of Chesterfields that were hidden up there. Defiantly, he lit one up, passed it first to Calvin, who took a deep drag without coughing and then passed it on to me.

Marvin spoke, "Let's see if you're a chicken."

Without thinking I took a puff and started coughing, but not before seeing the look of horror on the faces of Tom and Beth. While I continued coughing, he and Beth turned abruptly and walked down the gravel path. I finally caught up with them. Tom was angry. Beth looked like she was about to start crying.

"What's wrong?"

It was Tom who spoke.

"Don't ever do anything like that again."

"Okay. I didn't think it would be that big a deal."

"It's a very big deal."

"Okay. Okay." What did he know that I didn't?

We walked in silence. I didn't know how to react. Somehow I felt that I had let them down by taking one puff of a cigarette. I felt as if I would never be able to make it up to them, that they were somehow way out of my league in social graces and knowledge of social taboos. In retrospect, maybe I was right about that. In the background I could hear Marvin and his bully buddies laughing at me.

"Hey chicken! Cluck, Cluck, Cluck!"

The three of us walked faster, me trailing behind Beth and Tom. I was sick that I had disappointed them.

I would never smoke another cigarette in my life.

As the summer wore on, we all celebrated birthdays and turned eleven, and our beginning of sixth grade drew closer, our bike adventures spread to newer and newer territory. We would eventually include our favorite fishing hole on Senator Buckley's property on North Main. Later, we'd ride up Phillip's Hill Road, Buena Vista Road, West Clarkstown Road, and when we were feeling adventurous, South Mountain Road all the way to Rte. 45. Then we'd head south to New Hempstead Road and head east to the top of the New Hempstead "Big Hill." Arms outstretched, we rode "no hands," building speed until we became almost frightened that we might take flight, the tips of our fishing poles we were carrying wobbling with the g-force. We became *airborne* and left the world all behind.

Some days, we'd stop on Congers Road at Clarkstown Junior-Senior High School where we would eventually wind up for six years, where so many significant events in our lives would take place. We'd walk our bikes across the grounds in amazement of the campus' beauty. And then we were off again across the Lake DeForest Reservoir, with just a moment to lament the loss of Sweet Clover swimming hole.

In the waning days of fifth grade during that late spring of 1957, I came to a realization. There wasn't a day that went by that Beth didn't make me laugh. Every day she made me laugh. She was so far out in front of the curve, in front of me, with her sense of humor, that sometimes I had trouble keeping up, understanding her jokes with oblique, obscure references. Even my dullness was fodder for her sense of humor.

As the summer of our first school year together came to a close, we all looked forward to leaving the Damiani basement and going back to the real New City Grammar School for sixth grade. But our last year at New City Grammar was to end sooner than we thought.

CHAPTER FIFTEEN

NEW CITY

1957-1958
Sixth Grade, Age 11

Our sixth grade year was to bring more surprises and more surprises. Some wonderful, some indicative of the changes that were taking place in New City and the world.

The first part of the sixth grade year started with us all going back to the New City Grammar School on the hill on Old Congers Road.

My own grandfather had left the original New City Grammar to be one of the first students at the new school on the hill in the late 1800s that my father would later attend in the 1920s and I in the 1950s. My sixth grade class would be the last one to ever attend the towering New City Grammar School on the hill, before moving to the brand new, New City Elementary School on Crestwood Drive. That summer and fall of 1957, construction was nearing completion.

I had mixed feelings about that. For me, personally, since my father and grandfather had attended the same school, it was like coming home for me. I was following in their footsteps once again. The downside was that we were not in our own private domain as we had been in the Damiani basement, away from the main school. There was a sense of independence in that.

Yet on the other hand, we were reunited with the other half of the class that we had been separated from in the fifth grade and friendships were rekindled. There were enough sixth graders for two classes, with two separate teachers and at least temporarily, held on split, morning and afternoon sessions.

My day would start by riding my bike north on Main to Twin Elms Lane, where I would meet up with Tom on his bike. We would peddle down Second Street to the bed of the abandoned railroad track right-of-way, head north to the site of the round-house that had been torn up and abandoned after WWII. It had been part of the Erie Railroad System, dating back to the 1830s. The black cinder roadbed would lead us in behind Vanderbilt's Lumber Yard that had taken over the old railroad station, and then to the base of the hill behind the school. There we would walk our bikes up the rutted, rock-strewn roadbed of "Vandy's Hill" to the rear of the school and join the other kids and hang out in the school yard. We waited for Beth to be dropped off by the school bus between the two huge Dutch elm trees guarding the front playground. We would talk and laugh until the morning bell rang. There were separate front entrances for boys and girls. Girls would line up on the west entrance, boys on the east. It had a huge basement where we all convened to duck-and-cover during air raid drills and to get our polio shots in the days when our parents were convinced that we were threatened by both a nuclear attack and a crippling virus. The building had stood proud and tall on the top of the hill, surrounded by gravel and tarmac playgrounds and a giant pine. The playgrounds had been the site of generations of field day events and marble competitions, a giant swing set, monkey bars, and bike racks.

On the ground floor, classrooms for first, second, and third grades had long been established, each room bearing a piano, desks with ink wells, and a mysterious cloak room, filled in the winter time with the smell of damp clothes and rubber galoshes.

Upstairs, grades four, five, and six were held. It all looked and smelled the same, down to the desks and chairs, sweeping compound and floor wax, as it had when my father had attended in the late 1920s and his father had in the early 1890s.

Our teacher that year was another surprise. Another male teacher, another WWII Vet, who had earned his degree on the GI Bill in the years following the war. Arthur Righetti was a tall, Italian, tough guy with a sense of humor and a heart of gold. Our perceptions about just women being school teachers were changing, and once again the classroom was proving to be a magical place for any of us with intellectual curiosity who cared to learn.

After school, most afternoons that fall, Tom and I would ride down the hill behind the school, Beth sitting sidesaddle on my crossbar, her books in the big wicker basket on my handlebars, and we would ride Tom home to the Florion estate. There, he would spend his three hours practicing.

Sometimes we would sit on the terrace and listen, quietly, while Tom's music would echo off the line of trees to the north. Sometimes we would wait in the woods and listen. I would try to envision his fingers racing along the keyboard, finding each destination precisely before racing on to the next assignment as proscribed by that right, Middle-C index finger. He did them all; Bach, Liszt, Tchaikovsky, Von Suppe, Rachmaninoff, and he did them masterfully. He wouldn't let us watch often back then. It made him too self-conscious, he told us. Later, that would change.

Other times, as the days become shorter, we would walk my bike to the big gate at the rear entrance of the estate and then I would pedal leisurely north on Little Tor Road, Beth astride my crossbar, the fragrance of her hair filling my nose. As we made our way to South Mountain Road, she leaned against my chest in the fold of my outstretched arms as I grabbed the handlebars. What a feeling that was, embracing her, in fact, without such an acknowledgment. How do we get those feelings back? Can they ever return?

Sometimes we would stop and we would just walk along-side the bike, talking about school, friends, music; a joke that Peter Tripp told on Your Hits of the Week the night before; a new song on the Top 40. I liked *That'll Be the Day*, by Buddy Holly and The Crickets. Beth was into *La Bamba*, and *Oh, Donna*, by Richie Valens, and Tom liked *The Fat Man* and all Fats Domino, or any piano rock for that matter.

At her driveway, I would drop her off at the top of the glen that fell beneath our feet. She would hop off, wave over her shoulder and smile back at me. "See you tomorrow!"

Then, she would turn and run down the shaded slope that crossed over her brook to her father's two-story cottage. It was a smile that would stay with me forever, a smile that had worked its way into my heart. Even at the age of twelve I sensed I would never see another smile like the ones she would give me on those autumn afternoons. I wanted to swing out the kickstand and fol-low her down the hill, past the cottage to the old barn her father had converted into his artist's studio where Beth would spend the rest of the afternoon and evening helping him and doing her homework.

As the Indian Summer ended and fall truly began, the shad-ows grew longer earlier each day. And every day I was filled with a sense that what was happening at each moment in the present was somehow contributing to a larger reality, a more significant reality that would pay off sometime in the future. Someday, the things I was feeling with my friendship with Tom and the strange, awakening feelings I was having for Beth would have some deeper significance.

But again, the biggest surprise of sixth grade came when it was announced that we would be leaving the New City Grammar School building after Christmas Vacation and moving down the street to a brand new Elementary School that was nearing com-

pletion on Crestwood Drive that backed up on the rear of the old
"Squadron-A Farm."

The school was designed to be a sprawling, one story, glass
and aluminum structure, modern 1950s' architecture, with tile
floors and bright lights and brand new desks, and wonder-of-all-
wonders, a "café-torium."

During Christmas break the books and furniture were transported from the late 19th Century to Post WWII. I wasn't aware
of its profound symbolism until much later with the passing of
the years. I was going through culture shock. Over the course of
a short winter break, I had moved from a 19th Century schoolhouse environment to a modern, mid-20th Century school house.
Although I was not able to articulate it, somehow I didn't feel like
I was "in Kansas" anymore. I wasn't sure if I liked the change.

On the first day at the new schoolhouse, Tom and I still took
the old route on the railroad tracks to Vandy's and then on to Congers Road.

Also on that first day, one of the construction workers finishing clean-up detail held up an old silver dollar he had found during the building. He hypothesized it was lost at the fairgrounds
racetrack that had once occupied the site in the early 1900s. To
me it signified the confluence of the old and the new. Perhaps my
grandfather had dropped that very same coin at the fairgrounds
one day and had spent hours looking for the lost treasure? Had the
loss of that coin caused some long-forgotten consequences to the
boy who had dropped it? And now, here it was being presented to
me for examination perhaps sixty years later by a workman building a school for me.

Within a week of that new winter term we had abandoned our
old bike route, another rite of passage. Now, from our rendezvous
point of Twin Elms and Main, we rode our bikes down Second
Street to Maple and north to Congers Road. Then down the hill
on Congers past the Revolutionary War-era graveyard and Jerry's
Tavern. There, instead of veering south down Old Congers Road

toward the old schoolhouse we continued on New Congers Road to Crestwood Drive and turned north behind the boundaries of the Squadron A Farm. It was a path to a new adventure.

In the sixteen months the three of us had become best friends, Beth had never showed favorites, treating us equally. Did she like Tom better? Did Tom like her as a girlfriend? I concluded that if Tom ever expressed a boyhood crush on her, I would be doomed. But one day on one of our bike rides to school, he surprised me.

After being quiet most of the trip, he popped a question as we coasted past the old Revolutionary War cemetery, cater-cornered from the back of The Elms Hotel.

"Have you ever thought of Beth as more than a friend?"

"What do you mean?"

"As a girlfriend."

"For you or for me?"

"For you."

"Never for me," I lied. "For you. Why do you ask?"

"I just always assumed she was your girlfriend."

"Why?"

"I just always had that idea. I can see how she feels about you. She even said something."

"Really? About me? What?"

"Sorry, can't betray a confidence."

"She said something about me? Come on!" A refrain of disbelief.

"Nope."

In reality, I wanted her to feel about me the way I felt about her. I just didn't know how to articulate exactly what that was. I would soon find out.

CHAPTER SIXTEEN

LAKE LUCILLE
NEW CITY

Winter, 1958
Age 11

My first date with Beth, if you could call it that, was on a bitter cold winter day in January of 1958, during our sixth grade year. It started out as just another day of ice-skating. I had been skating for about five years. Francis had taught me. He and I had made the rounds each winter, since he wanted to be sure I knew all the good spots.; Vanderbilt's Pond, Taggart's Pond at the end of First Street, Damiani's Pond, New City Park Lake, even the forbidden Greenberg's Pond. The frozen surfaces of woodsy lakes appeared magically while we slept. At morning's light they had become a winter wonderland.

But then, that sixth grade January, Beth invited Tom and me for an afternoon of skating on the private Lake Lucille, along South Mountain Road. I had never been there to skate, just to swim.

Tom's chauffeur, Max, drove us up Little Tor Road, hooked a left on South Mountain Road, and on to Beth's. From her house we headed east and there, nestled in a glen, was Lake Lucille, surrounded by refurbished summer cottages that had been winterized and were now serving as year-round residences. Looking across, it was like staring into a Christmas card; the roofs of the bungalows piled high in white fluff, the snow-laden branches dipping low, and all around, silence. Overhead, the sky un-mistakenly sighed, *"More snow is on its way."*

We sat on the edge of the bridge and changed out of our boots and into our skates, shivering against the cold. Max left and the three of us had the frozen lake to ourselves. At the dam I looked down at the stream flowing east. Where is it headed, I wondered?

The three of us skated the hours away, arms interlaced at the elbows, Beth in the middle. What I wouldn't give for a photograph of that.

Max returned later in the afternoon to pick up Tom. He had to go home to practice the piano under the direction of his grandmother and Mero. The chauffeur handed us each our own tan thermos Frau K. had filled with hot chocolate, and we sat sipping it as we all started to remove our skates. She had also fixed us a picnic basket. Inside, sandwiches with thick ham slices and dark brown mustard on pumpernickel bread, and *pfeffernüsse*, dusted with powdered sugar.

"You two don't have to leave now. Why don't you stay?" Tom asked.

I looked to Beth. "Is that okay?"

"That would be great. I'm in no hurry to get home."

I thought for a moment of the implications and logistics of that. "Max doesn't have to come back. We can get back okay."

"You sure?"

Beth looked to me and nodded to Tom. "We can walk it."

And so it was settled. Beth and I would stay and skate, and Tom would leave.

I turned away from the blue exhaust, as the limo, Max behind the wheel and Tom's head silhouetted in the back seat, drove off into the snow alley created by the low hanging boughs.

I helped Beth finish re-lacing her skates, my freezing fingers trembling. "Race you to the other side," She yelled over her shoulder. She sped toward the opposite side of Lake Lucille, almost fifteen hundred feet to the west.

I barely caught up with her as she sped ahead, gliding on her blades as they cut through the surface of the ice.

I'm alone with her, I thought.

As we arrived at the lake head, fed by the stream that passed under her own driveway two miles to the west, she slowed and I caught up.

"Slowpoke," she laughed.

Is it possible for a sixth grader to feel such love without having it labeled puppy-love? I don't know. I did know that day I wanted to spend the rest of my life with Beth.

What little sun there was disappeared behind dark clouds over the tree line by late afternoon and we stopped skating. Beth's cheeks were bright red and her lips were shiny from the gobs of Chap-Stick she kept smearing on them. She handed me the tube and I rubbed my cracked lips. This tube has been on her lips, I thought, and now it's touching my lips. Does this count as a kiss? *A prelude to a kiss?*

On this first day we were alone, it was a winter wonderland. And what do I remember of that afternoon?

Tying Beth's skate laces, wanting to hold her hand;

Frozen air bubbles beneath the crystal ice;

Winter birds flying overhead;

Grabbing her as she fell, scarf around her neck;

Beth wearing faded jeans and her Dad's WWII Navy pea coat;

Her wool hat with matching mittens. A perfect choice;

Black branches against a dark gray sky;

Aching ankles;

An ice skate whip, holding hands, laughter, laughter, laughter, round and around and around the edge of the lake.

We discussed Tom.

"He's my best friend."

"You and Tom are my best friends."

Girls in sixth grade are so much more socially adept than boys at that age; at strategies, and planning, while boys just go through wishful thinking. What it is and what it could be; what it *will* be? The girls already know those answers.

The world was made for just us that day, no one else mattered. It could have been 1800 or 1850 or 1900 or 1936, instead of 1958, for all we knew of the world; what was going on in the rest of the world. Whereas *our world* was standing still. Wanting it to never stop but be frozen in time just as the water beneath our blades was frozen, not moving, held precisely in the one perfect moment in time. Preserved. How many times in the passing forty-four years have I wanted to somehow relive that one perfect cold winter day? We came close one winter night at Lake Lucille, but that would require another six-year wait until the night of our Senior Christmas Ball.

With dusk approaching, another family came down and built a small fire on the shore and we roasted marshmallows and S'mores, the melted chocolate oozing through our frozen fingers and chapped lips. More parents arrived, shoveling snow off the ice, making room for their kids to skate. We sat on a fallen tree trunk and laughed at the smaller children skating as their parents waited, with knowing smiles, as if remembering something long ago in their own pasts, as I would eventually do myself, years later. Across the campfire, I admired Beth's face through heat wave lines, while framing her head was the smoke rippling from nearby fireplace chimneys. When I circled to my left just a few degrees it looked like smoke was coming out of her ears. I made her swap seats and look at me and she laughed. "You're thinking again."

The temperature dropped and we shivered in tandem and the sky began to close down. First snowflakes fell and landed like teardrops on the end of her long, fine nose. Crossing her eyes, in exaggerated surprise, we doubled over in laughter again. She knew exactly what to do to make me laugh, but anything that day would have made me laugh. I laughed to mask my feelings, my fear it would all somehow end.

We skated around, our heads angled up; our mouths open trying to catch the puffy flakes as we whirled in circles, hand-in-hand. How close can you get to a kiss without it becoming a kiss? I tilted my head straight to look at her and almost, in my sixth grader's desire, took her in my arms. Is it unseemly for a man nearing sixty to reminisce about wanting to kiss a sixth-grade girl? If it is, I don't care. I wanted to hold her face in my hands. Hold her face in my hands for the rest of my life.

How is this for perspective; for irony? Instead, I would eventually hold her face in my hands that one final time while kneeling over her body in the chill autumn waters of the Demarest Kill so many years later.

On that winter day of sixth grade, as snow fell deeper, slowing our skating, we lay back flat on the ice, head to head, making snow angels that disappeared within moments of our standing. While all around us the branches complained in screeches and moans as they accepted their new-fallen burden.

We changed into our hiking shoes as we sat on the icy bridge wall, the snow coming heavier now. Our own huffing and puffing and the racing, pounding of my heart was all that I could hear.

We gathered our skates and laced them over our shoulders and began to walk toward Beth's house, a good two miles away. The flakes dropped softly to her hair and wool pull-over cap, and she brushed them away with her oversized mittens.

In the sixth grade it isn't easy to articulate what it is that is drawing you to this person. All I knew is that I wanted to hold Beth in my arms and have her smile at me like that forever. The excitement of walking a girl home at that age is not measurable in any empirical terms. Sometimes as you get older, the memory is the only thing that makes the days worthwhile.

Don't take my word for it. Try this before you die. Walk South Mountain Road with someone you love on a late afternoon in winter with the snow falling and see for yourself how it feels. The snowflakes drift down in search of you both, darting, changing direction before they find you and land on your wool scarf. Each flake seems to be reminding you, *Pay Attention.*

We kept to the side of the road as we walked west on South Mountain Road, passing Little Tor and beyond. My feet were freezing and our breath was coming out as little puffs of smoke as we shivered our way forward.

And all around us the only sound was the muffled silence of her breath through her scarf and that pounding in my chest that wouldn't go away.

The light was fading as we made our way around the bend and to the top of the drive that led to her father's cottage and barn studio beneath us in the small valley. You had to cross that small brook to get to it. That very same brook that fed into Lake Lucille. The very same brook that would join the Demarest Kill and later the Hackensack River before they poured into Lake DeForest. Looking down and seeing the water gave me an odd sensation. It was a feeling I would remember six years later when we were both seniors in high school, on another night when the snow was falling heavily and my feet were frozen and my heart was filled to bursting.

At the top of her drive she turned to me.

"My father can drive you home."

"No, that's okay. It's really not that far. I like walking in the snow." It was true. I did. If only I had been dressed for it.

"Are you sure? You'll freeze."

"I'm fine. Thanks for inviting me. Us."

"It was fun. We can do it again. Well, see you Monday."

She nudged me on the shoulder with her own, a gesture that

surprised and confused me. She turned and shoveled her feet and skidded down the hill toward her cottage.

I watched her for a moment before turning and heading toward home.

Walking home, trying to keep from freezing, I was energized as never before. I sensed before this that I was in love with her, but this was a depth I had never before experienced. My heart was pounding again and it wasn't from trudging through the drifts.

The sounds of tires on a snow-covered country road; awakening feelings never felt before left me giddy; hyper-charged as if I could do anything. I was invincible. Unable to think of anything else. Obsessed with the blossoming love.

On the way home my feet were freezing, my fingertips were numb, my mind was racing, and I felt alive and happy for the first time since "Francis' Day" seventeen months earlier.

Tramping through the woods at Greenberg's Pond and then the Florion estate I could hear Tom at the keyboard. Hours after he had left us, he was still practicing. I was falling in love and he was on his way to infamy. I stopped and listened for as long as I could take the cold, exposed to Chopin, Satie, Rachmaninoff. Somehow, when I finally walked on, toes and fingertips frozen, I felt like I was leaving Tom behind, but perhaps the opposite was true. I ran into the Dutch Garden because I preferred to take that route to cutting through the estate. For some reason, The Garden always made me feel closer to Beth.

It would be another half-hour and two inches of snow before I made it home, exhausted, shivering, toes near frost-bitten. I stopped by Steinman's to check out the new Classic comic books and buy a Turkish Taffy and a Three Musketeer bar and bask in the warmth of the store. Henny was closing early that day because of the snow, so I didn't linger at the comic rack as long as I usually did. It was a day I would not have missed for anything.

Arriving home after that first skate together, my boots wet from the snow, I hung my skates on the peg in the pantry and stepped into Francis' room to share my joy. My father had a look of objection on his face as I passed him in the living room. I lay next to Francis and held him close to me. He breathed in the scent of cold air lingering on my flannel shirt and corduroy pants. Could he tell that I had changed, that I was happy and sensed that somehow, between my new friend Tom, and my new love Beth, that I was taking a first step in my journey to leave him behind? Was my new-found love a defense mechanism to protect myself from the constant mourning I was going through for Francis? Was I moving on, as my parents could not, would not? Did Francis sense any of this in any way? Did he know as I lay there holding him, drawing his warmth into my frozen bones, that I was actually leaving him?

This day was the start of another six weeks of Saturday ice-skating with Beth and Tom on Lake Lucille, except for those times when Tom was at the piano keyboard. We skated from early morning until dusk every Saturday that January and February, and into March, until the surface turned to slush. The last couple of times Beth took pictures of us with her Brownie, and handed it over to some parents to take shots of all three of us. The persistent vision of a young boy's heart is apparent if you look at those pictures carefully. And although Tom was with us most of the time, it was probably obvious to him that our attention was on one another. All the while I kept wondering, why was she interested in me and not Tom?

And what do I remember most of those days on the ice during the winter of our sixth grade? Beth's smile and the sound of her laughter, as it echoed against the muffled tree line across the horizon. The smell of wet wool. Her hands in mittens holding mine.

How can we ever recapture that feeling? Sometimes revisiting the person can make it happen, but rarely. You've both moved on too far in other directions. We see similarities, even as an adult, through gestures, phrasing of speech, but cannot recapture it.

Sometimes revisiting the location will work. But really,

you're just revisiting a place, not *a place in time*, and *"aye, there is the rub."*

I was to find out later, Thomas Wolfe was wrong. You can go home again. But Thomas Wolfe was also right. You *can* go home again, but the home has changed and the cast of characters who originally made it home has moved on, leaving behind a stage with new, unknown players.

As winter was ending and spring, 1958 approaching toward the end of sixth grade, things were starting to change. Our nature walks continued with Beth behind an old Nikon 35mm SLR camera, peering through the eyepiece, documenting our trips on slide film and TRI-X. It was a new hobby for her. One day, in the late winter of 1958 she took a picture of me kneeling at the water cress-laden spring-head behind the Dutch Garden, where a parking lot now sits. I'm wearing a red and black plaid lumberjack jacket, about to dip my hands under the pipe that flowed from the grotto.

Other changes included the new school along with new routines, accompanied by new songs. *At the Hop*, by Danny and the Juniors was my favorite, until I started thinking about *April Love*, by Pat Boone in April of that sixth grade year. Beth liked *Catch a Falling Star*, by Perry Como, and Tom was crazy about *Tequila*, by the Champs. They were the sounds of a new world.

As the days grew warmer and the ice on Lake Lucille was no longer safe for ice skating, I knew we had to do something to replace those Saturdays on ice. What would it be? More trips to the Dutch Garden? Gardening in the Dutch Garden? More springtime bike rides, expanding our itinerary far beyond where we had traveled heretofore?

I wanted it to get freezing cold again, at least for one more Saturday. One more Saturday in our own little winter wonderland.

My wish came true when we woke up one Saturday morning in the middle of March to find over twelve inches of snow blanketing New City.

Our yard and barn looked like a Christmas Card, but it was March. It was only eight o'clock in the morning but I called Tom. "Have you looked outside?"

"I've already built two snowmen and I just came in from an hour of sleigh riding down the front hill."

"Seriously. What are we going to do?"

"Hope it's this bad on Monday so we can have a snow-day?"

"Seriously."

"Seriously, I already called the guys. Snowball fight starts at two this afternoon in the cornfield across Little Tor Road. A bunch of big shots are coming over from Chestnut Grove for the challenge. Call Beth and tell her to bring her mittens. Max will be there in twenty minutes to pick her up. I'll wait for you here. Frau K. already has the hot chocolate brewing. Enough for fifty."

I called Beth and told her the plan.

By nine-thirty, Chestnut Grove had shown up and eight of them were rolling giant snowballs up and down the corn rows to build their fort. By stacking five alongside one another, and then putting four on top of that stack, their fort was almost six feet high.

By the time Tom and Beth and I showed up, Tim, Jimmy, Pat, Bobby, Richard, and Willy had already rolled up the nine giant snowballs to establish our fort almost five feet high. Our flag was an old Conger's High pennant I had grabbed from the barn. All of us sported garbage can lids to act as shields during the inevitable onslaught, as we tried to capture Chestnut Grove's flag, posted on a mast behind their snow fort wall.

Tom and Beth were laughing, rolling the softball-sized snow-balls that would serve as ammunition. It was all new to them. For me, it brought on a sadness at the familiarity. Twice in the past four years a great snowball fight had convened on this very same corn field on Little Tor Road, but then Francis had been the commander who led the charge. Today I would fight for his honor.

As two o'clock approached, each team had hundreds of snowballs stacked in pyramids behind their fort walls. The rules were simple. Each team had a flag to defend. The first team to get their opponent's flag back behind their own fort wall was the winner. No snowballs aimed at the head were to be thrown. Body shots only.

Charlie from Chestnut Grove stepped forward with a bottle rocket with a long fuse. He would light it, run back to his fort a hundred feet from ours, and we all would wait. The skyrocket would take off, and when it reached its apex and exploded, it would signal the start of the battle.

Beth stood on the sidelines trying to keep warm near the trunk of the limo, where Max had placed the thermos filled with hot chocolate. She had been joined by other girls from both schools. Phyllis, Bonnie, Sue, Linda, Betty, Nancy, and the twins, Laura and Barbara.

As the long fuse sparked closer to the skyrocket, everyone began to cheer with war-whoops. And then there was a whoosh, as the rocket took off into the threatening sky. There was just a brief moment of silence and then the explosion as the colors lit up the overcast daylight.

The battle was on. Some of us wore football helmets, others WW II helmets from our fathers. Some even sported Nazi helmets later adopted by biker gangs. The strategy was simple: as part of your team moved forward to capture the enemy flag, they would be bombarded by snowballs in a head-on maneuver meant as a diversionary tactic. Smaller teams were sent out into the flanks to circle around and close in from the sides. Since both teams used the same tactics, smaller skirmishes broke out near the cornfield's perimeter.

I deflected a hit with my garbage can lid and the wet snowball sprayed my face with icy slush. My hands and face were freezing, but we fought on, ducking, bobbing and weaving.

In a surprise move, Charlie raced from the Chestnut Grove wall, his shield before him. He was flanked on either side by two allies, also bearing shields. They raced for our flag, and before we knew it, they had stormed our wall and taken our flag. In doing so, they had won Round One.

That day the snowball fight would last until dark, fought in the headlight beams of Max's limo and the cars of those few parents who showed up to watch battles that had their roots in their own childhoods.

The fight ended with the last of Frau K.'s hot chocolate.

CHAPTER SEVENTEEN

ROCKLAND COUNTY COURT HOUSE

Wednesday, 8 a.m.
October 18, 2000
Age 54

Jimmy called at ten o'clock the Tuesday night after Beth's murder. "Will, we're going to review the autopsy report tomorrow morning at eight. Henion and the other guys wanted me to tell you that you are welcome to attend, but to remind you that you could not be part of this investigation. He's doing it as a personal and professional courtesy to you because he knows you knew Beth."

"I'll be there."

By Wednesday, it had been two days since I had been to the Courthouse. I just couldn't pull myself out of bed and go to work, so I had taken up Henion's earlier offer to stay home. And so Tuesday I had stayed in bed, unable to watch television, read, or even raise my head off the pillow. Delores was patient, understanding, comforting, but I sensed a feeling of defeat in her look that I didn't have the time or the insight to consider.

So I set the clock for earlier than usual on Wednesday, because I knew it would take me longer than usual to get ready. Longer than usual to walk to work. And I still had to stop in, as I did almost every day, to say good morning to my mother and Francis.

My mother had a searching look on her face when I arrived, trying to determine my present state of mind. I put on the stoic face, probably more effort than I had put forth for Delores. I helped her bathe Francis and then was on my way after gulping down some of her coffee.

The investigation team was headed up to the conference room for the autopsy review with the D.A. Jimmy's assistant was setting up the computer projector when I arrived at the Board Room and he quickly muted the light to prevent me from seeing any of the photographs before the others arrived. We exchanged hellos. I knew because of my presence, and his friendship with Beth, that Jimmy's presentation was going to be more difficult than usual for him, more guarded.

Carl walked in followed by Ray and Dave and Jeanette, who prepared a tape for the recorder.

Carl began. "Will, I suppose Jimmy told you that you're here out of a professional courtesy. Nothing else. You have no role in this investigation."

"Like you said the other day."

"Correct. The other thing is, since you knew her, some of this may not be easy to take. You're free to leave if it becomes too much."

"Got it."

"Okay, Jimmy. Let's begin."

Jimmy opened his file and turned on the projector again. On a cold, stainless steel slab was a woman I had been in love with for over forty years. I had told myself earlier I would not crack and now I was working to keep that promise to myself.

Jimmy turned to his first page of notes. Jeanette nodded, began to both record and type. "Let the record indicate on the morning of Wednesday, October 18, 2000 at 8:05 a.m we are going over the autopsy summary of murder victim Beth VonBronk who was killed sometime between ten p.m. on Sunday, October 15 and two a.m. on Monday, October 16.

"My initial examination indicates that the cause of death was strangulation from behind before she was pushed over the edge. She was likely already dead when she was pushed down the hill. There was no water in her lungs. Her neck probably snapped in the fall after she was dead. She had had intercourse, probably forcibly, in other words raped, within about two hours prior to her murder. We surmise this from the bruising and abrasions of the labia and vagina walls due to forced entry while she was still alive. Semen was found in and around her vagina from at least one man, and a DNA screening is pending. Since there is no evidence of her defending herself, such as, the skin of the assailant under her nails, she may have been raped while semi-conscious during the intermittent, yet what we hypothesize was, a prolonged strangulation. Again, at this point, I am sorry to report that she was strangled slowly, almost tauntingly, and died a slow, painful death, perhaps during which time she was raped, or prior to when she was raped."

Jimmy clicked the projector and a close-up of Beth's upper torso appeared on the screen. "Her collar bone was broken in a way that makes me think the attacker was behind her the whole time. Even if she had survived, she may not have been able to identify him. She may never have seen his face."

Jimmy looked to me. "Raped while she was dying slowly," I repeated.

Ray answered, "That's what it looks like so far. Also, there were no clothes found at the scene and no evidence indicating that the crime was committed elsewhere and the body dumped there. Dave has a report on the parking lot video in a minute. Whoever did this approached her at the location."

"Someone she knew?" I asked.

"Or she didn't hear him approach."

"And the missing clothes?" Carl asked.

"My guess is souvenirs, trophies, taken after the rape and murder."

Jimmy continued. "Another interesting thing. She had bruises on her left bicep that look like they were made by a man's right hand and fingers, probably while facing her. And get this." He changed to a new slide. "She had older bruises on her upper arms and back consistent with punching, but not in the last few days. Maybe a week or two ago."

Again, everyone exchanged glances, wondering where this evidence was pointing.

Carl interrupted. "I'm sure our boy Rainer will be able to shed some light on that latter question when he gets here. When is he getting here?"

Ray checked his notes. "He's supposed to arrive tomorrow morning, Thursday, the 19th, with the funeral being held the next day, Friday the 20th. We'll bring him in for questioning Monday, the 23rd. Give him some grieving room."

Carl turned back to us all. "The question then becomes, what was she doing there at that time of night, if she wasn't murdered elsewhere and carried there?"

Dave turned to us. "We're bringing in Tom Hogenkamp later today. He may know something. There's a path that leads from the gazebo to his place."

We all looked at one another.

Dave continued. "We have some indication to corroborate that her murder was at the site. The morning her body was found, we found her car parked outside the courthouse. We checked the security surveillance tapes and there doesn't appear to be anyone else in the car when she arrived and got out a little before seven p.m., so that leads us to believe that she came to the Courthouse on her own. Another security camera picks her up exiting the basement door and heading south. In looking at the archived security tapes, her car had also been parked there earlier this week, two nights ago, around seven p.m., and she's seen walking into the

Courthouse and out the rear basement door toward the Garden alone on that clip, also. We're still trying to piece it all together from the surveillance videos. We're going through all the tapes to see if there's any pattern.

Ray referred to his notes. "Her car has also shown up numerous times in the last year, and on these earlier tapes Beth is again seen entering the main door of the courthouse during business hours and then leaving the main door and returning to her car several hours later. We checked a lot of personnel in the Court House, Business Licenses, DOT, Probation Office, Building and Zoning, tried to determine a reason why she would have parked there so often, since it doesn't appear that she had any business reasons for coming to the Courthouse.

Dave broke in. "This is very time-consuming. These surveillance tapes have not been a priority item in the past, so the filing is a little, shall we say, 'lax'?"

Carl turned to me. "Was she coming here to visit you, Will? No one in the office remembers her visiting you here."

"No, she never came here to visit me." That was true.

In recent years, when she was living in the U.S., I had seen her come into the court house on several occasions. The first time I wrote it off as business, some task or errand for her land developer husband, but the second time I saw her I tried to follow her but she eluded me. I walked the corridors looking for her, but she seemed to have disappeared into thin air.

Ray continued. "But when we initially talked to Tom Hogenkamp the other day, he told us that she recently started parking there when she came to visit him at his boathouse."

Carl interrupted. "Why would she park there? Why not drive up to his house?"

"According to Tom, it seems that in the last few years, or so, her husband had become jealous of Tom, convinced they were having an affair. Klein told her not to visit anymore. He threatened her."

"Threatened her, how?"

"Not sure yet. We still have to talk to Klein. There are those bruises on the body that were not done the night of the murder. Like Jim said, maybe within the last seven to fourteen days.

"Anyway, according to Tom when we first talked to him at the boathouse, Klein had sicced a private detective on her, followed her."

"How did he know that?"

Ray referred to his notes. "She told him. That's why she didn't park out in front of the estate. So she would park in our parking lot, enter the building in front, then leave through the basement and head through the Dutch Garden and make her way to Tom's boathouse. The investigator didn't have the sense to follow her into the building, or didn't want to be seen in the Courthouse, so he never knew that she was just passing through.

"According to Tom the night she was killed, she parked there and walked to his house as they had planned. She stayed there awhile and then left. "

Henion interrupted. "Why was she going there all those times?"

"They were friends."

Jimmy chimed in and corrected Ray. "They've been friends over forty years."

"Lovers." The D.A. stated it as a fact, not a question.

I winced at the thought.

Jimmy answered again. "Not likely. Just friends. Confidants."

"Why do you say that?"

"It's just not likely. I know them both. It's highly unlikely. Let's just take that at face value for now."

Carl looked at Jimmy. "Are you protecting your old friend? Do we have to pull you off this case, too?"

"No. I've just known them for over forty years and I would bet my job on it." Jimmy wasn't about to let Henion run him over, despite the fact that Henion was his superior.

I looked at Jimmy. How could he be so sure, I wondered?

Ray continued. "Okay, so she parked her car, walked through the courthouse, then the woods to his boathouse, stayed there two hours, which according to Tom is what she usually did, and then never made it back to her car. That's probably when she was murdered. On her way back from Tom's to her car. No one else can be seen entering or leaving the parking lot on the surveillance video, so whoever killed her came in from the south."

"Or west," I said.

"No. There are security cameras on that parking lot, as well."

"But not in the woods along the Kill."

"So that leaves Hogenkamp as our suspect?"

Jimmy shook his head. "No, no, no. Not likely. Like I say, they've been close friends, more like family, for over forty years."

Ray continued. "Hogenkamp said the bruises may have been from Klein. Klein was threatening her and she wanted to leave him. So when he gets back, we'll know more."

I looked to Jimmy. Rainer beat her? I was sickened.

"What about the security tape from the nights before the murder?"

"We haven't looked at all the tapes yet thoroughly. Like I say, they're a little disorganized, to say the least. We're going through everything. Very thorough. We started with the murder night. Then they started going back thirty days to confirm Hogenkamp's story. They should be caught up in the next two-three days."

"Maybe Rainer's detective found out what she was doing, told Rainer, and he ambushed her."

"He was in Hong Kong. Airtight."

"He could have had someone do it. Maybe just scare her, things got carried away," Dave hypothesized.

Carl shook his head. "Private investigators don't murder and rape the wives of their clients. I don't care how sleazy they are. What did I tell you about watching too many cop dramas on TV?"

There was muffled laughter, until they remembered I was in

the room.

"Anyway, Rainer's due to arrive tomorrow for the funeral on Friday. We'll pull him in for questioning Monday."

Barry stood. "Okay. Keep me posted with what's going on."

Everyone stood for the mandatory papers-into-files-before-leaving shuffle.

Jimmy caught me before I left. "Sorry you had to sit through that."

"What makes you so sure they weren't lovers?"

"Will, don't ask me to compromise this investigation, okay?"

"What are you saying?"

"I'm not saying anything. I know this is troubling for you."

Then, instead of becoming more angry, Jimmy softened. "At the expense of sounding like my mother, why don't you go see Father Carrick?"

"You sound like *my* mother."

"I'll take that as a compliment."

"Been there already."

"I mean, where is your head on all of this?"

"Where do you think it is? Someone I've loved all my life has been murdered."

"And things aren't going fast enough for you?"

"What am I supposed to think, Jimmy? I mean how long can the list of suspects be?"

That stopped him short. "With Rainer out of town? I'm not sure if the list suddenly got longer or shorter."

"What's that supposed to mean?"

"I don't know what it's supposed to mean. My question is, who would want Beth dead? Answer that. This was no random encounter. That's not even a consideration."

Jimmy hesitated, then "Go see Father Carrick again."

Carl was walking out of the room and I stood in his way. "I have a question for you."

"Really? What makes you think you can ask questions at all?"

"Whose semen was it in the autopsy report?"

"That will take time to cross reference the rest of the male population of the world. Get out of here, Will. We already have your DNA on file. Now let us do our job. Like I said, you need to watch your step. Oh, and if I find you've been pestering your friend, Jimmy, here, for information, like I said the other day, you and I are going to the mat."

CHAPTER EIGHTEEN

ST. AUGUSTINE'S CHURCH

Midday, Wednesday
October 18, 2000
Age 54

Father Carrick was shuffling papers on his own desk when I arrived unannounced thirty minutes later.

"To what do I owe this honor?"

"I just got back from the autopsy report."

I told him what Jimmy had discovered.

Father Carrick closed his file and rubbed his tired eyes. "Why did you go? Trying to inflict more damage on yourself?"

"Tell me about Tom."

"Why?"

"Tell me about my friend. About what happened. About the man he became."

"Why don't you ask him yourself?"

"He wouldn't tell me."

"You mean you're too embarrassed to ask him because of your shoddy behavior for the past thirty-two years. If you were so interested, you've had plenty of opportunity."

"Please tell me about my friend. I want to know who he is."

Father Carrick stood and joined me in the armchair next to mine. He took a deep breath and sighed, as if questioning his judgment over what he was about to tell me.

"I'm not speaking as your priest now, but as a mutual friend. Anyone in town could tell you the same thing. Tom gets up at dawn and heads out for his morning jog. He follows the path along the Demarest Kill to the Dutch Garden and through the Courthouse parking lot to Main Street. He goes north on Main Street and jogs over to Congers Road, past Clarkstown High School, across the Lake DeForest reservoir, south on Waters' Edge Drive through Valley Cottage and West Nyack and back north on Strawtown Road, to Brewery Road. On Third Street he heads west to Main, and then here to St. Augustine's for confession."

More confession, I wondered? It's just over ten miles, every day for thirty-two years, the loneliness of the long distance runner filled with the sights and sounds and smells that were ever-changing as our little town grew up. It was a similar path as the bike route adventures that he and Beth and I had taken dozens of times. What did he think about on those runs? Father Carrick's story intrigued me. Our paths had never crossed in all those years, even when I was walking myself from New City Park to the Courthouse. Was Tom still in Church when I walked by? Had he timed his runs to intentionally miss me as I walked to work?

What did he think about when he ran past the school that shaped our brains for six years from seventh through twelfth grades? What was he thinking about as he ran, plodding one foot in front of another as he jogged past all the important historic places that marked our lives? Did the same memories crop up every day? Was his daily pilgrimage to those places a way of implanting those memories forever in his mind? Was he trying to recapture something himself, as I had for so many years? Was he running to remember or was he running to forget what had happened in the intervening years? His daily running routine somehow mirrored my father's walk toward oblivion. Was Tom trying to run away the pain he had endured in his life? To somehow overcome what it was that forced him to live the reclusive life he now lived?

Like my father, was he paying penance? If so, why?

"So go ask him yourself who he has become. He said he wanted to talk to you."

"He did?" It took me by surprise.

"He said he has a question for you."

I hung my head in defeat. Father Carrick remained speechless, not giving up anything.

"He wants to know if I killed Beth, doesn't he? Do you think I would do something like that?"

Instead of answering my question, he had his own. "I don't pretend to know any answers anymore, Will. Do you know what something like that would do to your mother?"

His non-answer surprised me. "So you think I killed her, too?"

"Will, if there's something we need to talk about, then better sooner than later."

I looked at him in disbelief. "Why was Jimmy so certain Tom and Beth weren't having an affair?"

"Beth was raped."

"Yes."

Father Carrick stood and breathed a sigh of relief. "Well then we can rule out Tom as a suspect, can't we?"

"How can you be so certain?"

"Because Tom is celibate, Will."

"What? You mean he can't have sex?"

"I'm saying it's a choice. It has nothing to do with his physical ability from his injuries. This isn't some Hemingway novel."

"So he is physically able, but chooses not to? That doesn't make any sense."

"And since when are you in possession of all the facts in life? It doesn't make any sense to you, Will. It makes perfect sense to me."

CHAPTER NINETEEN

**THE HISTORY OF FIRE
IN NEW CITY, NEW YORK:
PART II**

As I grew older and we explored New City, I became more aware of my family's history. In 1857, my great-great-grandfather Henry came over from Erfelden, Germany. With his new bride, they took a riverboat up the Rhine from Darmstadt to Rotterdam on the North Sea, then a small ship to the French port of LeHavre, then boarded a steamer to New York. Whether or not it was his objective when leaving, or he found the work after arriving here is not clear, but he started to work as a horse trainer on the farm of General Louis Ludwig Blenker, a German political revolutionary who had been thrown out of Germany in 1848.

My great-great-grandfather first worked on the farm that stretched from New City Park lake area on the south to New Hempstead Road on the north, on the west side of what is today called Little Tor Road. This is essentially the same property where the snowball fight had taken place in Middle March of 1958, a century later. Blenker would eventually join the Union Army to fight for the north during "The Rebellion," leaving my great-great-grandfather to take over the horse training facility. General

Blenker was known for his flamboyance, having a large entourage, and keeping his troops, all of them German, in beer. A man of excess, he was criticized for leading a torch-light parade in Washington, D.C., in honor of General Sherman. He was later wounded at the Battle of Keys in Virginia in 1863, and mustered out. He returned to New City where he died later that year after declaring bankruptcy.

My great-great-grandfather Henry would then move to the farmhouse on the hill overlooking the present day courthouse and Highway Department and sire eleven children with his wife, Barbara, his bride from Germany.

Some of his descendants would grow up to start two shoe factories in New City, others would remain farmers, some would open a general store and deli counter that would remain open for over sixty years. Others would become mailmen. Some had apparently made some people in town very angry. A series of barn fires, and later, fires in the shoe factories, were all probable arson.

THE ROCKLAND COUNTY TIMES
VOL. XV, NO. 26. HAVERSTRAW, N.Y.,
April 2, 1904.
PRICE FIVE CENTS

FIRE AT NEW CITY.
Flames Destroy Barn and Stock
of Mr. John Eberling

An unkind fate seems to be pursuing the Eberling family of New City unrelentingly.

During the last few years this family has been sorely stricken in many ways, and it seems as if their burden of trouble was never to end.

A fierce fire broke out early on Sunday morning in the large barn of Mr. John Eberling, at New City destroying the building, with its entire contents, consisting of grain, hay, farming utensils and livestock.

Neighbors who saw the flames hurried to the assistance of the Eberling family and were successful in getting the horses out. But owing to the heat of the fire it was impossible to save the cows, and the whole herd of fifteen were consumed in the flames. The bellowing as they perished was terrible.

There was a small insurance on the barn and contents, but the loss to Mr. Eberling is a severe one.

This fire on the Eberling property has forced upon the people of New City and vicinity the inevitable conclusion that the Eberling family are being pursued by some unrelenting, bitter and unprincipled enemy. It is only a short time ago since the Eberling shoe shop, owned by Charles Eberling, was burned.

Twice have the smokehouses on the Eberling farm, where the fire took place, been burned and only a short time ago the barn of Henry Eberling was destroyed by the fiery monster.

These fires are entirely too coincidental, and, as in every other case, the fire broke out about the same time, when most of the residents of the vicinity were sound asleep.

In addition to all these suspicious circumstances, there was delivered at the Eberling barn on Saturday five tons of hay and five tons of feed for the cattle.

The total insurance on the property amounted to $1,500.

Who had done it? Why? What was it like to hear the cattle as they screamed out while being burned alive in the confines of the barn, waiting to be rescued by their trusted masters? What was going through the minds of my ancestors? Did one of them know the cause of some neighbor's anger? Felt guilt for having instigated such anger? Did the arsonist look on innocently, perhaps even helping put out the fire, wearing a face of dismay while his heart raced with adrenaline?

After the fire, did my own grandfather clear out of the farmhouse, move his new wife to Main Street to get away from whatever or whomever was causing the fires of both the barns and the shoe factory and the smokehouses, thereby distancing himself from the rest of the family? Did the fact that I grew up on a piece of property on Main Street in the 1950s have anything to do with barn arsons in 1904?

That same shoe plant owner, Charles Eberling, a son of my great-grandfather, would become the county coroner. He would be in charge of the dead after the massive clay slide in Haverstraw that claimed the lives of twenty-two on the night of January 8, 1906, burying them during a blinding snowstorm.

NEW YORK TIMES
January 9, 1906
HAVERSTRAW, N.Y., Jan. 9, (1906)

> The bodies of twenty-two persons are buried under thousands of tons of clay and quicksand as the result of the disaster which overwhelmed the northeastern part of this village last night.

The clay slide was caused by brick makers in the lower valley digging out clay from a hillside for the one million bricks the three hundred laborers made each day. For years, their clay extraction undermined the ground on the property above it, eventually making it unstable.

On that bitter cold night in January of 1906, the ground gave in and thirteen houses slid down 150 feet. Only one house was vacant. A dozen more would later fall into the clay pit.

Some parents evacuated their children to safety, then ran back to salvage their possessions and were in the homes when they toppled over and slid down the embankment and burst into flames.

Firemen arriving on the scene realized water mains had been broken by the slide and water gushed out over the pit, turning the scene into an ice slide.

One of the victims, age sixty, had fought the encroachment of the brick makers for over thirty years, finally succumbing to an "I-told-you-so moment."

The brick makers would make a profit however, as about $200,000 worth of clay slid down the embankment into their pits. According to legal precedent, the clay that slid onto the property of the very people who had undermined the cliff, was now owned by those perpetrators of the slide. Crime does pay.

According to a coroner's investigation conducted by the Coroner, Charles Eberling, twenty-two people perished in the disaster. One of those who perished that night was Delores' grandfather. He retrieved Delores' mother from a house that was about to slide over the edge, then went back to retrieve the family's photo album and never made it back. His body, along with about a dozen others, was never found. Her grandmother was pregnant with Delores' father, who would grow up to be one of the brick masons who created the original Dutch Garden in the mid-1930s under the direct supervision of Mary Mowbray-Clarke. Mowbray-Clarke would pick them up each morning in Haverstraw in her own car and drive them to New City to lay brick.

By 1950, the bricklayer's wife became pregnant with Delores, the woman who would grow up to teach at Clarkstown High School and with whom I would live for twenty years.

CHAPTER TWENTY

NEW CITY

Spring, 1958,
Sixth Grade, Age 11

That spring of 1958, as the frigid air turned mild, I led two expeditions to High Tor, the local mountain peak that helps cir-cumscribe the northern edge of New City and separate us from Haverstraw. The first hike was from near the 9W intersection with Old Rte. 304. Max dropped us off at the base and we began the more direct, closest route up the mountain from that southeast access. My second trip was from the west from Little Tor, walk-ing along the ridge line and seeing the vineyard on the hillside below.

On our third trip to High Tor, Beth had led us through the Dells and the old Zukor property and up through the vineyard.

As exciting as those trips were, Tom was about to come up with something different. Something that would change our lives. He wanted to trace The Demarest Kill from its headwaters near where the Palisades Parkway and West Clarkstown Road and Red Hill Road all converge, all the way down to the north end of Lake DeForest. But he didn't tell us about his plans right away. First he did his research, and then he dropped the idea on us.

CHAPTER TWENTY-ONE

THE DEMAREST KILL

June, 1958
Age 11

As school was letting out that first June, 1958, in the new, New City Elementary School, Tom ran up a pile of dirt twenty feet high that the construction crew had bulldozed to the west of the new school. From that elevation he was gazing out toward the barn of Squadron-A Farm, and site of the abandoned race track.

Flowing through the Squadron A plain was a stream and a placid farm pond.

Beth and I joined him at the top of the dirt pile and followed his gaze.

"You see that barn down there?"

"Yes. Sure. It's The Squadron-A barn."

"That's right. Squadron-A. The mounted unit had a colorful history. In 1898, the squadron supplied a troop of cavalry in the Spanish American War."

"Remember that film in Mr. Righetti's history class a few months back?"

Beth and I looked down at the barn and we both recalled

the film we had been shown in history class. It was a film from The Library of Congress, footage taken by Billy Bitzer in Tampa Bay for Edison's Biograph Company, as the troops and horses embarked on steamships, enroute to Cuba. When they arrived in Havana Harbor, there were no accessible docks and the horses were pushed off the troop ship into the water and made to swim to shore. The filmmakers were not there for that. Billy Bitzer would later to go on to be cinematographer on over 300 short narrative films with D.W. Griffith, and would eventually finance and film *The Birth of a Nation* for him in 1915.

Tom nodded, then recited, as if reading from a history book. "The Squadron A Farm was so named after the summer of 1915, when Squadron-A encamped that year on 140-plus acres that had belonged to the successful businessman Florent Verdin. He built his mansion across North Main. Squadron-A was again called into federal service in 1917, and they became the 105th Machine Gun Battalion before going to France and Belgium to fight in World War I. Their motto was *"Boutez en Avant,"* or *"Push Forward."*

We both stepped forward to flank Tom. The look of the Belgian front was in Beth's eyes. *"Push Forward."*

"Yes. You see that stream down there?"

"Yes."

"That's the same stream that runs behind my house and Will, the tributary that runs behind your house, flows into it, as well as the water from Greenberg's Pond."

"I think you're right."

"It's true. I asked my grandfather. He says all the streams flow together on their way north to Lake DeForest.

Beth interjected, "Even the stream that passes in front of our cottage."

"Yes."

I thought about it for a minute. "So that means that my property and your property and Beth's property are somehow all connected."

"Yes. It's all very metaphorical, of course."

Beth and I exchanged glances. *Metaphorical indeed.*

"Where does the stream end?"

"They all flow into the Hackensack River and then into the new reservoir. Lake DeForest."

It was during this first day of summer vacation after sixth grade that we decided to follow the motto of Squadron-A, and "Push Forward." We were going to walk the Demarest Kill from its headwaters south of Davies' Lake to its pouring into LakeDeforest.

And so in the closing days of June, 1958, as we all approached our twelfth birthdays, following information from Tom's Grandfather and some old hydrological maps dating back over sixty years, we traced a route of our journey of the Demarest Kill, starting upstream at its headwaters.

The first day, Max and Tom picked up Beth and me and then we headed back toward New Valley Road. He let us off south of Davies' Lake, up near where Addison Boyce Drive and Red Hill Road and West Clarkstown Road all come together. With our wading boots and maps and gear and a new Nikon S3 rangefinder camera around Beth's neck, we looked like we were taking off on a safari.

Stepping into our boots with thick rubber treads, we were off. And what a journey it was to be.

Beth snapped photos along the route, winding through rolls and rolls of Tri-X and Kodachrome slides.

We would eventually take detours and follow the tributary behind my house, the upstream waters that fed Greenberg's Pond, and later the stream that started up near Sawmill Road that flowed past Beth's cottage on South Mountain Road.

What the three major tributaries all had in common was that they flowed northbound past our respective houses, converged at the Hackensack River near Old Rte. 304 and Christie's Airport, dumped into Lake DeForest, and eventually found their way through New Jersey to the kitchen sink taps of Hackensack.

We were Sacajawea and Lewis and Clark on an expedition just as important and surely of equal historical significance. Over the first two weeks after school ended we hiked the entire route. We slogged, tripped, fell, got soaked from head to foot, suffered numerous minor sprains to our ankles, and learned what it was like to be truly alive in a small town without equal.

On the first day we waded down and around Davies' Lake, through Cropsey's Farm, and New City Park Lake.

The second day we started at Collyer Avenue at the New City Park Lake dam and we wound our way past a bend we nicknamed "Stomach Pond" for its curled shape, toward Shriever Lane and onto the Florion Estate, past a spring with potable drinking water and then to the waterfall at Greenberg's Pond.

On the third day we had Max drive us upstream along Little Tor Road near Gail Drive to the headwaters of the Greenberg tributary and walked down to the pond. We then walked behind my house and followed that tributary to Damiani's Pond and the dried up pond to the north where we found a crumbled dam of sandstone where the water spilled into the main tributary of The Demarest Kill.

On day four we backtracked to the Greenberg's waterfall and walked to where those three tributaries came together behind the Dutch Garden near Tom's boathouse and just west of the gazebo. At the tea house, Max was waiting for us with a picnic lunch prepared by Frau K. After lunch we walked to the wooden bridge behind the Courthouse, headed north under New Hempstead Road, and through the concrete tunnel built when they made the supermarket parking lot, dumping us out south of the farm pond on Squadron A. We moved onward. *"Boutez en Avant."*

By day five we were exhausted, blistered, sunburned, yet determined to move on.

Max dropped us off south of Senator Buckley's place near

Phillips' Hill Road at North Main, and we followed the oxbows and switchbacks, north into unknown territory. Up until this point we were relatively familiar with the terrain and the hydrology. The next few days would bring us into the unknown, north of town.

Day six brought surprises as we found where Zukor's stream converged with the waters we had traipsed up until then, and then the stream took an abrupt turn south, circled back north with the gravitational flow of the gently rolling foothills, and headed toward Christie's Airport on Old Rte. 304. We waded north until the convergence of Beth's stream east of the Country Club. The joining of those two streams meant we were close to Lake DeForest and that we now had to make another detour and backtrack. Calling it a day, we walked through the woods to Christie's where Max had dropped off our bikes earlier.

Day seven we took one of our detours west of Beth's house on South Mountain Road near Buena Vista Road. The beauty along South Mountain Road reflected what we knew the Native American Ramapaughs must have witnessed. It was all untouched wilderness. Who had meandered here last, before us? What young girl or boy had been curious enough? By lunchtime we were ready to stop for food. On Beth's back deck, her housekeeper, Consuelo, had left sandwiches. We were tempted by the beauty of the day to stop after lunch, but knew we had to carry on. By late afternoon we were on the eastern shore of Lake Lucille, right where we had started ice skating only months before, and we knew our journey's end was in sight.

Day eight brought us to the convergence of where we had detoured two days earlier, and it was literally all downhill from there. Although unfamiliar, the tree branches reached out to embrace us; to urge us onward toward the finish line like encouraging parents. We trod slowly, spinning in circles at the beauty we beheld. Overhead, a Piper Cub from Christie's circled lazily.

Another two days of fighting heavier underbrush and deeper

waters and we finally made it to the widening of the waters and the first indication of the stream being identified as The Hackensack River on the old maps. The water here was too deep to wade, so we made our way through the marshy banks filled with cattails, put on hip-boots attached to inner tubes and floated out into the lake. We made our way to shore, stripped to our bathing suits and went for a swim, even though we knew it was illegal.

By day ten, we had made it. We had walked The Demarest Kill. We had not yet turned twelve.

If we had continued, we could have followed the Hackensack River under the New York Thruway to Lake Tappan, the Oradell Reservoir, and into the New Jersey Meadowlands. But we had accomplished what we set out to do. It was a trip that stayed with us a lifetime.

Those ten days seemed to mark a turning point in our existence and our friendship and brought us into new territory. Without trying to sound like a pun, it was a watershed event in our lives. Whatever happened after these ten days, we had a common bond that was irreversible. Like the bike rides the previous summer, I would reflect on our first ten-day hike countless times in the coming years. It was a bonding experience shared by no one that I would ever know, or even hear about. It was metaphorical in so many ways. Tom taking the lead, scouting out the rocky bottom, navigating; Beth next, following Tom's lead, using her hiking stick to step gingerly over the submerged rocks, and me following up, catching Beth as she fell, urging her on in the sometimes chest-deep waters, my palm flat against her shoulder blades offering support.

Our laughter filled the leaf-covered dome above our heads as we took each step downstream, stumbling over the submerged boulders. Other times there was no human sound to be heard, and we would stand in the water and listen for moments at a time to the natural sounds of the water, the birds, the breeze in the trees. We would close our eyes and just listen. Just listen for long minutes.

And like before, on that day skating on Lake Lucille, during those times, it could have been 1800 or 1850 or 1950 and there would have been no difference whatsoever. We could have encountered Chingachgook and Leatherstocking along the way and not been at all surprised.

In the near silence, we were all realizing, concluding something. What was it? *What was it?* The ephemeral nature of life on this planet? A brief moment of perfection in time than can never be repeated? Or were we too young to have that perspective? I don't know. I've thought about it every day since and I still cannot articulate what we all felt simultaneously. I almost started to cry from the overwhelming emotion, and when Beth sensed that from me, she reached out to a nearby maple and pulled a whirlybird seed pod from a branch, split it in two, and spread the sticky pod apart, gluing it on the end of her nose like a bird beak, and crossed her eyes looking at it like the day she had stared at the snowflake on her nose earlier that winter. She looked so foolish we all started laughing, breaking my melancholy reverie. When a childhood is filled with such perfection, can subsequent adulthood only bring disappointment and a sense of anti-climax?

I'm a believer that our DNA has memory for more than just physical characteristics and traits. I believe DNA has a *memory of events;* DNA memory of *events* that your grandfather and great-grandfather and great-great-grandfather experienced are passed down to you in the chemical stew of your brain pan, and recall of such events can be triggered as surely and randomly as the recessive trait for blue eyes. How else would you explain that as I walked the Demarest Kill and the tributaries during those ten days I was overcome with the overwhelming sense-memory that I had already done this before? I am sure of it. No coincidences, or similarities, or easily explainable, common *deja vu*, but vivid memories of what lies beyond the next bend in the stream as we worked our way north. I, (or some chemical component part of me that had been passed down to me through the generations), *had been here before.*

My DNA remembered!

But with no primary source witnesses still alive at that time, with the possible exception of my father, and no written journals to record such a hike by one of my ancestors, I am left to wonder who it was that had walked these footsteps before me in the 100 years since they had settled here in New City and then passed on their DNA memories to me through the family lineage. For surely at least one of them had done it. It was all so invigorating and unsettling at the same time. How to explain it?

Just as the streams converged at the junction of the Hackensack River, so had our lives. Just as my grandfather had probably settled on the property that ran from the stream to Main Street because of a fire in 1904; and Tom's grandparents had settled on The Kill and built Dove Cottage as a result of enormous radio success in the 1930s; and Beth's father had settled on a tributary along South Mountain Road to assuage the pain of his wife's sudden death, the need to raise his daughter in a safe environment, his need for a studio in seclusion in a beautiful area; so were the three of us now coming together. And where would we wind up? How would we wind up? If I knew then, could I have done anything to stop what loomed ahead?

CHAPTER TWENTY-TWO

SECOND FIREMAN'S CARNIVAL: NEW CITY

July 4, 1958
Age 11

That July 4th, 1958, right after sixth grade, was a Friday. Beth had turned twelve, two days earlier on July 2. It would be another two weeks before Tom turned twelve and another five weeks for me.

We were still exhausted and exhilarated from our ten-day adventure down the Demarest Kill. Such was our excitement that all considerations for sprained ankles and aching muscles and mosquito bites were ignored. We were proud of our accomplishment, and Beth dropped her film off at Steinman's to be processed. We couldn't wait to see the photos, but in those days, delivery would be the next week.The trip along the Kill seemed to accelerate our lives, not just that summer, but forever after. Everything changed so quickly. We were growing up. Our elders had trusted us enough to go on a ten-day hike with little intervention or interference, and that trust, although not articulated by any one of us, was sorely appreciated.

But in wading downstream, perhaps we had left something behind us forever. In following the Demarest Kill, we had waded into our respective futures.

The Annual July 4th Fireman's Carnival started that Friday at dusk, and we made the rounds from booth to booth, the smell of hot cotton candy filling the air, spending our dimes on wheels of chance, the ring toss for red spindled walking canes topped with ceramic dice and bulldog heads, and the ping-pong ball toss for goldfish. Any fish we won were passed on to the next kid in line. We didn't want to have to lug them around for the night. As the sun went down on the horizon, we ran to the Ferris wheel for our trip to the top of the world; our world. As the sun disappeared behind the tree line behind the Courthouse, we again gazed down at the hustle and bustle of New City life. A new generation of kids falling in love with the carnival, while mingling with some of the old-time, firehouse pioneers.

As nine o'clock approached, we walked north on Main Street to the far field of Squadron A, where a crowd was gathered to watch the fireworks display. As we approached the group, Beth broke from us and raced forward to a lone man walking through the crowd, hands in his work corduroy pants pockets, a Camel cigarette dangling from his lips. He was a dead ringer for Dylan Thomas, I would later appreciate. He walked with not quite a swagger, but an air that said he was just an observer here, not a participant in the festivities. She ran to him and when he saw her he opened his arms and embraced her.

Tom turned to me. "Beth's Father."

I had seen the works he had created in his studio when I had ridden Beth home on my bicycle handlebars, and seen photographs of him on the wall, but this would be the first time I would meet him.

"Dad, these are my two best friends in the world, Tom and Will." He greeted us with a nod and a handshake, his hands rough and callused. He reeked of cigarette smoke.

"Tom of Dove Cottage fame and Will, the son of Marion and Francis, my mailman. Of course. Evening, gentlemen." Then, pulling her to him, they walked on ahead to claim their space for the fireworks.

Beth and her father stood side by side, arms around each other's shoulders. Their eyes were identical in a family resemblance way. As the moments of anticipation wore on, all her attention and her smiles were on him. The pop of a single skyrocket marked the beginning of the show, accompanied by applause and "ooohs" and "aaaahhs" from the onlookers. I walked in front of Beth, so I could turn and watch her face light up in the muted glow of the fireworks, soft blues and reds, the colors and flashes of the star sprays reflecting off her cheeks, her shiny hair, and in the sparkling of her eyes. I couldn't take my eyes off her face. It was mesmerizing.

Tom elbowed me and whispered hoarsely, "Hey lover boy, the fireworks are over there." He was wrong.

After the grand finale, the crowd began to break up and Beth and her father started walking north to where he had parked his '51 Ford Country Squire, a woodie station wagon. Tom called after them. "See you guys Sunday afternoon. Hope you didn't forget." Without turning around, Beth's father waved affirmatively over his shoulder. Beth turned and gave us a thumbs up and a smile.

"Max will be by to pick you up around three o'clock."

I couldn't really hear Beth's father because he was facing away, but I think he said, "I'll be ready with bells on." Whatever he said, Beth punched his shoulder and laughed and they disappeared into the traffic jam of North Main.

Earlier that week, wading the stream as Beth's birthday and July 4th weekend had approached, Tom had invited Beth and me to a celebration party at the Florion Estate for that Sunday afternoon, the day after the fireworks. He didn't really say what it was to be a celebration for and we figured it must have been his grandparents' Independence Day Party. In a way, it was.

As the fireworks crowd dissipated, Tom and I headed back to the carnival and our bikes. That was the tradition. Carnival, fireworks, carnival again until midnight. "I hope you didn't forget the party."

"I tried, but my mother wouldn't let me. The tuxedo fitting and all."

"Very funny."

Walking our bikes home we went our separate ways at the Esso Station, Tom heading to Dove Cottage, me to my home.

He was halfway down to the Damiani stream before he turned his head and yelled, "Same thing tomorrow night?"

"I plan to win every goldfish," I called back.

He rode off into the night.

CHAPTER TWENTY-THREE

DOVE COTTAGE, NEW CITY
THE FLORION LAWN PARTY

July 6, 1958
Age 11

When I look back over the childhood I had, I often think of how and when I became part of the history of the world. Did I have any brushes with infamy? Although I would later do a hitch in Vietnam, I never felt that as anything other than two years of going through the motions, one day at a time, while in a semi-comatose state of denial.

But there was something that happened that summer after we finished sixth grade and were awaiting our start at seventh grade at Clarkstown Junior-Senior High School. It would happen in a matter of a few hours; such a brief time that I never even gave it much thought until I matured. And when I did realize the historical significance, it's almost as if it is something I might have imagined.

Certainly things like this didn't happen to a boy like me, from my background. It was all a part of our rush into the future at breakneck speed.

It had been arranged that on Sunday,Tom's Limo would pick up Beth and then come and get me to drive us to the party. My mother made sure I was in freshly ironed good pants and shirt, with a tie. Church clothes. I couldn't really understand what the big deal was, and having no dress shirt and tie of my own, I had to wear one of my father's, probably from about 1940, gauging from the size of the collar and the width of the tie.

The first surprise came when the limo drove up Main Street and pulled into our driveway and Max got out to open the door for me. My mother stood at the front door and waved to Max, and he smiled and waved back. "Tell Francis I said hello, please, Ma'am. Both Francises, that is."

My mother laughed. "I will, Max. Have a wonderful afternoon."

"Oh, and Ma'am, I've seen Mrs. Florion's dress and it looks lovely."

"Why thank you Max, what an unexpected compliment."

I had known my mother had sewn the dress that Mrs. Florion would wear that afternoon. What did she feel about not being good enough to be invited, but yet her son was?

As Max opened the door I saw Beth in a pale yellow summer dress, her long hair in matching ribbons. All dressed up, she was breathtaking to behold. The fireworks were still in her eyes from Friday night. Sitting next to her on the long bench seat was her father, smoking a cigarette with the same, bored look on his face he had worn the other night. I had almost forgotten he was coming.

I looked back to Beth. "You look nice."

"Thank you. So do you. Wow, a tie."

"Yeah, my dad's."

"Dad, you remember Will."

He turned to look at me and a half smile crept over his face.

"Well it has been almost forty-eight hours, but I suppose I remember him."

He extended his hand and when I shook it, it felt like dried shoe leather, his palms calloused and his nails filthy from the clay and oil paints he worked with. He was dressed in brown corduroy pants, ragged at the cuffs, a plaid lumberjack shirt, and a tan blazer. It didn't even look like he had shaved or bathed for three days.

"Did you know my dad is friends with Tom's grandparents?"

I nodded. Of course my parents knew Tom's grandparents, as well, but my parents had not been invited. Why? I wouldn't find out until another year how famous Beth's father was on the art scene. His sculpture and paintings were internationally known, and he was considered a somewhat reclusive genius from what I had heard.

Max drove north on Main and left onto Twin Elms Lane at the Esso Station, where it finally ended on the gravel drive to the mansion. At the bottom of the hill we drove past ten limousines, Cadillacs, Lincolns, a few Chrysler Imperials, and a Mercedes Benz 220 Cabriolet A, their chauffeurs all milling about smoking cigarettes and digging their heels in the gravel drive.

As we got out of the car Beth's father said, "Don't forget to tell Will about Florida."

I turned to her.

"Oh, yeah, we're going to Florida for two weeks to visit an old friend of Dad's who teaches at the University of Florida."

She was excited and I didn't want to ruin it. I was in shock.

"That's great. Sounds like fun."

"I'll send you a postcard.

I was blind-sided with her announcement. Two weeks without Beth. How would I survive?

As we walked up the hill I looked up and saw a huge white tent that had been erected on the plateau on the east side of the house. Women dressed in pale summer dresses, big hats with ornate floral designs, all sipping cocktails, were listening to Paul Whiteman's Orchestra playing *Wang-Wang Blues*, a tune I remember my father listening to on the hand-made radio in his shop in our basement. "The King of Jazz," my father had mumbled, while soldering wires on the short-wave radio he was building.

At first I didn't understand. This was just a band playing a Paul Whiteman tune, right? But then there he was, standing before me and fronting his ten-piece orchestra sweating but smiling in his white dinner jacket, a small baton bouncing up and down absently. Pop Whiteman himself. He dabbed his face with a hand-kerchief and yelled across the room, laughing, as Tom made his way across the tent to greet Beth and me.

Tom was dressed in a suit, hair slicked back, looking very dapper.

"Excuse the formality."

"Is that really Paul Whiteman?" I asked."

"Sure, Pop is old friends with my grandparents. They used to do a lot of radio work together. These are all friends of my grandparents. I'd like you to meet them."

I looked at all the strange faces before me, and as I did, some of them took on a surreal familiarity, as if I knew them even though I had never met them. Half in a daze, I asked, "Why?"

Beth was aghast. "Why? So someday you can tell our grandchildren that you met them, silly."

"Met who?"

Tom laughed and dragged us across the tent to meet his grandparents.

"'Whom', met 'whom'. What, are you a hillbilly?"

Tom's grandparents had created a dynasty on the radio in the 1920s, 1930s, and 1940s. By the early 1950s, as television forced radio back into the obscure corners of the nation's radar screen, they had already made their fortunes over and over again, so the transition was seen as a mildly humorous inconvenience, instead of the tragedy that others in their profession perceived. Now, most of their time was spent with investments and philanthropic concerns, helping those in the radio business less fortunate.

Although both Beth and I had met Tom's grandparents many times, at today's more formal setting, it was all handshakes and good manners. His grandmother, who dressed like she was about to attend a ball at Buckingham Palace in the dress she had commissioned my mother to sew, was all smiles. All I could see was the work my mother had put into the dress and then had not been invited to the festivities.

"Beth, Will, so glad you could come. Beth, I see your dad has made his entrance. Please be sure to send him over. And Will, how are your parents? Please tell your mother I love my dress."

"They're fine."

"And your brother, Francis?"

"Getting by."

"He was such a beautiful young man. You're so lucky to have him as a brother. Please tell your family I said hello."

"I will."

"Tom, why don't you introduce Will and Beth to our other guests. I know they would all like to meet your friends."

"Okay, Gram."

"And don't forget, we'd all like to hear you play something later, after Yolanda. Maybe you can get together with Oscar and put a smile on our faces."

"I'll go tell him now. Be right back, guys."

Tom excused himself, leaving Beth and me alone for the first time since the limo picked me up.

"I can't believe I'm actually going to Florida. Isn't that exciting?"

"Yeah."

"Oh, my god!"

"What's the matter?"

"Is that Bob Hope?"

All I could do was stand and stare across the tent. It was indeed, Bob Hope.

"What's he doing here?"

"I guess they're friends."

"He's talking to Jack Benny."

"Is this for real? There are such things as celebrity impersonators," Beth joked.

We started looking around the tent. The faces were somewhat familiar, but not always instantly recognizable. Then Tom was back.

"Tom, what's going on here? I feel like I'm at a Hollywood Party."

"You are at a Hollywood party. But it's in New City."

"Who are all these people? I mean besides the obvious."

"Well, there's Mr. and Mrs. Jim Jordan, otherwise known as Fibber McGee and Molly, you don't recognize them because they're on the radio. There's Dorothy Kilgallen. Myron Cohen.

"Do they live in New City?

"A lot of them are just visiting my grandparents. But most of these other people have homes here. Myron Cohen up on New Hempstead Road. A lot of them up on South Mountain Road near you, Beth. There's Maxwell Anderson, the playwright; writes his plays in 'blank verse'."

"Blank verse?"

"Like Shakespeare."

"Why?"

"I don't know. Ask him."

"And Burgess Meredith, the actor. John Housman from the Actor's Studio. There's Lotte Lenye. She lived up there with Kurt Weill."

"Who's that college kid?"

"Oh, that's the local babysitter, Rene Auberjonois, says he wants to be an actor. He went to Clarkstown High."

"That old guy? Adolph Zukor, he's the one who started Paramount Pictures and built Dellwood Country Club."

It was my turn to chime in.

"My father used to caddy for him. It used to be Zukor's Country Club back then. In fact my father was invited to a caddies' party one night and they screened *It Happened One Night*, before it was released to the public"

"There's Helen Hayes, she lives over in Nyack. You'd recognize her if you went to the '*theatah*.'"

"So over there we have Bennet Cerf. And there's Yolanda Mero, my piano teacher, she's going to play the piano before Oscar and I do."

"Oscar?"

"Levant. Old friend of George Gershwin's."

"And of course I know you know the guy with the big cigar."

I looked over and saw a round-faced smiling man with jet black hair slicked back, and a big bushy mustache. I couldn't believe my eyes.

"He just bought his mother a place on South Mountain and comes to visit her on weekends."

"Who's the guy holding the comic strip panels of *Steve Canyon*?"

"That's Milton Caniff. He lives over near you on South Mountain, too. And that's Alan Lerner. He wrote *Brigadoon* and *My Fair Lady* with Frederick Loew."

"South Mountain Road?" I wanted to make sure I heard him right.

"All down the street from Beth."

"You never told us you knew all of these celebrities."

"They're not celebrities. They're friends of my grandparents."

I stood and looked around the tent and it slowly began to dawn on me that I had entered another world. A world of wealth and power and influence and genius of a kind I had never imagined. I was a boy of an earlier century thrust into the modern world and floundering to keep up.

I turned to Beth and looked at her as she stood peering around the tent with me.

"Your father is friends with these people too?"

"Most of them. A lot of them have commissioned work from him. They're his friends and clients, both. His stuff, his sculpture and his paintings are all over their houses both on South Mountain and in Manhattan."

It was then I realized that Beth and Tom, as close as friends as they had been to me for the past two years, were actually from another world, a world where people like my parents and me were rarely invited. It had a strange effect on me. It wasn't a feeling of anger or jealousy. It was more of a feeling of an awareness, a hopelessness; of being an outcast, someone who didn't belong; would never belong. Someone once described it as the "poor-boy-at-the-party" syndrome: An outsider.

Suddenly I became very self-conscious of wearing my father's stiff, starched white shirt my mother had so carefully ironed that morning trying to disguise the frayed collars with heavy starch, and the gaudy, wide, out-of-fashion tie. It was a feeling I was never truly able to overcome in Beth's presence. Was I not giving myself enough credit? Was I not giving her enough credit for see-ing beyond all of that?

We drifted through the crowd, everyone making a big fuss of Tom, the grandson of the hosts, and Beth, the sweet young girl with the long brunette hair in the pale yellow summer dress. Wasn't she VonBronk's daughter? Indeed, she was. And who is this other young man with her? Do we know him? Is he *anybody*?

As the afternoon wore on, I became increasingly uncomfort-able. I wanted to go home and talk to Francis, tell him who these important people were that I had met.

All the while, The King of Jazz and his combo kept up the soundtrack of my life, *Lady be Good, I Got Rhythm, Strike Up the Band, Let's Call the Whole Thing Off, Nice Work If You Can Get It, Love is Sweeping the Country.* During *Someone to Watch Over Me,* Beth turned to me and said, "Why don't you ask me to dance, numbskull?"

I was petrified. I didn't know how to dance.

"I...I don't know how."

"Follow me. No, I don't mean follow me. You have to lead, and I'll follow you. Come on. It's slow. You can fake it."

She dragged me onto the dance floor, where beet red, I made a fool of myself.

Tom sensed my discomfort and came to my rescue. Halfway through the song, he tapped me on the shoulder, "May I cut in, *monsieur*?" He purposely mis-pronounced it *"mon-sewer"*

He whisked her away and I stood in awe, heartsick. He was *watching over her*, while I stood by, paralyzed.

Finally, when Paul Whiteman took his cue for a break, Tom's grandmother tapped her cocktail glass with her spoon.

"Thank you all so much for being here today to help us celebrate two wonderful milestones.

"And 'Thank You' to Pop Whiteman and your orchestra for all the lovely music you've been playing all afternoon. It brings back such fond memories for all of us. Ira, I'm sure you'll agree." The crowd grew silent. Ira Gershwin smiled and nodded.

"Our first wonderful announcement is that we have decided to spend most of our time back in Manhattan, and have sold the acreage at the bottom of the hill to a developer who will be turning the property into some lovely homes. Let me introduce him to you." She mentioned his name, but I wasn't really listening. I was still reeling from her announcement. My private domain, where we had flown model planes, spent days sleigh-riding down the hill, stuffed ourselves with Concord grapes my grandfather had planted and tended, was being sold off to build houses.

"He has promised us he will build the loveliest of homes," she said, repeating the adjective as if trying to convince herself.

A cocky young man in his early-thirties walked forward as if he had stepped out of the pages of a European fashion magazine. He spoke with a soft Dutch accent I mistook for German.

"Thank you Mrs. Florion. And she is correct, we will be building 'the loveliest of homes' and you have my promise we

will always be good, responsible neighbors. I look forward to seeing you all again at the groundbreaking ceremony."

I had the vague sensation that I didn't like this man. He was
invading our demesne. Was that a word I would have used in the
sixth grade? Yes, thanks to Mr. Righetti.

Mrs. Florion again took center stage. "Of course we will be
keeping the hillside property and Dove Cottage and the boathouse
down in the woods, and we will continue to be your neighbors, at
least on the weekends when we come in from Manhattan to get
away from it all.

"We'll have a second announcement in a moment, but as a
special treat, one of our guests has agreed to pay tribute to your
brother, Ira. Please join me in welcoming Miss Yolanda Mero, and
also a warm thanks to her husband, Hermann Irion who provided
us with this beautiful Steinway for this afternoon's celebration."

An older, short woman perhaps the same age as Mrs. Florion,
walked forward to explosive applause from the group.

She stood at the piano and spoke softly. "Ira, I'd like to invite
you and our guests to take a journey with me back in time to that
very cold afternoon in February of 1924. That day we gathered
at Aeolian Hall to listen to your brother premiere his masterwork
with the orchestra under the baton of another wonderful guest
here today, Mr. Paul Whiteman, who we all know commissioned
the piece.

"I almost feel like an imposter playing this, but to Ira and Paul,
and Oscar, and to all of us who knew and loved your brother, I'd
like you to accept it as my way of saying thank you, for his genius
and for his contributions to our American culture."

She turned and sat at the bench and glanced at Whiteman.
Her fingers poised over the Steinway. And then, I heard the most
explosive beauty I had ever heard in my life as the clarinet player
lifted his licorice stick and began the opening plaintive wail of
Rhapsody in Blue.

For the next eighteen minutes, I stood spellbound at what was transpiring before me. The King of Jazz was a professional. The man known as Oscar took a deep drag from his cigarette and hung his head and closed his eyes, as if remembering something. The man referred to as Ira was smiling while holding back tears.

Tom never took his eyes off Mero's fingers. The sunset began to peek under the tent roof and turned Beth's skin into a golden tan. Upon reflection, it was all so surreal, but at the time, I had no perspective to understand the importance nor uniqueness of the moment.

And then in just under twenty minutes it was over. We had become a part of history known by few.

When Mero finished, there was silence in the tent, as the vibrato of the piano strings disappeared into the treetops on the horizon. And then Ira Gershwin stepped forward and extended his hands and began to clap. Mero stood and walked to him for an embrace as the rest of us gave a standing ovation.

"Thank you so much Yolanda for that brilliant interpretation. And Paul, what more can be said for your contributions."

Again, the applause before Mrs. Florion spoke.

"Our second big announcement is that our grandson, Thomas Hogenkamp, will begin his first summer tour of Europe, starting next week, and between now and the middle of August, he will be performing in Vienna, Amsterdam, Berlin, Paris, Copenhagen, and London."

I exchanged glances with Beth. "Did you know anything about this?"

"Something. A little."

Why didn't I?

"To get things started, we've asked Thomas to sit down and play another tribute to George, this time with our other wonderful guest, Mr. Oscar Levant, who will join Thomas for a four-hand version of *Rialto Ripples*.

The man who had been chain-smoking all afternoon stepped forward to join our friend Tom at the piano bench. He turned to

Ernie Kovacs, who stood with his arms folded, chomping on his cigar.

"Put out the stogie, Kovacs, you're stinkin' up the joint.

"When you put out that cigarette, Oscar.

"When there's ice in hell three feet thick, bo-hunk.

"You started stinkin' up the joint when you walked in here this afternoon. And by the way, I might just steal this song for my closing theme music on my new show."

"This guy. . . Always hustling his show. Why don't you get a cigar maker to sponsor your show?"

"Maybe I will."

The tent erupted in laughter at the exchange.

"Least I got a show to plug, has-been."

More laughter.

Ira stepped forward. "Ladies and gentlemen, *Rialto Ripples* by my brother, George Gershwin, soon to be re-named *Ernie Kovac's Closing Theme Song.*"

Another burst of laughter.

"Kovacs, just make sure those royalties keep on coming in, big-shot."

The tent went wild.

And then as the sun went down, my best friend became a part of history himself at the ripe old age of twelve. He extended his hands, the index finger on his right hand brushing the ivory Middle C as if becoming oriented. I was so proud of him I almost began to cry. But the happiness and the goofiness of the song, along with watching Ernie Kovacs using his cigar as an orchestra baton, keeping beat to the music, while dreaming up wild television schemes, had us all laughing.

We said goodbyes to Tom, knowing we wouldn't see him for almost six weeks.

The ride home in the limo didn't last very long, since I lived just a few hundred yards away.

Beth smiled at me. "That was a great party."

"I guess. Pretty fancy."

Beth's father was quiet, intense, semi-drunk, but not sloppy. He turned to me.

"Do you know who those people were?"

"I recognized a few of them."

"They're some of the greatest creative minds of the 20th Century, all gathered under one tent, is what it was. Someday, when you look back on all of this it will make an impression. You'll wish you had been able to sit down and talk to each and every one of them; hope that some of their stuff would rub off on you.

"When you are older you will look back on this day and amaze yourself. But whatever you do, don't ever tell anyone about it. They'll never believe you. They'll think you made up the whole thing."

"Dad," Beth chastised.

There was a lot of truth to what he said. Who would ever believe such a gathering had occurred?

The ride was short, so I had to get it out soon. "I can't believe Tom is leaving tomorrow for a month. He didn't even say anything."

"He mentioned something to me."

"He did?"

"Yeah, he was pretty vague about it, off-hand. 'No big deal', he said."

"A month long concert tour in Europe, no big deal?"

"You know how Tom is."

"When are you leaving?"

"Wednesday morning. We're driving. Three or four hundred miles a day. It will take us almost three whole days to get there. We have to be there next weekend for a showing in Gainesville."

"Will I see you before you leave?"

"I don't know. Dad would that be okay?"

"Sure. But you have to pack."

"I will. I'll meet you at the lake tomorrow morning. That sound good?"

The limo pulled up in front of the house.

"Nice to see you again, Mr. VonBronk."

"Likewise, I'm sure."

"See you tomorrow morning, Beth."

"New City Park. I'll pack a picnic lunch."

And then the limo took a left on Third Street and was gone.

Later, I would learn more about Beth's father, see his works displayed. "VonBronks" would eventually be worth millions, I would find out.

I walked up the front sidewalk and up the two steps of the front porch. My parents were sitting on the sofa watching television. The Ed Sullivan Show had just started.

My mother stood to greet me. "How was it?"

"Fun. It's still going on, probably until the wee hours of the morning, according to Tom. They even had a full orchestra there. That bandleader you like."

My father rose from the couch, turned down the volume knob on the television, and walked to the back porch. My mother joined him first, and I followed. He looked in the direction of Dove Cottage. Our view was blocked by the barn my grandfather had built, but you could hear the music on the mild breeze of the early July evening.

He turned from the northwest and walked inside and a moment later I heard the window to the dining room slide up, next to where my brother spent his life. He wanted Francis to hear. A moment later my father returned to the porch.

As Whiteman played a slow tune I didn't recognize, my mother touched my father on the shoulder and he turned to her. She held her hands aloft in a wistful plea. Apparently not able to find a reason to say no, he accepted her invitation and they began to dance, danced a full three minutes for the first time since the night before the attack on Pearl Harbor, seventeen years earlier.

The slow tune stopped and White segued into *Whispering*, and they started to dance again, but then my father stopped suddenly and withdrew. Embarrassed to dance in front of his son? Unable to accept the fact that he was allowed to enjoy himself?

He went back inside to comfort Francis, leaving my mother and me on the porch alone. In a moment, the dining room window slid down. I turned to my mother. "I didn't know you knew how to dance."

"Before we were married we danced every weekend."

"To the King of Jazz?"

"Yes. Sure. Him and Bunny Berrigan and Benny Goodman and all the others."

"I met Whiteman today."

"Do you know how lucky you are? Your dad is jealous."

"Beth's dad said the same thing. I guess I understand."

"That means probably not. I recognized his music the moment I heard the band begin to play. It's unmistakable."

"Hey, Mom."

"Yes, Will."

"Tom's leaving for Europe for a month. He's going to be performing all over."

"He's a very talented young man."

"And Beth is going to Florida for two weeks."

"I've always wanted to go to Florida. Maybe someday. These hands of mine seem to freeze up in the cold. They get raw. What will you do without your friends for a few weeks?"

That was a very good question, and it had me concerned. "Do you think you could teach me how to dance while they're gone?"

"Ah, yes, Will. The need for social graces. Every young boy needs to learn to dance. We can have our very own private finishing school. I'll even teach you how to hold your knife and fork properly and how to hold the door open for Beth. We can start now."

As we danced to the distant strains of Paul Whiteman, as she had done earlier that evening and a lifetime ago, and as I had tried and failed so miserably to do earlier in the afternoon with Beth, I thought of her, and then I thought of Francis.

"Mom? Do you think Francis will ever be able to dance?"

My question broke the magic spell. She fell to earth in ribbons. "No. Francis will never be able to do anything more than what he does now. You need to accept that, Will."

"Do you think Dad will ever get better, be himself again?"

We danced a full thirty seconds before she spoke again.

"Will, your father died during the war. I don't even know the man who came back in his place. I always hoped he would come home again. I thought maybe he would. I think what happened to Francis, whatever shred of hope there might have been for your father, was lost that day. So, no, I don't think he will ever come back."

"What are you going to do?"

She hesitated, but not for long. She had already figured out the future. "I'm going to take care of him until the day he dies and I'm going to take care of your brother until the day he dies. And...."

"What?"

"And, I'm going to teach you how to dance."

"Thanks, Mom. For everything."

"That's all I needed to hear."

"Oh, and Mrs. Florion said 'Thank you' for the dress."

"That's nice. But that's not really important to me now."

The next day at New City Park Lake was uneventful, as Beth and I swam out to the raft and talked about Tom and Europe and then her trip to Florida. Beth was quiet for a while. I assumed it was because she was thinking about her trip.

Later, we sat in the shade by the brick barbecue pit and ate the picnic lunch Beth had prepared. Tuna fish sandwiches with lots of relish and celery mixed in, the way she knew I liked it.

But her thoughts were on Florida, and as the afternoon wore on, she became increasingly restless.

"I guess I need to go home and start packing. I'll miss you."

"I'll miss you, too."

"More summer fun when I return."

As she drove her bike out of the parking lot to Hall Avenue I yelled to her.

"Don't forget the post card."

"I already wrote it."

It was to be the first time we had been apart in almost two years.

The next two weeks I was lost. But I learned how to dance.

CHAPTER TWENTY-FOUR

BETH'S FUNERAL
ST. AUGUSTINE'S CHURCH,
GERMONDS CEMETERY

Friday
October 20, 2000
Age 54

I walked from my house in New City Park Lake and met my mother at home. "Delores called. She's going to be delayed. She'll meet us at the cemetery."

My mother nodded in silence, asking no questions, as she adjusted her hat at the front hall mirror. Francis remained behind, attended by one of the nuns from the Maple Avenue apartments. We walked across the street in silence.

St. Augustine's was filled to capacity for Beth's funeral. Beth's father stood off to the side. Her husband Rainer, their daughter Alison, and all of his business associates became the center of attention. Tom was there, along with Frau K. and Max, now approaching their eighties. Many of Beth's high school and college friends were there, as well as Karen and Jimmy, all of the investigators, my mother, and me.

At the appointed time, Father Carrick walked to the pulpit and bowed his head in silence for what seemed forever, trying to compose himself. Finally, he looked out over the congregation.

"We are gathered here today to celebrate the life of one of the most special human beings that God has ever let me have the opportunity to know."

There was another long pause. "And I must interject here, this is the hardest thing I have ever had to do, so please bear with me."

Members of the congregation who related to what he had just said nodded silently in affirmation. My mother reached out and put her hand over mine.

"Who was Beth VonBronk? Loyal friend, student, New City adventurer. Wife, mother, accomplished, award-winning photographer and photojournalist, artist. But she was so much more than that, if that's even possible. It makes it difficult to know where to even begin.

"I watched this young woman grow and mature from the time she was ten until the time she grew into adulthood and moved away. God granted me the privilege of being both her priest and her friend. For those of you gathered here today who may have befriended her in recent years, let me tell you there is so much about Beth VonBronk you probably don't know. Although she grew up never knowing 'want' and marrying into wealth, Beth always insisted on being her own woman. As a successful entrepreneur and art gallery owner, and as an acclaimed photographer in great demand, with her own entrepreneurial skills, she amassed her own wealth. Surprised?

"Ordinarily, it is not considered good manners to talk about wealth in polite company. And even though Beth never revealed much about this to others, I don't think it's inappropriate to share with you what Beth shared with others less fortunate.

"In Africa, in China, in South America, she established reading programs for children, paying salaries of village teachers out of her own pocket. She bought books, built schools.

"Why? I asked her why. She said it was to share her joy of reading. She wanted other young children to feel the joy she felt, holding a book in their own hands. Many of the villages she visited didn't have clean drinking water. Now, thanks to Beth, they do. Closer to home, in a place called Pahokee, Florida, she worked with the local diocese and parish to do the same. Teachers, books, clean water. She shared her magnificent mind and her gifts with so many.

"And then sixteen years ago, she and her husband, Rainer Klein, decided to become parents." He smiled.

I hung my head in shame.

"And so they adopted an infant, named her Alison, and raised a wonderful human being to walk among us."

Father Carrick tried to go on, but it was becoming increasingly difficult. There was a silence of thirty seconds while he stepped forward, looked down to place his hand on the coffin. Then he looked up and addressed the congregation.

"What have we become? Things like this don't happen in New City. Yes, things like this are commonplace all around us in this country that we have become. Every day, scores of senseless murders all around us. But New City? Things like this don't happen here.

"So what have we become? What has New City become? Once a safe haven in a world gone mad, we can no longer count on that. I am sickened. My body, my mind, my heart, my soul, are sickened by what we have become."

Again, there was a long silence as he returned to the pulpit.

"I'm sorry, I had many more words to share with you today. But I just can't seem to find them. I know I'm repeating myself here, but one of my greatest joys in life was knowing her, watching her grow. Watching her become the woman she became.

"My job is to offer consolation and solace to you who have gathered here today. But I'm afraid I'm just not up to it, so I'll have to ask your forgiveness."

Father Carrick caught himself, choking, shaking his head in his attempt.

"On behalf of Beth's father, her husband, and her daughter, I thank you for coming today to pay your respects. I thank God for allowing me the privilege of knowing such a person. I, for one, will never be the same, knowing she is no longer walking amongst us. Can never be the same.

"So until that time we will all meet Beth again, kneel together with her and touch the hem of His garment, let us all rejoice in her life and the lessons she shared with us and thank God for allowing us to share our time on earth here with her, by saying, 'Our Father, who art in Heaven. . .'"

The congregation joined in on The Lord's Prayer. Father Carrick turned and walked from the pulpit toward his office before they were finished.

The choir quickly recovered and began to sing *In Paradisum*. The congregation exchanged nervous glances. The service had lasted less than ten minutes. They finally stood and walked out awkwardly, pouring onto the sidewalk. Rainer watched as Jimmy, Tom and four other pall bearers I didn't recognize stepped forward to do their job.

I escorted my mother out onto the sidewalk. She was distraught and not just for Beth.

"He took it very hard. You were all his children," she said into my shoulder.

A thousand million memories flooded my mind as we stood on the sidewalk when the casket passed by and was lowered into the hearse. Karen walked to me and took my hand.

Jimmy turned from closing the door on the hearse and joined us, taking the three of us in his embrace.

I rode in Karen and Jimmy's car to the cemetery. At the last minute, Beth's father had invited my mother to ride with him.

Delores drove directly from Clarkstown High School on Congers Road.

At Germonds' Cemetery, near where my father and our ancestors were buried, Beth's plot had been prepared. Jimmy and Karen
and our other classmates and Beth's colleagues from Manhattan
completed the large circle of mourners. Many, surprised, or possibly even dismayed by the brevity of the service at St. Augustine's
had elected not to come. The murder investigating team stood at a
distance, not very discreetly in the background.

That morning at church, I had not seen Beth's father in the
thirty-two years since our break-up, except in the arts magazines
where photographs of him and his artwork appeared regularly.
Now, as I looked at him standing at the grave site, he hadn't
changed much. He was still dressed in crumpled corduroys and
a plaid flannel shirt, brown work boots, hands stained from his
work; still appeared mysterious, lost, his wild, thick shock of hair,
now turned from jet black to heavy salt-and-pepper. What Dylan
Thomas would have looked like had he not drunk himself to death
at the age of thirty-nine. He was still chain smoking Camels, had
one now in his nicotine-stained fingertips. He appeared as if the
graveside memorial of his daughter was just some inconvenient
interruption of his work schedule. Or maybe there was just no
emotion left.

He looked at me as if trying to place me, although he had
looked right at me earlier at the church. Now having placed me,
he walked to my side with resignation in his voice asking me why
this had to happen. He was delirious. "She should have stayed
with you. She was always so happy with you. You fucked her up
really bad, kid." He turned abruptly and walked away.

"Wait, what do you mean?"

He turned back to me, squinting, and returned the few steps.
"You were her life, and you ruined it. She never got over you."
He turned and walked off toward the parking lot across Germonds
Road. He walked past Tom, who was standing on the periphery.
Tom never cried or showed emotion during the funeral service or
graveside ceremony. He stood off on the perimeter, never walking

closer, while his limo awaited, Max behind the wheel.

I wanted to stop Beth's father, but couldn't move. "Always so happy with me?" "Ruined her life?" Then why did she run away and marry Rainer and avoid me like the plague for the rest of my life? I wanted to chase after him, demand answers.

Instead, before I could take a step I was accosted by Beth's husband, Rainer Klein. Like Beth's father, the press was always filled with photographs of Klein, but I would have recognized him anyway, even though the first day I saw him was forty-two years earlier when I was only in the sixth grade.

Rainer approached, wearing a black suit, crisp. He looked like the greedy land developer he was, originally from Holland, who had inherited family money and quadrupled it on numerous land deals; some honest, some shady. At his side was their sixteen year-old daughter, Alison, weeping silently. Did she recognize me from the luncheonette check-out line at Tor's from last year? Rainer was looking at me angrily, as if I had been responsible for what had happened to her.

"What are you doing here? You have some nerve."

Before I could answer, he continued loud enough for everyone to hear. For a brief moment I thought he was going to attack me physically.

"I'd better not find out you had anything to do with this, you creep. Beth told me you were stalking her for years."

"What are you talking about?"

"You know exactly what I'm talking about. You could never get over her so you wouldn't let her alone."

"What?" I looked around nervously. If Rainer were trying to attract an audience, he was succeeding. The investigators were being baited.

"Following her around, accosting her in public with inappropriate displays of emotion. Saying all kinds of things."

I continued to stare in disbelief.

"Don't look at me like you don't know what I'm talking

about."

"That was years ago, when we were kids."

"Oh, really? And when did you stop being a kid? A few months ago? A few weeks ago? A few days ago?" How could he have known this?

"What? Wait, what happened a few months ago?"

"Last Christmas, in the luncheonette. You accosted her at the cash register, embarrassed her in front of our daughter." Alison looked in my direction without making eye contact, then back to her father. "Wouldn't stop bothering her after all these years."

"I wished her a Merry Christmas, that's all. How is that a problem? Alison was there. She can tell you, right, Alison?" She did not reply.

"Don't you dare speak to my daughter. Beth told me everything about you. Everything. And you know what? Now your boss is going to know, too. You know why? I think you had something to do with this. I think you couldn't deal with the fact that she didn't love you after all these years and so you killed her."

"You're crazy." I looked around. My mother was staring at me and Jimmy was walking toward me at a rapid clip.

"We'll see."

"We'll see what?"

"We'll see after I tell your boss and your colleagues what she's been telling me for years."

"Which is what?"

"That you've been obsessed with her and never let it go. She told me a lot."

Father Carrick stepped forward with a comforting hand on Rainer's shoulder. "Mr. Klein, I know you're very upset. Why don't we just try to remember why we're here today. To pay tribute to your wife and the beloved friend of all of us. Let's not dishonor her memory. I'm sure this can all be hashed out on another day. There are others here who want to remember Beth as she was. Please, this is not the right time or place."

As the crowd began to thin after the service, Delores walked up to me.

"I have to go back to school for a little while. You want me to drop you off at home?"

"No. I'll walk."

"Okay. I'll see you at home." She started toward the parking lot and then turned back. "Will, try to take it easy."

"Okay."

I left the cemetery with the others who had parked in the rectory parking lot. We all walked in silence. At the stone gates they all proceeded across the street. Jim and Karen left with the others. Father Carrick, along with a carload of nuns, drove my mother home.

I headed west on Germonds Road, on foot, to the intersection where Middletown Road becomes Little Tor Road, passing the entrance to the Palisades Parkway, and turned north. At Old Middletown Road, I cut over to Chestnut Grove Elementary School and just stood there looking at it. For what reason? I don't know. Except for a few friends from my school days, I had, or should I say, Beth and I had no connection to the old fieldstone building. It was just a part of New City history I had always wondered about. A Clarkstown Patrol car entered the parking lot behind me and the cop behind the wheel, a long-time local, gave me a tip of the hat when he recognized me.

"Everything okay, Will?"

"Yeah. Just taking a little walk down memory lane."

"I thought you went to New City Grammar."

"I did."

"Oh. Okay. So. See you around the courthouse."

I walked on. Down past New Valley Road, past what remained of Davies' Lake, past Cropsey's Farm and Red Hill Road. At Lake Drive I turned right, walked past the yellow Hetherington house, and headed home.

Delores' Chevy was in the driveway. She beat me home.

Inside, she was sitting in an armchair in the living room. She sat upright, determined, waiting for me.

"What are you doing?"

"Will, I've packed a few clothes in an overnight bag and I'll come back later this weekend to clear out my things."

"What is this all about?"

"You know how you felt about Beth all these years? Well, that's how I've felt about you. So I know what you're going through. Let's just leave it like that for right now, okay? I'm tired of living alone."

"What do you mean? We've been living together for twenty years."

"No, Will. I've been living with someone who is never here, even when he's here. Your body has been here but you've never been here. You're not even here now.

"And now that Beth is dead, it's not going to get better. It's going to get worse. Now, instead of mourning the living and what could have been, you're going to spend your time mourning the dead and what should have been. I just can't live my life that way anymore. You and I have no future. I thought someday you would be able to move on, but that's never going to happen. I'm tired of playing second fiddle. You'll never marry me.

"I love you, Will. I love you and I've never heard you even say it to me."

"Where will you go?"

"My mother's house in Haverstraw. At least for starters."

I didn't know what to say. I didn't feel anything. I started to protest, just to make a show of it, but she must have sensed that's all it was; a show.

"Will, don't. Don't say anything. Just let me go. Maybe some-day I'll feel differently. But for now, I just want to be alone. I'll come by later in the week and pack up my stuff."

She left me there.

I sat in the armchair and didn't stop her.

Five minutes passed before I stood in the living room in the gathering darkness. I was paralyzed. Delores was right, of course. Right about everything.

Eventually I found my way to the kitchen and stood at the window over the sink and looked out into the back yard toward the lake. I had been lying to Delores since we had first moved into this house together.

I stood at the counter top and looked out the back window to the lawn where Beth and I had conceived a child on a summer night thirty-three years ago. I couldn't think of Delores leaving. All I could think of was Beth.

I went outside without a jacket and leaned back against the tree next to where we had lain. What had I done, I wondered? What was I going to do about all this? Was I going to continue to spend a life of regret?

CHAPTER TWENTY-FIVE

ROCKLAND COUNTY COURT HOUSE

Tuesday
October 24, 2000
Age 54

The Monday after Beth's funeral, Rainer Klein was interviewed officially for the first time by Barry Henion, Carl Betts, Ray Cicci, and Dave Sherman. His attorney, some oil slick from Manhattan, was by his side.

Later that same day Tom was called in and interviewed formally for the first time since Ray and Dave had questioned him at his boathouse, the day he discovered Beth's body.

Although I wasn't allowed to be present at the interviews, I know what was said because I went on-line at the office on Tuesday and opened the files. Once transcribed, the files are accessible to anyone in our office. Anyone with a password.

Even though I wasn't present, I could read enough between the lines to imagine Rainer's arrogance as he spoke to the investigators.

RE: BETH VONBRONK HOMICIDE, OCTOBER 15-16, 2000. FROM

THE TRANSCRIPT OF MONDAY, OCTOBER 23, 2000, 9 a.m. INTERVIEW WITH RAINER KLEIN, HUSBAND OF VICTIM, CONDUCTED BY LT RAY CICCI and LT DAVID SHERMAN, CPD. OBSERVED BY BARRY HENION and CARL BETTS from DISTRICT ATTORNEY'S OFFICE and JAMES CAPOBIANCO from the CORONER'S OFFICE. ALSO PRESENT IS MR. KLEIN'S LEGAL COUNSEL, WALTER TATE.

RC: Let the record indicate that we are interviewing Rainer Klein, husband of the murder victim, Beth VonBronk Klein. He is represented by his attorney, Walter Tate.

Mr. Klein, for the record, please state your name and residence.

RK: Rainer Klein. Our legal residence is in New City, over by the reservoir, but we also have residences in Manhattan, Hong Kong, Heidelberg, and London.

RC: Is that part of the old Dr. Davies' Farm property?

RK: Yes.

RC: Are you here of your own volition?

RK: Of course. I want you to find out who killed my wife.

RC: What is your occupation?

RK: I'm a land developer. Developed a lot of property in Rockland as a matter of fact.

RC: How long were you married?

RK: Just over twenty-nine years.

RC: Would you say you were happily married?

RK: Of course. We spent the last twenty-six years traveling the world together. I developed properties and managed my investments. My wife was involved in philanthropy and a lot of photography.

DS: Philanthropy?

RK: Yes. She supported several children's charities dealing with literacy and clean drinking water.

What Father Carrick had referred to in the memorial service. I immediately thought how fitting that was. Beth was the most voracious reader I've ever known. As for the clean drinking water, all I could think about was the springs; the spring behind the Dutch

Garden where Beth had taken my picture kneeling, the springs on the Demarest Kill below the ridge line on Tom's property that we drank from so many times; that we had taken for granted. It all saddened me so much to continue reading.

DS: Can you provide us the names and contact information for those charities?

RK: I'll have one of my people get it to you.

DS: Where were you on the night of Sunday, October 15 of this year between the hours of 7 p.m. and 7 a.m. the next morning, Monday, October 16, New York Time?

RK: I was in Hong Kong. My attorney has prepared a list of witnesses, including three from the diplomatic service.

DS: Do you know of anyone who would want to kill your wife?

RK: Her two old friends come to mind.

DS: Would you state their names for the record?

RK: Tom Hogenkamp, her current confidante, inamorato, or whatever you want to call him. They were together for years.

And then he spoke my name.

RC: And what can you tell us about the latter?

RK: He's been pursuing her for years.

DS: What do you mean?

RK:Theybrokeupthirty-twoyearsago,aftercollege,andhejustcouldn't let go, move on. She did. He didn't.

DS: How do you know?

RK: She told me everything. He stalked her at her gallery before he left for Vietnam. In the Seventies, before we were married, she told him to back off. And when he got back from Vietnam she told him she and I were going to get married and he freaked out. Went ballistic. Started crying in the middle of the street, making a scene in Greenwich Village.

DS: Where was this?

RK: Washington Square Park where she walked to lunch every day.

DS: Were there any witnesses?

RK: I told you she witnessed it. That's how I know.

DS: Besides her.

RK: You can talk to her co-worker. I'll get you a name.

DS: What else?

RK: He phoned her for years, or kept trying to. Ask her father. The Christmas before we were married, he came back from Vietnam and begged her to change her mind. Go back with him. She was so upset we moved to Europe for seven years after we were married, just to get away from him. She figured when we got back enough time had passed, but he saw her driving through town one day around 1978 and called her at her father's house.

DS: What did he want?

RK: Typical stalker stuff. Just wanted to talk to her to explain his side of the story. You know, work his way up from there.

DS: Did he ever say anything threatening to her? Threaten to harm her, or himself, or you in any way? Your daughter?

RK: Could be, but she never told me that. She was just very upset. So we moved to Hong Kong. It just so happened I had a project over there anyway, so it worked out.

DS: At any time did you hire a private investigator to follow your wife when you were living in New City?

RK: Yes.

DS: What's his name?

(inaudible with attorney)

ATTORNEY WALTER TATE: What is this about?

CH: This is about trying to find out who killed your client's wife.

RK: Never mind. Okay, I hired a guy to follow her.

DS: Why?

RK: Because I thought she might be having an affair.

DS: With whom?

RK: Tom. Maybe Will.

DS: Why did you think that?

WT: You don't have to answer that.

DS: Okay, what did he find out?

WT: That's privileged.

RK: He followed her all around town. She would park in the parking lot out front here and walk in the front door and not come out for hours.

DS: So that's why you thought she was having an affair with Will. You thought she was visiting him at the Courthouse?

RK: Yes. Either that or the guy at the Building and Zoning counter.

DS: Your investigator never followed her inside?

RK: He did a couple of times but he could never find her.

DS: Any of you guys ever see her around this office?

(inaudible mumbles from CICCI and HENION)

CICCI & HENION: No.

DS:So to get back to our original question, do you know of anyone who would want to harm her?

RK: I told you, the stalker from your own office. What's so hard to figure out? He wanted her back, she wasn't interested, he gets angry, she pulls away, he goes crazy. Simple stuff. Elementary, is what Sherlock Holmes used to say, right?

JD: According to the autopsy, she had bruises on her chest and arms that look to be about a week to ten days old. Possibly from being punched. You know how that happened?

RK: She was very clumsy.

DS: You know nothing about the bruises?

RK: Sure. She fell down the stairs carrying some stuff to her car. She showed them to me after her fall.

DS: You weren't skeptical?

WT: My client has answered the question.

RK: For all I know, either one of those creeps could have beaten her up a couple of weeks back.

RC: What were her plans for the immediate future? Do you know?

RK: She and Alison were going to meet up with me in Hong Kong. She was packing for an extended stay.

RC: Extended stay? Why? More harassment?

RK: Mostly because that's where we live now. I have several projects underway.

CH: Okay, Mr. Klein. That will do for starters. Will you be around for the next week or so?

WT: My client has to be back in Hong Kong for a closing next week. If you need him you can get in touch with him through my office.

(inaudible)

CH: Just make sure we know how to reach you. We will want to talk to you some more in the next few days.

RC: This ends the preliminary interview with Rainer Klein. Time out is 9:40 am on Monday, October 23, 2000.

CHAPTER TWENTY-SIX

ROCKLAND COUNTY COURT HOUSE

October 24, 2000

Tom's first official interview had also been transcribed.

RE: BETH VONBRONK HOMICIDE, OCTOBER 15-16, 2000 FROM THE TRANSCRIPT OF WEDNESDAY, OCTOBER 18, 2000, 11 a.m. INTERVIEW WITH TOM HOGENKAMP, FRIEND OF VICTIM WHO FOUND THE BODY. CONDUCTED BY LT RAY CICCI and LT DAVID SHERMAN, CPD. OBSERVED BY BARRY HENION and CARL BETTS from DISTRICT ATTORNEY'S OFFICE and JAMES CAPOBIANCO from the CORONER'S OFFICE.

RC: Let the record indicate that we are interviewing Thomas Hogen-kamp, friend of the murder victim, Beth VonBronk Klein for the second time. The first time being an informal interview at his boathouse on the day he found the victim's body, October 16. At that time he was inter-rogated by myself, Lt. Ray Cicci, and Lt. David Sherman. Hogenkamp is not represented by an attorney.

RC: Please state your name and address for the record.

TH: My name is Thomas Hogenkamp, and my address is Dove Cottage, New City, 10956.

RC: Mr. Hogenkamp, how long have you known the victim, Beth VonBronk?

TH: Forty-four years.

RC: How would you describe your relationship with her?

TH: We were very close friends. Lifelong friends. Confidantes.

RC: When was the last time you saw her?

TH: Alive or dead?

RC: Let's start off with alive.

TH: The evening of October 15. She came by to talk.

RC: Where?

TH: The boathouse where I live. Behind Dove Cottage.

DS: Let's hold off a minute. Do you know how she got there?

TH: She drove to the Courthouse parking lot and then walked through the Dutch Garden and then along the pathway by the stream.

RC: Why wouldn't she just pull up to Dove Cottage on Muller Court and walk down the hill? Wouldn't that have been easier? Wouldn't get her feet wet?

TH: Yes. But like I mentioned the other day when you were at the boathouse, her husband had a private investigator following her and she was tired of it, so she would park at the Courthouse, walk through the front hall and out the basement door, and then back through the Dutch Garden to throw him off.

RC: How do you know he had a private investigator following her?

TH: She told me.

RC: Do you know his name?

TH: No.

RC: Why was he having a private investigator following her?

TH: I suppose it was because he thought we were having an affair.

DS: And were you having an affair?

TH: You mean were we sexually intimate?

DS: Yes. Were you sexually intimate?

TH: No.

DS: At any time in the forty-four years that you knew her?

TH: No.

DS: And why is that?

TH: It wasn't that kind of friendship.

DS: What kind of friendship was it?

TH: We were emotionally and intellectually intimate.

DS: But not sexually.

TH: That is correct.

RC: You'll have to excuse me a minute, Mr. Hogenkamp. Call me old fashioned, but I'm a little skeptical. Two attractive people, very close friends for forty something years, "emotionally and intellectually intimate," and what, no sparks?

TH: It wasn't that kind of friendship.

RC: So you said. Help me to understand. Are you gay?

TH: No.

RC: So. . .?

TH: Were you in Vietnam, Detective?

RC: "Lieutenant." What's that got to do with anything?

TH: It's got everything to do with anything. I'm celibate. It's the answer to your question. I'm celibate.

RC: Wait, because of Vietnam, you can't get it up?

TH: I didn't say I was impotent. I said I was celibate.

RC: I'm not following. I don't get it.

TH: I didn't suppose someone like you would.

RC: What's that supposed to mean?

TH: You're the smart guy. You should be able to figure out that last part.

DS: Okay, guys, let's stay on point. Tell us about the morning of October 16.

TH: I go out jogging every day at dawn. Down the path to the Dutch Garden. Down Congers and across the reservoir. Down the east side and then north on Strawtown.

DS: So on this day in question? October 16, 2000?

TH: I hadn't gone more than about two-three hundred yards down the path when I saw her in the stream under the gazebo.

DS: And what did you do then?

TH: I approached her body and knew immediately it was her. I looked around to see if anyone was still there, lurking, watching, whatever. Then I took my cell phone out and dialed 911. Then Ron and Bill got there.

DS: Faber and Johnson?

TH: Yes. I talked to them for a few minutes and they said you and Ray would catch up with me later, which you did that afternoon.

DS: They didn't ask you to hang around?

TH: No. I've known them for forty-odd years, too. We went all through school together.

BH: Let the record indicate I'm speaking to Lts. Cicci and Sherman. Ray, tell your guys that I don't care if it's their mothers who discover the next body. Everyone sticks around, doesn't leave the scene until we get a chance to talk to them.

DS: Right. Did you touch the victim's body? Move it?

TH: No. I stayed about six-eight feet away.

DS: So it was exactly the way Detective Cicci and I found it a few minutes later?

TH: I don't know how you found it a few minutes later. I wasn't there when you got there, remember? I never touched her. After Ron and Bill arrived they said I could leave. They said they knew where I would be. Whether they touched her after I left, I don't know. I would have no way of knowing.

DS: Did you identify the body for them at that time?

TH: No.

DS: Why?

TH: They didn't ask.

BH: You knew who it was and didn't tell them? That sounds preposterous.

TH: Maybe I was in shock, denial.

BH: Or maybe you were hiding something?

TH: I have nothing to hide. I'm here of my own free will.

DS: Let the record show that we are passing crime scene photographs to the interviewee, labeled 10152000-dash-1 through 6.

(Pause on tape while interview subject examines photos)

DS: Does this reflect what you saw?

TH: Yes. It doesn't look like anything was disturbed.

RC: Okay, let's go back to when Beth was at your house. How often did she show up using that back path?

TH: When she was in town. A couple of times a week. Usually during the daytime Courthouse office hours, sometimes at night.

RC: And on the night in question, what was her demeanor?

TH: She was upset about something. She said that she was leaving Rainer and taking Alison and going to live in New Zealand indefinitely. She asked me if I would go with her.

RC: And what did you say?

TH: I told her that I was going to Vietnam and that I could join her later or they could join me.

RC: And why were you going to Vietnam?

TH: I'm building a school, or actually schools there. And an orphanage.

RC: So you would join her when?

TH: In about a month or so. Then I would have to go back and forth after that.

RC: To Vietnam?

TH: Yes, to monitor the schools' progress.

RC: What did she tell you about her relationship with Rainer? Why was she leaving him?

TH: He was physically abusive.

RC: Meaning what?

TH: He punched her. Beat her up a few weeks ago. She was waiting for him to leave town and go back to Hong Kong, and then she was going to make her escape.

RC: Why was he physically abusive?

TH: He was convinced she was having an affair with someone.

RC: Who?

TH: Like I said, he accused her of having an affair with me. Possibly Will.

RC: Do you think she was having an affair?

TH: Highly unlikely. With Will or anyone else.

RC: Why do you say that?

TH: She wasn't that kind of person. She had exceptionally high moral standards. A code of conduct.

RC: Did she tell you any other reason he might have beaten her?

TH: Yes. It was an accumulation of things. He thought she was spending too much of his money philanthropically. He wanted her to cut back. She just spent more. He also felt she had betrayed him. In a business deal.

RC: What business deal?

TH: He wanted to buy up the rest of my Dove Cottage estate. The woods. Greenberg's Pond, and my property along the Demarest Kill. He wanted her to convince me to sell it to him. Instead she told me what he was trying to do.

RC: How did he find out she had betrayed him?

TH: I can't be sure he really did find out. She just said he acted as if he knew something. He accused her of ruining the deal with me.

RC: How could he have found out?

TH: I'm not sure.

RC: Do you know anyone else besides her husband who might want her dead?

TH: No.

RC: What about your friend, Will?

TH: Ex-friend. What about him?

RC: Rainer told us he was stalking her.

TH: Stalking? That's not how she put it to me.

RC: How did she put it to you?

TH: She said Will was still in love with her and was trying to convince her to go back with him. She said he was persistent. She was concerned for his emotional state.

RC: She didn't feel the same way?

TH: She loved him, but there was no way she was going to go back to him.

RC: Why?

TH: She had moved on. He hadn't. Look. I'm getting kind of tired. Can we continue this another time?

(inaudible)

JC: He has a medical condition. The medications cause fatigue.

CH: We'll need to get you in here again in the next day or two. Let the record indicate the interview ended at five minutes before noon.

Beth still loved me?

I knew they were going to interview Tom another time on tape, so I would have to wait.

I downloaded, saved, and printed the files and stuck them in my briefcase so I could read them again later. I headed to Father Carrick's.

CHAPTER TWENTY-SEVEN

ST. AUGUSTINE'S CHURCH

Tuesday
October 24, 2000
Age 54

Father Carrick looked like he was expecting me. Maybe he was always expecting me. Why did I go to see him? Confirmation of what I had just read, perhaps. Corroborating evidence.

"What did they do there at the boathouse? Were they intimate?"

Father Carrick looked at me and shook his head. "Let's not beat around the bush, eh? Let's cut to the chase. Is that what is bothering you? Again, I'm not talking as a priest, here. No. He cannot be intimate. I told you that the other day."

"Why not?"

"I should have said, *will not* be intimate. I told you already. After Vietnam he became celibate, asexual."

"Gay?

He shook his head in disgust. "Why do people always jump to such conclusions? Never mind, I already know. *'Black or White Fallacy'* from Logic class. No, he's just completely asexual. Celibate. He committed to living under a vow of chastity. He told me they would hold one another like old friends, even lie on the bed together and take naps embraced in one another's arms, so yes, they were intimate as far as their emotional intimacy, but not sexually intimate. They held each other like the dear old friends that they were."

"I don't get it."

"Yeah, I bet the D.A. didn't get it either."

"He told those guys he didn't expect someone like them to understand."

"How do you know that? He told me you weren't allowed in the interview."

"I just know, okay?" I couldn't tell him I had downloaded and read transcripts I wasn't supposed to see.

"Granted, it's not a very common behavior. But perhaps a lot more common than you think, choice or otherwise. But it's his behavior. He became what some people call an esthete. A Tantrist is what he would be called in the world of Yoga. Kind of like me being celibate."

"Esthete?"

"He focuses on other things."

"Like what?"

"His music. If you look on the walls of his home you'll find shelves of his recordings. Over four thousand on reel-to-reel tapes, DAT tapes, memory cards, whatever the latest technology is these days. I can't keep up."

"What did he talk about with Beth?"

"They talked about her child, her marriage to Rainer. Stuff that old friends catch up on. They often talked about you, Will, and the events that brought us to this situation."

"What situation?"

"Beth told Tom you were bothering her, demanding meetings over the years and she didn't want to meet. The situation where she just wanted to leave everything behind and leave Rainer and take their daughter and go somewhere and start anew. Europe. Italy.

Greece. Australia. New Zealand was the latest. She was going to meet Rainer in Hong Kong, but I think her long-term plan was to leave him once he started that big project over there and became really busy. Rainer was becoming increasingly paranoid, jealous, accusatory, verbally abusive. Physically abusive."

"Jealous of what?" I knew Tom and Rainer's version from the interview transcriptions. I wanted to hear from Father Carrick.

"Their meetings. His suspicions about you. She was convinced he had a private detective tailing her to see if she would go to Tom. Or tailing you. Or both."

"Tailing me?"

"He saw her go into the Courthouse on many occasions. Never could find her though."

"She never came to see me there. She was going to Tom's through the woods."

"I know."

I continued to play dumb. "So some guy was tailing me?"

CHAPTER TWENTY-EIGHT

DAVIES' LAKE

Summer, 1958
Age 11

While Tom and Beth were gone, I was lonely, walked around the house, hung out in back yard, lay down in the shade of the sugar maple by the chicken coops as Francis and I had done so many days, but this time looking as the weeds and saplings began to take over the baseball field that my father had built for Francis and me. I was waiting, killing time. Waiting for what?

One day, I saw Marvin and Sparrow getting ready to get on their bikes and were putting paper bag lunches in their carrying baskets.

"Hey, dipshit. You wanna go swimming?"

"New City Park?"

"Nah, they won't let us in. We're going to Davies'."

I had been swimming at Davies' Lake with Francis. As Beth and Tom and I had discovered firsthand just days ago, it was actually a part of the Demarest Kill waterway. I asked my mother if I could go.

Knowing I was lonely, she said, "Yes, but watch out for that Marvin. He's trouble. If he starts to bully Calvin, come straight home."

Like father, like son. What did that pose for me, I wondered?

She packed a quick sack of peanut butter and jelly sandwiches and filled a thermos with cold milk, and we were off.

We rode in silence south on Main Street past Collyer, almost to Germonds. I had never been this route before. At King's Highway we headed west to South Little Tor.

Davies' Lake sat on a broad, gently sloping valley. Like New City Park Lake just a few hundred yards to the north, a dam had been set up along the Demarest Kill at the north end of the gully, and the result was a swimming lake surrounded by giant oaks and maples. A narrow strip of sand had been trucked in to form a beach on the southeast perimeter.

By the time we arrived, the parking lot was filled with Red and Tan Line buses dropping off families from the City and I didn't see any of the kids from school. Everyone was a complete stranger. It was a citified version of New City Park Lake, filled with new faces. Somehow even those two lakes were a metaphor for something. I just couldn't figure it out.

After paying admission, we pushed our bikes through the gate and locked them in the bike rack. The smell of grilled hot dogs and frying onions filled the air, along with the smell of sun tan oil and kids screaming, all set to the tune of *Tequila, Sweet Little Sixteen, At the Hop*, and *Great Balls of Fire*.

Marvin was swaggering about, showing off to the other boys who had newly arrived and who seemed to know him. Calvin and I spread out our towels.

"You ready to go in and get wet?"

Calvin nodded and after looking over his shoulder to see if Marvin was watching, we waded in the water through the splashing children.

"You want to swim out to the raft?"

"Nah, I can't swim."

"Francis taught me when I was seven. Does Marvin know how? How come he never taught you?"

"He doesn't come here to swim."

"What do you mean?"

"He's got other stuff on his mind. Let's go down here to the other end by the dam."

Calvin took off his tee-shirt and I looked at his tiny frame and fragile bones. He looked like a skeleton, and the name he had chosen for himself seemed ever more fitting. He had the tiny bones of a frail little bird. His pale skin was blotched with dark soft bruises.

I pointed. "What's that?"

"Nothing. I fell down the basement steps a few weeks ago."

We waded to the north end, close to the dam and the lifeguard tower. Calvin kept looking over his shoulder, nervously, as if at any moment Marvin would attack.

"What's wrong?"

"Nothing. Just checking."

"What?"

"Marvin usually gets into a fight when he comes here. It's like he picks a fight on purpose."

"Why would he do that?"

"I don't know. Show how tough he is."

We waded into the water. "You want me to show you how to swim?"

"Yeah, I guess."

Do you know how to hold your breath?"

"Yeah."

"Well stand out here and bend over and put your face underwater. You're gonna hold your breath and then turn your head and let the air out and take in some new air and then turn your head and put it under the water again." I demonstrated.

"It kinda scares me."

For the first ten minutes Sparrow bent at the waist and turned his head to the left and right, regulating his breathing like he would have to while swimming. Each cycle we went to deeper water. When he caught the knack of that, I held out my arms and he stretched out flat across the crook of my elbows, face down, parallel to the surface. Holding him aloft was like holding a handful of twigs.

"Okay, good. Now keep your knees straight and kick. Do the breathing thing." He kicked. He started laughing and choking and kicking and sputtering all at once.

"Doggy paddle."

"What?"

"Doggy paddle. Paddle your arms like a dog swimming."

"I can do that." He doggy paddled. And before he knew it I lowered my arms and he took off, laughing, petrified and filled with uncertain glee at the same time. He began to sink but kicked off the bottom without me telling him.

"Keep your lungs filled with air as much as you can. It will help you keep buoyant."

He lifted his head and filled his mouth with air and water, coughed it out and came up for another gasp. He was creating a lot of turbulence, and was going nowhere fast, but he was learning how to swim.

I stopped him, just as Francis had stopped me years earlier. While he caught his breath I demonstrated how to put it all together with an Australian crawl.

"Why do they call it that?"

"Because some guy crawled all the way across Australia to learn how to swim."

"Really?"

"No. Try it." My jokes were starting to sound like Beth's.

He kicked off, began kicking and doggy-paddling and before long he was over his head in the water and started the overhand stroke.

"You're doing it! You're doing it!"

And he was. Just as I had learned from Francis at Sweet Clover, I had passed it on to Calvin. I remember how patient Francis had been with me and how happy it had made me when I finally caught on, just as he had shown me how to ride a bike during those early days. I was proud of Francis for helping me teach Calvin how to swim. His delight moved me in a certain way and in that moment I understood something. No one had ever loved Calvin enough to teach him how to swim. I couldn't wait to get home to tell Francis.

"How am I doing?"

"You're doing great!"

It wasn't exactly great. Great was still a long way off. But he was motor-boating and doggy-paddling his way to a crawl.

He swam over to me, still coughing up water, but less and less with each lap. He was building self-confidence.

"You wanna swim out to the raft? Are you ready for that?"

"I wanna try it. Will you swim next to me in case I can't make it?"

"Yes. If you feel yourself going under, go all the way down to the bottom. It's only a few feet over your head and kick off the sand and shoot up out of the water and grab some air like a whale. You can do that over and over again until you reach shallow water."

"I want to swim the whole way."

And he did. When he got to the raft he was too winded to lift himself up onto the deck and I had to hang on and push his butt up the ladder. He collapsed on the wooden planks for a moment before bouncing back up and looking toward the shore.

"Marvin! I can swim! Marvin!"

But Marvin wasn't on the shore.

"Marvin!"

He looked to the opposite shoreline, but Marvin was nowhere to be seen. He slumped back down in a heap and began, again, to catch his breath.

"I don't believe it. I can swim. I always wanted to learn and now you taught me."

I looked up and around the shoreline. No Marvin.

"I'm gonna catch my breath and swim back and find him and tell him. He's not gonna believe it."

"Can he swim?"

"I don't think so. But he doesn't want anyone to know that. Just the doggy-paddle, maybe."

I lay flat on my back, my folded hands behind my head. With a choir of screaming kids playing in the background, and the sun beating down on my face, I became drowsy and began day-dreaming first of Francis and then of Beth and Tom. I wondered where they were and if we would ever swim at Davies' Lake together. I was probably only asleep for a minute before Calvin stood and jumped into the water.

"I'm going to find Marvin and tell him," he called over his shoulder.

Groggily, I got up and jumped in after him, heading toward the shore alongside of him, just in case. We walked the sandy beach back to where we had left our towels. Still no Marvin.

"Maybe he's in the bath house."

"You're right. I'll go look."

"I'll go with you."

"No, that's okay. I'll just go tell him and come right back."

"But I have to go to the bathroom."

Calvin looked around. "Maybe he's behind the hot dog stand at one of the picnic tables and we just can't see him. You go look there."

"Okay. I'll look for him on my way to the bath house."

Calvin stood looking around, trying to find Marvin. "Maybe he's over on the other side of the lake. Why don't you look there?"

"Okay, I'm just going over to the bathroom first."

Calvin looked off toward the horizon. Something was bother-ing him. I headed off toward the bathhouse near the east gate. It was a one story plywood structure with the men's side on the west nearer the water. Inside the long narrow area was a gang shower-stall, a few changing booths and some toilets surrounded by more plywood booths. Running laterally down the middle of the rectangular building was a plywood wall running from the floor to the peaked roof rafters.

Calvin followed me from a distance. As I approached the door, a kid I didn't recognize held up his hand and stopped me.

"Hey Marvin. Some kid wants to come in."

Marvin and a couple of his friends were in front of the last toilet booth at the far end of the bath house, almost like they were standing guard, laughing about something, and when I crossed through the door they became silent.

"That's okay. I know him. Let him in."

I approached slowly, warily, remembering what my mother had told me.

"Well look who's here. It's the mama's boy. Come on over Will and let me introduce you to a couple of these Jersey boys."

I walked forward reluctantly. "Hey guys, this is Will. Will, say hello to all these mopes. They just came up on the bus and they're not exactly here to go swimming."

The group of four other guys broke into laughter. I couldn't figure out what was going on and finally Marvin grabbed me by the arm.

"Come here. We're going to let you in on a little secret. Initiate you into the Davies' Lake Club."

The other guys laughed again.

"What do you mean?"

"Follow me."

I resisted.

"Come on. This don't hurt."

More laughter. He looked toward the main entrance to see if anyone was coming in. He opened the stall door and knelt down beside the toilet. He put his face to the wall and put his eye right up to a tiny knothole and held up his hand for me to hold still. A few seconds later he waved me forward and whispered.

"Look through that knot-hole and don't say anything."

I knelt down next to him and put my face up to the thin plywood, where it abutted another sheet, sharing the 2x4 wall stud. Holding my eye up to the knothole and supporting myself on my hands and knees, I peered through.

On the other side of the thin plywood was the women's changing room. Three women, one middle aged and two in their twenties were either getting into their bathing suits or drying off to change back to their street clothing. All three faced me, naked.

It took me a few seconds for all of this to register and to figure out how I was supposed to react. My heart started pounding and I drew in a gasp of air and became paralyzed in disbelief. Kneeling there, frozen, I couldn't make myself move.

"Okay, pervert, that's enough."

Marvin had me by the scruff of the neck and pulled me to my feet.

"Not too much at one time. You might go psycho on us."

He pulled me away and I tried to say something, but couldn't. He pulled open the door and the Jersey guys were all laughing.

"Hey pervo!"

"Hey Peeping Tom!"

"Hey jerk-off.

I pulled away and ran for the entrance, passing Calvin, who was looking past me toward his brother. "That's why I didn't want you to come in here. This is what I meant when I said Marvin doesn't come here to go swimming."

I ran to my beach towel, humiliated and ashamed of myself for staying longer than a split second at the knot hole.

"Wait! I want to leave with you."

We grabbed our stuff and headed for the bike rack. As we were pulling out, another busload of city people was pulling in. I wanted to get home as fast as I could. I wanted to get away from Marvin and his friends. I pedaled down Little Tor. Just past Cropsey's Farm I turned right into Lake Drive and rode right up to the clubhouse at New City Park Lake. I felt safe there.

It was fairly empty for a midsummer day. The crashing of the water over the dam was tempered by the sounds of AM radio tuned to WABC playing Eddie Cochran.

George, the lifeguard, nodded to me and looked over my shoulder as Calvin struggled to keep up. He was an older boy from C.Y.O. and I had known him for years. The club allowed him to have non-member guests come for a swim, if he knew them.

He looked to Calvin. "Friend of yours?"

"Yeah."

I hopped off my bike and swam to the float, all the while I kept thinking, what would Francis do if he ever found out? What would Tom do? They would both be so disappointed in me.

And finally I thought of Beth. What would Beth do? She must never find out. How could I protect her from anything like that ever happening to her in a place like Davies' Lake? I closed my eyes, sick with self-disgust, and nodded off to sleep.

A splashing sound a few moments later woke me up. It was Calvin, breathless, struggling and spitting to make the last few feet to the float. I stood and pulled him up the ladder and he collapsed in a heap like he had at Davies'.

"I'm sorry, Will. That's why I didn't want you to go in there. I'm sorry. Please don't tell your parents."

"No need to worry about that."

"I swam out here."

"Yeah."

"Thanks to you."

"Yeah."

"Thanks for teaching me to swim, Will."

I spent the rest of the afternoon sulking, listening to *Sum-*

mertime Blues wafting its way from the tiny speaker on the dam played once an hour, every hour, on George's AM radio, until it was almost dinnertime.

CHAPTER TWENTY-NINE

NEW CITY

August, 1958
Age 12

When Beth got back from Gainesville a few days later, she couldn't stop talking about how much she loved that town and the University of Florida. Her father had introduced her to his friend, Jerry, who ran the photography department in the fine arts program and had given them both the grand tour of the campus and the town. Beth was set on going there after high school, six years down the road. It was all she could talk about until Tom returned. It made me think of where I would wind up going to college, or if I would even go to college at all. What was in my future? Would I become a mailman like my father before me and his father before him? Would I endlessly plod the streets of New City, looking down at my footsteps, never looking up at all the world had to offer, never leaving town?

When Tom arrived back from his European tour, he seemed a little different; distant, reflective, driven by his music. It was almost as if he, too, were leaving our circle of friendship; had changed, with more important things on his mind. He wasn't quite sure what to make of the international crowd's reaction to his playing.

But with the passing of the summer vacation days, they both turned back toward our own circle and life went on as it had before.

As we got ready for seventh grade, we were all invited to a back-to-school party that coincided with the hostess' birthday at the home of our classmate, Ellen, on Phillips Hill Road.

There, in a basement filled with more crepe paper twirls and balloons than I had ever seen accumulated in one place, were thirty, sixth-going-on-seventh-graders, ready to party. In the closing days of the summer of 1958, after much anticipation, I asked Beth to dance for the first time. She looked at me, surprised, as if to say 'You want to put yourself through this humiliation?' Instead, she smiled and said, "Sure."

Tom reached out to stop me. "It's my obligation as your friend to prevent you from any further embarrassment. I thought you had two left feet?"

"I got rid of one of them."

"Hey, Beth, if your feet get crushed and you need me to come rescue you, just give a little wave. I'll call an ambulance."

And then we danced, really danced this time, slowly, to *All I Have To Do is Dream*, by the Everly Brothers.

We danced fast to *Peggy Sue* and when we danced to *Queen of the Hop*, I got the "yellow dog blues," just like Bobby Darin had.

We danced the cha-cha to the calypso sounds of *Susie Darlin'*, and by that time people had stopped to watch us in disbelief. Even amusement.

Tom called from the crowd. "Hey Will. When school starts you'll have a topic for your first essay."

"What's that?"

"How I spent my summer vacation: Losing my two left feet."

Raucus laughter broke out from everyone in the crowd, but I

didn't care.

Beth pulled me closer. "Just ignore them. They're jealous."

We danced slow again to *Lonesome Town*.

I never wanted the music to stop.

We spent the rest of the summer exploring; exploring our yards, our woods, our neighborhoods. We took more bike trips along my paper route so I had something to remember the next day on my solitary ride at daybreak. We talked about walking the entire Kill again, but decided it should wait until after seventh grade was over. We would make it an annual, first-week-out-of-school ritual. We would become the Demarest Kill Waders. It sounded good on paper, but I was doubtful it would ever come about. Things had a way of getting in the way of good intentions: Life.

The last day before school started for seventh grade, the Tuesday after Labor Day, we sat in the shade near the dam at Greenberg's Pond, next to the three-foot plaster statue of St. Mary, and listened to the water cascade over the spillway. We had discussed plans of how we would spend our last day together before starting Junior High School, but when it came down to doing anything, we all just decided to do nothing but lie on the cool, green grass in the shade of the sugar maples that lined the south bank of the pond. We had all brought a book to read. Beth brought *Little Women*. Tom was half way through *The Adventures of Huckleberry Finn*. I was reading *Penrod* for the third time. I heard my father's voice narrating it. Occasionally, the silence would be broken by our laughter from the novels. Good belly-laughs, followed by the others asking, "What? What part?"

A quick description would follow, accompanied by nods and knowing chuckles of recognition.

"I love that part," Beth would always say after Tom's or my contributions, remembering back to when she had read those same passages.

It's a day I think back upon often for the sheer, simplistic enjoyment of the pleasure we all derived from each other's company, the beauty of the unspoiled, as yet undiscovered environment, the sharing of the great minds of the writers; Alcott, Twain, Tarkington.

It could be argued that specific day that Beth, Tom, and I were then enjoying, had actually been conjured up intentionally, years before, just for us, by those three minds whose works we held in our hands. The authors knew of this convergence on this specific, future day, and had prepared for it, just for us.

It could also be argued that that specific day, just two short years from when we had first met, was actually the start of our eventual separation; that from this day forward, when we stood up and dusted the twigs off our jeans, we would stop becoming closer and start drifting, ever so subtly, and ever so slowly, apart.

It could be argued that that specific day marked the end of our childhoods.

If, in fact, all those arguments are true, my one consolation is that we had that one specific day, together, when we sat *"breathing the pure serene air,"* there were no other sounds except the splash of the water on the spillway, the rustling of leaves overhead, the rustling of the literary leaves we held in our fingertips, the roaring in our ears of impending adolescence and the inevitable pain that brings.

CHAPTER THIRTY

CLARKSTOWN CENTRAL
JUNIOR-SENIOR HIGH SCHOOL

1958-1959
Seventh Grade, Age 12

As could be expected, seventh grade brought enormous changes of just about every kind. Tom and I were growing taller, stronger, more athletic, and Beth was becoming a woman.

It was to be a year of dances, sponsored by the Catholic Youth Organization, in the basement of St. Augustine's; a year of basketball both at the Jr. High school with Coach Beecraft, and C.Y.O basketball with Father Carrick as coach. It was to be a year of new experiences at every level and we faced it with excitement and fear and trepidation. For me, it was to be a year of sheer horror following an event I have never told anyone about, that happened in a matter of seconds, but which still leaves me shaking and feeling ill about the human condition.

In the fall of 1958, Clarkstown Central Junior-Senior High School was in its fourth year of operation. It was supposed to have been built adjacent to where Lake DeForest Reservoir now sits, but after a land-switch deal with the Spring Valley Water Works in 1951, it was instead built on the grounds of the old Carnochan Estate.

The Carnochan Mansion was built in 1915 by Frederick Carnochan in a neo-Georgian style. When it was built, the three story concrete and steel building had a swimming pool, marble baths, eighteen rooms and seven fireplaces. It was all preserved during the construction and served as the administration building for the school and the district.

As a result, it may have been the most beautiful public high school campus in the country, with its thirty-three acres of towering elms and oaks and maples and broad lawns that became the tennis courts, soccer fields and football field. The whole environment made the place feel safe, secluded, special, like a New England Prep school. Not knowing any different, we took its special beauty for granted, perhaps never fully appreciating its uniqueness, nor what a truly special place it was until later in life. It provided us with a place of safety and solitude. Compared to the prison-like architecture of so many high schools today, we lived and learned and studied in something out of the 19th Century English Countryside. It kept us grounded in early 20th Century New City history before thrusting us out to catch the treacherous ride on the 21st Century Express.

It housed grades seven through twelve in the one building, which meant we were going to school every day with high school seniors from the very first day of seventh grade.

The student body was no longer made up of two classes full of students from New City, but as a centralized district, we were now mingling with students from Street School on North Main; Bardonia and Chestnut Grove to the south; West Nyack and Congers to the east. Although some of us knew students from the other schools through church and family connections, for the most part it was open season for making new friends.

With all those new social opportunities available, some of us thrived and others were lost in the shuffle. Tom came under the wing of Doc Carney, the legendary orchestra leader at the school who changed the lives of thousands of students. Tom's time was taken up every afternoon with marching band practice where he played the trombone and later his own piano practice at home.

Beth was immediately a hit with her newly expanded circle of girlfriends, while Jimmy, Charlie, Ken, and Vinny and I were grunts on the football team. We all seemed to be going our separate ways, and for me it was frightening. It wasn't as if the friendship between the three of us weakened, it was that we were just growing, however slightly, apart. I shouldn't have worried about it, but I did. As the year went on, our friendship actually strengthened, since we sought solace with one another when we would spend most of every weekend together.

The fast-paced social whirl was not for everyone however. Some kids, the quiet, shy ones, seemed to get lost.

My next door neighbor, Calvin, was the first casualty. Ever since "Francis' Day," I had spent less and less time with Marvin and Calvin. I just couldn't face them because of the painful memories of that day and because Marvin never seemed to stop bullying his younger brother. After Tom and Beth arrived on the scene in the beginning of Fifth grade, I would only go next door two more times; the day of the Davies' Lake incident and one night after school that would be the very last time for many years. After that last night, Calvin, who everyone in seventh grade now knew as Sparrow, could never look me in the eye for years after because of his deep shame.

In science class one day, Calvin sat next to me, sketching from memory, illustrations that would make Audubon proud. It was his very own private science project, far more important than the rock formations the rest of us were studying.

No one looking at any of Calvin's sketches would have believed this young boy had drawn them. As Mr. Carr, the science teacher droned on about the differences between igneous and sedimentary rocks, he wandered the classroom, slapping his palm with a yardstick, blathering on as if it were the ten thousandth time he had given the same lecture. He circled around the back of the room as we all took notes. All of us except Calvin, of course, who was sitting next to me at the lab table working on one of his meticulously detailed sketches on an artist's sketchpad using simple #2 and #3 pencils given to him by Miss Palermo, the art teacher. When he got behind us, Mr. Carr stopped abruptly and slapped his yardstick down on the black surface of the lab table. Everyone jumped at the noise.

"Calvin! Are you taking notes?"

Calvin shuffled his papers quickly to hide his work.

"What are you doing? Let me see that."

He examined three or four of Calvin's sketches, spreading them out on the lab table.

"Where did you get these?"

"I drew them."

"You drew them? I think not. Who did you steal them from?"

"No, I drew them. This is a. . ."

The yardstick crashed against the table top, just inches from Sparrow's fingertips.

"Silence! I will take these and return them to their rightful owner before you ruin them."

I tried to interject, to defend Calvin. "Mr. Carr?"

"Silence!' He gathered them up and tucked them under his arm and walked to the front of the class.

"Now the igneous rocks of Rockland County came to us through the courtesy of the Triassic Age, that's T-R-I-A-S-S-I-C Age and can be seen in the outcroppings of the Palisades over-looking the Hudson River."

Calvin sat in silence for a few moments, his head down, his shoulders trembling in what I thought was embarrassment. Within moments, he stood, squared his shoulders, and walked directly out of the room. Was he crying?

"Calvin? Calvin! Return to your seat immediately. Calvin!"

It was the last time I ever saw him in a classroom. When the bell rang I waited until the others had left and Mr. Carr was filing his papers in his briefcase. I approached slowly.

"Yes? And what may I do for you?"

"Mr. Carr. Those sketches. Calvin drew them. I watched him. I've seen him do hundreds more like it. Ever since third grade."

Mr. Carr withdrew the four sheets from his folder and examined them each, one at a time, his face a mixture of disbelief and anger at the accusation of being wrong. Finally he whisked them at me.

"Well, you tell your little friend that his *Spizella Monticola* needs attention."

"His what?"

"Just tell him. *Spizella Monticola*. He'll know."

I gathered the four sheets and ran out the door, repeating to myself, *Spizella Monticola, Spizella Monticola, Spizella Monticola*, so I wouldn't forget it.

That evening after dinner I walked behind the barn, hopped over the fence to Calvin's yard, and walked up the rear sidewalk to his back porch. I knocked softly on the kitchen door, trembling in fear. I hoped that his father or Marvin would not be home.

Calvin answered, and I breathed a sigh of relief and tried to be lighthearted when I handed him the sheaf of papers.

"Hey, Calvin, I told 'Mr. Protozoam' that you had really done those pictures. He got mad and said your *Spizella Monticola* needed some work."

It may have been the only time I had ever seen him smile besides that day that I had taught him how to swim. He looked at his papers, going to the illustration of a Sparrow, the *Spizella Monticola*. He examined it closely.

"He's probably right."

"Is that what *Spizella Monticola* means? Sparrow?"

"Tree Sparrow. That's why I always favor drawing *Spizella*

Monticola. That's how I picked my name. *"His eye is on the sparrow and I know He watches me."* That's a hymn my mother used to sing. Jesus is watching over me. He's never gonna let anything bad happen to me. That's why I picked that name. I'm protected."

I looked down again at his illustrations.

"You want to come in? I can show you more pictures I drew."

I glanced nervously over my shoulder. "I'm not sure. I think my mother's about to put dinner on the table."

Sensing my trepidation, he widened the door.

"It's okay, Marvin and my parents went over to Sloatsburg. They won't be back for a while."

"Okay."

The house smelled of a kerosene stove, even though it was still early fall, and I wondered if I would ever be able to get the smell out of my clothes. In Sparrow's tiny upstairs room he pulled a scrapbook out from under the bed. It was two pieces of corrugated cardboard torn from a box and held together with a bootlace, but it contained one of the most remarkable things I have ever seen. A collection of over one hundred sketches, in an almost photo-realism style, of robins, jays, orioles, cardinals, crows, just about every bird Rockland has ever seen, and all drawn with the precision of a surgeon. I was unable to speak, such were their beauty. I looked to my friend as he talked about each one, but it wasn't pride I saw in his face. It was fear. How could such works of art spring from such a troubled soul?

After a half-hour of his talking about each sketch, we heard the front door open and the voices of Marvin and their drunk father. Calvin turned to me and for a moment I thought he was going to cry.

"Quick. Hide this."

I looked around the room. There was no door on his closet. I grabbed the scrapbook and slid under the bed, knowing instinctively, immediately, that I was just making things worse. A few of the illustrations remained behind on the bed where I had left them.

Calvin's father banged on door of his bedroom, then slammed it open. "What are you doing in here?" What's this? Those stupid drawings again? What did I tell you about that? Is this what the school called about today?"

There was a moment of silence where I couldn't really hear anything except what sounded like Calvin trying to struggle out of harm's way. I couldn't hold my breath any longer, and I exhaled into my sleeve. And then his father did the unthinkable, while I hid under the bed in fear with my eyes closed. After the assault, his father slapped his face and flung him across the room where he ricocheted off the beaded-board wall siding and into the space between the wall and the bed. He landed in a crouch next to where I lay clutching the scrapbook. His face was inches from mine.

"Do what I tell you to do, goddammit," his father yelled as the bedroom door slammed shut. I finally opened my eyes. Calvin's bloodied face filled my view as I huddled in fear. I was close enough to smell the blood. There was also another unfamiliar smell that I couldn't identify at that time. The blank look in his eyes was so intense that for a moment I thought he was dead.

"Are you....Are you okay?"

"Go. Take the scrapbook with you. Climb out the window. Shinny down the drain spout."

I retied the bootlaces around the cardboard bindings and stuffed the scrapbook into my jacket, closing the hooks, and was out the window as fast as I could move. I turned back and all I could see of my friend were his spindly arms and elbows as he braced himself to rise up. He struggled, blubbering through snot and bloody lips and tears, his eyes averted. Then he looked at me. "Just go."

Although we would speak from time to time, it was the last time for forty years that Calvin would ever make eye-contact with me. I slid down the drainpipe, as I had done from my own back porch roof many times. It would be the last time I ever visited his house.

Inside, just a few feet from the drainpipe, Calvin's father was in the kitchen, bellowing in a drunken rage.

CHAPTER THIRTY-ONE

NEW CITY
SEVENTH GRADE

Fall, 1958
Age 12

After the abuse incident, Calvin withdrew and became reclusive, focusing on his amazing pencil sketches. I would find portfolios on my doorstep, bound again just in cardboard and string. But inside were the most beautiful illustrations. It was like he was leaving the pictures for my safekeeping. They still reside on a shelf of my boyhood bedroom closet on Main Street. I never saw him in school again.

I believe there are some types of kid who will succeed in spite of his parents' efforts to turn him into a complete failure. I'm not sure Calvin was one of them, depending on your definition of happiness and success. He could have hung around me, I would have been his friend. But because he was probably embarrassed by what I knew, he chose to hang out with other kids, kids who would lead him into a life of crime. It wasn't until I was much older that I realized that Calvin had probably saved my life that night. If he had revealed that I was hiding under the bed at that moment, his father most certainly would have killed me.

Of course I never told anyone about the bedroom incident. I was afraid of what his father might do to my family, and there was just no getting around that, no matter how I tried to sort it out.

Later, Calvin would keep to himself, rarely speaking or acknowledging those around him. During his teen years, his slight build made him the victim of many bullies, especially his brother.

He withdrew, eventually drifting into a life of petty crime and car theft. His first arrest came at Andrews' Five-and-Ten. He was caught shoplifting a box of #2 pencils and a sketchpad. Later, he stole a car on an icy night, spun out of control on the Congers Road curve past the high school, and knocked out every window of the old Dodge with his head as the car skidded toward the reservoir. He was not critically injured, but he spent the next three years in reform school upstate. He would never be the same person again.

During those early days of Junior High School, whenever Beth and Tom had time off we continued to explore our surroundings. We had already taken our bike circuit over and over for weekends at a time, so it was time to branch out. We had traced the Demarest Kill. We gave each other assignments: Ask our parents for the most unique location in the New City area and we would explore it together. Beth re-introduced us to the Dells on the old Zukor property with its elaborate bridge and arched stonework. It was something out of a fairytale. Had Zukor brought in Hollywood crews to design and build it? The walls of the Dells were filled with ancient carvings, some of it dating back to indigenous peoples from centuries ago; Native American artifacts and hieroglyphics on the sandstone walls leaving stories behind for all who wished to read them. A stone pump house stood at the stream's edge. It had been used for irrigation in the early days of the golf course.

That fall we took more expeditions to High Tor, once again from near the 9W intersection with Old Rte. 304. It's a steeper, more abrupt climb, and once from the west from Little Tor, walking along the ridge line, up and down for two miles. A third time we repeated the trek through the country club property.

I felt I had to come up with something new so I came up with Hook Mountain. We pedaled our bikes across the Lake DeForest reservoir that Thanksgiving weekend, through Congers to Rockland Lake and to the site of the old ice-harvesters' building. Although not as ambitious as the climb to High Tor, the view of the Hudson below is just as spectacular.

As our seventh grade winter approached and we settled in and sought new activities to pursue, we continued ice skating at Lake Lucille, and expanded our itinerary to all the other lakes in the area, leaving our blade marks on Greenberg's, Congers Lake, Rockland Lake, Swartout Lake, the shoreline of Lake DeForest. Some nights, Max would drive us to Garnerville to the rink up there. New City Park Lake was drained most of that winter.

Those winter nights in our seventh grade years were busy. Tuesday and Friday nights we would be at the school's varsity basketball games. School dances were on Friday nights after the game, dancing to the music of Glenn Miller, as interpreted by The Sophisticated Swingsters, under the baton of Doc Carney. Tom would stand close to the piano player on-stage and watch and evaluate. The player, a senior, was a careful study in 1940s-style decadence: a wrinkled suit, including a fedora that kept the cafeteria fluorescent lights from shining in his eyes, and a Sam Spade attitude. It was as if his choice of wardrobe and film *noir* demeanor were necessary to carry the full meaning of the music he was playing.

On Saturdays during this seventh-eighth grade time, it wouldn't be unusual to find us in the basement of St. Augustine's playing basketball in the basement during the daytime and attending dances at night, both activities sponsored by the Catholic Youth Organization. Unlike the school dances, at C.Y.O. we danced to the music from our own era: Richie Valens, The Big Bopper, and Buddy Holly. Father Carrick officiated over both Saturday events, the earlier in those black P.F. Flyer sneakers, the latter in standard issue black oxfords. The dances had probably been set up as a place where young Catholic boys and girls could meet and mingle with others of their own faith. None of that inter-faith dating going on here like Friday nights at the High School. Who knew what that could lead to?

On the Sunday morning of February 9, 1959, that winter of our content, Beth and I were standing in the kitchen of Dove Cottage, talking to Frau K., waiting for Tom to come down and join us for breakfast. Frau K. turned on the radio, and we caught the opening strains of a song we had never heard before, *True Love Ways*.

Tom rounded the corner at the bottom of the staircase, walked up to the radio and silenced us. "That's Buddy Holly singing. But with violins. That's an uncharacteristic choice. Something new. That's odd."

We stood listening in silence until the song ended, Tom's left ear cocked in a special way we would later come to recognize as his "memory ear."

There was a pause and then the disc jockey came on. "Once again, we are saddened to report the death of Buddy Holly, who died in a plane crash late last night during a snowstorm in Clear Lake, Iowa, along with two of his friends on the Winter Dance Party Tour. Hit recording artists J.P. Richardson, known as 'The Big Bopper', and Ritchie Valens also perished in the crash. We'll continue to update information as it comes across the wire."

Then in a voice that came close to halting, the DJ continued. "In the meantime, let's listen to *Come On, Let's Go*, from the late, great, Ritchie Valens."

Frau K. wasn't sure what to make of the looks on our faces.

Beth was fighting back her tears, her hand over her mouth. I couldn't swallow. Tom turned the volume down on the radio and raced up the spiral staircase at the back of the kitchen. We followed him. What else could be wrong?

We found him at the piano bench. His eyes were closed in concentration. He was stumbling, faltering his way through *True Love Ways* on the keyboards, singing in his god-awful singing voice. But except for a few lyrics where he substituted his own, "something-something-something," he got it. Beth and I could only look on in astonishment.

"You were able to play that after hearing it once?"

With his eyes still closed, he waved to us. "Shh-shh-shh. Don't talk." And he started again from the beginning, this time with less faltering, less hesitation. It was to be the first time we experienced Tom's "memory ear," but far from the last time. Is it possible to perform an audio version of "sleight of hand?"

That day I also was beginning to understand that I was developing my own "special talent," perhaps not as overt as the ones Beth and Tom had been developing, but one that I would be reminded of for the rest of my life. Just after hearing the song once by Buddy, a second time with Tom's stumbling through it, I knew all the lyrics.

Just you know why,
Why you and I,
Will bye-and-bye
Know true love ways.

Even though it had been recorded two years earlier, *True Love Ways* was not released publicly until the spring of 1960 on Buddy Holly's Greatest Hits 2 album. What the radio station played that morning must have been a bootleg. Whenever I hear it I think of the day Tom played it, and the look of astonishment and sadness on Beth's face.

As late winter of 1959 was disappearing with the melting snow, and before that last seventh grade spring was coming into full bloom, we were back in the woods again, taking in the beauty of the Demarest Kill flood watershed.

We had started that Saturday morning near Tom's Boathouse and headed west, upstream. Patches of melting snow remained on the banks, flooding the Kill. There we passed through a familiar stand of white birches, the bark peeling off like sunburn on a tourist. We had explored this area a million times before, but now, at the end of seventh grade, we had a new perspective on all that we beheld. We had recently learned we were not the only ones who embraced our beloved environment in reverence.

Tom stood, squared his jaw, and recited, "*When I see birches bend to the left and right across the lines of straighter, darker trees, I like to think some boy's been swinging them. . . .*" On cue, I climbed to the top of the nearest one, shinnying up the snow-white trunks, using my ankles, *pulling myself up through the empty black branches until I reached the top.* I was careful, *keeping my poise, using the same care you use filling a cup up to the brim, and even slightly above the brim.* Below, Beth joined in the recitation we had learned from Mrs. Handley in Lit. class. They raised their voices for me to hear them *as I climbed toward heaven.* Then, on their cue, I threw my feet outward, kicking as if swimming upstream, until the treetop swayed, then dipped down and lowered me to my waiting friends. We spent the rest of that snow-melt filled afternoon, laughing and climbing and *getting away from earth for awhile. One could do worse.*

As we made our way south along the stream, walking upstream toward what was now known as Twin Elms Lane, our galoshes unbuckled in spring-time carelessness, we approached the spring head we knew so well. Above it, the cliff rose steeply fifty feet straight up. If we had climbed it, we would have wound up in the back yard of a house on Irion Drive, one of the forty houses built by Rainer Klein on the dwindling Florion Estate.

Just to the south of the spring head we saw something we had never noticed before. Jutting out of the bottom of the cliff was a concrete pipe, three feet in diameter. What was it? More important, what did it mean? We were determined to find out. We approached it slowly, peering into the mouth of the pipe that was opened to the east. The canopy of the maples and elms offered scant light and we were only able to see about ten feet into the pipe looking toward the west.

Tom looked at us both. "Next time we'll bring flashlights and candles. I want to know what this is."

Within a week we were back. After a stop at Moore's Hardware Store on Main Street to pick up some flashlight batteries and some plumbers' candles and a box of wooden matches, we were ready to explore the concrete pipe.

On our hands and knees, with Tom taking the lead and Beth in the middle, just like our Demarest Kill treks, we crawled west several hundred feet until the pipe branched off into a "T" to the left and right.

We sat at the intersection in an inch of water, our cramped backs against the concrete pipe wall. Tom looked both ways. "Just as I suspected. It's a storm drain for the new development."

Beth looked concerned. "You mean when it rains, all that sludge can wash down through here into the brook?"

"Yes."

"But it's right upstream of our spring. Will we be able to drink out of the spring anymore?"

Tom furrowed his brow in the candle light. "I don't know. I just wish my grandparents hadn't sold this property."

"I just hope it's rainwater."

I turned to Beth. "What do you mean?"

"It could be septic tank run-off. Are these places hooked to the new sewer line?"

Tom looked off into the darkness of the pipe heading south. "I don't know. It's too late now, anyway." Too late.

Tom turned, knelt, and crawled a few feet north. "Come on. Let's get out of here before it starts raining."

Beth and I detoured, crawled south to let him squeak by, then we backed out to the north, so Beth could be in the middle again as we followed Tom. Wanting to have nothing more to do with it, we made our exit from the concrete pipe that would befoul our playground and our Demarest Kill.

By the end of seventh grade we had matured considerably. We had learned so much more about one another. I had danced with Beth a hundred times, falling in love with her a hundred times. All set to the Friday night Big Band music of Glenn Miller and Bunny Berrigan and The Bunny Hop. But we had also experienced the death of one of our idols, something that had never happened to us before. It was as if a trial balloon had been sent up to see how we would react to the death of a beloved public figure, how we could prepare ourselves for more to come.

And then there had been the incident in Sparrow's house. An event that I would never share with my two friends, but that had a shivering impact on my view of the adult world, the more I began to understand about it.

CHAPTER THIRTY-TWO

1959-1960
Eighth Grade, Age 13

By the beginning of eighth grade we had all just turned thirteen and were now officially teenagers. The three of us had become even closer. We had ice skated on various ponds of the Demarest Kill from New City Park to Greenberg's to Damiani's to Lake Lucille; the same lakes where we spent our days swimming. There were trips to movies; The Lafayette in Suffern, The Broadway in Haverstraw, The Rockland in Nyack, all three Skouras theatres. Transportation was provided by Max, who also took us to mini-golf in Nanuet.

Meanwhile, while we were lost in fun land, New City was growing up before our eyes.

Although I had met Beth's father that first time at Fourth of July Fireworks and two days later at the Florion tent party and had visited his studio with Beth in the past, I had never seen the artist at work in his studio.

One spring day Tom and I rode the late bus home with Beth and followed her to her father's artist's studio. It was a huge, gutted barn with exposed post-and-beams constructed in those rough-cut timbers a century earlier. Soft light came through a huge glass window with a northern exposure and fell on a model's raised platform. Later in the afternoon, he could turn on theatrical lights and flood the area with naturalistic lighting. All around the perimeter of the interior, paint splattered canvas covered up partially completed works of art.

At first we saw her father working alone, then I noticed a nude model in the distance. She was a woman of about forty, not especially attractive or well built. Almost like an older, suburban housewife. Of course this was not my first glimpse of a naked woman but certainly the first since Davies' Lake. I averted my glance, and Beth tried to hide a smile. Her father and the model were very nonchalant about the nudity, as was Beth. The studio was filled with sketches and sculpture of nudes. The nudity would eventually become commonplace.

Beth and I drifted around the huge studio space, while Tom stayed behind to talk to Beth's father and listen to the music coming from a Wollensak reel-to-reel tape deck. I hardly noticed what was playing, some old-fashioned piano music.

As I walked from picture to picture, I tried to figure out what it would take for me to duplicate such an effort. On one wall was a charcoal of Beth, so beautiful in its rendition that I stood spellbound in front of it. In the sketch, Beth stood in the doorway, schoolbooks in hand, white blouse with her Peter Pan collar, plaid skirt and black tights.

"Is that you?"

"Yes."

"How old are you here?"

"Six."

"It's beautiful. You're beautiful."

"Thanks, he just did it for fun."

"Fun?"

"Yeah, I came in after school one day and when I walked through the doorway he just told me to stand there for him for a few minutes."

"A few minutes later and this was done?"

"Yes."

The charcoal sketch captured perfectly the essence that was Beth.

While I was looking at that sketch, Beth pulled a pastel work from the frame rack.

"This is my mother."

I looked at the pastel sketch of her mother's face. It could have been a sketch of Beth at a later age, they looked so similar. It was a picture that would come back to haunt me as we grew older, almost as if it were a premonition of Beth's future look when she became a mature woman.

"She's very beautiful."

"I wish I had been old enough to know her." She placed the frame back carefully in the rack.

At the sound of Tom's laughter, I turned as he was finishing a conversation with Beth's father. I looked around at the pastels and charcoals and sculpture that surrounded us in the converted barn and took it all in. I was overwhelmed by her father's creative work. Did such a place really exist in New City?

Later that spring day we meandered through our Dutch Garden.

When the Dutch Garden was funded by Roosevelt's Works Progress Administration and designed by Mary Mowbray-Clarke, a renowned landscape architect and philanthropist who lived in West Nyack, it was the only WPA project overseen by a woman. The garden was to be a tribute to both the Dutch Heritage of the County and the Haverstraw brick industry.

Mary would get in her car near Rte. 303 and drive up 9W to Haverstraw, double back to Garnerville and pick up the team of Sicilian bricklayers headed up by master mason, Biagio Gugliuzzo.

Three or four other Sicilian men would ride with her, including Delores' father, the infant spared in the Haverstraw mud-slide of 1906, who was then about thirty.

They would drive through the cut in the mountain near Trap Rock to New City and on to The Dutch Garden, where Haverstraw bricks had been delivered, stacked on pallets in the parking lot. On a sheet of plywood across two sawhorses Mary would spread out her roll of blueprints and renderings for the men to follow. There, they would painstakingly place brick upon mortar, using wooden block jigs to brace up the latticework in the walls until the mortar had cured and the bricks were locked in place. Sometimes my grandfather would watch, my father tagging along and to volunteer as a hod-carrier. And then just over a few weeks' time, the masterwork of the craftsmen grew before their eyes.

On the east side was a tiny table surrounded by semi-circular brick benches. On the north side was the tea house. If you look closely you can still see some of the facades of the bricks representing the sense of humor in the men. There is an old Dutch Cleanser Lady, and even a depiction of Popeye, now worn by time and weather and chipped away by vandals. And of course there was a pergola on the south border leading to the hexagonal gazebo facing the stream on the southwest. Mowbray-Clarke called the gazebo "The Summer House" on her original renderings.

In the late 1940s the Dutch Garden became quite popular and weddings were held there as well as many other civic meetings, hosting Eleanor Roosevelt and Burl Ives, and special spring meetings of my mother's Girl Scout troop.

Over time, winters of frost and thaw had their way with the walls and columns, and by the early 1960s the walls were starting to tumble, the mortar cracked like the brittle teeth on an old man, and the Dutch Garden fell into disrepair. By the time Beth and I left for college, more local vandals had done their work, and like an abandoned graveyard, the brick headstones, created thirty years earlier, were turned over for a laugh.

That spring day during the eighth grade when we were drifting through the Dutch Garden, Tom stopped along a flower bed near the sundial. He knelt and then pinched off a few buds of a deep purple, flowering ground cover. At first I thought it was some kind of violet. He lifted it to his nose, and took in its fragrance. Standing, he put the tiny cluster behind his back and then turned to Beth, bowed, and with a dramatic, gallant, sweeping gesture, presented her with the flowers.

"What is it?"

"A *heliotrope bouquet*," Tom said impishly.

She looked at it, smelled it, looked at him questioningly. What?

He looked at her in silence.

Then she broke in to a broad grin, gasped in a breath of air in understanding, and laughed. "Oh, I get it. Very clever. *Heliotrope Bouquet.*"

Something had passed between them. She got the reference, I did not. I could only stand there dumbfounded; helpless. The feeling was both agonizing and hopeless.

I stood there, trying to understand. Would I ever understand? "What?"

"This morning, when you and Tom were in my father's studio. Dad was playing it on his tape deck."

I thought back. Her father had a tape playing on seven-inch reels on his Wollensak tape recorder. It was something he did all day long as he worked. The song was some convoluted, complex piano music that Tom had admired. He had spoken to Beth's father at considerable length about the tape and the music. I couldn't remember what was said, but Tom had his head cocked in his "memory ear" position. Beth and I had been engaged in conversation on the other side of the barn studio, she sketching me, and me standing there.

"Playing what?"

"*Heliotrope Bouquet*. It's a rag by Scott Joplin."

"Who?"

"Scott Joplin. You know his music."

"I do?"

"Think silent films. Kind of New Orleans boogie-woogie stuff."

I was lost. "*Heliotrope Bouquet?*"

Yes. That's the name of the song. She extended the flowers to me. And this is your *heliotrope bouquet*." She turned and laughed with Tom. The joke was now on me.

"It's usually found in warmer climates. Someone must have planted them here some summer."

So there it was. References I didn't recognize about things I didn't understand. Something passed between them that day and I cannot think of how to characterize it other than as an immutable truth: Beth and Tom were more suited for one another than Beth and I. Tom had his piano, Beth had her art, her photography, her vast, intellectual curiosity. They had hopes and dreams and college plans and career goals. What did I have? I started to feel sorry for myself. Then I realized I had things neither of them would ever have. I had both Beth and Tom. I had Francis. I was also beginning to suspect I had something else, as I had that day the previous winter as we listened to the Buddy Holly lyric, but that realization and its implications would only come later.

I looked down into the nearby shrubbery, a thick yew fanned out like a palm, low to the ground. Inside the branch system I saw something that didn't belong. I reached down into the spiky cluster and pulled out a rusted garden tool, the four sharp fingers reaching out, finger knuckles bent, as if to break up the clumps of topsoil and grab some unwanted weeds.

I recognized it as a hand cultivator, four metal tongs bent into a frozen, scratching grasp. Something on the wooden handle caught my eye, an identifying mark, almost like a cattle brand had been burned into the hickory handle. It was the initials of my grandfather, my father, my brother. I shook off the mud and rust and stuck it in my hip pocket.

Later that day I would carry it home. How had it been left behind? Lost? Maybe my father would know. Like the silver dollar lost at the horse track, maybe my grandfather just left things behind.

That evening, when I gave the hand cultivator to my father, he took in a deep breath, shook his head. "Come with me."

I followed him out to the barn and there, on the wall, was a hand trowel with an empty peg next to it. On the trowel's wooden handle were the initials branded into the hickory exactly like on the cultivator.

"Your grandmother was given these tools. She died planting some ground cover. We found the trowel, but could never find the cultivator. Where was it?"

"By the sundial."

"What type of plants?"

"A ground cover. Yew."

"And *Heliotrope*?"

"Yes."

"It's poisonous, but she loved it." He took a rag and wiped the mud from the handle and the bent fingers. "She loved digging in the garden like that." He hung it on the hook next to its mate. "Your grandfather would be glad to know you found it. It was given to him and your grandmother by Mary Mowbray-Clarke to say thank you for volunteering at the Dutch Garden. He liked everything in its place."

"How come you never use these tools?

"I'm not a plant person. Not a garden person like my parents."

I wanted to ask him what kind of person he was.

"I'm more of a bookworm, you might say. I guess I'm cultivating other things."

"What things?"

"Things in my head."

"Do you know a song with heliotrope in the title?"

He looked out the barn window across the driveway to the house, to Francis' window. Spider webs and cob webs on the panes blurred his view.

"Yes. An old Scott Joplin tune. About 1906."

"*Heliotrope Bouquet?*"

"Yes. How would you know that?"

"Beth and Tom were talking about it today. Beth's father was playing it on his tape deck in the studio where he sculpts and paints."

"I'm not surprised. He has a brilliant mind. It never rests."

Just like his daughter, I thought.

My father continued to examine the hand tools hanging on the wall. "If I asked you to name a song that was popular ten years before you were born, could you name one?"

I thought about that. Ten years before I was born in 1946? A song from 1936? I had no idea.

CHAPTER THIRTY-THREE

NEW CITY

Tuesday Afternoon
October 24, 2000
Age 54

Alone, at home in New City Park, I paced the floor wondering what the interview transcripts meant. Did Rainer really think I was stalking Beth? Had he hired a private investigator to follow me? There was only one way to find out. I called him.

"Rainer, this is Will."

"What do you want?"

"I wanted to talk to you."

"I was told you are not a part of the investigation."

"I'm not."

"Then we have nothing to say to one another."

"I disagree. Do you really think I was stalking Beth?"

"That's what she told me."

"I don't believe you."

"That hardly makes a difference at this point. None of this is any of your business."

"A private investigator following me? That's my business."

"I wouldn't know anything about any private investigator. Why would you say that?"

"I think you're lying. Why would you lie about something like that? Try to throw suspicion my way?"

"I don't know what you're talking about. But your boss can probably shed some light on the matter for me when I call and talk to him."

"While you're at it, tell him I had nothing to do with Beth's death."

"Now it's time for me to say 'I think you're lying'. And also to say, 'this conversation is over'."

Jeanette called the next morning. "You better get in here, Will. The boss-man has steam blowing out of his ears, he's so agitated."

"What happened?"

"Something about a phone call"

Barry Henion and Carl Betts were pacing his office floor when I arrived twenty-five minutes later.

"Any results on the identity of the semen in the autopsy report."

Barry stepped forward. "That's none of your business. Did you talk to Tom again?

"No. You told me not to."

"Anyone?"

"Yes. Father Carrick.

"About what?

"That's privileged.

"Who else?"

Somehow I figured he already knew the answer to that question. "I called Rainer Klein to offer my condolences. Apologize for any misunderstanding. You saw him. He was agitated at the funeral. Tried to get him to calm down."

"Calm down? He was ballistic when he called my house last night at ten o'clock. How did he get my home number? Did you give it to him? Rainer called me to complain about you. He said you denied stalking Beth for years and now you were stalking him.

"What?"

"Will, if I have to warn you again, it could cost your job. You have to stop this now. You are way out of line here. And might I add that from what I've been hearing, you really need to watch your step."

"What's that supposed to mean?"

"You're a smart guy. You can figure it out. In the meantime, we will not tolerate any meddling. Whatever it is you are doing, just stop. Don't go see Tom Hogenkamp or ask him any questions."

But there were so many questions I needed the answers to. And from where I stood, only Tom had the answers. Even if Beth hadn't died, which was a pretty big "if," only Tom had the answers. The time to reunite with my old friend was long overdue.

CHAPTER THIRTY-FOUR

**THE HISTORY OF MUSIC
IN NEW CITY, NEW YORK:
PART IV**

1960-1961
Ninth Grade, Age 14

In 1960-61, while other ninth graders across the country were listening to *Save the Last Dance For Me, The Twist, Tossin' and Turnin', Quarter to Three, Blue Moon,* and *Please, Mr. Postman,* at their school sock hops, we were probably the only high school in the United States of America in the year 1960 where Rock and Roll was still not allowed to be played. Instead, Beth and I and all the other fourteen year-old couples at Clarkstown Junior-Senior High School danced and fell in love to the sounds of Doc Carney's Sophisticated Swingsters. We were in the school basement cafeteria, listening to *String of Pearls, Moonlight Serenade, In the Mood, Tuxedo Junction,* and *American Patrol.*

The only thing that saved us from complete agony of the music we scorned then and love now, were the C.Y.O. dances, where on Saturday nights, I could hold Beth while dancing to *This, I Swear, is True,* by The Skyliners.

Then one night in that fall of 1960, there were more surprises to discover. At a school dance one autumn Friday night, Doc Carney stood before The Sophisticated Swingsters and introduced two, new, underclassmen into their ranks. Tom took the stage and played *Blue Rondo Ala Turk*, from Dave Brubeck's 1959 album *Time Out*. I would find out later he had learned it in two days. Someone yelled out from the crowd, "Hey play something we can dance to!" So he played *Take Five*, and we still couldn't dance to it.

After some mild applause more in amazement than appreciation, Doc Carney called Beth to the stage, and accompanied by Tom, she sang *A Nightingale Sang in Berkeley Square*. The blue spotlight on her face reminded me of the fireworks light from summers before, but now, over two years later, it had a much more profound effect on me. Beth was beautiful, yes, but she was changing before my eyes.

On autumn weekends we were always off for more adventures, back to High Tor and Hook Mountain like we owned them. Our bicycle routes continued to expand. One trip along South Mountain Road to Rte. 45 took us past Conklin's Apple Orchards and we stopped to pick apples, before heading south on Rte. 45 to Hillcrest, then Spring Valley to Rte. 59. There, we headed east to old Rte. 304, past St. Ann's Catholic Church and Rockland Monuments, a place we nick-named, "tombstone territory," where the headstones of my ancestors had been carved.

We were now freshmen in high school and were thrilled to follow in the footsteps of our predecessors, following traditions and precedents that dated back who knew how many years? If not at Clarkstown, then at Congers High. How many years? We didn't know and didn't care. Every Saturday was a football game in the fall. During basketball season we were courtside two nights a week, Tuesdays and Fridays.

Tom and I rode our bikes to school and Beth took the bus

from her house past Centenary Store and down Ridge Road. After school, when I wasn't involved in football practice or track in the spring, I would walk Beth to the bus line in front of the school where we waited until the last minute before she boarded. Or sometimes I would take the bus home with her and then walk home before dinnertime. We would spend time in her father's studio, watching her father with one model or another, or with Beth showing me his work if he was working in his studio in the city.

Scholastically, we never questioned the authority of our teachers, teachers we would eventually appreciate, who were dedicated to us with a fervor. Every school year our reading list always included at least one play by Shakespeare and several novels. In seventh grade it was *Romeo and Juliet*, and *Treasure Island*. In eighth grade it was *Julius Caesar* and *Ivanhoe*. By ninth grade we were up to *The Merchant of Venice* and *Silas Marner*.

During trips to the barn studio Beth would do charcoal sketches of me, with me only eventually realizing it. She would photograph me when I was talking to her father or Tom, then sketch me from photos she would develop herself in her father's darkroom.

One day out of the clear blue sky she gave me a sketch. In it, I'm leaning up against a doorway frame, staring off into space, my left knee bent at a ninety degree angle, heel to the frame behind me, my hands in my pockets. I don't even ever remember standing like that. She handed it to me nonchalantly without comment. I didn't know what it was at first. Was that me? Of course. It was my face and body etched in charcoal.

She has no idea the impact that small gesture had on me. It was one of the most important gifts she ever gave me. I still have it, of course. I never touch it. The charcoal dust on it was shaded into place by her fourteen year-old fingertips.

At the end of ninth grade it was another summer; another end-of-school dance with Beth; another hike down the Demarest Kill all together. It was our fourth complete trip down the Kill. By now, we were old-timers.

What we didn't realize was that trip after our ninth grade year would be our last complete trip down the Kill together. Something that had stood as some unnamed turning point in our lives would occur during those four summers after sixth, seventh, eighth, and ninth grades. Something so precious. Why did we stop? Had we outgrown the trek? Was becoming an active teenager more important?

Tom's summers, starting after ninth grade, were more consumed by his tours than ever before. His European performance schedule became more hectic, starting earlier in the summer and lasting later. Early summer again marked another month without Beth. She was spending parts of every summer in Florida now. Where was this all leading?

While they were gone I spent my mornings with Francis, reading *From Here to Eternity, Something of Value, The Adventures of Augie March*, and *The Sun Also Rises*. My mind was being reshaped by the masters.

The rest of that summer, when Beth and Tom returned, we hung out whenever we could at New City Park Lake, swam, and listened to Top 40 radio, surrounded by Jimmy, Charlie, Vince, Bobby, and the rest of our group. As we continued to mature, we all remained inseparable, but inevitably, in subtle ways, we were all beginning to find our own way.

That same post-ninth grade summer, when Beth returned from Gainesville, she found work as an arts-and-crafts counselor at Candy Mountain Day Camp on Phillips Hill Road and would spend her days cutting construction paper and smearing it with white paste, supervising the making of pot holders, and the weaving of key chains and lanyards out of plastic and rawhide.

By late afternoons she would ride her bike down the hill and the momentum almost allowed her to coast down the entire length of New Hempstead Road, take a wide swing onto Little Tor Road, and south into New City Park Lake compound without a lot of pedaling.

We would spend our late afternoon and early evening hours on the dam as I helped the official lifeguard by watching the kids and closing up for the night. We would talk about the craziest things, with her making me laugh until my sides hurt. What were we doing, I often wondered, besides killing time before Tom came home from Europe? Was more going on here? Then, that ninth grade summer, before we all earned our learner's permits and later drivers licenses, I would bike home with her before dark, say goodnight at the top of her driveway, and make it home as the sun set over the Ramapos.

I don't think any one of us would have admitted it, but we were actually looking forward to the start of school and our soph-omore year at Clarkstown High School that fall of 1961.

Although earlier that summer we had taken our last hike together on the Demarest Kill, in the days and weeks and months that would follow, we would explore new vistas that became available to those in their mid-teens.

We wouldn't forget the Demarest Kill, we just had what we thought were new priorities.

CHAPTER THIRTY-FIVE

**THE HISTORY OF MUSIC
IN NEW CITY, NEW YORK:
PART V**

1961-1962
Tenth Grade, Age 15

> *And in case she gets a notion,*
> *I'll jump in the air*
> *and come down in slow motion.*
>
> Twist, Twist Senora
> Gary U.S. Bonds

Like many kids in New City in the early 1960s, the music came to us via several radio stations, all out of Manhattan; all AM.

Starting at the low end of the dial on the left hand side there was WMCA, 570, with the WMCA Good Guys. The WMCA jocks included Joe O'Brien, Harry Harrison, Jack Spector, Dandy Dan Daniel, and B. Mitchel Reed, and their play list was sort of good-time, middle of the road stuff, with a bunch of guys trying to be funny, and fake laughter. Not my cup of tea, but a lot of the girls seemed to like it. If you look in our yearbook, the 1964 SAGA, there is a picture of Nancy Robinson standing next to a trampoline, wearing a WMCA Good Guys sweatshirt. Nancy, I just saw on e-Bay they're selling for $50,000. Just kidding.

Next stop on the dial was "*Seventy-Seven, WABC*," at 770. Herb Oscar Anderson ran the morning drive, Big Dan Ingram, a truly hilarious DJ, was on in the mid-afternoon, and Bruce Morrow, "Cousin Brucie," a recent émigré from WINS, ran the night shift. Their play list was also severely limited, with two songs followed by about eight commercials and talk, and the mandatory playing of the top three songs every single hour.

My personal favorite was "*Ten-Ten WINS*," with a less polished approach first led by the legendary Alan Freed, who was fired amidst a payola and tax-evasion scandal in the late 1950s. Freed's play list included the more raw, real music, and was heavy on R&B, Doo-Wop, and the early pioneers of Rock & Roll, regardless of their position on the charts. He played the good stuff. He was also receiving "pay-to-play" cash from promoters. I once heard him play Jackie Wilson's, *I'll Be Satisfied*, seven times in a row without stopping.

WINS also had Murray "The K" Kaufman, an aging hipster with a trophy wife who ran his nightly show, "The Swingin' Soiree with Murray-The-K." Kaufman's musical choices were eclectic. He started the show every night with a Sinatra song. His picks were not always taken from the Top 40, and included lots of "Golden Gassers for Submarine Race Watchers," a code phrase for making out in the back seat of your parents' car while listening to Oldies but Goodies. Kaufman had lots of comical schtick, his own pig-Latin style language, and played Doo-Wop and lots of Girl Groups like the Shirelles, the Ronettes, and The Crystals. With Freed and Kaufman, there were no manufactured pop stars coming from Dick Clark's milquetoast sphere of influence. No Fabian, Frankie Avalon, Bobby Rydell, or other cookie-cutter mush. WINS played the real deal. Both Freed and Kaufman pro-

moted Holiday Shows at the Brooklyn Fox and Brooklyn Paramount, and would bring in up to a dozen acts. I vowed to get there
one day, but never did.

At 1050 on the dial, WMGM broadcast Peter Tripp's "Your
Hits of the Week," a countdown of the Top 40 between seven and
ten p.m.

For late night listeners who were up past eleven and were serious aficionados of Doo-Wop and more obscure R&B, the only
place to go was WADO, 1280 on the dial. There, the legendary
"Ace from Outer Space," Jocko Henderson, hosted his nightly
"Rocketship Show." A black hipster, whose rhyming patter pre-
dated hip-hop by at least twenty-five years, Jocko played roots
Rock & Roll and an assortment of amazing, heavenly Doo-Wop
that couldn't be found anywhere else. I heard *Twist & Shout*, by
The Isley Brothers on Jocko's show weeks before it was played
on the other stations.

Hank Ballard had written and had a minor hit with *The Twist*,
and it was later covered by Chubby Checker. For him it became a
hit in 1960 and again in 1962. But they were far from the best of
The Twist songs. That title would have to go to The Isley Brothers
or Joey Dee and the Starliters or Gary US Bonds. But no matter
who was singing it, the dance craze became huge and we were all
a part of it.

I listened to Jocko whenever I could, but my preference at
ten p.m. was to take a break and join my father and Francis listening to Jean Shepherd. On some nights, my father would lie
alongside Francis with the table radio on, and listen to the tales of
Jean Shepherd coming through the airwaves from WOR in New
York. On those nights, I would slide the door aside from where
I sat outside the room, and listen in on stories about growing up
in Depression-era Indiana, of BB guns, and plastic lamps in the
shape of a woman's leg, of Flick, of getting tongues stuck to frozen flagpoles in the dead of winter, of taking Wanda Hickey to the
prom for a "night of golden memories." It was all punctuated by a

sly, partially subdued laughter from Shepherd. He would improvise these stories in a relaxed, off-the-cuff manner, and would later collect them into several anthologies of short stories. I even heard my father laugh once at Shepherd's shenanigans. "Shep" had actually made my father laugh. Then, he was brought back down to earth and off on his nightly walk.

At the start of tenth grade we settled into a routine for our school days and after school activities. On tap were *The Taming of the Shrew* and *A Tale of Two Cities*, and *David Copperfield* for reading. Homework for Beth, orchestra for Tom, and JV football for me. We would all take the late bus home, dropping Beth off first, then Tom and me at the top of his drive off Little Tor Road. Varsity Football games on Saturday afternoons provided the highlight of each week.

By early that fall we would spend Sunday afternoons on the rear deck of the boathouse, or wandering over to the O.B.W., listening to Tom practice all afternoon upstairs in Dove Cottage while waiting for him to join us on our adventures. By then he was an astounding performer.

And he lived in a mansion on a hill.

CHAPTER THIRTY-SIX

THE DUTCH GARDEN

Halloween Eve
October 30, 1961
Tenth Grade, Age 15

By late autumn of 1961 we were in the full swing of tenth grade. We had taken our last hike along the Demarest Kill earlier that summer and it was disappearing into a distant memory. Many in our circle of friends had been together for almost eleven years, if you count kindergarten. Tom and Beth and I had been our own family for five years, working on our sixth. In the week leading up to Halloween, we had decided to all get together with everyone in the group for what was called "Gate Night." Gate Night was a long-standing tradition in our New City neighborhood, where kids would get together on the night before Halloween and tilt over any remaining outhouses, soap up storefronts and car windows, and then toilet-paper trees and hedges in residential neighborhoods. Gate Night had apparently started in the late 1800's where it got its name when kids put front gates on the porch roofs. It was still a tradition when we were in high school. In past years, storefront windows had been soaped with innocent graffiti, and the trees in front yards had been draped with dozens of rolls of toilet paper, the tissue strands hanging in the breeze as if they had been hung by goblins.

The plan was for Tom and Beth and me to rendezvous with some of the other school kids at the Dutch Garden. From there we would spread out and with bars of soap and candles, soap or wax any car windows we encountered, as we soap-barred all the store-fronts along Main Street. It was just mischievous fun, we thought, so innocent compared to some of the things that are done today.

At six-thirty, before dinner, Tom called to say he wouldn't be able to make it. He had to drive into Manhattan with his grandfather on some mission and couldn't beg off. He apologized and I was disappointed, but didn't think anything more of it.

At eleven o'clock I slid up the window in my bedroom on its frame, careful not to let the lead sash-weights rumble against the wall studs and wake my mother. My father was already long gone on his nightly walks, and I only had to make sure that we didn't bump into him, as we had planned to hit every storefront from the Knick-Knack-Knit Shop in the old post office next to the Elms, all the way south past Steinman's General Store and the Rexall Drug Store. We would have to post guards to keep watch for patrol cars or any traffic. Although at that time of night, in October of 1961, there was little traffic passing through New City. The only late night bars were The Elms on Main Street, Jerry's Tavern on Congers Road, and the Town Tavern a few miles down South Main down by Germonds Road.

By leaving via the back of our field and keeping to Capral Lane and sneaking through the back lot of Dr. Feldman's, I was able to avoid being seen on Main Street.

> *The night was clear,*
> *and the moon was yellow,*
> *and the leaves came tumbling down.*

At the brick lattice wall on the south of the Dutch Garden I put the toe of my boot in a hole and hoisted myself over. The moon was so bright it cast shadows on the lawn and as I passed the sundial in the center of the garden it was bright enough to read. The sundial, covered in a crusty patina of verdigris, read *"my time."* There was an autumn chill in the night air, but not cold enough to be uncomfortable. Just enough to let us know that fall was underway and the world as we knew it was settling into its winter dormancy.

As I approached the tea house on the north end of the Garden, my feet crunching on the gravel path, Beth stepped from the shadows. She was alone.

"Hi."

"How did you get here?"

"I rode my bike."

"All the way from South Mountain?"

"Did you expect me to ask my dad to drive me?"

"Who else is coming? Everyone we asked?"

"I guess so. Where is Tom?"

"He called around dinner time when I got home from football practice. He can't make it."

"Why? What happened?" She asked innocently.

"I don't know. Said he had to go into the city with his grandfather. Maybe he just chickened out."

"Maybe."

"Did you hear from anyone else? Any of the girls who are supposed to come? Susan? Phyllis? Ellen? Betty?"

"No."

I pulled two bars of Ivory Soap from my jacket. "This should get us started. Did you bring any?"

"No, I thought I would just use yours."

Odd, I thought. I expected Beth to lead the pack, using her artistic skills to draw pumpkins and ghosts and witches on the storefront windows. Wouldn't the store owners and police be surprised? Instead of the usual graffiti, there would be artistic jack-o-lanterns and goblins all over their window fronts, just in time for trick-or-treat.

The moon shone in from the southeast, casting light and creating deep shadows in the interior of the tea house. Silence surrounded us. There was no traffic on Main Street, but once in a while the screams of an agitated prisoner from the nearby jail would echo through the darkness.

I sat in silence on the brick steps and leaned back against a brick pillar that framed them. Beth leaned against the pillar opposite and drew up her knees. We sat that way in silence for a good ten minutes, listening for any sound of footsteps approaching on the footpath or wooden bridge behind and beneath us.

"What time is it?" I wondered aloud.

Beth glanced down to her watch and then grabbed her ankles again.

"About twenty after eleven. Won't be long before the '*we-bitching hour*,' I mean 'bewitching hour.' "

"Very funny."

I was becoming annoyed by our friends. First Tom had called and chickened out, and now it appeared Beth's friends had chickened out as well. I was running a thousand things through my mind about being dependable and on time. A thousand things I would use in school the next day to reprimand my friends. Beth finally met my eyes, then looked down.

"They're not coming." She sounded like she was confessing, not making a prediction, and it confused me.

"I'm beginning to think that. They're almost a half-hour late. We have to get started soon, or we'll be up all night."

"No," she shook her head. "I mean no one else is coming." She said it with a self-assuredness that surprised me. Now I was really confused.

"How do you know that?"

"Because I asked them not to come."

"What do you mean? Tom was…."

Beth looked at me intently, as if afraid to say too much. "Tom was one of my co-conspirators."

"What are you talking about? This was supposed to be a group meeting…"

"This isn't about Tom or any of the others. This is about you and me."

She stood and walked toward me and pulled me up on my feet.

We were standing foot to foot, our faces inches apart. I didn't know what was happening. "What do you mean?"

But before I could finish my question, she had her arms wrapped around my waist and was pulling me toward her and had encircled me in her warmth, her head cradled against my chest. I could smell the clean shampoo smell of her hair and in the deep breath I took to catch my breath I almost inhaled her entire being into myself. She smiled up at me and her brown eyes were black and her black hair was shining in the moonlight and before I knew it she was kissing me and the warmth and the wetness of her mouth on mine almost made me faint and my teeth started chattering and my breath was coming in gasps.

"I love you so much, Will. How can you be so blind?"

So there I was, fifteen years old, never having kissed a girl, and there she was in my arms squeezing me as tight as she could. A girl I had fallen in love with five years before at the age of ten and who was now professing her love to me, was making my mouth wet with her mouth and our faces wet with our tears.

I could hardly believe it was happening. Something I had wanted for so long was now being offered to me.

"So you got me here alone to tell me that?"

"Call me old-fashioned. I told Jimmy and Phyllis and Sue that it was canceled. Come on, Will. Haven't you known all along how I feel about you?"

All I could do was sputter. "I feel that way, too. I've always felt that way about you."

"Well why didn't you say something?"

"I don't know. I was afraid."

"Afraid of what?"

"I don't know. That you would laugh at me, dismiss the idea. I thought you liked Tom."

"I do like Tom. He's one of my best friends. I love him like a brother.

"But I love you, Will. I love you so much. I love you like a woman loves a man. I've always loved you since that first day in fifth grade when I walked into class in those goofy, shiny, patent-leather shoes. That very first day I knew I wanted to be with you forever. How could you not know that?"

How? I could think of a thousand reasons why. What was there to love about me, for starters? A poor kid, average looking, going nowhere? What was there to love about me?

Girls always know what to do and how to do it. Boys are stupid. She kept kissing me so tenderly. She never closed her eyes and she never stopped smiling and she never stopped holding me tightly.

"I want to be with you forever, Will. Tell me that you'll be with me forever."

"Yes, Beth. Yes. I want to be with you forever, too. Forever."

She pulled from me and sat me down on the steps and sat on the step beneath me and half turned so her torso was between my legs and her face was in my chest once again. My heart was racing and I couldn't catch my breath. I had to force myself to speak.

"So you told everyone not to come tonight?"

"Yes."

"You told them it was canceled?"

"No, I told them I wanted it to be just you and me. Alone."

"And Tom?"

"Tom knows."

"Tom knows what?"

"Tom knows how I feel about you."

"He's not jealous?"

"Jealous of what? He doesn't like me that way. He likes a new girl every week. This week it's the new cello player in the orchestra. Next week it will be first violin. He's known all along how I feel about you."

"He has?"

"Of course. He even jokes about it. How could he *not* know? It's so obvious to everyone but you. How could you not know?"

I had been thrust into an entirely new world in a matter of seconds and I was reeling from the shock. A world of love. A world of affection. A world of kissing and holding someone I loved. I was fifteen years old and the girl I loved more than anything in this whole world loved me and was kissing me so hard I thought I was going to pass out. I didn't know how to act or conduct myself, how to react, how to behave. And worst of all, I wanted to cry with happiness. I thought back to the first day of ice skating with Beth at Lake Lucille and the happiness I had felt. Now, the feeling was magnified exponentially.

"I don't know. It's . . . It's like it's too good to be true."

"It's more than 'too good', Will. It's perfect. We're perfect. We're perfect and we're going to stay that way. And it is true."

"Yes. Yes. That's what I want. That's what I've always wanted. I've always wanted you to like me."

"I do like you, Will. And I love you, too. I love you so much. Can't you feel it?"

Yes, I could feel it. But it was something so foreign to me, so uncharacteristic of my life up until that point, that I didn't know how to respond, how to react, how to accept what Beth was telling me. And if I did accept it, what if she changed her mind later? Where would that leave me? I knew if I tried to stand I would fall over. So I sat there, holding her, holding her as if it could prevent the night from ever ending, all while thinking, I'm in tenth grade, the girl I love and have always loved, loves me, and she keeps kissing me and I don't ever want it to stop, and it's quite impossible that I can ever be this happy again in my life and if I can, I don't know how. Nothing I could think of could ever make me this happy again, I knew. And at that time, I was right. It was the happiest moment of my life up until that night. But there would be even happier days and nights yet to come, days and nights filled with unspeakable joy and contentment, when my heart was filled to bursting with my love for Beth and her love for me.

We held each other for another hour, murmuring to one another between long kisses. I didn't even know how to kiss a girl, but I followed her lead and did what she did, kissing my lips, my cheeks, my eyelids, the tip of my nose, my ear lobes; touching my face and caressing my neck and caressing my head, and all the time smiling, smiling at me, drawing me in with her smile, holding me a captive to her love for eternity.

Another hour went by, and then another. We were shivering now, and I had inhaled her essence into deep within me.

She stopped to look at her watch.

"It's three o'clock. I have to get going."

But I didn't want her to.

She turned to me. "Do you know what it means when I tell you I love you?"

"I...I..."

"Don't worry. I'm going to spend the rest of my life showing you. I love you."

"I love you. Beth, I've never felt this way before. I've never felt so happy before. I don't know what to do. I don't know what to expect."

"Don't worry. It's never going to go away. It's going to last forever. And we'll make each other happy forever."

We kissed one last time in the archway of the tea house, the moon low on the horizon now, and I didn't want to let her go.

"When I see you in school tomorrow, just remember how much I love you, Will. I want you to know I'll be thinking about you every second of every day until forever. Every second of every day, forever"

She seemed to sense my newfound fears.

"Don't worry. Don't worry about anything, Will. Don't worry. Nothing can happen to us. You'll see. I love you."

Her warm, wet mouth was on mine again and her eyes glistened in the moonlight.

She hugged me one last moment, stood and grabbed her bike from where it was leaning against the fireplace in the tea house. She flipped on the light and turned to me.

"I love you, Will. You'd better get used to it. I'll always love you."

And then she pushed her bike down the steps, and turned to me in a moment that remains frozen in my mind. She smiled and spoke in just above a whisper. "I'll love you to my dying day."

She walked her bike toward Main Street over the brick pathway and down past the WW II monument. I followed, walking quickly alongside her. Suddenly I felt so unworthy.

"I love you, Beth. I'm so glad we were together like this. I'm really glad you told the others to stay home. Thank you...thank you for loving me."

She stopped and swung her leg over the bike seat. "You're so beautiful, Will. How could I not love you? How could I not love you forever?

"Meet me at O.B.W. Saturday morning at ten. I have a plan."

She pushed off and I watched her coast down the embankment and across the sidewalk and onto the empty street. At Congers Road she looked over her shoulder and waved and smiled one last time. In the darkness I could follow the tail light on her bike's rear fender and the headlight on her handlebars all the way up North Main. The streets were empty and the streetlights were sparse, but in each little pool of light they created, I could see her heading north. I ran to the rise where the WWI monument sits on the north lawn and watched her head toward Squadron-A Farm. Unexpectedly, her light wavered as she swerved suddenly to avoid hitting something in the road, and in the dim light from her handlebars I caught a brief glimpse of my father, making his way southbound toward town, his head down, his hands pushed down in his pants' pockets, walking toward oblivion.

But then in a flash of recovery of her balance, Beth continued north, and my father was lost in the darkness. Did she know it was my father? Did she know of his walking? Was it something people in town talked about?

I turned and ran back through the tea house and disappeared into the nighttime Dutch Garden. As I approached the pergola and scaled the brick wall, the only sounds I heard were that of my heart and the racing of the Demarest Kill.

Suddenly the near silence was broken as an alley cat screamed at the top of her lungs and my heart leapt in fear. It was a piercing scream from down behind me near the wooden bridge. I stopped to catch my breath, then continued on, my heart racing in a way it never had before; pounding still. It was Halloween Eve, after all. A screaming cat was somehow fitting.

I paused in the silence that followed. Nothing. I half expected to hear Tom practicing at three o'clock in the morning. It would not have surprised me.

What Beth had said to me that night was a new concept. Someone who loved me for myself. My father was spending all of his love on Francis, and my mother was spending all of hers on my father and my brother. Not that I would ever begrudge those facts, but there was nothing left over for me. I was just a spectator of the family drama that was being played out under our roof. But for now, with what Beth had told me, my outlook on life was about to change, if only temporarily.

For filled with life-long self-doubt, there was still no denying I was still the poor boy at the party. Was it even fair to take up her time and energy when I could never be the man that Tom was or her father was? I was just going to be the son of a lost mailman and a seamstress mother and the brother of a hopeless cripple, doomed to live out my life as a drone. Why should I hold her back? Unable or unwilling to think of myself as someone Beth could actually love, what was the point of going on with it? It would only end up in disappointment for the woman I loved. This was to be the overriding doubt which would eventually plague my future and lead up to the fateful day with Beth.

If only I had accepted her at her word. If only I had taken her simple statement of love at face value, how different my life would be; our lives would be.

What does a tenth grader know about love? Or any man, for that matter?

I raced home to beat my father's arrival.

CHAPTER THIRTY-SEVEN

O.B.W. CEMETERY

Halloween Week
1961
Age 15

I found out about Beth's O.B.W. plan the following Saturday, when, as instructed, I met her there at ten in the morning. We hugged we kissed and her smile overwhelmed me. She took my hand and led me down the hill to the sandstone and earthen dam on the east side of the dried-up lake in front of Tom's boathouse.

She pulled a pocketknife from her jeans and knelt down at the foot of the dam remains. She unfolded the blade and swept away some vines that covered the sandstone facade, almost like sweeping away the long dark hair from her face. There, with the knife point, she etched *her name and mine, inside a heart, upon the wall. They found a way to haunt me, though they're so small.*

"We'll come here every Halloween week to celebrate. By the time we're old, there will be dozens of these hearts here. I picked a stone big enough, especially, to last for years."

How did she think of such things, I thought, as she leaned back on her haunches to gain some perspective and admire her work? What had I done to deserve such love?

Our visit there together would be a Halloween-week ritual, at least for a few years.

CHAPTER THIRTY-EIGHT

NEW CITY

Christmas
1961
Tenth Grade, Age 15

That Christmas we started a tradition that would end just four years later. The three of us decorated a tree at Beth's house, while her father stood and watched silently, a tumbler of Scotch in his hand. Then we moved on to Tom's and sipped homemade eggnog with Mr. and Mrs. Florion, Frau K., and Max, as we all put the final trimmings on an enormous tree. We wound up at my house helping my mother decorate our tree, as my father and Francis watched through the sliding doors where my brother lay. Three trees in one day. Three different lifestyles blending together. I was dizzy from stringing the lights around the trees.

As Christmas Vacation ended and 1962 began, I was looking forward to everything. I wanted to be awake 24 hours a day just to take it all in.

We had just defeated Haverstraw in basketball in early January. In the gymnasium that night along with Beth and Tom, another dark-haired young woman sat on the hometown bleachers and cheered for her Haverstraw Raiders. I would later find out her name was Delores.

Saturday we spent yet another day ice skating at Lake Lucille. I was so much in love with Beth I couldn't focus on anything else.

CHAPTER THIRTY-NINE

MAIN STREET, NEW CITY

January 13, 1962
Tenth Grade, Age 15

On Sunday morning, January 13, my father stood at the bottom of the stairs and called up to my room. This was unusual for him. I didn't know what to expect. I stood on the landing.

"I have some bad news for you."

My heart raced. Was something wrong with Francis? My mother? He stood with the *New York Daily News* clutched in his hand. "A friend of yours died."

Beth? Tom? Jimmy?

I ran down the stairs in a panic as he walked down the hall to the kitchen table and put the newspaper down in front of me. There, on the front cover, was a photograph of a white Corvair, the driver side door smashed into a utility pole. I opened the front page and read the article. Ernie Kovaks had died in a crash on the way home from a party with Jack Lemmon and Milton Berle and other friends. He lost control of the car. In his left hand was an unlit cigar.

"I'm sorry, Will. He was a great man with a great mind.

Someday I hope you'll understand just how great." He turned and walked into Francis' room. I was surprised. For him, it was an uncharacteristic display of emotion. For me, another one of my heroes had died. Someone I had actually met at a cocktail party when I was just eleven years old. We had watched him on television during every erratic opportunity, laughing at his silliness in our living room. Later that winter I would see him in an Italian film, *Five Golden Hours*. He played a con artist, perfectly cast, perfectly portrayed. But I had once stood in his presence; stood in the presence of his greatness.

Tenth grade continued, as did our routine. In the outside world, in the world of music and culture, everything was changing. We seemed to be entering a new age. We could all sense something.

We were poised, waiting.

CHAPTER FORTY

**THE HISTORY OF MUSIC
IN NEW CITY, NEW YORK:
PART VI**

Winter, 1962
Tenth Grade, Age 15

Late one Saturday afternoon at dinnertime, Tom called me.

"Get on your tie and a sports jacket. Call Beth and tell her to dress up in her nightclub outfit. We're going someplace."

"Where?"

"I'll tell you when I see you. Max and I will pick you up in two hours. Tell Beth we're coming for her, too."

By eight o'clock, we were headed south on the Palisades Parkway to Manhattan along with Tom's date from Spring Valley High School named Madelon, an oboe player he had met in a recent orchestra competition. After badgering Tom until just north of the George Washington Bridge, he finally gave us an answer.

"One word. '45th Street'."

Beth and I looked at one another. "That's two words, maybe three. What's on 45th Street?"

"Don't you guys ever read the newspaper? Listen to the

radio?" He sang, *"Meet me baby down on 45th Street."*

"The Peppermint Lounge?"

"Bingo."

Beth and I exchanged looks of disbelief.

"They won't let us in there. We're not twenty-one."

"Stick with me, kiddos."

Another half hour of heavy traffic and Max pulled the limo up to the front door and got out. Two hundred people were standing in the freezing weather, waiting their turn to get in to dance. Mounted policemen sat on their horses, the breath of the beasts coming out in snorts of snot-filled white mist. The doorman rushed to open the limo door for us and we poured out onto the sidewalk where he ushered us under the canopy.

We paused as a photographer called out. "Picture, sir! For your grandfather."

The flashbulb lit up our faces.

"How did you pull this off?" I yelled in Tom's ear as we were whisked inside by the doorman's associates.

"Can you say 'Genovese'?"

"What?"

"Never mind. I'll explain later."

Inside was pandemonium. Joey Dee and the Starlighters were playing *Ram-Bunk-Shush* to a packed house. On the stage dancing the twist were three beautiful black women from a singing trio. They had arrived as a group to see Joey Dee, were mistaken by the management for a dance troupe, and ushered onto the stage to dance. The following year they would sign a record deal with Phil Spector and become famous as The Ronettes. The song ended and with a split second pause they broke in to *Hold It*.

The Hammond organ got my attention hammering out a heavy bass line through the rotating propeller of the Leslie speaker.

Beth stood next to me staring at the bandstand. "Am I dreaming this?"

"No," I said, wanting to add, but holding back, *I'm dreaming it.*

Beth started dancing, following the movements of Ronnie Bennett and the Ronettes. Had Beth been practicing?

The next week we were the talk of the school. Tenth graders at the Peppermint Lounge? How was it possible? How would we ever be able to top that?

The answer was just weeks away.

CHAPTER FORTY-ONE

**THE HISTORY OF MUSIC
IN NEW CITY, NEW YORK:
PART VII**

May, 1962
Tenth Grade, Age 15

It was getting near the end of our sophomore year. In early May, we were sitting on the deck of Tom's boathouse listening to him practice. Finally, when it was over, he ran down the hill to join us and reached in his shirt pocket and pulled out four stubs that looked like theater tickets.

"What?"

"Do you guys like piano music?"

Beth laughed. "We hate it. That's why we spend our afternoons down here listening to whatever it is you are doing up there."

"No I mean real piano music."

"Sure. We could use some real piano music." Beth again.

"Enough to come with me to Carnegie Hall in two weeks?"

"Carnegie Hall? You're performing at Carnegie Hall?"

Beth reached out and grabbed the tickets out of his hand. She shook her head in disbelief. "You're not going to believe this."

The suspense was killing me. She held the tickets up to where I could see the performer's name: Ray Charles.

On the Sunday afternoon of May 13, 1962, we were again in the back seat of the limo, Max at the wheel, and Tom's new date squeezed in next to us: Suzanne, another piano virtuoso Tom had met on his travels, and who was now living in Nyack.

The four of us watched from the balcony as a part of musical history took place before our eyes. The Ray Charles' Orchestra played for an hour before the man himself was led onstage by an assistant. At the corner of the piano he followed the edge to center stage, reached out and picked up a saxophone from a stand. Three songs later, he turned, retraced his steps, and sat down at the keyboard. He played everything that day, but the highlight was *You Are My Sunshine*, with Margie Hendricks growling her lyrics in a raw sexual way I had never heard before. Tom and Suzanne watched, analyzing keyboard technique. Beth and I sat, mesmerized that we were a part of this. As a tenth grader, I quickly realized you can never be the same person after witnessing something like what we saw that day. You're different somehow. Were kids like us even allowed to see stars like this?

CHAPTER FORTY-TWO

**THE HISTORY OF MUSIC
IN NEW CITY, NEW YORK:
PART VIII**

Summer, 1962
Age 15

TOP HITS OF N.C.P. LAKE 1962
Twist and Shout, Isley Brothers
Hey Baby, Bruce Channel w/ Delbert McClinton
on opening harp
Duke of Earl, Gene Chandler
Peppermint Twist Pt. II, Joey Dee and the Starlighters
Dear Lady Twist, U.S. Bonds
Green Onions, Booker T. and the M.G.s,
with Steve Cropper on lead guitar
Uptown, The Crystals
Surfin' Safari, The Beach Boys
I Wish That We Were Married, Ronnie and the Hi-Lites
The Wanderer, Dion DiMucci

My summer job after tenth grade started the week before

Memorial Day Weekend, as a lifeguard at New City Park Lake. Bill, the chairman of the Lake Committee, saw to it that I would get my Red Cross Badge. We finished school the third week in June, and after that I was pretty much committed to the job. Tom was leaving early for his European Tour, and Beth was scheduled to start at Candy Mountain Day Camp again, as soon as she got back from Gainesville.

With Tom getting ready to leave for Europe, and my time with Beth limited prior to her leaving for her now annual Florida trip, she and I still made attempts to hike Demarest Kill for the fifth time. We even completed some of it, hiking in fits and starts. But it seems we had temporarily lost interest or maybe were merely distracted by visions of earlier trips. Without Tom as a companion, it was beginning to get old, even though by that time, Beth and I were spending every waking moment together. We had, at least so we all thought, just moved on to other things more suitable for students about to enter their junior year of high school. Upon Tom's return from Europe, he would join me at the Lake on his few days off, although he was beginning to spend an increasingly more amount of time at his grandparents' apartment in Manhattan during tour breaks. But our long absences apart would soon be forgotten as each new school year began.

Most summer Mondays I had off from the Lake. During those long afternoons Beth and I sat by the O.B.W. cemetery and listened to Tom practice for his trip. We joked about our assigned designation on the tiny tombstone. Suppose it really did stand for *Old Bird Watcher*? At first as we listened we were convinced Tom was tricking us by playing albums of other pianists on a record player near the window, cranking up the volume loud enough to hear in the woods. Of course we realized it was really him playing as he first struggled through, then mastered, *Rhapsody in Blue*. Beth leaned back against the tiny tombstone reading *Arrowsmith*, while I half dozed, my fingertip keeping my place in *The Magnificent Ambersons*. I was only half listening to the music. She stopped, closed her eyes.

"Felix."

I looked around. "Felix? Felix The Cat? Where?"

"No."

"Felix Festa?" I ventured, naming the superintendent of the Clarkstown School District.

"No."

I was out of Felixes.

"Mendelssohn, goofy. Felix Mendelssohn."

I nodded. "Sure."

"Tom's so good."

I looked toward the house where the music was playing. "Yes, he is."

"I want to be good at something. Really good. Art or photography or something like that. Like my father. I want to be really good at it. Have you ever felt that way?"

"Yes."

"What do you want to be good at?"

I thought long and hard about that. "I don't know."

She looked back to the house. "I know. I know what I want." She listened for another minute, really staring off rather than looking at the house. Then she looked at me for a moment and then returned to her book.

I thought about my answer. Would I ever be able to match them? Was there anything I wanted to be good at? Was I good at something already but hadn't realized it yet? Yes. I had a highly developed skill, but it would be years before I truly understood what it was and the impact it would have on my life and my mind.

CHAPTER FORTY-THREE

NEW CITY

1962-1963
Eleventh Grade, Age 16

Another summer passed.

By the beginning of the eleventh grade in the fall of 1962 we were all sixteen years old and were on the road to being convinced we knew everything of life there was to know. My two friends and I, who had been together for six years, were like old family members. Tom and Beth and I would spend our junior and senior high school years, inseparable in mind and spirit.

But there was a haunting impression of anticipation, a feeling difficult to describe. We could sense the momentum building in our lives as we raced toward graduation just short of two school years down the path. The eleventh grade fall was filled with band and football practice for Tom and me, while Beth began to concentrate on her art and photography in earnest. While Tom was mentored by Doc Carney, and I by Coach Morrow, Beth fell under the spell of Miss Palermo, an art teacher with a hip sense of humor and sarcasm that complemented and nurtured Beth's own.

As I spent my after-school hours hitting the tackling sled and Tom marched endlessly up and down the field pumping a trombone slide, Beth was becoming an accomplished photographer. She roamed the halls and the campus of the Carnochan Estate developing an eye that would eventually land her work in galleries and magazines and books around the world.

There continued to be a change in the feel of the music. Something was happening. The originals like Chuck Berry and Little Richard and Fats Domino were being pushed aside by all the newcomers and the manufactured acts coming out of the Dick Clark circle of influence.

We had already witnessed Hank Ballard being pushed aside by Chubby Checker with *The Twist*, which had led to a lot of great twist songs by our new idol, Joey Dee, and others like U.S. Bonds, The Isley Brothers, King Curtis, and Sam Cooke.

We fast danced to the music of Dion DiMucci and Bruce Channel.

We slow danced to Ketty Lester, Don and Juan, Henry Mancini, The Shirelles, and The Drifters. I couldn't quite put my finger on it, but the music was changing, getting better, more sophisticated, moving us out of the past and into the future. Each week brought an onslaught of new music.

Fall football practice clearly demonstrated we were getting better; better skills, teamwork, and strategies. Some of my Junior Varsity team members were moved up to Varsity, but we would all dress out for every Varsity game on Saturday afternoons. I looked around and saw guys who had been playing together for four years. I noticed something else. With few exceptions, all of the guys on the team were not what you would think of today as typical jocks. All of us were smart. Many of us were in advanced classes, taking math and science classes a year ahead of the requirements. Could that possibly have an impact on the future of the team?

Beth and I would spend every available moment together in

one another's arms. It never once occurred to me that our making out would ever move beyond that until when, or should I say if, we were to ever marry. It wasn't even on my radar screen. I was satisfied to cradle her head in my arms as she leaned against me under a giant oak or on a blanket and we gazed into an unknown future. I was too frightened or too insecure to risk going further.

That fall in the beginning of the eleventh grade, on Sunday afternoons, we found something to do before the winter that would usher in our ice skating trips. While Tom was practicing, Beth and I would ride our bikes to the back of Conklin Apple Orchards with a lunch basket on the front of my bike, pull up under the Macintosh trees, spread out a big plaid blanket and talk and nap the day away and watch the sun go down behind red and golden MacIntosh apples. The black of Beth's hair was tinged with deep orange against the autumn twilight.

At the first big snowfall, Max picked up Beth and me, and along with Tom, and an ancient oak toboggan sticking out the back of the limo trunk, drove us to the first fairway of Dellwood Country Club on Zukor Road.

Tom told us the history he had heard from his grandfather. We knew the old man had been friends with Zukor for years, had even seen him at the lawn party four summers earlier. It was originally called Mountain View Farms because it sits in the basin underneath High Tor. When Adolph Zukor, founder of Paramount Pictures, moved to New City in the 1920s, he bought the three hundred acres of land that already had a nine-hole golf course on it. A few years later he bought another 500 acres and built guest houses and a movie theatre, greenhouses, and reconfigured an eighteen-hole golf course.

Some of the history I knew myself from my own father. Zukor would hold movie parties for the club members and the neighbors and the caddies. One night in 1934, my father, then eighteen, and Zukor's personal caddy, was invited along with my grandfather, who did part-time lawn maintenance there as he had for the Florions, to attend an advance screening of *It Happened One Night*. Although the film was produced by Columbia Pictures, Zukor had loaned out Claudette Colbert from Paramount to show her what it was like to work on a low-budget film.

My father's familiarity with movies was slight at that time. Since there was no movie theater in New City in 1935, the only other movie my father had ever seen as a boy was the film, *Whoopee*. He had seen it across the street from our house at the Forrester's Hall building that would eventually become St. Augustine's Church in 1934. But on an earlier night, in 1930, when my father was fourteen, the itinerant projectionist making his rounds around Rockland County set up his projector and showed the Eddie Cantor hit comedy based on his Broadway show that Flo Ziegfeld sold to Sam Goldwyn.

Later during the Depression, after he had lost his fortune, Zukor opened the golf course to the public and eventually sold it in 1948 to Bernie Nemeroff, who named it after the nearby Dells on the west side of the property.

For whatever reason, the owners of The Dellwood Country Club let the local kids toboggan in the wintertime of 1962-1963 on the first hole fairway, a hill on the west side of Zukor Road. On moonlit nights kids would toboggan down the hillside and then scramble up to the top for another ride.

As the sun disappeared behind the line of trees to the west, the full moon lit up the dark blue-black sky, and the first fairway that crossed the road was filled with a hundred neighbors, their squeals of glee filling the night.

Tobogganing by moonlight, my arms encircling the girl I loved and who loved me, the smell of the old pea coat she still wore, mixed with the smell of the snow, put me in a trance. My hair and eyebrows would freeze up and form icicles and Beth would nibble-kiss them off. Tom was always with a different girl, and without exception they were always among the smartest and prettiest and most talented in the class. It was as if he had had the key and unlocked the padlock on the local schools' brain trust.

"Do you make them take an IQ test before you ask them out?" Beth once asked him.

"Yes, how did you know? I asked them not to tell."

We would toboggan for hours and then Max would drive us to Dove Cottage for warm cider or cocoa prepared by Frau K. By this time, Tom's grandparents were getting older and spending more and more time in Manhattan. They would come out on an occasional weekend, but most of the time, Tom rattled around the house by himself, attended to by Frau K. and Max.

When we left at the end of each evening, Max would drive us all home, Tom's date first, then Beth, and then head to the home stretch before dropping me off. We knew the time was quickly approaching when we would all have our drivers' licenses, and maybe even our own cars to drive. I had been saving money for years, delivering the *Rockland Journal News* before dawn, shoveling snow off sidewalks from in front of just about every merchant in town, and mowing lawns in the neighborhood.

Tom would rely on Max and the limo for the next few months. Later, Beth and I would be his chauffeurs as our double-dates continued.

Tom and I had both caddied at Dellwood Country Club for several early seasons in the past, not an easy job to get, unless, of course, the owner knew both of your grandfathers.

In the springtime of our eleventh grade year we caddied again, when it didn't interfere with track practice and his piano routine, earning good money in tips for carrying bags two rounds of eighteen holes each, shagging balls on the driving range, and in the late afternoon, cleaning the pool.

One day, much to our surprise, Calvin and Marvin showed up to caddy. They lasted one day and were banned. Calvin was too frail to make it even nine holes, and Marvin was rude to the players.

Sometimes, Beth would meet us afterward and we would

swim in the country-club pool. We were treated like guests because of who our families were. That spring of 1963, it would become our designated home away from home as had New City Park Lake, both in the past and in the future.

That same spring, late in our junior year, we had all earned our driver's licenses, and were poised for the next great chapters in our lives, as drivers of our own cars. Beth was first. One day she roared up in the 1950 Willys Jeepster she inherited from her father. It was a really cool phaeton-style car. Her father had been keeping it for her in storage in the garage next to his barn studio. It was maroon, with a big back seat, but the heater never worked.

I was able to barely afford a 1960 Volkswagen Beetle, after learning how to drive a clutch transmission in Driver's Ed. A new one would have cost $1,600. My three year-old blue one cost $400.

During the closing days of eleventh grade, just before Memorial Day when New City Park opened, Tom and I both secured lifeguard jobs for the next few weekends, and later, when school got out, every day of the week.

Sometimes, I would even ride over in the morning to listen to him practice for a while, starting at six a.m.

Frau K. would make us pancakes or omelets to prepare us for our trip. By ten we were at the lake, bag lunches in hand, watching little kids as we split our time, alternating between the north and south ends. And then in the early days of July, Jimmy replaced Tom temporarily, so Tom could go on his annual European tour.

CHAPTER FORTY-FOUR

NEW CITY

Summer, 1963
End of Junior Year
Age 16

With the ability to drive instead of bike that summer of 1963, before Tom was to leave for Europe and Beth left for what had become an annual trip to Florida, our adventures went farther afield.

Heading south, we double-dated in my car to Palisades Park. It was illegal for us to drive in New Jersey, but we took the chance.

On this night, Tom's date was Inez, another cello player he'd met in County Orchestra. She lived in Nyack and we crowded into my bug and drove down the Palisades Parkway, got lost in Ft. Lee, and finally found our way to the Park. Getting lost was part of the adventure, a guaranteed increase in the laughter level, and we were expanding our horizons, spreading our wings. We were growing up.

From high atop the Ferris wheel, just like we had at the New City Fireman's Carnival, we could see the future. But this time when the wheel came to a stop, and as the buckets swayed, we could see across the majestic Hudson to the Manhattan Skyline. What did that Skyline portend for our future? Would any of us wind up there?

"Someday I want to own an art gallery over there. I want to sell my father's work. My work."

"Your work?"

"Yes."

In one way I was so proud of Beth. But another side of me felt fear. Where did I fit into this picture?

When Tom left for Europe, I continued to lifeguard at New City Park Lake with Jimmy filling in on the lifeguard stands. For me, it was getting harder to imagine what those European tours must have been like. I was watching the kiddie pool in New City Park and Tom was headlining venues with standing room only audiences in Vienna. It just all didn't add up.

On my day off from life guarding, Beth and I decided we wanted to travel a little bit, so instead of climbing High Tor, we climbed Hook Mountain as we had years before. This time in Beth's Willys, we drove over to Rockland Lake, a once thriving town due to an ice-harvesting industry, that was now dying. We parked next to the Fire Station and climbed up to the crest for a spectacular view across the Hudson. Although I felt something then, I was never able to really articulate it. It was only later I would reflect on how much natural beauty there was within just a few miles of our homes.

That summer, with the top down on Beth's Willys, we explored Seven Lakes Drive in Harriman Park, Lake Tiorati, went swimming at Lake Welch and Lake Sebago. We drove to the top of Perkins' Memorial Drive and climbed the tower. Every day was a new adventure, and every day we left fewer and fewer breadcrumbs behind. We were on the road constantly that summer, even at night. Having outgrown the C.Y.O. Dances and Doc

Carney's cafeteria soirees, we went in search of wilder fare. We started from nightclubs like Perunna's and Villa Lafayette in Spring Valley, The Wayne House in Haverstraw, and Brophy's in Grassy Point. Looking for new excitement, a bigger dance floor, a more sophisticated crowd of nineteen year-olds, we branched out and headed northwest and went as far as The Long Pond Inn on Greenwood Lake.

It was all a part of exploring new worlds, far from our cradle of New City.

When Tom returned from Europe and Beth from Florida, Tom and I convinced her to spend her time with us during our summer days lifeguarding. While I was working, Calvin would show up, and under the skeptical eyes of the Club President, would be allowed to stay as my guest. He had never returned to school after that day and night in seventh grade, dodging the truant officers by constantly moving back and forth between relatives in Sloatsburg and Suffern. Then he had spent almost three years in a reform school after the theft. But in the summer of '63, he would spend those summer days swimming the length of the lake from the dam to the lighthouse and back. He was becoming a strong, disciplined swimmer. It was something he could be proud of. Just when I thought he might somehow turn his life around, he went to jail for grand theft auto. Was he in the wrong place at the wrong time, or was this the beginning of his own pattern of recidivism? His erratic behavior prior to this left me wondering, and mourning for him.

Our routine at the lake was more like a social gathering than a real job. The radio was on constantly, and all of our friends came by to hang out. It was party time every day. Who needed the surfing beaches of Southern California when you had New City Park Lake?

TOP HITS OF NEW CITY PARK LAKE 1963
Be My Baby, Ronettes
If You Wanna Be Happy, Jimmy Soul
Surfin' USA, The Beach Boys
Wipeout, The Surfaris
Wild Weekend, The Rebels
Mockingbird, Charles and Inez Foxx
Pipeline, Chantays
Heatwave, Martha and the Vandellas
Marlena, The Four Seasons
Da Doo Ron Ron, The Crystals
Just One Look, Doris Troy
Memphis, Lonnie Mack
You've Really Got a Hold on Me, Smokey Robinson
and the Miracles
Pride and Joy, Marvin Gaye
One Fine Day, The Chiffons

All the fun we were having was a distraction. Once, while I was talking to Beth, Tom jumped in and saved a young boy's life. Witnesses said we jumped in at the same time, but I know for certain I was at least five-ten seconds behind, having had my attention diverted. Ten seconds that probably would have meant that the boy would have gone down for the last time without being rescued, had not Tom been there. The boy's mother came running from where her blanket was spread out in front of the brick fireplace and couldn't thank me enough. I was too shaken, too frightened of the implications, to acknowledge that it was actually Tom who had saved her son's life. Could he have saved Francis if he had been there that day?

Beth had come back from The University of Florida after her summer '63 trip and announced she was applying to go to art school at UF with a minor in photography. I was delirious with concern. I was expecting to go to Rockland Community College, and maybe, if lucky, become a teacher. But what about tuition? My mother told me that my grandfather had left money for my college tuition and that I should not worry about it. So I announced, somewhat hurriedly, impulsively, that I wanted to go to UF and major in pre-law. What I really wanted was to be with Beth. So my mother agreed and Beth was ecstatic that I would be able to join her. Beth's father was not so excited about it. In the back of my mind, the fear and trepidation was beginning to build.

To our surprise, Tom announced he would be applying to Dartmouth. Was this the correct choice for him, we wondered? Should it be Peabody, or some other prestigious music school? Julliard? New England Conservatory? Boston Conservatory? But Tom was adamant. He wanted a law degree with music as a minor. So, at the end of the following summer, he would be heading to Dartmouth.

Later, as we raced toward the future, our hiking trips expanded into more elaborate overnight camping trips. On the night of August 15, to celebrate my seventeenth birthday, we camped out on High Tor, our three pup-tents dangerously near the edge of the palisade.

We looked down to the majestic Hudson River, the northern extremity narrowing of the Tappan Zee, the setting sun casting our shadows first down to Haverstraw at our feet below, then across the river to Croton Point Park and Van Cortland Manor.

As the sun disappeared behind the Ramapos, the jagged edges of the Trap Rock cuts were bathed in the geometric slashes of golden sunset. How many nights had Maxwell Anderson spent observing the similar splendor of what we now were witnessing, in order to write his landmark play, *High Tor*?

From our sequestered homes in the New City valley, we were now able to see the outside world and all it represented. Standing, facing north, our vision was filled with the history of The Revolutionary War.

We all faced southwest. I walked to the edge and looked down into the valley. I held up my arms in a wide embrace, facing New City, and stood there taking it all in. Beth and Tom joined me, staring in wonder.

Beth looked at me. "What are you doing?"

"It came to me that every significant event in my life has taken place in the purview of my outstretched arms. Everything. I've never been anywhere else."

Beth and Tom exchanged looks, then looked out at what we all beheld.

"That will change before you know it," Beth tried to reassure me.

I wasn't convinced. But of course, as usual, they were right.

Turning south, the skyline of Manhattan clearly visible less than thirty miles away, we faced the future. It was as if every day of our lives, every moment of our lives was presenting us with a profound revelation of what life was, and a warning of what life was to become. If only we had listened. If only we had paid attention. Would it have made a difference in our thinking and our behavior that late summer evening in August of 1963, just before the world lurched and spun off its axis? Why didn't we listen? Why didn't we pay heed?

As we said goodnight to one another and crawled into our respective pup-tents, I didn't want the night to ever end.

It was Beth who broke the silence with her words that traveled through the darkness to our nearby tents.

"Hey, I just thought of something."

Tom groaned. "Here we go."

"You guys don't sleepwalk do you? I would hate to have to scrape you off the rocks down there in the morning."

"Very funny. Go to sleep"

"One last question."

"Now what?"

"Where did you put the chamber pot?"

As that summer of '63 drew to a close, we were all seventeen. Was there anything that could have prepared us for what was to come in the next twelve months? The changes would be so profound there would be no going back. We would all enter a state of shock from which some would never recover for years.

We stood poised for what we thought would be a standard issue senior year at CCHS, trying to follow in the footsteps and traditions of our predecessors. But the world didn't care. The world was making its own plans for our futures, and was not sharing those plans with us.

Two musical events signaled change. A twelve year-old blind kid from Detroit released *Fingertips*, and we all sat up and took notice. We listened to the young voice and we listened to the harmonica flourishes.

One song we overlooked was recorded by Del Shannon that climbed up the charts as "just another Del Shannon song." Shannon had been on tour in England earlier that year. One night he played a gig with fourteen other bands, heard the song, and decided to record it for himself. It became a modest hit for him in this country that summer of '63. What made it different was that it was written by two young men from Liverpool. The song was, *From Me to You,* and the young songwriters, unknown in the U.S., were John Lennon and Paul McCartney. But who was listening? Who was paying attention? Certainly not the three friends from New City. The world was setting the stage for other surprises, surprises like Ernie Kovaks and Buddy Holly, designed especially for seventeen year-olds.

We were about to be blindsided.

CHAPTER FORTY-FIVE

THE HISTORY OF MUSIC
IN NEW CITY, NEW YORK:
PART IX

Fall, 1963
Senior Year, Age 17

> "We become what we behold."
>
> II Corinthians, 3:18
> & Marshall McLuhan

Our senior year started out as a long, humid Indian Summer began. The temperatures remained hot through our pre-school football, two-a-day practices. Several of my teammates and I were close to suffering from sunstroke on more than one occasion.

There was unprecedented excitement in the air because after a seemingly endless six years, we were now on the top of the heap. We had finally made it. Now here, we were clueless as to what to do, but we had finally made it and most of my classmates were busily making plans for college. I had taken the College Boards and sent off my application to the University of Florida at Beth's urging.

The music that fall was among the best out and had seemed to reach an apex up to that music invasion we were about to experience; Doris Troy, *Just One Look*; *Mockingbird*, by Charles and Inez Foxx; *Be My Baby*, The Ronettes; *Dah-Doo-Ron-Ron*, The Crystals; *Heat Wave*, Martha and the Vandellas, and *Surfin' USA*, by the Beach Boys. A little bit of everything to keep me happy and on the dance floor with Beth whenever I could.

In accordance with all the unwritten senior class traditions, we made sure we followed in the footsteps of our predecessors. We planned to go through the motions of what it meant to be a senior and then passing the baton to the underclassmen.

Whatever cliques there had been in the earlier grades seemed to melt away as all of us knew, at least subconsciously, that when this year ended we would probably never see one another again. We were all joining forces, circling the wagons, in our last onslaught of high school life.

Just about every day, I picked up Tom for school and we drove over in my bug. Some days Beth would pick up both of us in her Willys. But that all changed when Tom called us both one Sunday night to let us know he didn't need a ride to class the next day.

"Why not?"

"I can't tell you until tomorrow."

It all sounded very mysterious.

As could be expected, Tom outdid us all when that Monday morning in early October of 1963, he pulled up in the parking lot with a 1960 Austin Healey 3000, Mark I. It had two seats in back and we nicknamed it the "two-by-two."

I had never been jealous of Tom's wealth before, but this car made me think twice. It was sleek, just three inches of clearance off the ground. It had wire wheels, brass knock-off caps that held them on, rear view mirrors that stuck out of the sides of the fenders just behind the headlights. It had side-curtains instead of roll-up windows. It was British Racing Green. But what did it for me was the sound.

Although Beth and I had had our own transportation for months now, our ride of choice from that day forward was the Healey. Forget about the back seat. The three of us squeezed into the front, Beth sitting side-saddle on the transmission hump, shifting her body weight toward me each time Tom moved through the gears.

That fall of 1963 we raced along South Mountain Road from one end to the other, driving at reckless speeds, laughing uncontrollably as the low-slung car hugged the roadway around each blind curve. A raccoon tail at the tip of the antenna wiggle-wobbled in the draft. As the autumn breeze blew through our hair, we never thought of it at the time, but we could have been killed, rolled over the edge of the road, killed others, a hundred times over. We were too full of ourselves, too full of life, to give it a second thought. And each downshifting of the gears brought that throaty muffler sound to my head, a sound I can still hear. A sound that still haunts me, associated as it was with Beth leaning her body against mine.

Although there was other excitement in the air, our thoughts and efforts were focused on football. There was a big bonfire on the north perimeter of the football field that first Friday night before the first game. The band marched around out of formation in rag-tag costumes, playing fight songs as we all sang along and cheered. I walked away from Beth to talk to some of my teammates for a moment, and when I looked up, through the flames and waves of heat I saw her looking at me, smiling. Of the millions of moments in the photo album in my mind, this is one of the many that stands out. Her knitted cap was pulled down over her dark hair and her hands were stuffed into the pockets of her pea coat and she was smiling at me. Her eyes had never left me.

Most years the first game of the season was an out-of-county team; some team from Westchester County or Northern New Jersey. Most of the time we lost. But this time we rolled over Goshen, 20-7, from Orange County, in the pre-season game and everything seemed to take on a new perspective. It was a perspective called 'hope'. Coach Morrow and Coach Sawyer were reluctant to get too excited about our first win.

The following week was another away game, this time against Tappan Zee. I was running and blocking as both offensive and defensive right guard, Tom was walking in formation with his trombone in the marching band, Beth was sitting in the stands. I knew my mother would be going to the game; she would attend every game to watch me play. We beat TZ, 14-7.

We proceeded with caution and that next week we beat Pearl River, 35-6. In in successive weeks we defeated Suffern/Away 30-0, Haverstraw/Home, 15-13, Nanuet/Away 19-0.

As the weeks progressed, we alternated between jubilation and numbness and disbelief. We were all holding our breaths, waiting for the disappointment of surely what would be our inevitable losing in the final weeks.

Two games out of the last three were the toughest: Spring Valley/Away and Nyack/Home. No one said anything because we were almost certain to lose both games. They were just too powerful and we were out of our league against them.

The days immediately before game days we never used the practice field at the bottom of the hill behind the school. On the Friday before the Spring Valley game, we walked in silence from the locker room past Doc Carney's orchestra room and tennis courts to the official playing field for our last minute walkthroughs. We were certain that if we showed any enthusiasm it would somehow jinx our chances.

The next day, November 2, 1963, we played Spring Valley on their home turf and we beat them 15-13, despite their fast running-back, Jimmy Ashcroft. It was as if the coaches and our quarterback, Bobby Lawson, had sat down and decided amongst themselves that we simply were not going to lose. The ride home on the bus after the game was a combination of jubilation and concern for what we faced on our home turf the next weekend against Nyack.

Nyack had always been the county powerhouse and therefore our biggest rival, although I'm sure they never felt that way about Clarkstown. I'm sure they thought of us as a group of privileged, rich, white kids, no matter how inaccurate a perception that was.

The last practice on the last Friday of my football career was filled with apprehension. I spent most of the day preparing myself for the inevitable; we would lose to Nyack, destroying our undefeated designation, and having us tie for the first place position with an opponent that was used to winning.

As usual, the day before the game, our practices consisted of just dressing out in our helmets and gym clothes, no pads. We would walk through each play to make sure everyone knew their blocking assignments. Everyone, especially the coaches, were subdued, focused. We went through the entire playbook, beginning-to-end, custom-designed to overcome Nyack's defense. We did it over and over again until it was perfect. Our big worry now was our defense. Could it hold back Nyack's aggressive onslaught?

At the end of the practice session we were exhausted from nerves, not physical exertion. Coach Morrow called us together in a circle and we all took a knee at the north goal post, near where the bonfire had been just weeks before. He paced in front of us for a few moments without saying anything, as if trying to formulate the right words. Was he trying to prepare us for what would surely be a loss the next day? Finally, he spoke.

"Boys, you are the finest athletes I've ever had the honor of coaching. This season has been the best of my career. I've always known you could do this, I've never doubted we could get this far. There is something about this team that sets you apart from all the others I've coached and from all the others in the county. I did some research up in the guidance office and what I found up there confirmed my suspicions. Although you are all fine athletes, we've won every game this season not because we're bigger than they are, or stronger than they are. You won because you are *smarter* than your opponents. This is the smartest team I've ever coached. So tomorrow, when you get out on this field I want you to outplay them, and the way to do that is to outsmart them. We're going to win because we're going to outsmart them."

The next day, November 9, 1963 the final day of our final football season, we played Nyack High School.

During the game warm-ups we took the field when Doc Carney and our marching band were blaring out the Notre Dame fight song, custom tailored for our school. After Doc's trumpet solo downbeat, the band went into full swing.

> *"Cheer, cheer for Old Clarkstown High.*
> *You bring the whiskey, I'll bring the rye.*
> *Send those freshmen out for gin*
> *and don't let a sober sophomore in."*

Once the game started I felt sick to my stomach. I blocked a pass downfield. Unable to intercept it because of the angle, I batted it to the ground. I looked over to the stands to see Beth and her father and my mother sitting together, and was surprised to see my father. He was in the space between the staircases that led up to the bleachers, behind the wheelchair with Francis slumped over. It caught me off guard, almost a shock. Whatever fears I had beforehand went away. What a player Francis would have been, the sheer athleticism of his early adolescence maturing along with him. He would have been a superstar. How much of all of this did he understand? My father would stand there next to Francis during the entire game, holding his hand.

When the referee blew the whistle to signal the incomplete pass, I trotted past Nyack's bench and approached the snow fence separating the players from the stands. I stood before my brother and mouthed the words, "Francis, this one is for you."

At the end of the day, we had followed Coach Morrow's simple request. We had outsmarted Nyack and beat them, 13-2.

Afterward, the team lifted our coaches on our shoulders and carried them off the field. I felt a hand on my shoulder and turned to see my father. "Good game, Will." He patted me twice on my shoulder pads and put his arm around me before I was dragged into the crowd separating us. It was the first time I remember my father expressing an emotion toward me. The only time after childhood he ever put his arm around me.

While the team made its way down behind the school to the locker room, the marching band led a contingent of screaming students down Congers Road to New City and back. I wished I could have been there to see it. The only account I have of what happened that day came from Beth and Tom, who told me about it later.

As for my teammates and me, we stood in the alleyway outside the locker room, taking off our pads and hanging them up, many of us, including me, for the very last time. I would never play football again. I wanted them to retire jersey #52. It was a rite of passage that lasted but a moment, but the significance of which has stayed with me a lifetime. In many ways it could be interpreted as my last action as a child, my first action as an adult. As a few of my teammates from that day have personally shared with me, life was pretty much all downhill from that day of victory. In many respects, but not all, I would have to agree with them. Never again would we feel the way we did that day.

For the first time in the history of Clarkstown High School, we were the undefeated football champs. Our class of '64 would also go on to hold the championships for basketball, baseball, tennis and cross country that year. Five championships out of eight county high schools in existence at the time.

Coach Morrow had been correct. The Class of '64 had outsmarted them all.

That night some parents had arranged for us to have a victory party at the Bardonia Clubhouse.

Tom picked me up in the Healey with a girl named Leila from Spring Valley in the front seat. We drove to pick up Beth and she and I scrunched in the back seat. Better to be uncomfortable in the Healey than to travel in the bug.

We all stood around drinking punch from a bowl that had been spiked with grain alcohol. The mood was festive, but I could sense an underlying feeling; Okay, so where do we go from here?

While slow dancing to *The End of the World*, by Skeeter Davis, Beth whispered in my ear, "I have a surprise for you."

"What is it?"

"If I tell you it won't be as surprise." And then she laughed.

Afterward, Tom dropped Beth off first, then me, then he and Leila took off for parts unknown.

The days were rushing past us in a blaze of autumn glory. The next day, Sunday, was one of the last Sundays during that last autumn in our own private, sheltered world. Beth and I squeezed into the Healey with Tom and Leila, his date of the week, and drove South Mountain Road to Conklin's Apple Orchard on Rte. 45. Under the MacIntosh branches at sunset, with my head drowsily reclining against Beth's shoulder, I could smell the first nip of winter frost. But there was something else in the air. The winds of history. Unknown to us, some people had lit a fuse and now we were all just standing around, waiting.

If we had been paying attention, we would have known more about our beloved President and his many enemies. We would have known about the Bay of Pigs' invasion force training on an off-shore oil rig owned by a future president, known about its eventual fiasco and its many implications and consequences. We would have heard of some places in Southeast Asia. But we were having too much fun to pay attention, almost as if a diversion had been set up to keep our attention on frivolous thoughts.

The following week it was almost impossible for our teachers to keep us all calm enough to get through classes. We were still high from the Nyack win. To say there was electricity in the air is a cliché, but we could all feel a certain tingling as if scuffing our feet on carpet on a cold day and touching a metal doorknob.

There was no time for recovery. The momentum was building and there was no stopping us. Up next, the Senior Class Play, another tradition. On Monday after school, my teammates and I went to the final rehearsals for *The Man Who Came to Dinner*. The senior football players were assigned walk-on roles for comic relief.

During class that final rehearsal week I caught Beth staring at me with a smile I had never seen before. When I asked her about it later she just grabbed my bicep and nuzzled her head against my shoulder. "It's nothing. I was just thinking how much I love you."

"Because I played for Clarkstown's very first championship football team or because I have a walk-on role in your play?"

"*Our* play. No, it's because your left sock is on inside-out."

I looked down. It was. A stray white thread stuck out over the edge of my chukka boots. The look she gave me when I looked up from my fashion misstep showed me she was miles ahead of me. Perhaps even light years. I pulled my right boot off and turned my right sock inside-out to match the left. "Happy now?"

She stopped smiling. "That's why. That's why I love you."

But there was something more on her mind.

I had never seen a stage play before, outside of the ones performed on the school stage, never knew about the backstage machinations or the beauty of the language from the wordsmiths. As I watched Beth and Tom from the wings during rehearsals and the weekend's performances, I was amazed at how good they were. Beth played the ditzy nurse, Miss Preen, and Tom played Banjo, the character inspired by Harpo Marx and played by Jimmy Durante in the movie. They played their comedic roles so well, I hardly recognized them. They had disappeared into their roles. They were so good, I was sure that this was the "surprise" Beth had alluded to at the victory party the week before. Charlie and I just had walk-on roles as dumb cops. Vinny played a messenger boy delivering penguins. Jimmy played a local reporter. The cast had been in rehearsals for six weeks and I had always wondered what all the fuss was about. Now I knew. Sharing the stage with Beth, Tom, Kenny, Jimmy, Don, Ralph, Sue, Jeannie, and with other friends I had known for over twelve years was a thrilling experience, especially when the audience broke into laughter.

We received standing ovations each night, and after the Saturday performance we went to a cast party held by Jimmy's parents. As a special treat Jimmy's Dad had invited two actors who lived in New City who had actually been in the audience that final performance night. Robert Strauss who had played Animal in *Stalag 17*, and Harry Belaver, who had played the bartender in *The Old Man and the Sea*, came to offer their well-wishes. Once again, I was flabbergasted about the people who lived in our community, and that one of our dads actually knew them.

To my surprise, Beth wanted to leave the party early, telling Jimmy's parents that she was exhausted from the performance. We stepped outside into the freezing November air, and got into my Volkswagen. The battery turned over, but not without causing me a little concern. It must have been the cold air, I figured. "Don't have to worry about antifreeze," I remember Beth saying to me.

To my further surprise, as we approached South Mountain Road and I turned on my left directional signal to head toward her house, Beth put her hand on my wrist. "Let's go up to 'The Hill' for a few minutes."

It was almost midnight.

CHAPTER FORTY-SIX

**THE HISTORY OF MUSIC
IN NEW CITY, NEW YORK:
PART X**

November 16, 1963
Age 17

What makes a woman decide?

That night, November 16, 1963, after our triumphant curtain call for the final performance of *The Man Who Came to Dinner*, and the cast party that included real movie stars, Beth and I made love for the first time.

What we didn't know that night was that the next five weeks would bring changes to our lives forever, with the impact of a high-speed, head-on collision.

That very same night in another part of the world, at the Winter Gardens Theatre in Bournemouth, England, three American television crews shot 16mm film segments of a concert. The out-of-control audience screamed so loud, the four mop-topped singers could barely be heard. Their footage would air on American television five nights later, on Thursday, November 21. I wasn't paying attention to the dates. Less than eighteen hours after that broadcast in the United States, the world would change, irrevocably, on November 22, 1963.

And what was happening to JFK on that same night of November 21? He was about to leave for his trip to Dallas, after looking at a list of the most recent American casualties from the ever-expanding war in Vietnam that we gave little pause for. Deeply disturbed, he turned to an associate and said, "This is going to change when I get back from Dallas. Vietnam is not worth another American life."

American teenagers were about to downshift into low gear before lurching ahead out of control into a future that would forever change the face of the American landscape. How could we have known that night, alone in the car, just one week earlier, when my life was about to change so profoundly, what would happen to the world in the next few days and weeks?

The fact that we lost our virginity that night was almost like it was pre-ordained; something that *had* to happen that night so the *rest* of the history of the world could commence.

Hire a novelist to write a story about the lives of this young boy and girl so it conforms to the rules and conventions of all the coming-of-age novels. Every sequence and plot-point perfectly in its place, happening when it is supposed to happen, in the precise, required chronology. Real life following tried-and-true narrative structure.

We drove to the top of The Hill and parked in our favorite parking spot on Low Tor. We listened to the sounds of Sunny Ozuna and the Sunglows covering an old Little Willie Johns' song, *Talk to Me*. If we had waited just another few weeks, we would have been a Beatles' couple. But it was in the final hours of the countdown before that British Invasion that took us by storm, by complete surprise, as we rushed headlong toward our destiny with fate. We were about to be blind-sided with a one-two-three punch that would knock us to the canvas. The music was somehow different then, in the waning days of American influence on the world of music. No less catchy or significant or meaningful, it was still a sound-track to our adolescence.

That particular night it was Murray the K on *Ten-Ten WINS*, playing all the songs for all the submarine race-watchers in the audience, of which Beth and I were included. It all happened in the space of three songs. *Popsicles, Icicles* by the Murmaids. *I Wonder What She's Doing Tonight* by Barry and the Tamerlanes; and of course *Talk to Me*, by Sunny and the Sunglows.

If I had to make up a way for it to happen, to design, plan, and control the circumstances, to create a better soundtrack, I couldn't have made it better than what actually happened.

What makes a woman decide when? Where? I'll never be able to figure out that calculus if I outlive Methuselah. What makes a woman decide? Would someone please explain that to me?

After, we lay shivering in each other's arms, watching the window fill up with an early snow. What had we just done? We dressed and pulled ourselves together in silence and I moved to start the car.

"No, wait. Ten more minutes. Turn off the radio."

How could I ever say no to anything she ever requested after what had just happened? She rolled down the window and we watched the snow fall slowly, silently, in giant flakes. The air was cold, but invigorating, and I had just come alive. I breathed in a lungful. The air was so pure. So pure.

She leaned her head back and out the window and caught a snowflake on her nose. Quickly, she nodded her head toward me, pointing to the tiny melting crystal that had so much wanted to make it to the ground with its companions. "Lake Lucille!"

"Yeah, sixth grade."

"You remember?"

"Of course." But the snowflake finished melting and the tiny droplet ran off the end of her nose onto her scarf.

"Do you ever wish a night like this could go on forever?"

I was so moved by her beauty that I couldn't speak. Paradise by the dashboard light, indeed. I couldn't speak. Another few minutes passed. The only sound was the snow falling, which was no sound at all.

"I'll always remember this night, Will. How I gave myself to a boy I loved so much and how happy he made me feel." She sounded mesmerized.

"Everything is perfect. A perfect football season; a perfect play; a perfect boy; a perfect night; perfect music. You were so gentle with me. You made it perfect. I'll always love you for that, Will. I'll always be thankful for how beautiful you made it for me our first time and how unselfish you were with me. I'll always love you for that. Nothing that happens or no one I will ever meet can ever change that. I'll always love you." She said it over and over again from her vantage across the front seat, the snow falling through the windows and landing on her hair, the vapor from her speaking forming a special shape as she said it over and over, "I'll always love you for that. I'll always love you." I could *see* her words in the frozen air.

She rolled up the window and breathed her breath on it, a long, throaty breath, "Huhhhhhhh." It immediately iced over. With her forefinger she wrote, "I love you" in the frozen vapor.

It was all I could do to maintain my composure. I loved her so much I thought my heart would burst. The pain was agonizing.

"You know what we should do? Let's see, twenty-five….no, *thirty*-five years from now we should come back here and do this again. No matter where we are in the world or what we are doing or who we're married to. Let's see, that would be November 16, 1998. We'll come back here and make love in the front seat of a car. Deal?"

"Deal," I said. Then, "You know that's never going to happen. A lot can happen between now and 1998."

"Yes. Yes it will happen. I promise. Even if I'm married to the President of the United States. I'll slip away from the Secret Service and come and make love to you here. I hope it's snowing then."

And then the ten minutes were over. Ten minutes that would live with me forever and make it impossible for me to ever achieve that level of intensity again.

I sat up and tried to start the car, but of course the battery was dead from the radio and the cold.

We pulled ourselves together and stepped outside to survey the scene around us. Three inches of snow had fallen since we first arrived less than two hours ago. Now, my car faced downhill toward New City. A row of three-foot boulders kept it from rolling over a sixty-foot drop. It was almost two o'clock.

Beth got in the driver's seat. I faced New City. With my back to the front hood of my VW Bug, I placed my body between the large rock retaining wall and the front fender, my butt on its hood, as Beth skillfully pushed in the clutch to shift into neutral, while carefully holding the brakes so the car wouldn't roll forward from gravity and crush me against the boulders.

I extended my legs out straight, pushing the car back enough to allow Beth to turn the steering wheel downhill to the right. No words were spoken. I jumped out of the way and she released the brake and the car eased forward until it was again just a few feet from the boulders. Again, I placed myself between the car and another boulder and straightened my knees as she straightened the steering wheel. The wheels inched back. This time, cutting her wheel sharply, again to the right, it was enough for the car to be facing downhill safely, aimed toward the bottom of the hill. She climbed over the gear shift knob and emergency brake handle into the passenger seat as I slid in the driver's seat, shivering uncontrollably out of both cold and fear.

 She wrapped her arms around me once again and kissed me with her warm mouth. My lips were rimmed with snowflakes, but her tongue was slow and probing. How can we ever feel that way again? Why does that ability to feel that sense of wonderment and joy leave us? Isn't there any way to ever get it back?

I put in the clutch and shifted into second gear and gravity eased us out of the parking lot and onto the treacherous, winding Little Tor Road. As the car built momentum, free-falling downhill, I popped the clutch and the engine staggered and choked and bucked to a start. It stopped almost immediately. It took us over twenty minutes to coast down the one mile stretch of switchbacks, crawling in first gear to stay in control as we crept along the sharp, slippery incline. As we approached the straightaway at the bottom of the hill at the blinker light, I popped the clutch and the engine caught and sputtered again. With the second popping of the clutch it started, this time the ignition catching. I turned on my directional signal to turn west onto South Mountain Road.

"No, don't turn." I could see her breath in the darkness.

"Why not? You're late already. You're father's going to kill me."

"It's too dangerous. You don't have snow tires. The car will stall again. You'll never get through. I'll walk it from here."

She was right, of course. Without snow tires the car would have slid off the side of the narrow road, for certain. Or, we would have been stalled and stuck before going another few hundred feet on the up-and-down drive. Had it been merely a downhill slope, that would have been different.

"I'm going with you."

I coasted into a vacant field alongside Little Tor Road and the car came to a stop in the snow near Smith Farms' cornfield.

We stepped out into the blinding snowstorm, oblivious to the danger of what we were doing. With just light jackets and loafers on our feet, we could have died from exposure before reaching her house. We just weren't thinking. Or at least not thinking of the danger. But we had just made love for the first time in our lives and so we were now invincible.

Less than two hundred yards from where we started, we heard the roar of a motor, the ringing of the tire chains, the scraping of the plow blade. We turned to see a Clarkstown Highway

Department truck plowing the road behind us, like a giant robotic monster gaining on us as we fled some ancient landscape. The bank of spotlights on the roof of the cab caught our faces as we waved frantically to flag it down. It was Gary Plunkett, a lifer in the Highway Department, out on his first plow of what would be a long winter's season.

"I thought that was your car in the field, Will. Get in before you freeze to death."

He drove us to Beth's steep, hillside driveway that plummeted over the edge of South Mountain Road. It was a driveway that presented a dangerous maneuver no matter what the weather.

Gary turned to us. "I can drop you off here. Will, I'll be back to pick you up on my way back. I've got to go all the way out to Conklin's on 45. It could take me an hour. Then I'll have to go back to fill up with sand.

"I'll be here," I said, as Beth and I stepped out into the storm for the third time that night.

Gary's truck disappeared into the blinding snow, leaving Beth and me to stand and look at each other as we never had before. She reached for my hand and led me down the hill to her cottage, taking short, choppy steps to keep from sliding, as she had that day of the other snowstorm that first day of skating at Lake Lucille in the sixth grade. Smoke wisps from a dying fire rose from the chimney and amber lights from the rear rooms of the house shone dimly through the front windows.

When we reached the front door she turned and kissed me on the cheek. "Will I see you tomorrow?"

"You'll see me every day for the rest of your life."

"That's what I wanted to hear. Come in and stay warm until Gary gets back."

"No, I'll wait for him on the top of the drive."

"You can't do that, you'll freeze. My father's sleeping or working in the studio. Come in and let me keep you warm."

She opened the door and the warmth from the smoldering fireplace engulfed us both. She took off her jacket and opened mine and slid her arms around my back. I buried my face in her scarf. We never moved the entire hour until the rattle of the chains on Gary's tires could be heard approaching at the top of the drive.

We kissed deeply and I turned as she smiled. "I love you, Beth."

"I know," she smiled. "Go."

Our fingers touched one last time as she shut the door behind me. I skidded up the hill to Gary. It was now almost three a.m.

I was lost in thought, sitting in Gary's cab as his truck blade scraped the surface of the road, trying to keep up with the falling snow. The cab smelled of stale cigarettes and coffee, mixed with anti-freeze. Gary squinted into the darkness, sipping on coffee from his red thermos top.

"Beth seems like a lovely girl."

"Yes. She is."

"You're a lucky young man."

"Yes. Yes I am."

At the cornfield Gary pulled over, dropped me off, and waited for me to try to start my Beetle. The battery was still dead, so he hooked a chain around my bumper and he towed me through the falling snow back toward the Highway Department. I sat in the VW steering and braking and sliding down Little Tor Road.

We slid down the treacherous S-curve of New Hempstead Road, the chains on Gary's tires biting into the ice, my front bumper banging off the hitch on the back of his dump truck, and crawled into the driveway of the Highway Department. Gary towed my car to the back of the lot that was now filled with drivers running back and forth to their cabs under the yard lights. There was an excitement in the air with these men. There were snow-covered roads to plow.

We unhitched the chain from the V.W.

"I gotta fill up with sand and head east on South Mountain. Maybe one of the other guys going down Main can give you a lift the rest of the way home."

"Thanks, Gary. I appreciate it, but I'll just lock up my car and get it tomorrow. I can run through the Garden. It's not that far."

"Your funeral. Stay warm. And hey, kid, take care of that girl-friend of yours."

"I will."

I got back in my car to lock up and as I leaned across the seat to make sure the passenger side door was locked, Beth's words written in frozen vapor on the window were backlit from the spot-light on the roof of the garage. The words had been preserved by the cold and would remain there through the night and until the next day when I came back with Tom and Jimmy to tow the car to the Esso station to replace the battery.

Now, as I ran across the field past the water cress sluice-way and up to the wooden bridge, the snow began to let up a little and the lights from town reflected off the dome of sky, casting an eerie, yet beautiful light and shadows across the Garden. Each brick column supporting the brick latticework bore a perfect snow cone from the last two-hour's fall. The same with the sundial in the center. The blade would cast no silhouette tonight, smothered in the fluffy whiteness. I was breathless from the events earlier in the evening, and exhilarated by the beauty of what I beheld before me. It was all so perfect as I ran across the open lawn beyond the sundial. It was indeed, a perfect world.

But then I noticed something that did not register at first, something I would not even give any thought to until much later. The footsteps of an earlier visitor to the Dutch Garden had crossed perpendicular to my path, heading south, sometime recently. Just another few minutes and the footsteps would have been com-pletely covered. But now, they were still there, quickly disappear-ing, but still bearing evidence to an earlier passer who had cut through the Dutch Garden, perhaps just moments before.

I stepped across the other person's path and continued run-ning, first over the brick wall, then cutting through the back of Dr.

Feldman's yard toward Capral Lane, too excited to even contemplate whose footsteps they might be and how recently they must have been made. Only later would I reflect on it. Why were there footsteps there and who had made them on a night such as this? Another boy from town, after saying goodnight to his girlfriend?

When I got home the house was silent. The sounds muffled by the snow outside seemed to mute the noises inside the house, as well. I took the stairs one at a time, stepping on the edges so as not to wake Francis or my mother. My father was still out walking, I assumed. I finally eased between my freezing sheets, my skin goose-fleshed in the cold and from what had happened just an hour or two before. My body tingled from what remained on me of her touch, her essence.

And then a strange thing happened. I started to cry, or sob really. Out of joy? Out of happiness? Out of a beginning of a new stage in my life and of leaving an old stage behind? Out of fear? I felt as if I were being torn apart, I was so happy. I was filled with exhilaration, and my body shook as I hugged the cold pillow to my chest. Is there any other feeling in the world like it, having just made love for the very first time to the woman you wanted to spend the rest of your life with? As happy as I had been that Halloween two years earlier?

Maybe I cried with the realization that nothing that had ever happened to me before would ever make me as happy as I was right then. Maybe I cried with the realization that nothing that ever would happen to me after would ever make me as happy. Now, as soon as I fell asleep, it would be over. Someday I would lose her and she would be gone forever. I cried because I loved her. I cried because what we had done was the most beautiful act that had ever occurred on the face of the earth, in the history of all time, in the entirety of the universe. I cried because my brother, Francis, would never experience such joy with a woman. And I would never be able to share my happiness with him; make him understand what it was like. I cried, because deep down inside me, something told me I could never keep her. That somehow, however beautiful this night had been, I had crossed a turning point, a Rubicon, and it somehow marked the beginning of the end. (Isn't that always the case?)

My joy and our shared secret would keep me through the coming week. Every glance we exchanged in school, every touch of our hands, every smile she made, now had a new, hidden meaning. Could anyone else tell? How could the entire school not see it? I remember other girls saying, "I can always tell whether or not a girl is a virgin by the way she walks." Was it all nonsense bragging, maybe even an ounce of jealousy, or was there an element of truth to it?

And then, the following Friday afternoon, just six days later on November 22, 1963, the whole world lurched, thrown off the tracks, and we jerked and stumbled, trying to regain our balance, grasping at any support, trying to absorb what had happened. The whole world changed once again, forever. Who knows what would have happened that next weekend, with the gathered momentum, the anticipation of being alone again for hours at a time driving us both to distraction? Who knows what would have happened that next weekend, instead of spending Friday night, Saturday night, Sunday night, at Mass in St. Augustine's, praying for a dead president, his family, our nation? Who knows what would have happened if we had not been forced to postpone our plans to return to The Hill on the end of Little Tor Road, that overlooked my little town, that late November in 1963?

Lying in my bed that night, between the cold sheets and the quilt my grandmother had hand sewn for me, crying with a happiness I had never before experienced, I did not know what was about to happen in less than one week.

As I lay in bed, fighting off sleep, re-living the hours that had just passed as the early snow had begun to fall, I sniffled and turned on the Silvertone radio next to my bed. Diffuse yellow light filled a small corner of the room as the tubes warmed up. And then, as

I drifted off to sleep, the sound faded slowly in from Symphony Sid's Show, thirty miles to the south, with another chapter of the History of Music in New City, New York. It was the voices of the Mello-Kings singing the last verse of their only hit song, written by the great Billy Myles, reflecting the voice that was crying out in my own heart with an ache and promise I would keep forever.

Tonight, Tonight,
May it never reach an end.
I'll miss you so,
'Til you're in my arms again,
With all of my heart,
I declare with all my might,
I'll love you forever,
As I love you, Tonight.

CHAPTER FORTY-SEVEN

NEW CITY

Friday
November 22, 1963
Age 17

That following Friday I was sitting in cafeteria, still in a daze from the past Saturday night. It was the study hall period after lunch. Beth came running in through the double doors to the school cafeteria. She had been up in the Guidance Counselor's office finalizing plans for college. Now, she was sobbing. I couldn't imagine what they had told her upstairs.

"Someone shot President Kennedy! I just heard it on the radio in the Guidance Office!"

Within seconds, everyone in the cafeteria knew, and as the bell rang we marched upstairs to Economics class, but not before stopping at the library where a television set was playing the news cut-in. Walter Cronkite was trying to compose himself.

It was all confirmed, the President was dead. As we walked to Economics, the halls filled with students in a state of shock. Before they dismissed us early to go home, the rest of the school day went by in a blur of disbelief.

Earlier in the week, Beth and I had made plans to go back to The Hill on Low Tor on that Friday night. But that was not to happen. Instead, we went to Mass after dinner that night and stayed through midnight. I drove Beth up Little Tor Road afterwards. At the intersection on South Mountain Road I hesitated, wondering what to do about The Hill.

"Let's just go home. I feel so terrible."

"I do too."

"It's not just the assassination. There's something else."

"What do you mean?"

"I don't know. I just have this sense of foreboding. Uneasiness. I can't explain it. Like something really terrible is going to happen to the world because of this. Like after what happened this afternoon, we can never be happy again. Who would want our president dead?"

"It doesn't have anything to do with last week, did it? You're not regretting your decision, are you?"

"Oh, no, don't ever think that. That was beautiful. That's the only thing keeping me going right now, wondering when we can be together again. I can't wait. No, it's something more. I feel like we've lost something and can never get it back. We, as a country, lost. Something. Maybe I'm just in shock."

At the top of her drive she turned to me and gave me a quick peck on the cheek.

"You don't have to walk me to the door. It's too cold. You know I love you, right? I just didn't want to go to The Hill tonight. I just can't think straight. You know I love you, don't you?"

"Of course."

I left her at the top of her drive. She got out and shuffled down the icy hill.

I drove slowly west to Rte. 45, taking the long way home.

That Saturday, everyone was still walking around in a state of shock. My parents were stuck to the television screen. It was the first time I had seen my father watch television since Ernie Kovaks had died. He just stopped watching television that day. But now, he couldn't move away from the screen.

I called Beth that afternoon, but she was still feeling low and didn't want to go out that night. My parents and I sat with Francis all that afternoon, next to him on the bed watching his small black and white screen. The four of us all crowded into what had once been the dining room and we watched in silence.

The next morning, Sunday, my mother was back at Mass presided over by Father Carrick, when my father and brother and I witnessed, on live television, the slaying of Lee Harvey Oswald by a man we would later know as Jack Ruby.

I watched in shock as Oswald flinched in the Dallas garage.

My father mumbled something and I had to ask him to repeat it.

"Mob hit."

"What?"

"Kill the patsy killer. Keep him quiet. Oldest trick in the book."

"What do you mean?"

"How stupid do they think we are?"

He got up and left the room as chaos ensued in the basement of the Dallas Police Station.

CHAPTER FORTY-EIGHT

NEW CITY

Late November – Early December
12th Grade, Age 17

In the aftermath of the JFK assassination, we lurched into a frightening, unknown future. Our plans for going back to The Hill on Low Tor the following week were thwarted. However, it could be safely said that we made up for lost time in a very short period in the ensuing weeks. I had no idea what pleasure and happiness life had to offer.

School simply couldn't return to normal the next week, a three-day week because of Thanksgiving Break. We were all in shock, but facing a four-day holiday weekend. By the time Wednesday rolled around Beth was becoming more affectionate and looking at me like she had the night on Low Tor.

As we walked to the parking lot after school, she turned to me.

"What do you want to do this weekend?"

"I guess we can hang out with everyone at that party Bobby's having. His parents are going to be out of town for Thanksgiving weekend."

"I mean after that?"

"What did you have in mind?"

She held my hand to her cheek in the frigid air and looked into my eyes.

Starting after Thanksgiving Dinner on Thursday afternoon, Bobby's party became a three-day drunk for most who showed up. Beth and Tom and I watched in surprise at the high school debauchery. Nothing like an empty house to bring out the worst in your classmates. As Tom engaged Leila in some deep political discussion surrounded by friends who were binge drinking expensive rare wines found in the wine cellar until they vomited and eventually passed out, Beth and I wandered the enormous home and found a quiet spare bedroom in the attic and snuggled together against the cold.

Our lovemaking sessions experienced on The Hill on Low Tor, which I was hoping to become a weekly adventure, would only last a few more weeks at that location. But that was a good thing.

As we approached Christmas Vacation the weather grew even colder and we had more snow. We had to decide whether to take Beth's Jeepster up to Low Tor with the bigger back seat, but with a convertible top that didn't hold the heat from the weak heater, or, take my bug up there with better heating but smaller accommodations. With Beth's snow tires casting the deciding vote, we opted for the cold back seat of the Jeepster. In an environment of freezing cold, surrounded by fogged windows and the sound of snow chains, we passed through our period of initial discovery, teaching each other how to touch; offer comfort, love.

That Christmas Vacation, our world, changing ever more rapidly, was now moving at unprecedented speeds, as if someone had set up an itinerary, with changes coming exponentially. With nothing to do but party and relax for two weeks around the holidays, Tom made plans to move into the boathouse and make it his own bachelor's pad. As Tom moved in, Beth and I practically moved in with him.

The first thing to make the trip down was the Steinway, which required four moving men to carry it out of the second floor of Dove Cottage. A special dolly was used to maneuver it down the hill through the snowy woods behind the mansion to the boathouse, where it would remain for the next thirty-six years.

While they struggled to keep it upright on the soft bed of the snow-covered woods' floor, Tom ran alongside shouting cautions. Beth followed them, snapping black and white pictures with her new Nikon F-1, an early Christmas present from her father that year, replacing her earlier Nikon. She pre-set the camera's controls and handed the camera over to Tony, the mover's son and a classmate of ours, and told him to fire off a few shots of the three of us.

Beth would eventually become a master with this camera, and these pictures of the men pushing the piano through the woods on a dolly with big balloon tires would eventually hang on the walls in the boathouse for years in the makeshift recording studio Tom set up.

In those photos taken by Beth and Tony, which I would not see for more than thirty-seven years, Tom and I can be seen in the background, Tom waving his arms around like a madman, cautioning the movers, while I stand by, laughing. In others, Tom and I pose as musclemen, our elbows bent at ninety degree angles. There we are, in another shot, posing, as Tony took a photo of all three of us all leaning against the Steinway on the deck of the boathouse, while the movers tried to figure out a way to muscle and maneuver it in through the doorway.

Eventually, they made it through by removing the center post in the French door frame and dipping it over the threshold vertically.

The movers and Tom then returned to the main house and carried down his bed and dressers and tables and chairs and two sofas that faced one another perpendicular to the fireplace.

Beth and I helped carry clothes and all Tom's other things the movers hadn't. When it was all over Tom was ready to set up housekeeping in the second floor of the boathouse, with a deck overlooking the now dried-up site of the millpond.

On our last trips down, we carried the reel-to-reel tape deck, audio mixer, sound blankets, microphones and microphone stands, for Tom's boathouse recording studio.

While Tom walked the workmen back to the moving van they had come in, Beth looked around the great room where a fire was now blazing in the fireplace. She looked from one sofa to the next, facing one another, and smiled, a smile with an ambiguous yet at the same time obvious meaning.

"What?" I said.

"Are you thinking what I'm thinking?"

"Depends. What are you thinking?"

"I'm thinking that it doesn't matter anymore that the heater in my Jeepster doesn't work."

She stepped back, spread her arms toward the sofa. "Tah-Dahhhhh!!!!!"

I laughed and she tackled me and we collapsed on one of the sofas. We were so in love that the happiest moments of our lives continued to eclipse one another on a daily basis. It was like we were banking the experiences for later withdrawal.

We heard Tom's steps on the deck stairs and we jumped apart, each taking a separate sofa.

"Completely innocent face," Beth hissed to me, wiping her palm in front of her face for the instant transition.

"You guys better not be doing anything indecent in there," Tom called from outside.

He stepped through the French doors. "Jesus, what took so long? I turn my back for five seconds...The least you could do was wait until I get Sandrine up here."

"Sandrine?"

"Who's Sandrine?"

"Another new one?"

"I can't help myself."

We carried firewood from the garage woodshed and stacked enough on the deck under a tarp to last us through the winter. Tom brought thirty-pound quilts down from the main house.

Finally Sandrine arrived, dressed as we expected she might be, in full beatnik attire, signaling the transition from that earlier bohemian era with influences that might have led us to label her a hippie, had that term been known to us at that time.

She was carrying a cello case over her shoulder like a baseball bat, and before we knew it she was one of us, laughing and drinking wine from the wine cellar and before long, as the fire crackled gently, she began sawing away at the cello while Tom, seated at the newly arrived Steinway, ripped through a spontaneous, *O, Come Emmanuelle*, in honor of Christmas. Had they practiced this before? They must have.

Beth and I closed our eyes to listen and maybe somehow to preserve another one of the most beautiful moments in all time, in the history of the universe. We drifted off in an alcoholic haze, under quilts a hundred years old, as outside the snowflakes floated, darted through the tree branches in search of us, looking for our upturned noses, our extended tongues.

The heat the four of us generated sleeping on our respective sofas was enough to keep us going without the fireplace and it wasn't until almost midnight, more than twelve hours from when we started, that we awoke from our snuggling, hibernation slumber. I drove Beth home and her hair was still sleepy and I straightened it before she got out of the car.

"That was a lovely day," I said, "Sandrine seems nice."

"Maybe Tom will keep this one."

"A perfect match."

"Like us," she said.

"Like us."

"Are you crying?"

I shook my head. "No. Yes."

"Why?"

"I don't want this to ever end."

"It doesn't have to ever end, Will."

I looked into her eyes as she said it again.

"It doesn't have to ever end."

Later that night at home, my mother had been waiting up for me. Her milk and cookies seemed like an incongruous anachronism. As usual, my father was out on his walk to oblivion; not rain, nor snow, nor sleet, nor hail, nor dark of night, stayed this courier from his appointed rounds.

"Are you okay, Will?"

"Yes. Sure."

"I don't see much of you these days."

"You know. School."

"I mean during this vacation."

"Well, Tom and Beth. We're just doing vacation stuff."

She sat down, putting her hand over mine. "Will, I want you to promise me something."

"Okay."

"Promise me you won't wind up like your father."

"I promise, Mom."

"I mean, if something should happen between you and Tom or you and Beth, you have to learn to move on. You have to pick up the pieces and move on. You can't let it destroy you like your father has been destroyed by the events in his life. Between the War and Francis. Well. . ." She couldn't finish.

"Nothing's going to happen Mom. Tom and Beth and I will be best friends until the day we die."

"You're all going off to college next year. Maybe you won't see each other as much. That happens you know. Sometimes friends lose touch. They grow in different directions. Drift apart.

It's very common."

It was something I tried never to think about. "It will work out. You'll see."

"I hope you're right."

The senior Christmas Ball was held in the school gym the Saturday night after school got out for the break. Beth and I had planned to double-date with Tom and Sandrine, but at the last minute Beth wanted us to go in my bug. After, I found out why.

That night, Beth and Tom stole the show. In the middle of Doc Carney's Sophisticated Swingsters show, Tom called Beth onto the stage and he accompanied her on piano as she sang a haunting, agonizingly slow version of *Have Yourself a Merry Little Christmas*. She was wearing a scarlet cocktail gown, tight at the waist and then flaring at the knees. She looked at me, through me, the entire song. It tore my heart out to hear her sing it.

Instead of having me take her home after, she surprised me by suggesting we drive by Lake Lucille. When we got there she reached into the back seat and pulled her ice skates from the bag she had brought with her. In a moment she had changed from her dancing shoes into her skates.

"What are you doing?"

"I'm going mountain climbing, smart guy."

"In your ball gown?"

"I could take it off."

She had me turn on the headlights and the radio as she hobbled over to the lakeside, and as a light snowfall began, she began skating in lazy circles to the music of Lenny Welch singing, *Since I Fell For You*. She disappeared into the darkness, out of view of my headlight beams. I stepped forward to look for her and she skated into view, a smile on her face, ice skating in a formal gown, wrapped in her pea-coat.

"Turn the headlights off."

I did as I was told. As my eyes adjusted to the darkness, Beth continued her swirling skating until she beckoned to me. I shovel-footed across the ice to join her waltz-like skating in a trembling embrace.

The remaining days of 1963, it felt like we were poised on the edge of a diving board, about to lose our balance. I had filled out the application for the University of Florida two months earlier, as Beth had suggested. Now I was still sitting and waiting.

CHAPTER FORTY-NINE

THE HISTORY OF MUSIC
IN NEW CITY, NEW YORK:
PART XI

Late December, 1963 – Early January, 1964
Age 17

There are insufficient words in the language to explain what happened; what the Beatles did to our culture. I can say that because many have tried. Looking back from a perspective of fifty-odd years, it's difficult to describe for anyone who did not witness it. It's probably impossible for them to comprehend.

How it changed the world of music and the world of American culture has already been described in ten thousand books and documentaries and narrative films.

On a specific level, it changed everything. Maybe it was because we were seniors in high school and it was our personal dose of the excitement of what the world had to offer. If so, the timing was impeccable. Maybe it was because we had gone through the excruciating heartbreak of having our beloved president assassinated and this was somehow compensation for that.

Perhaps it was a way of softening us up with a gift from the galaxy before the realities of Vietnam came home to roost. Or in my case, perhaps it was timed to coincide with the loss of my virginity and the beginning of my understanding of what the world was all about, and how deep my love was for Beth.

The day after Christmas, 1963, *I Wanna Hold Your Hand* was released in the United States.

Beth had gone to Manhattan with her father that day in late December. It was uncharacteristic of her to miss our days together that vacation, but in a moment of foreshadowing in the novel of my life, he wanted to show her his new gallery that he hoped someday that she would run. While in midtown, they passed a record store where thousands of kids were trying to get in to buy a record, any record by this new group from England that most of us had never heard of before.

That night, when she returned from Manhattan, she called me to tell me of the wild scene, similar to what we had witnessed with adults outside the Peppermint Lounge not two years earlier. When she told me the name of the group, I thought she had mistaken them for someone else.

"You mean The Crickets, Buddy Holly's old group?" They were still recording, weren't they?

"No," she said. "It's definitely 'The Beatles'."

It was definitely The Beatles.

CHAPTER FIFTY

Senior year, PART II

Winter-Spring, 1964
Age 17

The British Invasion arrived and held us all prisoners. There was no escape. We were simply overwhelmed and defenseless to resist the onslaught.

That winter we went to every basketball game and supported our team as we headed for another County championship. Every Tuesday and Friday night was a big deal. After the game on Fridays, we would go to Perunna's or The Wayne House and with our newly acquired fake I.D.'s that said we were 18, nurse a beer or two while some of our classmates got trashed, and then we would go back to Tom's and sit by the fireplace, Beth and I on one sofa, Tom and his Lucky-Girl-of-the-Week on the other sofa, all to the sounds of The Beatles.

By late winter we were all talking about the impending end to our imprisonment at CCHS. The truth of the matter is, unlike all my friends, I didn't want to leave school, leave town, go off to college. I wanted everything to remain the same, just keep going to high school, forever. Little did we know that in future days some of us would wish we were back here. Imagine that, continue going to high school forever.

Our final spring at Clarkstown was a whirlwind of anticipation, final exams, saying good-byes. Some of the guys were trying to start bands and become the next Beatles.

Track season started in March and we were off and running. First, in the warmth of the gymnasium and later when the March cold turned to spring rains we would be out running in the cinder track in our ponchos and gold sweat suits, the frigid air burning our lungs, seeing our breath with every stride.

Tom ran the mile, and I, the 180-yard low hurdles. Together, with Jimmy and Vinny, the four of us ran the 880 relay. Charlie and Rocky were setting county records with the shotput and discus. On cold spring afternoons, maybe thirty people would watch our track meets, and front row, center, was Beth.

On March 15, I received my acceptance letter from University of Florida. Beth's acceptance had been a fait accompli for years. The letter was waiting for me on the kitchen table when I got home that afternoon after track practice. My mother handed me the letter. "Dad brought this home today."

"What does it say?"

"It's for you to open, not us."

I opened it with shaking hands.

"Well?"

I wriggled my finger under the flap, unfolded the letter. The UF letterhead was revealed to me. I read down. "I've been accepted."

"Congratulations, Will." She stepped forward to hug me.

"Are you and Dad going to be able to afford this?"

"Even with the out-of-state tuition, there's enough in your grandfather's fund. It's still a lot cheaper than New York colleges. We'll figure out a way to do it. Your job is to go to college. Eventually get a good job. Build a future, a life for yourself."

"You don't think I should go to Rockland, stick around here to help out?"

She stopped, adamant. "Rockland Community College? No. Definitely not. Florida is a much better opportunity."

I handed the letter to Beth later that night. She opened it nervously and read it. She threw her arms around me. "Will, this means we can be together, forever. No interruptions. You know that don't you?"

"Yes."

"That's what you want, isn't it?"

"More than anything."

That spring raced by all too quickly. Time seemed to accelerate like the winding up of some massive engine that would drive us into the future.

As we approached final exams, there was a mixture of excitement in the air, along with a feeling of apprehension. Something was winding down while everything else was accelerating. It was dizzying. Friends we had known for a dozen years were making other plans without us.

A feeling of *"the end of something,"* as Hemingway once put it, hung over us. Like the change that had occurred at the beginning of seventh grade. There was a sadness involved in all of it. At least for me. I had been going to school here for thirteen years and now it was all over. Safely ensconced in the protection of our community, we would soon be facing the real world. The days raced by gaining in momentum.

Some of us took it in stride. Others, like myself, saw it as a time of dread.

We followed in the footsteps of our predecessors, with a Senior Class Picnic at Platzl Brauhaus up in Ladentown on Call Hollow Road.

Baccalaureate services were held at the new Episcopal Church on Strawtown Road, the old one down the street from my house on Main Street having finally closed its doors.

After graduation rehearsals in the auditorium, as the orchestra packed up and we checked out our caps and gowns, Beth invited me backstage. We walked to a dark corner and she slid out a canvas flat from the scene storage rack. She turned it around, the back facing us. She pointed to the corner of the frame.

"I forgot to show you this."

There on the canvas, in Magic Marker, was a heart with an arrow through it with the inscription, *"Beth and Will, on our own stage, together-forever."*

"I did this when a bunch of us were painting the scenery for the class play. You were at football practice."

I held her to me. "Thank you," was all I could get out. While I had been on the practice field that preceding fall, Beth had been thinking of me.

Our class was the first class too big to graduate in the school auditorium, as the ten senior classes before us had. After hastily installing stadium lights that had been a gift from our senior class the first weeks in June, we now would march out onto the field, where only months before we had won unprecedented victory and untold glory. We would march forward to the goal line to get our diplomas.

Like that last football game against Nyack, as we marched across the field to our seats to Doc Carney's orchestra playing *Pomp & Circumstance*, I scanned the bleachers for recognizable faces. Off to the side, was my mother standing next to my father. He had a look of reminiscence on his face, a look of "Don't let life do to you what it did to me." He again stood behind Francis in his wheelchair, my brother with a look of fear and happiness on his face, not really even sure where he was or what was happening. And there, in my cap and gown, ready to receive my high school diploma, I burst into tears again. Not so much for myself, but once again for Francis, the little boy, now approaching the age of twenty, who would never be anything more than that little boy of twelve who had carried me to safety on that fateful day; who would never share what I had experienced, could never share whatever life was about to hand me. Instead, he had been handed down a life sentence, through no fault of his own.

As my classmates looked on, I tried to maintain my composure. They were all getting emotional, so they hardly noticed the tears of another classmate.

After, once again, there was a huge party at the Bardonia Club to celebrate graduation. Beth and I made an appearance, anxious to leave for our own celebration. What we weren't even thinking about was that this was probably going to be the last time we would see a lot of our classmates for perhaps years. We had taken their friendship for granted for so long.

We slipped out, left without saying goodbye.

CHAPTER FIFTY-ONE

**THE HISTORY OF MUSIC
IN NEW CITY, NEW YORK:
PART XII**

Summer, 1964
Age 17, 18

For a split-second after graduation the world stopped and we reevaluated what was going on. *Now what?* After that was a quick acceleration into the unknown.

> *Well, it's been building up inside of me for*
> *oh, I don't know how long.*
> *I don't know why*
> *But I keep thinking*
> *Something's bound to go wrong.*
> *But she looks in my eyes*
> *And makes me realize*
> *And she says "Don't worry baby*
> *Don't worry baby*
>
> DON'T WORRY, BABY
> by Brian Wilson

Brian Wilson's song, released just before our graduation from high school, became my theme song that summer. It kept building up inside of me, this idea that Beth and I would go away to school, she would find a new boyfriend, and I would be left behind. And yet every time I broached the subject, she acted as if she didn't know what I was talking about.

"Don't worry baby
Everything will turn out alright."

I'm sorry, Brian, but when you're wrong, you're wrong. And you were wrong.

CHAPTER FIFTY-TWO

FINAL SUMMER IN NEW CITY

1964
Age 17, 18

Our final summer together in New City started with two weeks of partying together before Tom left for his annual European tour. The partying was fun but it was exhausting. Staying up late and drinking and then getting up early to lifeguard at New City Park was wearing me down.

Beth spent her days preparing and planning and packing to go to the University of Florida for our three day mandatory Mid-Summer Freshmen Orientation Session, prior to our actually attending there when the trimester would begin in late August.

She was shipping down her easels and darkroom equipment and clothes and everything else, so she could travel light. She had hoped to go to school straight through without stopping for summer breaks and then start working in an art gallery in Manhattan after graduation. She would be representing her father's art work.

Her Willys was in the mechanic's for a week while they determined whether or not it was terminal. It was fourteen years old and hadn't been working right since the spring. It was decided I would pick her up on at her place and drive down to New City Park Lake, where she would read and sketch and paint while Tom and I worked.

The previous summer after our High School Junior year, between school getting out in late June and July 4th weekend, there wasn't much of a daytime crowd at the lake. Tom and I had spent the early mornings painting picnic tables and the club-house and cleaning up the winter debris and raking leaves on the grounds.

That summer after graduation we painted the wooden row-boat and the twenty-foot fake lighthouse on the south end. We painted the south end picnic tables and replaced the rope floats. We even towed the raft to the side of the wall and painted it all down to the water line, being careful not to drip paint into the lake or rock the raft until the paint dried. Within a week everything was covered in a dark, forest green enamel and sparkling white. A new aluminum diving board replaced the old rotting wooden one, and we were ready to go for the season.

Once again, we strung out speaker wires from the radio in the clubhouse to the lifeguard stand. Then, when the swimming crowds drifted in, Tom would take the deep end in the morning and the beach end in the afternoons, and I would do the opposite. When there was no one there, I would sit in the guard tower and pull out my copy of *From Here to Eternity*, or *Raise High the Roofbeam, Carpenters*, and when there were no kids in the water I would hold it on my lap and with my sunglasses on, no one could tell I wasn't watching the water.

When Tom had gone on his European tour after our junior year, Jimmy filled in for him, and the same was planned for this summer after our senior year. The only difference was that this summer Jimmy subbed for Tom first, and we got Vinny to sub for me while I was in Gainesville for a few days of Freshmen Orientation.

In one sense that last summer in New City was uneventful.

In another sense it marked a rite of passage of our last summer in town together. And for that, the dread that I had felt earlier continued to get worse.

The night before Tom left to go on his summer performance tour I picked up Beth in my VW and we sat on the dam at New City Park Lake and listened to the sound of the water rushing over the top of the spillway.

Tom came roaring up in his Austin Healey and skidded to a stop on the gravel. His big smile could be seen as he walked past us in the last moments of twilight and he hopped up and sat next to us on the dam.

"Well, I guess I'll be back in a month. Same thing every summer. Moscow, Berlin, Vienna, Copenhagen, Paris, London, Heidelberg, Rome. What a drag."

Beth threw a wet towel at him. "When you get to Vienna, pick up a couple of cans of sausage for us, okay?"

"They don't sell it there."

"You know I don't ever remember getting one postcard from you. What's it been, what, six summers now?"

"Yeah, they must have been lost in the mail," I said.

"Maybe next summer you both can travel with me if I go?"

"Wow. That would be great! Can you imagine, Will? Traveling all over Europe for six weeks?"

I tried to show my excitement. "That would be great. Fantastic. Pretty expensive."

"Not for you guys. My grandfather would pick up the tab. I'll tell him you're my trusted assistants. Roadies. He'll get a laugh out of that. That's if I tour next summer. Not sure yet."

Beth and I looked at one another, confused. Before we could ask why, he interrupted.

"Oh, before I forget, I have a going away present for you guys."

"Wait a minute, you're the one who's going away."

"That's right, so I have a going away present for you."

He pulled his Austin-Healey keys out of his pocket and said, "Here, take these. You can share it while I'm on tour. Beth you can drive it until your car gets fixed and then Will can have it the rest of the time. Keep it under 120 though, will you? It has a little shimmy in the front end if you go any faster than that."

I sat in disbelief. His hot little roadster was the coolest car on the planet, and he was letting us drive it. Before we could comment further, Tom shucked out of his jeans down to his bathing suit. "Time for a swim." He dove in.

Beth and I joined him out on the raft as the summer moon came up. The only sound was the occasional car passing by on Collyer Avenue. As we stretched and looked up at the night sky, we all must have been thinking the same thing.

Tom broke the silence. "What's going to happen next year guys? Are we going to be typical high school friends and just drift apart after spending every day of our lives together for the past eight years?"

"No way, I said. That's what air mail stamps and long distance phone calls are for. Before you know it, it'll be Christmas break and we'll be home and we can do the usual stuff. Then, summer will be here again and we'll be back here life-guarding, business as usual." Did I realize how hollow my words sounded? Did they?

There was a long pause and then Tom said, "I won't be coming back here next summer. I think I'm going to go to school every summer term, see if I can finish up in three years."

Beth looked over at me. "That's kind of what I've decided, too."

I was shocked. "Well, what's good for you guys is good for me. We'll all finish in three years and after we graduate we'll all be back together again." Even I could hear the lack of reality in what I was saying.

Beth looked from Tom to me. "I thought you two guys were going to law school after."

I looked at Tom. "Yeah, but that can wait until that following fall."

Again there was a silence as the realization came over us that this moment in history might be the last moonlit summer night we would ever spend on the raft together.

Tom sat up, his back to us, facing the clubhouse. We couldn't see his face.

"You guys have been like a brother and sister to me. I don't know what I would have done without you both. I never had a real family. You're my family."

Beth sat up and wrapped her arms around him and rested her head against his back. "Will and I love you, Tom. We're never going to stop being friends. We'll always be here for you. You're gonna be, what, three hundred miles from here and we're a thousand miles south. Even if we're fifteen hundred miles away from you in Florida we'll be here for you."

There was a roar on the gravel in the driveway and an Austin Mini-Cooper pulled in and a tall, thin blond with her hair cut short stepped out of the car.

"That would be Louise."

"Louise?"

"First violin, Nyack Conservatory." He called to her in the darkness. "We're out here. Come on out."

Louise looked to us on the raft. "You didn't tell me to bring a bathing suit."

In the light from the moon she stripped down to nothing and dove in the water and swam to the raft.

We yelled out hellos as she approached the raft, and then without the slightest bit of self-consciousness Louise hoisted herself up the ladder and stretched out on the raft next to us.

"Louise, say hello to my two best friends in the whole wide world, Beth and Will."

We exchanged small talk, me trying not to stare at her nakedness in the moonlight. She and Beth started laughing at some Tom foible as I stared across the water to the lighthouse.

After five minutes, Tom stood. "We're gonna take off. Louise will drive me home.

"Beth, I left the Healey keys on your towel. Take good care of it. Use only Castrol-Girling products for the hydraulics on the brakes and clutch. No petroleum-based lubricants or it will eat through the slave-cylinders. If you need to get it serviced, take it over to Cecil at Foreign Cars of Rockland in West Nyack. He knows what to do.

"Well, guys, I guess this is it."

Beth and I stood. "We'll swim in with you."

Tom turned to Beth.

"No, you guys stay here. I love you Beth." They hugged.

Then he surprised me.

"I love you, Will. You're my brother." We hugged awkwardly.

And with that they jumped in the water and swam off in darkness toward the clubhouse. We sat and watched them towel off and get dressed in the dim light. Then, just as he was climbing into the tiny front seat of the Mini-Cooper, he turned and waved.

"Say hello to those Gators for me."

And then Tom was gone.

Beth was silent for a moment and started to cry.

"He's the best friend we'll both ever have in our entire lives, you know that don't you?"

"Besides you."

"And besides you. But you know what I mean, don't you?"

I did.

"We must always treasure that friendship and protect it."

"I know."

"He really doesn't have anyone else. His grandparents are getting so old. When they're gone it's just Frau K. and Max."

We lay in the moonlight and watched the stars pass by and thought about the future.

Finally, Beth turned to me and put her palm on my face and

looked into my eyes.

"You know how much I love you, don't you?"

"Yes."

"And you feel the same way about me?"

"Of course."

"You know that will never change, don't you? Never, no matter what happens in Gainesville or when we get older, right?"

"Of course." I wanted it so much to be true.

"Our life adventure begins tomorrow morning."

"I know."

"Will you be there for me, Will? Will you help me? I'm going to need your support."

"I want to be with you forever, if you'll let me."

"I want that."

"Train leaves early tomorrow. Are you packed?"

"Yeah."

"Come on, let's go."

"Wait."

"What?"

Beth took off her bathing suit. Naked in the moonlight on New City Park Lake raft. "You, too."

I shucked out of my bathing suit. "Feels natural."

We held hands and jumped in the water, our bathing suits held in our opposite hands.

"Feels great."

"Much better. Louise had the right idea."

"Yeah, but what would you do if Tom were here?"

"I'm not self-conscious. I pose in the nude for my father's paintings all the time. What about Louise? You're the one who would be hiding the goods." She laughed out loud.

Skinny-dipping would become routine for the two of us from then on.

We swam to shore and toweled off.

"I can't believe he's letting us use his precious car."

"You're the one with the broken car, not me."

"When we get back from Gainesville my car will be fixed, and then the Healey is yours until he gets back."

"I guess."

We both had driven Tom's car a million times before, so Beth hopped in like a pro. She turned on the ignition and waited for the familiar click, click, click of the electric fuel pump behind the seat and pressed the starter button on the dashboard.

"Wow! I feel like some hot chick."

"You are some hot chick!"

"Then aren't you the lucky guy? I'll see you at six."

She leaned over and kissed me and I watched her pull off into the night. She was a perfect fit for the coolest car on the planet.

As I drove away from New City Park Lake without Beth beside me in my bug, having just said farewell to Tom, what I didn't realize was, for all intents and purposes, our lives together as The Three Musketeers in New City were over. It was too enormous a concept to realize, let alone dwell upon.

When I got home my mother was waiting up.

"Tomorrow's the big day."

"Yeah."

"My little boy is all grown up. It happened so fast."

Suddenly, I didn't want to leave for Gainesville in the morning. I wanted to stay in New City and commute to Rockland Community College over in Viola in my beat up bug every day. I wanted to stay with my brother and be a "townie." That would be plenty good enough for a guy like me.

"Are you sure you and Dad can afford this?"

"We've been saving."

It was only later I would find out what this really meant.

"Go say goodbye to your brother. Your father will say goodbye in the morning. He knows when you're leaving."

I slid open the door to my brother's room and he was snoring softly. Without turning on the overhead light I pulled the chair up to the edge of the bed and covered his hand in mine. I was only going for five days; three days of orientation with a day of train travel each way, but it felt like I was betraying him. I sat there in the darkness for a few moments before I left and slid the door closed. What would happen to Francis at the end of the summer when I left to go to Gainesville for an entire trimester? For three or four or more years?

Upstairs, my small bag was packed for the five-day trip. I looked at the inexpensive, gaudy plaid suitcase my mother had bought for me and packed, and knew that I was about to pass an important milestone in my life. But I didn't want to pass any milestones.

Although it was just for three days of orientation, I was leaving New City. I couldn't begin to grasp what that meant.

The next morning at six a.m. , Beth's father dropped her off at our front porch where my mother and father and I stood waiting. She had two suitcases and I helped her get them out of her father's trunk.

"Hello, Marion. Hello, Francis." He said it like he had known them all his life.

My parents waved and smiled.

"Our kids are all grown up."

"Indeed they are."

"You take care of Beth now, Will. Those fraternity boys down there can be pretty sly. And say hello to my friend Jerry. He runs the photography department. One of the resident campus geniuses."

He kissed Beth on the forehead and drove off.

My mother turned to Beth. "You look very pretty this morning, Beth."

"Thank you."

Before she could say anything else, an old Red and Tan Line bus spouting smelly diesel fumes pulled up to the Third Street intersection and opened the door for us.

"See you in five days, Mom."

She reached out to hug me and slid four twenty dollar bills with cookie jar wrinkles into my hand. "Have fun. Learn a lot. It's going to be your new address for the next seven years.

And then we were on the bus heading south on Main Street toward Penn Station in Manhattan. When we arrived, Beth led me through the cavernous building and down into the tunnels like she had taken the trip herself a thousand times. She was to be my tour guide in this new world.

By noon we were passing through the Jersey flats south of Newark, headed for Waldo, Florida. Our adult life was beginning and I didn't really want it to.

CHAPTER FIFTY-THREE

FRESHMEN ORIENTATION
UNIVERSITY OF FLORIDA
GAINESVILLE, FLORIDA

July, 1964
Age 17

Almost twenty-four hours later the train pulled into the little station at Waldo and as we stepped down onto the platform we were engulfed in a blanket of heat and humidity I had never experienced before. It took our breaths away.

Four taxicabs sat in the parking lot awaiting students. An air-conditioned ride to Gainesville, seven bucks apiece.

"We'll take it," I said, and carried our luggage to the open trunk.

The ride in through the North Florida piney woods and scrub palmetto was unlike any terrain I had ever seen. This was a new world for me.

Gainesville, Florida, was once known as "Hogtown." In the piney rolling hills of north central Florida, it was in the middle of an agricultural belt that went back hundreds of years.

Over the centuries it was settled by various indigenous peoples, including Alachua cultural inhabitants. When DeSoto passed through in 1539 he brought the two standard killers, European diseases and Christianity. Later the Miccosukees and Seminoles lived there under the leadership of Micanopy.

The town was named after General Gaines, who distinguished himself in the Second Seminole War, if you consider slaughtering Native Americans an honorable pursuit worthy of posthumous recognition.

The taxi took us to the faculty friends of Beth's father. Jerry and his wife lived in a tree-shaded house on the northeast of town. We put down our luggage and showered, and they drove us to the UF campus to register for orientation. The campus was huge, with brick, collegiate gothic architecture, set on a bluff. It was empty for the summer, populated almost exclusively by hordes of incoming freshmen going through orientation in staggered starts. All around campus, pine trees and live oaks covered with Spanish moss shaded the common areas. Even though I was uneasy, I couldn't deny the beauty of the place. I was excited because Beth was excited.

We checked into our dorms, Beth in Rawlings Hall, named for a famous author as yet unknown to me. I was to be in Hume Hall. The dorms in those days were not air-conditioned and the air inside was stifling, some might even say oppressive. I put a window fan on my wish list. Beth considered spending the night at Jerry's house. It was air-conditioned.

They marched us around campus to show us the highlights; from the Auditorium to the Bell Tower, to the live alligator cage to the stadium to the gymnasium. We signed up for all the basic classes together. Everyone took the foundation classes for most of the freshmen and sophomore years; American Institutions, Logical Thinking, Freshman Composition, Physical Science, College Algebra. Since The University of Florida was originally established as a land grant school, freshmen boys were required to take Reserved Officers Training Corps, or "ROTC." I would be in an

Army uniform marching in the heat every Thursday afternoon. They handed us our schedules in the gymnasium and from where we were seated, told us turn to the left and right and look at the students next to us. "One in three will drop out their freshman year," was what they said. Beth and I determined that would not be us.

On the first evening, during designated free time, Jerry and his wife drove us back to their home for a dinner party in our honor. Or, should I say in Beth's honor? Somehow, a half-dozen faculty members present either knew Beth's father or wished they knew him. In our four years there we would visit Jerry's home often, and later that summer after we drove our cars south, we would park them there during the freshman year because as freshmen we were not allowed to have cars in Gainesville.

The rest of the time during the three days of orientation was filled with yet more walking tours and informal fraternity parties. I was not interested in joining a fraternity, but Beth seemed interested in joining a sorority. She said she was not interested, but was obviously flattered by all the attention. What would she ultimately do? At the end of three days, all in all, it seemed like campus life looked like it might be exciting, as much as I didn't want to admit it. But it wasn't New City. It was a new world with new rules.

We returned to New York on the train after three days of Freshmen Orientation, leaving out of Waldo and arriving at Penn Station late in the afternoon. We took the Red & Tan home, and when we stepped down from the bus at Third and Main, even though it had only been five days, New City seemed different. After years under our stewardship, had our town turned its back on us for our desertion, or just marched forward to spite our indifferent abandonment?

Francis seemed to sense I had been gone, marked by his enthusiasm upon my return. In the days to come, my mother busied herself with preparing all my clothes, complete with marking all of everything with indelible laundry ink, like I was going to summer camp.

As usual, my father had little to say, except to ask me what I planned to major in. I thought he knew. When I said pre-law he only said "that's a long seven years."

Later that summer, Beth and I made it a point to skinny dip in every swimming hole and swimming pool we could access that summer: Davies' in the middle of the night, along with New City Park, Lake Lucille, Greenberg's, and even Lake DeForest. We skinny-dipped in the Dellwood pool, and Bobby's pool. Everywhere we could think of. It was like we were making the pools our own, somehow, marking them off a list like in a John Cheever story.

CHAPTER FIFTY-FOUR

NEW CITY

Late Summer, 1964
Age 18

New City Park Lake was beginning to take on a new feel as time passed that summer. It started to transition from a place where we had spent so many happy times to a place where we 'used to go' to have fun. I would eventually spend a lot more time there in the coming years, but without the old crowd, which was dwindling away with every passing day, it would never seem the same.

When we got back from Freshman Orientation, instead of Jimmy staying and Vinny leaving, Jimmy moved on to get ready for a short summer vacation in Lake George before heading off to Villanova to get into pre-med.

Tom's European tour was extended and we only had a week together before Beth and I headed out for University of Florida and Tom, to Dartmouth. Those nights were filled with bar-hopping at all of our old haunts and some new ones, as well. The Wayne House in Stony Point, Brophy's in Grassy Pointe, Scotty's in West Nyack, Perunna's in Spring Valley, any place that would not ask for I.D.s of anyone who was still seventeen but looked eighteen. Beth and Tom had turned eighteen earlier in the summer. I had to wait until August 15.

Before long, everyone was heading out for their own freshmen year all over the country and Beth and I would take our final swim out to the raft before heading off to Gainesville. Those school bells were breaking up that old gang of mine.

That last night, I put the top down on the Healey where it was parked in my barn where my grandfather had once stabled his mail route horses. I drove it to Tom's and picked him up. Climbing out, I handed over the keys. "Thanks. I got to drive my dream car for the summer." He threw a few duffle bags and a cardboard box in the back seat. I didn't think much of it. He was leaving for Dartmouth early the next morning, and if truth be told, I really didn't know if I would ever see him again.

We drove to New City Park Lake. Before long Beth pulled up in her Jeepster.

The three of us sat on the wall in silence. Beth spoke to Tom. "No hot date tonight?"

"Wanted to spend the last night with my best friends."

Beth looked around. "When are they arriving?"

"Very funny."

"We're glad."

"We have something special, don't we?"

"Yes. Will and I have talked about it."

"I don't want us to change." Tom looked at us both.

Beth looked at me. I finally broke my silence, and once again with false bravado, exclaimed, "We're not going to change. At least I'm not going to change."

"Good."

More silence followed.

"What's out there?" Tom asked no one in particular, staring off toward the Pape's garage and the lighthouse on the south shore.

"The future," Beth said. "A great future for us all."

Tom reached in his backpack and pulled out three tiny champagne bottles. "Almost forgot. Let's give a toast to our futures."

We unscrewed the caps from the bottles with a fizz, touched one another's bottles, and drank.

Beth gagged and spit hers over the dam. "Uggghh. This is awful. Where did you get this?"

"I gave some to my doctor to analyze and when the lab report came back it said my camel had diabetes."

Beth and I laughed at the old joke and we all chugged down the two tiny gulps and then we all threw the small bottles over the dam onto the rocks below in the Demarest Kill.

"Sorry. Best I could do on short notice." Tom looked down as if trying to figure out what to say, then looked both of us in the eye. "Thank you for being my family."

Beth and I didn't say a word.

"When you come home for Christmas I'll have some real champagne chilling by the fireplace."

"Along with another new girlfriend."

"One can only hope."

"With any luck."

There was another awkward silence.

"Well, I'm off. I decided to drive to Dartmouth tonight. I'm leaving straight from here. You guys have a long drive tomorrow and I've got to figure out how I'm going to get my Steinway into the back seat of the Healey. Thanks for taking care of my car all summer."

Tom handed me a second set of keys. "These are for the Healey and the boathouse. Just in case."

He reached out his left hand to Beth and his right to mine and squeezed them. "Until we meet again."

He gave us both a brief hug and hopped into his car without opening the door.

He pulled out onto Hall Avenue, hooked a left on Collyer and roared past us on the dam, off toward the Palisades Parkway and into the future, to the sound of a throaty rumble of his Healey muffler.

Beth and I were silent. I'm not sure, but I think she started to cry after a moment. She turned her back to me, slipped out of her clothes and hopped into the water on her way to the raft without showing her face. I watched her in silence and then I joined her on the raft. She lay on her stomach, her head face down resting on her wrists.

On another night, not too many years away, we would spend our final night on this very same raft, but on this night, it somehow seemed like it would be the last night.

"Big day tomorrow."

"Our adventure begins, Will. I'm so excited I can hardly contain myself."

"It's a little bit daunting."

"But think of what it means for us. A new life, a new beginning."

"We're leaving a lot behind."

"I know."

"I hope my brother will get along. I'm going to miss him. And my mother, too."

"I know Will, how hard it must be for you to leave Francis. And I don't want to give you advice, but you have to do what is best for your future. Your mother has made the choice to stay with him and keep him at home and not send him to a nursing home somewhere."

"She would never do that."

"I know she wouldn't. "

"I would never do that to Francis."

"But you have to go and live your life, Will."

"You're beginning to sound like her."

"Because it's the right thing to do. I know it's very hard for you, but you have to move on. We have to move on."

"I know."

"The Willys is all packed. What about you?"

"I just have to stuff a few duffel bags in the bug after you drop me off."

That night on the way home from the lake, instead of stopping at my house, Beth surprised me. "Let's drive through town."

I knew better than to ask. "Okay."

"I know we're going to be gone for just a few months, but I want to take a look at some things."

"Okay."

We cruised slowly in the Jeepster and when we reached the Courthouse we turned into the parking lot.

"Let's walk."

"Okay."

We walked to the tea house in the Dutch Garden and inside to the front of the hearth. Beth looked at all the intricate brickwork, the figures of Popeye and The Dutch Cleanser girl worn smooth by time. She stepped out onto the steps that faced the garden. The site of our first kiss. She took my hand and led me to the steps where we had sat shivering that Halloween night almost three years earlier. She kissed me.

"They built this tea house just for us, you know."

"But . . ."

"Even though it was completed a dozen years before we were born, they built it just for us. It's ours. It will always be ours."

I looked up to the slate tile roof and all the countless hours of work that had been put into its construction.

"It's ours and someday, when we get out of school we're going to come back here and get married on these same steps and then we're going to move in here and take it over. We'll fix up all the gardens and they will be our front yard. And we'll have twenty babies and we'll all work together all day long making the flower beds beautiful. And your mother can have her Girl Scout meetings here again."

My mother had given up her Girl Scout leadership after "Francis' Day." I looked out and imagined all that Beth was saying. I could *see* it all, as if all her plans had come through on the same day and the Garden was filled with hundreds of smiling people.

"Yes."

"Follow me."

I followed her down the path past the sundial and the bed of dormant heliotrope to the old pergola and gazebo. By 1964 vandals had already started knocking things down in the Dutch Garden. At the pergola leading to the gazebo she held me. "We've spent so much time here I wanted to come back one more time before we left town and make sure you keep your promise."

"Which one?"

"The one to meet thirty-five years from last November 16. That would be November 16, 1998. Only thirty four more years to go. If we round it off and make it in the year 2000, that would make it thirty-six years. Just a few from the original promise. I meant it when I said it. I meant it last fall, and I mean it now. We'll do it. Deal?"

She looked at me, waiting for my response, her eyes bugged out in her goofy way.

"Deal," I said. "I promise."

"No matter what?"

"Yes."

"What if you're the President?"

I thought of my chances. "Not likely."

"What if I'm the President?"

"Much more likely."

We stood in the gazebo and gazed west across the Kill.

"Is the key to the boathouse on Tom's key ring?"

I pulled the key ring from my pocket and twirled them around. "Yes."

"He did say he was leaving for Dartmouth right away, didn't he?"

She took my hand and led me through the woods to Tom's

boathouse. There was no need for a flashlight. Our feet knew the way by heart memory.

In the darkness of the boathouse, on a sofa that had become our second home, I pulled her to me and could smell the smell of New City Park Lake on her still-wet hair as we made love in the empty, silent boathouse.

Two hours later she dropped me off and headed home to prepare for our first trip to Gainesville as official students, this time in our two cars.

I knew the year 2000 would be here before we knew it and I would keep my promise. What I didn't realize at the time was the gut-wrenching impact it would have, leaving my friends and my New City behind.

CHAPTER FIFTY-FIVE

FRESHMAN FALL
GAINESVILLE, FLORIDA

Late Summer, 1964
Age 18

That night I said goodbye to Francis for what I thought would turn out to be the better part of seven years, assuming I managed to get through law school. The last eight years I had spent every moment I had been home, in his room with him; doing homework, watching television, reading to him when my father was not at home. And now, I would not see him for months on end. The next time would be during Christmas break four months away. How would he change?

I tried to be strong for him, but I could not. I had lived "Francis' Day" every day for the last eight years, trying desperately to put it out of my mind. I had held hundreds of one-sided conversations with him where he just lay and looked at me, a bemused look on his face. If only I could tell what was going on in his mind. But that last night was different. That night I made a solemn vow to him and to myself that I would succeed in school if only so I would be financially better able to take care of him as an adult. I knew someday my parents would pass on and I would be responsible for him and I was more than willing to accept that responsibility with no regrets. "This is what God has given us," my mother always used to tell me. But in order to do that I was going to have to be successful. So even though I had never spent much time thinking along those lines, except as they pertained to Beth, I made a commitment to take care of Francis to the best of my ability, until death us do part.

The next morning at six a.m. I kissed Francis goodbye in his wheelchair on the front porch and then my mother. She and I had had our long talk in the days leading up to my departure and there was little more to say. As for my father, he stood behind the wheelchair and blinked and said, "Do good work, son. You'll make us proud, I know."

It was the first time I had heard him make a positive remark in years, and I felt a sudden urge to hug him goodbye. He stiffened at my touch and repeated his words. "Do good work. Use good judgment."

Despite my mother's earlier references, it never occurred to me at any time who was paying for all of this beyond my father's meager postal worker's salary and the small inheritance from my grandparents. I never questioned it. Like so many others my age, I just took it all for granted.

As Beth pulled up in the Jeepster, her back seat stacked to the roof with her suitcases, Father Carrick stepped down the front steps of St. Augustine's for a final wave. He didn't walk across the street, not wanting to intrude on a family moment. Earlier in the week, Beth and I had said our goodbyes to him in what became an emotional scene for him during his final prayers for us in his office. He had said some brief comments about "God will be there to protect his precious children every day that you are to be gone. He will be there as you grow in your ways." I had never seen his composure falter before that day.

Beth left the motor running and ran up and hugged Francis and my parents in turn. Francis smiled in his own way. "I'll take good care of your New City boy," she told my parents and then we were off.

That first day we drove in tandem as far as Richmond, stopping every two hours to talk and hug and kiss our excitement away. Finally, after dinner, we checked into a motel and instead of sleeping the night away, we made love until past midnight.

The next day we drove the remaining six hundred miles down U.S. 301, stopping at some souvenir stands and *South of the Border Motel* to buy postcards for everyone on our mailing list.

As midnight approached our second day on the road we drove through Waldo and passed by the little railroad station where we had disembarked from the train less than a month before for Freshmen Orientation. We left U.S. 301 and cut over to S.R. 24 for the fourteen mile trip into Gainesville.

CHAPTER FIFTY-SIX

THE HISTORY OF MUSIC
IN GAINESVILLE, FLORIDA:
PART I

University of Florida
Freshman Fall Trimester, 1964
Age 18

> *My dearest, my darling, tomorrow is near,*
> *The sun will bring showers of sadness I fear.*
> *Your lips won't be smiling your eyes will not shine,*
> *For I know tomorrow that your love won't be mine.*

It's Almost Tomorrow
Gene Adkinson, Wade Buff
Performed by
THE DREAM WEAVERS

In 1954 a group of students had a nightly radio show on the school's radio station, WRUF. To sign-off-the-air at night, they composed a song, called themselves The Dream Weavers, and recorded *It's Almost Tomorrow*. When a Jacksonville record producer heard the tune, he invited them over to record it in his studio and the 45 r.p.m. record began to be played all over the state.

Decca Records picked up the license, re-recorded the song, where it became a Billboard Hit for 21 weeks, climbing as high as #7 on the charts. What happened to The Dream Weavers that night on their trip to Jacksonville? What was the conversation in the car; the level of excitement? Did they know that Florida back roads' trip would change their lives forever? What happened in the recording booth? On the way home to Gainesville after the recording session? The next day on campus?

That fall of our Freshmen year, 1964, was a difficult time for me and a time of enormous maturing for Beth. I was in culture shock on a massive scale, trying to fit in. I was in pain. She thrived.

From our little school with a graduating class of 265, we entered a world of 18,000 students far more sophisticated than I ever would have imagined. With a sprawling campus we had only just started to explore during orientation week, we discovered a whole new world of adventure.

Beth and I lived in dormitories, as required by all freshmen, separated nights, except for the darkened corners where we snuck off to hold one another before a strictly enforced dorm curfew. Our cars were hidden off-campus in Jerry's driveway. We had to take a city bus to the east of town to get to them. Most of our weekdays were spent walking the broad campus, taking it all in.

Some of our classes had more than three hundred students; brilliant, driven students, and of course, the party animals. One of the hardest things to deal with was the rich, smug fraternity boys filled with entitlement; the guys all over Beth. I was petrified. Beth's girlfriends invited her to a sorority rush party where she was surrounded by a dozen, slick, rich southern fraternity boys, all on a tight, highly competitive deadline to get laid by as many incoming freshman women as possible in the first month of the semester. They hit on her hard and at first Beth was confused by their forwardness, then flattered, then amused, then annoyed. I was petrified. She would come home from the parties angry and frustrated by their advances and tell me stories of their drunken passes and lame pick-up lines. She tried to laugh it off.

I was a Liberal Arts major enroute to a pre-law degree, Beth was Commercial Art, who was headed toward a Fine Arts degree. As an incoming freshmen, we all took the same required classes and thanks to Beth's strategizing during freshmen orientation earlier in the summer, we took most of our foundation classes together. As a result, as I struggled through the first trimester, Beth carried me.

Walking around campus, surrounded by Beth's new friends, women more beautiful than I had ever seen, I knew I would never be able to fit in here. I was ready to go home. It was all too much for me. Francis needed me, my mother needed me, I needed Tom's strength and friendship, and Beth was maturing into a brilliant, talented woman with her photography and sketches, covering everything from fashion design to landscapes and architecture. I was floundering. Without her pushing me every night to study, I would have flunked out that first trimester. But the more we got into the trimester, the more her time became scarce. She was in the darkroom for hours on end, developing and printing, organizing and attending fashion design and art shows, and worst of all, she was being rushed by every sorority on campus. They recognized immediately her beauty, her intelligence, her poise, her presence, her talent.

I did my best to hide my fears but they were becoming over-powering. It was just all too new, all too overwhelming, all too self-fulfilling. The bottom line is that she fit in perfectly and I was just some small town country bumpkin. By leaving New City, I felt I was being ripped out of the early 20th Century and being plopped down in some alien world of the future. The irony for me was that these students from the south were the sophisticated ones and I, the New Yorker, was the rube. How can that be possible, I wondered? How could I have been so misinformed? *So ethnocentric?* (a word I learned in American Institutions that first trimester).

The one break in routine during the week came every Thursday afternoon during the required R.O.T.C. march. We called it "ROT-SEE." Since Florida Freshman and sophomores were required to take either Army or Air Force R.O.T.C., I had chosen the Army. Bad mistake. As we marched endlessly up and down the field, our M-1 rifles over our shoulders in the insufferable heat, Beth stood on the sidelines, proud of me in her own way.

On one Thursday afternoon, some smart-ass came up to her and started flirting very obviously and I almost broke ranks and ran to her side. My rage was becoming uncontrollable as my jealousy grew and my self-confidence dwindled with every passing day.

The Gator Football games on autumn Saturdays were a thing to behold. It was the first time I witnessed a football game in person that I wasn't playing in. All the guys in the stands wore blazers and ties, the girls, semi-formal dresses. We sat in a stadium with a population larger than our home town. It was all so new to us.

The cultural events seemed to come several times a week, providing us with plenty of chances not to go to the library and study together. One night, enroute to the library, as we walked past the Bell Tower and the old Auditorium, we were drawn in to see *Mark Twain Tonight*, with an unknown actor by the name of Hal Holbrook.

On another Saturday night, an older couple Beth knew from the faculty picked us up for a surprise night out. "Beth, Will, you have got to see this to believe it."

They drove us north of town and then west into the woodsy wilderness. They turned off the paved road and followed a dirt road for a few miles through palmetto scrub and cow pastures.

Beth turned to me and raised her eyebrows. "Are you guys kidnapping us?"

"You'll thank us on the way home."

We came to a one-story cinderblock building with neon beer lights in the windows surrounded by cars parked haphazardly under the live oaks.

"What is this?"

"This is Cunningham's Bar, part of the 'Chitlin Circuit,' and you've never seen anything like it." They were right and they were wrong. Cunningham's was a mostly all-black bar with a band playing the best rhythm and blues music we had ever heard. A few years later, a scene in the movie *Animal House* could have been based on what we saw that night. The similarities to the movie were uncanny, a direct reflection of what we actually experienced that night. When we walked in, everyone tried to ignore us, but it definitely put a damper on the patrons' excitement. A skinny black woman, Hester, (named after Hawthorne's Hester Prynne, I wondered?) wearing a tight, white, dress, was wailing out the lead solos and we might as well have been listening to Irma Thomas or Betty Wright or Ronnie Bennett (soon to become) Spector. When she sang a slow version of *Stand by Me*, it reinforced my suspicion that we weren't living in New City anymore. And why wasn't Hester world famous with a voice like that?

This was part of what the world outside of New City had to offer. Later, when I saw *Animal House*, I came to realize this was just another one of the common rites of passage for white kids, the same as if an earlier generation was whisked off to The Cotton Club for a night of Duke Ellington.

The football season ended and the basketball season started and our first trimester away from home was drawing to a close. We began to reflect on what it all meant.

The basketball games weren't as formal as the football games, but it was sure different than watching our Rams play, and that somehow summed up how I felt. I kept trying to feel for the Gators the way I had for the Rams. I kept waiting for those old feelings, but they just weren't happening. We didn't really know any of the players, so it was all so impersonal. I couldn't find a connection. No authentic reason to cheer the home team.

As our first trimester neared its completion, our evenings were filled with late night cramming, but without the Dexedrine assistance so many of our classmates seemed to depend on. Christmas Break was upon us and the anticipation was driving me crazy. We decided to drive home in one car, the VW, because the Willys probably wouldn't make it.

We drove up U.S. 301 in near silence in my bug, trying to absorb all the stimuli we had experienced in the last four months. On the radio we listened to Petula Clark singing *Downtown*, over and over, along with new cuts from the new album, *Beatles '65*.

We were not the same two kids who had driven this same road just four months earlier. It was all so hard to take, disorienting, confusing, exciting, and disappointing at the same time. We vowed to go home to New City every summer, no matter what, Beth re-thinking her earlier plan to go straight through school in three years. We were also disappointed to find out that Tom could only be home in New City part of the time that Christmas because of his performance bookings in Manhattan.

CHAPTER FIFTY-SEVEN

NEW CITY

Christmas Break, 1964
Age 18

That first Christmas break we came to realize how much we had grown; how much our perspective had changed; the bleakness of my parents' lives, the hopelessness of Francis' existence. Life wasn't fair. I looked at my house, not through the distance of four months' absence, but in some sense from some indefinable time in the future. It made me feel as if my life had jumped off a time-line and skipped ahead, leaving behind all I felt dear.

We reunited with old friends. Jimmy was at Villanova, Charlie at Gettysburg, Vinnie at Memphis State, Ken at Clarkson, and a lot of the other guys at R.C.C. Most of Beth's friends were attending SUNY colleges around the state. Although happy to be home, it was tempered with a sadness that we all knew it was ending in just another two weeks and Beth and I would be off again. All the old friends were now leading different lives.

Beth helped my mother and me set up the Christmas tree as she had in years past. We opened the dining room sliding doors so Francis could turn his head and watch us work and so we could pretend he was all a part of what we were doing. When we turned on the tree lights, he looked up at us and smiled without lifting his chin off his chest, the lights reflecting pinpoints of colored sparkles. How much did he understand?

Bobby's parents, not having learned their lesson from Thanksgiving '63, allowed him to throw a huge New Year's Eve party. Another evening of debauchery conducted by my friends since kindergarten, and some underclassmen who got wind of it.

Except now we were listening to *BEATLES '65*.

On the second of January, 1965, the scene on my front porch was as it had been that past August: the start of a long series of good-byes.

CHAPTER FIFTY-EIGHT

GAINESVILLE

Winter, 1965
Age 18

On the return drive to Gainesville after the winter break, we vowed to return home to New City in May. Sure, Gainesville had its strong points, but nothing could beat New City in the summertime, right?

As we neared Gainesville, Beth turned to face me and reached for my hand. I pulled off into the parking lot of the railroad station in Waldo. There was something on her mind.

"Will, I'm worried about you. I want you to try harder this trimester."

"I know, I know. I will. It's all just so overwhelming."

"It is for me, too, but it almost seems as if you're resisting it. Fighting it."

"Fighting what?"

"I don't even know what I mean. 'Change' maybe? Like you're hanging on to the past, afraid to let it go."

"I'll try harder."

"Try harder to hang on or try harder to let go and change?"

"To change."

"I'm worried about you, Will. Maybe because I'm not originally from New City like you are, but I feel like you're not willing to let go of your old hometown."

She was correct in her perceptions. I was actively resisting the change. As if I could somehow hang on to the past by not accepting what I was supposed to be learning in class.

It was the start of the new trimester with new challenges and new distractions. The more Beth stayed out at her activities at night, the more I stayed home drinking beer smuggled into the dorm. We would meet outside her dorm fifteen minutes before curfew to say goodnight and seeing me drunk did not please her. At ten o'clock, she was locked in for the night.

Having spent almost every waking hour of my life with Beth for the past eight and a half years, it was almost as if we were being weaned off of one another, spending hours apart with her studies and new friends and me in the library trying to keep up with the academic demands. The women there were distractingly beautiful, not that I ever would have considered even talking to one of them. But Beth talked to all the cute guys. It was just natural for her.

Upon our return to Gainesville that first winter, Beth and several of her classmates formed a co-op and rented store-front studio space on Main Street for an Art Gallery. It looked like a smaller version of her father's on South Mountain Road, with a retail capability. She started spending a lot of time there, leaving me lots of time to study.

As one of the University of Florida's rites of passage approached, we planned to spend the Valentine's weekend of 1965 in the infield at the Daytona 500. Again, my world and my worldview were expanding. What better Valentine's gift than to get trashed with thousands of drunk rednecks? At the last minute, Beth decided to stay in the art studio and work on an art project.

"Want me to stay and help?"

She laughed. "You'll only get in the way. Go have fun with your dorm buddies. The sound of engines racing doesn't appeal to me, not to mention the fuel smell."

By early March, it was time for another rite of passage. We drove over to New Orleans during Mardi Gras, an eight-hour drive. We could almost have driven home to New City in just double that amount of time but chose not to. Were we losing our apron strings?

By then it was almost the middle week of April, Spring Break, and we spent three nights in Daytona Beach, sharing a room with fifteen other freshmen friends at the Thunderbird Motel on the beach. We slept, or should I say "passed out" in shifts. We had officially become Florida college students, along with over 100,000 other students who filled the beach that Spring Break. Were these rites of passage getting in the way of schoolwork? Absolutely.

That spring we also discovered the magical Ichetucknee River, an hour's drive northwest of Gainesville, and despite what could be said for Lake Lucille and High Tor and The Dells, we discovered there was another world out there. If you've never tubed the Ichetucknee River, you can't call yourself a true Gator. I think it's some sort of unofficial prerequisite to graduating. From a giant springhead near Fort White, the Ichetucknee flows southwest at one mile an hour. The water is a constant 72 degrees, too cold for alligators, but warm enough to park your butt in an inner tube and float leisurely down the river through a prehistoric cypress jungle.

Despite all the distractions, I managed to bring up my G.P.A. to a respectable level. I was beginning to recognize and accept my "special talent," my ability to remember facts and dates, events and other minutiae and retain it all, holding on and never letting go. Once I started applying myself, my retention skills surprised even myself. I was beginning to make it work to my advantage. I had even begun to allow myself to assimilate into the campus scene. Beth, although she looked almost the same, the person she had *become* was almost unrecognizable to me.

CHAPTER FIFTY-NINE

**NO DIRECTION HOME
NEW CITY**

Summer, 1965
Ages 18, 19

We kept our vow to go home to New City that summer of 1965, but it was not without reservations. Should we have stayed in summer school?

By the time the second trimester was over in early May, Beth and I were more than ready to drive our two run-down cars up Route 301 back home to New City once again. When we had made that vow to return, and when we kept that vow, we had little inkling how our minds would change as we all turned nineteen. I had already secured my post on the lifeguard stand at New City Park Lake and Beth's father had helped her arrange a job in the Fashion District in Manhattan. That should have told me something right there. I was returning to the past. She was off to the future.

When we came home, we saw our little home town in an entirely different light. What I had suspected over the dark, dreary

Christmas was now coming to fruition in the bright light of late spring. Our world had changed. Our world-view and perspective had changed, our address had changed, and now everything looked old and drab and empty and lonely. What had once been accepted as the norm, now seemed out of place. Part of an old world. Or was it just us? From our childhood friends we heard dozens of wild college stories about their freshman days; new friends, new adventures, new special places. There was another universe out there. Life in New City had gone on without regard to three little friends who had grown up there.

Just as he had told us that night on the raft a year before, Tom announced upon his arrival home the first night for a brief visit, that he was just home on a break before heading back to summer classes at Dartmouth. The annual European Tour was being put on hiatus for a few summers. He planned to finish his degree in three years and then go on tour again before heading back to start Law School. Did we want to drive up with him to see the campus? Of course we said yes. We made plans to visit him in a few weeks.

Every Monday morning, Beth drove her Jeepster and parked it in my driveway and took the bus at Third Street into Manhattan, where she would stay at her father's apartment with another woman from the garment district. I would spend the next few hours with Francis before walking to New City Park Lake and starting my lifeguard days. I walked up to the Lake, a walk I had already taken hundreds of times and would eventually make thousands of times. On Friday evenings I would be at the Third Street corner to greet Beth when she arrived by bus from Manhattan for the weekend.

Although my days life guarding were relatively easy and stress-free, starting at ten in the morning and ending at dinnertime, Beth's job in the city was filled with stress and book-ended by two long commutes by bus on Monday mornings and Friday evenings. Most weekend evenings when she was home in New City she tired early. She was becoming a sophisticated woman of the world, exposed to some of the most brilliant minds in the design and art world, her own talents appreciated and in demand. Did she tell her colleagues she was dating a summer lifeguard? I was just a mediocre, liberal arts major with a dream of going to law school that he could probably not finance, while working a high school-level summer job. What had once been a routine for us as high schoolers had been replaced by a newer routine in our lives as we became college sophomores. Even though we repressed those feelings, I knew we both felt them. Our new home town was Gainesville.

Despite that, we settled into a temporary, summer routine. Weekend nights, we would make the rounds of Perunna's, The Wayne House, Brophy's, and Long Pond Inn on Greenwood Lake. We headed over to Villa Lafayette in Spring Valley to see Ray Murray and the Travelers. One night when we got there, it was The Belmonts performing, without Dion. Another night, we even went to White Birches, Spring Valley's answer to Gaines-ville's Cunningham's, to see Bobby Blue Bland. For some reason, having gone to the clubs in Gainesville, including Cunningham's, these local haunts had lost their *caché*. We would spend hours in them, but the excitement was over. The friends were gone. Even Brophy's, dancing to *I Can't Help Myself,* wasn't the same as dancing had been in the high school years with our fake I.D.s. *How you gonna keep them down on the farm, after they've seen . . . Gainesville?* We went to those places expecting the old crowd to be there, but when there even was a crowd, it was comprised of much younger, unsophisticated kids. Had we been that way just one year before? Our friends had moved on. Why hadn't we? Had we been away for more than just one year and hadn't realized it yet, somehow looking from down the road even farther?

Without Tom and Beth at my side on a daily basis, the life-guard job took on a whole new feeling of boredom, something I had outgrown, a kid's job. I sleepwalked through my days and remained aloof to the underclassmen who came to swim and hang out, and to the other lifeguard who had been hired to replace Tom after his decision about summer school became reality. I spent the time reading *The Magus* when kids were not in the water.

According to my mother, my father's routine had not varied in the nine months since I had gone. He walked his postman's job during the daytime and walked his penance at night. With me, aside from a few perfunctory questions when I first returned home, our conversations had been non-existent.

My mother was worried. "I don't know what's going to happen to him," was all she would say when I asked her about it. "He won't go see Father Carrick."

"What about a doctor?"

"No."

But Beth and I went to see Father Carrick. We reminisced about the old days and he asked a thousand questions about life down south and about how we were adjusting to adult, independent life. He tip-toed around the question, "Were we thinking of getting married someday?" I saw no other future for myself, and I assumed she felt that way, as well.

In the first week of July, Tom came home again to work a gig in Manhattan and we made plans to go to Dartmouth with him when he returned for the long Fourth of July Weekend. We were also celebrating Beth's nineteenth birthday. As usual, the three of us fit perfectly into the front seat of the Healey, Beth sitting side-saddle on the drive train and transmission hump.

The drive to Dartmouth took over six hours. We took the Thruway up to Glens Falls and then took Route 4 across the rolling hills and state parks to White River Junction and finally Route 10 into Hanover. In a way, it was like old times, the three of us together, the rumble of the Healey droning in our ears, reminding us of earlier trips, but somehow we were all different. Now, we all had secrets unbeknownst to the others. At least I felt Tom and

Beth had. Why weren't we still together every day? It made no sense. When we first rode like this in the Healey, every shifting of the gears resulted in Beth's body leaning against mine in unfamiliar excitement. Now we felt comfortable together, and with each shifting, she would lean against me in an exaggerated swaying, intentionally teasing me and reminding me of our earlier, awkward, innocent contact.

We all had experienced new lives and friends that put our own relationship in an entirely different context. Beth had become a woman and Tom had become a man in just a few short months. And me? Somehow I felt as if I had been left behind while they went on ahead.

We spent that holiday weekend at Tom's in an old two-story Victorian boarding house behind Main Street in Hanover and the nights at a nearby, smoky Ratskeller, catching up and regaling one another with tales of our Freshmen years. Just about everyone who came into "The Rat" said hello to Tom, and he introduced us as "a couple of ex-friends from high school," until Beth stopped laughing at that and punched him in the shoulder and told him how unfunny that was. We would never be his "ex-friends."

He also introduced us to our waitress, Ramona, who we would find out later in the evening was Tom's love interest that week.

From the other side of the room came the call of "Hey Beethoven, Hey Chopin, get up and play us some tunes."

Tom walked up to the upright piano in the corner and was surrounded by his new friends. Beth and I peered over their shoulders as Tom sat down and launched into a set that included Little Richard, (*I Hear You Knockin'*) George Shearing (*I'll Remember April*), Ray Charles (*Drown in My Own Tears*), and Dave Brubeck (*Blue Rondo ala Turk*).

Later, Professor Longhair. The crowd chanted "Monk! Monk! Monk! " and he broke into some obscure Thelonious Monk that I will never "get." This was all new stuff to Beth and me. Another of Tom's secrets that through modesty or embarrassment or "no big deal," he had kept from us. Or maybe he didn't think we would get it? His friends threw quarters into a tin cup. He closed off his set doing an imitation of Tom Lehrer singing *Poisoning Pigeons in the Park*, something we had never heard him do before. Our best friend was changing, opening up, becoming more gregarious, more of a social butterfly; a performer.

When the weekend was all over it was a letdown among the joys of seeing him, since I had plans for us all being together for what I hoped would be a carefree summer before we started our sophomore college year. I wanted to extend the weekend; insist upon it no matter how unrealistic I knew that would be. What I didn't know at the time was that it would be the last time we would spend any length of time with Tom before we all entered yet a new phase of our lives and of our friendship.

Beth and I took a bus back to Manhattan that Sunday afternoon. Beth stayed in the city in her father's apartment and prepared for work the next day. I caught the last Red & Tan back to New City late that Sunday night.

Overall, it had been a quiet, yet eventful weekend. We knew Tom was an extraordinarily talented classical pianist. What we didn't know was the extent of his diversity in musical accomplishment. We also discovered that either through some careless oversight, or procrastination, or through willful neglect, or maybe even civil disobedience, Tom had never registered for the draft when he turned eighteen the summer after high school graduation.

By midsummer Beth and I surprised ourselves by both admitting that we couldn't wait to get back to Gainesville. It was almost blasphemous, but it was true. In a way, for me, it was an act of acquiescence; an admission of defeat.

That first week in August, 1965, three weeks before classes were to begin, Beth and I decided it was time to return to Gainesville.

On my front porch that final morning, it was a repeat of what had happened in August a year before. But this time if almost felt that we weren't leaving home to go away, we were leaving a place we were just visiting to return to our new home.

Francis was in his wheelchair, my father standing behind him stoically in his mailman's uniform, ready to walk his daytime job, and my mother looking at me as if to wonder how her little boy had grown up so fast. Except this time my mother whispered in my ear something that came as a surprise. Instead of telling me she missed me and hoped to see me soon, she said, "Go live your life Will. Forget about us here. If you never want to come back here to this, I will understand." Her words shocked me. *To this?* She squeezed my hand in emphasis. *"Go."*

The Willys and the Bug were packed and ready. We said our goodbyes and headed south for our second year of college.

This time we made it to *South of the Border Motel* before we stopped. We had seen all the billboards, had bought fireworks there, and decided we would make it a rite of passage to stay in the gaudy, rundown motel. With the new I-95 bypassing its old Route 301 location, I figured it would be only a matter of time before it closed, like so many other motels on the old highway.

CHAPTER SIXTY

UNIVERSITY OF FLORIDA

Sophomore Fall Trimester, 1965
Age 19

When we arrived back in Gainesville for our sophomore year, when dormitory residency requirements were no longer in effect, we moved into what was known as "The Ghetto" on the north side of the campus, across University Avenue. Actually, it was a Craftsman house Jerry owned and had arranged for us to rent. We would share it with two other art students, Leonora and Melanie. Suddenly, when the trimester started, I would be living with three distractingly beautiful women.

For the three weeks before our sophomore year started, Beth and I fixed up the place, made love in the stifling, August Gainesville heat, and made plans for our future.

We were back in our new hometown. I was still a little unsettled after leaving New City, and by what my mother had said to me. The past summer had taught me that time marches on and that I had to change, or turn into another lost dinosaur, another *schlub*, going back home to try to recapture the glory days of high school. I determined that I would fit in this time and get with the program.

And as I did, the more Beth seemed to fall in love with me, so I worked even harder to deserve that love. I had begun to recognize and understand my "special talent" that I had discovered.

We had both turned nineteen over the summer, and we were in our glory right in the here-and-now. Our days and nights were filled with classes and study, and as the Gainesville autumn slowly crept up on us, our weekends were filled with football games on Saturdays. On Sundays, it was off to the Ichetucknee until the weather turned too cold. Other than that, it was unending hours of study. I welcomed the escape from reality.

We cruised through that first trimester as sophomores, watching with amusement the difficulties of the incoming freshmen that we had experienced just a year before, a sense of homesickness, even dread.

As Thanksgiving approached, we had to decide what to do for the upcoming Christmas break, and we decided to stay in Gainesville. When I went next door to call my mother to tell her the news, she started to cry, and then regained her composure. "It's all right, Will. We haven't had a real Christmas here in a long time anyway."

When late December rolled around and our roommates left for the holidays and the town emptied out, Beth and I were alone in our little love nest to spend the holidays on our terms. The first surprise was when Beth asked me to come out to the car one evening where a Christmas tree was sprouting out of the rear seat of the Jeepster. I carried it in and stuck it in the hole of a cinder block, and with a few scraps of lumber from the tumbledown garage out back, I was able to prop it up. For ornaments, Beth pulled out her school bag and took out enough color paper ornaments to decorate the tree. It was a homemade tree of a very personal kind, and it moved me.

As we sat in the darkness of our first Christmas Eve alone, the candle light was just enough to see the tree. Our windows were open to let in the December breeze and the streets outside were silent. Beth turned on the radio to a station playing Christmas Carols and we held each other all night long on the sofa. As she cuddled up in my arms she spoke softly to me. "Can you believe we've been together for almost nine years? Since fifth grade when I first fell in love with you."

"Wow. Does this mean we're adults now?"

"Will, I want to be serious. I want us to be serious. I want to spend the rest of my life with you. You know that don't you?"

"What about all the frat boys here? Not to mention every professor you meet?"

"Will, be serious. It's you that I want. Not them. You have to always remember that."

"What about all those sophisticated Madison Avenue types that have been chasing you all over Manhattan with their martinis?"

"I'm not interested in them. They have nothing on you, believe me. I'm not interested."

"How do you know?"

"I've always known what I've wanted."

There was silence except for the carols on the radio.

"I am worried about my New City Boy, though."

"Why?"

"I don't know. I. . ."

But she stopped and refused to continue. What did she mean by "my New City Boy?" Did she have another boy from another town? Was she concerned that I would never outgrow that horrible affliction known as, "New City Boy?"

CHAPTER SIXTY-ONE

UNIVERSITY OF FLORIDA

Summer, 1966
Ages 19, 20

That summer of 1966, between our Sophomore and Junior years we stayed in Gainesville to go to school as we had originally talked about two years earlier. Hogtown had become our home now. We turned twenty.

CHAPTER SIXTY-TWO

UNIVERSITY OF FLORIDA

Fall, 1966
Junior Year, Age 20

By our junior year, in the fall of 1966, the entire world was changing.

The campus look, the student look, were different. Now, as the incendiary war in Vietnam forged ahead, student activists filled the Plaza of the Americas with protests, draft-card burning, flag burning. No more Bass Weejuns and khaki pants and Gant shirts. No more blazers and ties for football games. Now it was ragged jeans and ragged tee-shirts and tie-dyes and plaid, flannel shirts. Many students were taking on the hippie look, the hippie dress. Even many professors adopted the look. Students openly smoked dope and the entire campus went through a metamorphosis, populated by this new group who was replacing the Southern good ol' fraternity boys that had held sway for so many years. It was revolutionary.

The New City influence in our lives, that which had shaped and formed us for so long, had all but disappeared.

CHAPTER SIXTY-THREE

UNIVERSITY OF FLORIDA

Spring, 1967
Junior Year, Age 20

By late May in the spring of 1967, we finished our Junior year. To our own astonishment, we hadn't been back to New City in two years. We remained in the Ghetto Craftsman house two blocks off campus.

After a week of goofing off, Beth and I started summer school. By this time I was really committed and digging into my studies every night. I was now motivated to go to law school and didn't want anything to stand in my way. Beth and I were committed to graduating early. My "special talent" was becoming more and more noticeable. What had been perceived as my easy recall of events and details in my life was now readily apparent in all of my studies. I was surprised, but not really surprised at what I had suspected all along.

One night there was a knock on our door. We weren't expecting anyone. It was Tom. He had flown down to Gainesville to let us know that he had graduated from Dartmouth in three years as he had planned, and to tell us he had been drafted into the Army. As he had confided jokingly during the Dartmouth weekend, he had failed to register for the draft when he turned eighteen. Even if he had registered, the fact that he was no longer an undergraduate would have made him ineligible for a II-S Deferment. We were shocked. They were trying to make an example out of him, he suspected.

Beth looked concerned. She asked a question that she apparently had already figured out the answer to. "You could have just told us over the phone. I mean we love it that you flew down to see us. It's a great surprise."

"You don't have a phone, in case I have to remind you. I'm headed for six weeks of basic training. Then it's off to 90-Day Wonder School. It's amazing what a grandparent's influence can do."

"An officer? That can't be too bad."

"Have any idea where you'll be stationed?"

"There's a war going on, Will. Or don't they have TV news down here?"

He didn't have to remind me, yet he did. Vietnam was all just an abstraction for us, despite the rise in campus protests. Was it time for Beth and me to reconsider what side we were on? I had gone through two years of R.O.T.C., which made me eligible for what, I had wondered? Did it make me in favor of the war? Weren't we protecting our country? "Stemming the tide of Communist aggression?" I couldn't decide.

That night we sat on the front porch of the Craftsman and sipped wine and listened to the traffic pass by on University Drive. There was little conversation between us. It started out with empty laughter and came to a stop when Tom looked at us and said quietly, "I just wanted to see my two best friends in the world one last time before I left."

"One last time?"

"Left?"

We sat there in silence, pondering the ramifications. What did all of this portend for my own future after graduation? I got up and excused myself abruptly, leaving them alone on the porch glider. One last time? Could forces outside of our control really do something like this? Destroy lifelong friendships?

There was an unspoken dread when he left the next day. Sometime during the night we became convinced we would never see him again. How could this possibly be? We were all just a couple of kids from New City, weren't we? And now the outside world had encroached on our lives and was swallowing us.

As Tom stepped toward the departure gate he turned to Beth and handed her the keys to his Healey and the boathouse. "Almost forgot. It's in the garage. Usual spot."

On the way back from dropping him off at the airport, Beth refused to speak about it, which was okay with me. It was just too upsetting to even consider. The triple shock of his surprise arrival, announcement, and quick departure were all too much to absorb that morning in June of 1967.

One morning, a few days later in that same summer trimester during June of our junior year, there was another knock on the door. Beth hopped up from our side-by-side desks in our bedroom.

As she walked forward she joked, "I guess Tom forgot something."

Beth answered the door and stepped outside, which I thought was unusual, and there was muted conversation coming through the open windows. After a few moments I got up from my desk from where I was studying, pulled the curtain aside, and looked outside in time to see Jerry returning to his car.

Beth sat on the stoop and it looked like she was starting to cry. I could not imagine what Jerry had said to her. What did it mean?

I stepped outside, the screen door slamming behind me, and sat down next to her. She looked at me with such a look of anguish that I felt sick. Before I could say anything, she buried her face in my shoulder and began to cry. "You need to call your mother. Your father has been killed in an accident. I'm so sorry, Will."

The shock went through me. I couldn't form words. How could that be possible? The man I had hoped to engage in conversation one day was gone. There would never be that conversation.

"He was struck by a hit-and-run driver last night. Your mother's been trying to get in touch with you. She finally asked my father to call Jerry."

I flew home from Gainesville right away to be with my mother and Francis. Beth would fly home in time for the weekend funeral.

CHAPTER SIXTY-FOUR

NEW CITY

The Funeral
Summer, 1967
Age 20

The funeral at St. Augustine's was a reunion of many of my old friends from high school who had driven in from their respective college towns and summer jobs, all our distant relatives, and people on my father's mail route. Girl Scouts from my mother's troop of twenty years earlier came to pay respects to my mother. Together, we pushed my brother across the street in his wheelchair.

Beth had flown in the night before, and her father was there. I hadn't known that her father and my father had spent many hours talking while my father was on his daily route. Tom was in basic training and could not come, but his grandparents, the Florions, came in from Manhattan to pay respects to the son of their gardener and cabinetmaker, my grandfather. Frau K. and Max sat respectfully in a rear pew.

Father Carrick did the eulogy, praising my father for his service to his country during the war and on his mail route, and for being a good father, and that is when I lost my self-control for the first time since hearing of his death. Upon hearing the news two days earlier, I had accepted it with stoicism, probably due to shock, and on the flight home I had managed to stay in control. But at the mention by Father Carrick of my own father's commitment to his sons, I couldn't take it anymore and I broke down for the first time. There was so much I had missed with him. I missed it all. Why had he withdrawn from us? What had happened to him? Was it fear of losing a second son?

At Germonds' cemetery, at the century-old family burial plot, we paid our last respects to my father, all of us wondering who this man had really been. Father Carrick had driven my mother and Francis. My brother sat at the gravesite, propped up in his wheelchair with pillows. What could he possibly understand of this?

Later, at a reception in my parents' home, my mother served tea and finger sandwiches and my father's classmates from Congers High School brought in *hors d'ouevres*.

After, I said goodbye to Beth and we agreed to meet up later that night and go to the Lake.

It was after all the guests had left the house; after the reception of tea and lady-fingers, that I helped my mother and Father Carrick wash out the teacups and scraped away the crumbs left on the embroidered tablecloth, and then excused myself.

I needed to get a breath of fresh air. I stepped into the setting sun. I wandered into the yard; the very same yard my father had wandered during his boyhood.

I found myself in my grandfather's barn as I began to wonder who my father was, trying to get a grasp on the enormity of it all; what had just passed, never to return. There was a smell of horses and rat dung lingering in the air.

I walked through the barn, seeing tools, gardening implements; their hickory handles smoothed to a shine from years of use; a hoe, a stone fork, a stone rake, an Italian grape hoe, a pick-ax to chop through the hardened Rockland County soil. Had any of these tools been carried over from Germany? Had any of these tools survived the barn fire of 1904 up on the hill? Had they been used to scrape through the remains of the livestock that had burned to death in the old family barn? There was a hand-hewn wheelbarrow my father used to drive Francis and me around the yard when we were kids. Against the wall, tilted on end, was a winter sled (always referred to as a "sledge"), and upstairs, was my grandfather's mail wagon. Had my father ridden the mail route with his father in the mail wagon and the sledge? What had they talked about on those days? On one snowy day my grand-father had attempted to take a short cut across a shallow frozen pond on Phillips Hill Road and the horse had broken through the ice and broken its leg. My grandfather had to put it down on the spot and with the help of neighbors, towed the sledge off the pond before he continued walking the rest of his route.

Against one wall were shelves of seed packets, chicken feed, animal traps for fox, beaver, and otter, all kept meticulously, yet neglected and abandoned since my grandfather had died.

One shelf contained shoe forms that survived the family's shoe factories' fires. My great-great grandfather and all the chil-dren he sired and all their cousins, as children, worked in the dim light of the shoe factories, stretching and tamping the leather over the beech shoe-lasts, until they took on the form of shoes.

The workbench had been crudely assembled and had a vise on either end. Had he stood at his own father's side as he worked in here, as Francis and I had done at our father's radio workbench in the basement?

On the shelf above the workbench, mason jars and coffee tins were filled with horseshoe nails and assorted bolts. Hanging above the bench I found the two matching hand tools given to my grandparents by Mary Mowbray-Clarke, and I thought back to what the hand cultivator had looked like the day I found it in the

Dutch Garden and brought it home. It didn't look like that any-more. I noticed that the tines on the cultivator had been scraped clean, rust removed, and that the hickory handle had been lightly sanded, bringing out the branding of my grandfather's initials, perhaps sanded recently, perhaps in preparation for something. What?

I was reminded of my father saying he wasn't a gardener like his own parents had been. My bookworm father had made a delib-erate choice not to follow in his father's footsteps. Or maybe it had just been a sign of the new generation of high school students who had graduated from Congers High School in 1933. I would later find out that Mr. and Mrs. Florian had paid for my father's NYU education when the time came to attend college.

Upstairs, in what was once a hayloft, in addition to my grand-father's mail wagon, were steamer trunks and wooden crates filled with books. The books of Dickens and Twain and Tarkington on the shelves inside the house were just part of this larger collection. There were hundreds trundled up in wooden bins and bushel bas-kets once occupied by green beans and peaches. Upton Sinclair's twelve Lanny Budd novels, starting with *World's End* and ending with *The Return of Lanny Budd*. The Horatio Alger series was there, too, and *Main Street* and Arrowsmith by Sinclair Lewis. One of his favorites, *Winesburg, Ohio*, by Sherwood Anderson, showed the most wear and tear. Many I'd never heard of, all popu-lar novels of the 1920s, 1930s, and 1940s, now unread, faded, along with their authors, into a regrettable obscurity.

And there on the top of the stack was the twenty-odd Jerry Todd and Poppy Ott series, by Leo Edwards. Most still had their dust jackets. These novels were special to my father, since he had discovered them in his pre-teen years. Dozens of adventures of good-hearted boys, roaming the fictitious Illinois town of Tutter in the Post WW I years, having laugh-out-loud shenanigans with a group of the most eccentric characters ever compiled in all of boy-hood literature. The imaginary town of Tutter, created in the mind of an obscure author, was a special place to him. Tutter reminded him of New City in his own boyhood days. Carefree, friendly, a highly idealized, safe enclave, where all boys should have a chance to grow up without fear or care. Now, since he was gone from this world, I would like to think of my father wandering those streets with his boyhood chums for all eternity. So happy. So innocent.

I noticed one of the books from the series was missing. Was it inside the house? Had he been reading it to Francis the night he was killed?

I left the barn, not knowing it would be years before I would return to it.

I walked down the garden path, past the barn and past our sugar maple where Francis and I had spent so many hours in its embrace. At the chicken coops I stopped to look inside, trying to imagine what my father must have imagined that day he so frantically searched for his little lost boy. I walked past the four blue spruce that lined the pathway to the top of the little baseball field my father had carved out of a weed patch when I was just five and Francis seven. I had not seen the field for the three years I had been away in Gainesville, and I didn't remember the last time I saw it during my final high school years. The last two years of high school, with a car, my walks from Tom's through the woods and baseball field had stopped. So it had been awhile since I had walked the path, and I expected to see a field overgrown in ragweed, goldenrod, Queen Anne's Lace, a few maple saplings and the spread of sumac.

But when I crested the rise past the chicken coops I saw something completely different.

Someone had cleared the field recently. Mowed it flat and smooth. The baselines were raked clean and a rough, patchy line of lime dust precisely described the baselines, just as it had been when Francis and I were growing up on our way to baseball stardom.

A section of rubber tire tread, painted white, had been nailed to a board and anchored in the ground and served as a pitcher's mound, and canvas bags, dusted white with the lime, served as bases. It was all just as it had been for the few years leading up to "Francis' Day." I stood there at home plate silently, not understanding what I was seeing.

Was time-travel possible on such short notice without advance reservations? If you were taking a time-travel trip back in time, when would you place the reservations? In the past? The present? Or would that be the future? Had my mother allowed the neighborhood boys to fix up the field for a place to play ball during my stay in Gainesville?

I walked quickly back to the kitchen. "Who cleaned up the field?"

"What do you mean?"

"It's a baseball field again."

She didn't know what I was talking about.

But then I realized the obvious. Turning, I walked to the sliding doors that separated the eyes of the outside world from Francis. He grunted in recognition, then in surprise, as I picked him up and carried him in my arms, just as he had carried me that day eleven years earlier. I carried him through the living room and down the hall. As we passed through the kitchen my mother looked at me in shock.

"Will, what are you doing? Put him back," as if he were an object to be replaced on a shelf.

I carried him through the small lobby and down the back porch steps, the same steps where he had sat me down with a twisted ankle on his day.

"Will, where are you going?"

I carried him down between the rows of catalpa trees, trimmed to perfection. "We're going to say goodbye to Dad."

Francis' breath began to quicken as we passed our barn and the chicken coops nearby where my father had desperately hoped to find Francis hiding that fateful day years before. Francis hadn't been outside the house very much in years. Could he sense the passing of the years? When we got to the bottom of the spruce slope, and he saw the little baseball field, the guttural sounds emanating from his throat became agitated, then almost a laugh. He looked at me and started rocking in my arms, violently at first, and then a sobbing, thrusting motion. He wanted me to put him down so he could get back in the game.

I gently placed him down at the base of the poplar tree and sat next to him, propping him up against me. As he looked from side to side, his spastic wails began to soften to a murmur. The footsteps behind me grew louder and then my mother was on his other side. At first she never said a word at what we beheld, only shook her head from side to side in bewilderment. Then, holding her son to her breast, she whispered softly, "Oh, Francis, Oh, Francis." I didn't know if she was beseeching my brother or my father, but then it became obvious. "Oh, Francis, what have you done?"

As the sun sank in our faces over center field, my brother slowly slumped toward my mother and his head drifted into her lap. Still mewing, his eyes remained open for a few minutes, still taking in the baseball field before him.

Is there someone who can tell me what was going through my brother's mind at that point? Could it be articulated in any language I might decipher? Or was it just some form of instinctive, primeval sensory recognition and response? Did he have memory? It would seem so from his reaction to seeing the baseball field. What did he want to say to me? Did he understand that our father was dead, that he had restored the playing field for his sons in what he knew would be one of his last acts before stepping in front of a passing car?

Did my brother understand what that concept even meant, that there would be no one there to read to him every night but me for the next few nights, and then, after I left, it would be my mother, already exhausted from his full-time care? Did he suddenly recognize, just as I had suddenly recognized, that sometime in the days before my father had died, he had cleared the field one final time as a reminder to his sons, a legacy of sorts. If that is so, then he must surely have known he was going to die. Or perhaps he had already decided that he had died on "Francis' Day" and life since then had simply been a postponement of what he knew he needed to do.

After the hit-and-run, after the funeral, three witnesses came forward and told police they saw my father walk deliberately into the oncoming car that had struck him. The witnesses had been leaving the New City Pub and were drunk at the time, but they all agreed and said he had abruptly stepped off the curb between Dr. Cohen's Craftsman House and Henry Steinman's General Store and into the path of a car leaving the Pub's parking lot. It was almost as if he were waiting for a *particular* car to drive away, they said. A *particular* driver. They never identified the driver. There was really no need to.

The coroner ruled my father's death a suicide.

I later reflected on my father's life and all it had been. Like all lives, it was remarkable in both its similarities and differences to his peers in the same environment in the same era. After four years at Congers High School, he had chosen to go to NYU to be an accountant. His daily train trips to Manhattan had resulted in both his meeting my mother and his college degree. Then when the war had broken out, he had chosen to join the navy and fight for his country. Just about everything since then had not been his choice: the unspeakable acts he had been forced to witness in the South Pacific as a pioneer radar technician, what it had done to the scholarly New City bookworm, his decision to take a passive job in the Post Office upon his return, and the birth of two sons. Since the start of the war had he ever been happy? He found some happiness with his namesake first son and had poured his attention on him. And what of me? Had I just been an afterthought? A mistake? The result of some effort to comfort him when he returned home from the war? Was he one of the men who led a life of quiet desperation? It made me question my own life and its meaning.

Eventually, it would all became clear to me; the walks, the locations, the reasons for his penance. He was taking the route his own father had driven on his mail route. He was re-tracing his father's path. It was as if by diligently walking my grandfather's mail wagon route every night, he was monitoring, protecting the territory from any change. He was standing guard to prevent any further development, reliving his own father's, my grandfather's, day-to-day life. That's why he had taken Francis on that mail route walk so many times before I was old enough to join them.

Maybe he was convinced that if he walked it long enough he could get enough traction with his footsteps to make the world spin backward, clockwise, to an earlier day when he had accompanied his own father on the mail rounds; make the world spin backward to the summer day before Francis Day, and know in his heart it was time to invite his two sons to accompany him on a walk of his postal route. In that way, on that very specific day in time, Francis and I would not have been playing in the brook and I would not have sprained my ankle in an attempt to capture a crayfish, and all the rest that followed would never have happened that day because there would have been no crayfish, no sprained ankle, no game of hide-and-go-seek, no Kelvinator. But maybe it was even more than that. Maybe he was making his rounds, standing guard to make sure nothing further ugly and bad would happen to New City. But with him gone, there was no one left to guard New City from all the brutal ugliness of the outside world.

Later that evening, I was glad to get out of the house. I simply could not stand to be in the presence of my brother and mother and their grief. It only amplified what I was going through myself, the collective weight fed upon itself, expanding my own grief exponentially.

When Beth arrived at the house, she left the Healey in the driveway and we walked up to New City Park. We sat on the dam through the late dusk and Beth tried to console me.

In between sobs she led me to the pathway on the east side of the lake and down toward the lighthouse where she undressed me first and then herself, never breaking eye-contact. She took my hand and we stepped down the roots to the water's edge and treaded silently over to the raft and climbed up.

In the darkness she held my head against her breast and stroked my tear-stained cheek. "My poor little New City boy. My poor little boy. Will, I'm so sorry for everything and everything you're going through."

Instead of making it better, it made it feel worse. We lay like that until my crying subsided and then she sat on the edge of the raft and lowered herself into the water. "Come with me."

I slid into the water next to her and we silently breast-stroked our way to the east bank and up the root trail.

She took my hand and we followed the path south, closer to the lighthouse, until we came to the old property that we both knew had been vacant for three years. Surrounded by high, unkempt hedges, we lay in the tall, uncut grass and she cradled me in her arms where in the heat of the summer evening, we shivered, naked.

After a moment she rolled over on her back and pulled me on top of her.

"I'm here, Will. I'm here for you."

And as I started to cry all over again for my father and for my mother and for my brother, she took me inside of her to offer the only possible, life-affirming comfort that she knew could console me at that moment.

After, we lay on the long soft sweet grass and gazed up at the stars. All was silent as I tried to regain my composure. I listened for the sounds of children splashing and swimming, but there was none at this nighttime hour. She looked into my eyes like she had done a million times before, but unlike any other time she had before. "You are a most remarkable boy and I want to spend the rest of my life with you."

I turned onto my side and pulled her face forward. How could anyone as beautiful and as perfect as she was love someone like me, I wondered? It's just not possible.

In the distance, we heard the siren atop the New City Firehouse wailing, and at first we gave it no thought, since it was something we had grown up hearing. But before long the sirens of the tanker and hook-and-ladder got nearer, and we sat up at the smell of smoke and turned toward the sound and realized the night sky was filled with the flames of the New City Park Clubhouse.

We rushed down the path and scrambled into our clothes and reached the parking lot just as the tanker pulled in and ran an intake hose to the lake.

Within minutes the fire was out, but the north end of the roof was lost. We stood behind the other bystanders, watching the firemen do their jobs until the last ember had been doused and the night air was filled with the stinging smell of smoke.

As the rubbernecks began to drift off, we watched the men begin to roll up their hoses. I walked over to Chief Freddy Hadley, now in his late seventies, whom I had seen just hours ago at my father's funeral.

"Will, sorry about your dad. He was one of our finest."

"Thanks, Chief Hadley. What happened?"

"Don't know. Got a call that the clubhouse was on fire. Caller wouldn't leave his name. You two see anything?"

"No. Nothing."

"Your hair is wet. Were you swimming?"

"Yes, down at the south end. But we didn't see anything going on up at this end."

"Funny thing."

"What?"

"It's almost as if the call was made before the fire started. Otherwise, in the time it took us to get here, the building would probably have been burned down to the ground."

"That's odd."

"Yes it is. Where's your car?"

"We walked."

"How come you were swimming down at that end instead of this end?"

I glanced at Beth before answering.

Beth took over. "We were skinny dipping. Less chance of getting caught down there."

Chief Hadley turned to the south toward the Pape's house, as if looking for something. Beth and I skinny dipping at the south end. A memory from his own past, perhaps? It seemed to make him sad.

"Okay. But you didn't see anything when you walked past earlier?"

"Nothing."

"Okay, Will, Beth. Will, tell your Mom I said howdy. Beth, same to your dad."

"You don't think we had anything to do with it, do you?"

Freddy looked at us in disbelief, as if I had said something to insult him. "*You're Francis' son*, aren't you?"

The next day I decided that rather than returning to school in Gainesville, I would stay in New City for the rest of the summer to be with my mother and brother, and to volunteer to help rebuild the clubhouse where I had spent so many summer days.

Beth was disappointed. She understood, but she had to get back to finish her classes for the summer term. She dropped off the Healey in my driveway, we hugged goodbye, and she took the bus to JFK airport from Third and Main.

The next day I helped my mother pack up all my father's clothing and belongings and take them across the street to St.

Augustine's basement, where they would be washed and folded and sold at the next Ladies' Auxiliary rummage sale or distributed to a needy family. Other than the Post Office uniforms, there were surprisingly few clothes. The shirt and tie I had worn to Tom's Fourth of July tent party with Pop Whiteman still hung there. Had it been my father's only formal attire?

In the barn were the steamer trunks of his high school yearbooks and college textbooks and all those novels. "I want to keep all those books that are in the barn," I told my mother.

I worked as a lifeguard and helped the other volunteers rebuild what remained of the clubhouse after the fire. I learned carpentry from the eighty-year-old Norwegians who had built the original structure. An investigator thought it was set by arson, but the results were inconclusive. The photographs of the Norwegian settlers on the interior wall would have to be replaced. Were there copies somewhere?

Beth was back at school, moving on with her life, accelerating her career.

I missed her, couldn't wait to get back to Gainesville. My decision to stay in New City had been a mistake. But I had dropped my classes already.

One morning in late July Tom knocked on my front door. His hair was short, his uniform crisp. He saluted when I answered the door. "Private First Class Thomas Hogenkamp reporting for duty, sir."

"Private? I thought you were a Ninety-Day Wonder?"

"Didn't take. Plus, they wanted a four-year commitment after."

We sat down on the porch glider and I looked at my friend with sorrow. In just a few short weeks they had obviously damaged him; he had become a broken man, a stranger to me. The differences were palpable. I recognized the symptoms. Instead of talking about himself, he insisted on talking about Beth and me.

"I've got this funny, uneasy feeling, Will. For the first time in my life I don't know what's going to happen. Will, promise me that you will do good in school. You owe it to your family, you owe it to Beth, you owe it to yourself to succeed."

"I know. I've done a lot better these last two years. It was getting through my freshman year that hurt my G.P.A."

"Beth's a keeper, Will. Treat her right."

He was talking to me like a stranger. Or like one of us had become a different person.

"I will."

We looked at one another. "You make it sound like you're not coming back."

He stood up from the porch glider to say goodbye.

"Next stop, Ft. Lewis, Washington, enroute to Vietnam. Ooops, I'm not allowed to tell anyone that. Send for the firing squad. Or maybe I'll just be court martialed."

I was positive I would never see him alive again. It could be argued that I was correct in that assumption.

That evening I was able to get through to Beth on the phone and tell her about the visit. I didn't tell her the details, and certainly not the tone of the conversation. I tried to keep it positive.

"Tom will be home in a year, safe and sound," I tried to assure her. "Things will be back to normal."

CHAPTER SIXTY-FIVE

NEW CITY

August, 1967
Age 21

Later that summer, in early August, 1967, I would take a train to Waldo, and Beth and I would start our senior year together in our little Craftsman cottage in the ghetto in Gainesville with our two gorgeous roommates. But now I was a trimester behind. Where had the time gone?

It would be another few weeks before Beth announced she was pregnant. We had only been together once that summer and that was in New City Park on the back lawn of an empty house the night of my father's funeral and the fire at New City Park Clubhouse.

"I thought you were on the pill."

"I stopped."

"Why?"

"They were making me dizzy."

"So you didn't tell me?"

"I was going to, but then your father. . .You were distraught and I didn't think. I thought that for sure everything would be okay *just that once. Just one time.*"

Things were not okay. Beth had been wrong for once, or so I thought at the time. It was uncharacteristic behavior.

At first I was petrified and then I became frantic, ridden with anxiety.

I was so caught up in getting into law school that I didn't want to allow the responsibilities of parenthood or planning a wedding to get in the way of my finishing undergraduate school and starting law school, or of Beth earning her degree. We simply could not afford to do that. We argued.

"Lots of people do it all. We can do it all."

"Oh really? And Manhattan after that?"

Another week went by. Finally Beth conceded reluctantly that, what I wanted, to terminate the pregnancy, would be for the best in the long run. Or was she just humoring me? We could always have children later when we got married, I argued.

We didn't talk about it for a few days and then one day sitting in class I realized that with Beth, *I could do anything.* I could work to support a child, ten children, if she were at my side. Besides, I reasoned to myself, with a child, Beth would never leave me and they would both be mine forever. I rushed home after class to tell her that I had reconsidered. We would keep the child, celebrate. But she wasn't there and didn't come home until after dinner. I was frantic with worry. Was there a project that had kept her late? Had she told me something and just half-listening at the time, I couldn't remember now?

Finally she came home and I rushed up to her and blurted out that I had changed my mind.

She sat down and started sobbing.

"It's too late. I had the abortion this morning and I've been resting on a friend's sofa since then."

The images of fatherhood, of wanting to be a great father that had filled my mind all of that day vanished in an instant.

I would later find out that the sofa belonged to one of her fellow students in the art department who had also found a place for her to have the abortion. It was on her sofa that Beth had rested. But it would be later before I found out about this part of her day.

She started bleeding right after dinner. I rushed her to J. Hillis Miller Hospital because of the hemorrhaging. The abortionist had damaged her uterus and they performed an emergency hysterectomy. She would no longer be able to have the children she always wanted; like we had always talked about.

The news had a strange effect on her. Beth knew she could never conceive again. At first she was in denial. It was just some sort of mistake. She tried to prove the doctors wrong with marathon sex. She was heartbroken, but after her initial shock, depression and recovery, she tried to drown herself in sex, as if some way trying to reverse the damage I caused her. It seemed to be the only thing that would console her. In retrospect, I should have sensed it was the beginning of the end for Beth and me. I knew I would always feel the same way I had always felt about her. But I sensed a profound change in her feelings toward me, as if she had thrown something away because of my carelessness and selfishness. In a way, she was right in her accusations. So even though she wanted sex constantly, I didn't sense it was out of her love for me anymore, but rather an attempt to heal the pain that I had caused her; an attempt to feel something, anything.

She changed radically that fall, seemingly re-examining her life and her future, but I really couldn't understand what she was going through. She was just changing; in school, her demeanor, her appearance, and her attitude toward me. She became silent, not as outgoing. Her sexual appetite had tripled, even as it became more impersonal. I almost felt as though she were thinking of someone else when she was with me. Like she wanted the sex, but she just didn't want me anymore.

A letter came from my mother about another fire destroying another New City landmark. The Elms. It had been a roadhouse since before the Revolutionary War, even boasted on the sign in the shape of a stagecoach out front that Lafayette had slept there. In recent years it had had its ups and downs, serving as a banquet hall, home to Pepe's Barber Shop, and last, but not least, a restaurant with a prophetic name, The Embers. Was it a kitchen fire? A gas leak? A cigarette left behind? A fraud perpetrated to get insurance money? Will anyone ever know? Probably not. But it was yet another mysterious fire. My mother and Father Carrick had walked down Main Street and joined the crowd of spectators as volunteer firemen struggled to put out the blaze. The property was deeded over to the town for a pocket-park.

CHAPTER SIXTY-SIX

GAINESVILLE

Spring, 1968
Age 21

That spring, as Beth's graduation approached I knew I would have to stay in Gainesville for the summer to finish up my degree. Having dropped out of school that previous summer term after my father's funeral, I was two classes short. I also had an opportunity for an internship at a local law firm. After my decision, I just assumed she would spend the summer in Gainesville with me, as she had in the past, but she announced she would be going to Manhattan to work in an advertising agency. It was a job her father had lined up for her.

The first week in April, Martin Luther King was assassinated. Like almost five years earlier, in another town, we walked the hallways and campus in silence. What was our country becoming?

After Beth's graduation, I prepared for my summer classes leading to my own graduation and move into law school in the fall. Beth abruptly packed up and drove her Willys to New City, assuring me that everything was all right, but never really convincing me. I was both shocked and dismayed. We had made plans to rent the house all summer. It was the first time in twelve years that we would be apart for any length of time; longer than the summer before. I sensed she was drifting away. I was correct to a degree, but I had no one to blame but myself. Our endless days in Gainesville, covered with sweaty sheets in stifling heat, were apparently over, at least for the time being. Wasn't she coming back after the summer job to join me for law school?

In May of 1968, the senseless bloodbath in Vietnam continued, the anti-war protests on campus and across the country became more vehement. As our four years together in Gainesville came to a close, it was a time of great turbulence in our country. Gainesville itself had changed so rapidly in the past few years, it would have been, in many ways, unrecognizable to any former students who happened to pass through. The saddle shoes and khakis and madras shirts that had started to phase out at least two years earlier, had given way to ragged bell-bottom jeans, sandals, tie-dyed tee-shirts, and long, greasy hair. It was less than a decade since Robert Frost had left Gainesville, after spending many happy days there lecturing.

On June 5th, Robert F. Kennedy was assassinated. A third idol gone. Not just dead. Shot in the head by forces unknown. A sense of mourning and dread seemed to pervade the campus.

And where were The Dream Weavers by then? Bubbling under the surface of this remarkable southern town, Harry Crews was dreaming of *The Gospel Singer*, and Padgett Powell and Carl Hiassen were teaching themselves how to write novels. It was not far off from the days before Dickey Betts would come up from West Palm Beach, join up with Duane and Gregg after they left Daytona Beach, pass through Gainesville in a battle of the bands and move on to Tallahassee; before they got tied to a whipping post on the way to meet Sweet Melissa and to eat a peach; years before Tom Petty leaned on a Mud Crutch on the way to finding an American Girl. Like our day under the tent in Tom's front yard in New City, we had little knowledge or appreciation of the cultural influences and events of our adopted Gainesville neighborhood. Maybe there's something in the water there.

It's Almost Tomorrow was playing on the radio as an Oldies Pick, when my next door neighbor, Marcy, knocked on the door to tell me I had a phone call from my mother. This could only mean bad news, I thought, as I ran across our adjoining lawns to Marcy's house. First King was killed, then Beth left, then Bobby Kennedy was killed. Was something wrong with Francis?

"Mom? What's wrong?"

"Will? Tom has been injured in Vietnam. He's already been airlifted to the Philippines."

"How serious is it? Where was it?"

"It's serious. His upper thigh and abdomen, with a lot of blood loss. They had to remove his spleen. But they expect a full recovery.

"How do you know all this?"

"Max called. He said Tom will remain in the Philippines until they can find room for him at a VA hospital first in San Diego, and maybe later, in a few months, on Long Island."

I was sickened by the news of Tom. And then for a brief moment I realized I was glad that he had been injured. Why? Because at least now he was coming home *alive*. In Vietnam, there would be almost 17,000 American casualties for just 1968.

The details were sketchy about how he had received the injury, and there was no further information available from his grandparents. I called Beth in Manhattan and she wanted to drop what she was doing and fly to the Philippines immediately, and just as suddenly realized the futility in that. She sounded like a stranger on the phone.

"He'll be in San Diego soon," I said. "We'll be able to see him then."

But whenever we called him in the weeks to come, he told us "absolutely not. I can't have visitors here." We would have to wait until he got to the Brooklyn V.A. Hospital. It would be another few months before a boy we had played with in our woods had been almost killed in a faraway jungle no one knew about or cared about.

I graduated in August of 1968. Law School started just a week later. I jumped in with both feet, eager and committed to doing really well. My desk files were never so organized. I spent days and nights memorizing details of case law. I would make Beth proud of me again. All would be forgiven and we would live happily ever after. The "special talent" I was reluctant to acknowledge I possessed to match the talents of Tom's and Beth's was kicking into high gear. Within the first few weeks at the law library I would realize how powerful a talent it was.

And then I got drafted.

Not graduating on time made me ineligible for my II-S student deferment. Now that I had graduated I had been reclassified I-A, or "ready to go." What had taken them so long?

I decided not to tell Beth. No need to get her upset. I would request an appeal, appear before my Draft Board in Spring Valley, and when I won the appeal, I would get my deferment extended for law school. Only when I was safe once again would I tell her. No need to make her worry.

I wrote the Draft Board to request a personal appearance for an appeal, but they were booked up for weeks. I would have to wait. As the date for my physical examination neared, I began to panic.

The draft lottery would not begin for more than another year. Eventually my number would be 102. If I could just hold out.

Beth was commuting to Manhattan as she had that first summer, staying in the City on weeknights, taking the bus home to New City on Friday nights. I would find out later that when the Art Director at the advertising agency had made a pass at her, she quit working there. She called to tell me. I wanted her to return to Gainesville, but instead she went back to work in her father's gallery. I planned to make her change her mind when I came back for my Draft Board appeal. I just knew I could talk her into it.

CHAPTER SIXTY-SEVEN

NEW CITY

October 15, 1968
Age 22

I received a letter from the Draft Board in Spring Valley the first week in October. There had been a cancellation in their appeals calendar. Could I appear before the Appellate Board on October 15? Of course my answer was, "Yes."

Before flying back to New City for the Draft Board, I called my mother to request that she be sure not to tell Beth I was coming home, if for some reason she saw Beth, or Beth called her. I wanted to surprise her in Manhattan after my meeting with the Draft Board, with what I was sure would be good news.

I flew into LaGuardia the night before and took a bus home. It was all I could do not to call Beth or drop in on her in Manhattan. But I wanted to wait to share what I was convinced would be good news. I figured I would be out of the Draft Board meeting by early afternoon and I could call Beth afterward and arrange to meet with her at the art gallery in Manhattan, or at home.

The next morning my mother and I went through our routine with Francis. She gave me a haircut in the back yard and then I drove my father's car to the showdown.

My Draft Board was in Spring Valley in the corner building opposite the old Congregational and Dutch Reformed churches. I parked my father's car in Memorial Park down by the old Tiger's Den, empty this time of day, and walked up the hill between the two churches.

I walked upstairs and sat in the waiting room, trembling, trying to rehearse my story of why my deferment should be extended. I dropped out of summer school because my father died and I had to come home. Isn't that a good enough reason for not finishing in four years? I was now graduated and enrolled in Law School. I had my father's death certificate and my law school acceptance papers and class registration with me in a folder, ready to make my case. I would try to reason with them. "You're surely not going to send me to die in Vietnam because my father got hit by a car and I had to drop out of school for one trimester and couldn't finish my degree in the allotted time?"

After a three-hour wait, I was finally called in. A parade of young men my age had walked in before me, each one looking as nervous and distraught as I was. Some even had their parents with them. One-by-one, they left in silence, as if they had just been notified of a death sentence: their own. Several were holding back tears.

An athletic looking young black man, flanked by his weeping parents, left stunned, bitter, and mute. Had I played football against him? No, he was too young to have been an opponent.

I came very close to walking out the door and driving directly to Canada. I was fully prepared to do that, if necessary.

When my name was called and I walked through the door, I was asked to sit at the end of a board table filled with old, white-haired men dressed in double breasted suits from the 1940s. I started to hold up my paper file, but one of them held up his hand. Instead, one-by-one the men who held my future in their hands reviewed their own file on me and then passed it to the next white-haired man.

Finally, my file reached the head of the table. The man read it over while packing a pipe with tobacco, tamping it and lighting it. All the familiar delaying tactics. In another ten seconds my fate would be sealed. I couldn't stand the suspense any longer. Finally he looked up from the folder.

"Are you Marion Summers' son?"

I was taken off-guard by his question. "Yes."

He sniffed perfunctorily. "Your deferment has been reinstated. You're free to go. We'll send confirmation in the mail."

"What? You don't even need to see. . ."

"We have a certain amount of discretion on these matters at the local level. Your deferment appeal has been approved. You're free to go, son. Good luck in law school."

I thanked them all and they didn't even look up at me.

The decision all happened so fast I became dizzy with relief. I decided I would get some late breakfast before returning home to call Beth. Too late for a surprise lunch meeting in Manhattan, it would be another six hours before she got out of work anyway. I drove over to Rockland Community College and looked around campus for any of my old high school friends, but they had passed through long ago. I took Route 202 over to Monsey and had breakfast at the 202 Diner. Up through Garnerville and Haverstraw and Stony Point and then over to Grassy Point to Brophy's, our old drinking and dancing haunts, where we had danced countless nights away, empty now in the midday light, framed against the Hudson River. I headed south on 9W and parked alongside the 9W Hudson overlook in the shadow of Trap Rock and contemplated my future with Beth. A giddy sense of relief had followed the loss of strength that seemed to have overcome me earlier in the day.

With the threat of the draft behind me, it would be clear sailing through law school. Life was good as I headed home to call Beth in Manhattan, tell her the good news, and see if she could come home early to spend the weekend with me before I headed back to Gainesville. I would try to talk her into returning to Gainesville with me. I needed her to get me through law school, I would tell her.

My mother was waiting for me on the porch glider when I pulled in the driveway. She stood to meet me.

"Tom called the second you left. He couldn't reach you in Gainesville. He's coming home today."

The timing could not have been better.

"That's great. I'll call Beth."

"I already called her. She knows."

"How come you called her?"

"Tom asked me to. He had to hurry to his connection in Dulles Airport. A guy was pushing his wheelchair."

"Wheelchair?"

"I asked him. It was just a temporary formality. For the airport."

"Can I use the car to go pick him up? Where's he flying to? Is it military or civilian?"

"That was four hours ago. Max is picking him up. He's probably already home. I didn't tell Tom or Beth you were home to appear before the Draft Board, just like you asked. What a nice surprise it will be for all of you. I'm sure he's home by now. Beth said she would get there as soon as she could."

I didn't even take the time to tell my mother about the Draft Board's decision, or the fact that the decision might have been made because some old man, probably a friend of her father's, had recognized my name.

I could have taken the short route down Capral and Twin Elms Lane, but it had been awhile and I didn't want to walk past those development houses. I wanted to take the scenic route to the boathouse. So I ran down Main Street, taking in the changes of the little town that was growing up without me. At the WWII Monument I cut across the Courthouse lawn, through the Tea

House, through the Dutch Garden, through the gazebo and down the slope to the water's edge.

It was October 15, 1968, another magnificent autumn day on the Demarest Kill.

My friend was alive and now I could see that he was safe and could come home and we could do all the things we had always done and the war was not going to take him, as it had taken so many other boys our age; continued to take them at hundreds per week for reasons no one could understand or even seemed to care about.

Even better, Beth would be joining us to celebrate Tom's safe return. I wasn't even thinking about my renewed deferment status.

The woods were alive with the movement and sounds of small animals and birds preparing for the winter ahead. The browns and golds that surrounded me were urging me to come home to stay, to not even go back to Gainesville.

I ran through the woods to the boathouse, retracing the steps we had taken a million times before that were so familiar to my feet. As I ran, I was going over my plans to convince Beth to return to Florida with me until I finished law school. I had been positive I could convince her. But now, with Tom there, might she want to stay and nurse him? Was I in danger of losing her to Tom now, as I had always feared?

I half expected to hear Tom playing the piano like we had heard him do so many afternoons before. The fact that he wasn't at the piano signaled a profound change. We would never be kids again, waiting in the woods with O.B.W., for Tom to finish practicing. I walked up the root-rutted pathway toward the boathouse and came to a bend in the path.

As I rounded the corner I saw something that made me stop in my tracks. Beth was reaching up, kissing Tom's face while they held one another in an embrace. Beth was crying and Tom's face was in a grimace as if holding back tears. A pair of wooden crutches leaned against the nearby railing.

I stepped forward from the cover foliage in shock and disbelief. Having caught my breath, I was now out of breath again, the air sucked from my lungs by what I had just witnessed. And what had I just witnessed? I was punched in the stomach. My mind raced. Neither one of them knew I was home. They thought they were safe, that I would never know. But I had to know. I took another step forward, my chest heaving. Beth turned, frightened suddenly when she heard an unexpected snapping of a dry twig behind her.

"Will, what are you doing here?"

"What's that supposed to mean?

"I didn't know you were coming home"

"I guess not, from the looks of things.

"What do you mean?

"What's going on here between you and my best friend?

I stepped forward, and Beth sought shelter in Tom's embrace.

"Will, Beth is here because I called your mother from D.C. I couldn't reach you in Florida. I had to catch to my connection. I asked her to tell both of you that I would be home. Max picked me up at Newark.

"Didn't your mother tell you? Well obviously she did, because you're here. I thought you were in Florida and was hoping you might be able to come up for a few days."

"Yeah. My mother told me you called her this morning."

"I called her because I didn't know how to get in touch with either one of you.

"Your mother called Beth for me and told her I would be home. Your mother agreed to call her as a gesture of friendship. She thought it would be a nice surprise. She didn't tell me you were coming home."

My voice was rising. "I was home already. I had asked her not to tell anyone. She just now told me Beth would be meeting you later. How convenient for you. You thought I was in Florida. So you thought you would be alone."

Tom was trying to follow my line of reasoning. "Why are you home?"

Beth turned to me. "Yes, why are you home? I thought you had mid-term exams this week?"

"I had to fly up and meet the Draft Board. I got a draft notice. I wanted to see if I could get my deferment extended. I thought it was going to be happy news for us and I wanted to surprise you. But instead you surprise me like this."

"Will, what are you talking about? When your mother called I came straight here from my job to see Tom."

"Thinking I was in Florida. Not knowing I was in New York."

"Of course I didn't know you were here. I even tried reaching you in Florida to talk about it. You never told me you were coming home. Will, I came to see my best friend, next to you. This guy, Tom, you remember him? Your friend who was shot in the war. Will what are you thinking? Are you thinking that there is something going on between Tom and me? How could you think that?"

"How? Because you thought you were alone with him and you were kissing him, that's how." I was raising my voice again.

"I was kissing him because I love him and I'm happy to see that he's home safe and sound and I was crying and hugging him because I was so happy to see him. I just fell apart." She began to fall apart again.

I was speechless. It seemed so obvious to me what I had stumbled across, no matter how much she protested. "You expect me to believe that?"

Beth was crying. Were the tears real? "Of course I expect you to believe that. It's the truth."

"Will, I couldn't wait to get home to see you and Beth. I've missed you both so much. Please don't do this."

"Do what, Tom? Ruin your little tryst?"

"Will, there is no tryst. There was nothing going on. We were hugging because I was so glad to see Beth, so glad to be out of Vietnam, out of the hospital. Back home. I'm alive, Will. Don't you know what that means? I made it out *alive*. I never have to go back."

Tom was starting to choke up now and Beth was sobbing in disbelief. She pulled from Tom and ran up the steps and across the deck and inside.

"I can't believe this." Tom was shaking. He reached for his crutches.

"You can't believe this? You're supposed to be my best friend and I come home as a surprise and I find this?"

"Will."

"After all we've been through?"

"Will. I'm sorry you think this. You are wrong. It's not what you think."

"Sure. You always were a womanizer."

He placed his crutches under his arms and started to hobble up the steps to the boathouse. "I think you'd better leave. I wanted us all to be so happy together. You're really upsetting Beth."

Tom and I had always spoken as equals. Now, as a Dartmouth graduate and a Vietnam War Veteran and Purple Heart candidate, I could hear the note of condescension in his voice.

"What, are you her protector now? Some big war hero comes home to steal his best friend's girlfriend and be some big shot now? Is that what's going on?"

He stood on the bottom stair. "Will, I want you to leave. I don't want you to say anything more that you might regret later. This is horrible what you are thinking."

"That's great. Leave you and Beth alone like you thought you were going to be. Fine. I'm leaving."

I walked off, angry, hurt, jealous, and disgusted with myself. Behind me I heard Tom use his crutches to get up the final stairs. I walked away from the two best friends I would ever have in the world without telling them I didn't have to go to Vietnam; that I could stay in law school; without telling Tom that I was glad to see him home alive and well and on the road to recovery; without telling either one of them that I loved them both and could never envision my life without them in it. I turned my back and walked away from both of my friends in anger.

I went home and said goodbye to my mother and to Francis. She could tell I was upset.

"What's wrong?"

"Nothing."

"Will, please tell me."

"Nothing's wrong. I have to get back to school."

"Is Tom okay? How did he look?

"He's fine.

"Did Beth make it? I called her, thought it would be a nice surprise."

"Yeah. A great surprise."

"I didn't tell her you were home. Like you asked."

"Did you tell Tom I was home?"

"No. Remember, you told me not to tell Beth, so I just assumed you didn't want me to tell Tom either. I called her. I thought it would be a nice surprise for all of you when you showed up. A surprise reunion."

I turned and walked toward the stairs.

"Will, did I do something wrong?"

"No, Mom."

"You never told me what happened at the Draft Board."

"You must know someone. They let me off."

"Of course. My father's boyhood friend. Mr. Conklin. White hair?"

"They all had white hair."

"I'm so happy for you Will. Now you don't have to go to that awful place."

I flew out that next morning to Jacksonville and caught a Greyhound to Gainesville. I got in late Thursday night and by then

I had decided what I was going to do. I would not talk to Beth or Tom for two weeks, until November 1. Make them contact me and beg forgiveness for what I was sure was their betrayal. How could they have done this to me? How long had it been going on? I was determined to find out. I thought a waiting game would be best.

On November 1, two weeks after not hearing from either one of them, I started to fold. What if they had been telling me the truth? Hadn't Beth told me time and again that they were just friends and she would never love anyone else but me?

That night in Gainesville, I called Beth at home in New City, and her father answered the phone.

"Beth doesn't come home on weekends, now. She stays with her friend in Manhattan."

"Do you have a number for her? Can I call her?"

"They don't have a phone. Can't afford it. Even if they did have a phone number I don't think I would give it to you."

"Why not?"

"She was very upset the last time she saw you. Might not be a good idea."

"Will you tell her that I called?"

"If she calls I'll tell her. I wouldn't expect a call back, though."

I had her number at work, but that was almost three days away. I didn't know if I could last that long. I even considered flying up in the morning, but as usual, money was tight and I had law school tuition to pay again before January.

Instead, an hour later, Beth called me on Marcy's phone. I raced across Marcy's lawn to answer.

"Will?"

"Beth?"

"My father told me you called."

"He said he didn't have a number for you. You don't have a phone."

"We don't have a phone. I just happened to call him from this phone booth and he told me you just called."

I wasn't sure whether to believe her.

"So you don't have a number."

"No. It's too expensive. I'm a starving artist. I don't have a phone. Like I'm a poor college girl all over again. Our apartment is the size of your mother's pantry. I'm in a deli on the corner."

" ' Our apartment' ?"

"Mine and Loretta's"

"Loretta? I've never heard you mention her."

"Will, if you're going to start making jealous comments again I'm going to hang up right now."

"I want to get together again."

"Even though you think I cheated on you with our best friend?"

"I'm willing to overlook that. Forgive you."

"Will, are you crazy? You really think I cheated on you? Would ever cheat on you?"

"I want to get back together again. Come live with me while I finish law school. Then we can move back to New City."

"No. I'm not leaving my job. Everyone loves my work and there are too many opportunities here for me."

"Can't it wait? It's just another two years or so. Or I'll come up there."

"No. I'm not leaving. And I don't think you should leave law school, either. You'll get drafted and go to Vietnam and get killed. Tom was a lucky one. You may not be so lucky."

"Beth, please."

"Will, no. Finish law school. Maybe the war will be over by then and you can come home and you can begin a practice and maybe if we can work things out we can live in New City and live happily ever after.

"But I need some time to be by myself, Will. You don't know how much you hurt me the other day. How much you hurt Tom. After all he's done for you."

What did she mean by that?

"Your behavior was inexcusable. That was the second time you've hurt me in just one year. I just need time to think. I need to think this through."

"Beth, we've been together for over ten years."

"I know, Will. But we have to stop. At least for now. I have to have time to think about this. I'm sorry."

There was silence on the phone except for her breathing.

"I love you, Beth."

"I love you, Will."

And then she hung up.

CHAPTER SIXTY-EIGHT

December, 1968
Age 22

> *Just one smile, the pain's forgiven,*
> *just one kiss, the hurt's all gone.*
> *Just one smile to make my life worth living,*
> *a little dream to build my world upon.*

> Gene Pitney (1966)
> Written by Randy Newman

This is all I wanted from Beth that November 1, after that phone call; *just one smile*.

My trips to the UF campus were now restricted to the Northeast corner where the law school was. Getting to class the past two weeks had become a huge effort. I had more important things on my mind. But the real problem began when I got there; paying attention to what was being taught, when my life had fallen apart. Between classes, when I was not in the Law Library, I would wander around the Plaza of the Americas, almost as if I were looking for Beth. But of course she would never be here again. I was looking at two years without ever seeing her. Maybe a lifetime if I couldn't get it right. I couldn't face a future without her.

After two weeks of waiting and then finally getting through on the phone and begging, I was ready to throw in the towel. What difference did law school make when I had lost the love of my life to my best friend? Or at least that is what I had convinced myself in my moments of hopelessness and despair.

In my infinite wisdom I decided to drop out of law school and get drafted for an unknown future in Vietnam. Getting drafted for two years was better than enlisting for three. Maybe if I became a war hero like Tom, Beth would take me back. That's how crazy my reasoning was.

I called the Draft Board and explained that I had changed my mind and was ready to serve my country immediately. When I first explained it to the secretary who answered the phone she put me on hold and the old white-haired man got on the phone.

"Is this Mr. Conklin?"

"Yes."

"My mother said you and her father were boyhood friends."

"That's correct, and I was on the train with him and your mother the day they met your father for the first time. He was on his way to N.Y.U."

I let that sink in.

"You don't have to do this, son. I would advise against it. Think of what it will do to your mother."

I had already thought about that when I'd received my defer-ment extension. Someone would have to go in my place. What would that boy's mother think? Or as the Kinks put it, *"some mother's son . . ."*

Finally, the old white-haired man relented. Although con-fused, they were ready to oblige and by early November of 1968, just weeks after my fateful day with Beth and Tom, I reported to the induction center in Jacksonville. I had left all my earthly pos-sessions and my VW Bug with Jerry.

Within a few days I was in basic training in Ft. Polk, Louisiana.

I was twenty-two years old and would be in the Army for two

years until December of 1970.

Just before Christmas, after six weeks of boot camp, I came
home on a weekend pass, in uniform, to see my mother and brother
on the last day of the last furlough, December 20, 1968. She was
on the front porch, waiting for me, as I stepped off the bus. The
bus pulled north, revealing me standing on the corner of Third and
Main, my duffel bag in hand, my heart on my sleeve. She looked
at me, trying to be proud, my short hair, my lean frame, my erect
status, my crisp uniform, but there was more fear in her eyes than
anything else. I could tell she was trying not to cry.

As for me, I was operating on auto-pilot, just making it through
each day, focusing on the ground two inches in front of my feet.

"Why don't you go see Father Carrick," had become my
mother's mantra by that time.

Francis looked at me in uniform, his face in a tight grimace.
What did he understand? Did watching television actually give
him understanding of the mindless debacle our country was
involved in?

I took my mother's advice. I went to see Father Carrick. He
looked me up and down. "You didn't have to do this, you know.
All you had to do was apologize to Beth and Tom."

"Apologize? They are the ones who betrayed me."

"Will, Will. That's simply not true. It can't be true."

"I know what I saw."

"It can't be true."

"Why are you taking their side?"

"Because I know it can't be true."

"How."

"I know Beth. And I know Tom."

"I know what I saw."

"You know what you *think* you saw. Apologize to them both
before you leave. You don't want to leave here without. . ."

He stopped. By "here" did he mean New City or this earthly

plane? But then he saw I understood what he was saying.

"Before you leave this planet, get it off your chest. You have no idea the hurt you have caused."

"My bus is leaving."

He must have realized that line of the discussion had ended. There was silence in the room as he evaluated his dismay. "Will, don't let anything happen to you over there."

"I won't."

"Don't come back like Tom."

"What do you mean?"

He hesitated as if wanting to tell me something, but maybe he had already told me too much.

"What do you mean?"

"Just be safe. Come back safe. Your mother and your brother need you, Will."

"And Beth."

"Just think of your mother and your brother. You have to come back home safe for them."

"What aren't you telling me?

"Don't think like that. Promise me."

"I will."

I stuck out my hand to shake hands with him, but he turned away from me, his shoulders shaking.

I actually did think about going to see Tom, but I wasn't sure what it would accomplish. Helpful tips for surviving in Vietnam? More lies about him and Beth? I stood in the back yard down by the chicken coops and looked at the ball field, now overgrown from neglect once again, and almost went to see him.

In the grand scheme of things it was just a few small steps. But I couldn't take even one step forward.

It would be thirty-two years before I ever spoke to Tom again.

Although I had wanted to see my mother and brother before I

left for Vietnam, my real reason for coming home between basic training and shipping out was to see Beth. I just assumed that she had heard I had dropped out of law school and had joined the Army. Maybe if she knew I would be leaving for Vietnam in a short time she would reconsider and take me back. At least then I would have something to fight for, something to come home to, something to rally around the flag for.

I said goodbye to my mother and Francis, going through the motions, trying to act nonchalant as if I were just going out to buy a quart of milk, unsuccessfully masking the fact that my never coming back was practically *a fait accompli.*

Under skies that were overcast in dark grey, with a signal for a snowstorm in the air, I took the bus into Manhattan and hung around the art gallery where I knew she worked. Everyone knew her father had bought the gallery to handle all of his work. It was the talk of the town.

Even under the dark skies, the city was alive with the Christmas spirit this December of 1968. Holiday decorations were everywhere and the shop windows were filled with lights and color. The pedestrians seemed to be in the holiday spirit and some pedestrians were even smiling. It still looked empty and bleak to me.

At lunchtime, Beth and a co-worker headed south to Washington Square Park, brown lunch bags in their hands. I followed from a distance until she sat down on a bench.

As I approached, she looked up from her sandwich with at first confusion, then surprise. She didn't recognize me in the uniform.

"Will, what are you doing here? Why are you in uniform? Why aren't you at law school?"

"You didn't know I quit law school and joined the Army? How could you not know? Everyone knows."

"Of course I know. Like I said, what are you doing here? Why are you in uniform? Why aren't you at law school?"

"Can you take a walk?"

She looked to her friend and around at the bustling crowd. "I'm eating lunch."

The woman co-worker she was sharing the bench with, who I assumed was Loretta, stood and walked off on cue. "I'll see you back at the gallery."

"What are you doing here?"

"I wanted to say hello. And goodbye."

"I don't understand."

"I'm shipping out. I can't tell you where, but the first initial is Vietnam."

"I'm sorry to hear that. After all the trouble we went through to get you into law school, I can't believe you dropped out. You were home free, Will. You didn't have to go."

I shrugged it off. "'We' went through?"

"Will, please be careful. Please promise me that however you feel about me that you'll be careful over there; that you'll be all right."

"I'll be careful. Will I be all right? That's a different story."

"You look different."

"I am different."

"I don't mean the haircut. You look different somehow."

"I am different. A lot different. I see the world from a whole new perspective now."

"I can imagine."

"Can you?"

"Will, I don't want to fight."

"I'm not fighting. Just trying to understand."

"Understand what?"

"The woman I love and my best friend?"

"Will, we tried to explain to you that what you saw was a hug and a welcome home kiss on the cheek between two old friends. That's all it was."

"Well if that's all it was, how come you won't talk to me?"

"Because you were being unreasonable. You were acting

childish. You insulted Tom. You insulted me. I needed time to think, Will. How can I live with someone who doesn't trust me? Who doesn't believe what I tell him?"

"I know what I saw."

"What you saw is not what you think it was. I don't want to go over and over this again." She paused and looked around the park before she continued. "Will, between what happened in October and what happened last year with the baby, our baby, it made me start to think that maybe this wasn't meant to be."

"This?"

"Us. Not meant to be, Will."

Even after all that had transpired over the last two months, I still could not accept that simple fact.

"Why?"

"Because I spent the first twelve years I knew you, loving and idolizing you and then I find out you're not the person I thought you were. Quitting law school we worked so hard for, to join the Army? That was a childish waste, Will. Were you trying to get back at me, back at Tom somehow for something that isn't even true?

I couldn't answer her.

She looked away before speaking. "I don't think I can live with what all this has done to me."

"What has it done to you?"

"What has it done? Well for starters I'll never be able to have children because of the botched abortion that you insisted I get, even though I wanted our child more than I've ever wanted anything in this whole world. *Our baby*, Will. Our precious child that we conceived in a beautiful moment of love. Do you know what that did to me? Of course you don't, and that's the problem.

"According to you, I would never be able to be best friends with someone I love and care about very much because you cannot trust me to be around him without thinking awful things are going on? Is that enough yet? I can't deal with it anymore. I'm tired of crying all the time."

I didn't know what to say.

"Will, I still love you and I feel like I've lost the best friend I've ever had. I don't even know who you are. I don't want anything to happen to you over there. I'm really worried. You don't look right. You look, I don't know, crazy."

"*I am crazy*, Beth."

"Right now, I don't think we'll ever be able to be together again like we were before. Maybe I'll feel differently in time. I just need some time. I'm sorry Will."

"Two years be long enough? I'll be back in two years."

She stood and wrapped up her brown bag. She started to cry.

"I'm sorry Will. Please promise me you'll come home safely. Don't let them do to you what they did to Tom."

I wanted to ask her, *what did they do to Tom?* That was the second time I'd heard that expression that day. What did she and Father Carrick mean by that? Instead I stood, my arms at my side, thinking only of myself.

"Please, Beth."

"You didn't even ask what they did to Tom."

"What did they do to Tom? You mean besides his leg injury? His stomach?"

"Yes, besides those."

"I don't know what you mean."

"They betrayed him, Will. That's what they did. We betrayed them all. He'll never recover from that injury."

"What do you mean?"

"You'll understand. You'll understand someday. It will all become very clear to you very quickly. I'm sorry, Will. I have to get back to work. Be safe, my love. "

She reached out and cupped my cheek in her palm for only a second. "You'll always be the one. You will never know how much you hurt me." Then she turned and was lost in the noon-day crowd before I could catch up to her.

In a Hollywood movie, a light snowfall would have started on this cue. But this was no Hollywood movie; no one was watching this sad scene unfold. All that happened was the skies got darker and everyone was too busy to pay attention and that she had told me that I would "always be the one."

The snow would fall later.

CHAPTER SIXTY-NINE

VIETNAM

1969
Ages 22-23

You don't even want to know the details of what happened to me in Vietnam. You've already heard the terrible stories from others, so why go on about it? With my R.O.T.C. and pre-law school credentials I got lucky. I became a high level clerk in an adjutant's office and spent the better part of two years in Vietnam helping clean up the legal messes and accompanying paperwork. I saw firsthand and up-close my share of what can happen from such an ill-conceived enterprise. I worked with the adjutant's office and spent most of my time in Saigon and nearby cities like Pleiku, and was not in the infantry and did not see much action personally. I was close enough to the front, close enough to the skirmishes, to be overwhelmed by the sheer violence and stupidity and arrogance of it every day, to live in abject fear. I became an *accomplice* to the countless atrocities of war we committed over there.

It was so much worse than anyone can imagine on so many levels, if you haven't seen it firsthand. The banality of evil, to use a cliché. My evil became average, routine. Our work there was truly an evil enterprise instigated by psychopathic men without conscience. But it was nothing like what I would hear about Tom's experiences before all of this would be over. That would be so much worse. Beth was correct. I would understand very quickly what they did to Tom, to me; what they did to every kid who was sent there. It was an unspeakable betrayal on a grand scale.

Sometimes the only defense mechanism that works at times like that is humor. We jokingly referred to the soldiers in the field as "The Howdy Doody Boys," my playmates and peers raised in an innocent age, playing with hula hoops and whiffle balls and collecting Davy Crocket bubble-gum cards and dancing the Twist one day; forced, or willing, to commit unspeakable horrors and spill entrails and witness depraved acts in the name of empty patriotism the next day, for absolutely no justifiable reason.

Why did we go so willingly? Why did we listen? Why did we obey inhumane orders? We wanted to be heroes like our fathers had been in World War II and like we saw in the movies. That was our incentive. We believed the propaganda because we were vulnerable and our leaders used our vulnerability and our desire to be like the men our fathers were, to convince us, and turn us into the killers we became.

Will our country ever learn they cannot do to their young people what they did to us in those times? We betrayed them all. We were all betrayed. Young boys from the ghettos and the farm-land and the bayous and the mountains and the suburbs, from sea to shining sea, it made no difference. The hearts and minds and very lives of the Howdy Doody Boys were considered acceptable collateral damage. What I had feared was soon enough validated when the stories began to emerge publicly, when the books began to get published, like *My Lai 4* and *Born on the Fourth of July*. We were all willfully betrayed and there's just no getting around it. Why would a country do that to its own young people? What kind of country would do that? What kind of country? There's something to think about. What was worth that price some of us paid?

Answer those questions if you have the guts.

I became an *accomplice*.

CHAPTER SEVENTY

**THE HISTORY OF MUSIC
IN NEW CITY, NEW YORK:
PART XIII**

Christmas, 1970
Age 24

> *Sam Stone came home,*
> *To the wife and family*
> *After serving in the conflict overseas.*
> *And the time that he served,*
> *Had shattered all his nerves,*
> *And left a little shrapnel in his knees.*
> *But the morphine eased the pain,*
> *And the grass grew round his brain,*
> *And gave him all the confidence he lacked,*
> *With a purple heart and a monkey on his back.*
> *There's a hole in daddy's arm where all the money goes,*
> *Jesus Christ died for nothin' I suppose.*

Written by John Prine
Performed by Swamp Dogg

By Christmas of 1970, my Army career was over and I was discharged, "honorably,' if that word can be so blatantly, so sickeningly misconstrued, in Ft. Dix on December 20, 1970 after the two years in Vietnam I've spent the rest of my life trying, but not capable of, forgetting. I'm not capable of forgetting, remember? But for now, it was all over and I was trying to look on the bright side. I would try to recover as much as I could in the coming years, but the enormity of the betrayal is one that can never leave you. The betrayal alone is incomprehensible, and the more you thought about it, the more you realized how transparent it had all been for anyone who had taken the time to notice. Like any betrayal, upon realization, you feel foolish, wondering how you could ever allow something like that to happen to you. The long denial sets in, and the betrayal from my own country that I knew was real, only exacerbated the betrayal I had perceived from Beth and Tom. The two, back-to-back, were like raw, bleeding, sucking wounds to my lungs whenever I tried to take a deep breath. Ever had vertigo? I had it, but not between my ears. I had it in my heart.

As the bus pulled into the Port Authority Terminal, I made a decision I had been trying to make for months.

Instead of transferring to a bus to take me home to New City, I caught a subway downtown to the Village. There, I retraced my steps of two years earlier, past the holiday shoppers and the Christmas decorations. This time a light snow began to fall. Now as I walked these streets my perspective and my perceptions were so different. What was this country now? I'm not sure I even recognized it. I didn't feel like I belonged here. I didn't want to be in such a country. I didn't belong anywhere. Everyone seemed oblivious to what was going on over there, not really caring, getting on with their lives. Why did they call us "baby killers" when we arrived back home? That answer is simple. *Because we were baby killers.*

It was so different than what I knew of WWII from the newsreels and family stories and Hollywood movies about sacrifice and all pulling together. It was like it was a make-believe war, and for those who were never there, I suppose it was a make-believe war. It wasn't until years later that I accepted the fact that even for those who were there, those who suffered in the jungles and rice paddies, and those who suffered when they got home and continue to suffer to this day, it really was just a make-believe war. It was disguised in empty, emotionally-laden words like "patriotism," and "glory," and "heroes." And to what end? It's really not so hard to figure out.

When Beth and Loretta left the gallery with their lunches in hand, I followed them again down to Washington Square Park. I kept a safe distance. I knew where they were headed. Their routine appeared to be the same.

This time, as I approached their bench, I wasn't in uniform, and it was Loretta, Beth's co-worker, who recognized me first and stood to leave abruptly. "Meet you back at the gallery."

Beth then stood to greet me and I stepped into a lukewarm embrace. "Will, I'm so glad you made it back alive. I didn't hear anything from you for two years. Tom and I were so worried. We've been calling your mother every week for an update. You're okay?"

"I'm alive. I guess that's asking a lot. 'Okay'? Maybe time will tell."

"But you're home. Safe. You're out?"

"Yes. Out."

"I wish you would have called and told us you were coming home."

"Two-year hitch. Two years ago the other day."

"But you haven't contacted Tom or me."

"No. Didn't want to disturb the little love nest."

"Will, please don't start."

"I'm not the one who started this."

"There is no *this.* You imagined everything."

"Have you had a chance to think about what I said two years ago? Had your 'time to think'? At this very bench, as I recall." I sounded so self-righteous.

"Yes, Will. Yes I have."

"And?"

She didn't hesitate, as if she had been rehearsing and had anticipated my arrival, this ambush conversation, my cue. "And I'm getting married."

I felt the bile rise in my throat. I took a deep breath trying to hold it back. My worst fears of the past two years, despite all I had been through in Vietnam, were now confirmed in this one moment.

The snow was falling heavier now. There would be a 'White Christmas,' just like the ones we used to know; like our days ice skating on Lake Lucille; like our night on The Hill, like our night of ice skating on Lake Lucille in the glow of the headlamps after the Christmas dance.

"You're marrying Tom." It was not a question.

"Tom? Why would I marry Tom? I told you, I've never felt that way about Tom. That's something you always imagined that was never true."

"Who?"

"Someone I met. Someone you don't know. Well, actually you have met him but you probably don't remember him."

I felt myself weakening so I sat on the bench next to her. She instinctively moved away, as if we were strangers. My mind raced back over our years together. Someone from Gainesville? A crazy art professor? A friend of her father's? Someone from New City?

"Who?"

"He's the man who bought the Florion property from Tom's grandparents. He developed the Twin Elms housing development. Do you remember him?"

Vaguely. I remembered him standing up and addressing the

group gathered there under the tent that day of Tom's lawn party, and promising in a slight, polished Dutch accent that he would never befoul the community in New City.

"How did you meet him?"

"He came into the gallery one day to buy one of my father's pieces. He said I looked familiar. We talked and then it all came back. I remembered him."

"He has to be thirty years older than us."

"Twenty four years older, to be exact."

"I don't understand."

"I don't really either. We started seeing one another and we fell in love."

"How did you start seeing him?"

"When he came into the gallery that day. It was a coincidence. We started talking. He's very charming. He mentioned how much he loves New City. One thing led to another and, well, it's a small world."

I did some math in my head. "He's forty eight?" The idea was preposterous to me.

"I don't care. I love him Will. You have to understand that."

"I can't understand that."

"You have to Will. I told you two years ago that I didn't think there would ever be anything between us again."

"Did you know him the last time we met here?"

"No. Just that day at Tom's tent party. This was all after you left. That following spring."

"Pleiku."

"I don't know what 'Pleiku' is, Will."

I shook my head. Did anyone? "While I was in Vietnam."

"Will, if you're going to be like this I'm leaving. I'm trying to tell you something and I want you to be happy for me."

"Happy for you? He's forty eight."

"He's exciting, He's interesting. He's fun. We're always laughing. He supports my work, my art. We travel. I love him

Will. He's taught me so much of the world."

"He's rich."

"Okay, Will. I'm sorry you have to be like this." She sighed, started wrapping her unfinished sandwich in the wax paper on her lap. "I wanted to tell you face-to-face when you got back. I wanted you to be happy for your old friend. I want you and Tom to come to the wedding."

"Old friend?"

"Yes, me. Your old best friend."

"That's what I've been reduced to after all we've been through? I'm your 'old best friend'?"

She finished wrapping her sandwich. "Can't you let the past stay there?"

"Apparently not."

I turned and walked away toward my own oblivion.

"Will. Please don't be that way."

I heard her but I didn't hear her.

I walked through the heavy noontime pedestrian traffic as the snowflakes began to get traction, and headed toward the Port Authority Terminal. In retrospect, I was taking my own first footsteps toward oblivion, just as my father had after "Francis' Day." But unlike him, I would not be walking in circles around New City in the dark of night. I would be elsewhere, in bright daylight, riding in circles while staying stoned twenty four hours a day for the next two years.

At the Port Authority Terminal I caught a Red & Tan to New City and got dropped off on Third and Main. As the bus pulled away my mother was wheeling Francis out the front door to watch the snowfall, her back to me. I stood at the corner and watched them go through their routine and found out what their life had been like in my two-year absence. Life had gone on for them. As she turned him around they both saw me. Francis craned his neck as best he could and his bottom lip started quivering and the tears poured from his eyes. I had not seen him in two years. I dodged around a snowplow driven by Gary Plunkett, his tire chains jangling as he passed with a wave and a honk, and I ran across the street and up the front sidewalk into my mother's embrace.

"Will, you're safe. You're safe. I prayed every day for you to come home all in one piece and now you're here. Somehow I knew you would be home today. We come out every day and wait, but somehow, I knew today would be the day."

Her tears began and her shoulders began to shake and even though I knew she had nothing in this life to hang on to, I also knew I had to leave her. I had to get out of New City.

"It's so good to have you home safe and sound, Will."

"It's good to be home, Mom."

"You're alive. That's all that counts."

She walked us inside and it was if I had been there yesterday. Nothing was changed except a new oilcloth on the kitchen table where my father had been born fifty-four years earlier. Her quilting frames were set up on chairs in the corner next to the bookcase near the open doors to Francis' bedside.

"I'm still doing all the reading now. We did all of Thomas Hardy. Now we're doing Sinclair Lewis and Pearl Buck and Sherwood Anderson again. We save Jerry Todd and Tutter for the summers."

She fixed us a late afternoon lunch and we wheeled Francis back to his bed. Now twenty six, I saw no improvement in his condition. Just his pale, almost transparent skin and the traces of acne and his same broken form. I ached for him, but I was getting to the point where I could no longer look him in the eye without falling apart.

"Don't let him see you cry, Will. It upsets him. He knows he's the reason."

As I helped clear the table, my mother turned her back to me, as if she knew she wasn't going to like my answer.

"Are you going to stay here with us? Do you have any plans?"

"I've been offered an internship at a law firm in Gainesville. They're going to pay my tuition to go back to law school.

"That's wonderful, Will. When do you have to leave?"

"Tomorrow morning."

She turned to me. It's difficult to describe the look that came over her face. She was torn between living an existence she faced every day without my being there to help, and the knowledge that she had to let go and let me live my life. She was resigned to the fact that all hope for me to return home soon was now gone.

"Your father would be so proud, Will. Law school."

My father wouldn't even notice, I thought.

"I'll come home whenever I can, Mom."

"I know you will. You mustn't worry about us. Francis and I are old pals and we love our days together. We start all the Edna Ferber next week after we finish *Winesburg, Ohio*."

She hugged me and my self-hatred only increased for having lied to her. I spent the night cradling my brother in the crook of my arm, watching game shows and sit-coms. By the time Johnny Carson came on, we were both out for the night. Early the next morning, I arose and changed his diapers like I had on thousands of mornings before, led him through the physical therapy regimen, kissed him on the forehead, hugged my mother goodbye, and headed for the bus stop.

It would be sixteen months before I saw them again.

CHAPTER SEVENTY-ONE

FLORIDA

Winter, 1971 – Spring 1972
Ages 24, 25

There was no internship. There was no law firm. There would be no paid tuition to law school from a private practice resulting in my earning a doctor of jurisprudence. I would not become an attorney. What I told my mother was all a lie.

Instead, the next morning I said my goodbyes and caught the seven o'clock bus to Port Authority and caught a Greyhound to Gainesville. Thirty-six hours later, I retrieved my VW from where it had been parked in Jerry's garage for two years. The car was stacked to the roof with boxes of books, my Smith-Corona type-writer, jeans, and work shirts.

After a brief 'thank you,' there was little conversation between us. He was a friend of Beth's and her father, first and foremost.

"I heard Beth's getting married. See you at the wedding?"

"Not likely."

The bug started with just a little push, and I headed south on I-75. At a rest stop near Paynes Prairie I made a few phone calls.

Six hours later I was in Palm Beach Gardens and filling out

paperwork to hire on with the lawn maintenance crew at P.G.A. National Golf Course. It was owned by one of the country's first billionaires, John D. MacArthur. A college buddy of mine, Rodney, had landed me the job.

After work I took P.G.A. Boulevard and headed east across U.S. 1 to Air Force Beach and turned south on Singer Island, where I checked into a flea-bag efficiency apartment Rodney had arranged for me. I threw my bags on the floor and crashed on the bed. The smell of insecticide was overwhelming, but the balmy air coming from the ocean through the open jalousie window slats was a change from the frigid night I had just left in New York.

The room was to be my prison cell for almost two years.

The next morning I arose at four a.m. and put on work jeans and my Army boots and headed back to the golf course where Rodney handed me a wide brimmed straw hat and walked me over to the garage that housed the lawnmowers.

He went over the rules and the controls and handed me a schematic diagram of the three golf courses and showed me where to mow on our upcoming tour.

By daybreak, we were squeezed onto a one-man seat and we headed out to the sunrise to mow the fairways and roughs on the golf course. He lit up a joint and passed it to me. "You're gonna need a lot of sunscreen and a lot of this stuff. Forget either one and your days and your nights will be miserable."

He was right. But my days and nights were going to be miserable anyway.

For the next sixteen months, I arose before dawn and drove circles around the golf courses mowing the roughs and fairways, and smoked bales of Columbian marijuana that were dropped out of low-flying airplanes after dark and tumbled to a halt on the far corners of the golf courses where there were no houses and no D.E.A. agents to be found. The planes would then fly back up onto the radar screens and land empty at PBIA. Before dawn we would pick up the bales and divvy it up and smoke what we could and sell the rest. I didn't ask any questions. I was stoned into incoherence most of the time and dizzy from riding around in circles, baked brown by the Florida sun.

At night I would drive back to my efficiency apartment and try to write short stories on the Smith Corona my mother had given me for college. In college my influences were Malamud and Updike and Jones. Now, I was reading Oates and Fowles and *The Adventures of Augie March* for the third time.

Seven days a week, for almost a year and a half, it was the same routine without ever coming up for air to go on a date or do anything but read, write, get stoned, and mow endless lawns to perfection. I was so stoned that I couldn't even mow the greens with a hand-mower, because that required walking behind the mower instead of remaining seated. The one time I tried it I was so loaded I gouged a hole near one of the cups. I tried to convince Rodney that it was a divot but he knew there were no divots that size on the greens.

Some days I worked with the carpentry crew that was building covered bridges on top of concrete pilings across the many canals on the courses. I remembered a little carpentry from watching my father and grandfather and the Norwegians at New City Park Lake, and it all came back to me in a hurry. "Plumb, level, and square." "Measure twice, cut once."

No matter how hard I tried to dull the pain and get lost in a haze of marijuana and the novels of Drieser, DosPassos, Bellow, Oates, Steinbeck, and Updike; and the fumbled fits and failed starts of my own writing, I still couldn't forget about Beth. I tried to follow the advice of Wordsworth and *recollect the spontaneous overflow of powerful emotions in moments of tranquility*, but it just never worked out. I couldn't find the *tranquility*, but I could recollect. That was the one "special talent" I had perfected. Detailed recollection was my curse.

Beth was the subject of all my musings and in my thoughts as I mowed up and down the endless grass of fifty-four holes of golf course every day. I couldn't leave her behind, no matter how hard I tried. But I couldn't get it down on paper. I couldn't get it out. It was all trapped inside, a million memories fighting to get out, fighting for priority; begging, pleading, to be forgotten. That would have been a welcome relief. My countless memories of Beth and Vietnam had buried me in an avalanche of despair.

In the meantime, that spring of 1971, six months after my last Washington Square Park encounter with Beth and my start at PGA, Beth and Rainer Klein were united in holy matrimony in St. Augustine's in a high mass presided over by Father Carrick on a June Saturday afternoon when I was riding in endless circles around a golf course 1300 miles away. All of our high school friends, including Tom, and many of Beth's college friends, were in attendance. I would find out later that even my mother was there, tucked back into a far pew with Francis in his wheelchair. What did he make of it? What had my mother been thinking that day? Beth and Rainer would leave for a honeymoon in Europe that would last almost seven years until 1978.

By the spring of 1972, my lungs were burning from the smoke and inhaling gasoline, insecticide and fertilizer fumes all day long. I thought I might go into anaphylactic shock at any moment. My skin on my face was brown and cracked from the endless sun, my fingers were raw from typing worthless, incoherent sentences into the night until I fell asleep, and my brain was fried. I was physically and mentally and emotionally exhausted. I didn't think I could spend another summer in the South Florida furnace. I needed solace and had no idea where to find it. I was seriously ready to call it quits on life, but I knew I couldn't do that without going home one last time to say goodbye to Francis. I knew I couldn't end it, with his life the way it was. It would have been an insult to him for me to waste my life in such a way. I couldn't put my mother through it. But I was going home to say goodbye.

I packed up the VW, said *adios* to Rodney and P.G.A. National, and my little ocean-side efficiency apartment and headed north.

I called my mother from a roadside stop somewhere in North Florida and spoke to her for the first time in two years. "Mom?"

"Will. Are you okay? We've been so worried about you. I showed Francis the postcard you mailed last year. It looks very pretty there. He asks for you all the time."

I knew what she meant. Unable to talk, he asked with his eyes. She had learned to interpret the gaze in his eyes.

"I'm okay. I want to come home."

"Francis would love to see you. Come home, Will. We need you here."

I headed back home to New City.

CHAPTER SEVENTY-TWO

NEW CITY

June, 1972
Age 25

Thirty hours later I pulled into the driveway on Main Street.

I came home because I missed my brother. I missed my New City, without realizing until it was too late, of course, that *my* New City was gone forever. It had changed into something different in the eight years since I first had left to go to the University of Florida. It now belonged to someone else.

For the first time there was a real movie theater in town. The New Rte. 304 had bulldozed its way through the spine of New City, knocking down landmarks like the railroad roundhouse foundation, Jerry's Tavern, Taggart's Pond. There were now strip malls and apartments on the old Squadron A property where the barn had burned to the ground, the property had been sold, and houses built on the site of countless horse races and county fairs.

In the time it had taken me to drive home, my mother had arranged for me to interview for a teaching job at Clarkstown High School, my old Alma Mater. Before I left, I shaved off my scraggly beard and my mother gave me a haircut, cutting my shoulder-length hair. It was a ritual long overdue.

As a boy, waiting my turn on the back sidewalk, sitting on a line of kitchen chairs between the catalpa trees, she would cut the hair of my grandfather, then my father second, then Francis, then me, carefully sculpting our haircuts better than any barber in town could have done it. After brushing our necks with a towel, my father sprayed us down with a garden hose, even my grandfather, and our laughter filled the back yard. My grandfather watched from his perch on the back porch stoop he had built fifty years earlier. Later, after my grandfather died, after "Francis' Day," the haircuts became a solemn ritual. No laughter. No hose. Instead, she poured water over our heads from a galvanized sprinkler can.

On the night before going to my draft board appeal in October of 1968, she had repeated the ritual, but now there was just me sitting on the same kitchen chair, as she made me "look present-able." I guess it worked. When the Draft Board Chairman had asked me that day if I was Marion Summers' son, I wanted to say, "Yes, can you tell by the haircut?"

Then, just a few weeks later, I got it all cut off upon my arrival at basic training. Except that time it all happened in less than twenty seconds. There was no kitchen chair in the shade, no lov-ing touch from my mother's hands, no laughter under the hose.

It wasn't the last time, but it was a memorable time, when she cut it before I went to apply for the job at the high school. All the haircuts were a marking of the time, benchmarks for important rites of passage. Walking down the row of catalpa trees where the haircuts took place, I can still hear my brother's laughter from his day on the seven-league stilts.

So I stopped smoking dope, bought a cheap suit and a couple of pairs of dress slacks, drip-dry shirts, and ties at Robert Hall's with my golf course savings. At my mother's insistence, I drove over to my alma mater, Clarkstown Central High School on Con-gers Road, and applied for the teaching job. Walking in the front door that day, I laughed at the irony. Six years of junior and senior high school there, for what? To come back and teach the next generation of New City kids, eight years later.

As luck would have it, my old social studies and history teacher, Mr. Gritmon, was now an Assistant Principal in charge of hiring new teachers and he hired me on the spot, pending the successful arrival of my transcripts.

There are now two Clarkstown High Schools. The original, now renamed Clarkstown North, is on the old Carnochan Mansion site where we attended for six years. Clarkstown South is down near Germonds and Strawtown Roads, near the southwest corner of the reservoir. As far as my classmates and I were concerned, there will always be just one Clarkstown High School: The old Carnochan Mansion.

CHAPTER SEVENTY-THREE

NEW CITY

Fall, 1972
Age 26

I was to start in the classroom in two months, just after Labor Day, 1972, teaching Political Science and Civics, two sections of American Literature, and two of Creative Writing. I was glad to get whatever I could. I knew all the subject matter content by heart. I was sure the job would keep my mind off the obsessive feelings I was having for Beth, and "the numbers" still racing through my head from Vietnam. But what happened that Fall was just the opposite. Instead of helping me forget, every day when I arrived to teach I would be reminded of yet another incident shared with Beth and Tom and the rest of our classmates. It was almost hysterically hopeless. The halls of my old high school were filled with laughing ghosts with smiling faces that ridiculed me. I relived every moment of my high school years, every conversation at an open hallway locker, every race up and down the tiled stairways, every joke and prank and homework assignment. When I walked the halls as a teacher, Beth and Tom were always at my side.

I found an old American Lit textbook in the book storage room and leafed through its pages. I could recall what happened the day of each lesson from the 1960s. What happened the day we read Dickenson, Whitman, Twain, Frost. What was the classroom dynamic during *"Mending Wall," "Birches," "The Road Not Taken"*? They were all bonded together, permanently; the recitations with the events in the lives of the trio of literary giants known as Beth and Tom and Will.

QUESTION: What happened the same day we learned of *the girls throwing their hair over their heads to dry in the sun?* The day that *Two paths diverged in a wood?*

ANSWER: (I bought Beth's Christmas present, the *Half Heaven, Half Heartache* album by Gene Pitney).

QUESTION: What happened after we read and learned about *"Birches"*.

ANSWER: We climbed our own Birches that day in the woods, trod our own paths.

QUESTION: What happened the night of the day we learned that Frost stopped by a woods on a snowy evening?

ANSWER: (The Spring Valley basketball game) The woods were owned by a man *whose house is in the village, though.* "Village?" That next day in 1962 I bought *Village of Love* by Nathaniel Mayer and *Washington Square by* The Village Stompers. They were all inexorably linked together.

And so now, as I *taught* each lesson and the words of the great American poets, I was drawn back to those earlier days of *learning.* The meaning of the poems and short stories were of secondary importance compared to the fact that Beth and I drove to Tom's boathouse after school and made love all afternoon on the day in the Spring of 1964 when we read The Open Boat, by Stephen Crane. When I taught it to my own students that winter of 1973, it made little difference to me that the story was conceived by Crane after a visit to a Florida whorehouse and after spending three days in a dinghy after a shipwreck off the coast of Daytona enroute to Cuba. No, while Crane's character was arguing with an oiler in the Atlantic on a December night in 1896, and my students were reading the resulting story on a March morning in 1973, I had been snuggling with Beth, in front of the fireplace on Tom's sofa nine years earlier in March of 1964. A year later, near that same Daytona coast Crane had described, I had puked my guts out while watching the Daytona 500 race from the infield during Valentine's Day in February of 1965 without Beth.

And so it went with every lesson. Every lesson had a present and two pasts. Every lesson, every work of literature, was a reminder of events that I was trying to forget.

High school students had changed in eight years. Instead of the naive, innocent sweetness that we had experienced as high school kids, the students of 1972-1973 seemed not to be connected with their pasts and from any ties to New City, or at least my ties and my past in New City. Few had roots here. Drugs, especially marijuana, were coming into widespread use and many students appeared to be stoned all day long. I couldn't decide whether to be tolerant because of my own past, or intolerant because I was living proof of how too much marijuana use could cobweb the brain. I tried to ignore it, but it was annoying.

Only eight years out of CCHS and I was starting to sound like an old fart. But the world of New City and the world at large had indeed changed during my four years in Gainesville, my two years in Vietnam, and my two years driving in endless, meandering circles in Palm Beach Gardens.

I must admit that some aspects of teaching at the high school from which you've graduated can be fun. All the teachers know you, but now know you as one of their peers and they open up and reveal secrets they would never share with you when you were a student. Most of the Clarkstown teachers were real people, with interesting lives, and most of them were egg-heads; intellectuals with keen perceptions and academic intellect, who somehow seemed to be seeking some protection, some solace from the harm the outside world could inflict. Perhaps they all had secrets like me. Perhaps they sensed, after our graduating class and the triumph of the Class of '64, that it all would be downhill from there.

My days were filled with trying to inspire my students, as my teachers had inspired me. I'd had great examples of inspiring teachers both in high school and the University of Florida. Most of my teaching peers had graduated from Ivy League colleges or schools in New England or the SUNY colleges. With a degree from UF, I'm not sure they were convinced I could even read, until they remembered I had graduated from CCHS just eight years before. One of the most skeptical was a young teacher named Delores from Haverstraw.

The kids seemed to like me. I was young, a veteran, and some of them even considered me hip with my reading assignments coming from a much more contemporary list than what they were used to.

My list of required reading in New York schools was something I never really appreciated while I was fulfilling it. Each year the class was required to read one play by Shakespeare. In the seventh grade it was *Romeo and Juliet*. In eighth grade it was *Julius Caesar*. By ninth we were reading *The Merchant of Venice*, with *The Taming of the Shrew* in tenth, *Hamlet* in eleventh, and *Macbeth* and *King Lear* as seniors. We read them and we understood them. My students would not have understood them if they had read them outside the classroom on their own.

We had been required to read at least one or two novels each year, as well; *Treasure Island, Ivanhoe, Silas Marner, David Copperfield, A Tale of Two Cities, Moby Dick, The Red Badge of Courage, The Scarlet Letter, The Citadel,* and *The Bridge of San Luis Rey.* I remember when Mr. Handley had told us Thornton Wilder was the only American writer to win a Pulitzer Prize as both a playwright and a novelist. We had been quite impressed in 1963. After all, *Our Town* was a high school literature and drama staple, and *The Skin of Our Teeth*, a Broadway favorite. In 1973, when I told my students about the double Pulitzer, it was met with indifference. It was not important to them. What was?

What were they reading in my classes in 1972? Mostly nothing, until I turned them on to J.D. Salinger, Kurt Vonnegut, Jr., William Goldman, Ken Kesey, Joseph Heller, John Nichols, Larry McMurtry, and other contemporary novelists of the late 1960s and early 1970s. But it wouldn't be long before high school students reading novels would become a rarity; one of the great, real tragedies in our lifetime.

Along with retracing my footsteps in the hallways of Clarkstown High, I become a regular at all the CCHS traditions; the season-opening bonfire and pep rally and parking lot dance. I kept looking through the flames to find Beth in the crowd. The only good thing to come out of my teaching days at CCHS is that I worked with Delores. It was during these school activities that I first met her. I had heard of her by reputation and had seen her in the pre-school faculty meetings. The kids loved their Creative Writing teacher who also sponsored the school's literary magazine. I had also heard that she distrusted this new arrival from Florida.

She was three years younger than I was, and had recently graduated from SUNY Purchase in 1971, after graduating from Haverstraw High School in 1967. I learned her father had been a bricklayer who worked on the Dutch Garden with landscape architect, Mary Mowbray-Clarke. Clay, bricks, brickwork, and the intricate designs were part of Delores' genetic makeup.

We would clash more than once before we became friends, and eventually lovers. We were friends the first year. Then we began dating, slowly at first. She was comfortable to be with, allowing me to get on with my life without the constant anguish of obsessive love. We shared interests, but not passions.

During that first fall, I looked forward to the football games, running up and down the field with the chain-gang in the crisp autumn air. Coach Morrow had moved on by then, and the football team wasn't very good. But it was fun to be on the field again anyway, despite the ghosts who looked on.

In mid-October of that year, not too far from the fourth anniversary date of my fateful day with Beth and Tom, the Clarkstown Rams were trailing and on the receiving end of a lot of bad calls by the referees.

Out of the corner of my eye I could see Marvin Hessian, striding the sidelines in manic gestures, screaming obscenities at the referees. After yet another bad call he hopped the snow fence and cold-cocked a referee, blindsiding him.

Coaches from both teams and Doc Carney pulled him off, and Clarkstown Police Officers Ronny and Bill walked him to the prowl car in handcuffs. He would eventually be sentenced to ninety days for assault. I would see Ron and Bill together twenty-eight years later at the crime scene on the Demarest Kill.

Marvin's father called Judge Sheehan, pulled some strings, and got Marvin out in two weeks, just in time for the final game of the season.

For retribution, Marvin broke into the football locker room the night before the next big game and stole all the Rams' uniforms, helmets, spikes, and playing equipment and dumped them into the swamp behind the practice field at the bottom of the hill. Thirty trips up and down the stairs, the final one just before daylight, gasping for breath. The stuff would not be found until the following week.

CCHS almost had to forfeit the game that day. They couldn't field a team without regulation uniforms, so they played in borrowed uniforms from Nanuet, taking the field in black and yellow uniforms instead of our traditional purple and gold.

We would later find out from Clarkstown Police that Marvin's favorite pasttime had become walking the corridors of CCHS in the middle of the night, speeding his brains out on crack, gaining access through the service catacombs that were underneath the building. One night he had stolen a janitor's master keys, ransacked teachers' drawers, pilfered objects from lockers, and stole a case of Country Club Black Raspberry ice cream cones from the cafeteria freezer. They caught him sitting on the top step of the practice field in the dark of night, polishing off the last of the twenty-four paper cones of ice cream.

CHAPTER SEVENTY-FOUR

NEW CITY

Summer, 1976
Ages 29, 30

In the spring of 1976, after teaching for four years and slid-ing into the boring routines associated with the job and walking the halls filled with too many memories, I started getting restless again. I had saved a little money, living at home, and considered returning to Gainesville to get my law degree. But New City kept calling my name. Even though I had started to hate teach-ing, something about the autumn days and the Saturday afternoon games wouldn't let me go. And so I started actively looking for something to do with my life, now that I knew that teaching was not for me, that I was never going to be the next Joyce Carol Oates no matter how many summers I devoted to writing, and that I would probably spend the rest of my life in New City. I didn't know it then, but I would remain in New City for the next twenty-five years.

When summer vacation neared during those four teaching years, I even considered taking on a job as lifeguard at New City Park Lake. But what would I do when Labor Day rolled around and I couldn't bring myself to go back into the classroom?

The mysterious fires in New City continued through these years.

One night after dinner in the summer of 1976, as the entire country was celebrating its Bi-Centennial, I got a call from Jimmy telling me that the investigator's branch of the D.A.'s office was looking for someone with a little law background to help out. It was a glorified law clerk's, civil service, entry-level position, but it paid more than teaching, and I got to go out into the field with investigators to learn and observe and collect evidence to help build the prosecution's cases. There was usually room for advancement, and who knew, Jimmy told me, maybe they'll pay for your law degree someday. With my pre-law degree and my two years as an Army Staff Judge Advocate's assistant, my credentials were perfect. Plus, Jimmy greased the wheels and made them hire a local guy.

Starting that summer of 1976, and for the next twenty-four years, I walked to the Courthouse each morning, first from my family home on Main Street and later my own home in New City Park, and put in my time. I learned the ropes and actually started trying to live again. There were no daily reminders of earlier days of classes and events and friends from my student days at Clarkstown High School. Now I had other things to keep my mind occupied; robbery, larceny, rape, drug possession, murder.

CHAPTER SEVENTY-FIVE

NEW CITY

1978
Age 32

In 1978, almost seven years after Beth and Rainer left for Europe on their honeymoon, they returned to the States and settled into a Manhattan apartment and a weekend house overlooking the north shore of Lake Deforest up by Dr. Davies' old farm.

I had heard about her return and began to think of a way I might speak to her. One day, I saw her driving past as I was leaving Tor's Luncheonette after lunch. I watched the car disappear up North Main. I assumed she was going to visit her father on South Mountain Road. If she had been headed to her new home, she likely would have taken a right on Congers. I waited twenty minutes, and called her father's house from the phone booth at Tor's. Her telephone number had not changed.

She answered the phone. "VonBronk residence."

"Beth."

There was a moment of silence. "How did you know I was here?"

"You mean in the US? It's the talk of the town. How are you?"

"Did you ever apologize to Tom?"

"No."

"It's been ten years and you never apologized."

"No."

"How did you know I was at my father's house?"

"I just saw you drive north past Tor's. I just assumed. . ."

"What do you want?"

"I would like to talk to you."

"About what?"

"About....everything."

"I don't think that would be a good idea."

"Not for even fifteen minutes?"

"Rainer is not the jealous type, but he doesn't want me talking to you."

"Me? Me specifically, or other guys?"

"You."

"You do whatever he says?"

"He knows it makes me upset."

"To talk to me?"

"Yes."

"So you won't talk to me?"

"No."

"Beth."

"Will, I'm going to hang up now. Please don't be angry with me. What you want can never happen."

"You don't know what I want. What I want to say."

"Goodbye, Will."

The next thing I heard was that Beth and Rainer were moving to Hong Kong. They would not return until 1988, or another ten full years. All that time Rainer was developing malls and sky-scrapers, in anticipation of the 1997 transfer of Hong Kong from Great Britain's control to the mainland government.

Or was there something else behind their move? Could she

have been annoyed, fed up, even frightened by my persistence?

In Hong Kong, in 1986, they would adopt a Vietnamese orphan and name her Alison.

I suppose it might have been easy to forget about Beth during those long years when she was absent from the country, first for seven years in Europe and then ten years in Hong Kong. But I didn't even try. I didn't want to try.

In the meantime, life went on in New City: the typical comings and goings of a suburban bedroom community, with established residents commuting to Westchester and Manhattan, and newer residents escaping the City to move to Rockland. It was the dream of so many, with no consideration of what impact it might have on the locals.

I continued to work and help win cases, worked my way up through the department achieving seniority, continued dating Delores, the literature dynamo from CCHS, and late in 1978 eventually bought a house on the southeast bank of New City Park Lake that I had been waiting for when it came up for sale. Near the Prendergast's house and across the lake from the Pape's house, I bought that New City Park house because to me, it was hallowed ground. I paid more for it than I should have, but you couldn't beat the view. In the background, through a line of Oaks and Maples was the shoreline of New City Park Lake. In the foreground, right outside the kitchen window, was the lawn where Beth and I had conceived our child on the night of my father's funeral in the summer of 1968, ten years earlier. Of course I never shared this with Delores, but she knew how I felt about Beth. Delores moved in and we settled into a marriage-like routine. Outside, on summer days, we could hear the gleeful voices of children in the Lake. Delores would sit on the deck at her keyboard working on her novel. We would eventually spend over twenty-two years together. She was in love with me. I would always be in love with Beth.

I still walked to work every morning, stopping by my mother's house to start Francis' physical therapy. Again on the way home; help feed him, read to him from *The Mill on the Floss*, the Crunch and Des fishing short stories of Philip Wylie, and John D. Mac-Donald's Travis McGee series that I had discovered in Florida. Did Francis understand what I was reading? Were my efforts to entertain him just a selfish act to assuage some guilt?

CHAPTER SEVENTY-SIX

NEW CITY

1979
Age 33

One of the most memorable crime scenes in my career was a murder we worked in the late 1970s and never solved. Most of the murders our office covered were domestics or the aforementioned stupid murders involving victims and shooters who knew one another: no mystery. This one was a little different, because we didn't even know if it was a murder. The body was found on an autumn Sunday morning by a security guard working in Trap Rock Quarry.

Trap Rock was a mining company that was excavating roadbed gravel on the mountain ridge facing New City. The sheer rock walls of the Palisades rose up from the Hudson River looked like staircases turned on end. *Lanape* Native Americans thought they looked like a line of standing trees. In seventh grade science class we had learned those cliffs were a type of basalt rock formed 200 million years ago during the Triassic Age.

At least a sideways staircase was what they looked like from the south east river side. Growing up, we would hear occasional explosions at noontime that were set off to mine the stone. Explosions had gone back as far as the early European settlers who recognized the rock's value for paving.

In the 1920s, concern over Trap Rock mining led to protests and laws preventing the mining companies from blasting on the Hudson River side of the mountain tops. Maxwell Anderson wrote one of his most famous plays, *High Tor,* about the environmental controversy. It was later made into a film with Burgess Meredith and later, as a live, Philco Television Playhouse presentation. A third adaptation became the first ever made-for-television movie with Bing Crosby and Julie Andrews in 1956. It was filmed ahead of time because Bing Crosby didn't want to do it as a live performance, as was the custom then, so they filmed it at Desilu Studios.

Today, from the riverside, the damage to the mountaintop from the blasting cannot be seen. From the southwest side, the results of the strip mining is obvious. Driving north on Main Street in New City in the early 1950s, if you looked to the northern horizon your eye was first drawn to High Tor and the High Tor Beacon. To the immediate right were the sheer scarred cliff sides of Trap Rock.

The death could have been an accident; she could have been hiking and wandered off the trail. But she wasn't wearing hiking clothes and from the looks of the exploded remains at the bottom of the quarry, she was not someone in the type of physical condition to go hiking, as her father would confirm. She was borderline obese. It could have been a suicide. There was no way of telling with what we found that first day. I first showed up in the bottom of the quarry where the dead body lay. It's not like you see in the movies or on television. It doesn't look like a Hollywood extra covered with fake blood lying there trying not to breathe while the camera is rolling. I looked down at the body. The impact from the 100 foot drop onto the hard rock surface had literally exploded the body into a bloody splatter.

We found a car with a Dutchess County tag parked in a pull-off on Long Clove Road that we eventually linked to the woman and used it to I.D. her.

There was marching band sheet music in the trunk of her car. What did it all mean? Without further evidence or meaningful information from her drunken father up in Beacon, the death was eventually ruled a suicide.

Details of the death scene were not made public.

CHAPTER SEVENTY-SEVEN

**THE HISTORY OF FIRE
IN NEW CITY, NEW YORK:
PART III**

1981
Age 35

One night in January of 1981, my mother called with heart-breaking news. The New City Grammar School was on fire. I ran out to Delores' car and drove over to the old building, now ablaze and surrounded by a crowd of people witnessing the scene in the freezing cold. We would later find out it started from an undetermined cause, and even through it was just a few hundred yards from the firehouse, it was a complete loss.

The school where my grandfather had finished his education, and where my father had attended before going to Congers High School in 1929 and where my brother and I had spent most of our early schooling and where Tom and Beth had gone for a few short months in sixth grade, had been turned into an ash pile. I mourned for the old building and the millions of lessons given there to thousands of students who had gone on to lead who knows what kind of lives because of the dedicated, committed teachers they had known there.

I stood and watched the flames reach up into the black sky and heard echoes of the screams of horses and cattle from a burning barn on New Hempstead hill in 1904.

Was this another arson? Some of the people watching mourned the building in silent memories as others, newcomers to New City, took it all in as "business as usual." No ties, no childhood moments of inspiration from a loving teacher they could reminisce about.

Beth was traveling abroad all those years, filling her life with new experiences that would shape the woman she would eventually become. I would find out later that she had traveled to twenty-three countries, studying art in Florence, Vienna, Moscow, Paris. And later, when her wonderful mind was filled with images from all the great art galleries of the Western World and her photographs became recognized, she began her philanthropic efforts. She didn't put her art behind her. She combined those worlds and traveled extensively in Central and South America, helping set up the literacy programs and clean water programs I would later learn about. Her remarkable, heart-rending photographs documenting her work tell the story. Every face in every photograph has a story to tell.

And all those years Beth spent living her adult life traveling the world? I stayed in New City retracing the footsteps of my own past, of Francis' and my father's past.

My "special talent" had become fully realized and acknowledged by me and eventually put my brain into overdrive. I discovered I could recall almost every day of my childhood and boyhood days with Francis, my father, and Grandpa, on an individual, day-by-day basis, complete with graphic imagery; my days with Beth and Tom. I could remember a million details, the names of all six hundred students of mine from Clarkstown High School, where they sat in my class during what periods, their final grades, the topics of every essay that they had written.

I could remember, without referencing files, all the details of cases from the very first day I started at the District Attorney's Office: names, addresses, charges, defense attorneys and their strategies; thousands of cases and their outcomes, their appeals, their sentences, the names of their brothers and sisters. This came in handy, for sure, because I received calls at all times of the day and night from cops and prosecutors asking questions for answers they could not remember and when they could not access the files. I was their go-to guy. My memory had become both a blessing and a curse.

Worst of all, I remembered and could not forget all that I had seen in Vietnam. All that I had seen firsthand, all that I had learned from my job during my special assignment. Facts, details, evidence in excruciating detail, details I could never forget.

All these memories haunted me to the point where it was like struggling to avoid an avalanche without an escape route. I became buried in the past and only survived the present by putting one foot in front of the other, marking time, concluding I didn't have a future as long as I was trapped in the past, plodding on a treadmill until my time was up or I just collapsed, gave up, and suffocated under the weight.

Like my father before me, I made my regular pilgrimages around town. His nightly journeys were likely attempts to obliterate the realities of his life while trying to protect the past of his boyhood haunts, perhaps even retrace his father's footsteps on the original mail route. Or am I overanalyzing things? Maybe it was all just a diversion to distract from his mental anguish brought on by his war and my brother.

My journeys, although not nightly, were also an attempt to obliterate my present while reliving the past. And so I would walk New City to celebrate anniversaries that were known or remembered only by me.

On Gate Night, the night before Halloween, I would sit on the steps of the tea house in the Dutch Garden in the middle of the night and relive our first kiss. On more than one occasion, groups of high school kids would gather there, their pockets stuffed with bars of soap, no doubt, as they fulfilled their obligations to carry on a long-term New City ritual. I'm sure they wondered what a middle-aged man was doing on the steps at that time of night, and frightened, they hurried off to gather elsewhere.

Every November 16, I would sit on the top of The Hill on the Little Tor overpass and remember the night we both cried from the beauty of what we had done, a dance of the eyes, while the VW car battery had gasped its last breath in the freezing weather and the snowflakes drifted down in silence like dried dandelion parasols. It was so bad I even made a tape of the three songs that ushered us into adulthood to play in my car and played it over and over and over again waiting for it to snow outside. *Can't Help it if I Wonder, Popsicles/Icicles,* and *Talk to Me.*

One night, a Clarkstown police car pulled up and a cop got out. It was Ron. He swung his light in my face and recognized me in the glare.

"What's up Will? Got a complaint from some teenagers that an old man was sitting by himself in the car up here. They thought you were doing some weird stuff."

"I am doing some weird stuff."

My answer surprised him. "What's that?"

"Trying to recapture my past."

He nodded slowly, walked to the boulders on the edge of the cliff and gazed out toward the lights of New City. He turned back to me, his mood changed. I couldn't tell if he was angry or thankful.

"Yeah, well, there's a lot of that going on. Join the club." He turned his flashlight off and again turned to New City in the valley below. "I guess we all had some times up here, eh, Will? We had it all. Feel kinda sorry for a lot of these kids these days."

"Yeah, we all had some times."

He turned to his cruiser. "Happy Thanksgiving, Will, if I don't see you around the Courthouse before." He turned off his blue flashing light and just before he drove off, leaving me alone in the night, he rolled down the window.

"If you figure out how to do that, let me know, will ya?"

"How to do what?"

"Recapture the past."

In late December, early January of each year I would sit on the stone bridge on the east end of Lake Lucille and stare across the frozen expanse of lake and watch sixth graders skate circles on the ice and make snow angels, just as Beth and I had done. I kept waiting for one of the young girls to catch a first snowflake on her nose.

As for New City Park Lake, since I lived on its banks it was a nightly summer routine to swim to the raft and lie in the moonlight. Delores would wonder about these nightly swims, and about why she was never invited to accompany me. Did she suspect what I was doing? What was going on in my mind as later, I lay in the grass in the back yard drying off in the summer night air?

On a certain summer night, on a date that I shall keep to myself, but that could easily be found by checking the obituary column for my father, I would quietly slip into the water at New City Park Lake, swim to the raft, lie on my back and look at the stars. If I waited long enough, traffic on Collyer Avenue would dwindle to just an occasional car and the night would be silent and I would listen for the far-off roar of an approaching Austin-Healey 3000.

Through rain or sleet or hail, through dark of night, I walked to work every day for the next twenty-two years, always leaving early enough to stop at the house on Main Street for my brother's morning routine, give him physical therapy, and have toast and coffee with my mother. Her daily life, for all outside appearances, had gone unchanged since my father died fourteen years before, in 1967

CHAPTER SEVENTY-EIGHT

NEW CITY

1988
Age 42

Another seven years passed.

By 1988, word had spread through town that Beth was back from the Far East with their adopted daughter, now two, living in Manhattan during the week, and on weekends at their Lake DeForest house overlooking the reservoir. Now that she was back in the country, every day when I walked to work I hoped to see her driving by on the way to the market. I just knew that someday I would see her.

All the time they were in Europe for seven years and Hong Kong for almost ten years, Beth actually owned the gallery in the Village where she had worked. Rainer had subsidized and expanded it for her father and her, and a series of managers ran it while they were traveling the world. Seventeen years she traveled the world, absorbing new ideas and experiences while I counted the cracks in New City's sidewalks, crack addicts on New City's sidewalks, along with uncountable unpaid child support cases, liquor store hold-ups, small time drug busts, and domestic assaults.

CHAPTER SEVENTY-NINE

NEW CITY

1993
Age 47

Another five years drifted by, I, imprisoned in my past.

I went about my job and my life, one day at a time. By day, toiling in the D.A.'s office. By night, trying to settle into some sort of domestic tranquility with Delores. The years flew by. It was the days that seemed endless.

On November 16, 1993, five years after Beth and Rainer returned to the country, I made up some pretense and took the afternoon off and headed down to Manhattan. I could have driven, but decided to take the bus like on the two earlier trips.

It was the first time I had seen Beth in fifteen years, since that one brief glance on Main when she had driven by Tor's in 1978, when we were thirty-two. We were now both forty-seven years old. I know that I had grown older physically, my graying hair beginning to thin just a little. My face had filled out, but I still looked fairly trim in a new suit I had picked for the occasion. A lawyer suit.

But I wasn't prepared for what I saw with Beth as I entered

the gallery and watched her for a moment from afar as she talked to some gallery customers. I watched in disbelief at how beautiful this forty-seven year-old woman was. She was just magnificent, her black hair gleaming in the sunlight that pored through the gallery's skylight. Her figure just as trim as I had recalled. Her face had not aged at all. Just as I had always known would happen, she was stunning as a mature woman.

I recalled the day in her father's studio when she had shown me the pastel of her mother that her father had drawn. Beth's resemblance to the details I remember from that portrait of her mother, drawn when she had been in her early forties, were uncanny.

I pretended to be looking at some artwork on the wall, my back to her, until she finished with her customers and then approached me.

"May I help you?

I turned and the smile disappeared from her face.

"Will?"

"Hi Beth. Welcome back in the U.S.S.A.," I sang, half-Beatle-like, in an attempt at a joke.

"Thank you. We've actually been back for five years. How are you doing? You're looking quite. . ." She was looking for a positive, yet neutral word. "Handsome. Successful."

"Same old, same old. Still at the D.A.'s office. Bought a house on New City Park Lake."

"Oh, really, which one?"

"Our house."

It took her but a brief moment to figure out what I meant.

"Oh, that cute little cottage with the red shutters near the lighthouse?"

"Yes."

"How nice."

"Yeah, I can walk to work."

"We have a house near the reservoir. We have a daughter now. She's almost eight."

"Yes, I heard. Congratulations."

"Are you here to look at some paintings? Sculpture? My father's new pieces are right over there. I can show you something that I think you might like. For the home? The office? A gift?"

"No. Actually, I came here to talk to you."

"Okay."

"No, I mean, somewhere private. Where we can actually have a conversation."

"A conversation about what?"

"About everything."

"I'm not sure I know what you mean."

"I've been thinking. I want to tell you what I've been thinking about what happened."

"Since I was in Hong Kong?"

"Since October 15, 1968, the afternoon we broke up."

"Twenty-five years. That's a lot of thinking."

"Yes, a lot of thinking. I wanted to share it with you. The thirtieth anniversary of our promise is coming up."

"Our promise?"

"Our promise of thirty years ago to reconnect on November 16, 1993. We made the promise the night of November 16, 1963. Again, on the night we left for Gainesville. August 15, 1964."

She glanced away and then back. She took a breath. More of a sigh. Suddenly I felt so juvenile.

"Will, it's been a long time. Thirty years is a lifetime. A lifetime."

Beth looked away for a moment, turned with a half-smile. "Anyway, I think we changed that. What we said was we would reconnect in 'thirty-five years'. That would make it 1998, five years from now."

"What are you saying?"

"I'm saying you're five years early." She was trying to keep it light.

"Okay, so I'll see you in five years."

She looked around the gallery, blinking. Was she looking to see if anyone was listening? Looking for protection from a security guard? An escape route? She started to turn and walk away. She turned back, polite but firm.

"Will, I have other clients I have to assist. It was nice seeing you. Glad you're doing well. Maybe someday I can meet Delores."

"You know about Delores?"

"Sure, Tom told me."

"I didn't realize Tom kept up with my life."

"Father Carrick."

"Huh."

"Life moves on, Will."

For some, I thought.

"So I'll see you in five years? November 16, 1998?"

She half-smiled in a non-committal way and politely turned away.

"Beth?"

She turned back. "Yes?"

"You look exactly like your mother in that pastel your father drew."

"Thank you. I'll accept that as a compliment. It was nice seeing you, Will."

I left feeling there was a ray of hope in what she had to say. But there is hope and there is false hope. Could I live another five or six years on false hope? What concerned me even more was the way she had treated me. As if I were some crazy person in off the street. As if I were a stranger. Was it annoyance I sensed in her? Fear?

CHAPTER EIGHTY

NEW CITY

1998
Age 52

Another five years flew by, and before I knew it, it was early November, 1998. And where was I? I was still at the D.A.'s office, drowning in details. My obsessive mind bleeding, disintegrating from thousands of stab wounds, still going through the motions with Delores, still changing diapers, and still trying to talk my mother into hiring help. Beth and I were now both fifty-two years old.

As November 16, 1998 neared, I remembered what Beth had said that night on Low Tor. "Even if I'm married to the President of the United States, we'll get together and make love." That had been thirty-five years earlier.

I took another trip to Beth's art gallery, and as I walked in the door, she looked down, half-smiling in near defeat, shaking her head, trying to keep it light.

"Has it been five years already? You don't give up, do you?

"Are you married to the President of the United States?"

"No, someone far more powerful."

"I can take down the Secret Service Agents."

"Well, it is thirty-five years, isn't it? I didn't think you were going to take this seriously."

"You were the one who said. . . "

She stopped me abruptly, trying to restrain her anger. She was a stranger.

"Will, we were children. I was a wide-eyed high school girl. Surely you didn't seriously think . . ."

"I just want to talk, Beth. Nothing more."

"Will. . ." A look of sadness came over her face. "Will, there's really nothing to talk about. I've tried to be clear about that." She hesitated with a faraway look in her eye. "Maybe someday. . ." But then she caught herself and stopped again.

"Someday what?" Was she just being polite as a delaying tactic?

"Talk to Tom. I think you should talk to Tom."

"What does Tom have to do with this? I just want to talk to you."

She was becoming agitated and it began to concern me. "Will, I don't want to have to call security, but. . ."

"Security?" I stood for a moment in disbelief. Is this what it had become? I turned abruptly and walked out onto the street. She was going to call security? For me?

Then, just over a year later, as Christmas, 1999 neared, I went into Tor's to buy lunch and a few holiday gift cards. As I approached the register on the way out, Beth and her daughter Alison, now almost fourteen, were talking to the cashier. Beth's back was too me. Alison looked up at me. I smiled at her.

"You must be Alison."

Beth turned, almost alarmed, put her arm around Alison in a protective reflex, then recovered with her half-smile, changing tactics. "Hello, Will. Merry Christmas. Yes, this is Alison. Alison, this is an old friend, Will."

Alison, gave me a distracted handshake. She was dressed in an Albertus Magnus school blazer and plaid skirt, horn-rimmed glasses. Her mannerisms in the few seconds I observed her were mirror images of a young Beth. She was reading a paperback edition of *Silas Marner*.

"Merry Christmas to you and Alison, 'old friend.' "

"How are your mother and Francis doing?"

"I'm heading there now to help put up the tree. She never misses. Want to come along and help?"

"No, we have to be on our way, but thank you for the offer. Please tell them we said 'hello.' "

"I will."

She turned to Alison. "Okay, Alison, you ready to see your grandpa?"

Alison nodded and they headed for the doorway.

"It was nice seeing you, Will. Sorry we have to rush off. Happy Holidays."

And then she was gone.

Eleven months later, on October 16, 2000, Beth would be found dead, not two hundred yards away from Tor's and just thirty-one days short of the thirty-seventh anniversary of our making love on The Hill on Low Tor in the middle of an early snowfall.

CHAPTER EIGHTY-ONE

NEW CITY

October 25, 2000

TRANSCRIPTION OF SECOND INTERVIEW WITH
Thomas Hogenkamp conducted on October 23, 2000.
Detectives Ray Cicci, Dave Sherman, with Carl Betz from
the District Attorney's office present.

RC: Let the record indicate this is a follow-up interview with Thomas Hogenkamp on Tuesday October 24, 2000, the first being conducted on October 18. So what more can you tell us about the victim?

TH: She was becoming paranoid in the last month or so. She felt that someone was following her. She felt threatened by his presence.

RC: His presence?

TH: The private investigator I told you about. And then there was the land deal.

DS: The one you referenced in the earlier interview about Dove Cottage?

TH: Yes. Her husband wanted her to use our friendship to convince me to sign over my property to him to develop. She knew what my land meant to me and so she revealed his plan to me. She had to pretend to her husband that she was trying to convince me, when in fact she was warning me against him.

RC: Why did he want to buy the land?

TH: Do you have any idea what that property is worth on today's market? That location? The woods? Greenberg's Pond? The Demarest Kill? All of it? It all belonged to my grandparents and it's belonged to me for almost thirty years. I've had hundreds of people make offers on it. Unimaginable prices. But I won't sell it and he knows it. That's why he allowed her to continue seeing me. What he didn't know is that she would never betray me like that. Maybe he found that out.

RC: That she was betraying her husband instead of you?

TH: It's possible.

RC: How would he find out?

TH: Good question. It was a private conversation at my studio.

RC: Do you think your friend Will could have murdered her?

TH: Ex-friend. I don't know. I do know he was . . . bothering her.

RC: Bothering her?

TH: Maybe that's too strong a word. Ever since they broke up in 1968 he seemed to be obsessed by her. He made a number of attempts to get her to reconcile, but she wasn't interested.

RC: That's what, thirty-two years?

TH: When she got back from another trip this last time about a year or so ago, he went to her studio again in Manhattan. He couldn't seem to drop it.

RC: What do you know about their encounter eleven months ago?

TH: At Tor's, or I should say the luncheonette across the street formerly known as Tor's. He was constantly pestering her to meet him. His gallery trip the year before was an anniversary date or something. I think he thought he could talk her into going back with him.

RC: Would she ever do that?

TH: I doubt it, even though she still loved him. When she was younger and we were all friends, she was very much in love with him. But he doubted her word on something and she never forgave him for it. I think it was a particular incident that was the final straw for her in something that had been building up.

RC: Like what?

TH: It was a year before their break-up. Fall of '67. They were just starting their senior year of college. I was enroute to Vietnam when she first got pregnant with Will's child. It was unplanned. He didn't want it. He talked her into having an abortion. It was illegal then and some back-alley butcher in Gainesville botched the job, almost killed her. She couldn't have children. She was devastated. Then, they got into another argument.

RC: When?

TH: October, 1968. She wanted a clean break. She got over it. He apparently never did.

RC: How do you know all this? Did she tell you?

TH: I witnessed the last part of it. I surmised a lot of the rest. I think by that time she was beginning to realize she had outgrown him.

RC: What does that mean?

TH: She was moving forward with her life. Had moved forward. He didn't seem to want to move forward.

RC: So you didn't see all of the aftermath?

TH: No.

RC: But she told you this in her own words?

TH: Yes, later, she told me everything, confirmed my surmising. The abortion was the beginning of the end for her and Will. She never completely forgave Will for making her go through with it. It was the beginning of the end.

RC: And the argument you referenced?

TH: Yeah, when I came home from Vietnam they got into a huge argument because Will thought that she and I had something going on.

RC: You didn't?

TH: Absolutely not. Like I told you before. We were very close friends. That's it.

RC: Lots of friends have sex.

TH: Okay, so she was like my sister. You going to tell me lots of brothers and sisters have sex? It never happened between us. What's with you guys?

RC: Where did she meet her current husband?

TH: We all met informally when we were kids at my grandparents' lawn party. Klein was the guy who bought my grandparents' acreage and developed the Twin Elms Lane homes. She met him again by coincidence at the gallery in Manhattan she now owns.

RC: It was just a coincidence Klein walked into the art gallery?

TH: So he claims. He swept her off her feet and the rest is history. She got on with her life. They traveled extensively. Lived in Europe for six, seven years, Hong Kong for ten years. They travel constantly. Homes in Buenos Aires, Paris, Hong Kong. Hong Kong's where they adopted their daughter, Alison, around 1986. She's in and out of town, in and out of the country.

RC: So what about lately?

TH: They're back and forth between their Manhattan penthouse and their Lake DeForest place.

CHAPTER EIGHTY-TWO

THE DUTCH GARDEN

Wednesday
October 25, 2000
Age 54

Jimmy called and asked me to meet him at the pergola. He was pacing when I arrived. Over his shoulder it was a few feet to the gazebo where Beth had been murdered. I couldn't help but glance down the embankment as I approached him.

"What's up? Something new in the case?"

"Were you stalking her?"

He extended a blue folder clasped at the top. They looked like interview transcripts. "I always considered you a brother, Will. I'm risking my job showing you this."

I sat down against a brick column and read the transcript of Tom's latest interview.

"I didn't think I was stalking her. I thought she wanted to talk to me, too. Maybe I was misreading her cues. I'm not very good at that. I thought she was encouraging our eventual meeting and discussion on a specific date we had talked about. "

"You went on a date?"

"No, the date of an anniversary. We were going to meet and talk on the anniversary date."

"Could it be she was just being polite? Could it be her demeanor was caused by her fear of you?"

"Fear?" I tried not to think about it.

"You need to tell me the truth. Why were you so insistent on seeing her?"

It was a question I had asked myself daily for years. "My reasons changed over the years. For a long time it was because I wanted to get her back and thought I would be able to talk her into it. I wanted to explain my side of the story, get it out, have some sort of closure, but she would never give me the satisfaction of even having a conversation. Yes, I tried several times over the years."

"Why did you want her back so badly?"

Was it an attempt to recapture the past? Relive happier times?

"I loved her, Jimmy. Why are you asking that? You know that."

But Jimmy didn't answer. He let me continue.

"Then, years later, after meeting up with her briefly a few times, one day I just realized that getting back together was never going to happen and that maybe we could just become friends again, like old times. I missed her friendship. I wanted her friendship. I wanted her to admire the person I had become as an adult, if that's even possible."

"And later?"

"I wanted to apologize and beg her forgiveness. Or at least that's what I told myself."

"You lied about seeing her at the luncheonette."

"No, it's true. I did see her at Tor's last Christmas."

That's not what I mean. That wasn't the last time, was it?"

His question surprised me. Caught me off-guard. Unnerved me. "No."

"When?"

I couldn't postpone the inevitable any longer. "The night before."

"Before what?"

"The night before she was found dead. How did you know that I saw her? Did Tom tell you?"

"Did Tom even know?"

"I don't know."

"We went back and looked at the security camera. It shows you leave the back of the courthouse and enter the Garden. And then a few minutes later, on another camera, her car pulls into the parking lot and she enters the Garden. You never come out. She never comes out.

"We think, but we're not sure she went to Tom's after you apparently left her here. Do you know if she went there?"

"No."

He let that sink in. "I talked to your mother."

I was starting to unravel. "You did? When?"

"I just left her house before I called you. Your mother told us you asked her to set up the meeting with Beth the other night."

"It's true. I wanted to meet on our "anniversary date, next month."

"What anniversary date? You keep talking about this 'anniversary date'."

"An important date for us. November 16th. It would have been our 37th anniversary together on November 16."

He calculated the dates. "That was the night of the after-play party we had. You knew her before that."

"It was the anniversary of our lifelong commitment. My mother called her on my behalf and Beth agreed to meet me. But she said she was leaving the country before November 16. It would have to be right away. She agreed to meet me at the gazebo that same night. October 15. We met around seven o'clock. I worked late in the office until just before then, then went to the garden."

"That's what the security camera shows. I'm glad you're finally telling me the truth."

"Why didn't you tell me this right away? Don't you know how bad this makes you look? How bad it makes me look?"

CHAPTER EIGHTY-THREE

THE SUMMER HOUSE
THE DUTCH GARDEN

Sunday, 7 p.m.
October 15, 2000
Age 54

It was true. Beth and I met at our gazebo in the Dutch Garden. I paced the hexagon's bricks while I waited in the darkness. Finally, a few minutes after seven o'clock, I heard her hurried footsteps on the gravel path. She was out of breath, in a hurry.

"I have to leave in ten minutes, Will. What is it you want?"

It would have taken me hours to answer that one. "I don't know. I wanted to meet on November 16. Do you know why?"

"Of course. I knew as soon as I heard your mother's voice on the phone. It would be what…thirty-seven years ago?"

"Yes. I've been wanting to speak to you for so many years, I've even rehearsed what I wanted to say. Now I don't know if any of it will make any sense."

"Why don't you try? I've got to leave in a few minutes. I'm leaving the country with my daughter tomorrow and I have to run some errands and finish packing."

"Where are you going?"

"It's not important, Will."

Maybe there was a sound of other footsteps nearby, but I didn't hear them.

Maybe there was a sound of a twig snapping, but I didn't hear it.

Maybe there was a sound of rustling leaves, but I didn't hear them crackling softly in the night.

Maybe there was the smell of cigarette smoke wafting in from nearby, but I didn't smell it.

I stood and looked at her and a sickening feeling came over me; a realization. Maybe now, with so many passing years, she was just not the same person I had known. There was no *young* Beth anymore. Just an *adult* Beth, whom I no longer knew. A different Beth. She was all grown up, had spent the better part of thirty years out of the country, traveling, living, changing; had lived an *entire lifetime* without me.

I could only hear Beth's impatience as I tried to find the words to tell her what I wanted.

"Look, Will. Maybe I should say something. Maybe this will help you somehow with whatever is troubling you. Whatever you thought happened between Tom and me that day you surprised us? It never happened. I was in love with you. I have never had feelings like that for Tom. And besides, he was not capable."

"What do you mean?"

On that Sunday night prior to her murder, this was still news to me. It would be another few days before I heard this from Father Carrick and read Tom's transcript. I was skeptical.

"I don't mean not capable physically. I mean he's celibate. It's his choice. It's all very complicated. All because of what happened over there. He's just not inclined. That component of his personality is gone. So even if in some bizarre, alternate universe I wanted to have sex with him, it would not happen. He's celibate. It's a commitment.

"So what you saw that day was me crying for a boy I loved like a brother, a boy that I had grown up with who I realized was now destroyed. Because that's what they did, Will. They betrayed him and they destroyed him with that betrayal. What you saw was my loving embrace of a little boy, by the friend who was sickened by what she saw in her friend. Nothing more than that."

"I realize that now. . . I."

"Stop, Will. Let me finish this once and for all. *You* were the one I loved. You were the love of my life, Will. Not him. You'll never know how much I loved you, Will. *You will never know.* You will never know what I went through because of my love for you. I don't think it's possible for a woman to love a man that much and maintain her sanity.

"I never would have betrayed you and you could just never accept that. Just like you never could really accept how much I loved you the whole time we were growing up. What you saw that day was my attempt to comfort a wounded soul. I know it might not have looked that innocent, but that's because you showed up at the wrong place at the wrong time. It was just a matter of bad timing and a gross misinterpretation. After what you and I had been through, I was hurt that you would think that I would be untrue to you. You just don't know I could never have done that. Tom has been like a brother to me since the first time we all met in fifth grade. I love him, Will. I love him as if he were a real brother I never had. What other family did I have then besides Tom and you?

"But you could never accept that. And then after all that happened the year before in Gainesville with the baby, the anguish, I knew I had to move on. I thought it would be the best thing for the both of us to go our separate ways for a while, and, with time, it proved to be the best thing for me. You know that old saw about women maturing earlier? It's true. I had become a woman, Will. You were still just a boy. I'm sorry if that sounds sexist. That young girl you fell in love with, Will? She doesn't exist anymore.

You don't even know me or who I am now. You only remember who I used to be. *That* young girl.

Her body language told me she was wrapping it up in preparation for leaving.

"I'm sorry that things didn't work out for you, Will. You were a big part of my life, but Will, that ended thirty-two years ago. Thirty-two years Will. You have to let it go. I'm telling you *as a friend* that you have to let it go because *nothing* is ever going to come of it. *Nothing.* You have to leave it in the past."

I couldn't say anything. I knew if I started to say anything, the sobbing would begin. I knew what she was saying was true. She was living in the real world, I was stuck in the past.

"Will, what are you doing to yourself? Look at yourself. I'm trying to be honest with you because you deserve it. I met you this one last time tonight against my better judgment, but you need to know that *nothing* will ever take place between you and me ever again. I don't say these things out of malice or to be cruel, Will, I say it because you need to accept reality and get on with your life.

"Delores loves you very much, I hear. Why don't you try loving her back? Go home to her and tell her you love her."

I thought about that.

"When my daughter and I leave tomorrow, I don't know when, or if, we'll ever be back to New City. But that's my life now and it's really none of your business. New City is not a part of my life anymore, except to see my father. I loved you back then Will, but we were *kids* then and we're not kids anymore. You've got to move on."

"We have a history, Beth."

"History is the past. You need to keep it there, in the past. And don't you go quoting Faulkner on me here."

I had, indeed thought of the quote from *Requiem for a Nun,* many times. But she stole my thunder, beat me to the punch. As usual, she was way out in front of me.

"I haven't been a kid for a long time. Can't you please just be happy with what we had? It was so perfect. Can't you stop ruining those memories I have of you?"

She stopped when she saw the look on my face.

"I didn't mean that. Just let those wonderful memories remain the most perfect part of both of our lives. Maybe if you had children you would understand."

I couldn't respond. I just stared down at the Kill.

"You're scaring me a little bit, Will."

She walked to the edge of the gazebo and peered into the darkness toward the Kill, then toward the path to Tom's, her back turned to me.

She spoke to the empty darkness in front of her. "You have to promise me you won't ever try to contact me again Will. You're making me feel awful and you're frightening me. It's like it's not even you. *You're really frightening me.*"

I don't know what I thought was going to happen when I asked her to meet me that night. I thought I could hold her one last time, look into her eyes and see that *'just one smile'*, while we held one another; somehow recapture, if only for a fleeting moment, a happiness that I had lost forever. I thought if I could hold her one more time on the banks of the Kill I could change her mind. But that was never to be. I was so ashamed of myself, so embarrassed, so emotionally drained. I turned and walked toward the tea house.

She called after me in the darkness. "I need to hear your promise, Will." Those were the last words I ever heard her speak.

But I couldn't make her that promise.

CHAPTER EIGHTY-FOUR

THE DUTCH GARDEN

Wednesday
October 25, 2000

Jim interrupted my thoughts. "So why doesn't she walk out through the parking lot on the surveillance tape? She was on her way to Tom's?"

"I guess. You'll have to ask him that question."

"That would make Tom maybe the last person to see her alive and maybe the first person to see her dead."

"So maybe you should be talking to him."

"Why don't we see you walk out of the parking lot?"

"I waited in the tea house for a few minutes for her to return, go to her car, but she never did. I went to look for her in the gazebo, but she wasn't there. I figured she probably had gone to see Tom. I hopped over the brick wall on the south end and went home."

"Will, why didn't you tell me all this before? Don't you know what kind of position this puts us all in? You said the last time you saw her was last Christmas season, not the night she was murdered. Why weren't you truthful? Why didn't you ever tell me? Didn't you even suspect it was her when you knelt down in the stream to turn her over?"

I had to think back to that morning. "The possibility of its being her never crossed my mind that morning. It would have been all too incongruous. The body, the hair, it was covered in mud and leaves. It was just beyond any possibility that it could be her. She was leaving the country, maybe even on her way to the airport at that time. How could it be her?"

"Despite the proximity and just a few hours since you had both been there?"

"It was simply never a possibility that crossed my mind. A coincidence, but not a possibility. I thought it was some random teenage girl. It looked like a teenage girl from behind. Kids hang out here all the time. I never thought it was her. Never Beth."

"And there wasn't another meeting, later that night, after her visit to Tom's? A meeting maybe she didn't know was going to happen?"

I turned to look him in the eye. "Like an ambush?"

"Like an ambush."

"No. Never. What are you saying?"

"Don't you realize where this leaves me?"

"You?"

"Now I'm going to have to go back to the office and tell them that you lied to me, Will. Now you're going to be 'Suspect #1'."

I looked at my old friend and thought of all the time we had spent growing up together. The snowball fights, the football games, the parties, the lifeguarding. He had been there for so much of it. Whenever it was more than just Beth and Tom and me, Jimmy had been there beside us with the rest of our gang. Now, I was compromising his integrity.

"So you want to tell us about it? I've got to ask you to follow me back to the Court House. I told them I could get you to come in voluntarily. It could have been ugly."

I couldn't blame Jimmy for what he had to do.

"Don't lie to Dave and Ray, Will. They're going to ask you

a lot of questions they already think they know the answers to. They're going to try to catch you in a lie, trip you up, and if they do, that will not be good for you."

Carl and Ray and Dave were waiting for us when we arrived and sat at the board table. Carl looked at his folder before he began. "So now it's your turn to answer some more questions."

"Okay."

"Jeanette, let the record indicate blah, blah, blah."

"You told Jim on that morning at the crime scene, that the last time you saw Beth was in Tor's Luncheonette almost a year ago, when she was paying for a Christmas card. You want to tell us about that?"

I started to tell them, in detail, what I had told Jim at the crime scene the first morning. "Her adopted daughter, Alison was also there at the luncheonette. Beth introduced us, and then she hurried away.

"What happened then? You didn't ask to meet up with her sometime later, or in the future?"

"No. Wait, that day I jokingly asked her if she and Alison wanted to come to my mother's house to help trim the Christmas tree."

I thought back to that day again.

"I just kept staring at Alison, thinking, *this could be our daughter, Beth, but I made you get rid of our child.* I had the feeling Beth and I were both thinking the same thing. I think it was making her uncomfortable."

When I was finished, Carl reviewed his notes from his yellow legal pad. "But is that really the last time you saw her?"

"Why do I have the feeling that you already know the answer to that?"

"Just answer the question without the editorializing. Is that really the last time you saw her?"

I exchanged glances with Jim.

Carl leaned forward. "Jim's not asking the questions. Answer Ray, Dave, and me."

"No, that's not the last time I saw her."

"When is the last time you saw her? And I mean the very last time you saw her….. *alive.*

Silence.

"So where was it?"

"At the gazebo."

"In the Dutch Garden?"

"Yes."

"The crime scene the night she was murdered?"

Again, I exchanged glances with Jim. I wasn't sure what he had told them. Whether he could protect me.

"Yes. The other night I asked my mother to call her and set up a meeting for next month, November 16. That's a special anniversary date for us. Beth told my mother she'd be out of the country by November and it would have to be that very night, October 15."

"So we're expected to believe that you met with her the night of her murder, at the exact crime scene location where her dead body was found, just hours later, and that when you left her that night she was still alive. Is that correct?"

"Yes."

"And why should we believe that?"

"Because it's true. I would never do anything to hurt her."

I knew my excuse sounded lame, weak, like so many other suspects before me that we had all interviewed together.

"Never do anything to hurt her except stalk her for thirty-something years and make her fearful.

"I never stalked her."

"Let's not quibble over semantics. You did make her fearful."

"I didn't mean to. I just wanted to talk to her. She was always polite during our conversations. I thought she was encouraging me, or at least pretending to be interested."

"Maybe out of fear? She was a polite person from what I've heard. She told at least two people you made her frightened."

"Tom and her husband, right?"

"We'll ask the questions."

So did you just happen to run into her at the gazebo? Like you ran into her at the luncheonette?"

"No. I just told you. My mother called her for me."

"Your mother."

"Yes."

Jimmy interjected. "I spoke to his mother. She confirmed."

"Why did your mother call her?"

"I told you. Because I asked her to. I didn't think Beth would take my call directly. My mother knew how I felt and she knew I wanted Beth back."

"Back after....what, thirty . . . years?

"Yes, thirty-two years."

"So your mother called on your behalf?"

"Yes."

"Will...."

"I know. I know it sounds crazy. But Beth agreed to meet me for ten minutes."

"Why there?"

"She suggested it."

"Beth suggested the location?"

"Yes, I think that's how she used to go to visit Tom, anyway.

"How do you know?"

"I surmised it." I couldn't tell them I had read Tom's transcripts.

"You surmised it, or you followed her there in the past, stalked her?"

"No. I just assumed that. We took that path ten thousand times as kids."

"Who else knew that she was familiar with that footpath?"

"No one that I know of. Just Tom and me. Of course any kid we grew up with."

Jimmy couldn't stand it anymore. He held up a hand. "Will. You may want to call a lawyer. I can call Richard for you if you want."

"I don't need to call a lawyer. I didn't do anything. Let's just get this over with."

"What did you talk about?"

"I wanted to tell her I was sorry for what happened thirty-two years ago."

"That's all?"

"I wanted to tell her I was a jerk."

"I think she had already concluded that and had already let you know."

"I wanted her to consider leaving Rainer, and for us to get back together."

"Really? And what was her reaction to that?"

"I never got around to telling her that. She looked at me like… talked to me like …I was crazy. Like I was scaring her."

"And so then what happened?"

"She wanted to leave. I asked her to stay for just a few minutes longer. I wanted to explain everything to her."

"What's everything?"

"Everything. How I felt. How it was a mistake. How I never stopped loving her all these years and it wasn't too late for us to start all over again."

"Did she want to listen to you?"

"At first, the apology part, but then I think she changed her mind and stopped listening when I started to talk about the future stuff."

"And when she wouldn't allow you to tell her all this?"

"She started to leave."

"And then what?"

I looked at Jim. I hadn't told him this part.

"And I reached out to hold her arm. To beg her to stay just one more minute."

Jim lowered his head and shook it in disbelief.

"Above her left elbow?"

"Yes. How did you know?"

"The bruise . . . "

"A bruise?"

"Yes, a bruise that was discovered during the autopsy. There were several bruises that were either not consistent, or older than those she received later at the time of the murder. One was above her left elbow. There were more. On her left shoulder, as if she had been punched. Did you punch her?"

"No, I swear. I just reached out for a second to try to get her to stay."

"Was there a struggle?"

"No. I let go."

"No punching?"

"No, of course not."

"Why did you let go?"

"She said I was hurting her. 'Hurting her again.' "

"What do you mean?"

"She was obviously referencing what had happened that day I came home and caught her and Tom, together. She said I had already hurt her enough and that what I wanted in the future would never happen. Never."

"So you did not punch her left shoulder before her murder?

"No."

"And then?"

I looked at Jimmy. He was losing his composure.

"And then I started to cry."

"Why?"

"She wanted me to promise that I would never contact her again."

"And then? What then?"

"I don't know."

"Did you promise her that?

"No. I walked away."

"Because you didn't want to promise her that, did you?"

"Yes. Yes. But I couldn't promise her that. I *couldn't* give up. I could never give up. I walked toward the tea house. I turned around and walked back to the gazebo, but by then she had already left. I assumed she went down the path toward the Kill.

"The Kill?"

"The stream. The Demarest Kill. She had walked up the stream and disappeared into the woods and that's the last I ever saw of her alive. I swear to God. That's the last I ever saw of her."

I was sobbing now.

"Why didn't you tell us this before?

"Why? Why? Because you would think I did it, that's why."

Jimmy leaned forward and interjected. He was crying now, not even trying to hide the tears streaming down his cheeks. He was angry with me. Angry at himself. He put his hand on my neck, his forehead against mine. Another brother. "And did you do it, Will?"

"You've known me for almost fifty years. What do you think?"

His anger overtook his tears. "It really doesn't matter what I think. Did you do it, Will? Just answer us and we'll do what we can for you. You're one of us. But you've got to answer truthfully."

Karl cut in. "Jimmy. Shut up. This can't get personal."

"No. No I didn't do it. I loved her. How could I do anything like that?"

Henion sat shaking his head. "I've been doing this for over thirty years, Will, and just about every homicide I've ever investigated was committed by someone who 'loved' the victim. As a matter of fact it was done *because* they 'loved' them. Is that how it was with you, Will? You loved her so much and she wouldn't come back to you and so you killed her because you couldn't stand it anymore?"

"No. That's not how it was at all." I tried to control my trembling. Fear? Anger?

"So let me summarize. You met her at the gazebo, where maybe you knew she used to walk to get to Hogenkamp's boathouse. And you three were the only people who knew that she used that route."

"I told you. Every kid we grew up with knows that path."

"Right. And that night after you met her there and bruised her arm, she rejected you and tells you she's leaving the country, and that you should never, *ever* contact her again. Right, so far? A few hours later she's found dead in the exact same spot, beaten, bruised, *raped*."

"No! I would never do that to her."

"Raped and killed. And you don't know anything about it. Is that your story?"

"Yes."

"When was the last time you had sex with her?"

"What?

"Answer me. When was the last time you had sex with her?

"May 10th, 1968."

"Thirty-two years ago, and five months, give or take."

"Yes."

"How do you remember that specific date?"

"It's the day she graduated from The University of Florida. She moved back to New City the next day. Started working in Manhattan, and I spent the summer in Gainesville finishing up for law school. We didn't see each other all summer."

"Whose idea was that?"

"Both. Like I say, I was getting ready for law school and she was busy working. We planned to get together again during Thanksgiving."

"And never since then?"

"No."

"So you wouldn't mind subjecting yourself to a DNA test?"

"Of course not. But you already have my DNA from other cases."

"On the morning of her murder, what did you pick up outside the gazebo when you were walking toward it?"

"What?"

"You stopped at the tipped-over brick latticework next to the pergola walk-way. What did you pick up and put into your pocket?"

I closed my eyes and thought back a few days. "A piece of brick from the original latticework wall. I heard they're going to take it down and rebuild it and I wanted a piece of it for a souvenir. For Delores."

"Who?"

"My ex."

"Your ex? Why?"

"Her father built that part of the original wall. I was going to give it to her before it all disappeared. That's on the security camera?"

"Never mind how we know. Where is it?"

"It's at my house. On my bureau. Or, she might have taken it when she left me, I don't remember."

"She left you?"

"Yes."

Carl and Jim exchanged looks.

"And what did you pick up and palm and put into your pocket from underneath the victim?"

"Something in the stream bed underneath Beth."

"What was it? Some sort of evidence you left behind?"

"No, it was a rock. A smooth, flat rock. There are no security cameras there."

"That's right. An officer saw you palm something. What was it? Evidence? Tell us now, Will."

"No, it was just a rock. I don't know why I did it. I was in shock. I wanted something from there. One of the last things she might have touched."

"Another souvenir?"

"No. I'm . . ."

"She didn't touch anything, Will. She was dying or more likely dead when she rolled down the hill. Dead for sure when she arrived."

"I wanted some contact. Something......some touchstone to her."

"Where did you go later on the night when she was murdered? Between say, an hour later at eight p.m. and two a.m.?"

"I was home."

"Home on Main Street or home in New City Park?"

"My mother can tell you I stopped by."

"And after?"

"New City Park."

"Can anyone corroborate that?"

My heart sank. "No. I don't think so."

"You don't think so. Where was Delores?"

"Haverstraw. She went to visit her mother. I was home typing on my computer. I suppose a forensic computer analyst might be able to confirm that."

I felt boxed into a corner of circumstantial evidence. I tried to remember everything that happened that night. Could there have been anyone there watching or listening to us? Could Tom have been there, waiting for Beth? Could Tom have murdered her for some reason I couldn't even imagine? Maybe she never made it to Tom's. Maybe he made up all of that, convinced police he found her body on his morning run.

Had I smelled cigarettes that night? Had Tom followed her back to the gazebo? Had someone lain in wait?

I even began to doubt my own sanity, asking myself if I could ever have done such a thing to Beth and had somehow blocked it out.

"So, the last you saw her, she was alive in the gazebo, then you walked past the tea house and went home to New City Park to work on your computer sometime say, around nine-thirty or ten."

"Yes. That's correct. No. I waited in the tea house for a few minutes, then went back to the gazebo. She wasn't there, so I hopped the brick wall and went home the back way down Capral Lane to see my mother and Francis. Then I went home to New City Park after stopping to see them."

"So if not you, then who? Help us out here, Will. I have to ask myself, 'Assuming it wasn't just a random killing, which is not likely, who would want to kill her?' She didn't have any enemies, did she? She's a philanthropist and an artist. Her husband is out of the country. So who does that leave? The guy who found her? Maybe, but not likely. What would be his motive? He's not in love with her. On the other hand, what about the guy who's been stalking her for over thirty years? Okay, now we're on to something. You see where I'm coming from, Will? You see where this puts us?"

I did see.

CHAPTER EIGHTY-FIVE

NEW CITY

Wednesday
October 25, 2000
Early Afternoon

I decided to follow my mother's advice again and go see Father Carrick. It was almost as if he had been expecting me when I walked into his study.

"Good to see you, Will. What brings you here?"

"I don't even know. I want to go to confession."

"I see, well, let's step into the isolation booth. Remember they used to call it that on the $64,000 QUESTION TV show?"

"Yes."

"When was your last confession?"

"Thirty-eight years ago."

"Tell me what's troubling you, Will."

"Everything is troubling me."

"What are you here to confess?"

"Everything. How I've made a mess of my life and hurt other people I never meant to hurt. How I hurt Beth. It was all a big mistake."

"Tell me about it. Is there anything specific?"

"I hurt Beth and Tom by not believing them. I hurt my mother and my brother by running away. It's ruined my life and it ruined theirs and now Beth is dead and they think I did it."

We walked toward the confessional and sat next to the booth. Mrs. Pyrcz, an old, longtime neighbor, was making her way down the aisle.

Father Carrick called out, "We're closed, Mrs. Pyrcz. You'll have to come back for evening confession."

"Closed? How can you be closed? It's a church. I come here at this time every day."

"Today we're closed. We're performing an exorcism."

"I've never heard of such a thing."

She turned and walked away.

"She comes to confession every day at this time. It's her only social life. Don't worry about it."

We waited until Mrs. Pyrcz left the building.

"Let's take this one step at a time. You didn't believe Beth and Tom even though they both told you that it wasn't true. I even told you that it wasn't true."

"Yes. I couldn't believe them."

"Why not?"

"I don't know."

"You know neither one of them would ever betray you like that. Beth loved you with all of her heart and soul. Do you know how many times she told me that? She even came to me and told me that the week before she got married."

"Why did she marry him?"

"She was mentally exhausted, Will. I guess he gave her respite for her troubled soul; a safe harbor after what you had put her through. A new life so she could focus on moving ahead whether or not she loved him. It was a place for her to escape from you, not worry about anything."

"Are you supposed to be telling me this?"

Father Carrick was becoming impatient with me. "Her soul is in Heaven, Will. She doesn't need my protection anymore. She loved you more than you can ever possibly imagine and you hurt her more than you can ever possibly imagine. What happened with the baby in Florida? You tore the heart out of her body. And then a year later you accuse her of lying? Lying to the man she loves? About being unfaithful? It was all too much for her. When she came to see me later that very same day, she was on the verge of collapse. She was so confused and hurt. You ripped her heart out, Will.

"And as for Tom, if you had ever, in all your selfishness, stopped to think about him, you would know what you thought happened, never could have happened. You don't know, do you?"

"Know what?"

"What happened to Tom."

"Please stop saying that. Just tell me. What happened to Tom?"

"Like I told you the other day, Tom is celibate. By choice. Like me. I'm celibate because it was part of my vows. I'm married to God. Tom is celibate of his own volition."

I already knew all of this from my earlier conversation with Father Carrick; the transcripts; what Beth had told me that last night.

"I know that. But why?"

He shrugged. "Like I told you before. It's not because he is physically incapable. It's his penance."

Father Carrick was about to join me in my crying jag. It was making him angry.

"Penance for what?"

He clenched his fists.

"That's for another place and time, Will. You just have to know that Tom could not and would not do the things you accused him of. Thirty two years he's been celibate. Since Vietnam. So no, it could have not happened back then and it could not have happened a month ago or a week ago or the other night."

"I'm not following you."

"You know about his foundation?"

"No."

"Tom has donated millions of dollars to the children of this parish."

"Why?"

"Again, it's part of his penance. That's all I can say right now. You're just going to have to take my word for it. Someday I'll tell you everything. Or Tom will, if that's what he decides. You just have to understand that a lot of things happened after you all went away to school and left New City; when you ran away to Vietnam and later were lost in Florida. You cannot expect the world to stand still while you were wallowing in your own sorrows and self-pity.

"So whatever it is you came here today to confess is forgiven."

He brushed his hand as if sweeping away crumbs off a tablecloth. "It's all forgiven, Will. No 'Our Fathers', no 'Hail Marys,' no 'Penance.' It's all forgiven. I don't care about, or want to know the details anymore."

"All of it? You haven't even heard what I came here to tell you."

"No matter. Forgiven. All of it."

He raised his fist above his head. "Forgiven. I'm grading you on a curve. Now get out of here before I lose my temper."

He stood from the pew and walked back to his office.

CHAPTER EIGHTY-SIX

COURTHOUSE

October 25, 2000
Afternoon

I went back into the office and carried on like it was a normal day. When the secretary went out for a coffee break I went into the transcription files again to find out the latest. I downloaded them to a floppy disc I had brought with me.

THISISDETECTIVERAYCICCI,WITHASECONDINTERVIEWWITHVICTIM'S HUSBAND,RAINERKLEIN,CONDUCTEDBYDETECTIVESRAYCICCIandDAVE SHERMANONTUESDAY,OCTOBER24.DISTRICTATTORNEYCARLHENION and CORONER DR. JAMES CAPOBIANCO were also present.

RC: Did you hire a private detective to trail your wife?
RK: Yes. I told you that the other day.
DS: What's his name?
RK: That's privileged.
DS: Why?
RK:That's the law.
DS: No, not his name. Why did you hire a PI?
RK: Because I thought she was cheating on me. I think I want to call my

attorney. I don't like the direction these questions are heading.

DS: Cheating with whom?

RK: Hogenkamp.

DS: Did you know that he is impotent?

JC: He's not impotent. He's celibate.

DS: Same difference.

JC: No, it's not the same difference from a medical standpoint.

RK: What? No. It doesn't matter. She was sharing…other intimacies with him."

DS: Like what other intimacies?

RK: Like what a woman is only supposed to share with her husband. I'm not talking about physical intimacies. I'm talking about her thoughts, her dreams, her emotions. She would not share them with me, only with him. And then there was her old boyfriend, the guy from this office.

DS: Will?

RK: Yes.

DS: So you had a private investigator track him, as well?

RK: Yes.

DS: Why?

RK: The reason we spent so much time abroad was because he was harassing her. We went to Europe and Hong Kong to get away from him.

RC: Was that her idea or yours?

RK: Both.

DS: So what did the P.I. disclose?

RK: Nothing, yet.

DS: Did he say she would go into the courthouse for hours at a time and you assumed it was to see Will?

RK: Is that what the investigation disclosed?

DS: I'll ask the questions. Did you suspect that she was having an affair with Will?

RK: I don't know. I don't think so. She didn't want to have anything to do with him, or so she claimed. I warned her.

DS: Warned her what?"

RK: I warned her that if I ever caught her with him she would be sorry.

DS: What did you mean, 'sorry'?

RK: I didn't mean anything by it. It was just an empty threat made by a husband trying to keep his wife in line. I think she was actually frightened of him.

DS: Did you have reason to believe she wasn't in line?

RK: I knew that she was seeing Hogenkamp on a regular basis.

DS: They were friends. So what?

RK: It was unseemly.

DS: "Unseemly?"

RK: She was behaving strangely.

DS: Why?

RK: I don't know.

DS: What do you know about the meeting that was set up by Will's mother for Beth to meet Will?

RK: What meeting? I don't know anything about it, I was in Hong Kong.

RC: Were your home phones tapped?

RK: That's privileged.

I printed out a copy before Jeanette's smoking break was over.

When she got back from her smoking break she was giving me an odd look. How much did she know?

"I almost forgot. You had a strange phone call earlier."

"What do you mean?"

"A guy called while you were gone. Wanted to talk to you. It sounded like he was in some sort of trouble. Said he needed to talk to you and some guy named Craig or something like that. Cary maybe? When I asked him what his name was, all he said was Sparrow. I asked him what the phone number was and he said he didn't have one. He said you would know where you could find him. Is he an informant? Does Carl or Ray or Dave know about him? If this is about the VonBronk investigation they're gonna have to know. You know I have to tell them. Who is he?"

"Nah. No informant. That's his nickname, Sparrow. He's my next door neighbor. Or should I say 'was' my mother's next door neighbor. He's just a kid I grew up with. I'll go by, see my mother on my way home, make sure everything is all right."

I dismissed it. I think she bought the lie.

CHAPTER EIGHTY-SEVEN

**SING SING CORRECTIONAL FACILITY
OSSINING, NEW YORK**

Wednesday
October 25, 2000
Late Afternoon

I headed toward the Thruway to take the Tappan Zee Bridge over to Westchester.

I hadn't thought of my old friend in some time. He was a tragic figure in my life, or should I say another tragic figure in my life, competing with my brother and father and now Beth, for attention. How could there be so much unhappiness in New City? In the world?

The last time I saw Calvin was at Beth's art gallery, two years earlier. I almost didn't recognize him because of what he was wearing. He was wearing a *smile*. In all the years I had known him I had never seen him smile except when I taught him how to swim and when I gave him the message about what our science teacher had said.

He was also wearing a tuxedo that night, which could not have been more incongruous.

The occasion was a showing of his work at Beth's art gallery in the Village. During his many years in and out of prison, about the only other constant in his life had been his art work. He had acquired several patrons and had become the darling of the art world.

On that night in 1998 Delores and I had driven down to Manhattan at Calvin's request. I had accepted the invitation half-heartedly, because in the back of my mind I actually was hoping to see Beth, even though I understood she was still out of the country at the time. When I saw Calvin I choked up immediately. It was the only time I had ever seen him happy, with hope in his eyes. He was surrounded by the guests and the media and I hesitated to step forward to say hello and break the spell. But when he saw me, he interrupted what he was doing and approached us.

"Will, Delores. Thank you for coming. It means a lot to me." He was actually trying to making eye contact.

"Congratulations on your big night."

"I never thought it would happen, Will. It's like everything that has happened in the past doesn't matter anymore. This is my life now."

I remember looking at him, hoping against hope that what he was saying was true. He had already been through more than anyone should have to endure. I guess deep down inside I knew it was all too good to be true.

"His eye is truly on the sparrow, Will. Remember I told you?"

"Yes. We're so happy for you, Calvin."

During an earlier jail term Calvin had "come out" at about the same time his drawings started attracting serious attention in the art world. His work started selling and the money started flowing in from a host of patrons who thought of him almost as a novelty act; a gay, jailbird-artist-genius. Along with the money came a series of male lovers who abused him and took advantage of him and spent all his money. Eventually, not long after this gallery opening that was supposed to make a change in his life, one of his lovers finally went too far. Calvin discovered that the man had been stealing from him for weeks.

Discussions led to constant physical and verbal abuse. Calvin was too weak to defend himself from the constant barrage, so one night he picked up a kitchen knife and killed his lover in a rage-filled moment while his lover lay sleeping with another man in Calvin's bed.

I had put in a call to Sing Sing to let the administrators know why I was coming. I had known a few of them from earlier investigations. I told them Calvin might have information in a pending murder investigation and they believed me. When I got to the guardhouse, I flashed my investigator's badge and was ushered through.

I was led to an interrogation room painted institutional tan and sat down, the smell of sweat and urine and disinfectant hung in the air. The smell of tobacco smoke lingered years after smoking had been banned.

They brought him in, half carrying him. When I saw him I couldn't believe my eyes. He looked emaciated and like he had been beaten recently. His face was swollen everywhere.

I looked at the guard. "What's this?"

"Your witness."

"What happened to him?"

"He slipped in the shower."

"My, God, Calvin, what happened to you?"

"Creative differences, I think is what they call it in the art world."

"Are you okay?"

His face was puffy and his eyes closed over from the recent beating. His nose looked broken, eyes swollen shut. He spoke through the corner of his mouth and sounded like a punch-drunk prize fighter.

"What's wrong?"

Calvin brushed me off.

"Who is responsible for this?"

"I guess you could say I am. I'm the captain of my ship. Or the captain of my *shit*, as the case may be."

"Calvin, this is no time to joke. You're hurt."

"Nuttin' I ain't used to. *Nuttin' I ain't survived before.*"

He spoke like an old-time movie tough guy.

"Stop joking. I'm going to call someone."

"You don't like my James Cagney? That's not why I called you here. I was sorry to hear about Beth. I know you loved her. I loved her too. She was always very kind to me. All those days at the Lake? She always included a sandwich for me. You probably didn't even know that. It meant a lot. And the gallery opening? I don't know if you ever knew she helped me get an opening. She arranged it all."

I didn't know that story, or much of it. I wanted to know more.

"I'm sorry you two never got together."

"We did, for a while."

"I mean for keepsies. For life. She was a beautiful person."

"I know."

"You're investigating her murder?"

"I'm not part of that team. Not allowed."

"Tell them they can stop looking."

"What do you mean?"

"I think Marvin did it."

"What makes you think that?"

"He's as much as told me over the years what's been going on.

"Over the years?

"Yeah. What's been going on."

"What has been going on over the years?

"He stalked both of you. All through school, summers at New City Park Lake."

I started to feel light-headed.

"So you think he's capable of that kind of violence? Against a woman?"

"Let me tell you some things," Calvin began. "I'll start at the beginning, then you can decide for yourself. You may wanna take some notes."

I took out a narrow reporter's steno pad from my hip pocket, and a ballpoint pen.

Calvin breathed as if the weight of the world was being lifted from his shoulders. In a way, it was. "That Gleason fire when we were kids?"

"We were what? Eight years old?"

"Yeah. He did it because he got in a fight with that girl's older brother. He put a copper penny in a fuse box because he heard my father say it would overheat and cause a fire. Other fires? A few years after that? Those were all Marvin. He did it for fun. He did it whenever something made him angry. He liked to watch the fire engines pull up and the volunteers go to work. He was angry all the time.

"Then when you and Beth were in Gainesville, during a Memorial Day parade, Marvin had become entranced by a Glockenspiel player in New City Fife & Drum. She was this big fat girl, she never washed her hair, but she became Marvin's obsession. You remember her? She was a year behind us in school. Used to be in the marching band."

I vaguely remembered the girl Calvin was referencing. Then I suddenly remembered the last time I had seen her. Or her body.

"After high school, she joined Middletown Fife. Marvin followed them on tour, up and down the Hudson River Valley, showing up at every parade. He was obsessed with her, watching her march. He begged to join the New City band, even started taking drum lessons, but Gunnar Pedersen refused to let him. He had no talent, and his ulterior motives were obvious to the leader.

"But he continued following her performances, like some groupie, never taking his eyes off her. She was grotesque. After six months of stalking her, watching her march up and down the streets of the Hudson River towns, he worked up the nerve to speak to her. Less than three sentences into the conversation, he lost control and proposed marriage. His compulsion frightened her and she stood to leave the park bench where they sat between sets of the competition she was playing in up in Beacon. He grabbed her wrist to comfort her and she struggled to break free. In his frustration he started slapping her, demanding that she listen to his pleas, finally graduating to full punches.

"They sent him to six months in Rockland State Hospital, gave him mega-doses of Thorazine, and he was back on the streets. But he had gained fifty pounds himself and was dangerous to himself and others. He went back to living in the barn trying to plan out his future, but most of the time he couldn't get any further than jerking off to *Playboy* all day long.

"You know that girl that jumped into the Trap Rock Quarry?"

"Yeah." It was all coming together now.

"Marvin forced her to jump."

"What do you mean?, 'forced her to jump'?"

"He told her if she didn't jump, he was going to push her."

"He told you this?"

"He laughed about it, like the Gleason fire."

"He did a lot of stuff like this?"

"Way before that he got an offer to do the bank job."

"What bank job?"

"Nanuet National. It was the same weekend as your father's funeral."

"Marvin had something to do with that?"

I thought back, trying to recall the details I read about in the paper after that already event-filled weekend.

"The bank or the funeral?" Calvin hesitated and gave me a look, as if he had let something slip, had given something away.

I didn't understand his question. "The bank job." What could he have had to do with my father's funeral?

"He was the getaway driver for the robbery. He needed the

money, so he agreed. All he had to do was sit outside of Nanuet Bank with the engine running in a car he stole in Nyack an hour before. Easy money. It was the same bank that was robbed in that play, *High Tor*."

"Maxwell Anderson's *High Tor?*"

"Yeah, I get a lot of reading done in here, broadening my literary horizons, when I'm not getting the shit beat out of me. Anyway, he parked the stolen car down the street from Rex Barber Shop. He told me he remembered Big Dan Ingram was on WABC playing Junior Walker and the All Stars. A perfect choice, considering what happened."

"What do you mean?"

"So this guy approaches from the opposite end of the street and gave Marvin a nod before walking in. Seconds later the guy is running out the door with canvas bag full of dough. Before he can even turn toward the car he is shot in the back of the head by the bank guard with a shotgun, no doubt inspired by the Junior Walker music playing on the radio, *Shotgun*. The song. Get it?

"The guy drops like a sack of potatoes. No dramatic gestures. No slow motion. Just an undignified, tangled drop. Bam! On the sidewalk. Marvin turns off the motor, wipes it down for prints like he'd seen in the movies, gets out of the car.

"He walked over and calmly joined the bunch of other rubbernecks standing over the body with a ground-chuck stump where his head used to be. He exchanged nods and shoulder shrugs, pretends he's an innocent bystander before the cops broke up the crowd and he wandered over to the bus stop. He catches a Red & Tan headed north up Middletown Road and he gets off at New City Park Lake.

"He was sitting on the dam contemplating his life when your lifeguard boss drove by, backs up, pulls into the lot and tells him he was on private property, and that he had to leave. Marvin left, all right, but not before vowing revenge. Then that night with you and Beth on the raft? That was a coincidence."

I couldn't get those images out of my mind. Marvin had invaded our privacy, our night on the raft, our intimate conversation, Beth's compassion.

Calvin continued, and as he did I sat there in amazement. The story made me sick to my stomach. He continued with his tale.

That night of my father's funeral, when Beth had given me solace in New City Park, Marvin had walked the stream bank south from Schriever Lane. He passed under the Collyer Avenue bridge and approached the dam. He was still stewing about being kicked off the property earlier that day by the president of the club, insulted, humiliated. So like he had on other nights, he entered the New City Park Clubhouse through an open basement window.

"This time he used cleaning solvents and old rags. His plan was to set down a short plumber's candle as a timing device. Then he planned to call the fire department before setting the fire. So when they arrive it's really just getting started and they can control it. Put a scare into them."

Black and white photos of Norwegian immigrants hung on the wall watched Marvin as he worked. When he heard Beth and me arrive he had apparently sneaked out of the building, circled around and quietly floated out to the raft where he hung, suspended, while Beth and I swam out and shared intimacies.

When Beth and I left and went up on the lawn, Marvin had followed us, then went back to the clubhouse, called the fire department, waited a minute, and lit the candle. It would give him about three minutes' lead time. Then, he swam out to the raft and hung from the barrel framework again.

The fire had just started when the fire trucks arrived. The photos on the wall curled up and turned black, fueled by the knotty pine bonfire. By then, Marvin was suspended under the raft in the middle of the lake, hanging by his fingertips in the water, watching it all from ringside. A fireman thought he saw something under the raft, but it retreated into the shadows when he swept his flashlight in that direction. Just a nesting muskrat, the fireman concluded. It was the reflection of golden flames off Marvin's jubilant face.

Calvin was staring at the wall now as he continued his story.

"Apparently it wasn't the first time Marvin had hung from under the raft while you and Beth lay on it at night, making out. He used to tell me about it."

How many nights had Beth and I spent on the raft, lying naked in the darkness sharing secrets? How many nights had she led me to the back yard of the vacant property near the lighthouse on the south lawn?

"The night he started the fire and watched from the raft, he could see your old lifeguard boss, Bill, sitting on a picnic table by the brick barbecue, trying to recall for the Chief the details of any conversation he had that afternoon. Could he describe the trespasser? Could it be related to the fire? Marvin had to stifle his laughter when he told me the story. He considered it all a form of his revenge against the world."

"Revenge for what?"

"That you had someone like Beth and he didn't. He used to brag about how he stalked Beth for years without her knowing it. He was always peeping in her windows when she was growing up in her father's art gallery. He still followed her through the Dutch Garden during her frequent visits with Tom, even after she was married to Rainer. Even after she was married and moved to that estate on Lake DeForest."

"Why was he so angry?"

"Like the night of the New City Park Lake Clubhouse fire the night you and Beth were there? He knew you and Beth were off in the woods somewhere making out. He was jealous. He just didn't want revenge for being thrown out. He wanted your attention so he set the clubhouse on fire. Like I say, he was there because they had thrown him out earlier in the day. That's the way he thinks. He was getting revenge for two slights from two enemies at once.

"Years ago, when he heard that Rainer wanted to buy the

property where the old schoolhouse was, he approached Rainer and told him he could help.

"He developed a plan. One night he snuck into New City Grammar School."

I, myself, had watched the fire that night consume the very same school attended by my father and grandfather. The history of the town was carved into the desktops of that school.

"He carried twenty cardboard boxes of files and schoolbooks to the basement where we got our polio shots in the early 1950s. He stacked them to the ceiling and doused them with gasoline. He used clothesline rope stolen from my mother's pantry and soaked it in a puddle of gasoline."

"He backtracked out of the basement window he had climbed through, stretched out the saturated rope along behind him. He disappeared into the Meyer's woods to watch the action that was about to start. One hundred feet down the hill he set fire to the rope."

The flames had raced up the hill on the rope and the citadel of thousands of childhood dreams erupted in flames, burning through the pages of old copies of *Dick, Jane and Sally*, and *If I Were Going*, pages which had once fueled the flames of a young boy's imagination, and now served as fuel to burn down a building we all held so dear.

The volunteer firemen were grief-stricken as they fought a losing battle. Many had gone to school there. They struggled desperately to save the old landmark, but it was too late. By daybreak, it is smoking black rubble. Two local firemen lost their lives when a fire escape collapsed on them. Marvin had stifled his laughter while hiding in the skunk cabbage in the woods before walking past Vandy's dump and down to the site of the old Dinky Line railroad bed, now covered by the New Rte. 304, toward his refuge in his barn.

"So this is something he did for Rainer?"

"He went to work for Rainer. Under the table. A few years

earlier The Elms was his audition piece."

"Doing what?

"Stuff. All kinds of stuff. Rainer wants a piece of property and the owners resist, Marvin takes care of it.

"How?

"Lots of different ways. His favorite was always arson. He gets off on fires.

"He did the same thing earlier down on Squadron A. When you were in Florida, the barn burned down so he could get the sale and build those condo apartments. When he did it for The Elms, that one didn't work out the way Rainer wanted it to."

"How so?"

"They turned it into a memorial park. Klein wanted it for commercial property. He lost that game."

I thought back for a moment. "What about the old Verdin Mansion?"

"Yeah. That was Marvin. More residential units."

"So why do you think he had something to do with Beth's murder?"

"Easy. He was jealous. He would follow Beth to the Court House parking lot, day or night, through the Dutch Gardens down the path of the Demarest Kill to Tom's house. He would peek into Tom's windows at the boathouse, hoping to catch a glimpse of Beth naked, but all she and Tom ever did was talk. Marvin eventually stopped tailing her to Tom's. Tom must have suspected something and installed a perimeter guard. Marvin tripped the lights on a couple of times before he realized what was going on."

"You're sure about this?"

"He laughs about it when he comes here. Beth was raped before she was killed, right?"

That fact had been kept from the press. "Yes."

"The dead fat girl in Trap Rock had glockenspiel music charts in her trunk, right?"

That fact had also been kept from the press. "Yes."

"Check for his D.N.A. He's wanted to have sex with Beth for years."

Calvin stopped talking for a moment while I absorbed all of what he had told me. It sickened me. It was almost too much to absorb at one time. Something, many things beautiful beyond description, had been despoiled by Calvin's tale.

What he said next caught me even more off guard and shook me from my thoughts.

"I love you Will. You're the only person in the whole world, in my whole life, who's ever been kind to me. Well, you and Francis and Beth. I'm so sorry about what Marvin did to Francis. For so many years I thought he did it on purpose."

My nose started burning and I lost my breath.

"Why?"

"He was jealous of Francis. And of your family. You were the All-American family and it filled him with rage to see you all so happy.

"And Will, I'm sorry about Beth. I know you still loved her. My guess? Rainer paid my brother to do it, time it out for whenever he was out of the country with a convenient alibi."

"Why do you say that?"

"Rainer knew how Marvin felt about Beth. He even knew Marvin was peeping in the windows at Beth. He allowed him to do it as a control measure, to keep Marvin on the hook, like it was part of a reward.

"Marvin knew Rainer was insanely jealous because she loved you and Tom. I think Rainer found out that Beth had betrayed him on some land deal. Rainer wanted to buy Tom's land and tried to get Beth to talk Tom into it. Marvin heard them talking and told Rainer that Beth was doing just the opposite of what he had asked her to do. I think it pushed Rainer over the edge."

My mind raced at what he was telling me. I sat there for a long moment in silence.

"Go talk to Marvin, Will."

"Thanks, Calvin. Hang on. I'm going to get you out of here. We're going to get you treatment and find a safe place for you."

Calvin stared off into space again, then directly back into my eyes. Eye contact.

"I love you, Will."

Thinking about that made me very sad.

"I love you, too, Calvin. We're going to get you out of here."

I later reflected on why I had told Calvin that. It was true. Kids who grow up in a neighborhood become so much more than friends. They become part of your extended family. Is that some form of love, or a form of pity for what I knew he had gone through growing up, or just another attempt to hold onto the past?

I got up from the table and we made a movement to hug one another, but the guard stepped forward and shook his head. Calvin had one last piece of information.

"Hey Will. The good news is that I'm HIV positive. It will all be over soon for me. My suffering will be over. I wanted to tell you about Marvin before it was too late."

I looked at this pitiable human form before me. It was all so sad. "You want me to send Father Carrick? "

"That's an idea. You think God will forgive me for all the terrible things I've done, Will?"

"Yes, Calvin. Yes I do."

CHAPTER EIGHTY-EIGHT

NEW CITY

Wednesday
October 25, 2000
Early Evening

I went to see Father Carrick again, to ask him to go see Calvin. The immediate necessity of last rites had crossed my mind more than once. I told him all that Calvin had told me.

"Do you think Marvin could have done it, Father Carrick?"

"While you were gone, Marvin was in and out of jail a lot. Lost his job at IBEW. His father got him a job on the Highway Department.

"He would sit on the steps in front of the Courthouse and drink Italian Swiss Colony by the quart. Every day for weeks he would sit there. I would try to talk to him but he was drunk, arguing politics with pedestrians and he would become abusive to the Courthouse crowd on their way to Tor's for lunch. Some arrogant attorney really told him off and he started to retaliate. The guy told him not to try anything, because he knew who Marvin was.

"In a blind rage Marvin headed south on Main Street just a few feet until he came to the World War II Memorial. Seeing his

father's name in bronze, he picked up a rock and tried to scrape it
off. Thirty days for vandalism of public property. The VFW guys
were outraged at the light sentence.

"In the County jail he would scream out the barred windows
at secretaries crossing the wooden bridge on their way to the new
Courthouse.

"The first night out of jail he decided to show them what vandalism of public property really looks like. He finished the job he
had started a dozen years earlier in the Dutch Garden. He over-
turned the brick lattice-work walls and scraped caricatures off the
brick facades with a cold chisel, smashed slate roof tiles, smeared
excrement on the brass plaques. He pulled up every flower planted
recently by the New City Garden Club."

"I guess a lot happened while we were in Florida."

"A lot."

"He was never punished for it?"

"No one could ever prove anything."

All these years and I had never heard these stories.

"I'll go see Calvin tomorrow. Before it's too late."

"One other request, Father. When was the last time you told
a lie?"

"Lying is a sin. Why do you ask, Will?"

"Tomorrow, when you go see Calvin he's going to ask you if
God will forgive him for all that he's done. You're going to tell
him 'Yes', right?"

"I don't have to lie for that."

I left the church and walked home to New City Park. Who did
I talk to now? Jimmy? No one?

CHAPTER EIGHTY-NINE

NEW CITY

Thursday
October 26, 2000
Evening

The next night, after getting the silent treatment at work all day, I walked home from the courthouse. I stopped by to see my mother and Francis, like I usually did. But this time there was another reason. I wanted to see if I could slip inside the barn where Marvin stayed to see if I could gather some DNA samples. Legal? No, but I really didn't care at this point. If I could convince Jimmy and Carl and Ray and Dave that I was not the killer and Marvin was, then we could all maybe find some peace over Beth's death.

My mother was sitting at Francis' bedside, spoon-feeding him his dinner as she had every night for the past forty-four years. I sat, putting in my time as they watched the news together. Then I excused myself and went upstairs to my old bedroom. It was plenty dark outside, but still, I made sure the lights were off before I peered out the window in the direction of the Hessian's barn for a bird's-eye perspective. The giant pine trees blocked most of the view. There were no lights inside and the house was dark in front, as well.

Back downstairs I made an excuse to my mother about looking for something in our barn and grabbed the flashlight from the kitchen drawer.

"While you're out there can you see if you can find a book I can't seem to locate?"

"Which one?"

"One of your father's favorites. *Jerry Todd and the Oak Island Treasure*. I know I put it back with all the others last year after I read it to Francis and now I can't seem to find it. I'm so careful about those books. Your father loved them so much. He hoped you would have a child to pass them on to someday since both you and Francis loved them so much. Will you look for it?"

"Okay." It was a momentary distraction for the task at hand, but I was willing to take the time.

Outside, I made my way down the catalpa-lined path and walked inside the barn and flipped on my flashlight. It looked as if nothing had been touched since the day of my father's funeral.

Had it really been since the day of my father's funeral, thirty-three years earlier, that I had been in the barn? Had my mother, other than to retrieve books to read for Francis? Had anyone? Or had those wooden walls just borne the passing of the seasons in lonely silence, home to memories and hand tools from a hundred years ago? The hand spade and the hand cultivator still hung on the wall, untouched on their own special places, and I was reminded of my father saying he wasn't a gardener like his own parents had been.

On the workbench, hand tools were arranged in neat and orderly rows beside the iron vise and the wooden vise my grandfather had made himself. Handsaws and block planes still held the evidence of sawdust and wood curls. The Mason jars filled with an assortment of nuts and bolts and washers and nails lined the back edge of the bench. It all made me think of the life my grandfather had led and what my own father had inherited from him. The history of those tools were the history of my life. And where had it all led me? Our lives were all so different.

Leaning up against the side wall was the old handmade sled my grandfather used with his horse to deliver the mail in the winter when the snow covered roads were otherwise impassable. It defined his winter days. I wished he had given me a ride in it, a link somehow, to the past.

I made a detour upstairs to look for the missing book. I opened the cardboard boxes that held the collection. It should have been in the third position, but it wasn't there. The book that I had remembered as missing that day of my father's funeral was back in its slot. My father had checked it out of his own library and my mother returned it, right?

I looked through all the other boxes. Maybe my mother had misplaced *Oak Island Treasure*? I would come back the next day and look in the daylight.

Back on the bottom floor I switched off my flashlight. I exited the barn through the rear window and lowered myself to the cinder pile.

Behind our barn I looked over into the empty field that separated our barn and its identical twin next door where Marvin had taken up residence. It was close enough to his family to be rent free, but he didn't have to encounter his father at every step.

At the fence line I waited in silence before hopping over and running silently across the small, open plot. I let myself in through the side door of Marvin's barn. Inside on the first floor was the familiar musty smell of the coal-ash strewn floor. I swept my flashlight beam across the room. In the corner was the old ice box that had been converted into a smoker that had taken the meaning out of my brother's life that June day so long ago. I wondered why they had kept it, but figured out that was just their way. Had Mr. Hessian actually used it to smoke venison in it after what had happened to Francis? What would prevent them? Surely not a conscience?

I stood in silence with the light off again, the only sound my heavy breathing from what I was about to do. What if he came in while I was there? Should I have told Jimmy what I was doing beforehand? I was on shaky ground career-wise, legally and certainly for my own physical safety.

Did Marvin leave DNA behind in the barn? I was hoping to find a hairbrush or toothbrush from which I could gather DNA samples, proving conclusively that Marvin had been the one who had raped Beth and then killed her. From there it would be a slam dunk for Carl's team to bring charges and have him arrested, maybe even Klein, as well. Could I have gone to Carl and asked him to get a search warrant? Probably. Should I have? Definitely. Would they have responded, deemed it probable cause, based on the word of Calvin, a convicted murderer?

I had heard some vague rumor that Marvin had spent countless hours remodeling the upstairs of the barn for his living quarters and winterized the open room and installed indoor plumbing, but I was not prepared for what I saw when I walked slowly to the top of the steps.

As I aimed my flashlight around the room, my beam revealed things that didn't make sense; didn't compute. As I tried to piece it all together my light revealed Marvin's chest. He faced me, standing with a shotgun pointed at my midsection. I thought my own chest would explode in disbelief. He flipped on the wall switch and the room became illuminated from track lighting off the ceiling beams.

"What took you so long?"

It felt as if someone had punched me in the gut. I don't know if I was more shocked by the shotgun pointing at me or what I beheld as I looked around the room. It appeared as if he had hand-sanded every board, every wooden surface in the place, in preparation for a photo shoot for *Architectural Digest*.

"Been doing some remodeling. You like it?"

He had meticulously rebuilt the room. The woodwork was magnificent.

It was such uncharacteristic behavior I really didn't know quite what to think. He must have been obsessive.

"Aren't you going to compliment me? No? At a loss for words? So, I don't need to ask you what you're doing here. I just need to ask you if you came alone."

"I'm alone. The others will be here in a few minutes."

"You're lying. You didn't tell anyone. You wanted to be the hero. Beth's hero."

He had figured me out.

"I had an interesting conversation with your brother yesterday."

"That faggot? What did he say? As if I didn't know. I thought you would have been here hours ago. You left me waiting around."

"He said he thinks you killed Beth."

He sneered. "Brilliant deduction. What would he know?"

"Would you be willing to give us a DNA sample?"

"What's that?"

"Like a blood sample."

"Never liked needles."

"We can do it with a cotton swab in your mouth."

"No thanks. Why would I want to do that?"

"Because you are now a suspect in Beth's murder."

"I should have killed that faggot years ago. He's an embarrassment. He just loves to gossip.

"You can't hurt your brother anymore. He's dying."

He glanced toward the house they grew up in.

"So what do you want to know about Beth? What else did he tell you?"

"How about everything? He told me some things, but I'd like to hear it all from you."

"You bet. Let's see. Where should I start? The night of the murder?

"Why don't you start in the beginning?"

"Oh you mean way back when? Sure, why not. Hmm. You sure you want to know all of this stuff?"

"Positive."

"Okay, it's your funeral, if you'll pardon the pun. Isn't that what they say? 'Pardon the pun?' "

"My funeral?"

"Your funeral. So, where to begin? How about Sixth Grade? That day up at Tom's house, that big garden party with the tent and the live orchestra and those muckety-muck friends of his grandparents."

"You were there?"

"Had a bird's-eye view of the whole thing from a tree branch looking down on the tent. I saw you and Beth in her pretty yellow sundress and all those old faggots smoking cigarettes and sipping cocktails with their pinkies stuck out. And then your buddy played the piano and got the boo-hoos from some of the ladies in the audience. It was all so touching. Kinda makes a guy like me feel bad not to get invited to a party like that. It's bad for my self-esteem."

I thought back to that day. I didn't know I was supposed to feel important, but I guess Marvin did.

"Then let's fast-forward the tape to another party I didn't get invited to. Gate Night in the Dutch Garden."

I felt sick. I wasn't sure I wanted to hear any more. "How did you know we would be there?"

"Calvin heard about it. Gate Night used to be big around here. My father said the kids would tear the gates off the front yard fences and throw them up on the roofs of the houses. I figured I'd show up and see what all the fuss was about, offer my services. Then I saw you two, and decided I'd do a little eavesdropping. It was all so sweet and innocent. I was moved. Deeply moved. I was able to get over the north wall and crawl on my hands and knees into the tea house. That's how close I was. And you never heard me. You were too busy swapping spit with Beth."

I wanted to strangle him then. But it only got worse.

"The funniest part was when you were leaving to go home."

At that point, Marvin let out the loudest, ugliest cat screech I had ever heard. Now, standing close to him, the visceral quality of it was nauseating.

"See that? You jumped three feet in the air again after all these years and it's not even Halloween."

I waited for my disbelief to sink in, and then as if to punctuate his claim, he let out with a second screech, that again recreated the cat scream from that Halloween in 1961. A chill ran through me as well as the realization that Marvin was crazy. Crazy and unpredictable and dangerous.

"You want more?"

"Sure."

"Let me set the scene. An early snowfall in 1963. Your car was being towed by Gary Plunkett. You got out of the car and talked to him just after I was getting out of work. I ran across the Garden and you followed me only a minute later. You stopped and looked at my footprints."

I remember the eerie feeling I had seeing them there and then sloughing it off as just another coincidence.

"There was quickness in your footsteps. Something nice must have happened that night. Something warm and cozy to put that smile on your face. Let me guess."

I didn't want him to guess.

"Let's see, there were plenty more. That day you moved the piano to the boathouse? I almost froze my ass off that day. What were you guys thinking? And that last summer before you all went off to college? Out on the raft at New City Park?"

"We were there lots of nights. Everyone knows that. So what? What if I don't believe you?"

"Oh, let's see. What if I dropped the name 'Louise'?"

"Louise?"

"Oh, sorry, I mean *naked* Louise. *Naked Louise*, the cellist from Nyack Conservatory. Her olive skin looked so beautiful in the moonlight. You remember."

Marvin had been there that night. He had heard the entire conversation. Watched us swimming.

Now, he continued to pace the room.

"Beth always arrived to visit Tom via the Courthouse. She used to pull in the courthouse parking lot, walk in the front door, then exit through the basement door and follow the path behind the tea house through the Dutch Garden to the boathouse. Very tricky. Fooled the private dick but it didn't fool me. That's what you get for not hiring locals.

"So I was there pretty much every night whenever she was in New City, waiting for her. When you two met the other night? I was there. I didn't realize you two had arranged a meeting. It was like old times. I was there for *her*. I got more than I bargained for. It was a lovely little soap opera. I almost started sniffling. *Ain't love grand ?*"

"You were smoking, weren't you?"

"Earlier that night. Yeah, I know. Nasty habit. A lingering stench. Trying to quit."

Marvin tossed me a pack of Chesterfields exactly like he had done that spring day when I took my first and last puff of a cigarette. Now, as he lit up I thought back to the smell the night of my last meeting with Beth.

"So, you never took up smoking? Still a wimp? You believe all that crap about cigarettes and cancer? It's all a hoax. Just scare tactics.

"When she was coming back from Tom's I was waiting for her. I stepped out of the dark from behind her and reached over and covered her mouth. She about peed her pants. She kept trying to scream, tried to see who it was. I wouldn't let her turn around. I wanted her to think it was you who had waited around for her to get back from Tom's. Anything goes wrong, she gets away, she tells the cops it's you. She even called out your name."

"She called out my name?"

Marvin covered mouth with his palm muffling Beth's words as he mimicked her. "'Will! Will!'"

I closed my eyes and hung my head.

"She started to struggle, and well, it was all downhill from there, if you'll excuse another pun. *Downhill*. I like that."

"So you killed her?"

"Not at first. Decided to have a little fun, first. I don't think she liked that very much. Kept struggling. Too bad."

"You punched her?"

"Things would have worked out much better for her if she had just kept her mouth shut and stopped struggling. Some women just don't wanna listen. A man's gotta do what a man's gotta do."

"Like the girl at Trap Rock?"

"Wow. My little brother was playing gossip-girl today. No, not like the girl at Trap Rock. I never punched her. I just pushed her over the edge because she started annoying me. She didn't want to marry me. I told her she could do it herself or I would do it."

He sat there in silent reflection for a moment. "She was the only girl I ever gave my heart to. Well, her and Beth."

"Where does Rainer fit into all of this?"

"Killing Beth? It was his idea. He just wanted me to wait until he was out of town so he had an iron-clad alibi."

Marvin was thinking back to earlier days. "That guy Rainer is one sick dude."

"What do you mean?"

"In addition to paying me to follow Beth around town, he let me take care of my somewhat voyeuristic tendencies by leaving the windows cracked at their home over on Lake DeForest. Kinda like the old Davies' Lake days, remember? You were such a pussy that day. A pussy peeping at pussies."

"So you are saying that Rainer knows you killed her?"

"I told you. It was his idea. Oh, and by the way, he didn't just meet Beth at the art gallery where she was working down in the village in some 'coincidence.' He always asked about her. I told him you guys had split up. He tracked her down and arranged for their little meeting to take place. Talk about stalking."

"Why do you think Rainer wanted her dead?

"She was becoming a pain in his ass. Spending all his money. "How?"

"How was she a pain in the ass or how was she spending all his money?"

"How was she a pain in the ass?"

"He wanted her to convince your old buddy Tom to sell him all the Demarest Kill property and the boathouse, Greenberg's Pond, Dove Cottage, the whole *megillah*. He wanted her to figure out a way to get the property. Sweet talk him out of it. Instead, she told Tom that Rainer wanted her to help him in his conspiracy to buy out Tom."

"How do you know this?"

"Rainer told me his side."

"And her side?"

"I heard them. I used to sit outside the boathouse and listen to their conversations. I told Rainer. Most of the time they were pretty boring, I gotta tell you. I kept waiting for them to fuck, but they never did. Never once in all these years. At least not when I was at the windows. Tom must be a faggot, too."

"He's celibate."

"Like a priest? Same difference. Speaking of which, your friend, Father Carrick, might have a little confessing to do himself."

"What do you mean?"

"That's for me to know and you to find out. All in good time."

It was all too much, but I had to let that go for the time being.

"So you told Rainer that Beth had spilled the beans to Tom."

"Sure, that she had decided to help her old buddy, Tom, instead of her own husband. That's what I was paid to do. Tell him stuff like that. Rainer was going to have me torch the Florion mansion, add a little incentive to his decision."

"Like with the other cases of arson?"

"So, Calvin told you about those, too, did he? Faggot."

"The Gleason fire?"

"That guy was picking on me in school. When I told my father, he suggested it. Teach the kid a lesson."

"The little girl had nothing to do with it."

"I think the military calls that collateral damage. You know about that, don't you, Mr. Vietnam War Hero."

"The Elms?

"Yes. For fun."

"The old schoolhouse?"

"Yes. I like to think of it as a catalyst for a quick land sale."

I asked one I didn't want to know the answer to. "New City Park Clubhouse?"

"That was just for fun. And revenge maybe. I got kicked out of there, so I wanted them to pay a price. I went back that night."

"The night of the bank robbery?"

Marvin stopped and thought back, as if trying to keep up. "He told you about that, too, did he?"

"Yes."

"Yeah, well I got kicked out of the lake by some old guy. He said I didn't belong there. So I came back later and crawled in the basement window and set it all up and then when I climbed out to wait around for the right moment and guess who was there? The love-birds, back home from Florida."

I didn't want to hear any more. He had been there the night of my father's funeral. The night Beth and I had conceived our child.

"Are you wearing one of those microphones or something to record this? You're asking a lot of questions."

He walked over and patted me down.

"Squadron A Barn?"

"Commission for a quick land sale."

"Verdin Mansion?"

"Sure. Hefty commissions for houses and apartments."

"The Sheriff's horse stable on North Main?"

Marvin paused to reflect. "Let's not go there."

"Because nine horses burned to death?"

"I said we're not going there."

"So why didn't you do it, the Florion mansion?"

"Rainer changed his mind when I told him that Beth was going to leave him."

"How did you know that?"

"The window treatment. Wow, I'm just loaded with puns tonight. I listened to their conversations for years sitting under the open windows. After Beth told Tom that Rainer would do anything to get the property, they also talked about Beth leaving Rainer for good, and of course, being the good soldier I am, I had to tell him that too. I got a bonus for that."

"A bonus?"

"Permission from Klein to fuck her before I killed her."

Suddenly, I was sick to my stomach.

"While Rainer was on a high profile trip to Hong Kong, of course."

Marvin walked to an oak filing cabinet and reached inside.

"He told me I could do it any time he was out of town and had a good alibi. When I saw you guys there together, I thought I could figure out a way to pin it on you."

He reached in his filing cabinet, grabbed a fistful of something. "Here's Beth's clothing. Shoes, handbag, scarf. I was going to keep them as souvenirs. Ooops, here we go. Don't forget the panties. Designer."

"Why are you telling me all of this?"

"There's nothing you can do about it because I'm going to kill you. I have to keep up my track record. I killed that little girl. I fucked up your brother real good, I killed Beth, and I killed your father. Now it's your turn."

I was trying to absorb all of this.

"You killed my father?"

"Well, he waited for me to leave The Pub and he stepped into the path of my car intentionally. So whether I killed him or he killed himself is really a, what's that phrase, a matter of opinion. *Conjecture*. Is that what you guys call it?"

"There are people who know I'm here. Who know what Calvin told me."

"Nice try. They'd be all over this place like flies on shit if they knew this stuff and knew you were coming here."

"I didn't say it was the police."

"Who then? Dear old Father Carrick? Another man full of surprises."

"If you kill me they'll know it was you. You'll spend the rest of your life in prison. Two murders."

"No, you've got that wrong. I'm going to kill you and drop these panties off at your house in New City Park and go tell your buddies that you did it. I'll tell them I witnessed the whole thing the other night. I'll tell them that you came up here and threatened me and I shot you in self defense. I've got it all figured out. It will be worth it to kill you. You've always been such a pussy."

I thought about that. What could I say to defend myself against those charges with someone who was going to kill me in a few minutes? I couldn't think of anything in my defense. Hadn't I ever done anything worthwhile in my life? Hadn't I been there for Francis except for those few lost years? Hadn't I served my country (if what you could call what I did, *service*) for two years? . Hadn't I ever helped a student reconsider a future life? I guess it's true. In your dying moments, your whole life rushes past you in fast forward.

"I'm a pussy? So what does that make you? You killed an innocent little girl. An innocent adult."

"White trash. That kid, her brother. He beat me up, like I said. My father gave me the idea."

"Those horses?" I thought back almost one hundred years to 1904 and my ancestor's barn fire on the hill where those horses were saved but the livestock perished, screaming in the night.

"I told you we're not going there."

I almost said something, but didn't. Instead, I shook my head. "Marvin, we've known each other for almost fifty years."

"This is gonna be good. I can tell. Yeah, so what?"

"I guess I find it hard to believe why you would do all of these things. You didn't have to do any of this stuff. Haven't you ever just stopped for one minute to think about it?"

"You gonna get all high and mighty on me now? Lecture me because I wasn't a nice little boy like you and your brother?"

"Marvin, I don't know what your life was like growing up."

Now he did pause. He started to pace. "Stop, already. I've always been sorry about the little girl, all right? It was just meant to scare them. I could smell her burning flesh for years after, like those horses. I felt more sorry for them than I did for her. So maybe I do have a conscience. Don't let the word get out. It will ruin my reputation."

He sat on the barstool, shotgun across his knees as he reconsidered his life. There was a long pause as he looked up to the smooth beams he had so meticulously refinished. "So how come?"

"How come what?"

"Guys like you get all the good stuff."

"What do you mean?"

"The only thing my father ever gave me was a knuckle sandwich. He used to keep shoving me down. Anytime I tried to speak to him he would shove me down. He saw me reading a book once and he slapped it out of my hands. He made me pick it up and then he slapped it across my face."

He sat silent, remembering, then stood and walked to the sofa where he sat again.

He nodded his head involuntarily in a couple of quick jerks. He looked around the room he had created. "You know how long it took me to sand-blast that wood?"

I looked up to the cross-members of the post-and-beam construction. "No."

Much to my surprise he started weeping. He picked up a bottle of Old Mr. Boston whiskey and took two deep draughts. "This is all so tiresome. I don't want to live like this anymore."

"Will you testify against Klein, in exchange for immunity from prosecution?"

"Do you have the authority to offer me a deal?"

"I'll get it, Marvin. Just hang on. You're going to have to trust me."

"So what happens? Explain to me how that immunity thing works."

"We make a deal. They don't care about you. They want the boss man, not the person who actually carries it out."

"You mean the 'small-fry,' like me."

"You testify, he goes to jail. You'll get a few years, for lesser charges. Your attorney will have to work it out with Henion. But you'll get out and you won't die in jail."

"So let me get this straight. The rich guy with a team of powerful attorneys goes to jail and the poor guy with fifteen minutes preparation by the Public Defender gets off easy? What world are you living in?"

"You're going to have to trust me."

"Why should I trust you?"

"Because I want to make this right, Marvin. You wouldn't have done this without him paying you and goading you all these years. He's the one who should be punished."

"What about the rape?"

The thought of it sickened me. "I'll have to find out about that. That one might be a little more difficult. You'll have to take your chances. Plea down. You got into a fight. She fell down the hill and broke her neck."

"She was dead before I threw her down the hill."

Beth. My Beth.

"You didn't know that. You could get manslaughter instead of first degree. Whatever happens, anything's better than what you're looking at, whether you kill me or let me try to negotiate."

"He'll go to jail?"

"I'll see to it personally. But you have to testify. We may even have you wear a wire. Let Rainer implicate himself."

"*I ain't no stoolie.*" He laughed. "Isn't that what they say in those gangster movies?"

I asked him something I hadn't been able to get off of my mind; that *I had to know*, especially if Marvin was about to kill me in cold blood. "Did Beth realize who was beating her to death and raping her? You said you snuck up behind her and did it, without revealing your face? She called my name?"

Marvin let out a sadistic laugh. "Why do you want to know that?"

I didn't say anything. He figured it out.

"Because you want to know if Beth thought it was you beating and raping her and not me? You want some reassurance? So you can die now in peace?"

I didn't answer.

"Tell you what, smart guy. I'm not going to tell you. At least not for now. Maybe Beth thought it was you killing her and before she was rolling down the hill she wondered why you were the one who was killing her and hurting her again. Why she kept screaming, 'Will! Will!' "

"She really said that? She was calling me to help her?"

"I told you before. She was calling *you to stop.*"

I had to persist. I had to know. "So did she think it was me?"

"All in good time."

"Marvin, you don't have to do this. I can talk to people. I can convince them that he was the brains behind all of this. Let him pay the price, not you."

He seemed to stop for a moment to think.

"Marvin, I know I should have been a better friend to you and Calvin all these years. We lived next door to one another. I should have been a better friend." I started to go on, but he cut me off.

"You don't know what it was like."

"You're wrong about that. I do know a little of it."

"How could you?"

"I was there the night your father beat up Calvin."

"That would have been a lot of nights."

"Okay, the night he told Calvin to stop wasting time on his drawings."

"That would have been a lot of nights, too."

"The first month of seventh grade."

He looked at me and understood. His vacant stare was frightening me. Now he would have to kill me for certain.

"You have no idea what it was like in my house."

"You're right. I cannot begin to understand. But if I talk to the judge."

He thought about that for a long moment; shook his head.

"No, that won't be necessary. I'm finished here."

He stood and looked around the room. He switched the shotgun to his left hand and ran his fingertips along the stock's wood surface. Was he thinking about Beth? My offer? His handiwork on the refinished barn wood?

"So you didn't answer my question. How come guys like you get all the good stuff in life?"

"What good stuff?"

"A life. Some kind of happiness."

He put the shotgun down and reached behind the designer sofa that sat incongruously in the middle of the barn loft. He pulled out a book and tossed it to me. "Here, take this with you."

I looked at the title: *Jerry Todd and the Oak Island Treasure.* It was the missing book my mother had been searching for in the box in our barn.

"Surprised? That must be the only thing Calvin didn't tell

you. That summer Francis. . ."

He stopped.

"That summer Francis got hurt. Calvin and I sat outside the screen window and listened to your father read to Francis every night. All those books. *Tom Sawyer, Huckleberry Finn.* Those Jerry Todd books. We were there every night listening to those stories outside the screen window. No one ever loved us enough to read to us. Never once. Our parents were drunk every night. So we sat out every night getting eaten by mosquitoes until your father turned off the light when he stopped reading."

I thought about that. I was just outside the dining room doors, just feet from Francis and my father reading. Marvin and Calvin were a few feet away outside the screen window, on the other side of the bed. Four boys listening to my father read to us.

"When it got cold and your father, and later you, put up the storm windows for the cold season, we had to wait all winter until the storm windows came down and the screens went up to hear the stories again.

"We would wait until you guys put up the screens and then we would be there every night. Then one night a few years later, when your father was reading *Poppy Ott and the Freckled Goldfish,* stupid Calvin got into a laughing fit and he started snorting. I punched him to get him to shut up. Your father stopped reading and I couldn't figure out why, so I stood up and peaked in the window and I looked right into your father's face. It was just inches away. He'd caught us."

"I don't remember that."

"Because he didn't say anything. He looked and saw us both out there. He didn't say anything. He just sat down and started reading to Francis again."

I thought long and hard about that one. Why would my father continue reading and not chase them away? Sometimes the answer is in the question.

"We did it for years until. . ."

"He died?"

"Yeah. Then your mother took over the reading. The same forty or fifty books all over again. Ever since. Over and over"

Marvin picked up the shotgun and paced back and forth shaking his head, as if trying to make a decision.

He pulled a five gallon jerry can filled with kerosene can from where it had been hidden behind the sofa and started dousing the room.

"Marvin, what are you doing?"

"Get out of here, pussy. Take Jerry Todd with you."

I tried to reach for the shotgun, but he was too fast. My fingertips only brushed the stock.

"You never quit, do you? Get out. The only reason I'm letting you out of this is because we're neighbors for fifty years and Calvin has a crush on you and your parents read stories to us every night during the warm weather. I'm being neighborly."

He held me at gunpoint as he continued dousing the room with kerosene, the fuel can awkwardly bouncing up and down under his arm as he hunched the fuel onto the furniture and wood floors.

He turned to me and said "Get out of here."

When I didn't move he said something so sorrowful it took me a split second to realize the implications of what he meant.

"See you in Tutter."

Tutter, Illinois, being, of course, the imaginary hometown of Jerry Todd and Poppy Ott, the boys who were the central characters in over twenty-five boys' adventure books my father had devoured as a child and had later shared with Francis and me. Tutter was a highly idealized version of New City in the 1920s, a small-town, middle-American place where every boy had a loving home, good friends, apple pie, and a happy ending. I had often thought of my father wandering the streets of Tutter with Jerry and the rest of his old friends after he had died. It's where he would want to spend eternity.

Marvin continued sloshing the barn loft, spilling kerosene all over his pants and shoes in the process. He stopped to drink more of the whiskey.

I turned and ran down the steps and to the front sidewalk and onto my mother's porch. She stood when she heard my footsteps, was standing, wiping her palms on her apron when I ran into the living room with the missing book under my arm.

"What's wrong?"

"Help me get Francis out of here."

"What's wrong?"

"Hurry. Call the fire department and tell them the Hessian's barn is on fire. Hurry."

I ran to my brother's room and carried him to the front room. His weight surprised me. There was nothing there. He whimpered in fear, sensing something was wrong.

I ran through the living room calling over my shoulder. My mother finished dialing and was waiting for the firehouse to pick up.

"As soon as you hang up, get out of the house. Run over to Father Carrick's."

Carrying Francis in my arms, I ran across the street and behind the church to Father Carrick's rectory on Maple Avenue and pounded on the door. In the distance I could hear the wail of the firehouse siren winding up, cutting through the night as Father Carrick opened the door.

"Go get my mother. Marvin's set his barn on fire."

He edged past me and Francis and raced down the street to my mother's. I put Francis down on the sofa and kissed him on the forehead. He looked at me with questions in his eyes.

I dashed across the street to the apartment complex where the nuns stayed. Two sisters in bathrobes who had known my mother for fifty years ran to the rectory to be with Francis, while I raced back to our house. Father Carrick was leading my mother across the street and the smoke from Marvin's barn began to fill up the night sky. Through the upstairs barn window, I could see the flames building, gaining momentum, destroying evidence.

I didn't care if Marvin's barn burned to the ground, or his house, for that matter. But I didn't want the same to happen to ours. In a desperate, laughably feeble attempt, I un-spooled the garden hose from the side of my mother's house and turned on the water and began to wet down the side. The heat was almost intolerable, but I knew I had to stay there. I watched closely as the flames began to build on the barn's second floor. It was frightening to see the flames. I knew even the slightest breeze would have sent sparks over to our barn and house, but the sparks were going straight up into the cold, clear night air. The heat was making the wet sides of my mother's house cast off steam. I pulled the extension ladder out of our barn and placed it against the side of the house. Grabbing the hose, I climbed to the front porch roof and scanned the sky for sparks. Across the yard the paint on the Hessian house back wall was beginning to curl.

The New City Volunteer Fire Department arrived with two pumpers two minutes later. Chief Howell yelled above the noise of the sirens.

"Anyone inside?"

"Marvin Hessian."

"He's the one who called it in. From the smell of things, we're too late."

"There's a loaded shotgun up there."

"Thanks."

"How did you get here so soon?"

"We were all at the firehouse for the carnival committee. You're lucky."

Three minutes later Hillcrest Fire Department arrived, and three minutes after that Congers arrived, having raced over the Third Street hill. A total of four pumpers were there, with two hosing down Marvin's barn, which was now burning freely on the upwind, north side, with the fire hoses aimed to control the downwind, south side. Two pumpers wet down the roofs of our barn and the two matching houses so none of the sparks could set off fires there. As the sodden roof of Marvin's barn collapsed, and the second story fell into the first floor, I caught a brief glimpse of the old Kelvinator ice box that had been turned into a smoker, before it all disappeared into a black, smoke-filled void.

The volume of water, arriving as quickly as it did, contained most of the actual fire to just the second story and the roof. The first floor barn walls and floors, and the remaining damaged infrastructure soon collapsed from the weight of the water.

CHAPTER EIGHTY-NINE

NEW CITY

Friday
October 27, 2000

The next morning the pumpers were still there, making sure the remaining barn and houses were safe. Main Street had been closed off all night. The paint had been melted off of some of the north side of our barn and the west side of the Hessian house.

Except for some minor smoke damage, and the smell of burning flesh that would linger another two days, my mother's house was mostly undamaged. According to Howell, if the pumpers had arrived another three minutes later, both barns and both houses probably would have been lost. What that means is that Marvin waited for the sounds of the fire alarm before he started the fire, had called it in just after my mother's call. Why the delay? Making up his mind what to do? Wanting to destroy evidence, but not wanting to endanger his parents' house? Just being neighborly again? Give the firefighters a chance to save everything but the barn? Maybe he did have a conscience. Whatever he decided, there was no way Marvin could have survived either the smoke inhalation, heat, or flames. He had heard his last siren wail. His charred body was found later that morning by the fire marshal. He was holding the shotgun to his head but had died before he could pull the trigger. It wouldn't have made a difference. The shotgun was not loaded. Marvin's DNA would be taken from his remains by Jimmy's team.

Any other evidence that may have been found in Marvin's possession was gone; gone in what only could have been a life-long arsonist's ultimate rush. Later, at the Coroner's Inquest, Jimmy confirmed it appeared Marvin had drenched his own body in accelerant, as I had witnessed.

My mother would spend the next few days with the sisters in their apartments, and Francis and I in the guest bedroom at the rectory.

The white icebox/smoker, smudged in black, taker of a young boy's dreams and aspirations, still stood out in the morning light.

The morning after the fire I called Klein's Manhattan office and they told me he was not in that day. I drove over to his house on Lake DeForest and knocked on his front door.

"You're not supposed to be here."

"I know you had Marvin kill Beth."

"I'm sorry, I don't know what you're talking about. I loved my wife. My wife. Not your old girlfriend. *My wife*."

"I know you'll never spend a day in jail for killing her, but I want you to know that I know you killed her. Marvin told me before he set himself on fire."

"You're delusional. And that man was a very sick individual."

"The feelings were mutual."

"I don't associate with known felons."

"How do you even know who Marvin Hessian is?"

"Beth told me all about him. He's a local legend."

I tried to imagine that conversation, but couldn't.

"You'll never get Tom's property."

"I don't know what you're talking about. Why would I want his property? My daughter and I are returning to Hong Kong. I'm not sure when we'll be back. We want to start a new life, away from all this ugliness. Away from you. I think you killed Beth and you made up this whole story about Marvin. I think you murdered him and set fire to the barn to cover up the fact that there was no evidence there, because he didn't murder her, you did. I've told the investigators that already this morning. They seemed very interested in pursuing that lead."

As he slammed the door in my face, he finished, "Losers like you are so pathetic."

Later that afternoon, I told Jimmy, Henion, Ray and Dave everything that I had heard from Calvin in Sing Sing and from Marvin before he torched himself. They went into a huddle to decide what to do. When they tried to call Rainer to come in, his attorney told them he would have to get back to them.

Father Carrick took his thirty year-old Cadillac with 12,000 miles on it from the rectory garage and drove to Sing Sing to talk to Calvin and offer last rites.

When he got back to town, we sat up in the rectory library. "I don't think he's going to make it."

"I put in a call to the State Prison System. They were going to intervene."

"He was in the infirmary when I got there, but he needs to be hospitalized."

"I'll have Henion call. They don't seem to care if prisoners die of AIDS. They figure they get what they deserve."

"Where is their humanity?"

"They don't have any."

"What's going to happen to Rainer?"

"I don't know. Without testimony, he could walk. It's all hearsay on my part. Henion tried to get in touch with him earlier today through his attorney. Later, his attorney called back and told Henion that Rainer already flew back to Hong Kong. Apparently his attorney convinced a judge he wasn't a flight risk.

I hadn't bothered to tell Henion and the others about my little encounter with Rainer earlier that morning.

"He'll get lost in China and they'll never extradite him, even if there was any evidence."

"What about phone records, anything?"

"They can try. From what Marvin indicated, they only spoke in person. So there's nothing."

"What about Calvin's testimony?"

"They are going to try to depose him."

"They'd better hurry. I don't think he has long. So what now?"

"Just wait and see, I guess. See what Marvin's DNA shows."

"What else?"

It was as if Father Carrick could read my mind. I felt as if my life were falling apart. The love of my life had been murdered and I was still a leading suspect, even after personally having heard the confession of the man who actually did it, a man who was now dead.

"Father Carrick, I want you to set up a meeting with Tom."

"I think that's long overdue."

"So do I. I want him to know I had nothing to do with it, even though Marvin is dead and Rainer will probably walk."

"Okay."

"I have to know what he knows and what he thinks. I want to warn him about Rainer's threat to burn him out."

"Would Rainer still do that now?"

"He told me he isn't interested any more. You never can tell. A guy like that would do it for spite."

"It's too late, anyway."

"What do you mean?"

"I'll let Tom give you the details."

"So you will you ask Tom to talk to me?"

"I will. Do you want me to be there?"

"Wouldn't hurt."

"I can stop the fist-fight.

"There won't be any fist-fights."

"That might not be your decision, Will. You've made a few people really angry. And there are some things you should know, first."

"Okay."

"You should know that Tom is not the person you think he is. Any preconceived notions you have of your friend as he is today, versus the kid you knew, are probably inaccurate and obsolete."

"Like my notions of who Beth became in recent years?" My question threw him off guard.

He hung his head. "Precisely."

"I'm listening."

"You only remember Tom as your friend. For what, twelve years? Age ten to twenty-two? You were children. Sometimes friends are blind to truth. You know the old expression, can't see the forest for the trees? Well, you're in the woods, my friend, and you can't see anything except an outdated misconception that you've carried around with you all this time.

"The first thing you should know is that Tom was the only surviving, legitimate heir to a wealth beyond counting. When his grandparents died they left him a fortune they had earned as radio celebrities for a generation. With their Wall Street connections they turned a tiny fortune into a huge fortune. Surely you must have known that growing up."

"I assumed. How could you not? A house on a hill? Property, servants, including my grandfather. But he never talked about it."

"The tip of the iceberg, my boy. And then when they died, Tom allowed their financial advisers to continue their work, which can only be described as miraculous.

"He never performed publicly after he returned to the States from Vietnam."

I hadn't known that. I never really kept track or thought about it all these years. I had just assumed he had continued the European tours and that I just hadn't heard about them.

Then, out of the blue, I asked what I really wanted to know. "What happened to Tom in Vietnam?"

Father Carrick broke eye contact. He wasn't being melodramatic. I had caught him off guard.

"Perhaps his experience there can only be described as a metaphor or a microcosm, for what happened to all you boys. Exposure to Agent Orange? Forced to do ungodly deeds in the name of who knows what? Who knows why? Injuries? Post-Traumatic Stress Disorder? Mental illness in all forms? Exposure to Hepatitis C in the hospitals? Years of homelessness and despair for thousands? All of those chickens had to come home to roost, Will.

"Are you familiar with Paul's Epistle to the Galations?"

"I don't know, a little, maybe."

"Galations, chapter six, verses seven and eight. I'm paraphrasing here. 'You reap what you sow.' We sent thousands of boys like Tom over there and they murdered almost two million civilians. I'm not talking Viet Cong or North Vietnamese or Khmer Rouge. Innocent civilians. When our boys came back, our society began to reap what was planted in the form of ruined lives. Lives filled with depression and extreme rationalization and defensiveness for what they had done."

"You're not telling me anything new. I was there, too, remember?"

"You're one of the lucky ones."

That was arguable. "What happened to him over there?

"Maybe I've said too much already. I should let Tom tell his own story."

"So you'll set up the meeting?"

"So you can tell him about Rainer?"

"No. I want to ask for his forgiveness."

"I think that's a good idea."

"Do you think he will forgive me?"

"Yes, Will, I do."

CHAPTER NINETY

THE BOATHOUSE

October 27, 2000

I had spent the night at the rectory with Francis. I told my mother over coffee and waffles with the nuns what the day held in store. For some reason, I had the feeling she already knew about the meeting.

"It's long overdue, Will. You need every friend you can get in this life."

We left Father Carrick's office after the noon mass and a light lunch and made our way north on Main to the Dutch Garden, then walked along the same Kill-side path that Beth had taken to the boathouse that final night.

Father Carrick and I didn't speak for the entire trip and I felt like I was a convicted murderer walking his last mile with his priest before the execution.

What Marvin had hinted about Father Carrick before he set himself on fire kept gnawing at me. What could he have possibly meant? I didn't even want to think about it at this point.

If the autumn mud got on Father Carrick's shoes on our hike he didn't seem to notice. The early afternoon was quiet with another brilliant blue, late October sky.

When we arrived at the boathouse, Tom was waiting for us on the bottom step as he had the other day when I had arrived unannounced. Father Carrick grabbed both us by the elbows and brought us together.

"Tom, I believe you know Will."

Tom looked at me without malice, unlike the way he had the other day, and extended his hand.

"Will."

"Tom."

Tom looked different this day than he did the other day. Tired? Worn out? Sick?

"I believe Will has something to say to you, Tom."

Tom led us onto the broad front porch deck that faced the wooded area that had once been the second mill pond, Simmons' Pond, in the tiered cascade of millponds leading to the Dutch Garden. We had spent countless hours there together with Beth; as children, teens, college students. Now, the sound of the Kill filled our ears.

"I have tea."

Father Carrick followed him to the door. "Let us help you serve."

Inside, the boathouse looked the same as it did when I had seen it last, thirty-two years ago, except for all modern recording equipment, microphones, cables, and a wall filled with thin white boxes and envelopes of varying sizes that I assumed were quarter-inch tapes and newer, digital media. But I wasn't prepared for what was thumb-tacked on the wall; something I had never seen there before.

There were about two dozen 8" x 10" black and white photos tacked to a bulletin board on the wall. One from our fifth grade trip to Ebbets Field. One taken during our tenth grade trip to The Peppermint Lounge, standing outside, just after we had climbed out of the limo on 45th Street. Another twenty or more taken the day we moved the piano from Dove Cottage to the boathouse that high school senior year Christmas Vacation of 1963. On an index card, someone, probably Beth, had typed a title card for the photo exhibit.

THE MYSTERIOUS MYSTERY
OF THE MYSTERIOUS
PIANO IN THE WOODS:
a mystery
(that's very mysterious)

Definitely Beth's sense of humor.

The photographs hypnotized me. My face from almost forty years earlier looked back at me, startling me with my own youth. Not many pictures have been taken of me in my life. My parents were not photographers, either due to lack of interest or lack of money. But there we were, the three of us, Beth, Tom, and I; the friends who vowed to remain inseparable. In another shot, we were posing, as the mover's son had taken a snapshot of us all leaning against the Steinway on the deck of the boathouse. It was taken during a break when the rest of the movers tried to figure out a way to muscle and maneuver it in through the doorway. I looked at the faces of the three young people in the photograph. What happened to them I wondered to myself?

"Life," Tom said from behind me.

"What?"

"You were looking at the photos and wondering what happened to those three kids in the picture, right? *Life* is what happened to them."

As usual, he was right.

Except for the piano photos showing Beth, Tom, and me in the frame together, the photos were all taken by Beth. I remember her asking one of our classmates, Arty, the boy whose father owned the moving company, to take a picture of all three of us.

Each time she set it up so all he would have to do is press the button. I looked at the three or four pictures Arty had taken of the three of us clowning around, while in the background, the movers pushed the dolly through the deep December leaves covered in early snowfall, struggling with the craziness of it all. Two of Arty's pictures depict Tom trying to play *Blue Rondo `ala Turk* on the moving piano, as if a movie soundtrack, as they maneuvered down the hill and up the steps to the boathouse deck. The movers looked perplexed and frustrated and Beth and I doubled over, laughing hysterically in the background. Arty's father can be seen waiting for him to put the camera down so he could get back to work. Arty's photos looked like tourist snapshots: tilted horizons, clipped head-room, slightly out-of-focus, blurred movement. I looked for Marvin, hiding in the trees, but I couldn't see him.

Even the group-shot Arty took of the three of us kneeling behind the O.B.W. headstone in the woods nearby shows his index finger covering part of the lens. The three of us were looking intentionally somber. It was supposed to be funny. Beth's idea. With his finger covering the lower left corner of the frame it's unintentionally even funnier.

Was Beth reminded of her mother at that moment, like she had been on our other trips to O.B.W., as she had once told me while listening to Tom practice?

Even if the photos had been taken in color, they still would have been black and white; the black piano, the white keys, the white snow, the black and white birches, Beth's black pea-coat, her black hair.

The other photos that were taken by Beth that day are works of art; perfectly composed, a careful choice of focal length, showing the dignity in each worker's face as he tried to move the monster piano to some place he was sure it didn't belong. Each face tells a multifaceted story: Dorothea Lange. Marion Post Wolcott. Each one could hang in a gallery alongside Walker Evans in order to *Let Us Now Praise Famous . . . Teenagers*. There is a series of shots of

Tom as he "conducts the orchestra" of the piano's journey, each mover, taking on an important role in the overall performance. In one, I can be seen in the corner of the frame, looking on in wonder, admiringly at Tom: Diane Arbus.

Tom now stood beside me with a china teapot. "Do you remember that day?"

Then, like the day a week earlier, it was all I could do to maintain my composure.

What I didn't tell him, had never told anyone, was that, of course, I remembered that day. I remembered *every day* because of my "special talent," my curse. He would understand completely. He could play literally hundreds of classical compositions from memory, allowing him to take flight at any moment he chose. I was imprisoned in my own memory, unable to escape, no matter how hard I tried.

What I wanted to say was, "You mean, do I remember one of the happiest days of my life?" Instead I just laughed, toughed it out, and said, "Those movers were not happy."

"I spoke to Arty the other day. He's going to come and help me move it back up to the house. You want to help?"

A Steinway round-trip ticket, *pianissimo*, thirty-seven years later.

"Sure, let me know."

"He inherited the moving company from his father. Now Arty's son helps him like Arty helped his own dad that day."

"Maybe we could take some more pictures."

Tom reached behind himself to a nook and pulled out Beth's old Nikon. "Here you go."

"How come you have this?"

"Over the years she kept graduating. From an F-1 to an F-2, to an F-3. She finally went digital. She gave me this old one a few years back. To go with all her negatives from those years."

"Are there a lot of negatives?"

"Thousands. See that cupboard? In there. They're all there,

black and white negatives and contact sheets, sorted by year and subject. Trays of Kodachrome and Ektachrome slides. There are hundreds from our walks on the Kill."

I would have to let that sink in later. Would he allow me to look at all of them? "Why are you moving the piano back to the house?"

My question caught Tom off-guard. Instead of answering, Tom thought about that as he walked to the deck with the teapot.

Father Carrick and I sat down on a glider on the deck and Tom served tea from the set on the deck table before sitting in one of the wicker side-chairs himself.

There was silence while I gathered my thoughts. An autumn breeze collected leaves from the nearby treetops and helped them on their journey to humus-ville. Finally I cleared my throat.

"Well, the first thing I suppose you should know is that Marvin murdered Beth. Calvin spoke to me when I went to see him the other day at Sing Sing and told me Marvin had practically bragged to him about it. And then I went to see Marvin. I actually broke into his barn to see if I could get some DNA and he caught me. He held me at gunpoint and confessed everything. The stalking, the murder, listening to your conversations with Beth through your open windows here, Tom. He said he was confessing to me because he was going to kill me and make it look like I had done everything. Then, for some reason, he changed his mind, dismissed me, and set fire to the barn."

I looked over to Father Carrick. "I'm sure you told him all about the barn fire."

"That's some story. I suspected as much. We heard things outside these windows from time to time. I told Beth it was raccoons. I recently installed an alarm system. If you were to come up here after dark in the past months, a dozen spotlights would go on. Like daylight."

"Anyway, a lot of what you discussed with Beth was reported back to Rainer. Including Beth's confession to you that Rainer wanted her to talk you into selling the land, and her plan to help you preserve it."

"Too late. I took care of all that. I signed the entire property over to The Diocese. When the time comes, Dove Cottage will house sisters from the Diocese and the remaining rooms will be used to help unwed mothers through their term, until they decide what they want to do. As for support, there's enough money in the coffers to run it for the next twenty years.

"As for the girls, there's enough money to give all those poor young moms college scholarships. I want to take care of all of it."

I looked around. "What about the boathouse?"

"The boathouse will remain mine and then it will go to the county along with what I already signed over. All the property from Little Tor Road over to The Dutch Garden, including all the property with Greenberg's Pond. It will become a county park, and the paperwork, it's complicated. The deed requires that it remain in the county's hands, in perpetuity. So you see, it's really untouchable by Rainer or whoever else wants to get his hands on it.

"Why have you done this?"

"I have to get my house in order, as they say."

"What are you telling me?"

Instead of answering me, he changed the subject.

"Let me hear more about what Marvin said."

"The bad news is that Marvin said he raped her and then killed her. Of course no one else was there to hear his confession but me, and he was planning to kill me from the start, so he had no compunction about telling me everything."

Tom deliberated, taking it all in. Was he skeptical or just having trouble absorbing it all. "So why didn't he kill you?"

"I convinced him, or so I thought, that we didn't want him, we wanted Rainer, and if he turned state's evidence to prosecute Rainer, we might be able to cut him a plea deal. We'd see to it that he got out of jail in a few years, while Rainer paid the price."

"Did you have the authority to tell him that?"

"Probably not. But he was going to kill me anyway, so I had to try something. A bluff's as good as the truth when you're being held at gunpoint. As long as it worked long enough to get me out of there alive."

"And then when you left he set fire to the barn destroying any evidence and killing himself in the bargain?"

"It appears so. When he allowed me to leave he was splashing kerosene all over the place."

There was a long silence. Then, Tom and Father Carrick exchanged glances, signaling what I expected would be a turn in the direction of the conversation.

"How do we know you didn't just kill him, set the barn on fire yourself, and make up this entire story?

My reading of Tom's earlier look had been accurate. "That's what Rainer was trying to tell Henion. Why would I do that?"

"So no one would think you murdered Beth."

I looked to Father Carrick and then back to Tom. "Do you think I murdered her?"

"I don't know, Will. All I know is that you frightened her in the past few years with your behavior. She seemed to think you were stalking her."

"I wasn't stalking her."

"The trips to the art gallery? The phone calls? The noises outside the window here?"

"Those noises? That wasn't me. I told you that was Marvin."

"How do we know? Following her into Tor's?"

"I didn't follow her into Tor's. I bumped into her there by coincidence as I was leaving after having eaten lunch there. Check the time-stamp on the receipts."

Tom was trying to decide if he believed me.

"I just wanted to have a conversation with her."

"To what end?"

"I wanted to apologize to her."

"For what?"

"For not believing her about that day."

"And do you believe what she told you back then?"

"Yes. I do now."

"I'm not convinced. I think that you still think there was something going on between the two of us. You believed it that day and for years after. What made you change your mind?"

"I don't know. I was just crazy for years."

"And now? Are you crazy now?"

"No, no. Not crazy now. Or maybe crazy now, but in a different way. I know that it probably wasn't true. What I thought about all those years."

"Probably?"

"Not true."

"Do you know why it isn't true?"

"Yes."

"Why?"

"Father Carrick told me you were celibate."

Tom looked to Father Carrick. Another betrayal?

"It's like a fire that's starting to go out. If there is something or someone there to re-kindle the tiny spark that remains, it may re-ignite. Otherwise it goes out forever. That's where I am. There's only a certain amount of emotion doled out to each person in a lifetime, and I used up all mine a long time ago.

"So your reason for believing us now is not really valid. How about because both your best friend, and the woman you supposedly loved, told you it wasn't true? That's not enough to convince you?"

"That, too."

"I'm not convinced you believe us."

"I do. I guess it's difficult for me to believe because I let it ruin my life for over thirty years."

"And hers."

"And hers."

"And you let it ruin our friendship."

I was ashamed. "Yes."

"And so for thirty-something years you believed your own lie and never let it go.

"Yes.

"And Delores?

"What about her?

"You kind of led her down the garden path, too. Didn't you?

"Yes.

"You lied to her?

"Lied?

"By not being honest.

"Yes.

"All because you refused to believe two people who loved you and told you the truth."

"I guess."

He stood at the rail, gazing out. "Beth was such a kind soul, Will. I really wish you could have known her when she was older. She became such a beautiful, magnificent human being as an adult. So giving. So selfless. It's a shame she spent so much time living in fear."

"Fear? Of what, Rainer?"

"Rainer and you. She was convinced both of you were dangerously unpredictable."

"She was fearful of me?"

Tom didn't answer. I looked to Father Carrick. He looked to Tom at the rail.

"Do you know the real irony of it all? You know how much of her own money and her husband's money she has given away to children? Countless millions of dollars. She made him do it. She forced him into giving it away. She basically was extorting it from him. 'Spend it or I'll leave.' That's another reason why he wanted to put a stop to her; all her philanthropy. So that's why I'm taking up the slack where she left off. I'm giving it all away. All of it."

He turned from the rail and sat down. His eyes were red.

"That day you thought you caught us 'doing something.' She showed up to welcome me home. She wanted to give me a welcome suitable for someone she thought was a hero, because she knew you loved me and couldn't be here to greet me yourself. We both thought you were in Florida, right?

"She wanted to be your representative that day, Will, your proxy. She was so happy and full of life. All she could ever do was talk about you and how great you were doing in law school. She couldn't wait for you to get home. When you walked up the path she had just finished talking about how happy you were together after what had happened the year before. She said you were rebuilding your relationship, and how she couldn't wait for you to come home over Thanksgiving. She was throwing her arms around me to kiss me, she was so deliriously happy.

"One second later, there you were at the bottom of the rise and it was as if she had seen a ghost. It was such a shock that the look on her face must have made you think we were doing something we weren't supposed to be doing. We were both speechless to see you.

"You know, I fully understand why you thought what you did. I get it. But it wasn't a look of guilt like you thought. It was the shock of seeing you. We thought you were in Florida. You just jumped to conclusions. If you had just shut up and listened, you would have known that I wouldn't have done anything, even if she had wanted to.

"But you were so pig-headed and said all those ugly things to her, she told me it reinforced a side of you she'd never seen until the year before."

"About the baby?"

"Yes. She was sick about it and she then decided she could never forgive you. By the time you flew back to Florida and took two weeks to cool off, Beth made her decision to move on to a new chapter in her life. I wanted to call you, intercede with her on your behalf, try to get you two back together, but she asked me not to, and so I honored her request, as did Father Carrick, here."

So Tom loved Beth as a friend only, and would never betray me, just as Beth had tried to convince me herself. Why couldn't I accept that Beth would never betray me? What I had caught them at was nothing more than a non-sexual display of affection between old friends, nothing more, seen from an unfortunate perspective, a perspective that included a lack of understanding and an acceptance that would determine the course of my life.

"Over the years, she tried to get over you and she got on with her life. You, apparently never did, from what she told me. She and I remained close. We became soul-mates, if I can use that clichéd term.

"Then she met Rainer. Or should I say he re-met her. 'Small World.' Do you remember him? When you first met him?"

"According to what Marvin told me, that meeting at the gallery was no freak coincidence. He remembered her from your tent party and tracked her down when she was old enough. Again, as Marvin told it, he had revealed to Klein we had broken up, so apparently Klein decided to make a move on her."

Tom stared at me and then looked toward the stream, trying to absorb the implications of all of that.

"That may be. If it's true, it explains a lot. He promised her the world. That's what she wanted and he delivered. She dictated the terms, and that's how she got all the money from him. They've spent years traveling all over the world doing what she wanted, helping kids. Reading programs, fresh drinking water for villages in Central America and Africa. All the things Father Carrick referenced during her service a few days ago.

"'Beth's Boat' Klein called her efforts, after the old joke about 'a boat being a hole in the ocean where you pour your money.' She started hemorrhaging his money and he told her she had to stop. She ignored him. He let it continue. He was torn, afraid of losing her and wanting to stop the money hemorrhage.

"But he told her if she ever initiated contact with you that it was over. She agreed. She was over you by then, had moved on, so it wasn't a tough choice.

"Then, last year, he tried to get her to use her influence on me to get me to sell him my land. It's true, she warned me about what he was up to and told me. She said if he had ever found out, he would have kicked her out. So I guess Marvin was telling the truth. He must have told Rainer about her betrayal. I had to pretend to entertain the idea, make him believe she had almost convinced me while working even faster to make sure he never got his hands on the land.

"He believed it at first, or at least acted as if he believed it. When he found out what I had done, he was furious."

I looked at Father Carrick. "Marvin said Klein considered torching Dove Cottage. I guess that won't be happening now."

"Klein's a businessman. He doesn't like to lose, and he and Beth got into heated arguments about it. He became abusive, physically. He beat her. Eventually he just went on to other business conquests."

The thought of anyone physically hurting Beth sickened me.

"The autopsy did show signs of a bruised collar bone, of old beatings."

"He punched her. Then he flew to Hong Kong suddenly."

"Certainly not because he was remorseful. According to what Marvin told me, Klein being out of the country was a window of opportunity for Marvin to kill her. Being out of the country was Rainer's alibi. She found out he had a private detective follow her around town."

"We know all that. She couldn't park in front of the Dove Cottage and walk behind it to get here. She couldn't park along Little Tor and walk here. Too obvious. She parked at the courthouse, walked in the front door and out the back to the stream. By the time he got in the Courthouse, she was nowhere in sight and he

couldn't follow her. He didn't know about the path here behind
The Dutch Gardens until Marvin told him.

"I did see her a few times in the Courthouse. I was hoping she
had come to see me. But when I tried to follow her I lost her. She
seemed to have disappeared."

"Those few times you saw her in the courthouse, she was just
passing through on her way to see me."

"I know. Marvin even laughed that he should have hired a
local guy. It was Marvin who told him everything. Klein flew out
of town for an alibi.

"Why didn't I see that coming? If only I had walked her back
to her car. She didn't want me to that night, despite the fact that
she always thought she was being stalked. She could sense it, but
she thought for years it was you. Maybe it was you stalking her?"

"No, never."

"That final night's visit, Beth confirmed she was planning
to leave Rainer. She was going to leave while he was gone. She
thought about going to live on South Mountain Road with her
father, or hide out at Jerry's, in Gainesville. She'd decided to fly
to New Zealand, meet up with me in a month in Saigon. She and
Alison had packed and were ready to get out."

"Did she tell you that we had met that final night?"

"No. That could explain why she was so upset when she
arrived. I just thought it was nerves from knowing she was going to
escape the next day with Alison. Maybe she was too embarrassed
to tell me. Maybe she thought I would interpret it as a betrayal of
some kind. She had always promised me that she would never
talk to you again if she could help it. I guess she didn't want me to
know, that it would be a sign of weakness on her part."

"So you didn't mention her visit with me that night to Ray and
Dave?"

"They never asked and I never knew that she had met with
you. But if I had known that she had met you earlier before coming here, had she revealed that to me, I would have insisted on

walking her back to the car. Maybe she'd be alive now. On her way to New Zealand. To Saigon to work on my project."

Tom was finished for now. He looked more drawn than earlier before when we had arrived. "I'm tired now. I need to rest. Just leave the tea service. I'll get it later after I sleep."

He started to go inside and I had to speak to his back. "Tom."

He turned to look me in the eye.

"I would like you to forgive me, Tom. That's why I came over today. To beg you for forgiveness."

"I forgave you a long time ago, Will. You hurt Beth and me deeply. It was Beth you had to worry about in the 'forgiving department,' and now it's too late for that. You're not the only one who loved her, Will, or who was 'in love' with her. I lost her, too. She was the only *true friend* I ever had."

He looked for more answers in the distant treetops, while I looked down at the deck, ashamed.

After a while, he spoke again, without turning. "Did Father Carrick tell you any more about why I have chosen to be celibate?"

"No. He just said you were paying some kind of penance."

Tom looked down at the deck, as if trying to find a missing piece of his past. "I suppose that's one way of putting it. Did he tell you what for?"

"Said he couldn't tell me."

"That's correct. '*Latae sententiae.*' Automatic excommunication from the church for breaking a confidentiality told during confession."

"He did say there had been lots of confession. Lots of confession, why?"

And so Tom told me his Vietnam story.

Thirty minutes later, when he finished, I couldn't speak. As much as it sounds like a cliché, I wanted to throw up over the railing. But that would not have been enough to purge what we had carried all these years. It was all so sickening. No, sickening is not quite the right word. Not strong enough. But I wasn't sick in my stomach. I was sick in my heart. Sick because it was revealing of so many deceptions. Sick because it was so disappointing. So horrifying. Sick because it validated my worst fears. I couldn't begin to label it. So I just sat there and looked at Tom, deciding whether or not to say them, say *the words*. Finally, I relented. Why? To let him know I understood how horrible he was feeling? To let him know I knew? A more selfish reason? I don't know, but I said them.

"*My Luoc?*"

Tom turned in disbelief and stared at me first, then blinked as a realization came over him. He looked down in defeat, then back at me. He stared at me for so long, Father Carrick looked at us, bewildered. Turning to me, Father Carrick mouthed silently, "What?"

I just nodded my head, indicating, "Not now. Maybe later."

Finally Tom began. "I never revealed those words to Father Carrick or Beth."

"I wouldn't know about that. Wouldn't know what you said to either of them."

"But yet *you know* somehow. '*My Luoc.*' "

"Yes."

He turned to me. "How is that possible?"

He stared at me from someplace far off he didn't want to be, shaking his head, while waiting for my answer that never came.

Finally, he spoke again when I didn't answer. "It's funny, when people ask me how long I was in Vietnam, I have to think about it. I had just turned twenty-one when I went there. I left that New City boy behind. In a lot of ways I never left Vietnam. That boy never came back to New City. I said that to someone once and they scolded me, 'Tom, don't be so melodramatic,' they said.

"'Melodramatic?' I told him, 'You think what we went through in Vietnam was a melodrama? You think it was some Senior Class

Skit over there?' ' "

He stopped to gather his thoughts. I stole a glance to Father Carrick. His eyes were closed, as if somehow he had to share the burden of guilt; was waiting to be stricken.

"What this country has been doing is madness. The Vietnam years? What they did in Iraq in '93? It is insanity."

Although I agreed with him I had to add, "The polls showed ninety percent of the people were in favor of what we did then."

"Thank God there are still ten percent of us who haven't lost our minds. There's still some small hope for this country. How many more 'Vietnams' do we have to endure, Will? How many more can this country endure and still survive?"

Again, even though I agreed with him, something made me play devil's advocate. "Are you saying, 'Desert Storm' in Iraq was another Vietnam? They kept telling us 'This is not another Vietnam.' ' "

" 'Repeated assertion.' "

'Repeated assertion.' It was a term I had learned in my Freshman year at UF in Logical Thinking class. An old propaganda trick. If a politician tells the people something over and over again, they begin to believe it, regardless of whether or not it's true. It's an 'assertion' that's 'repeated.'

" 'Repeated assertion,' like, 'This is not another Vietnam.' "

"So you're saying Desert Storm was another Vietnam?"

"It was a meaningless war, fought for no valid reason at all, other than as a political ploy to satisfy the ambition of another mindless, corrupt politician, and to make lots of money for his cronies.

"Bush had no more *principles* or rationale beyond winning the next election and raking in millions for his pals. He couldn't see beyond that. Nothing else mattered to him. He sentenced thousands of people to death, innocent civilians, while the rest of the world stood by powerless to do anything about it. *Powerless*! There are thousands of people who died because somebody

watched too many Rambo movies. Somebody was afraid of being
called a 'wimp.' What was the rush? Will you tell me that?

"We were not protecting our country. We were not defending democracy. We were not 'stemming the tide of communist
aggression.' They couldn't even use that tired old justification any
more. That's obsolete. So now they have to create a new enemy to
justify more military spending, justify their existence.

"That wasn't a war, Will, it was a 'Trade Show' for Defense
Contractors. Who's to say they won't come up with another prov-
ocation in a few years and a few years after that? It's endless cash-
flow for them.

"How old do you think those kids were over there in Iraq?"

"Those kids wanted to be there. They weren't drafted, like us.
Volunteer Army, remember?"

"I don't believe that. I believe the only ones who wanted to be
over there were the ones who don't have any sense anyway. No
sense or no options. They were nineteen year-old illiterates, for
Christ's sake. Sorry, Father."

Father Carrick gave him a dismissive wave.

"What did they know about reasoning things through? Marine
boot camp was probably the best thing that ever happened to a lot
of them. The most fun they ever had in their whole lives. They
said they wanted to be over there because that's what they'd been
told to say. That lack of critical thinking is dangerous to them and
dangerous to this country.

"Did you see the television interviews with those kids?
They've been brain-washed. They don't have the intellectual
capacity to reason things out. They're all muscles and no brains.
Their necks are thicker than their heads, for Christ's sake. They
didn't even realize they were nothing but mercenaries for special
interest groups.

"Those poor kids were convinced by a bunch of high-paid
congressional lobbyists, *thugs*, that they were doing something
patriotic.

"The Kuwaitis had a New York Public Relations firm writing the scripts. We sent a bunch of know-nothing kids over there to die for no reason. We're no better than the guy we went to fight. Our own President used political extortion to get that war off the ground. We had absolutely no choice in the matter. No choice! He over-committed us while no one was watching. Painted us into a corner. We had no choice! Why? What was the rush? What wasn't he telling us? What was the real reason?"

Tom stood to pour himself another cup of tea.

"Will, have you ever been to the Vietnam War Memorial in Washington?"

"Yes. I have."

"Did you touch the face of it?"

"Yes. Did you?"

Instead of answering, he changed the subject. Or so I thought at first.

"You know, in front of the Courthouse, the World War II memorial? On the south side? The big granite boulder with the bronze plaque on it? All those names of the ones who served in World War II from our little home town?"

Of course I knew it. The first time I ever remember thinking about it was when my father showed it to Francis and me after the Memorial Day Parade when I was in first grade. That day in a speech on the Courthouse lawn they talked about Midway Islands, Omaha Beach.

"My father's name is right up there on the plaque with all the rest, Tom. He took my hand and Francis' hand and touched our fingertips to his name. My hand was so small in his. He just held my hand there for a minute, touching his name, and Francis and I were so proud of him.

"Some of the names had stars next to them, and I asked him what they meant.

"He put his arm around me and didn't say anything for a minute. He was off, thinking. Finally, he said, 'Those stars are for the ones who never came home.'

"I looked up and asked him, 'Did you know any of them?' He didn't answer me. He just kept staring at that plaque.

"Every Memorial Day, after the parade, I used to go back and stare at that big granite boulder. I would stand there and stare at that plaque and extend my fingertips, and wonder what it would be like to 'never come home.'

"Our father's name is the seventeenth one down from the top in the first of three columns. There are four names with stars before his, and twenty-one names with stars after his. I could tell by the way he looked at them that first day when I asked him, that *he knew them all.* Maybe not personally...maybe he never even met them....but he *knew* them all."

Tom listened to my story intently, as if it reinforced what he was about to say.

"I have never been to the Vietnam Memorial. Are you surprised, Will? Don't be. I will *never* go to that place. Never.

"That first Memorial Day I was home? It was in May, 1969. I had been home about a year. *Life* magazine published the pictures of all the American soldiers who were killed in Vietnam in the *one week* period leading up to that Memorial Day."

I remembered it well. Someone had handed me the issue when I got off duty at the end of that day when I was in Pleiku. He wondered if I had known any of the guys in the pictures.

Tom continued. "Beth called me and told me about it. I stopped at VonThaden's and brought the magazine home at nine o'clock in the morning, and at six o'clock that night, I was still here at this table staring at those pictures.

"There were over three hundred pictures of guys, nineteen and twenty-years old. They were all American kids, just like me and you, Will, eighteen, nineteen, twenty years old, and they were all dead in just one week. Their lives simply did not matter. It had nothing to do with being patriotic or doing their duty fighting for our country, or to protect our way of life. It was to win votes and to make money. These were guys we went to high school with and went on double-dates with and played hockey with. A lot of them probably never even got laid before they went over, and their lives were taken from them because some fucking politician got a great idea. Some politician convinced them it was their patriotic duty. They were *expendable*."

Tom looked off to the sound of the Kill.

"And you know what, Will? They left one picture out of that *Life* magazine issue. One they didn't even know about."

He didn't have to tell me. I already knew what he was going to say. I had said it to myself a million times already. Every day since.

"They left out my picture, Will. It's been thirty-two years, and I still have a little star next to my name that's never going to go away.

"So don't try to tell me what's 'Another Vietnam' and what isn't. I'm like a buzzard. I can smell shit from miles away, and I smell it every time those politicians open their mouths.

"They should be made to pay for every life they've taken needlessly."

"Now you're talking crazy."

"I *am* crazy. Father Carrick here will tell you that I am the first to admit it. They made me crazy."

After, when the three of us had sat in silence, and the autumn afternoon wore on, and the enormity of Tom's story and the impact it had had on his life began to sink in, he rose to pour us more tea. He put the teapot down and turned to take a leak off the edge of the deck. I joined him at the railing, silently, almost in ritualistic fashion.

"How many times did we do this as kids whenever Beth wasn't around?"

"Five thousand, two-hundred and eighty."

"I believe you are correct. Except you forgot to count

leap-years."

Father Carrick joined us, relieving himself over the rail. "I'll pretend I didn't hear that."

I pulled up my fly and sat back down with Father Carrick while Tom remained at the railing and became reflective again. I tried to absorb the magnitude of what Tom had revealed to us in detail earlier that day, but could not. Still cannot. It was all so sickeningly familiar. His anger, although seething, remained hidden from view from the world. I have forever since remained in a state of shock. We were just a couple of boys who wanted to build forts in our woods; throw some snowballs, pick some apples. Laugh again.

Tom looked out over our woods. "Do you remember reading *A Catcher in the Rye?*"

"Every year in high school. Every year in college, thanks to you. One of my favorite books by one of my favorite authors."

"Did you know Salinger landed on Utah Beach during The D-Day Invasion?"

"No, I didn't."

"He was one of the lucky ones. He only got to see about two hundred of his brothers die that day. If he had been a few hundred yards away at Omaha Beach, he could have had the privilege of watching *three thousand* brothers die. He would have run up the beach flanked by Burt Reynolds' father and the actor Charles Durning. True story. Salinger fought his way through the hedgerows and eventually helped liberate a concentration camp. Did you know that?"

"No."

"Can you imagine what that must have been like? All that death? All that inhumanity being played out right in front of you? What it would do to you?"

"No. I can't. I don't know what it would do." Tom's silence and what I had just found out about his connection to past events told me he could imagine it. As for me, I was lying. I did know what all of that death could do to you.

"Do you remember the significance of the title, Will?"

I shrugged, struggled for a one sentence synopsis. "Holden Caulfield wanted to be a 'Catcher in the Rye.' To help little kids from running off the edge of a cliff. He wanted to protect the little children from harm."

"Harm?"

"The harm of growing up, turning into adults." I thought of what that process of turning into an adult had done to my two friends and me.

"Salinger wrote a short story during the War where Holden's younger brother, Vincent Caulfield, goes to visit a friend on their last furlough. In the story Vincent mentions to his friend that his older brother Holden is missing in action. Presumed dead. Have you ever read that story?"

"No. I never knew."

"You should read it. It was published in the *Saturday Evening Post* on July 15, 1944. One of the greatest literary characters ever created was killed off before we, his reading public, generations of readers, even knew Holden was alive. Very few fans of Holden Caulfield know that. It was heartbreaking for me when I discovered it. Like so many other readers, he was a real person to me. And then I found out that he had been killed during the War. He was dead before we had even met him. Salinger was writing about a dead kid and we didn't even know about it until later."

Tom turned and faced us. "Unless you take into consideration that Salinger actually created *two* Holden Caulfields. One that was missing in action in the war, presumed dead, mourned by Vincent in *Last Day of the Last Furlough*. The other went on to star in *A Catcher in the Rye*, written years later."

"Why did he do that?"

"Good question, I'll ask him next time he grants an interview."

Father Carrick looked to me, confused.

"Salinger doesn't grant interviews," I explained.

"I see."

Tom continued. "Now that you know about Salinger, does the title take on a new meaning, Will? Do you understand that what Salinger wrote was a war novel, thinly disguised as a coming-of-age novel?"

"I'm not sure I understand, Tom."

"Where was our *'Catcher in the Rye,'* Will?"

I could tell it was a question he had been harboring for a long time. He turned back and continued to stare off toward the tree-muffled roar of the Greenberg spillway.

"Where was *our 'Catcher in the Rye,'* Will? Ever wonder that? Where? Who was there to prevent us from going over the cliff? They not only didn't prevent us from going over the cliff, they shoved us over the cliff for a big, fat lie; a deception of immeasurable proportions. Think of what that means in the grand scheme of things, Will."

I couldn't. It was too big to think of right now, and even if I could, I'm not sure I wanted to know the answers.

"Why hasn't anyone apologized to us for this? What will stop them from doing it again? How do we know this Desert Storm thing a few years back wasn't the same thing all over again, 'another Vietnam'? What's to prevent it from happening again?

"The answer is, no one will stop it. No one will say, 'No, you're not taking my son.' It was all a myth, Will."

He paused and hung his head. "I want to go back to the days of our innocence. I want to go back to the land of *The Sterile Cuckoo,* when we were all so young and innocent and wandering our domain here. I know we cannot do that so I'm just not interested in anything anymore. I think if there is a God he has a sense of humor."

I looked at Father Carrick. "Why?"

"Because I think at a certain point in your life, as you get older, you stop worrying and fearing death and begin to embrace it. It's when you've had enough. *When life becomes a pathless wood.*

You remember that line?"

Indeed, I did.

"I've had enough, Will. Because when it's time to go, you don't care anymore; it doesn't frighten you anymore, you *embrace* the idea. Is that where you are?"

I hadn't thought about it quite like that. But it didn't take me long to answer in light of what had happened in the last ten days. "Yes. I guess that's where I am, too."

"I can't change anything. I can't get our political leaders to stop lying to us. I cannot save our kids from getting killed in end-less-war-for-profit. I cannot change New City back to the way it was when we grew up. It was there that way just once. It was that way just for us. *Just once, for us.* And now it's no longer there."

I, too, wanted to go back to those days. Relive those New City and Gainesville days. Whoever said we never appreciate our younger days until it's too late knew what they were talk-ing about. So, yes, I want to go back to the days of *The Sterile Cuckoo.* Don't know what I'm talking about? Google the author, John Nichols; read the book; see the movie. It won't take you back, but you'll know what I'm talking about. Maybe you'll even begin to understand.

And Tom was right about God's sense of humor, too. It was time to embrace his idea.

He went on. "I will never participate in the activities of this country again, no matter what it does. I have never been to the Vietnam Wall in Washington and will never go there. We were all betrayed. We were so trusting. We believed every word of that patriotic tripe they fed us. We were 'Born on the Fourth of July.' You know that book? The title of that book and movie are so apt.

"We weren't patriots. We were dupes. All the while we were just cannon fodder, bullet catchers, making them money as long as the American public was willing to put up with it, until they could figure out how they could back out and save face and make it all look justifiable, plausible. Kissinger convinced the North

Vietnamese to delay the Paris Peace Talks until after the '68 election. He convinced them they would get a better deal if they waited for Nixon."

"I was there, too." I signed up that same week as the Kissinger deception, I would find out later.

"Of course you were. That willful, deliberate delay in the peace talks killed twenty thousand more American boys like you and me, Will. Our friends. *Twenty thousand*. One hundred thousand more of our classmates were wounded. And then the brave Americans killed another *million* innocent civilians in that little country in those months that followed, fellow human beings who wanted nothing more than to control their own destinies, grow a little family, play with their children, watch the sun go down over their rice paddies. Instead, this monster from another century descended on their lives like aliens from another world and destroyed them. Annihilated them for a political ruse. They were convenient, and oh, so easy. Kids were being born without eyes and with stumps for legs because of the tons of chemicals we rained down on them and their farms and their water. They had no voice. So then what did the world do? They awarded Kissinger the Nobel Peace Prize.

"It wasn't some mysterious group of rogue bad guys or commies who killed most of those women and children. It was us. You, me, our classmates. The death squads we supported. We killed two million women, children, old people. That's a big number, Will, and it's all on us. PTSD? It isn't caused by what our soldiers *saw*. It's caused by *what they did*. You and I killed them and there's no denying it, no matter how much of the evidence was destroyed to keep from the American people. We did it because we like to kill people. Plain and simple. Americans like to kill people and any excuse will do. Add money to the equation and we become giddy. It's just easier if they're '*gooks*' or '*towel-heads*' or whatever other ugly names they create to make us hate fellow human beings. That makes it okay to hate them. Think of how easy it is for the arms merchants to have us do their dirty work. We're such an easy sell. So easy to convince."

The irony of it all overwhelmed me. "They defeated us, Tom."

"They did, indeed, but only because the folks back here in the States were catching on to the con-job, so we just stopped and pulled out. So yes, they did defeat us, but at great cost to them. We deserved to be beaten. We were the enemy. Does that sound unpatriotic? Good. You're listening then. You're paying attention.

"I don't blame or hold responsible our friends on the front line who had no choice where they were placed. I mean the top of the food chain. They were the ones who deserved to be beaten. But they were untouched. *Unharmed.* Unaccountable. *Unwounded.* A shrug of the shoulders and an 'Oh, well.'

"What people don't understand, or don't realize, or refuse to accept, is that we were not there to 'win.' "

"I got that feeling myself while I was there, too."

"Do you know why we were there?"

"Tom, I was there for almost two years and could never figure it out."

"One very simple, transparent reason. We were there to spend enormous amounts of money in unaccountable ways, as quickly as possible. Killing people and providing big numbers for the weekly body count presented the rationale, the justification. 'That little four year-old girl playing in the village might have been the one who carried the hand grenade last week, so kill her.' "

He was right, of course. He was always right.

"And they want me to be patriotic? They want me to believe all of their self-serving lies? No, Will. I have my own little, self-contained world right here."

"You keep saying that. What's wrong, Tom?"

"I'm a short-timer here. Hasn't Father Carrick brought you up to speed? But that's okay, Will. Someday you will understand. Not today, probably, but someday. It's all okay.

"Then Dove Cottage and the grounds will go for the nuns and

the children's home. Every kid who has to live there will never want for anything. They want to go to college? They get a free ride.

"How much am I worth? I don't even know. A hundred million? Five hundred million? Probably somewhere around there.

"It all goes to the kids who don't have Moms or Dads. Can you image what it's like to grow up without the comfort of a mother and a father in a home? They'll never have the basic fundamental birth rite that every creature ever born should have? What's it like never to be held by a mother or a father? I know, because that was my life. They may not have had that fundamental experience like I never did, but if they want to go to college, they'll go to college. There's enough for hundreds of them. Father Carrick, here, will see to it when I'm gone.

"I'm planning on returning to Vietnam next month. I'm going to build a schoolhouse near the *My Luoc* site. Beth was going to meet me there with her daughter and we were going to live there together, teach, but now I'll have to go alone. That's okay.

"And this property we're on now? Clarkstown can call it the Demarest Kill Park or the Dutch Gardens Park. It will be restored and maintained in perpetuity. It will always remain the way we remembered it. The way *we* remembered it. And where Beth was found? There will be a stepping stone path across The Demarest Kill. Maybe even a little plaque.

He took a long pause again, the pain welling up inside of him, the reflections of it all showing on his face.

"You know, Will, this country is about to jump off a cliff again. I can sense it. We are ripe for it. We are ripe for another war. I can smell it. 1993 was just a taste of things to come, a trial balloon. The next one is going to be big. As soon as they can find a bad guy that everyone can hate. My guess? 'Desert Storm Part II.' But this time it's not going to be over in a few days or even a few weeks like that one was. It will last for years. Maybe forever if they can sell the rationale. Imagine that. You know why? There's too much money to be made to let the opportunity slip away. I don't want to be around to see it happen."

"So I pose the question once again. Where was our *Catcher in the Rye*, Will? Didn't we deserve a catcher, too?"

The question hung in the air for a moment before he turned and walked inside.

With trembling hands, Father Carrick started to stack the tea cups and then stopped himself abruptly, awkwardly. "We should be leaving."

The sun was low in the west. We walked back the front way, past Dove Cottage, through the estate grounds and down the hill to Muller Court and to Twin Elms Lane, through where the vineyards and the apple orchards and the rhubarb patch planted by my grandfather *should have been*. Past where the Twin Elms had been before falling victim to Dutch Elm blight in the early 1950s.

Father Carrick seemed reflective, philosophical, resigned to the spot, whatever spot that was that we were all now in.

"What was it you said to Tom back there? I've never seen him react that way."

"*My Luoc*."

"*My Luck*? Is that what you're saying? '*My Luck*'? That's a Vietnamese phrase? Slang, I take it?"

"A village."

"He never mentioned it to me. How did you know then? Did Beth tell you?"

"No."

"How then?"

"*Latae sententiae*."

He was not surprised at my response. "Okay. Fair enough."

"Are you allowed to tell me about Tom's health prognosis?"

He thought of a way to couch it. "What Tom said about going to Vietnam to build a school?"

"Yeah?"

"It will never happen. Some of his money may wind up there, but he'll never make it there himself."

"Why?"

Father Carrick hesitated. "Tom is dying. It's finally caught up with him. My poor boy is still paying the price; the ultimate price. Tom is dying from a form of cancer."

"What kind?"

"It doesn't matter where it started. It's metastasized throughout his body. More poison from Vietnam. Agent Orange, exacerbated by the Hepatitis-C he got from all those blood transfusions in the Veteran's Hospital. He lost his spleen so he has a compromised immune system. He is very sick. The doctors don't even care about the source, it's so far along. Only has another few months, probably, at the most. There's so much more to this story, Will. I'll have to sit down and tell you all about it."

"How can you reveal such personal information? Isn't it breaking the priest's confidence?"

Father Carrick shrugged philosophically.

I could wait no longer. "Father Carrick. Marvin mentioned something the other night."

He slowed his walk and turned to me. "That Marvin really got around."

I hesitated, fearful of where my question might lead. "Is there something you want to tell me?"

He laughed out loud at what I soon found out would be from the irony of my question.

"It hardly makes any difference now, Will. I was planning on telling you later today. I'm retiring from the priesthood. I'm divorcing God."

"What? Why?"

"What happened to Francis, Tom, your father, Calvin, now Beth. What kind of loving supreme being would allow all that to happen? It's all just a bunch of bunk."

"How long have you felt this way?"

"I quit my job the first time on 'Francis' Day,' in June, 1956. I didn't fully realize it that day, but I quit. I've just been going through the motions ever since. Forty-four years of faking it. It's all over but the paperwork, as they say. I quit again when Tom first got back from Vietnam and we started to talk and he told me what was going on over there. I quit when your father died. I quit again the other day, when they found Beth. And I finally quit again yesterday for good, when I visited Calvin, that poor sweet boy. He never stood a chance. He grew up steps from where my office is and I never fully comprehended the extent of his suffering. He confirmed to me everything he had told you about Marvin. He told me about that night you hid under his bed in fear for your life. It's all so sickening. How do children survive?

"I told Tom and I'll tell Jimmy and I'll tell your boss. They'll know it was Marvin. It may be hearsay, but we all know it's all true. The DNA will prove it.

"I guess you could say I am finally 'firing myself.' I cannot in all honesty tell people what I no longer believe my own self. What kind of loving God would allow those things to happen to you and your family and friends? The last forty-four years of my life have been a lie. Based on a belief of 'wishful thinking.' I so badly wanted it all to be true."

I waited for a further explanation. Instead he offered another surprise.

"Will, now I have a confession to make."

My heart stopped. I didn't know if I could take much more trauma on this afternoon.

"Your mother and I are going to get married."

I was so shocked it took me a moment to realize how happy I was for her.

"Well, that is a surprise." The implications took a moment to sink in. "My mother is over eighty."

"In the prime of her life, I might add. And I'm seventy-five. It's never too late to have a happy childhood. That's something you should think about. We have been seeing one another for many years."

He immediately held up his hand like a stop sign as we passed Capral Lane.

"She was both loyal and faithful to your father until the end, Will. No worries there, in that department. When your father drifted off into oblivion because of what happened to Francis and was killed, she came to me for advice and I fell in love with her strength and her spirit and her soul. I still honor the sanctity of marriage, and so does she.

"The period of mourning has gone on long enough and we don't know what tomorrow will bring."

That made me stop and think.

The next day Calvin died all alone in his hospital room at Sing Sing from Kaposi's Sarcoma and internal hemorrhaging, already weakened by Auto-Immune Deficiency Syndrome and pneumonia. On his bed next to him was a pad with a pencil etching of his last sparrow, only partially completed in a shaky, weak, sketch-hand. In the corner he had written. "For Will, my true, real brother."

As I caromed back and forth between grief for Beth and Calvin, fear for Tom, and happiness for my mother and Carrick, I was called back into the D.A.'s office when I arrived for work the next day.

Carl Henion sat us all down at the board table. "So here's the situation. You say that Calvin told you that Marvin killed Beth, and then Marvin later confessed to you in the barn that he did it. He confirmed it."

"Yes. He bragged about it."

"Here's our dilemma: All we have is your word that's what happened. How do we know that you didn't make up all of this?"

"Why would I do that?" I already knew his answer.

"To cover up the fact that you did it. How do we know you

didn't do it, Will?"

"You must have been talking to Tom."

"As a matter of fact, we have."

"Well, talk to Father Carrick."

"Hardly a reliable witness. It would be hearsay, anyway. He spoke to Calvin, not Marvin."

"Are you going to talk to Rainer?

"He's got an alibi. He was out of the country. He's out of the country now. He won't be back from the interior of China for a year, maybe he'll never be back. He's with his daughter, looking for properties to develop."

"What about extradition?"

"Extradition for what? No phone records to Marvin. *Bupkis*."

My mind was wandering. Was I delirious? What else would have brought on this non-sequitur? I had to ask the question. "You know what happens to 800 Chinese people every month?"

Carl looked confused. "No. Is this a joke?"

"This is no joke."

"Okay, so what happens to 800 Chinese people every month?"

"They become millionaires."

"Maybe you should join Rainer over there."

"I'll be taking a leave of absence. But I won't be going to China."

"Oh?"

"I have over seventy days leave accumulated."

"As you wish."

CHAPTER NINETY-ONE

NEW CITY

March, 2001
Age 54

My mother and Carrick got married four months later in March of that following year, 2001. They were married by a Justice of the Peace on the tea house steps in The Dutch Garden where Beth and I had shared our first kiss. I was there with Francis in his wheelchair and Tom. Delores, who had spent many hours talking to my mother was there and we were cordial to one another. Jimmy and his wife Karen were there, as were all the nuns and priests from the diocese, my mother's friends from St. Augustine's Auxiliary, and over thirty former Girl Scouts she had led on walks on the Dutch Garden pathways there in the late 1940s and early 1950s. Her scouts were now all in their sixties and seventies; faces changed by the ravages of everyday life in the suburbs; faces filled with the ebbing and flowing of happiness and disappointments. On this day, faces filled with joy, for my mother, getting married in her eighties. She had remained in touch with most of them. I am happy to report that they are all still good Girl Scouts.

After the service, when it was time for Max to drive my

mother and Carrick to the airport for their honeymoon in Italy and Ireland, she had to say goodbye to her wheelchair-bound son sitting on the deck of the tea house with a look of confusion on his face. He kept tugging at the stiff starched collar irritating his neck with atrophied hands curled into a ball. The look on my mother's face was a mix of happiness, maybe even relief, and concern for leaving my brother's side for the first time in over forty-five years. Francis sat slumped in his chair, trying to figure out what was going on. Or maybe he knew and just didn't know how to tell us he knew.

Their parting was painful, my mother torn between the love of the two men in her life. I assured her I could and would take care of Francis. She paced back and forth on the bricks, as if convincing herself she needed his permission to go. Carrick waited patiently until she could finally pull herself away.

"Not too much butter on his oatmeal. And just a little cinnamon, Will."

"I remember, Mom."

When everyone had departed, Delores and Tom walked Francis and me back to the house to help Francis get situated. Tom headed home. Delores hung around for just a few moments of small-talk. There was an awkward goodbye, and then she left.

I stayed at the house on Main Street, spending my days and nights with Francis, reading Dickens, Tarkington, Twain, Franklin W. Dixon, and Leo Edwards. Stretched out on his bed, his head in the cradle of my shoulder, we worked our way through them all once again.

Most nights, Tom came over, looking weaker and weaker with each trip. We would make a simple meal together and he would tell me about the school he was building in Vietnam. After, we would take Francis through his physical therapy regimen, bathe him and sit around joking, Francis looking at Tom with a sense of wonder and love on his face. How much did he know about the past?

CHAPTER NINETY-TWO

NEW CITY

April, 2001
Age 54

In April my mother and Carrick, who had returned from their honeymoon in Europe and Ireland, and Tom invited us all to move into Dove Cottage in the coming weeks. I went to the house on Main Street and collected all the storybooks and carted most of them off to my house on New City Park Lake for safekeeping. Our house on Main Street would be vacant for some time.

It would be a full house at Dove Cottage, with Francis under the care of three, full-time nurses, giving my mother a rest and a chance to do a little gardening, a hobby she had all but given up forty years before. There would be a rhubarb patch on the property once again.

Carrick spent his days administering all the new arrangements and the financing and welcoming the nuns and young, pregnant women who arrived distraught, only to find the gift of a place of peace in a country manor. In the late afternoons Father Carrick would join my mother in her garden.

Tom and I took walks in the woods and even started to retrace the path of the Demarest Kill, as we had done forty-two years earlier with Beth. We started up by the intersection of Burda Avenue and Red Hill Road and walked a mile until we were on the shore of what was once Davies' Lake beach. We stared across the marshy area to the far shore where the bath-house had once been.

Tom started laughing. "I patched up the holes in the bath house, you know."

I looked at him. "Marvin told you?"

"Marvin told everyone you were a pervert. Peeking into the hole in the wall at Davie's all summer with all the rest of the guys."

"That's not true. It was just once. A fleeting glance." I started to say, "Ask Calvin, he'll tell you," but caught myself in time.

"I didn't think so."

"Just that once. And that was because he tricked me into it."

"I plugged up the holes one night."

"You did?"

"Yes."

"When?"

"That fall after it happened. The start of seventh grade. I snuck in one night. Beth and I hopped the fence with my little can of drywall mud."

"How humiliating. I'm ashamed that Beth knew."

"A silly boyhood prank. Nothing to get worked up over."

"Still."

"Calvin said you ran out of there, horrified."

"True."

"A little drywall mud and some paint, and you'd never know the holes were there. But your reputation remains tarnished."

I looked at Tom then out toward the marsh and he laughed again.

"They drilled new holes the next summer, from what I hear."

CHAPTER NINETY-THREE

NEW CITY

May, 2001
Age 54

In the weeks to come we would spend a few hours a day walking a mile or two on The Kill. That's all Tom could handle in his weakened condition. We had to prioritize, so spent our days at New City Park Lake, Greenberg's, the fishing holes north of Squadron A, the stream that passed in front of Beth's. At each location we would recall our walk in that first summer of '58, forty-three years earlier, remembering every detail. Remembering the songs playing on the jukebox at Whitey's during our celebratory cheeseburgers. Remembering our best friend, Beth.

Now, MacMansions blocked access to the stream at many locations.

On one of our final days on the Kill, we were following the stream as it merged with the Hackensack River east of The Dellwood Country Club. The near silence was one of its greatest appeals.

Just north of Haverstraw Road where the stream actually starts flowing south, Tom waded over to a large flat rock on the bank and sat down. He looked exhausted. It was a long moment before he spoke. The silence was filled with the sound of water bubbling over the stream stones. I joined him on the rock. I could tell he had something on his mind. I couldn't imagine what he wanted to say.

"There's something I need to clear the air about."

He sounded like he was talking to a stranger.

"I know Carrick didn't tell you and I know Beth didn't tell you. So how could you possibly know about *My Luoc*?"

And so I told Tom my Vietnam story.

It was complete with thousands of scenarios I have never been able to forget or share with another human being. Details that haunt us both. When I was finished Tom remained silent. I got the feeling he had died at that moment. He was still alive for all outward appearances, but he had died before my very eyes. He stood from the boulder on the bank and looked upstream for a long time, listening to the water gurgling over the rocks, before he spoke.

"I want to go home."

I pulled out my cell phone. "Let me call Jimmy. He'll come and get us at the underpass and drive us home."

"No. That's not what I mean." He looked upstream toward the headwaters once again.

"I want to go home. I want to go back up there. To the way it used to be. To that very first day when I first saw you across our Kill."

I stood and joined him.

"Yeah. Me too. After where we've been, I just don't know how to get there anymore. I'm not even sure we deserve to be there."

"That's okay. I'm going to be there before you know it. You know that Woody Guthrie tune, *I Ain't Got No Home In This World Anymore?*

"Yeah, I know it."

"Do you believe in an afterlife, Will?"

"Haven't given it much thought."

"Nonsense. We all think about it. Hope that it's true. As for me, it doesn't really make a difference. And it really shouldn't for you."

"How's that?"

"We grew up in Heaven, Will. Then we descended into hell. We left Eden or whatever you want to call it. It doesn't get any better than what we had, what we experienced in our own little Eden. Then we went to a place where it couldn't get any worse. The countless atrocities. I don't have to tell you. Now we're all condemned to hell for all eternity."

Indeed. I never counted the atrocities. I don't have to. They're all in my head where they won't go away. I had never told anyone what I did over there before I told Tom just a few moments ago.

No one ever asked.

We walked up the slope to the guardrail near where the Kill passes under Haverstraw Road and Jimmy picked us up and drove us toward home. He sensed our need for silence.

I sat in the back seat. Jim reached over and put his arm around Tom as Tom slumped next to him, head on Jim's shoulder, staring blankly through the windshield. He reached over and put his hand on Jim's, his way of saying "thank-you." For some reason it had never occurred to me that Tom and Jim had remained friends during the intervening years. Why had I not realized that?

By early May, Tom became very sick and would eventually spend hours in bed. Like the second half of a round trip, he returned to Dove Cottage and had movers carry his Steinway through the woods from the boathouse to his upstairs room as he had told us in October that he would. Arty, our classmate who had taken our pictures with Beth's F-1, and who had inherited the moving company from his father twenty years earlier, showed his men how to maneuver the piano out the doors and up the path.

We showed Arty and Arty III the pictures on Tom's wall and gave young Arty the ones that showed his father and his grandfather in the background. When they saw the men in the pictures they didn't react like I thought they would. Arty turned and looked away quickly to recover in front of his son.

I took some more pictures of Tom supervising the piano's return trip. The recording equipment and all the recorded masters came next.

Tom never told me why he had never performed publicly after his return from Vietnam, details of which Carrick had alluded to earlier. It was Tom's form of revenge, I suppose. But I would learn later that he would rehearse his 'recitals' every weekday and weeknight and then 'performed' on Saturday nights to an audience consisting of two microphones and his Nagra reel-to-reel tape deck. Later digital technology took over and then he used the state-of-the-art equipment. His recording regimen was obsessive, and contains a diverse collection of some of the great keyboard composers who ever lived; all for what he knew would someday be his posthumous audience.

The only time he ever made it to Carnegie Hall was that day in 1962 when the three of us witnessed the performance of Ray Charles.

As Tom's strength waned, he worked in a flurry to record as many concertos as he could before he became too weak to record any more. Somewhere in the collection I would later find him playing Rachmaninoff's *Piano Concerto #3*, among the most difficult piano works ever composed.

Just as Carrick had cautioned me, Tom never made it back to Vietnam. The children there will have to learn to read and drink clean water without the helping hands of Beth and Tom. Toward the end, we spent a lot of time together, reminiscing about our boyhood hikes, our ice skating adventures, climbing High Tor, our bike riding expeditions, our long nights in front of the boat-house fireplace; about our friend, Beth.

He lived long enough to oversee the beginning of the remod-eling of the Florion Estate and the boathouse to accommodate the nuns and unwed mothers and children that would eventually be housed there. There was also a permanent room for Francis with a small balcony on the east side that overlooked the giant spruce. Through a break in the branches, if you looked closely, you could see the treetops of our overgrown baseball field. Francis spent his days, propped up in a wheelchair, overlooking his domain.

By mid-May, true to Carrick's prediction, Tom succumbed to the poisons in his body. The war in Vietnam claimed the life of yet another American boy, twenty-six years after it was supposedly over.

On one of the last bright spring days when Tom was strong enough, we walked the woods once again and watched as Clark-stown developed his property into a town park. In another era, on another May springtime day, we would have been at track prac-tice, sprinting on the cinders of CCHS with Coach D'. But this May, one day he was making plans, the next day he was in and out of a wheelchair. The next day he was dead.

On that last day Tom was upstairs in Dove Cottage, rehearsing a piece by Chopin on the Steinway that had found its way back home through the woods.

I was in the kitchen with Frau K., now almost eighty, and Max, eighty-five. They had spent their lives caring for the child prodigy. I sat at the kitchen chair looking up to where the piano music was wending its way down the circular back staircase. I just kept looking up at the ceiling, listening. For some reason, perhaps the look on my face, perhaps an acknowledgment that the end was near, Frau K. and Max flanked me and put their arms around me as we all listened to the beauty that was being created upstairs.

Tom collapsed during the final movement of the composi-tion he was playing. You can hear him on the tape deck he used for recording. On the tape playback there is a pause and then his footsteps on the hardwood floors. You can hear the piano bench scraping as he sits and adjusts himself at the keyboard, arranges the sheet music, and slates it.

"This is a rehearsal take only, of Chopin's *Nocturne, Opus 48, #1 in C Minor.*"

There is a pause and then he plays for a few minutes, flawlessly, then begins to falter as the piece picks up in tempo, and he weakens during the difficult effort. You can hear the bench scrape against the wooden floor as he collapses.

We were downstairs in the kitchen listening and I heard him falter, heard the piano bench slide out from under him as he heaved forward, biting his tongue as he clipped his jaw on the keyboard before his head fell to the floor and the bench skittered across the room behind him. As we ran up the rear circular staircase and into the room, the old, analog reel-to-reel tape deck was spinning at seven-and-a-half inches per second, the V/U needles spiking as we ran across the hardwood floors yelling his name. I could hear the alarm in my voice when I later listened to the tape playback. You can hear Max's frightened begging.

Later, I looked up the musical reference. Many consider it to be one of Chopin's most difficult and emotional pieces to play for its required energy and aggressiveness. He must have worn himself out playing it.

We had all been in a state of hopeless mourning for his impending death for months, so there was no shock, just relief that his suffering was finally over.

After Tom died, Carrick and I made attempts to contact his parents. With information from the family attorney, and Max and Frau K., we were able to track them down, or at least Tom's father. They had been living in Vienna, until his mother had died two years earlier. No one ever told her only son his mother had died. The estate managers didn't even know. To our knowledge, his father never attempted to contact anyone in the family about her death, because he knew if he did, the financial support from the Florion estate they had been living on all those years would likely have stopped, had Tom ever found out. Tom and the estate had apparently been supporting his parents ever since the elder Florions had died in the late 1970s, due to a codicil in the will. Despite this, according to Carrick, his parents had never contacted Tom to thank him. Tom's father just assumed he was entitled to the annuity for being the husband of Florion's daughter.

Tom kept his promises. And, there were some surprises in his will. Others, not really surprises. He left most of his money for the home for unwed mothers and the kids' college fund as he promised. He willed all of the remaining Florion property over to the county, to take effect after the death of my mother, Carrick, and Francis. Dove Cottage and the boathouse would remain open for orphans and unwed mothers, supported by an endowment that had no limits.

Demarest Kill County Park will be a place where boys and girls would fish and skate and go on great adventures; a place for people like Francis, who although trapped in their physical prison, still dream of flying through fields chasing their friends and wading through streams, and who then must suddenly awake to ask why they can't be like other people.

At that time, it will all be connected to the Dutch Garden. And yes, there will be a plaque and a stepping stone bridge across the stream beneath the gazebo, as Tom promised.

Tom left behind over 4,000 piano performances on half-inch tape and digital media. It's the work of a world-class pianist. His name and music were already known throughout the world to true connoisseurs; the recordings will continue to generate revenue for his estate. He is considered a cult figure to those in-the-know.

Carrick remains in charge of Tom's endowment. A healthy salary. Carrick hired me to administer the endowment. I quit the

DA's office. There will always be enough money.

When Carrick and my mother were getting ready to leave for Ireland for a few week's respite, my mother handed me a letter that was part of Tom's will.

"What is it?"

"I don't know. The note on the envelope says you could find something on the pitcher's mound. He said you would know what that means."

I walked down Twin Elms to Capral and then south to the property. What I saw took me back almost fifty years. Like my father before had done himself, twice, Tom had paid someone to have the overgrown lot groomed into the baseball field in its original state. It was all there, with the exact precision my father had undertaken first when Francis and I were six and eight, and again in the days before his suicide.

On the pitcher's mound was a box with an envelope attached, addressed to "My second best friend, Will"

Inside the envelope was the automobile registration and the key to the Austin-Healey 3000, Mark I, with a note. "Remember, Castrol-Girling fluid only," referencing the vegetable-based, not petroleum-based clutch and brake fluid, required to preserve the the integrity of car's hydraulic slave-cylinders.

Inside the box were three items; Tom's handwritten journal tied up with black sash-cord like you would find backstage at a theatre, and a fielder's glove with handwriting in green ball-point pen, overwritten in black ink. It was Tom's glove from our child-hood baseball days.

When we moved the piano to the boathouse that Christmas Vacation of 1963, his glove, hanging on a peg in what was to become his music room, had been filled with even more writing, some of it by then in black ballpoint overwriting the green. I understood the words and recognized some of the quotes, but I couldn't link the quotes to the authors. As we played our last pick-up games in that last spring of 1964, as Tom stood in the outfield of the Dutch Garden ball field, or at the New City Park Church Tabernacle ball field when the Catholic Youth Organization played the Free Church Youth Fellowship, or at the Clarkstown High ball field, waiting to catch a fly ball, was he reading what he had written on his glove?

I realized I had not seen the glove since that high school graduation spring, watching Tom play our last baseball games of our youth. The leather was as oiled and supple as it had been then. He had obviously been using his Neatsfoot oil regularly.

As I read over the quotes on the glove, they all came back to me; a Browning quote, apropos a baseball glove, a life, *"A man's reach should exceed his grasp."* It was all in keeping with Tom's sense of humor and all in keeping with his Salinger influences, for the green and black writing was Tom's allusion to the gift from Allie Caulfield to his older brother Holden, taken to another level. In Salinger's first short story reference, the glove had green ink. Later referenced in *The Catcher in the Rye*, the ink color had changed to black, leaving readers, and Tom, and now me, to wonder *why*? Did it make a difference?

The third item in the box was a key with a string label attached reading, "Boathouse studio cabinet."

I walked back to the Dove Cottage carrying the boxed manuscript and glove and envelope. I opened the garage door on the west side of the mansion. The Austin-Healey 3000 was there under a white muslin cover. Underneath, it was gleaming, having obviously gone through extensive restoration in recent years. The convertible top was down and the side-curtains stood at attention in the corner of the garage. The *tonneau* cover was unzipped allowing me to sit behind the wheel. I put the key in the ignition and turned it. Behind me, the electric fuel pump clicked like a racing clock. I waited, then pushed the starter button on the dashboard with my thumb. It roared to life with its deep-throated rumble. I sat there, and for a brief moment I was racing along South Mountain Road on a crisp autumn day, Beth's head on my shoulder, my wedding ring on her finger, a liver-spotted Springer Spaniel on her lap. I had to turn off the motor.

I wandered down to the boathouse and used the key Tom had given me in 1964 to open the boathouse doors. Inside, I stood at the studio cabinet not wanting to open it, knowing all too well what was inside. The key Tom had left for me at the pitcher's mound stuck at first, perhaps from lack of lubricant or oxidation of the tumblers, but with a little bit of spit, I was able to jiggle the lock open.

As I suspected, the cabinet was filled with over twenty slide carousels and forty albums filled with Beth's photo negatives. In the front of each album, a sleeve of contact sheets, all meticulously identified in her fine hand. I went through the first three contact sheets, but then had to stop. I remember Beth always having a camera strapped around her neck, but I never thought for a moment the extent to which she had documented our lives. It was all there captured on over 6,000 negatives and transparencies. I closed and locked the cabinet. This would have to wait for another time.

I lifted Francis into his wheelchair and I wheeled him down the street to where the fence was accordioned-down, surrounding the restored ball field. I lifted him out of the wheelchair and carried him to the line of poplars behind the pitcher's mound. He looked around, trying to understand, trying to figure out how it was tied in to what my father had done, not once, but twice in our lifetimes, and more recently, to what Tom had done. Did Francis have a sense of time?

And then he looked at me and he was at peace. The older brother who as a little boy had promised our mother to always take care of me and had carried me in his arms to safety, was now my big brother to keep.

With Francis at peace, my mother could be at peace, I knew.

I put Francis back in the wheelchair and wheeled him up the hill back to Dove Cottage and returned him to the twenty-four hour care by the sisters and nurses, supported by Tom's generosity.

Tom's generosity was apparently boundless. I learned from my mother and Carrick that at the Florion's initiative and later at Tom's insistence, they had paid for my college education and had set up a long-neglected endowment for my law school tuition. How else would my parents have been able to afford out-of-state tuition at the University of Florida on my father's mailman salary? My mother had alluded to the trust Tom's grandparents had provided.

"Why did the Florions want to do this?"

"It was an agreement they made with your grandfather for Francis during the War. Free college tuition. When it became clear that Francis would not be going to college, they transferred the endowment to your name. They had paid for your father's education at NYU in the 1930s, as well."

"Why?"

"Because that's the kind of people they were. Part of the arrangement was that you would not know about it until after you graduated."

Now, all those years of my estrangement from Tom made me feel even worse. In the days before his death, he had never mentioned it.

"Why didn't Tom tell me? Why didn't he want me to know?"

"He felt you would be embarrassed."

"How did this all happen?"

"His grandmother approached me while I was sewing for her. She told me that she and Mr. Florion had made provisions for all of your college, just like they had done for your father."

"She hardly knew me."

"Like I say, they did it to thank your grandfather. She told me they never had time to thank him for all of his work before he died. I thought you would be glad to know."

"I'm thinking about how I didn't trust Tom. The things I said about him and Beth. All the while I was ugly to him."

Carrick raised a hand. "You have to put that behind you, Will. They're at peace now. It's time for you to find that same peace."

"Did Beth know?"

They exchanged glances. "Yes."

"How do you know?"

"We discussed it. She said it saddened her because she knew that someday you would find out and that it would make you feel awful."

Beth had been right.

"Don't let it make you feel awful. She didn't want you to go through that. Tom wouldn't want that either."

Too late. The enormity of that gesture took a long time to sink in. The implications and consequences were overwhelming. This is what Beth had meant when she had said, "After all Tom has done for you." I heard her say it, but I wasn't listening. How obvious it all was now.

The month of May slipped by, and I spent time with Francis every day and it was only there at his bedside or on the terrace that overlooks the boathouse to the north and the baseball field to the east that I, myself, could begin to find peace. I kneaded his hand feebly as his strength drained away and the dreaded decubitus ulcers in his emaciated flanks began to take their inevitable toll.

Once, near the end, my mother and I sat on the balcony with Francis on a brisk, late May morning. Below us, the daffodils lining the beds beneath the windows of Dove Cottage wavered in the breeze. I stood and looked north into the woods.

"What are you thinking about?" my mother asked.

"The Gershwin Party."

"Aha. Some of the greatest minds of the 20th Century, gathered together."

"I remember." I didn't really remember. It's just that I *never* forgot.

Possibly we were like that group that had gathered that February afternoon in 1924 at Aeolian Hall to listen to Gershwin introduce to the world his masterpiece of amalgamation and improvisation that still moves me to tears every time I hear it. The pleading theme of the closing strains was written for me.

But my version is not played by Gershwin, or Mero, but by twelve year-old Tom Hogenkamp, the index finger on his right hand giving the marching orders to the other nine. He hadn't played it that day of the party after sixth grade, but in the days that followed after he returned from his first European tour, we heard him play it all the time. A thousand times.

Then, like so many before them, time marched on and pushed these eggheads aside, to be replaced by a newer generation of artists. Now, Gershwin's *Rhapsody in Blue* is used to sell airline tickets, and VonBronk's paintings and sculpture are used by collectors for bragging rights.

And what of those people who had been there that day? What do we know of them now? Who even knows of them? What is their legacy beyond a few faded memories rattling around in the brain pan of a young boy now grown older? That day they were all so stately, so self-assured, so confident. No one remembers the driven genius of Oscar Levant or Ernie Kovacs or Pop Whiteman.

Standing out on the balcony of Dove Cottage, could you still hear the music of Whiteman reverberating through the treetops? I listened for the music in the tree branches many times, but the only thing I heard was the echoes of Tom working his way through a difficult Chopin piece before he left for Europe before we started ninth grade.

On one of the many days Beth and I had sat at the O.B.W. Cemetery plot between Dove Cottage and the boathouse, we listened to him struggle for two hours, before getting the Chopin piece right. He played it again and again. Through his careful manipulation of the sustain/forte foot pedal, the legato effect was still overlapping and resounding forty years later in a sound that lingers to haunt the trees and anyone who suspects it might still be there and who cares enough to know what to listen for.

I wished Marvin had never told me that he had been there, peering down from the treetops to witness it all. His presence ruins the memory of that moment in history. I never told Tom about this. Why ruin the party for him as it had been ruined for me?

"I can still hear it, Will."

I turned to look at my mother. She joined me at the railing.

"I can still hear Pop Whiteman playing that song. That Sunday night you came home and we all stood on our back porch listening was the last time your father and I ever danced together. So I can still hear it."

"I can too, Mom." I looked at her as she gazed into the woods, listening.

"Why weren't you and Dad invited to the party? You were good enough to sew her dress, but not good enough to be invited to their party? I could never understand that. It really hurt my feelings."

"Oh, no. We were invited. It was your father. He didn't feel as if he would fit in with all those important people."

I looked off into the woods and thought about my father.

"You know what else I can hear?"

I wasn't sure what she meant. "What?"

"I can hear the promise you made to me on another night, Will. Do you remember? Just before you went off to Gainesville?"

"Mom."

"I want you to keep that promise to me, Will. I want you to keep that promise to me and to Francis. I don't want you to ever be like your father anymore, Will. You have to stop. You must promise me you'll never be like your father that way."

"I promise, Mom."

A question lingered on her face. "That night of the barn fire you came rushing into the house to warn us. You had *Oak Island Treasure* in your hand. You found it. Where was it? I looked all over for it."

I had to decide whether or not to tell her.

"It was in one of the other boxes. Just misplaced, I guess."

"I don't know how. I was always so careful. Francis loved those books so. I didn't really appreciate them until it was my turn to read them to your brother. They were so delightful. No wonder your father talked about Tutter being like New City all the time.

"I usually waited until it was summertime to read them, school vacation time. That's when your father said he enjoyed them the most. So I kept up the tradition. I loved reading them. Sometimes I would hear noises outside the window, probably an old, stray tom-cat or raccoon, I suppose. I used to wish it was you come home from the university, or Vietnam, or Florida to surprise me. But it never was. Wishful thinking, I guess."

I could have told her then, but I didn't. It made me think of a question.

"I was thinking the other day. After Dad died, and I was away at school, or in Vietnam or Florida, who took down the storm windows and put up the screens every spring?"

She gave me a funny look, as if to say, *What made you ask that question?*

"Let me think. Father Carrick and the sexton at the church volunteered that first spring. And then, the strangest thing. I haven't thought about it in years. That first spring they started doing it again and then Marvin and Calvin came over and started helping. They did it for all those missing years you were gone. I always thought it was uncharacteristic behavior, but I never questioned why. Why are you asking?"

"No reason. Just doing some reflecting about those years I lost."

Two weeks before Francis faded away, he stared into my eyes

longingly until I got his message in a way that only brothers can communicate. Somehow he must have known he was on borrowed time and there is no mistake what he wanted. Sister Regina helped me lift him into a wheelchair and I rolled him down the hill once again to our old property. Would he remember from a few days ago? From thirty years ago? From forty-five years ago?

The field is maintained to professional ball park precision now by caretakers paid by Tom's endowment, similar to a cemetery plot on the perpetual care plan. Like before, I lifted him carefully and we sat at the row of poplars behind home plate and stared out toward second base at the legacy both our father and Tom left for us. Now for the last time, we were together in our field of dreams.

And then he looked to me and to beyond the lilac arbor and the bent forsythia hedge-tunnel we had spent so many hours crawling through on our hands and knees. It was time to go to the narrow stream behind our property where it abutted the Florion estate. Another goodbye.

On the bank of the brook behind our house, near the spot where I had sprained my ankle forty-five Junes earlier, I removed his slippers and socks and rolled up the cuffs on his pajama pants, then lifted him out of his wheelchair and sat him on the bank. Francis giggled at the feel of the icy water on his feet and rocked his head back in delight, the Bill Haley twirl in his Bill Haley curl falling back off his forehead. He looked north down the brook that flowed through the Damiani property and would eventually join the Demarest Kill on the south perimeter of the Dutch Garden.

Across from us and upstream just a bit, a hundred feet away, two young boys about ten and twelve squatted on the bank to discover what could be found. Pollywogs? Water Spiders? Crayfish? Salamanders? Or maybe there weren't two young boys actually there, but merely just another echo of what had been there so many years before.

Francis lifted his head and turned to the sounds of the splashing water and then back to meet my eyes and in that moment I knew he was still alive inside; in that moment I knew he had seen those two young boys also, whether or not they were really there. He was still alive and had spent over forty-four years reliving the memories that were starting to fade from ever being accessible to him again. Was it these memories that were keeping him alive?

Then, as I splashed his feet up and down in the stream, his Bill Haley spit curl fell once again across his forehead and his feet tickled with the gurgling of the water and the water spiders, he began to laugh his laugh. It was sounds others would likely find ugly and grotesque as he contorted his mouth, but to me now, they were the most beautiful sounds on earth; my brother laughing. His feral howling grew louder and his body spasmed with happiness and his grunting laughter echoed off the canopy of trees that hovered over us. I hugged him tightly to my chest and sobbed for what would have to be one more final time. Never again could I allow myself to feel this hopeless.

In a moment out of Steinbeck, I briefly considered pointing to the far bank and talking to him about raising rabbits on his own farm someday, but the implications of such a discussion were actions that I would never have been able to fulfill.

We sat there with our feet in our own little tributary of the Demarest Kill. No one knows about or cares about the days we spent wading these waters. Behind me now is an endless stream of traffic on Main Street and New Hempstead Road and the new Rte. 304. You can't find a parking space in the lot they made in the town baseball field behind the Court House Annex. My little town is growing. New people are moving in all the time without an appreciation for the history that has gone on before them in my little town. It won't be too long before a lot of what we remember will be torn down, rebuilt.

The New City Grammar School and the old Elms Hotel are long gone. St John's Episcopal Church on Second and Main is gone. St. Augustine's, the site where my mother took us to endless Sundays of early mass and where my father saw an early Eddie

Cantor movie, and where we played endless games of basketball and slow danced to the Everly Brothers in the bouncing sparkle of the mirror ball, has been placed on the short-timer's list. The sanctuary will be torn down and replaced in the near future.

But the waters leading into the Demarest Kill will continue to flow around the rocks and rills, beneath the lush canopy of oaks and maples, past the Dutch Garden, and through the enchanted meadows and wooded glens, for other boys to explore and discover the beauty of my stream.

A few days later, in early June, almost forty-five years to the day since "Francis' Day," my brother sat overlooking his demesne from the second floor terrace of Dove Cottage, where he drifted off into a world of peace while I sat next to him, holding his hand. I tried to cry one last time, but could not. Perhaps he was the only one out of all of us who was ever truly happy.

After we buried him in the plot next to my father in Germonds' Cemetery, my mother and Carrick moved to a small cottage on the seacoast in Ireland near where Carrick had been born and where they had visited during their honeymoon. They would remain there the rest of their lives and would eventually die there just three months apart in 2004.

CHAPTER NINETY-FOUR

HEADIN' SOUTH

Early September, 2001
Age 55

Sort of like the lyrics in a Billy Joel song, I moved to Florida, intending to go back to Palm Beach Gardens or Singer Island. I left New City, driving Tom's 1960 Austin Healy 3000 Mark I that he had left for me in his will. Jerry Todd and Poppy Ott and their Tutter friends, along with Penrod, and Frank and Joe Hardy, were in the front seat next to me. I had packed up Beth's enormous photo archive, ready for shipping, and left the boxes with Jim and Karen until I had a forwarding address.

As I left New City for what I thought would be the last time, I headed toward Clarkstown High on Congers Road. It was the start of another school year. I drove by my beloved high school one last time.

There has always been a sense, a very strong sense, that just as before; before we started our lives as adults and we left six carefree years of Clarkstown Junior Senior High School behind, that now, as the end approaches, we would be privileged to return to walk those halls. There would be a phone call from the school, inviting us to return, and early on a Monday morning, all of my classmates, now in our mid-50s would show up to renew those old friendships, retake the daily classes. Miss Hicks would struggle to remind us of what Pythagoros meant about the square of the hypotenuse being equal to the sum of the squares of the other two sides; Mr. D'Innocenzo would struggle to remind us of the importance of the signing of the Magna Carta at Runnymede; Miss Fitch would help us dissect a frog, and a red-faced English Lit. teacher would struggle to help us understand what Petruchio meant in Shakespeare's *The Taming of the Shrew*, when he said to Katherine, "with my tongue in your tail."

We would relive some of those adventures, laugh again, thank all of our wonderful teachers for their selflessness, and listen to the music in wonderment one last time before it was time for us to go on ahead. What fun that would be, knowing what we know now.

That's what I was thinking on my last morning in New City. I drove past Clarkstown High School. The parking lot was filled with laughing kids. It was the Friday after Labor Day, 2001.

Two afternoons later, I pulled into *South of the Border Motel* in South Carolina and took Tom's Vietnam Journal into the room with me. He had told me that day on the deck of the boathouse, in brief sketches, what had happened, his head hanging in a combination of self-loathing and bitterness. I wanted to read the details. Or so I thought. I popped a can of cold beer from the six-pack I had purchased at Pedro's Pantry Convenience store, and settled in.

CHAPTER NINETY-FIVE

MY LUOC MASSACRE
VIETNAM
"THE POET and the PEASANTS"

May, 1968
Age 21

Tom's journals from his days in Vietnam relate scenes of unspeakable horror told almost with a coroner's precision, and thoroughness.

Details of the massacre near *My Luoc* orphanage are difficult to comprehend. The children were scavenging for food, picking through scraps in desperation at a garbage dump at dawn. There were over sixty children involved, living in the orphanage, slowly starving to death, their parents killed by a war that did so much to rend our own country asunder a half a world away.

It was foggy, with almost no visibility. Tom's platoon came upon them by accident just before dawn. To Tom's 1st Lieutenant, they looked like Viet Cong; small, thin, dressed in black pajamas, their child-like faces obscured by their conical straw hats. Tom's lieutenant, under pressure for ever-higher numbers, *"body count,"* told his men to kill them all. Except they weren't Viet Cong.

The 1st Lieutenant didn't bother to take the time to give them a second glance and determine that they were actually children, not the slightly built enemy his company feared. They were alive and they were not Americans, so his orders were to "kill anything that moved. Kill anything that breathed. Get *the body count* up." He turned to Tom as his second in command and gave him the order to start the killing. When Tom hesitated, unsure of the targets, whispering protests, raising the possibility that they might be children, the 1st Lieutenant grabbed his .45 automatic sidearm and held it to Tom's head. He ordered Tom to commence firing or he would personally kill Tom on the spot.

Petrified, Tom intentionally aimed his M16 above the children's heads and fired off a burst. The children ran, screaming. The lieutenant, furious, grabbed Tom by the collar and told him to lower his barrel and begin killing or he would die right then and there.

Tom closed his eyes in silent prayer, prayers we learned together with Father Carrick, and with that same right forefinger that had discovered the magic of Middle C at the Steinway keyboard when he was only four, that same right index finger that lead the march through vonSuppe's, *The Poet and the Peasant,* and later Thelonius Monk, he pulled the trigger, and within ten seconds, thirty children under the age of ten lay dead, shot as they fled, ripped to bloody shreds by Tom's weapon; by Tom's right index finger.

In fear, the other four American soldiers remaining in Tom's platoon quickly killed another ten children. One boy in the platoon from Eau Claire, Wisconsin, refused the order. He stepped toward the Lieutenant who still had his pistol at Tom's temple and Tom's collar in his grip. The Lieutenant turned to look at him and the Wisconsin boy shot his own Lieutenant in the head point blank with his M16. As the 1st Lieutenant fell dying, he dragged Tom down on top of him, discharging the .45 automatic he held in his hand. The second bullet entered Tom's upper thigh and exited, leaving little damage. The first one had nicked his spleen. The wound would be enough to air-lift Tom to the Philippines within hours and eventually back to the States.

The Wisconsin boy, the only other one with a conscience in the group, was shot in the chest with the third .45 caliber bullet from the 1st Lieutenant's handgun that was intended for Tom. The bullet passed up through the nineteen year-old Wisconsin boy's trachea, chin and skull, and he died instantly, trying to help Tom.

The surviving children continued to scream and run in panic. Tom's platoon, now reduced to three still able to fight, confused, frightened, nervously *laughing*, killed twenty more children within seconds. Actual Viet Cong in the area, by now awakened, retaliated, firing back from a tree line across the dump. Tom, bleeding, radioed for aerial assistance. He didn't realize that within minutes the sky would be filled with helicopters. In the melee, the remaining members of Tom's platoon were killed by fleeing VC.

When the slaughter was over and the sun rose and the mist burned off, Tom looked toward the dump and realized he and his men had killed sixty defenseless children in addition to the VC. Another 160 nearby villagers, who had nothing to do with anything, were killed by gunships called in as the dawn broke. A few bursts from an overhead aircraft armed with a "Puff the Magic Dragon," spewed one hundred rounds per second, shredded homes, livestock, and humans into tiny pieces. By then, Tom was the only American survivor on the ground. A helicopter crew picked him up and evacuated him. It had all happened in less than twenty-five minutes.

Although Tom pleaded with his commanding officers afterward, no thorough, truthful, official accounting of the skirmish was reported further up the line of command, except for some perfunctory paperwork to make it look like someone actually cared. From rumor and talk amongst the grunts on the ground, who arrived via helicopter another five minutes later, and possibly the helicopter pilot, the story became legendary, almost mythical, and it was talked about for months before other atrocities overshadowed the lower-level discussions. It was dismissed and forgotten, never made public.

As far as the battle that ruined his life, and caused the death of over two hundred human beings, five of them U.S. soldiers? Tom was forever changed. His own personal My-Lai-Massacre-that-Seymour-Hersch-never-found-out-about? There is no one left to talk about it. It was all so "Viet Nam," so "America."

No one knew about Tom's story, the story of *The Poet and the Peasants* for years except Father Carrick, then Beth, then finally me. Tom had never told them the name of the village, so they could never have told me. When Father Carrick died, the secret was left to die with me alone.

Tom spent thirty-two years eating himself up inside, thirty two years of penance for a country that doesn't even care about what did or did not happen on that day in Vietnam. Why should they? Some got their cut of the billions in war profiteering. Other Americans got to feel patriotic, feel special, despite the costs to all the rest of us who pay every day. What form of humanity have we become? You may not wish to address that question. I already know the answer.

CHAPTER NINETY-SIX

PLEIKU,
VIETNAM

March, 1969
Age 22

I said I wasn't going to tell you my Vietnam story, but now, this little boy from New City must share his own experience.

Music Cue: *Gimme Shelter*.

Of course when Tom told me his story that day on the deck with Father Carrick sitting beside us, I recognized it immediately as the *My Luoc* orphanage massacre. Not all the details, and certainly not with his name attached, but I had heard enough through the rumor mill about that mindless, barbaric slaughter, and a lot of the other stories like it in my daily job in Pleiku. Tom's story, without specific identities revealed or remembered, was the talk of the town. Or, at least the town where I was in Vietnam. I knew of Tom's *My Luoc* story by reputation, and by some few scraps of paperwork, mostly redacted, that had survived almost a full year, that would cross my desk and would eventually come to the attention of my "*special talent.*"

Having a pre-law background, the Army considered me a good

fit for the job I did for over a year. During my initial interview they must have sensed my distraction, my fear, my vulnerability, so as soon as my top secret security clearance sailed through, they put me to work.

I spent every day of my first few weeks in Vietnam in the outside hallways of secured rooms in Pleiku. The 1st Lieutenant would come out with a cardboard box filled with reports and I would stand at a machine and feed the contents of those boxes into the machine and thin strips of paper would come pouring out the other end and tumble into a large plastic garbage can on wheels. The First Lieutenant would stand there to make sure I didn't read the reports, reports shredded like the hundreds of shredded bodies their stories told, before I fed the hungry maw.

When the garbage can was filled, I would take it outside to a yard where a group of privates would scoop the shreds out with pitchforks and put them in one of the fifty-five gallon drums that acted as incinerators and filled the daytime sky with diesel smoke, all under the watchful eyes of my 1st Lieutenant and me.

It took less than a week in Vietnam to conclude who the real enemy was. It was us. We were the enemy. You can put all the lipstick you want to on that pig, but the fact remains, *we were the enemy.*

After a month I was given a promotion and taken behind the closed doors to where a roomful of officers and non-coms were pouring through what I would soon discover were incident reports. Duplicate copies, I assumed, of those already passed on to Washington. I would then pack them in a box and carry them to my replacement at the shredding machine; watch my subordinate do the job I had done; shred and carry the strips outside; watch them go up in flames like the Vietnamese farmers' hooches they were written about. There was a clipboard with a checklist. I was very thorough.

I finally got to read some of the backlog. As the weeks went on and their trust in me grew, I became part of the team that sat at the desks and reviewed the documents to be shredded and burned. There was never any eye contact or conversation in the room.

One day it finally dawned on me what my job was. I was destroying evidence from primary source eyewitnesses. The countless folders, thick with reports, were not duplicates. They were the originals and the only remaining copies, all heavily redacted. At some point it might have become obvious that redaction was not enough. Evidence tampering definitions changed from simple redacting to complete eradication of primary-source witness accounts. The entire reports had to be destroyed.

My job was to cover up, systematically eliminate evidence and testimony, and erase the record of these atrocities, so word would not get back to the States to the press, so they could then tell the public what was really going on in Vietnam. I couldn't work fast enough to keep up, even at assembly line speed. It was a bloodbath of incomprehensible proportions; wholesale slaughter of old people, infants, children, women. And it went on and on.

And who was doing all this slaughter? Nineteen and twenty year-old American boys carrying out obscene orders for a meaningless cause they had somehow been convinced was related to patriotism and protecting our country from an abstract ideology.

The worst part of my job? I was a *collaborator*. I was an *accessory* in the deaths of a million or more civilians committed by my peers. *Body count*. Reports would come in with numbers that didn't add up. Sixty VC killed, four weapons retrieved? Really?

As Tom had said that day on the deck, the all too common PTSD so many of them suffered from in the years that followed was not a result of what they saw. It was the result of *what they did. They knew it was morally wrong and they did it anyway.* Ever since, some of us have been paying the consequences.

I became an accessory after the fact to the murder of what would eventually be verified as two million innocent civilians; women, children, babies, the elderly. I was erasing how they had been murdered in cold blood. I had become an accomplice. Yes,

I had figured out who the enemy in Vietnam was. It was us. By us I mean the United States Military and the people who control our government. For a while it seemed that we killed anything that moved; water buffalo, pigs, chickens, ducks, infants, pregnant women, old men, pre-teen children, innocent farmers in rice paddies. We were saving their country by killing everyone in it.

I was erasing the details and any evidence of any atrocities. I didn't know what I was doing at first. But then the paperwork increased, the evidence mounted, the stories circulated, the rumors hung on, the worst stories passed on like a party game of "telephone," Tom's story being a prominent one; one of the most gruesome ones. Had I been there nine months earlier, if I had taken the time to look closely at the names redacted by thick, black, Magic Marker, I might have seen Tom's name. Instead, I just remembered the details of that report's slaughter passed on through the rumor mill and filled with obscene descriptions. Details that included American soldiers, who had rescued Tom, while wearing the ears of the dead children strung on rawhide necklaces.

Tom's orphanage incident was soon replaced. There were hundreds of other atrocities ready to take its place on the gossip mill. I remembered the details of all of them that I was able to read. I could hardly bring myself to read another one.

I was able to rationalize everything because of my obsession. I really didn't care what was going on there. I just wanted to go home. If I could survive just one more day, it didn't really matter what I was doing in Pleiku. I just wanted to see Beth. My days were filled with images and memories of her, worry about her, imaginings, *can't help it if I wonder what she's doing, tonight, tonight.*

Later, they used me to type and mail letters back to the States. Threatening letters. Letters that told soldiers that if they ever revealed their stories to anyone they would face court-martial and spend the rest of their lives in Leavenworth, all in the interest of national security. I would type for days on end and then once a week a general would come in and sign those threatening letters, and out they would go, no postage stamps required.

I would find out years later one such letter had been sent to a New City boy. Its message was simple. Tom kept it in its original envelope in the back of his journal he left for me. It was dated before I had arrived in Saigon, but it was similar to the hundreds of letters I later typed. I recognized the letterhead, the words of threat, the *feel* of the paper it was typed on. But it had been typed before my arrival by some other poor, nameless, frightened, emotionally numb boy like me.

Two years later, in April of 1971, another Vietnam Veteran, John Kerry, would testify before Congress about the atrocities committed by American soldiers that were so commonplace; about the frequent and flagrant raping of women and young girls; of the cutting off of ears and limbs; of electric shocks administered to the genitals; the poisoning of food; the shooting of livestock and dogs and innocent civilians; all for shits-and-giggles. When he ran for President of the United States, they tried to get him to recant his Congressional testimony, and when he wouldn't, they ruined him; labeled him a fabricator and a traitor. But he didn't lie to Congress. It wasn't just the Americal Division or the Tiger Force who went on killing sprees, it was all of us.

As for me, I've spent over thirty years dwelling on what sent me there in the first place. Trying to forget the unimaginable body count numbers, incident reports, pregnant women, old men and women and young children slaughtered, while citizens of the United States allowed themselves to ignore it, fearful of being called unpatriotic. Did we "make the world safe for democracy?" Did we make Americans safer? Did we protect our own future?

Compartmentalizing, I think they call it. Denial.

I closed the journal and stepped outside onto the sidewalk at *South of the Border* and into the dusk, another beer in my hand.

In the distance, traffic on I-95 never stopped and two young, pre-teen brothers were twirling sparklers and throwing lady-finger firecrackers in the parking lot, laughing in delight as their father looked on, a broad smile of wonderment on his face, as if asking, *what will become of my boys?*

EPILOGUE

THE DUTCH GARDEN
NEW CITY

Fall, 2006
Age 60

> *Your name and mine inside a heart upon a wall*
> *They find a way to haunt me, though they're so small.*
>
> Walk Away, Renee
> The Left Banke

So, "Ladies and Germs," as Uncle Miltie used to say, that was my life. I've been living in North Florida for the past few years, but my life has really been over for quite some time.

By 2006 I had retired to a house on the Ichetucknee River, near Branford, Florida. After leaving New City after Labor Day Weekend in 2001, enroute to Palm Beach Gardens, I detoured to the University of Florida to look up some old friends and drive by the old Craftsman house Beth and I had shared in Gainesville. Later that week I spent a lot of time tubing down the Ichetucknee. I had forgotten how beautiful it was and decided to stick around the neighborhood. I was on the river by 8am on the morning of 9/11 and did not hear about the events of that morning until four hours after the fact. The contrast between the isolated, prehistoric river, and the abrupt, irrevocable change in the world, was startling. I was thrust out of a prehistoric world and into a *Brave New World.*

I never got as far as my original Florida destination, Palm Beach Gardens, to look up my old friend, Rodney. After fixing up a stilt-house on the riverfront where The Ichetucknee joins with the Santa Fe and the Suwannee in the Three Rivers area, I spent my days tubing the river and hanging from a hammock suspended between the stilts, re-reading Hardy Boys and Jerry Todd novels. Tutter was still the same. Tutter will always be the same if my father has anything to do with it.

When I left New City, I had already come to a conclusion: I had lived the only life I was going to live, and now it was over. My early life had been perfect. My later life had consisted of my daily care of my brother and my friendship with Tom and my love for Beth. They were all gone now. There would not be much else in my life worth noting. The rest was all formality. Florida is "God's Waiting Room," and I was on line with hordes of others, except I didn't believe in God. My expectations for the upcoming years were low. Florida is a state filled with people looking toward the end with a sense of relief that it will all soon be over. Life is simply too hard.

As Florida novelist Marjorie Kinnan Rawlings said, "It's not death that kills us, it's *life.*"

In mid-October in the fall of 2006, six years after Beth was murdered, after Marvin had committed the ultimate arson, after Calvin had drawn his last fragile bird and drawn his last fragile breath, after my mother had married Carrick and moved to Ireland, after Tom had died at his Steinway keyboard, after Francis had died peacefully in his sleep on the veranda at Dove Cottage with Tom's glove in his lap, and after I had moved to Florida, I came back home to New City and made my last visit to the Dutch Garden. Jimmy had called to tell me what was going on and why I needed to come home right away. Something was happening to the Dutch Garden.

In the past, I had always returned to New City because of Francis. Now, Francis was gone and so was just about everything else.

The day was filled with mixed emotions.

Jimmy picked me up at Newark airport late on a Tuesday night and drove me to his house. Before dawn the next morning, his wife, Karen, made us a gourmet breakfast and he offered to drive me downtown. I declined, told them it was a trip I had to take alone. He understood. I said farewell to my loyal friends. We had all spent so much time together.

What I discovered on my journey is that it's no longer my New City as it had been for so many years. Who does it belong to now? I don't know. It's as if someone had come through and rounded up all the families and shipped them out of town and replaced them with strangers like in a Ray Bradbury short story, and then bulldozed the buildings and replaced them; flattened the hills and valleys; straightened all the curves in the road; homogenized the landscape until everything had no distinction, was not recognizable anymore. It was just another suburban sprawl without any distinguishing features. Nothing seemed to be mine anymore, like I had once felt for so long.

I walked south on Little Tor Road to Germonds' Cemetery and spent an hour there in the autumn chill with my father and brother, my back leaned up against the tombstone they shared in our ancestral family's plot; the plot where someday I hoped to be laid to rest. Just like the headstones in Edgar Lee Masters' *Spoon River Anthology*, each headstone told a life's story.

After an hour of what can only be described as apologizing to my father and brother for not making something more of myself, and being a failure despite their efforts, I walked back Little Tor Road to the Demarest Kill County Park parking lot off New Hempstead Road. From the parking lot looking south, a trail takes you into the new park. I walked through the woods to Greenberg's Pond. Nowadays you can do that without fear of being chased by a shot-gun toting guard with a German Shepherd on a leash, like when we were kids.

In the pond, boulders still rise above the surface of the leaf-strewn water and a few mallards float like decoys in the breeze and there is the unmistakable smell of autumn that I had missed so much. The scent hangs in the air. Chlorophyll, exhausted now from a long summer of work converting carbon dioxide to oxygen, was giving way to reds and yellows and ochers, purples and oranges.

A light drizzle began to fall on this autumn morning as I followed the path and walked to the south side of the pond, then followed the stream beneath the spillway. The first cold bite of autumn air rushed up my nose and embraced my cheeks.

I followed the stream south toward the fresh water spring and the drainage pipe that had provided our early adventures together. Above, homes spread across the top of the curved ridge line, their backyards filled with weeping willows standing guard. The leaves on the Chinese Maples were turning from crimson to black-red like dried blood.

I took a quick detour to the tiny cemetery hiding in the woods. The O.B.W. headstone was still there. I thought of Beth's mother as I knew she had on our trips here. I then headed north toward the jut of man-made stone walls and earthen dams that crisscross the landscape, and then down to the remains of the second-tier dam.

High above, squirrels ran along the tree-branch highways. The leaves were ablaze in crimson and orange and yellow, their damp smell a sweet clean spicy smell tinged with chill; oak, maple, poplar, pine, each competing for your attention with their own distinct fragrance. With a light breeze, hundreds of leaves whirly-birded to the wood's floor. I tried to split one and paste it on the tip of my nose, but the sap-glue had dried out.

A few yards east I saw Beth's name and mine scratched into the remaining, derelict sandstone wall on the second-tier mill-pond dam. I had almost forgotten about the etchings and the dates that followed. But I can't forget anything, can I? I ran my fingers across the moss-covered boulder. What a day that had been when we carved it in 1961, that Halloween weekend after our first kiss.

In the days that followed after Gate Night, we would start a ritual that lasted for what I thought was seven years. On our walk to the boathouse, as we passed the sandstone and earthen dam, Beth pulled a pen knife from her pocket, opened it, and cut some of the vines that were covering the face of one of the flat rocks close to the ground. There, she etched a small heart into the sandstone and our initials inside the heart. Underneath, she wrote, 10/61. An arrow through the heart finished the scraping.

"Every year we'll come back and I'll do another one to celebrate our anniversary. Deal?"

"Deal."

So we would, for a few years at least. Halloween, 1962 brought us back to the sandstone block near the foot of the boathouse. A year had passed since we had first kissed, and Beth again took out her pen knife and did the honors.

On that second visit, I noticed that there was plenty of space on the block to carve many hearts over many years. I was looking forward to it.

Halloween, 1963, was right in the middle of our victorious football season. I was concentrating on football; Beth and Tom on *The Man Who Came to Dinner.* But Beth and I took the time for another carving. *Her name and mine, inside a heart, upon a wall.* How long had it been there before the songwriter stole the idea from Beth and me, because that is surely what happened?

Even when away at Gainesville, when we came home, we would always find time to go back with the point of the knife blade from her father. One of our first stops while in New City for Christmas Break that first year was to continue our tradition with HEART '64. We would repeat the scrapings until our last year of college. The scratchings on the wall and the dates etched in my mind did not run into one another. My fingertips remembered each distinctive day; what we were wearing, what we said, where we had walked from, where we went afterward. When was it scratched in. How many seasons had it weathered?

Over the next two years, we would go there whenever we were back home. HEART '66 was the last one we carved together.

We never made it there in the fall of 1967, but on that fateful day in 1968, I thought about walking past the dam later, after we would be leaving Tom's, to carve HEART '67 and HEART '68. By then, there would be eight hearts. I even had a pocketknife from home that I had brought with me in anticipation, but it never happened.

But on this day in 2006 when I pulled the vines away I was shocked to find something I never expected.

HEART '67, dated 10/31/68. A catch-up etching.

HEART '68 from Halloween of that year, also dated 10/31/68. Did she do it before or after the confrontation? Halloween? The day before I called, after my self-imposed two week wait to contact her? While she was waiting? Was she alone?

Buried behind more vines, HEART '69, dated 10/69, and finally HEART '70, the last one, dated 10/70. They were done while I was in Vietnam.

By June of 1971, she had met Rainer, married him, and our hearts carved on the wall stopped. What did it all mean? Had it been done by some kids as a prank? No. I recognized her handwriting, the imprimatur of her father's pen knife told the truth. But why had she done it?

Across the phantom mill pond was Tom's boathouse, framed in leaf boughs, quiet on this day. I could have been hiking through the Adirondacks from the boathouse's appearance. I stood below and looked up to the deck where that meeting had taken place with Tom and Father Carrick six years earlier. I reflected on all the times on that deck; wrestling the Steinway inside; snuggling with Beth on the deck glider; listening to Tom practice hour after hour, day after day; and that last day when Tom and I peed over the railing for the 5,281st time. I thought of all he said that day and the prescience contained in his words. I climbed the stairs to the deck and peered in the cobwebbed window. It was empty inside.

I'd had almost six years to reflect on what he'd said toward the end of the conversation and what I'd later read in his journal. Tom was right, of course, like he usually was. We weren't warriors and we weren't heroes, and we weren't brave and we weren't courageous. Those are just empty, diabolical words to hide lies and to make fools believe, rationalize, feel good about what we were doing; about what we did. All the basic training, all the tours of duty, all the flag waving and marching band music and campaign ribbons and sharpshooter patches and medals in the world are not going to change the facts; not going to make us feel good about killing innocent civilians. Our actions were based on fear.

The facts are, we were, indeed, Howdy Doody Boys. We grew up in the Peanut Gallery, watching and laughing and enthralled by an ever-smiling marionette dangling from some strings. You don't like that term? Okay, we were Hopalong Cassidy Boys or Roy Rogers Boys or Yancy Derringer Boys or Davy Crockett Boys. Are you getting the picture? We were just little kids watching Sky King and East Side Kids' movies, forced, cajoled, shamed, guilt-tripped into a great evil endeavor, for that's surely what it was. The war didn't change the boys that we were into men. The war changed the boys that we were into *damaged boys*; boys never allowed to grow up; boys filled with a lifetime of bitterness and resentment; filled with anger and hopelessness and confusion;

filled with a constant struggle to get by. Boys unable or unwilling to understand, to cope with or accept the enormity of the deceit that had been perpetrated upon them. We cannot accept the magnitude of it all, so it's easier to be in denial; make believe it never happened. Get enraged and pick fights with doubters. Shoot the messengers. Be surprised when people show up to jeer at our homecomings. It simply cannot be true. We deny, even though we are looking it in the eyes.

Some made it back and got on with their lives; or they pretended to get on with their lives because they were too proud to admit they'd been duped, or unwilling to ask for help. Others were unable to get on with their lives and were ignored by their country.

Still others could not accept the fact that they were accomplices in the cold blooded murder of two million innocent civilians. Who killed them? Tom and our classmates killed them, and then I covered it up. Scapegoats and patsies. It was us. We wanted to be war heroes like our dads before us, so we were easy to persuade. We were all willing, susceptible victims of an elaborate hoax.

Tom was right about something else as well, as melodramatic as it may sound. I really never left Vietnam either. There is no *Farewell to Arms*. It never leaves. When we do leave we're going straight to hell.

Back down at the water's edge, the Demarest Kill, a living, breathing entity that gets along just fine without my daily monitoring that it had benefitted from during my boyhood, sweeps downstream and disappears behind the denseness of the leaf canopy shroud. From the looks of the flow, it had been a dry autumn so far. The water was slow, completely different than after a spring thaw or a wet summer, or after a heavy rain, when the showers of autumn fill the headwaters. Every season it sounds different, but still the same.

I walked to the confluence of the three streams, where the water from Greenberg's joins the flow from the Demarest Kill and the tributary from behind my old house. My shoes squished out water from The Kill. If I had the strength and energy I could have joined Beth's tributary on South Mountain, but I was too tired now. Just as our streams had converged, so had our lives, and now everything was slowing down.

Just as my grandfather had settled on that property because of a fire in 1904 and Tom's grandparents had settled there as a result of enormous success in the 1930s and Beth's father had settled there as a result of his need for a studio in seclusion in a beautiful area, so had our lives eventually converged. Could our predecessors ever have imagined the consequences of their choices to live alongside the Demarest Kill?

In the distance I could hear the heavy equipment from the Highway Department Garage starting up in the morning stillness, behind the new Sheriff's Department and County Jail; the beep of the Highway Department's front-end loader backing up, stockpiling sand for the snow that would fall on the streets in another month or so.

The new courthouse is where it is today because the Eberlings sold them the land after their shoe factories burned down. More arson? All of the land where the courthouse and Highway Department, Sheriff's Department, and Greenberg's was owned by those family patriarchs. The newest Rockland County Courthouse has replaced the old jail; a new giant forever on the hill to overlook the parking lot.

Behind the new courthouse annex I made my way across the Demarest Kill on the new wooden footbridge. From the bridge you can look south and see giant boulders and sandbars dividing the stream; oval rocks worn smooth by the rush of water nonstop since the glaciers receded; sandstone ground into sand by the currents in the oxbows. I recognized those rocks, now more moss-covered, but unmoved in almost sixty years, maybe a thousand years. It never stops, it's constant.

The tree trunks were black from the morning's light rain, the leaves, now tired from their task of oxygenating the air, hung limply on the brittle branches. They kept the damp smell from fading.

All around was a silence disappearing, as the town awoke and the flow of traffic on Main Street and the New Rte. 304 and New Hempstead Hill caused an endless hiss of wet tires.

At the top of the rise above the bridge, I approached the tea house from the rear; *The Tea House of the. . . October Moon.* The tea house of the first kiss. I stood on the steps and looked south. Most of what I had remembered had been bulldozed. It made me heartbroken, but hopeful. The original plan by Mowbray-Clarke in 1933 had been much more elaborate, ambitious, than what was eventually done. In addition to the Dutch Garden, in 1933 she had also planned a Wild Garden, an Alpine Garden on the eastern slope of the Kill, and a picnic grove where the baseball field once was and where the annex parking lot is now. I don't know what happened. I asked my father once why she stopped, but he didn't know.

As I looked south from the steps, I wondered, do boys still play here anymore? Is it still an integral theater in the lives of those who grow up in New City, or has the outside world encroached too heavily on their hearts and minds to allow them the freedom to explore its banks? Have video games in virtual worlds taken the place of these actual realms of solace?

I wanted to go back to the Dutch Garden that day to find the boy who accompanied his mother and brother on Girl Scout meetings, who ran through flowers and down the gravel footpaths with joy in his heart. The boy who fell in love with the girl of his dreams in the years before 1961 and sealed it with a kiss on the night before Halloween that year, and later said his final goodbyes to the only woman he ever loved while she was still alive in the gazebo, and again, one final time, the very next morning, as her body lay face down in the stream in a final moment of indignity.

Whatever happened to that little girl I loved? Whatever happened to the little boy I was? Their footsteps in the gravel are still echoing out in space somewhere, sounds made with excitement in the heart so many years ago.

What if I had been the one and it wasn't Marvin? *What if I had been the one?* What if during the course of our discussion that final night in the gazebo, I had reached out to Beth's arm to try to make her listen to reason, to listen to what I had wanted to say for so long? What if she had pulled away and I had only grabbed her wrist even tighter? What if she had swung out to push me away, pleading with me to let her go, starting to scream loud enough to be heard on Main Street, and I had swung back punching her in the face and in the struggle she had fallen off the brick terrace of the gazebo, dropping six feet, landing on her skull, snapping her neck? What if I had jumped down to see if she were all right, realized she was dead, and then had done the unspeakable before taking her clothes, pushing her down the embankment to the stream bed and racing for home? Could I have done that? Could my obsession for her have led me to commit horrible crimes in my desperation? I've asked myself that a million times.

Maybe Tom suspected me all along, and wanted to protect me and told the investigators Beth had come to his house when in fact she had never made it there because I killed her on the way? Or maybe I just ambushed her upon her return from Tom's, lying in wait in the darkness until she came through the gazebo on her way back to the parking lot.

Could I have approached her from behind where she wouldn't have even known who it was, and in a moment of anger and passion after years, decades of frustration and hopelessness, had punched her, snapped her neck, ripped her clothes off and taken her for the last time before she left the country forever, leaving me behind?

Could I have made up Calvin's story knowing he was dying

in prison and made up Marvin's confession before catching him by surprise in his own barn, overpowering him, staging the arson to cover up my own murder of Beth, blaming it on a likely suspect, as the police and even Tom had suspected me of doing? Could I have fabricated such a story? Could I have done all of that and then covered my tracks? I had become an expert at covering tracks.

The answer is *maybe*. Maybe, in one moment of a loss of all control, knowing I couldn't live without her any longer, I'm the one who did all of those things to Beth. *I'm the one who did it.* And then through some psychiatric sleight-of-hand, forgot, or blocked it all out through some convenient amnesia, and convinced myself and others that it was Marvin after all, because didn't he fit the profile?

But then I realized, of course, that it could not have been me. As frustrated as I was, as much as I wanted to hold her one last time, I could never do that. Why? The answer is simple. Because of my mother and Francis. I wouldn't have been doing that to just Beth. I would have been doing that to my mother and Francis. Although possibly quite capable of doing it myself, both emotionally and physically, because of them, I knew that I could never do that, because of whatever it is in this life that forbids us, prevents us from making decisions like that.

The DNA tests had come back. It was Marvin. Nevertheless, I was responsible. I was responsible for her being there at that time and place.

The hexagonal gazebo known to old-timers as "the summer house," survived the bulldozer's blade, the floor still a hatch-work of herringbone-placed bricks. Were there Chesterfields hidden in the eaves of the roof beams? No, only spider webs, with morning daylight back-lighting, illuminating the fragile, wispy hairs.

There was a stillness to the soft drizzle as I stood in the gazebo at the top of the hill and looked around. Trees had fallen across the switchbacks, and falling acorns now popped on the terracotta roof tiles, shaped to resemble slate.

In the days before Jimmy's recent call and my arrival in that autumn of 2006, bulldozers had raked through the Dutch Garden plowing to the side the remains of the brick latticework. When I turned south from the gazebo I noticed there was a construction trailer in a parking lot behind Dr. Feldman's old offices.

Near that construction trailer on the south end of the park, orange polyester flags on stakes were stacked all around. Re-bar sticking out of the new footers were capped with plastic tops and pink fluorescent plastic ribbon warning others away. Apparently, the first time the brick walls were built in 1933, there were no sufficient footers poured, and so with every freeze and thaw, with every shift of ground, as the earth trembled and groaned in pain, the mortar had loosened and the bricks tumbled from their nesting place.

The light rain had become more persistent, and the construction crew was now huddled under a small tarpaulin to the south of the pergola waiting for it to stop.

The foreman, having watched my plodding through the rubble stepped forward and yelled out. "The park's closed."

"Yes, I know."

I wondered, why must I be so obsessive in my love for Beth? Why not just move on and enjoy the love from a wonderful woman like Delores who tried for over twenty years to put a smile on my face and then left when she concluded her efforts were futile?

What if Beth and I had married? Would it have made my life different, or would I have spent those years wasted on jealousy, self-doubt? Would we have settled into the bland domesticity of a lawyer and his wife? From Beth's eventual accomplishments, it would seem doubtful.

Would she have pursued and excelled in her photography, her art work, like she had done while living with Rainer?

As for her philanthropy, I probably would not have been able to keep up. Would we have adopted children? When you get right down to it, I would have done anything she wanted. The question is, would life with me have bored her? Did she need the resources of someone like Rainer to realize her true dreams? Was it in the final analysis better for her that she had married Rainer? As much as I hate to admit it, the answer is that probably up to a point, yes. She was happy traveling the world, exploring new horizons, helping illiterate children, providing clean water to entire villages, rescuing an adopted daughter from who knows what horrors. Could she have done all that married to me? No, I would have been a restraining factor to all that with my limited resources. So in some way can I be happy for her for at least that? Is there any solace in that at all? I'm trying.

And, now as lights-out approaches, what will my final moments of thought contain? Will I remember my years as a brother to Francis? Of the love he gave me? The kindnesses of my mother? The mute stoicism of my father walking behind my grandfather as he hoed row upon row of vegetables? His long nights of walking in an attempt to erase the past? Or would my final moments of thought be of Beth? The first smile in the fifth grade, the first kiss in the tenth grade, the first intimacy in the twelfth grade?

My greatest horror that will remain forever unanswered was that since Marvin had approached her from behind that night, she never knew exactly who it was, and might have suspected it was me who was brutalizing her during a moment of frustration and rage. Did she really cry out my name, during what Jimmy called "a slow painful death"? Marvin had told me she called out my name. Was he telling the truth, or was it just some sadistic taunt? Was she crying out to me to beg me not to kill her? Or to come to her rescue? That she would take me back? Was she remembering the tender moments that had characterized our love for one another? Only Marvin could have answered that question. On this very spot where I was now standing, as she was slowly watching the world fade away, *raging against the dying of the light,* in the hands of a monster, did she give even a second's thought to me? And to our glorious days together?

I edged my way down the hillside. Above, crows were cawing as if afraid of what would lie in the days ahead.

On the bank, as Tom had promised, a stone footpath led across the stream to a plaque in the hillside where Beth's body had been discarded. I bent over to read the inscription:

In loving memory of my friend,
BETH VonBRONK
who lived and died on the Demarest Kill
1946-2000

I reached into my hip pocket and pulled out a worn piece of notebook paper, one of the few I saved from my eighteen-month golf course exile in South Florida after two years in Vietnam.

A clumsy attempt at a poem, I wrote it one night in a dope-filled haze. It was an unsuccessful attempt to forget.

Don't want to remember
Just tryin' to forget.
I know I'll be there, someday,
but I'm nowhere near there yet.

I put away the albums
Couldn't get past the very first song,
Trying to erase our music
Didn't think it'd take this long.

Our pictures are in boxes,
Stored on the shelf for now.
Don't wanna think of that smile of yours,
But I just don't know how.

I want to turn my back on us
and wash away all the years.
Just go somewhere new and strange,
Slow down and shift the gears.

But I don't think it's gonna happen.
At least not any time soon.
If I could just get part-way there,
Even once in a very blue moon.

Cause then I could get on with things
and start to heal my heart.
But I can't even get you out of my mind
and that's the hardest part.

That day you said goodbye to me
I thought my life was through.
But since that time I've thought a lot
And it's time to start anew.

So forgive me if I don't look back,
I just can't stand the pain.
There aren't too many summers left,
to play out in the rain.

Gimme another autumn or two,
to walk my woods and dream,
To watch the leaves turn color and fall,
to watch the sunset gleam.

To stand in snowy woods again
and take in winter skies
And wait by mending walls and heal
Until my spirit flies.

With eyes that burn but somehow see,
Through pathless wood and stinging branch,
I'll keep walking forward toward my home,
Accept the fact there is no chance.

What we two had was something,
My half-life once made whole,
You took me in and gave me love
Gave shelter from the cold.

But it's over now, you told me,
Get on with things, you said,
So I'll take your advice and walk away
and try to keep my head.

I'll try to forget the old times,
I'll try to lose the blues
I'll try to take one step at a time,
but I've worn out both my shoes.

Forever is a long, long time,
But that's how long it takes,
To forget the past and start anew
before my poor heart breaks.

So don't expect to hear from me,
I don't want to be your friend.
I've got to go back home for now
and let my spirit mend.

Someday when we're much older
If our paths should somehow cross.
I'll look away, hope you don't see,
And try to forget my loss.

But if the stars should align again
Through some strange calculus of time
And the world starts spinning back to then
To the days which were sublime,

I'll reach back my hand to hold you
Like when we met at first.
You pulled me to your shoulder
And made my poor heart burst.

By then I'll try to be happy,
It won't take someone new.
It will only take what's left of life
To not remember you.

I folded the poem one last time, the only copy, and placed it beneath a flat rock in the water where I had last touched Beth's face.

Back on top I walked to the edge of a gash the bulldozer had made in the ground.

Sticking up from the mud was a fragment of the original brick lattice wall. I picked it up and put it in my pocket. I walked back up the gravel path and sat on the steps of the tea house where Beth and I had first kissed and now felt the cold of the previous night trapped in the bricks seeping through my wet corduroys.

When I could take no more, I turned and walked back toward Main Street. My ex-town was coming alive. I considered going across the street to grab a morning coffee, but then I would have to stand at the cash register where I had seen Beth and Alison that Christmas Season morning and I didn't want to do that.

At the WWII monument on the South lawn I paused briefly to touch my father's name embossed on the bronze plate one last time before leaving behind my Beth and leaving behind my New City.

As I pull my fingertips away from the embossed bronze letters of my father's name on the monument and walk out of frame, the camera pulls back in a fluid Point-of-View move to reveal the rain has stopped and the courthouse is bathed in bright autumn morning sunshine and we hear *September Song* as sung first by Lotte Lenya and then Walter Huston, the actor the song was written for by Lenya's husband, Kurt Weill, and New City resident, Maxwell Anderson. The camera holds for just a beat before it dollies its way forward, retracing my footsteps to the brick path to the tea house and there it sweeps past the DUTCH GARDEN plaque filling most of the screen before panning first left, then right, moving into the tea house and then the camera heads south through the brick archway, where it reveals in the foreground Beth (aged fifteen) and myself (fifteen) as we sit on the steps and then stand for a first kiss and as we do, the camera floats between us on its tracking shot south through the garden, down the gravel path bordered by the hens-and-chicks and the deep blue morning glories, and the daffodils and the pansies and the peony buds crawling with ants and the arborvitae topiary and yes, the heliotrope, and there a twelve year-old Tom hands a bouquet of same to a twelve year-old Beth and she laughs as she gets his joke. The camera floats past the sundial and up to the opening of the pergola and down to the hexagonal gazebo where the lens peers due west through the now afternoon sunsprays dappling the autumn-colored leaves, and then finally tips slowly down toward the stream, and then as if changing its mind before revealing what's below in the stream, just out of the bottom of the frame, it tips back up to the horizon, where the sun sets in behind the leaves now in golden silhouette and we hear the sounds of scurrying squirrels and watery ripples and we can see only in the right-and-left extremities of the ultra-wide angle lens, but not the bottom center of the lens, the lazy, endless flow of The Demarest Kill.

THE END

AUTHOR'S AFTERWARD

to
DEMAREST KILL

Summer, 2016
Age 70

Readers who are looking for the real New City, New York, on these pages are apt to be disappointed.

What I've tried to capture here is the geography and spirit of the New City of my youth, and the youth of those of the five generations of the Eberling family who first arrived there in 1857, lived on a farm where New City Park now is, and later moved to another farm on the hilltop overlooking the County Courthouse.

My New City as depicted on these pages is a perfect, highly idealized, set-piece. I lived there during the Post-WW II years, a perfect moment in history, with perfect parents and grandparents, sister Bonnie and brother Ray, and cousins, perfect friends, and perfect days. Has anyone else spent as many days wandering these woods and hills and fields, the streams and lakes, as I have? If so, I would love to talk to you. We can share obsessions.

When I was leaving New City in the summer of 1964 to move to The University of Florida after graduating from Clarkstown

High School, I climbed High Tor and looked southward. I realized every significant event of my life had occurred in that valley within the purview of my outstretched arms. I was leaving the home of my childhood and my ancestors, and although I didn't realize it at the time, except for brief visits, I was never to move back.

Over the next fifty years, as a documentary filmmaker, I traveled to many parts of the world, and explored the far corners of Florida extensively. But my heart and soul have never really left New City, that little house on Main Street, and my days wading The Demarest Kill.

My brother, Ray, and I have made several attempts to compile a series of essays under the title, *A New City Boyhood*. I came to the conclusion that few readers would be interested in such a book. After being inspired by novelists such as Robert McGammon in *A Boy's Life*, and Stephen King in *Hearts in Atlantis*, I realized that if I wanted anyone to read about my hometown New City, I would probably have to put it in the form of a mystery novel.

For those readers who wonder if this story is autobiographical, the answer is both yes and no. It is autobiographical in the sense of real places and historical events. It is autobiographical in its sense-memory. It is autobiographical in light of the fact that one day I locked my younger brother, Ray, in an abandoned ice box in our barn and walked away and forgot he was trapped in there. My cousin, who just happened to walk by a short time later, heard my brother yelling and pounding and saved his life. I've lived the rest of my life with knowledge that my own carelessness and selfish distraction almost killed my brother. It's autobiographical in the sense that when I left New City and my friends behind to attend the University of Florida, it was a gut-wrenching experience for me, ripping out my heart and soul.

As I write this in the spring of 2016, I understand it may be impossible for some readers to imagine such a time of innocence and simplicity. What has become of our country, even in the years leading up to 9/11, is enough to make anyone mourn. But such a place really did exist.

The fall of 1963 changed all that perfection. It started in a blaze of autumn leaves and the exhilaration of a victorious, undefeated football season for the Clarkstown Rams. We were at the pinnacle of our youth, falling in love, invincible, invulnerable, "studyin' hard and hopin' to pass," and immeasurably happy. It ended in changes that lurched us about in a whiplash of events that would forever alter our lives; the JFK assassination, the arrival of The Beatles, and the escalation of the war in Vietnam. We started our senior year as innocent, care-free, babes-in-the-woods and some of us ended it shell-shocked and adrift and frightened. We didn't slowly evolve out of our New City childhoods and land safely on the far shore. Those days came to a screeching, lurching halt when we were yanked abruptly out of paradise by the convergence of history and fate.

As for the orphanage massacre in Vietnam described on these pages, it is inspired by a true event related to me by a young U.S. Army veteran who had lived it and came home to New City, broken by it for the remainder of his life. He described it to me in detail, including the threatening letter he received when he arrived home. Although I will not identify him or relate to you all he said to me during our conversation, what he conveyed without speaking was even more disturbing than what he said. He was a small-town boy who refused direct orders to commit the unspeakable. For those of you who doubt the commonplace nature of the atrocities we committed over there, I refer you to *Kill Anything That Moves*, by Nick Turse and *The War Behind Me: Vietnam Veterans Confront the Truth about U.S. War Crimes*, by Deborah Nelson.

It should be understood that I do not place the blame for what my peers did over there on their shoulders. They were either forced to go over there against their will or lied into believing it was the patriotic thing to do. It is the Lyndon Johnsons, Robert

McNamaras, William Westmorelands, Henry Kissingers, Richard Nixons of the world who led us down that path of inhumane evil. They are the ones responsible for the deaths of an estimated two million innocent civilians at the hands of my peers.

In response to the Thomas Wolfe assurance that "You can't go home again," Brother Ray sums it up, "I don't want to go back to a *place*. I want to go back to a *place in time*."

And so it is with my New City. I have often considered moving back. Could I be happy there with all the changes? Now that most of the people I loved so dearly have either passed away or moved on, could I ever really find what I was looking for? Or would I be overcome with heartbreak? Perhaps it is just better to revisit when the leaves of the sugar maples turn red and yellow, the October sky is a brilliant blue, and I can take my shoes off and wade aimlessly, while listening to the rustle of my Demarest Kill as it flows northward around my bare feet.

Frank Eberling
Jupiter, Florida
Spring, 2016

ACKNOWLEDGEMENTS:

To my grandparents and my parents, aunts, uncles, and cousins, who brought me up in a highly idealized fantasy world, filled with love, intellectual curiosity, great literary works, and family traditions. My parents, recovering from their own wartime experiences, taught me a love of reading, a love of piano music, a love of the typewriter keyboard, a love of still photography, and a love for a special place in a special time.

To my older sister, Bonnie Eberling Dilts, a piano prodigy from the age of five, she filled our days at home with her playing of classical music and was my childhood idol. She taught this awkward, extremely shy, younger brother, how to dance so I could ask the girls at the junior high dances.

To my younger brother, Lt. Col. Raymond Eberling, USAF, Retired, for his encyclopedic, photographic memory of our New City childhood. For his forgiveness of the Kelvinator incident. The three of us made our first film together in 1962 and we have made a feature film since. For his review and input of this novel's drafts. And for being a good brother.

For Karen and Jim Damiani for their lifelong friendship, hospitality, lodging, and gourmet meals during my frequent visits and writing stints in New City. They also offered insights into the novel.

For my childhood friends, some of whom I have known for almost seventy years, Charles Pape, Tim Blauvelt, Pat and Bob Damiani, Richard Liebowitz, Willie Forlow, George Feldman, and the rest of us who spent our childhoods wading the Demarest Kill.

For my high school friends, Vincent Burns, Ken Conners, Ken Barkin, Simon "Rocky" Levinson, Bob Raspanti, Richard Connolly, Michael Talaska, and Tore Heskestad. It was Tore who allowed me to film his comedies that brought laughter to our friends and turned me into a filmmaker.

For our two beloved brothers, Bob Doscher and Erich Goerditz, who found this world too difficult and painful a place in which to survive, and who have gone on ahead. For the girls in the CCHS Classes of '63,'64,'65. I was madly in love with every one of you.

For the women in my life who have held me and given me joy and comfort and guidance and laughter in times of need.

For our inspiring teachers in the Clarkstown School System, Mrs. Seward, Mrs. Barrett, Miss Copeland, Miss Knopczyk, Cornelius "Pete" Dennehy, Arthur Righetti, Bill Morrow, Betty Hicks, Mrs. Marks, Mrs. Korn, Donald Grider, Joe D'Innocenzo, and dozens of others who gave us their best, while demanding the best from all of us.

For my cousin, Bruce Rogers, who spent hundreds of hours editing this third edition and cleaned up dozens of typos.

For all the New City residents who made growing up in that era such a special, memorable place.

For my wife of over forty years, Sammy, for her patience with my insanity and her literary critiques.

And finally, for our beloved son, Frank Henry Eberling IV. May you learn all of our family's history to understand from whence you came, and someday take another opportunity to return to New City as a sixth generation Eberling, to wade with me in my Demarest Kill.

KEEP READING
for the opening chapter of
Frank Eberling's

ensueño

a story of Palm Beach, told in the noir tradition,
now available at www.amazon.com.

When a beautiful woman climbs aboard Jimmy Phipps' 40-foot sailboat one night and tells him, "I know who killed your wife," Jimmy's long journey into the dark past begins. The unimaginable truths he discovers force him to confront a world of deceit and betrayal that bring him to the breaking point, and long for simpler times.

PALM BEACH.....
Balmy breezes, sunny days,
tropical nights, exotic women,
pristine beaches,
riches beyond belief.

A world so far removed from the
realities of life,
it's almost like...
...a dream.

ensueño

a novel by

FRANK EBERLING

*"The genesis of all art is the pursuit
of the irrecoverable"*
John Fowles

CHAPTER 1

I sit, typing, filling up a canary yellow second-sheet with my story. The words flow from me and spill onto the page as effort-lessly as if I had taken a razor and sliced the veins in my wrists and allowed the blood to flow onto the keys.

As I type in the darkened room, I feel his hand fall upon my shoulder. It is a touch of comfort, approval, love perhaps. He keeps his hand on my shoulder for a moment, then taps his cupped fingers twice, slowly, and walks away.

I finish the sentence on the page before I turn. But, by then he is gone. I walk to the door and as I step over the threshold he disappears into the darkness before I can call his name. I am too late. I am too late.

Then like a drowning victim filled with gasses, I ever-so-slowly rise to the surface and awaken from my dream.

JUNE 20, 1986:

The full moon in June cast a long shadow on Lake Worth as it rose over the Flagler Museum on the Island of Palm Beach. From across the water on the West Palm Beach side of the Intracoastal, I lay aboard my forty-foot Morgan sailboat, half dozing from my dream. There was not a breeze in the air, and as I stared dreamily over the water toward that mysterious, palm-laden island paradise, I kept waiting for the familiar lapping sound of the water against my boat's wooden hull. But the sound wasn't there. The water was as flat and still as a table top. As black and motionless as death.

I had been thinking a lot about death lately. How it comes so unexpectedly and leaves you with such mixed feelings: sorrow, regret, an empty longing than can never be filled; pain, and sometimes, even relief. At least those were the feelings I had felt about my late wife, Nikki: dead at the age of thirty.

I was trying not to think of the events of the last two months: all the changes I had gone through; the emotional turmoil, the "going through the motions" of work at school; ignoring my students and waiting for the school day to end.

Trying to forget about those Spring days was not possible, even now that it was early Summer and school was out and I had nothing to do but sit on my sailboat in the almost empty downtown marina and decide what to do with my life.

Suddenly coming into a lot of money is not all it's cracked up to be. Not when you were as confused as I had been lately.

So I just sat there in my sling chair on the shortest night of the year and stared out at Flagler's "Whitehall" and wondered what life had been like for the railroad tycoon eighty years before in the big white palace across my watery front yard. And still, there was no lapping sound against my hull. Not so much as a ripple.

Half asleep, I climbed down into the hold and pulled another beer from the box and rolled the icy bottle against my forehead. The cold felt good against my sunburned skin. One more beer in this heat and I would be asleep again before I knew it. Another chance to dream.

A yacht sounding its horn went by out in the Intracoastal as it motored north toward the Palm Beach Inlet. The bell on the drawbridge rang, announcing its intent before the red lights started blinking and the black and white gates swung down and the steel roadway cracked open and pointed toward the black sky like a trap door. In a moment, the passing boat's wake would reach me and I would feel the lapping of waves I had been waiting for all night.

As I climbed up the gangway, the gentle rocking began, and I had to grab onto the rail to steady myself as I pulled up the ladder. And then it stopped and I was once again alone on the hot, motionless water.

There were only a handful of boats roped to the three T-docks in the Downtown Marina. Four months earlier, at the height of the tourist season in February, over one hundred boats had been moored, and the make-shift city afloat, made up of the finest boats from the North, had been a bustling winter community of its own. But now, the boats were all in their home berths in Newport, Providence, Baltimore, Annapolis and Martha's Vineyard, and I was here to sweat out the summer with the few remaining permanent residents.

I don't know how long I had been dozing when the rippling sound began somewhere out in the channel. I was so used to hearing the water break in my sleep I didn't think much about it until I remembered there was no breeze and no boat to cause it.

And then I could hear the coarse breathing, of what could only be a person, swimming closer to the end of the dock where I was moored. I sat up in my sling chair and squinted my eyes into the moonlit darkness. Behind me, no one was about on the few boats nearby. Whoever was swimming toward me was coming from out in the channel. Unusual. No one swims in the fouled Intracoastal, at least not on purpose, especially at night.

And then I saw it wasn't a *whoever,* it was a woman. She had dark hair and a dark tan to match, but even in the bright moonlight I had trouble making out her features until she was holding onto the rope attached to my dive platform. As she pulled herself up hand-over-hand over the transom, gasping for air, I could see what looked like a pure white, two-piece bikini. But then as she walked over to where I was sitting, spellbound in my chair, I could see it wasn't a bathing suit after all, just pure white skin with dark tan lines. I glanced down to the glistening black patch between her legs and then up to her white breasts and dark nipples and then to her face. When she opened her mouth to speak, her teeth were so beautifully white, I almost didn't hear what she said in a breathless, urgent whisper.

"I know who killed your wife."

ensueño
by Frank Eberling

AUTHOR'S NOTE:

ensueño is the result of my forty years traveling through Florida filming thousands of documentaries and television programs. Being involved in such an endeavor gives you an appreciation for the history of the state, its people, and its landscape. One of the greats I got to spend the day with was John D. MacDonald, who shared his story with me on-camera. Out of this love and experience comes a story that is close to my heart, and one I hope you will enjoy.

I was also fortunate to meet and interview several surviving members of THE FLORIDA WRITERS' PROJECT, Stetson Kennedy and Charles C. Foster. Thanks to them for sharing their time and their memories with me.

THE FLORIDA WRITERS' PROJECT was a division of the FEDERAL WRITERS' PROJECT from Franklin D. Roosevelt's WORKS PROGRESS ADMINISTRATION, 1932-1943.

Two hundred men and women, including Zora Neale Hurston, Veronica Huss, and John and Alan Lomax roamed the State of Florida collecting folklore, recording oral histories, and preserving for our collective memories a forgotten Florida of long ago.

I wish I could have been there with them all during those days, but this is the next best thing.

As Stetson Kennedy told me, "We were on a great treasure hunt, in search of nuggets of historical lore."

Treasure, indeed.

We are all following in your footsteps.

We are all heirs to your fortunes.

KEEP READING
for the opening chapter of
Frank Eberling's
classic Country & Western comic novel,

SWEET CITY BLUES

SWEET CITY BLUES

a novel for film
by
Frank Eberling
Available on AMAZON

For
LARRY McMURTRY
IRVING RAVETCH
HARRIET FRANK, Jr.

and for
MARTIN RITT
and
PAUL NEWMAN
PATRICIA NEAL

for bringing to life their brilliant film collaboration,

HUD

CHAPTER 1:

SWEET CITY, FLORIDA, 1979
"And it's not even Monday"

Coming out of the turn at Twenty-Mile Bend, Goodtime Charlie McGill pushed his foot to the floor and leaned back against the cracked leather upholstered seat.

It was a straight drive into Sweet City from the bridge, and if the suspension in his '59 Caddy convertible held up on him, he would make it to work just in time. Lately the shocks had felt like they had been filled with warm Jello, and he had to grip the steering wheel extra tight whenever he took a turn or went onto the shoulder to avoid an armadillo or a pothole, to keep the car from swerving over the center line and into the path of an eastbound semi. At this time of year there were a lot of the big trucks, it being the cane harvesting season, and he didn't want a load of somebody's sugar futures forcing him off the road into the canal.

If that happened, "Night Train" would *really* get angry, because then, instead of being *almost* late for his on-air shift for the third time in a week, he'd be a "no-show," and Night Train's workday would be extended four more hours; keeping the housewives company via their A.M. radios after they sent their kids off to school and sat, drinking their third cup of coffee, while trying to decide when, if ever, to take the rollers down out of their hair and exchange their bathrobes for a housedress, at least.

Yes, Night Train would definitely be pissed, and not only would Charlie be dead from drowning in the canal, but he would also get fired for being "almost late" again; which at this point in time would be worse than being dead.

So he held on to the wheel for dear life and kept his bloodshot and mirror-shaded eyeballs on the road in front of him, only glancing once into the rearview to see the sun make its first appearance over West Palm Beach, thirty miles behind him.

The cardboard carton of Coca-Cola on the seat next to him was already getting warm as he reached over without looking and grabbed a bottle. In one motion, he grabbed his third tall-boy of the day, popped its top on the dashboard-installed bottle opener, took three long quick pulls, and heaved the empty bottle over his shoulder where it caromed twice off the rear seat and landed with a tinkling sound against the growing pile of other bottles on the floor.

He turned up the volume on the radio, drowning out the first word or two of Night Train's voice with his own liquid belch that almost landed on the front of his cowboy shirt.

"And in just a few moments the old Night Train is going to be saying *'Hasta Mañana'* for another day to make room for Good-time Charlie McGill to come on in and help you wake up and get the kids and husband off for the day."

Shit, Charlie thought, *if* I make it on time. He swerved out into the passing lane to pass a blue migrant-filled school bus and dodged back in front of it just in time to miss scraping his tail light off on the bus' front fender. "The *time*, Night Train, the *time*," Charlie said aloud as the commercial ended and Night Train came back on the air.

"And right now it's eighteen minutes before the hour, so if you have to get up at six o'clock like I know a lot of you out there do, you have time to roll over one more time and listen to a little more good country music before you get up and get ready to face the world."

Eighteen minutes, Charlie thought, looking at his surroundings. On either side of the road a heavy low-lying mist was beginning to dissipate on the horizons, and in the foregrounds the sugar cane fields stretched as far as the eye could see before the green stalks disappeared into the fog. And there, just ahead, was Clifton, cutting cane right down off the edge of the highway with two dozen other cutters. Charlie beeped his horn, and the Jamaican lifted his broad-bladed machete. Showing off his big white teeth, Clifton waved to him. "Hey Mon."

Another fifteen miles, Charlie thought. No sweat if I don't run into any heavy traffic or deputies. He shifted his foot around in his gila-hide boot and put more pressure on the gas pedal. Behind him in the east the sun was rising quickly, getting itself ready to scorch the pool-table-flat-muck-farmlands another long November day.

A half mile ahead a small frame house sat down the embankment on the far side of a wooden bridge that crossed the canal. On the front porch stood a slim, attractive woman, wearing an apron and double-checking the contents of a brown paper lunch bag of the boy who stood in front of her. She handed the bag to the boy and knelt down to straighten his collar.

Out on the highway, a yellow school bus slowed and put on its flashers and a small "stop" sign swung out from near the driver's window.

Shit, Lulu, don't do this to me, Charlie thought, looking down at the mom as he lifted his foot off the gas and started pumping the brakes of the Caddy. It felt like he was trying to stomp all the water out of a wet sponge. For a split second he thought about running the stop sign on the bus. No one was getting off, and Lulu's kid was too far away from the road. *No one will get hurt*, he thought. But then he saw the front end of the deputy's patrol car squeaking out from behind the rear end of the bus and he just knew Boggs would be waiting for him to make such a stupid move.

Shit, Lulu, you're going to see the kid again at three o'clock, he thought as the woman ruffled her son's hair and hugged him one more time. Kids had been sent off to an entire summer-full of overnight camp with less of a good-bye than that.

He was out of the car and down the embankment in a flash, breathing heavily before he even got close to the porch. "Running late, Lulu" he smiled to the woman, jerking her son's hand out of her grasp, spinning him around and reaching over his own shoulder to plant a kiss on the face of the surprised woman. "Talk to you later."

The kid's feet were churning up the dust, trying to keep up with Charlie's quick strides as he was dragged across the wooden bridge, up the hill and across the highway. The bus door swung open, and Charlie heaved the boy up the stairs by the belt loops.

He was burning rubber before the kid had a seat and before the stop sign swung back with a slap against the side of the bus. As the hood of the big pink Caddy ran even with the deputy's open window, Charlie leaned on the horn and flashed Boggs a smile. Maybe next time Boggs, he thought to himself, as he settled in and popped another Coca-Cola for the final stretch into Sweet City. Somewhere deep within, the sugar and caffeine mixture was beginning to do its job. Charlie felt a surge bubbling from inside.

Ahead he could see the stacks of two sugar mills punctuating the horizon, emerging from the mist as sunlight warmed the black earth. He took off his hat and stuck his head out the window, inhaling deeply the moist muck musk. And for a moment, however brief, he forgot his troubles.

I can't stand any more of this. Either Caroline's husband is going to have to stop going on the road selling Kerby's, or she's gonna have to visit me out here in Sweet City, he thought to himself.

In the eight months since he had met her, Caroline's husband, Harlan, had been out pushing vacuum cleaners and attending motivational lectures all over the state for long stretches at a time. His billing as top salesman in a twenty-three county area kept Harlan on the road a lot, en-route, no doubt, to some vacuum cleaner sales coup of the century. That star-studded billing thrust Charlie into his bed with his wife Caroline as soon as Harlan's car, packed with demo-models, left the city limits of West Palm Beach. The fact that Harlan was out hustling sucking devices all over creation when he had one of the very best models Charlie had ever met sitting at home by the pool every day knocking off cartons of Russell Stover chocolate turtles, was an irony that Charlie had not overlooked.

But the fifty mile drive from Sweet City to West Palm Beach every night, and then back again to Sweet City for his six a.m. radio shift was beginning to take its toll, not only on his car and his friendship with Night Train, but on Charlie, as well. Sleeping, correction, being in a strange bed every night, and then getting up at four-thirty to go to work had put small, black satchel-like protuberances under Charlie's eyes that were bad for his public image. Not to mention the fact that he was starting to have to wear his underwear inside-out since he hadn't had time to visit the laundro-mat in almost three weeks. The last time Harlan had returned from an extended sales trip, providing Charlie with a reprieve from Caroline, Charlie had filled every available washing machine at the same time at the Dixie-Wash by the time he finally had a chance to do his laundry. The last few days before that, he had spent without socks.

He felt the weariness in every muscle, and he finally understood what they meant by "bone tired." *It's time to get my shit together,* he kept telling himself. *But, first I have to get to work on time.*

He glanced down at his watch, but then remembered the battery was dead. "The time, Night Train, the time," he said aloud. He plucked off his mirror shades and rubbed his swollen eyes again. *I can't go on like this,* he thought.

"Six minutes before six o'clock. Six minutes before Goodtime

Charlie McGill comes along to give you all the latest music and chatter to start off your day on what looks to be another beautiful Sweet City morning. Six minutes before six." Charlie understood that Night Train was talking directly to him over the public airwaves.

And, then, like every other day for the past nine years, Night Train played the closing song of his show as a reminder for the audience to stick around for Charlie's program. A few plucks of the pedal-steel guitar before the plaintiff voice of Danny O'Keefe started it off.

(*)Author's note: I'd love to quote Danny Okeefe's lyrics here, but copyright laws prohibit me from doing that. Please go to YOUTUBE and listen to GOODTIME CHARLIE'S GOT THE BLUES by Danny O'Keefe. Let them worry about the copyright issues.

Over Danny's whistle that ended the song Night Train finished his sign-off.

"And our own Goodtime Charlie will be along in just another minute, right after the latest news and weather, so stay tuned, and we'll be back again tonight at midnight for another night of music with yours truly, Night Train, and The All Night, Train Ride Show. Until then, have a nice day."

The outskirts of town were fast approaching as Night Train punched a commercial for Hardy Grain and Feed, and Charlie slowed down. *Shit, it's gonna be tight.* First, thirty seconds for a commercial, and then two minutes of headlines and weather, and then there would be another thirty seconds for a commercial and Charlie would have to be on the job. He tried to remember where he was on the highway the first time he was as late as he was now. It was going to be very tight.

"WELCOME TO SWEET CITY, WINTER VEGETABLE & SUGAR CANE CAPITAL OF THE WORLD: The Sweetest Little

Town in Florida," read the sign that Charlie whizzed past as Night Train's friendly voice on the radio lowered an octave and became serious while he read the Morning News and Weather.

Just beyond the sign, the big Caddy slowed, and Charlie turned through a gap in the guard rail and drove across the gravel driveway of the station. The building was a converted white clapboard house with a big picture window in the living room for the jock to sit in front of while on the air. Behind the building was a rusted tower, 140 feet tall, with "W-G-A-H COUNTRY RADIO" stretching down its length in white, plywood letters.

Charlie screeched to a halt and his front tires bounced off the white painted telephone pole that lay on its side to mark the edge of the shell-rock parking lot. He hesitated for a second to let the dust catch up to him and pass the car before he opened the door and hauled his ass inside, just as Night Train ended the news and punched up the last spot. As the audio cart started, he jumped out of his seat and ran out of the booth as Charlie came bursting through the door.

"Goddammit Charlie, this is the third time in a week. This last-minute-arrival-shit is gonna have to stop." Night Train followed him around the reception area while Charlie peeled off his shirt, grabbed another from a collection heaped on the floor of the front closet, picked up the station programming print-out from Maria's desk, and poured himself a cup of Mr. Coffee.

"Sorry, Phil. I got stuck in traffic again. You know how slow those sugar-semis move when they're coming back from the Port."

"Well, I don't know how much longer my nerves can take it, you coming in just before air-time like you've been doing. I never know when, or even *if* you're gonna make it."

"I'll always make it, Phil, you know that," Charlie said, that faraway look in his eye that he got whenever his professionalism was put into question. Charlie stepped into the booth, and dumped the ashtray full of cigarette butts and crumpled coffee cups into the trash bucket next to his console. He reached under the turntable cabinet and pulled a warm Coke from a carton. He popped the top on the counter's edge, gargled with a swig, and then spit it out into the bucket. Slowly, he craned his neck, rotating his head on every axis, and as the commercial ended, not even a hint of his current mood could be detected.

He opened his microphone. "And a good morning to all you wonderful Sweet City folks. Well, it looks like we've got another nice winter day here in town. I'm Goodtime Charlie McGill, and we're here to keep you company until ten o'clock this morning right here on Sweet City Country Radio, W-G-A-H."

As he spoke into the mike suspended from the gooseneck device in front of the console, he reached up and pulled an audio cartridge from the rack in front of him, glancing down at the title. "And now let's get this morning started with a little music from nearby Pahokee's own favorite native son, Mel Tillis."

He poked the start button on the cartridge machine, potted down the microphone, and collapsed into the swivel chair. Night Train opened his fifth pack of Camels for the day and lit a new one off an old one. "You ought to seriously reconsider your lifestyle, old buddy. Otherwise I might suffer from a nervous breakdown or fatigue before my time, just worrying about you."

Charlie ignored him, and sat with his head in his hands only long enough to hear the first verse of Mel's new song. Then, in one slow sweeping motion he pushed Night Train's paperwork onto the floor and spread his own program log in front of him. It was all there: anecdotes, jokes, promotions, commercials, playlist, and school lunch menus ("It looks like mystery meat and powdered potatoes again today, kids. And what's this, no Jello? Rice pudding for dessert? I guess nobody liked yesterday's Chinese menu.") All Charlie had to do was rip-and-read wire-copy for the headlines, check the weather updates when necessary, and pour on the charm between the records.

How many songs in a row can I play without talking and still get away with it, he wondered? Maybe this would be the time to introduce some new album sides instead of just playing one song at a time and being personable between each song. Better not, he thought. Frank would get mad at him for jacking around with his precious programming concept which was designed to squeeze in as many commercials as possible without alienating too much of the audience.

Night Train broke his concentration. "And don't fall asleep too soon after you get off the air, because there's a big staff meeting at ten-thirty, and everyone is required to attend."

Charlie looked up at him through swollen eyes. "Why, what's so important?"

"Beats me. Frank just told Maria to spread the word to everyone here and to call everyone who works on the late shift to come in early." This was no mean feat, since Maria spoke only about four words of English: "Hello," "Please Hold, and "Goodbye." She spent her days answering the phone and then putting the caller on hold while she tracked down anyone available to handle the call in discernible English. That and practicing her typing. At last estimate she had just broken into the early teens in the words-per-minute department, and rumor had it that Frank was going to double her salary as soon as she broke into the low twenties.

Charlie remained immobilized until Mel was finished singing, and then slid a commercial into the slot for 'Hiway 27 Unlimited, Used Cars and Trucks City', providing himself with another thirty seconds to get himself psyched-up for the rest of the show.

Finally he spoke. "Okay Phil, I'll be there. Something real important, no doubt, like delinquent coffee dues. By the way, are there any of those stale doughnuts left over from yesterday?"

SWEET CITY BLUES
by Frank Eberling
AUTHOR'S NOTE:

I wanted the title of this novel to be, GOODTIME CHAR-
LIE'S GOT THE BLUES.

Although the story content was not in any way inspired by
Danny O'Keefe's wonderful, classic song, I felt the after writing
the novel that the tone of the song happened to match the bit-
tersweet tone of the story.

However, when I checked with Warner/Chappell about
licensing the name they wanted huge amounts of money. So I
thought I'd better change the name back to the working title,
SWEET CITY BLUES.

If the novel is ever made into a film, I hope they use O'Keefe's
song and the title. Maybe he'll get a little dough out of the deal.

The name of the town in the book was originally GLADES,
since it takes place in Western Palm Beach County, but I didn't
want it to be confused with the recent cable television series of
that name.

The town of Sweet City, Florida, exists only in the imagination of the author, however, Palm Beach County, the other towns
mentioned, and the State of Florida are believed to actually exist.

Although specific references to recording artists and movie
stars refer to real people, all other characters and events in this
novel are imaginary, and any resemblance to events or to any
other persons, living or dead, is purely coincidental.

Most of the events in this work of fiction take place in the
1970's.

The incidents, attitudes, and situations depicted reflect those
of that more irresponsible, carefree, bygone era.

You know, when sex was good, clean fun.

LOW TOR

A novel by Frank Eberling
Set in New City, New York
Available on AMAZON, Winter, 2018

SYNOPSIS:

New City native, Abby Traphagen was a local kid who made good.

A high school football star in the early 1960s who went on to sports fame with a full scholarship to Florida State University, he was later drafted by the NY Giants, where he spent ten years as a wide receiver. Hired as a television network football commentator, he capitalized on his fame and became a bestselling mystery novelist.

Now, in 2008, his life has fallen apart. His wife has died of acute alcohol poisoning, his 20 year-old son has disappeared, and he's been diagnosed with terminal brain cancer.

Alone in his remote, 200 year-old ivy-covered sandstone cottage on South Mountain Road, he's made a decision. He will take a last "walk into the woods" on his beloved promontory, Low Tor, and watch his final sunset.

But on his first night there he witnesses a senseless, brutal murder of a young woman by two men. After he reports the shooting to the police, they find no forensic evidence that a murder ever took place. When the body is eventually found on his remote hillside retreat near Lake Tiorati, he becomes the primary suspect.

Told through the eyes of his estranged son, LOW TOR is novel of small town aspirations come true, of lifelong resentments, secrets, and dreams, and a murder mystery, partially based on true events, that defies the conventions of the genre.

Like in his first New City novel, DEMAREST KILL, fifth-generation New City native Frank Eberling combines local history and lore with an intriguing crime story. Told partially in flashbacks that go back almost one hundred years, it weaves together four separate stories that explore the genesis of Abby Traphagen's obsessions, and how he came to live the complicated life he did.

Frank Eberling graduated from Clarkstown High School in 1964, moved to Florida to attend the University of Florida, became an educator, then an Emmy® Award-winning documentary filmmaker, producing over 3,000 television programs over the course of forty-four years. He lives in South Florida.

From the opening pages of LOW TOR, by Frank Eberling

PREFACE:

NEW CITY, NEW YORK, 2016
8 YEARS AFTER THE MURDER

When all is said and done, my father was a difficult, complicated man.

Like the sons of many difficult, complicated men, I grew up bitter, filled with anger and resentment. Was my hostility fueled by his neglect, or the fact that I knew I could never measure up to his accomplishments, his standards, no matter how hard I tried?

I knew that unless I changed my own name, disappeared, I would be forever associated with this complicated man, unable to climb out from under of all the weight his name carried, and become my own person.

It was not until the last year of his life, when he was accused of murdering a young woman, that I came to understand who he had been, who he was, and how and why he was like the person he had become.

By that time I was twenty years old and thought I had left my father behind forever; the man who had started out as a local high school football hero in New City, New York, went to Florida State University on a football scholarship, was drafted by the New York Giants and was their star for ten years, went on to be a television sports journalist, and eventually a world famous, best-selling author of four works of non-fiction and over a dozen mystery novels. Is that accomplished enough for you? It was for me.

Growing up, I just had a vague sense of his fame, no real

concrete details. Just the stuff you could glean from seeing the photographs, news articles and magazine covers framed on the walls, the trophies in the glass cases, the books on the shelves. It gave me a sense of the big picture without me having to bother to discover the specifics of what a person would have to do to earn a place on the cover of both Sports Illustrated and the New York Times Book Review.

Growing up,

I never watched his game films.

I never watched his broadcasts.

I never read his books.

But then, when he was in his early-sixties, he was charged with the murder of some poor white-trash woman who had apparently made some stupid decisions and was found buried on a remote piece of property my father owned. I thought about coming back home, despite my desire to never see him again. Could someone who had risen from such humble roots and accomplished so much, have done the horrendous things the police reports described?

By then it was almost too late. I say almost, because I made it back just in time to have some long-overdue conversations.

I remembered back to the last conversation I had had with my father the night before I ran away from home, two years earlier, in 2006, determined never to speak to him again.

As I stormed out of the house, I turned to face him directly and asked him, "Was it really worth it to lose your wife and your son to write a bunch of second-rate novels? Was it worth all the pain and suffering you caused us by your neglect and lost opportunities, to accomplish that?"

The fact that he paused to consider his answer to my question told me volumes. I turned and disappeared into the night. He didn't know where I was for two years.

Between what he told me when I returned, and what I later learned from his friends, I didn't know what conclude. Maybe it was time to change my mind about my namesake?

Abram Traphagen, III
New City, New York
Summer, 2016